Maxi [...] nd editor. He was be [...] wing a career in book publ [...] mous Murder One bookshop in London. He now writes full-time. He has edited a series of fifteen bestselling erotic anthologies and two books of erotic photography, as well as many acclaimed crime collections. His novels include *It's You That I Want To Kiss*, *Because She Thought She Loved Me* and *On Tenderness Express*, all three recently collected and reprinted in the USA as *Skin In Darkness*. Other books include *Life In The World of Women*, *The State of Montana*, *Kiss Me Sadly* and *Confessions Of A Romantic Pornographer*. In 2009 he published *American Casanova*, a major erotic novel which he edited and on which fifteen of the top erotic writers in the world have collaborated, and his collected erotic short stories as *Hotel Room Fuck*... *'s For Lust*. He compiles two annual acclaimed series for the Mammoth list: *Best New Erotica* and *Best British Crime*. He is a winner of the Anthony and the Karel Awards, a frequent TV and radio broadcaster, crime columnist for the *Guardian* newspaper and Literary Director of London's Crime Scene Festival.

THE MAMMOTH BOOK OF
BEST
INTERNATIONAL
CRIME

EDITED AND WITH AN INTRODUCTION
BY MAXIM JAKUBOWSKI

ROBINSON   RUNNING PRESS
PHILADELPHIA · LONDON

Constable & Robinson Ltd
3 The Lanchesters
162 Fulham Palace Road
London W6 9ER
www.constablerobinson.com

First published in the UK by Robinson, an imprint of Constable & Robinson, 2009

A copy of the British Library Cataloguing in Publication
Data is available from the British Library

UK ISBN 978-1-84529-957-6

Di...

US Library of Congress Control Number: 2008944132
US ISBN 978-0-76243-725-2

Running Press Book Publishers
2300 Chestnut Street
Philadelphia, PA 19103–4371

Visit us on the web!

www.runningpress.com

Printed and bound in the EU

Contents

vi   *Contents*

Acknowledgments

"A Crime for a Crime" by Giorgio Faletti, copyright © 2008 Giorgio Faletti. First published in CRIMINI ITALIANI. Reprinted by permission of the author's agent, Piergiorgio Nicolazzini Literary Agency.

"Rumpole and the Christmas Break" by John Mortimer, copyright © 2004 John Mortimer. First published in THE STRAND MAGAZINE. Reprinted by permission of the author's agent, United Agents Ltd.

"The Temp" by René Appel, copyright © 2002 René Appel. First published in ALGEMEEN DAGBLAD. Reprinted by permission of the author.

"Serum" by Jo Nesbø, copyright © 1999 Jo Nesbø. First published in MISTANKEN BRER SEG. Reprinted by permission of the author's agent, Salomonsson Agency.

"Huxley" by Chad Taylor, copyright © 2009 Chad Taylor. Reprinted by permission of the author.

"Among Partisans" by Carmen Korn, copyright © 2004 by Carmen Korn. First published in DU SOLLST NICHT TOTEN. Reprinted by permission of the author.

"Ethnic Cleansing" by Dominique Manotti, copyright © 2007 Dominique Manotti. First published in PARIS NOIR. Reprinted by permission of the author.

"A Really Shitty Day" by Camilla Läckberg, copyright © 2005 by Camilla Läckberg. First published in NOVELLER FOR

"Angel Child" by Tove Klackenberg, copyright © 2005 Tove Klackenberg. First published in NOVELLER FOR VARLDENS BARN. Reprinted by permission of the author.

"All For Bergkamen" by Sebastian Fitzek, copyright © 2008 Sebastian Fitzek. First published in GRAFIT VERLAG. Reprinted by permission of the author's agent, Tanja Howarth.

"An Urban Legend Puzzle" by Norizuki Rintarō, copyright © 2001 Norizuki Rintarō. First published in English in 2003 by ELLERY QUEEN'S MYSTERY MAGAZINE. Reprinted by permission of the author.

"The Duel" by Jacob Vis, copyright © 1995 Jacob Vis. First published in SPANNEND GEBUNDELD. Reprinted by permission of the author.

"The Deepest South" by Paco Ignacio Taibo II, copyright © 1988 Paco Ignacio Taibo II. First published in RAYMOND CHANDLER'S PHILIP MARLOWE. Reprinted by permission of the author.

"Escalator Obstructors" by Juergen Ehlers, copyright © 2008 Juergen Ehlers. First published in In KÜRZE VERSTORBEN. Reprinted by permission of the author.

"Voices in the Head" by Altaf Tyrewala, copyright © 2001 Altaf Tyrewala. First published in THE LITTLE MAGAZINE. Reprinted by permission of the author.

"The Christmas Present" by Jeffery Deaver, copyright © 2003 Jeffery Deaver. Reprinted by permission of the author's agent, Curtis Brown Ltd.

"Scars" by Daniel Walther, copyright © 2005 Daniel Walther. First published in NOIRS SCALPELS. Reprinted by permission of the author.

"Staring At The Sun" by Leonardo Padura, copyright © 2007 Leonardo Padura. First published in HAVANA NOIR. Reprinted by permission of Achy Obejas and Akashic Books.

"The Sword of God" by Josh Pachter, copyright © 2009 Josh Pachter. Reprinted by permission of the author.

"Now Let's Talk About Laura" by Andreu Martin, copyright ©
2008 Andreu Martin. Reprinted by permission of the author.

"My Vacation in the Numbers Racket" by Howard Engel,
copyright © 1989 Howard Engel. Reprinted by permission of the
author and his agent, Beverley Slopen Literary Agency.

"Night Over Unna" by Bernhard Jaumann, copyright © 2006
Bernhard Jaumann. First published in MORD AM HELLWEG
3. Reprinted by permission of the author.

"The Big Switch" by Mickey Spillane & Max Allan Collins,
copyright © 2008 Mickey Spillane Publishing, LLC. First
appeared in THE STRAND MAGAZINE. Reprinted by
permission of the author's Estate.

"Hitching in the *Lodos*" by Feryal Tilmac, copyright © 2008
Feryal Tilmac. First published in ISTANBUL NOIR. Reprinted
by permission of the author.

"It's Not True" by Diego De Silva, copyright © 2008 Diego De
Silva. First published in CRIMINI ITALIANI. Reprinted by
permission of the author and the author's agent, Marco Vigevani
Agenzia Letteraria.

"Tell Me Who to Kill" by Ian Rankin, copyright © 2003 John
Rebus Limited. First appeared in MYSTERIOUS PLEASURES.
Reprinted by permission of the author and the author's agent,
Peter Robinson Literary Agency.

Introduction

What with the world-wide popularity of crime and mystery fiction written in the English language – and how can one argue about the iconic heritage of Sir Arthur Conan Doyle, Charles Dickens even, Edgar Allen Poe, Agatha Christie, Raymond Chandler, Dashiell Hammett, etc. all the way to the many modern paragons of the genre that we all love and admire – foreign language fiction has often been overlooked by readers and critics alike. Setting aside the economics of the publishing industry in which the added cost of translation remains a negative factor and the de facto imperialism of the English language, there has always been a feeling that we produce enough interesting stories and novels and have a slight prejudice against culture from different countries. The same applies to the cinema, where Hollywood still rules the roost to a large extent. But it is an unfortunate state of affairs.

One might even argue, at a stretch, that crime fiction began with the slaying of Abel in the Bible, which was of course not written in English, and the dreadful passions and emotions which give rise to crime, both fictional and real, are a factor which is inherent to the human condition. As a result, crime has dominated history and parallels the rise of civilization everywhere, from the massacres and plots of Ancient Greece and Rome, the bloody Middle Ages, the Borgias, the rise of gangsterism in the American Depression; the examples are countless. And far from a British or American phenomenon. Crime is, sadly, universal.

As a result, there has always existed a vital stream of crime and mystery writing in almost all languages and cultures, but all too often it is we who have been too preoccupied with what was happening in our homes and countries who have chosen to partly ignore it. This lack of interest became self-generating and for many years it proved increasingly difficult for foreign authors (and not just in the crime area) to get their books translated into English, thus shielding us generally from an immense reservoir of talent. Some prominent names managed to break through such as Georges Simenon, Sjowall & Wahloo, Friedrich Durrenmatt, Boileau-Narcejac, but they were the exceptions, and similar major crime talents including Jean-Pierre Manchette, Friedrich Glauser and Giorgio Scerbanenco were overlooked.

Over recent years, the fortuitous success and acceptance of occasional Scandinavian writers in translation (Henning Mankell, Stieg Larsson) have somehow opened the doors wide and a grateful crime-reading public has for the first time in ages been able to enjoy foreign writers like never before. Fred Vargas, Boris Akunin, Jean-Claude Izzo, Arnaldur Indridason and Andrea Camilleri are also now widely available and enjoyed. There are now even some, admittedly small and independent, publishing houses who have generously decided to devote their efforts to exclusively promoting crime in translation, both out of intellectual curiosity and the well-known fact that success breeds success.

As someone who has for several decades vociferously supported genre writing from other countries, I personally find it difficult to explain why this has happened now, rather than earlier. Maybe Scandinavian sleuths ring a familiar chord in the souls of English and American readers who find their habits and preoccupations reflected in their travails and investigations; maybe globalization has made us more aware of foreign mores; maybe we were growing tired of our familiar sleuths; maybe the exotic attraction of foreign and alien shores and cultures has been a determining factor? And here I remind you of the undoubted success of English and American writers like HRF Keating, Donna Leon, Michael Dibdin and many others who set their books in foreign countries – as well as US authors such as Elizabeth George, Martha Grimes or Deborah Crombie who write about England while, conversely, many Brits (and Irish) mostly set their books in the USA: Lee Child, John Connolly, Ken Bruen, even myself . . . At any rate, it is a state of affairs we can only be grateful for and which, as I write, appears still to be flourishing as we continue to discover the talent of so many new writers with fascinating characters, locales and plots.

But there is a long way to go: a high proportion of English and American crime writers is translated into foreign languages, while the reverse movement is far from true. It might appear to the untrained eye that every single Scandinavian mystery writer is now available to us, when in fact we are still only seeing the tip of the iceberg. And from my own knowledge of the French, Italian and Spanish writing scene, I am painfully aware of how many major authors remain untranslated. There is a whole world of crime out there begging to be discovered by us. Which certainly whets the appetite.

For several years, I have been editing an annual anthology of the best of British crime writing in this series, and I was delighted when Pete Duncan and Nick Robinson at Constable & Robinson invited me to edit this volume, and broaden the scope to international crime writing. I am often invited to crime writing festivals across Europe and have met many foreign writers on these occasions and this affords me a way to get some of them published in English for the first time. It has been a fascinating book to edit, in so far as I was naturally limited to reading stories in the handful of languages I knew, so I recruited a group of advisers, all wonderful writers in their own right, to recommend some of the best stories they had recently come across in their own language. I must therefore thank Juergen Ehlers in Germany, Camilla Läckberg in Sweden, Paco Taibo in Mexico who advised on Spanish crime writing, Hirsh Sawney in India, Carla Vermaat in the Netherlands, as well as Johnny Temple at Akashic Books, who provided contacts and encouragement and, of course, publishes an increasing number of foreign writers himself in his Noir Cities series. I'm also grateful to Trisha Telep and Helen Donlon for advice on translators and Janet Hutchings at *Ellery Queen's Mystery Magazine*. Without all of them, this volume would not have been truly international.

I am customarily reluctant to highlight any particular story in an anthology as part of the introduction, and even more so in the present instance. How can one compare a story from Italy to one written in Russian, one from New Zealand to another from India, a Canadian story to a British one? They all have one thing in common: they are excellent crime stories which will grip, fascinate, intrigue, often surprise and trick you ... which is the virtue of the best of crime and mystery writing. You will also find here some British and American authors, many well-loved and familiar: how could an anthology truly be international if we didn't include ourselves on the basis of the universality of crime writing? Some of the foreign authors I've been privileged to select have already had books translated, while as many others haven't yet (but hopefully will). I hope this sampler of their immense talents will encourage readers to open their investigative nets even wider in times to come and help us make foreign crime authors even more widespread and popular.

Maxim Jakubowski

A Crime for a Crime

Giorgio Faletti

The station is the usual small town railroad stop.

Tracks behind and tracks in front, cables striping the sky and rust-brown ties coloring the ground as far as the curve that can be pictured back there. Alongside, a long, low building which from its design and color could only be a station. The blue sign hanging there suggests "ASTI" to passengers going by on trains and inflicts it on those who stop there. The train's brakes and iron screech until it grinds to a stop and the doors open.

Passengers step off as a voice announces connections. Names that don't arouse dreams, ordinary nearby towns, merely places to return to. The end of a journey which in places like this is hardly ever an adventure. They are simple everyday events that in recompense offer the rigid, ineluctable monotony of a pendulum.

Tic, toc, tic, toc . . .

One oscillation going and another coming, the same each day, until the momentum winds down and all that's left to do is to ascertain if the final second corresponds to a tic or a toc. As he steps off the train, the man who made his decision thinks that fundamentally this is also his life, a train in the morning and one in the evening, uninterruptedly, until he is too tired to go on.

Or until life decides that he is too tired to go on . . .

In any case, the man who made his decision promised himself that today would be a special day. The day when tears would be justified and pain would find a semblance of payback. The day when he will go in search of a smile, not for himself but for someone who is dead. Or for everyone who is dead.

If things were better, if things were just, if things came close to even a semblance of that law which should be the same for everyone, there would be no reason to do what he has decided to do.

If things had been different . . .

These thoughts are so powerful inside that he instinctively clenches his jaws. So clear are they, and so clear is his motivation, that he wouldn't be surprised if it were stamped on his face. He's amazed that his determination isn't a color or height or size that would make him stand out among the people around him like an abnormal character in a grotesque cartoon.

Instead his face, his expression and his height are what they always are, and he sails through the crowd like a tempest-free ship without a flag. No one pays any attention to him. They all have their minds on something they have found or are about to find at the beginning or end of their brief or long or easy or boring trip. To them he's just another anonymous passenger grappling with time and space, who melts into the piazza outside the station.

As soon as he steps out, he stops and with an accustomed gaze looks around at a town that he has seen numerous other times.

There and elsewhere.

A small town, a railroad station panorama: trees, taxis, buses, a fountain, shops on either side. The coolness of an ice cream parlor for summer days. A spurious population that is the sum of that station and of all the stations in the world. At the other end of that daily trip which for years has been his life lies a scene just like that one. The name on the sign where the train pulls in changes, the theater changes, the actors change, but not the characters. All it takes is a minute or so to figure out who's who, if one has the desire or will to do so. He shrugs faintly and starts walking, unhurriedly because he has no deadline to meet, only a result to accomplish. As he crosses the piazza, the town his sole objective, he thinks that the following day, when he will again board that train, he will leave behind a stopped clock. He doesn't know how his stride will be and what his breathing and his thoughts will be like, but he is certain that they will not be the same. He moves off, his anonymity protected by the unremarkable overcoat he's wearing, though it does not manage to enliven his step or conceal his slightly curved back.

In the right-hand pocket of that coat, the man who made his decision is hiding a gun.

1

The Sloth had two voices.

One was for everybody, the one he used when speaking to the world: he called it the Good Voice. It was the voice that discussed, that greeted people and said thank you and excuse me, but was nothing more than a kind of sonorous mask, a screen to hide behind during those times when he had to go out among people. And then there was the voice reserved for him alone, the one he heard inside him, which argued and talked as if it came from an autonomous part of his brain. In all that time he had been so good at hiding it that no one suspected it existed. That was his real voice.

It was the Bad Voice.

The one that was now moving wordlessly on his mouth, as he watched the girls and licked his lips.

He left the car in the parking lot behind the hotel and emerged from the dark on foot along the tree-lined avenue in front of the stadium. He turned right and left the hotel behind him, the glare of the lights from the salons like a stamp on his leather jacket. Walking slowly and staring straight ahead of him, he crossed the street and approached the mesh fencing only when he was away from the fire house.

He wasn't doing anything wrong but, given his prior record, he wanted to avoid attracting attention in any way. The fire house was still, but the station might come to life at any moment, and then, too, there was always some bored fireman glancing out the window once too often. They were people trained to see, as well as watch. And he didn't want to be either watched or seen.

Not in that place and at that hour, at least.

He crossed the street only when he reached a clump of oleanders that marked the boundary between the fence and the wall, where the avenue curved and the wall became the archway of the stadium's service entrance. He hunkered down in such a way that those shrubs found in the brief grassy stretch that bordered the pavement would protect him as much as possible from the eyes of anyone who happened to be passing by, on foot or by car. Even though it was no longer the season for going out for walks. And at that hour of the evening cars drove straight ahead, square bodies and round wheels carrying people home to dinner. He turned up the collar of his leather jacket and leaned his hands on the wire-mesh coated with green plastic. With hooked fingers he clung to the fence like a parasite to its host. On the other side of the fence was the bright green grass of a soccer field, glittering with moisture under the lights. On the other side was the world that each day populated his fantasies. In front of the door nearest to him, the members of a female soccer team were training under the lights of the reflectors. Almost all of them wore tracksuits but a few, despite the cool evening, had on shorts, and their firm, naked legs shone under the almost brash glow of the scoreboards riddled with floodlights, high above.

There was one in particular, taller than the average height of her companions, with a sweet face and a lean, lithe body that was more reminiscent of a model's figure than an athlete's. At that moment she moved off from the group which stood listening to the coach's words, accompanied by lots of gestures. She was a few yards away and was dribbling the ball with amazing skill, bouncing it easily from her left foot to her right, to her knee and back to her foot, with a movement which lent that technical action a strange sensuality, the color of a dance beneath the white light.

She was still tan, though summer was by now a memory, and the Sloth thought she must go under a sunlamp in a tanning salon every so often to maintain that amber color. He imagined her taking off her clothes and entering the tanning booth naked, her firm tits and unripe buttocks open to being frisked by the violet fingers of the UVA rays.

The Sloth ran his tongue over his lips again. He got no relief from it, because his mouth was dryer than his lips. He felt the bulk of an erection swell his pants. He would have liked to enter the tight space of that booth with her, naked and furtive, and talk to her with the Bad Voice while he shoved it in her. The sudden thought that she might be a virgin made a hot flush rise from his stomach to his temples. It would be even more satisfying to take her feverishly, without any regard for her, knowing that the rough act would cause her a little bit of pain . . .

Jerk off, the Bad Voice said.

Not here, he answered in a half-hearted murmur using the Good Voice.

He barely resisted the urge to unzip his pants, pull out his prick and masturbate to the rhythm of the girl's dribbling. What the Bad

Voice said shouldn't always be done. He had already gotten into too much trouble because of it and had had to learn to restrain it.

At least a little. At least in public.

On the field the girl stopped dribbling, as if rousing herself from an intimate moment, from that exclusive dialogue with a ball which in that situation perhaps represented more than what it should logically represent. With a nimble flick of her foot she lifted the ball off the ground and squeezed it between her hands. Tucking it under her arm she turned her back to where the Sloth was stationed and went back to the group, which hadn't noticed her absence.

As she walked away, the jiggle of her buttocks under the light fabric of her white shorts was almost hypnotic to the Sloth's rapt eyes.

She spotted you and wants to get you aroused, that bitch the Bad Voice said, screaming and silent.

The Sloth was undecided. Maybe this time the Bad Voice was right. Maybe that young girl possessed the cunning naughtiness and provocation of a grown woman. Of one of the prostitutes whom he managed to fuck occasionally, when he had the money to afford it. The Sloth was plagued by a series of problems when it came to satisfying his various lusts: he was ugly, he didn't have a cent and he liked beautiful women. His face with its protruding, watery eyes, pronounced incisors and almost no chin had earned him the nickname that he now bore like an epitaph. As far as everyone was concerned, Lucio Bertolino had died on that cursed day when he was in prison and someone said he looked like the three-toed sloth in the cartoon, the *Ice Age*.

He entered prison as a man, and came out a caricature.

This hadn't changed his life, at least not in any official sense. Just as before, whether he was Lucio or the Sloth, the only women with whom he managed to have relations free of charge revolted him. And he was revolting to the ones he really wanted.

The only way he could get laid was to pay. Whores were the only women capable of satisfying his desires and realizing his fantasies. He sought them on the Internet, on the numerous sites full of suggestive photos, bare buttocks and breasts displayed for the viewing, and sometimes faces, slightly blurred in an attempt to disguise features which could be surmised all the same and were even more exciting because of this. They were young girls, high class call-girls, and the fee was often beyond the Sloth's means. Sometimes, when his pockets were empty, he made do with watching those illuminated images on the screen and masturbated while letting his imagination run wild, creating in his head a film of what he could do with any one of them.

The next time he would choose a girl who looked like the one who, shortly before, had been bouncing the ball around on her foot with that hypnotic movement, almost a sexual allusion.

Up, down, up, down, up, down . . .

He would buy the right clothes and ask her to dress up like that girl, and he would make her undress in the bathroom and take a shower, like all athletes do after training. Then . . . The lights on the field went out, at the same time turning off the mental screen on which he was projecting his images. The woman stripping for him dissolved and was left floating in a yellowish spot before his eyes.

The Sloth was left alone in the dark, as always.

He stayed clinging to the fence for a few more seconds, as if electrified by his excitement. Then he let go, left the protection of the shrubs and crossed the street to go back to his car. As he walked he thought about what he could do to get some money. At that moment he was broke, but he would think of something. He always managed to get by somehow and he would do so this time as well. A friend of his had just introduced him to some guys who assured him that there was money to be made in drug peddling, that drugs were now a universal commodity with a market open to all social classes.

Weed, coke, heroin, ecstasy . . .

A guaranteed high for every budget and every type of addiction.

He had always stayed out of that circuit, not because of any moral compunction but simply because he had never had the opportunity to break into it. He had always made do with small apartment robberies, dismal muggings of retirees outside the post office, purse-snatchings and stuff like that. Little things for which he had hardly ever been caught. The major thing that had brought him to the attention of the police had been the complaints of harassment by some girls, complaints that had come to nothing when he stopped haunting them.

The only time he attempted something big, it went as expected. Maybe he and his friends bit off more than they could chew. As a result they ended up in the slammer with more counts against them than fleas on a dog.

And yet everything would have been smooth as butter, if only there hadn't been that damned curve and that damned car . . .

Nevertheless, in prison the Sloth had learned how the world works. A certain world, at least. The real guys in the know had explained to him how money is made. And he had learned that the law is a net with rather large meshes. According to the code he should have stayed inside for a number of years. But what with plea bargaining, clemency, and reduced time for good behavior he got away with less than three.

And now he decided to get serious about it.

To pay for all the whores he wanted and for all the good lawyers he needed, the kind who make it possible to go to jail in the evening and get released the next day.

Step by step he was back in front of the hotel. From inside the brightly lit reception hall came the sound of voices and the clink of china. Maybe it was one of the numerous social affairs sponsored by the Rotary, Lions or other such organizations. Rich people, rolling in dough, the kind that didn't have any problems and maybe had never had any. The ones who drove by Praia, the disreputable neighborhood where he lived, in their shiny, polished cars, glanced around appalled or preoccupied, and continued on toward their fine houses on the hills or in the historic center.

Bastard dickheads, the Bad Voice said.

He left the Bad Voice looming over the windows shouting out his fury. As he turned the corner, his mind erased what he was seeing and went back to what he had just witnessed. His renewed arousal obliterated that inkling of rage. Now he would go home, turn on the computer and go trolling on the Internet to find a girl who looked like the unknown soccer player. Once he found her, he knew his Bad Voice would be there intact so he could talk to the image on the screen, while waiting to talk to her in person.

Maybe he might even phone her, to hear her voice and find out how much she wanted to satisfy his fantasies.

Excited by that idea, he quickened his stride and reached the car, which he had left at some distance from all the others, its nose up against a laurel hedge that marked the edge of the parking lot. He was searching for his keys in the pockets of his jacket when, from the side, the figure of a man stepped out of the shadows, revealed by the flutter of an overcoat. Even before he was able to make out his features, he realized that he was holding a gun in his left hand.

The man's voice was deep and emotionless.

"Good evening, Mr Bertolino."

Instinctively the Sloth took a step back.

"Who the hell . . ."

"Shhhhh" the man silenced him. "Don't make a scene and get in the car."

As the Sloth took out his keys and unlocked the door, the man, with the gun still aimed at him, went around the car to get in on the passenger side.

They climbed in the car and the light from the dashboard fell on the face of the man with the gun. The Sloth had a shitload of bad memories and found himself sifting through them.

"I've seen you before. You're . . ."

The man interrupted him.

"Who I am doesn't matter. What matters is who you are."

The Sloth didn't have the sort of brain that enabled him to do too many things at the same time. He set aside all the questions he was asking himself and began to be afraid.

"What d'you want?"

He noticed that what came out of his mouth was a trembling Good Voice.

With the hand that was not holding the gun the main pointed vaguely beyond the windshield.

"Let's take a little drive. Start the car. And drive slowly."

As he turned the key in the ignition, the Sloth suddenly felt his throat go dry and was unable to find another word to say with either of his two voices.

2

As he made his way through the underbrush, Carlin Bonomo couldn't help but feel a little annoyed. His son, who talked the way young people talk, would have said pissed off, and maybe it would be the more correct term. If things went on this way, it would be his second night roaming around the countryside in vain. The season had been what it was and the meteorological logic that governed his second job was proving to be an exact science. It had not rained during the summer and the sun and heat had not had any kind of opposition. Thus, according to the accepted rule of thumb, a very good year for wine. And consequently a shitty year for mushrooms and truffles. Carlin recalled the blissful expression stamped on the faces of those who had just harvested a grape capable of becoming a great product over time. He remembered how they rubbed their hands together eagerly while waiting to put their labels on bottles that would end up on the tables of restaurants in Italy, America, Russia and Japan.

What pissed him off was that there wouldn't be any of his truffles on those tables, at least not that year. It mattered for his own personal satisfaction and not just for economic reasons, though these however counted for something.

His vocation of *trifulau*, as truffle hunters are called in those parts, had over time been a substantial supplement to his work as a car electrician. For years he spent his days in the repair shop changing batteries, replacing burned-out bulbs and restoring electrical systems. Every day from eight in the morning to seven in the evening, in winter, spring, summer ... But in autumn, in the right season, every night he took the car and Tabuj, his dog, and went out. He went to places that only he knew about, the secret, exclusive spots that every truffle hunter worthy of the name has on his private map and which he visits only under cover of darkness, to avoid raising a flag that would signal what is in fact an unauthorized personal domain.

Carlin smiled.

On television he had heard about a king, he didn't remember which one, who said that on his lands the sun never set. By contrast, on his small seasonal kingdom the sun never rose. All of a sudden the dog who was walking somewhere ahead of him whimpered quietly. It was their signal. A kind of code established over time by which Tabuj let him know that something had aroused his interest. Carlin's hope lit up along with his flashlight and both headed in the direction from which the dog's whimper had come. Carlin saw him sniff the ground and make digging motions with his front paws. The dog stopped almost immediately and turned his head toward him, expectantly. His body seemed to be electrified by a contained frenzy, as Carlin bent down, gently moved him aside and began carefully digging at the spot the dog had indicated.

Little by little he realized that once again the animal's nose had not been wrong. Slowly but surely he uncovered a truffle which, held in the palm of a hand that over time had become almost as accurate as a scale, displayed an approximate weight of almost two ounces.

Not bad at all.

Given that year's scarcity it was a fine specimen, which by the end of its journey would end up costing up to seven thousand euros per kilo. He wrapped the truffle in a piece of paper that he always carried with him and put it in the canvas bag he wore over his shoulder. Tabuj stared at him, wagging his tail slowly. He let out another yelp, this time with a different meaning.

"Okay, okay, I understand."

He dipped his hand into the pocket of his jacket and the dog's tail quickened its rhythm. He gave a faint sign of impatience, rising up slightly on his hind legs. Each time Tabuj did his job, Carlin rewarded him with a tasty piece of raw meat. He pulled out the morsel and held it out to him, waiting for him to take it gently between his teeth and chew it slowly. He patted him on the head. A truffle dog could be worth a small fortune and, if it was gifted as his was, the size of that fortune increased significantly.

However, profits aside, Carlin would never be without his companion, that medium-sized mongrel who over time had enabled him to earn some considerable sums. In this case too economic reasons weren't the only thing that mattered.

He had trained the dog personally, patiently, day after day, to make him achieve his present level. They had grown old together and together they would remain, even if that heap of fur were suddenly to lose his keen scent and were no longer able to earn his keep.

If it's true that man does not live by bread alone, it was equally true that he does not live by truffles alone . . .

Sighing he shut off the flashlight and let the dog roam about as he pleased. He waited for his eyes to become reaccustomed to the brightness of the night with its waxing gibbous moon. He raised his head up toward the sky and that shining crescent, one of many in his lifetime, was impressed upon his eyes. Through quarter moons and new moons, the time had passed almost without him being aware of it.

Now, to use an expression in his dialect that he generally resorted to, *l'era pù nen in fanciot*, he was no longer a kid. He was nearing the time when he would leave his small auto repair shop to his son. He was a good boy and had learned the trade well. Now it was almost time for him to stand on his own two feet. Carlin, over the years, had built up a modest pension and had put aside a tidy nest-egg that would see him and his wife through any kind of difficulty. He owned the house in which they lived and had a couple of shops rented out that ensured additional income.

The extra earnings represented by that part-time evening job in search of what they called "white gold", besides being an enjoyable pastime, could still guarantee him many enjoyable and profitable nights, now that his wife slept more and more and he slept less and less. He turned onto a path and headed towards a thicket covered by the leafy branches of a group of trees. When he reached it, he had to switch the flashlight on briefly to make out the trail he intended to take. A glittering on his right stirred his curiosity. He aimed the flashlight in that direction and a car appeared in the beam of light, half-hidden among the boughs. The light reflected off the rear window. Carlin hastened to turn off his light source. It was a maroon colored compact in pretty rundown condition and its presence in that area could only mean one thing. It was certainly not another *trifulau*. A fellow truffle hunter would hardly have parked in that area. He would do what he did. He would leave his car far away from there, in a rest area along the road, so as not to disclose his presence. It was probably a young couple who had gone out of the way in search of that privacy that only darkness and the steamed up windows of a car could provide for adolescents who didn't have the money to be able to afford the comfort of a motel.

He went away trying not to make any sounds. He didn't want to alert them to his presence for a number of very good reasons. The first was that he wasn't keen on being taken for a maniac. A friend of his, a fellow truffle hunter in a similar situation, found himself facing a hefty bruiser who mistook him for a voyeur and gave him a sound beating. All the other reasons decidedly paled compared to the possibility of returning home with two black eyes. At that instant, somewhere to his left, Tabuj began barking furiously.

Strange.

Habit had made him a silent dog, during the truffle search. The dog sensed, in a way that Carlin could not explain to himself, that it was better not to make their presence known. The only sound he allowed himself was the quiet, funny whimper when he scented a truffle under the thick layer of soil. And over time, he had proved to be entirely indifferent to the wild animals that they occasionally encountered during their nocturnal wanderings. An instinct for the chase was not part of his store of talents.

Carlin set off in the direction of the barking, working the button of the flashlight and sending brief flashes of light into the darkness to avoid putting his foot into a hole.

"Shhhhhhh. Be quiet!"

He issued the command in a low voice toward the spot where the barking was coming from, but Tabuj continued his frantic doggery undeterred. When he reached the place where the dog was, he saw him under a tree, barking, turning in circles, pausing only to rise up on his hind legs every so often, his snout pointed up, as if that little acrobatic feat helped him better express his agitation toward something that was above him.

Carlin pointed the beam of the flashlight up above and felt faint. He leaned against the trunk of the tree closest to him and felt his legs go limp, as if there were no more bones inside. A reflux of acid rose to fill and defile his mouth. He struggled to keep down the remains of his supper, which was trying to rise back up the walls of his stomach.

Before him, caught between the light of the moon and that of the flashlight, which vied for the openings between the branches, was the body of a man, hanging by the neck with a rope tied to a sturdy limb.

3

Where until recently there had been darkness, there was now a blaze of lights. The police squad that had arrived on the scene had mounted floodlights that lit up the site as if it were day. Commissioner Marco Capuzzo lit a cigarette. For the moment he was satisfied to remain on the sidelines, observing the spectacle of composure and frenzy which together usually animated the scene of a violent death.

For the moment it was premature to call it a crime scene.

As he watched, the men from the crime lab completed their data collection and began removing the body from the tree, swift shadows caught against the violent glare of the floodlights. From his vantage point he could see the man's face, which was swollen, the wanton open mouth revealing a glimpse of tongue.

The Commissioner turned to Lombardo, the agent who was his close aide and who was standing to his right, like him waiting.

"Who found him?"

Lombardo nodded vaguely towards a spot to the right.

"A *trifolao*."

The Commissioner smiled despite himself. Regardless of his geographically indicative name, Lombardo came from southern Italy, and no matter how many years he'd spent in the north, continued to have an unresolved personal conflict with words in the Piedmontese dialect. Not that it was important but at times, in the past, Lombardo had been a source of very amusing phonetic interpretations.

"He was out with his dog and found him there, hanging that way. He called us right away, with his cell phone. He seems to be a good man and almost dropped dead when he saw this sight in front of him. Bussi is questioning him now."

Capuzzo pointed to the body that had now been placed on a stretcher.

"Do we know who he is?"

"We haven't examined him yet. We were waiting for the crime lab guys to finish up, before going over there. So as not to contaminate the scene."

Capuzzo smiled again, this time with a trace of bitterness. That was CSI language. Agent Lombardo watched too much TV. Still, the Commissioner had to reluctantly admit that sometimes you could learn more from a television series than from the Police Academy. He stubbed out the remaining half of his cigarette and stored it in the empty packet.

So as not to contaminate the scene . . .

He sighed.

"Let's go see who this poor devil was."

They approached the body. Capuzzo pulled on a pair of rubber gloves, and as he bent over the corpse, he had the impression that he had seen the face of that lifeless man on the stretcher before.

Death had altered the features a little, but not enough to prevent this feeling.

He rummaged through the pockets of the leather jacket, then quickly continued his search in the inside pocket.

Nothing.

"Turn him on his side."

Finally he found what he was looking for, a worn leather wallet that was difficult to extract from the pocket of the tattered jeans. Inside there were only a couple of ten euro bills and a creased driver's license. Commissioner Capuzzo unfolded the document, turning it toward the floodlight behind him.

"Lucio Bertolino" he said quietly, with a trace of a question mark at the end of it.

That name and the crumpled face in the photo said something to him. Something that had to do with his work. At that moment he couldn't remember, but if the man had been a previous offender it wouldn't be difficult to find out who and why at a later time.

He was about to straighten up again when a detail attracted his attention. The collar of the dead man's shirt was stained with blood at the back of the neck. He ran a hand through the man's hair and withdrew it smeared with red. He examined the body more carefully and discovered a laceration on the scalp, which seemed to have been caused by a blow inflicted with a blunt instrument. He raised his head to study the branch from which the body had been hanging shortly before. It would have been quite difficult for him to have caused his own death. The corpse had been hanging too far from the tree's trunk and the length of rope was too short to assume that its swaying had sent him banging into the trunk. Capuzzo got up, took off his gloves and relit the cigarette butt that he had slipped into the packet.

He sucked in a mouthful of smoke and for an instant remained lost in thought. If it was true that every policeman harbors an animal instinct, his at that moment had its nose to the ground and was sniffing the scent of trouble.

Lombardo's voice roused him. The aide had remained silent the entire time the body was being examined.

"Parked a little further on is an old Polo. It's probably the car which he used to drive here. We haven't inspected it yet because we were waiting for you."

The Commissioner nodded to show his approval.

"Good. Let's go take a look at the car. Then we'll talk to the crime lab guys to see what they've found. Footprints and such."

As they walked over to the car, Lombardo allowed himself to voice an opinion, perhaps feeling authorized by the Commissioner's silence.

"Of course it's odd that someone would leave Asti and come all the way here just to commit suicide."

The Commissioner seemed to reflect for a moment, as if he couldn't decide whether to compromise himself or not by making a premature assessment.

"I'm not entirely sure that this poor devil really had such a strong desire to die . . ."

He left the sentence hanging for Lombardo to pick up on.

The agent turned toward him, a puzzled expression on his swarthy face. He knew the Commissioner for far too long to know that it was unlike him to make rash assertions.

"What do you mean?"

The Commissioner looked at him with a bitter smile on his lips.

"If you ask me, there was someone with him who *suicided* him, if you'll pardon the expression."

4

Back in his office, Commissioner Capuzzo was going over the summary results of the lab analysis with Superintendent Vanni and Bertone, the director of the crime lab. It was the latter in fact, a young, stocky man whose incipient baldness made him appear older, who was explaining what had emerged from their findings.

"It appears from initial assessments, that the footprints on the ground reveal the presence of a single individual. The soil was quite soft and from a summary examination the prints appear to have been those of the dead man's shoes. They begin at the car and go as far as the tree. There are no footprints of any kind going in the opposite direction, other than those left by the dog and the man who found the body."

"No traces of any kind?"

"Not a one."

The Superintendent stroked his graying whiskers with his fingers. He glanced over somewhat uncomfortably at Capuzzo, who was leaning against his desk, his arms crossed and an impassive expression on his face.

Sensing that he was being watched, he turned and went to the window. He remained silent, gazing at the traffic, practically non-existent at that hour, on Corso XXV Aprile.

The Superintendent continued exchanging information with Bertone.

"So you're saying that the suicide theory remains the most probable."

Bertone, as far as he was concerned, did not burden himself with opinions that went beyond his expertise.

"I'm not saying anything. I'm simply reporting what we found at the scene of the . . ."

He stopped himself an instant before uttering the word "crime", which in itself would have been an expression of a specific opinion.

". . . around the body," he concluded evasively.

"And the head wound?"

"You'll have to talk to the medical examiner to get a more accurate opinion on that. The autopsy will certainly clarify a number of things. As far as we're concerned, we found signs of slipping on the ground along the way and traces of blood and hair on a rock. Probably the dead man fell and struck his head as he was heading for the tree from which he hung himself."

"So it all seems fairly clear. The suicide theory seems the simplest and therefore also the most probable."

Generally this concept, applied to a violent death, never failed to demonstrate a high percentage of reliability.

The Commissioner turned around and spoke up for the first time since Bertone had entered the office.

"Did you measure *how deep* the footprints were on the ground?"

Bertone looked at the Superintendent, embarrassed, almost as if he were seeking his support against an unfair accusation. Then he looked at Capuzzo with a hint of bewilderment.

"Excuse me, in what sense?"

It was clear that he had no idea what the Commissioner was driving at and was going on the defensive. Capuzzo came away from the window and went over to the man he was addressing at that moment.

"I was simply asking you how deep the prints of the dead man's shoes were on the ground."

"Oh, well, I couldn't tell you. But I don't see what . . ."

Capuzzo cut him off with a wave of his hand.

"There's a reason why I'm asking you this. If it weren't for that head wound, everything would be clear enough. Nevertheless there's that detail that I'm not entirely at ease with, despite the signs of slipping, the blood-stained rock and all the rest. Everything seems too simple even."

He paused and then added, maybe only to himself.

"Too simple . . ."

Now both the Superintendent and Bertone watched him in silence, waiting to see what was stirring in the head of that man who was speaking and moving about the room as if they were no longer present.

"Let's formulate a theory, as far-fetched as you like. Far-fetched but not impossible. Let's imagine that the guy gets there accompanied by someone who obviously remains in the car, on the passenger side. Or in the back seat, it doesn't matter. As soon as they stop, this hypothetical passenger knocks Bertolino out with a rock that he's brought with him, and when he's no longer able to react, takes off his shoes and puts them on. He ties a rope around his neck, hoists the body over his shoulder, carries it to the tree and hangs him without any problem. Bertolino had a rather slight build and it would not have been an impossible job for a strapping man. Then, walking backwards in his own footprints, he goes back to the car and gets two pieces of cardboard or something like that. Laying them on the ground, he's able to move about as he pleases without leaving any prints. He stages the bit about slipping, and places the rock he used to strike his victim on the ground. Using the same method he returns to the tree and puts the shoes he had taken off back on the dead man. Still using the cardboard, he goes away, leaving not a trace."

Capuzzo finally looked up at his audience, as if only at that moment did he recall having one.

He directed his gaze at Bertone, catching an astonished expression.

"In your opinion, would all this be possible?"

"Well, in theory, yes. But . . ."

The Commissioner interrupted him again. Quietly and without a trace of authority, but holding firm to his position.

"Fine. If it's possible, I ask that you check to see if the prints left on the ground by the victim's shoes correspond in depth to those left by a man of his weight or if we can theorize that they were left by a man carrying another man on his back. Is it too much to ask?"

For a moment poor Bertone found himself wearing the expression of a man who comes out of the noon Mass on Sunday and realizes he's naked. Then he chose to replace this expression with the faint condescension of someone who knows he's dealing with a whacko.

"All right. We'll check."

Without waiting for anything further, the director of the crime lab took his leave from those present and left the office. He knew that someone in that room had just made a fool of himself. And in any case he didn't want to be there when it was clear who it was.

As soon as the door closed behind him, there was that split second of silence in the air that always precedes significant moments.

Then Superintendent Arnaldo Vanni looked Commissioner Marco Capuzzo right in the eye.

"As I was listening to you speak, a thought came to me."

Capuzzo waited in silence to hear what would come next.

"I suspect that you are not the right person for the position you hold."

Still Capuzzo remained silent, his gaze merely taking on a note of interest.

The Superintendent went straight to the point.

"If what you've just theorized is true, it's not right for you to be merely a Commissioner. You would deserve much more. If it were just a fantasy, in that case too the role of Commissioner would not be right for you . . ."

Arnaldo Vanni, Asti Superintendent, paused for effect. He was a man of the world and knew well how to rouse the attention of those he spoke with.

"You would have all the recognition you deserve as a script writer."

Capuzzo didn't need to come up with a suitable reply. Someone knocked at the door and immediately afterward Lombardo made his entrance into the room. He was surprised by the presence of the Superintendent. He stopped beside the open door, uncertain, a manila folder in his hand.

"I'm sorry, I didn't . . ."

"It's all right, Lombardo. What is it?"

"I have the file on that Lucio Bertolino. He has prior convictions."

Capuzzo held out his hand to the agent.

"Let me see."

The agent crossed the room and handed the Commissioner the folder he had in his hand. Capuzzo opened it and briefly scanned the contents. Then he pulled out a page and read it with particular attention.

"That's why I thought I knew him."

"What do you mean?"

Capuzzo raised his eyes to the Superintendent. He looked at him but it was clear that his mind was already elsewhere.

"I mean that in addition to the matter of the prints, there's another curious thing to note about this Bertolino."

Intentional or not, his pause was much more effective than that of the Superintendent a short while ago.

"It's not so much about how he died, but *where* he died."

5

From his balcony window, Mario Savelli stood gazing out at the small piazza below his house. Piazza Medici was certainly one of the most beautiful spots in Asti's historic center. All the houses were of the same period, restored as they should be to keep them that way. Nothing was out of place. To his right was a red brick tower constructed in the period between the thirteenth and fourteenth century, which gave the overall scene a noteworthy aspect. There was a time when he had stood at that balcony accompanied by his wife and son and together they had lovingly looked out at that small panorama inscribed between the walls that enclosed the city's rooftops above.

Then cancer had taken his wife away, and his son . . .

He came away from the window, which connected the balcony to a room that was at the same time a library and TV room. He moved into the adjoining room, a much larger living room whose prominent feature was a shiny black Steinway grand piano. He shifted the stool and sat down. He waited a moment before opening the lid that encased the keys like a coffer. Savelli liked that image. The ivory and black like precious jewels from which sprang, depending on skill and mastery, that great gift to mankind that was music.

When he was young he had been part of a band, a a combo, as they called them then. Then without any regrets he had abandoned his career as a musician for the more levelheaded one of banker. He knew he did not possess the talent necessary to go beyond local circles, but his passion, without any frustration, had remained. When the opportunity arose, he bought that piano as a tribute to a career he had never had and played for anyone who cared to listen to him, or just for himself.

Like now.

He played an ascending scale as if to check the tuning. He arranged the score of "Rhapsody in Blue" on the stand in front of him. He had just placed his hands on the keyboard when he heard the doorbell ring.

In advance of the housekeeper, he went to open the door himself. Another ring. It was an inconsequential sound, normal, everyday. But, when he found the vigorous figure of Commissioner Capuzzo framed in the doorway, he knew immediately that this was not a day like any other.

"Good day, Mr Savelli."

"Good day, Commissioner."

Between them lay the silence of words not spoken, concealed within the clamor of all the words they had been forced to say at one time.

"I need to speak with you a moment. May I come in?"

"Of course."

Savelli stepped aside. The Commissioner came in and took a look around without seeming to. The house was as he remembered it, the house he had once entered in very painful circumstances. Elegant, substantial, luminous. Furnished with the warmth that only affluence and good taste together with love could provide.

He took off the jacket he was wearing and Savelli hung it on the coat rack opposite the entrance. Then he followed his host along the corridor to the room where he had been at a time both of them would rather forget. Savelli took a seat in a leather armchair with the window behind him. He gestured Capuzzo toward the chair opposite him.

"Please, sit down."

The Commissioner sat down and didn't think he should beat around the bush. He knew what kind of person he was dealing with and didn't consider it necessary.

"Lucio Bertolino is dead."

Against his will he found himself emphasizing the words more than he should. And watching for the other man's reaction more closely than he would have liked.

Savelli remained impassive. As if the news weren't just hours or days old, but years.

"I know. I heard it on the news report."

He paused as if undecided whether or not to add something more. Then he decided that the answer to his interior question was yes.

"I can't say I'm sorry about it."

The Commissioner kept silent. Even if the man hadn't said it, he was certain that would be how he felt.

"How did he die?"

"A truffle hunter found him hung from a tree."

"Suicide?"

"It would seem so. We're not one hundred per cent sure."

Capuzzo gave Savelli time to consider this. To realize, while savoring and appreciating the fact, that in either case a kind of justice had intervened, be it human or divine.

"Did he suffer?"

"I don't know."

"If he didn't suffer, I'm sorry to hear it. If he did suffer, I'm sorry he didn't suffer more." Capuzzo ignored this merciless epitaph. He had heard others over the course of his career. They were the voices of people who no matter how much time had passed would never leave behind one iota of pain, victims of memory as well as of violence and circumstances. He changed the subject and his tone.

"I didn't feel it was necessary to summon you to Police Headquarters, but this meeting between the two of us had to take place somewhere. I think you understand me."

Mario Savelli nodded his head imperceptibly. He added words that weren't needed.

"Of course. I understand."

"So then, I don't think you will have any problem telling me where you were last night, say between nine and midnight."

"No problem at all. Would you like some coffee?"

The Commissioner did not take the question as a diversionary tactic, a brief interval to put off the moment of having to respond. He took it as a small fulfillment of a desire. He could really use some coffee.

"Sure."

A Filipino woman materialized at the door, as if evoked by the mere word "coffee".

"Ghita, will you make us two espressos, please?"

As if by tacit accord, they remained silent, each absorbed in his own thoughts, until the housekeeper returned carrying a tray with two demitasse cups. She set the tray down in front of them and went away in silence, gliding soundlessly on the cloth slippers she was wearing.

When the Commissioner raised his cup, Savelli finally spoke.

"My day was extremely simple yesterday. I arrived from Turin by train in the late afternoon. I would guess toward evening. Since the last time we saw each other, a few things have changed. Now they say that I've become a rather important manager of my institution and I work in Turin."

Capuzzo understood that there was no egotism behind those words. Only a trace of bitter self-irony, to hide the distress of a man who felt he had lost everything that was worth living for. And who had thrown himself into his work to delude himself that his life still had purpose.

"I didn't feel like moving. I chose to commute. My life, my friends, my attachments are all here."

He did not say "My wife and my son are buried here" but the Commissioner had the distinct impression that he was able to read those words in the mind of the man sitting before him. A man who calmly continued his account of what they both knew very well to be the statement of an alibi.

"I got home and took a shower. I played the piano for half an hour, as I do every evening."

Savelli gestured toward the instrument that could be seen through the door. The Commissioner remembered noticing it earlier, at the time of his previous visit. Music must be a genuine passion for that man, at one time perhaps a reason for the family to gather together, now a refuge certainly from solitude.

"At eight-thirty I went out and from eight-forty-five until past midnight I was at a meeting of the Palio Committee of San Silvestro. When we were through, we went to Francese's for a pizza. We stayed late because we started tasting some wine he recommended and to be honest when I got home I was slightly intoxicated. But not to the point of not being able to remember that I did not kill Lucio Bertolino."

Savelli finally allowed himself a pause to drink his coffee. He uttered his next remark an instant before bringing the cup to his lips.

"Even though I would really have liked to be the one to do it."

Capuzzo knew that Mario Savelli was a lonely man. And now that justice had been done, in one way or another, perhaps he would be even more alone.

"Commissioner, I understand. I mean, I understand the reason why you came to see me. I had a more than valid motive to hang that bastard from a tree, not once but a hundred times."

He paused, enough to clear his mind. He had probably pursued that thought as a much more concrete plan numerous times in the past.

Savelli roused himself and set the cup on the tray with a faint clink of china. He rested against the back of the armchair. He stared once more into the eyes of the police officer with whom he was now speaking as if to a friend.

"You see, Commissioner Capuzzo, I've always been a guarantist of the law, a fervent upholder of the principle that it's better to have a guilty man go free than put an innocent man in prison. At present however we have gradually lapsed into the theater of the absurd. Everyone is so concerned that no one touches Cain, forgetting an important thing."

Another pause. Cold as a tombstone.

"Justice for Abel."

The Commissioner looked at his hands a moment, before replying.

"Speaking of which, there's an odd detail that perhaps the news reports did not mention. I don't know if it was a coincidence or not, but Lucio Bertolino was found hung a few hundred yards from the curve where your son died four years ago."

Capuzzo would never be entirely certain of it, but for an instant he had the distinct impression of having seen the fleeting suggestion of a smile in the other man's eyes.

6

The Commissioner found himself back in Piazza Medici with a bit of confusion in his head. It was the confusion that always clogged the thoughts of a policeman engaged in pursuing a slippery hunch.

The evening before, reading through the file on Lucio Bertolino, an old matter had turned up, one which had led him to the interrogation he had just concluded. That dubious individual had always been a local felon, a figure who was more sleazy than criminal. The small stuff of suspended sentences, petty theft, charges of harassment by women who wanted nothing to do with him and his pressing attentions. And judging from his physical looks, no one could blame them. All in all a character much more suitable for intence psychiatric observation than for detention in a penal institution. In fact he had never been convicted of anything serious, until he decided to attempt a big leap, to make his entrance into the world of real criminals.

Almost four years ago, with two accomplices, desperate delinquents like him, he had attempted to rob a post office in a town near Asti. They were fleeing after having snatched some small change, and after a few kilometers, because of their speed, the driver lost control of the car as they entered a curve. And struck a car, head-on, that was coming in the opposite direction.

The driver of the other car died instantly. He was twenty years old and his name was Paolo Savelli. The son of the man he had just finished speaking with.

That death caused quite a sensation because the boy, a brilliant physics student, was a promising young man in the world of science and culture, and not just nationally. Bertolino availed himself of summary procedure and his lawyer, through plea bargaining and clemency, managed to get him off with just under three years.

Once again the Commissioner was forced to recognize the incredible irony of life. There was every likelihood that, if he were still in jail, the guy would still be alive now. From there, his thoughts returned to the man he had just left. He didn't know if Mario Savelli was a believer or not. If not, even if he wasn't convinced that the ways of the Lord are infinite, he must certainly be thinking that at times they can be infinitely winding.

He lit a cigarette and started across the piazza. Lombardo had parked the police car on the other side, in front of a bar in the shade of the tower overlooking the square.

His cell phone rang someplace, who knows where, in his heavy jacket. After repeatedly looking for it in the wrong pocket, he finally managed to find it and bring it to his ear.

"Capuzzo."

From the other end came the voice of the director of the crime lab. They all called it that, though Asti's police department lacked the adequate equipment to perform sophisticated analyses, for which they had to rely on other labs.

"Commissioner?"

"Yes."

"It's Bertone. We did the computations you asked for and I think your theory is more than plausible."

"In what sense?"

"In the sense that the depth of the footprints is excessive for a man of that weight. We are still verifying the data and I can't be more precise than that, but I think your observation was correct."

There was enough embarrassment in that voice to be in itself synonymous with atonement. The Commissioner did not consider it necessary to hit a man when he was down.

"All right. Let me know as soon as possible."

He had the impression that Bertone was ending that conversation with a certain relief.

"I will."

With an interior smile that was not without some satisfaction, Commissioner Capuzzo put the phone back in his pocket. He thought back to the words of the Superintendent. Now that it was no longer necessary to imagine a career as a script writer, he was curious to find out what life and his fellow man would propose as an alternative.

If, as it seemed, his theory wasn't based on thin air, there had been another man in the car with Lucio Bertolino the evening before. A man strong enough to carry him on his back from the car to the tree. That man certainly could not be Savelli, who definitely did not have the physique to accomplish such an endeavor. He was a rather thin man, with a delicate look: pale skin and slender fingers that gave the impression they might fracture at any moment. Much more suited to gliding along the keyboard of a piano than to tying a rope around a man's neck. Besides which, he could certainly not be described as being in his prime.

Capuzzo really couldn't see him performing such a strenuous task.

Of course, he might have hired a hit man to do it for him. But those were people in the trade, professionals, men with no scruples and no refinement. Maximum results with a minimum of effort. They show up, fire a shot to the head and off they go, making no concession to a creativity that they certainly do not possess. Then too, experience had taught him that when ordinary individuals get mixed up with certain people, they act so badly that they leave traces that are more obvious than a plane's vapor trail in the sky. They would investigate Savelli along those lines, though without a valid motive to substantiate this theory, Capuzzo was certain that nothing would come of it.

He joined Lombardo, who seeing him coming opened the door and got behind the wheel.

He waited for Capuzzo to get in beside him before speaking.

"I just talked to Bussi. There are new developments."

"What kind of developments?"

"They searched the Sloth's house."

"Who?"

"That Bertolino. A pal told us that they pinned that nickname on him in jail.

Thinking about those features, the receding chin and protruding eyes, Capuzzo decided that whoever had given him that nickname must be someone who had a good sense of humor. Evidently Lombardo was insensible to such considerations. He went on with his account of the facts.

"They found hash and heroin, concealed in a waterproof box in the toilet tank."

"Our friend must have decided to join the big leagues."

"Seems so."

"Okay. Then I'd say that to find out who killed him, we have to look in that direction."

Without any hurry . . .

The Commissioner added this mental note for his own benefit.

As the car went around the monument in the center of the piazza, Capuzzo fastened his seat belt and looked up at the balcony of Savelli's apartment. He thought he saw him standing behind the glass door, watching the car as it drove away. Then the sun's reflection turned the window into a luminous splotch and the Commissioner wondered if it hadn't been just his impression.

He found himself thinking that, without dragging the Lord into it, life sometimes closes its accounts in mysterious ways. In the case of banker Mario Savelli and his son Paolo, who died through no fault of his own except for being in the wrong place at the wrong time, justice had been done.

Abel had had his vengeance.

7

From above Mario Savelli watched the police car leave the piazza and then moved away from the window. He liked that man, Commissioner Capuzzo. He was a policeman but he was also a human being. He had understood that at the time of their first meeting when the Commissioner came to his house and informed him that his son Paolo was dead. That earlier impression had been confirmed by what had just taken place.

He loved his job of course but he was not possessed by it. He was a fair, sensitive man. Savelli knew all too well how much such a man was needed given the period that rotten world was going through.

"I am going now, Mr Savelli."

Ghita's voice surprised him from behind. He turned and saw her standing in the corridor, in front of the kitchen door. She was wearing her coat and scarf and was ready to leave.

"Of course. See you tomorrow."

His housekeeper had asked for the afternoon off to go and see a fellow countrywoman who was visiting relatives in Alessandria; they had all emigrated to Italy where they had found work and were trying to build a life.

He had willingly given her the time off. It was Saturday and the thought of being alone in the house was a pleasant one.

"I left you something to eat in the refrigerator. If you decide to eat at home, all you have to do is heat it up. Good afternoon, Mr Savelli."

She was a woman who was no longer young but had the shy smile of a young girl. She had been with him for several years and Savelli had never had any reason to regret hiring her. He watched her as she went to the door at the end of the hall, opened it and left the apartment. He waited for the sound of the elevator reaching their floor and only when he heard it go back down did he go toward his study.

There was no reason to be relieved by temporarily being the complete master of his house. Ghita was an invisible, discreet presence, and besides, all he had to do was lock himself in his study to have all the privacy he felt he needed.

Nevertheless, today was a special day.

An unusual circumstance for an equally unusual occasion.

He reached the room which many years earlier he had chosen as his personal domain, before the requirements of Paolo's studies grew to the point that he had to share it with him. From that time on it had become "their" study, something that bound them over and above affection, consanguinity and cohabitation. A place where each of them could find traces of the other, when one of them occupied it.

Now it was his personal study again. Mario Savelli had always thought that this would happen one day, when his son got married or left home to build a life of his own. But that room had become his exclusive property again in the most terrible way. And he had paid for it with days of tears and nights with eyes wide open in the dark, waiting for sleep which never came.

He went determinedly towards a painting depicting a still life, hanging opposite the door.

He turned it on lateral hinges and revealed the hidden safe.

They had laughed about it, at the time, he and his wife. They had joked for days about the predictability of disguising a safe with a painting. They had spent hours going over various alternatives but, all the same, in the end they were unable to come up with a better solution.

And the painting had remained.

As he dialed the combination, he could visualize Lorenza's

face. Her smiling face as a young girl and the racked face of an ailing woman. How much pain he had experienced, attending her day after day during the course of the tumor that literally devoured her in six months. And how much he had envied her afterwards.

Because she had been fortunate enough to die without having to suffer the agony of outliving her son . . .

He opened the door of the safe and took out a dark oilskin box. He went and placed it on top of the desk and sat down. He turned on the table lamp and when he lifted the lid, he found before him an object wrapped in a beige cloth. He took it out, moved the box aside and laid the bundle on the leather desktop in front of him.

He unwrapped it gently and revealed its contents to the light. As if seeing it for the first time, he stood staring a moment at a splendid example of a Luger, the pistol issued to German officers during the Second World War.

It had belonged to his father, who had never revealed how and under what circumstances he had obtained it. He had shown it to him when he was old enough to understand the sinister importance of that object. Mario knew that it had not been reported, that the pistol was kept in a particularly unlawful way, since apart from everything else it was a weapon of war. Nevertheless, it had remained in the house, a little secret to be shared between father and son, the sole incursion into misconduct on the part of a family of adamantine honesty.

His father had taught him to disassemble and reassemble it, he had taught him the right way to oil it and maintain it in perfect working order. And in all those years he had continued to do so, more out of tradition than necessity. And he would have taught his son Paolo to do so as well, if what happened had not happened. He didn't know when the pistol had last been fired. But now it was about to be fired again and Mario Savelli was certain that it would not betray him.

He began disassembling the firearm, calmly and deftly. As he did so, his hands moved of their own accord, guided by the threads of experience. He had time to go over that strange story, in his memory, from the beginning to what would soon be its end.

8

It had begun two years before.

He had gone to Capri for an important Credit Institutions conference. A lot of smoke and mirrors, but, in the end, the usual things. Training seminars for young executives and managers, prominent speakers on this or that subject, positioning in new and old markets, indications of new and old strategies.

And only on the last day a meeting of high-level European managers, concerning one of those extremely secret interbank agreements, the kind that are discussed behind closed doors, which the public is unaware of but which determine the future of a segment of the economy, the one linked to disbursement and the cost of money.

Savelli had gone there as a promotion, his first real prestigious assignment, his official entry into the world of high finance. Then that Tower of Babel had found the common language of food and drink and everyone assembled for the traditional end-of-conference reception, in the banquet room of what was one of the most sumptuous hotels on the island. A five-star deluxe convention center large enough to accommodate everyone, with a splendid view of the sea. But no room was luxurious enough to make him forget that it was still a hotel room.

And that he was occupying it alone.

Mario Savelli left the reception hall and went outside. He was able to take part in everything that concerned his work, but he had always had a kind of idiosyncratic aversion to forced cheerfulness, for what in his own mind he called "The New Year's eve syndrome", being sentenced to prescribed merriment.

He walked along the pool and was leaning against the wall that surrounded it, captivated by the eternal spectacle of the full moon on the sea.

The sound of a match, the spark of a flame and the smoke of a cigarette signaled a presence at his side. Then the man leaned against the wall a few yards away from him, the red glow of his cigarette occasionally interrupting the silver gleam of the moon.

For a time they remained that way without speaking, as if mesmerized by the panorama.

Then the man broke the silence, speaking in a very low voice, almost as if fearful that too loud a tone might break the spell.

"Beautiful, isn't it?"

"Exquisite."

The man approached and held out his hand. Standing with his back almost against the balustrade, his face was hidden in shadow.

"Pleased to meet you. I'm Alberto Medori."

Savelli too held out his hand.

"My pleasure. "I'm . . ."

"Mario Savelli" the other man concluded for him. "I know who you are, I know all about you."

He gazed back toward the sea and his profile turned to silver again.

"And not just about your professional skills. This is, after all, a small circle. Successes, as well as failures, get around. And apparently you have had very few of the latter."

Savelli observed the man more closely: strong build, taller than he, with slightly coarse features outlined in the moonlight as if by the stroke of a pen. The man went on speaking, giving him the strange impression that he had prepared his speech at length.

"You and I have something tragic in common, Mr Savelli. Something that just as tragically keeps our hands tied. And if you agree, we can untie them for one another. And find some peace. If you'll allow me a few minutes I will explain what I'm referring to . . ."

9

Mario Savelli finished reassembling the pistol. He wiped off the non-existent dust for the umpteenth time, dabbed away the excess oil, checked the release on the safety lock, and inserted the cartridges in the magazine. Then he slid it into the gun butt and heard it click into place with a sharp, metallic sound. That was the pistol's voice, it was a mechanical and impersonal way for the weapon to confirm to him "I'm ready".

He wrapped the Luger in the cloth again, placed it back in the box and went to lock it up in the safe.

That evening two years ago, when he sat down at a well-lit table with Alberto Medori and was able to get a good look at his face, he recognized the man immediately. Barely a year earlier he had appeared on the various news broadcasts a number of times, the unwilling protagonist of a tragic news item. For a time it was a popular face, he had been a guest numerous times on several talk shows, a symbol of a justice that is not fully attainable. Then gradually he was hidden away by the media in that limbo where little by little everything becomes naught.

The event that had brought him celebrity was tragically similar to Savelli's.

His mother and his eight-year-old daughter had been struck and killed by a hit-and-run driver in Salerno, where he lived. The story had a certain scathing, chilling predictability. The driver had decided to get behind the wheel of his car after having one too many and smoking a number of joints with his buddies. He hit the woman and girl who were walking on the side of the road, panicked and fled.

After a brief investigation, he was identified and arrested. Afterward, the course of events was very similar to that which attended the judicial proceedings of Lucio Bertolino.

Essentially, he would get off with little time. Savelli recalled the expression on Medori's face perfectly.

"There are things that come and go, because we're human and we manage to forget. There are others that never fade. For the same reason. Because we're human and *don't want* to forget."

At that moment Mario Savelli realized that it was like that for him too. Despite the passing of time, the pain and anger had not diminished. The pain was disguised by throwing himself headlong into his work. The anger was an inexhaustible fuel that kept him going day to day, more so than the food he ate and the water he drank.

Alberto Medori had looked into his eyes as he uttered the words that would bind them together for all time.

"I know your story, Mr Savelli. I know that you are a decent man. And so am I. However, there are cases where this can and should be of secondary consideration, compared to the enormity of lives shattered without reparation. I know that no act of justice can bring my mother and daughter back to me. Just as nothing can bring back your son. Still, there might be some relief in knowing that everything was resolved in accordance with the rules that distinguish the innocent from the guilty."

He paused. Then he went on in his faint accent that recalled the inflection of the south. His eyes were brimming with tears.

"And I, if I can't have justice, am prepared to settle for vengeance."

For a moment silence descended upon them with the same effect as the moonlight. Then they talked throughout the night, and in the end they made a pact. Savelli had been amazed at his own readiness, as if that encounter had suddenly yanked off a blanket that was too short, revealing his restless sleep. He had been amazed at the serenity with which he had found it all quite natural, just as he had found it natural a short time before to slide a magazine of bullets into the butt of an old pistol.

Since that time, he and Alberto Medori had not seen or talked to each other again. Their only communications took place the old-fashioned way, by letters written strictly by hand and immediately destroyed upon being read. No e-mails, no cell phones, no computers: all things which left behind traces as obvious as a snail trail.

They had made careful preparations, and when Savelli learned of the death of Lucio Bertolino, he understood that the other man had kept his promise, his part of the bargain. He knew that Medori had gone to Asti by train and that he had left there by train without staying in a hotel or taking a taxi. Undoubtedly he had gotten around using public transportation, an anonymous face among so many others. He had arrived and departed the same way, leaving behind vengeance after having tried in vain to obtain justice.

Exactly what he would do, once he got to Salerno.

A crime for a crime, he told himself.

Just as Hitchcock, and a shared passion for films, had taught them. If at times reality became a film, this time a film would become reality . . .

He left the study and walked through a house flooded by the sunlight of that strangely warm autumn. Its luminosity was one of the reasons why he and his wife had chosen this apartment. He felt a pang in his heart remembering that Lorenza, citing Quasimodo, had described it as being "impaled upon a ray of sun".

Never imagining that it would suddenly be night.

He returned to the French door, opened it and went out on the balcony. Once again he found himself observing the comings and goings of the cars and people in the piazza. People who confronted their everyday lives never imagining the heedlessness with which fate could shatter them. Children who would one day grow up and become men, something which his son had been denied.

He stood there for a long time, reflecting on these and other thoughts.

Then he left the sunny balcony and went back to the shadows, as every man does when he's made his decision.

Translation © 2009 by Anne Milano Appel

Rumpole and the Christmas Break

John Mortimer

I

"We must be constantly on guard. Night and day. Vigilance is essential. I'm sure you would agree, wouldn't you, Luci?"

Soapy Sam Ballard, our always-nervous Head of Chambers, addressed the meeting as though the forces of evil were already beating on the doors of 4 Equity Court, and weapons of mass destruction had laid waste to the dining hall, condemning us to a long winter of cold meat and sandwiches. As usual, he longed for confirmation and turned to our recently appointed Head of Marketing and Administration, who was now responsible for the Chambers' image.

"Quite right, Chair." Luci's north country voice sounded quietly amused, as though she didn't take the alarming state of the world quite as seriously as Ballard did.

"Thank you for your contribution, Luci." Soapy Sam, it seemed, thought she might have gone a little further, such as recommending that Securicor mount a twenty-four hour guard on the Head of Chambers. Then he added, in a voice of doom, "I have already asked our clerk to keep an extremely sharp eye on the sugar kept in the coffee cupboard."

"Why did you do that?" I ventured to ask our leader. "Has Claude been shovelling it in by the tablespoonful?"

Claude Erskine-Brown was one of the few barristers I have ever met who combined a passionate affection for Wagner's operas with a remarkably sweet tooth, continuously sucking wine gums in court and loading his coffee with heaped spoonfuls of sugar.

"It's not that, Rumpole." Soapy Sam was getting petulant. "It's anthrax."

"What anthrax?"

"The sugar might be. There are undoubtedly people out there who are out to get us, Rumpole. Haven't you been listening at all to government warnings?"

"I seem to remember them telling us one day that if we went down the tube we'd all be gassed, and the next day they said, 'Sorry, we were only joking. Carry on going down the tube.' "

"Rumpole! Do you take nothing seriously?"

"Some things," I assured Soapy Sam. "But not the government."

"We are," here Ballard ignored me as an apparently hopeless case, and addressed the meeting, "especially vulnerable."

"Why's that?" I was curious enough to ask.

"We represent the Law, Rumpole. The centre of a civilized society. Naturally we'd be high on their hit list."

"You mean the Houses of Parliament, Buckingham Palace, and number 4 Equity Court? I wonder, you may be right."

"I propose to appoint a small Chambers emergency committee consisting of myself, Claude Erskine-Brown, and Archie Prosser. Please report to one of us if you notice anything unusual or out of the ordinary. I assume you have nothing to report, Rumpole?"

"Nothing much. I did notice a chap on the tube, a fellow of Middle Eastern appearance wearing a turban and a beard and muttering into a Dictaphone. He got out at South Kensington. I don't suppose it's important."

Just for a moment I thought, indeed I hoped, our Head of Chambers looked at me as though he believed what I had said, but then justifiable doubt overcame him.

"Very funny," Ballard told the meeting. "But then you can scarcely afford to be serious about the danger we're all in, can you Rumpole? Considering you're defending one of these maniacs."

"Rumpole would defend anyone," said Archie Prosser, the newest arrival in our chambers, who had an ill-deserved reputation as a wit.

"If you mean anyone who's put on trial and tells me they're innocent, then the answer is yes."

Nothing alarming happened on the tube on my way home that evening, except for the fact that, owing to a "work to rule" by the drivers, the train gave up work at Victoria and I had to walk the rest of the way home to Froxbury Mansions in the Gloucester Road. The shops and their windows were full of glitter, artificial snow, and wax models perched on sleighs wearing party dresses. Taped carols came tinkling out of Tesco's. The Chambers meeting had been the last of the term, and the Old Bailey had interrupted its business for the season of peace and goodwill.

There was very little of either in the case which I had been doing in front of the aptly named Mr Justice Graves. Mind you, I would have had a fairly rough ride before the most reasonable of judges. Even some compassionate old darlings like Mr Justice "Pussy" Proudfoot might have regarded my client with something like horror and been tempted to dismiss my speech to the jury as a hopeless attempt to prevent a certain conviction and a probable sentence of not less than thirty years. The murder we had been considering, when we were interrupted by Christmas, had been cold-blooded and merciless, and there was clear evidence that it had been the work of a religious fanatic.

The victim, Honoria Glossop, Professor of Comparative Religions at William Morris University in east London, had been the author of a number of books, including her latest, and last, publication *Sanctified Killing – A History of Religious Warfare*. She had been severely critical of all acts of violence and aggression – including the Inquisition and the Crusades – committed in the name of God. She had also included a chapter on Islam which spoke scathingly of some Ayatollahs and the cruelties committed by Islamic fundamentalists.

It was this chapter which had caused my client, a young student of computer technology at William Morris named Hussein Khan, to issue a private fatwa. He composed, on one of the university computers, a letter to Professor Glossop announcing that her blasphemous references to the religious leaders of his country deserved nothing less than death – which would inevitably catch up with her. Then he left the letter in her pigeonhole.

It took very little time for the authorship of the letter to be discovered. Hussein Khan was sent down from William Morris and began spending time helping his family in the Star of Persia restaurant they ran in Golders Green. A week later, Professor Glossop, who had been working late in her office at the university, was found slumped across her desk, having been shot at close quarters by a bullet from a revolver of Czech origins, the sort of weapon which is readily and cheaply available in certain south London pubs. Beside her on the desk, now stained with her blood, was the letter containing the sentence of death.

Honoria and her husband Richard "Ricky" Glossop lived in what the estate agents would describe as "a three-million-pound townhouse in Boltons". The professor had, it seemed, inherited a great deal of money from a family business in the Midlands which allowed her to pursue her academic career, and Ricky to devote his life to country sports, without the need for gainful employment. He was clearly, from his photograph in the papers, an outstandingly handsome figure, perhaps five or six years younger than his wife. After her murder, he received, and everyone felt deserved, huge public sympathy. He and Honoria had met when they were both guests on a yacht touring the Greek Islands, and she had chosen him and his good looks in preference to all the available professors and academic authors she knew. In spite of their differences in age and interest, they seemed to have lived happily together for ten years until, so the prosecution said, death overtook Honoria Glossop in the person of my now universally hated client.

Such was the case I was engaged in at the Old Bailey in the run-up to Christmas. There were no tidings of great joy to report. The cards were stacked dead against me, and at every stage it looked like I was losing, trumped by a judge who regarded defence barristers as flies on the tasty dish of justice.

Mr Justice Graves, known to me only as "The Old Gravestone", had a deep, sepulchral voice and the general appearance of a man waking up with an upset stomach on a wet weekend. He had clearly come to the conclusion that the world was full of irredeemable sinners. The nearest thing to a smile I had seen on the face of The Old Gravestone was the look of grim delight he had displayed when, after a difficult case, the jury had come back with the guilty verdict he had clearly longed for.

So, as you can imagine, the atmosphere in Court One at the Old Bailey during the trial of the Queen against Hussein Khan was about as warm as the South Pole during a blizzard. The Queen may have adopted a fairly detached attitude towards my client, but the judge certainly hadn't.

The prosecution was in the not altogether capable hands of Soapy Sam Ballard, which was why he had practically named me as a founding member of Al-Qaeda at our chambers meeting. His junior was the newcomer Archie Prosser.

These two might not have been the most deadly optimists I had ever had to face during my long career at the bar, but a first-year law student with a lowish IQ would, I thought, have had little difficulty in securing a conviction against the young student who had managed to become one of the most hated men in England.

As he was brought up from the cells and placed in the dock between two prison officers, the jury took one brief, appalled look at him and then turned their eyes on what seemed to them to be the less offensive figure of Soapy Sam as he prepared to open his devastating case.

So I sat at my end of counsel's benches. The brief had been offered to several QCs (Queer Customers I always call them), but they had excused themselves as being too busy, or unwell, or going on holiday – any excuse to avoid being cast as leading counsel for the forces of evil. It was only, it seemed, Rumpole who stuck to the old-fashioned belief that the most outrageous sinner deserves to have his defence, if he had one, put fairly and squarely in front of a jury.

Mr Justice Gravestone didn't share my views. When Ballard rose he was greeted with something almost like a smile from the bench, and his most obvious comments were underlined by a judicious nod followed by a careful note underlined in the judicial notebook. Every time I rose to cross-examine a prosecution witness, however, Graves sighed heavily and laid down his pencil as though nothing of any significance was likely to come.

This happened when I had a few pertinent questions to ask the pathologist, my old friend Professor Arthur Ackerman, forensic scientist and master of the morgues. After he had given his evidence about the cause of death (pretty obvious), I started off.

"You say, Professor Ackerman, that the shot was fired at close quarters?"

"Yes, Mr Rumpole. Indeed it was." Ackerman and I had been through so many bloodstained cases together that we chatted across the court like old friends.

"You told us," I went on, "that the bullet entered the deceased's neck – she was probably shot from behind – and that, among other things, the bullet severed an artery."

"That is so."

"So, as a result, blood spurted over the desk. We know it was on the letter. Would you have expected the person, whoever it was, who shot her at close quarters to have had some blood on his clothing?"

"I think that well may have happened."

"Would you say it probably happened?"

"Probably. Yes."

When I got this answer from the witness, I stood awhile in silence, looking at the motionless judge.

"Is that all you have to ask, Mr Rumpole?"

"No, my Lord. I'm waiting so your Lordship has time to make note of the evidence. I see your Lordship's pencil is taking a rest!"

"I'm sure the jury has heard your questions, Mr Rumpole. And the answers."

"I'm sure they have and you will no doubt remind them of that during your summing up. So I'm sure your Lordship will wish to make a note."

Gravestone, with an ill grace, picked up his pencil and made the shortest possible note. Then I asked Ackerman my last question.

"And I take it you know that the clothes my client wore that evening were minutely examined and no traces of any bloodstains were found?"

"My Lord, how can this witness know what was on Khan's clothing?" Soapy Sam objected.

"Quite right, Mr Ballard," the judge was quick to agree. "That was an outrageous question, Mr Rumpole. The jury will disregard it."

It got no better. I rose, at the end of a long day in court, to cross-examine Superintendent Gregory, the perfectly decent officer in charge of the case.

"My client, Mr Khan, made no secret of the fact that he had written this threatening letter, did he, Superintendent Gregory?"

"He did not, my Lord," Gregory answered with obvious satisfaction.

"In fact," said Mr Justice Graves, searching among his notes, "the witness Sadiq told us that your client boasted to him of the fact in the university canteen?"

There, at last, The Gravestone had overstepped the mark.

"He didn't say 'boasted'."

Soapy Sam Ballard QC, the alleged Head of our Chambers, got up with his notebook at the ready.

"Sadiq said that Khan told him he had written the letter and, in answer to your Lordship, that 'he seemed to feel no sort of guilt about it'."

"There you are Mr Rumpole." Graves also seemed to feel no sort of guilt. "Doesn't that come to exactly the same thing?"

"Certainly not, my Lord. The word 'boasted' was never used."

"The jury may come to the conclusion that it amounted to boasting."

"They may indeed, my Lord. But that's for them to decide, without directions from your Lordship."

"Mr Rumpole," here the judge adopted an expression of lofty pity, "I realize you have many difficulties in this case. But perhaps we may proceed without further argument. Have you any more questions for this officer?"

"Just one, my Lord." I turned to the superintendent. "This letter was traced to one of the university word processors."

"That is so, yes."

"You would agree that my client took no steps at all to cover up the fact that he was the author of this outrageous threat."

"He seems to have been quite open about it, yes."

"That's hardly consistent with the behaviour of someone about to commit a brutal murder is it?"

"I suppose it was a little surprising, yes," Jack Gregory was fair enough to admit.

"Very surprising, isn't it? And of course by the time this murder took place, everyone knew he had written the letter. He'd been sent down for doing so."

"That's right."

The Gravestone intervened. "Did it not occur to you, Superintendent Gregory, that being sent down might have provided an additional motive for the murder?" The judge clearly thought he was onto something, and was deeply gratified when the superintendent answered. "That might have been so, my Lord."

"That might have been so," Graves dictated to himself as he wrote the answer down. Then he thought of another point that might be of use to the hardly struggling prosecution.

"Of course, if a man thinks he's justified, for religious or moral reasons, in killing someone, he might have no inhibitions about boasting of the fact?"

I knew it. Soapy Sam must have known it, and the jury had better be told it. The judge had gone too far. I rose to my feet, as quickly as my weight and the passage of the years would allow, and uttered a sharp protest.

"My Lord, the prosecution is in the able hands of Samuel Ballard QC. I'm sure he can manage to present the case against my client without your Lordship's continued help and encouragement."

This was followed by a terrible silence, the sort of stillness that precedes a storm.

"Mr Rumpole." His Lordship's words were as warm as hailstones. "That was a most outrageous remark."

"It was a point I felt I should make," I told him, "in fairness to my client."

"As I have said, I realize you have an extremely difficult case to argue, Mr Rumpole." Once more Graves was reminding the jury that I was on a certain loser. "But I cannot overlook your inappropriate and disrespectful behaviour towards the court. I shall have to consider whether your conduct should be reported to the proper authority."

After these dire remarks and a few more unimportant questions to the superintendent, Graves turned to the jury and reminded them that this no doubt painful and shocking case would be resumed after the Christmas break. He said this in the solemn and sympathetic tones of someone announcing the death of a dear friend or relative, then he wished them a "Happy Christmas".

The tube train for home was packed and I stood, swaying uneasily, sandwiched between an eighteen-stone man in a donkey jacket with a heavy cold, and an elderly woman with a pair of the sharpest elbows I have encountered on the Circle line.

No doubt all of the other passengers had hard, perhaps unrewarding lives, but they didn't have to spend their days acting as a sort of buffer between a possibly fatal fanatic and a hostile judge who certainly wanted to end the career of the inconveniently argumentative Rumpole. The train, apparently as exhausted as I felt, ground to a halt between Charing Cross and the Embankment and as the lights went out I'd almost decided to give up the bar. Then the lights glowed again faintly and the train jerked on. I supposed I would have to go on as well, wouldn't I, not being the sort of character who could retire to the country and plant strawberries.

When I reached the so-called "Mansion Flat" in the Gloucester Road I was, I have to say, not a little surprised by the warmth of the reception I received. My formidable wife Hilda, known to me only as "She Who Must be Obeyed" said, "Sit down, Rumpole. You look tired out." And she lit the gas fire. A few minutes later, she brought me a glass of my usual refreshment – the very ordinary claret available from Pommeroy's Wine Bar in Fleet Street, a vintage known to me as "Château Thames Embankment". I suspected that all this attention meant that she had some uncomfortable news to break and I was right.

"This year," she told me, with the firmness of Old Gravestone pronouncing judgement, "I'm not going to do Christmas. It's getting too much for me."

Christmas was not usually much of a "do" in the Rumpole household. There is the usual exchange of presents; I get a tie and Hilda receives the statutory bottle of lavender water, which seems to be for laying down rather than immediate use. She cooks the turkey and I open the Château Thames Embankment, and so our Saviour's birth is celebrated.

"I have booked us this year," Hilda announced, "into Cherry Picker's Hall. You look in need of a rest, Rumpole."

What was this place she spoke of? A retirement home? Sheltered accommodation? "I'm in the middle of an important murder case, I can't pack up and go into a home."

"It's not a home, Rumpole. It's a country house hotel. In the Cotswolds. They're doing a special offer – four nights with full board. A children's party. Christmas lunch with crackers and a dance on Christmas Eve. It'll be something to look forward to."

"I don't really think so. We haven't got any children and I don't want to dance at Christmas. So shall we say no to the Cherry Picker's?"

"Whether you dance or not is entirely up to you, Rumpole. But you can't say no because I've already booked it and paid the deposit. And I've collected your old dinner jacket from the cleaners."

So I was unusually silent. Not for nothing is my wife entitled "She Who Must Be Obeyed".

I was unusually silent on the way to the Cotswolds too, but as we approached this country house hotel, I felt that perhaps, after all, She Who Must Be Obeyed had made a wise decision and that the considerable financial outlay on the "Budget Christmas Offer" might turn out, in spite of all my apprehension, to be justified. We took a taxi from the station. As we made our way down deep into the countryside, the sun was shining and the trees were throwing a dark pattern against a clear sky. We passed green fields where cows were munching and a stream trickling over the rocks. A stray dog crossed the road in front of us and a single kite (at least Hilda said it was a kite) wheeled across the sky. We had, it seemed, entered a better, more peaceful world far from the problem of terrorists, the bloodstained letter containing a sentence of death, the impossible client, and the no less difficult judge I struggled with down at the Old Bailey. In spite of all my troubles, I felt a kind of contentment stealing over me. Happily, the contentment only deepened as our taxi scrunched the gravel by the entrance of Cherry Picker's Hall. The old grey stones of the one-time manor house were gilded by the last of the winter sun. We were greeted warmly by a friendly manageress and our things were taken up to a comfortable room overlooking a wintry garden. Then, in no time at all, I was sitting by a blazing log fire in the residents' lounge, eating anchovy paste sandwiches with the prospect of a dark and alcoholic fruitcake to follow. Even my appalling client, Hussein Khan, might, I thought, if brought into such an environment, forget his calling as a messenger of terror and relax after dinner.

"It's wonderful to be away from the Old Bailey. I just had the most terrible quarrel with a particularly unlearned judge," I told Hilda, who was reading a back number of *Country Life*.

"You keep quarrelling with judges, don't you? Why don't you take up fishing, Rumpole? Lazy days by a trout stream might help you forget all those squalid cases you do." She had clearly got to the country sports section of the magazine.

"This quarrel went a bit further than usual. He threatened to report me for professional misconduct. I didn't like the way he kept telling the jury my client was guilty."

"Well isn't he guilty, Rumpole?" In all innocence, Hilda had asked the awkward question.

"Well. Quite possibly. But that's for the jury of twelve honest citizens to decide. Not Mr Justice Gravestone."

"Gravestone? Is that his name?"

"No. His name's Graves. I call him Gravestone."

"You would, wouldn't you, Rumpole?"

"He speaks like a voice from the tomb. It's my personal belief that he urinates iced water!"

"Really, Rumpole. Do try not to be vulgar. So what did you say to Mr Justice Graves? You might as well tell me the truth."

She was right, of course. The only way of appeasing She Who Must was to plead guilty and throw oneself on the mercy of the court. "I told him to come down off the bench and join Soapy Sam Ballard on the prosecution team."

"Rumpole, that was terribly rude of you."

"Yes," I said, with considerable satisfaction. "It really was."

"So no wonder he's cross with you."

"Very cross indeed." Once again I couldn't keep the note of triumph out of my voice.

"I should think he probably hates you, Rumpole."

"I should think he probably does."

"Well, you're safe here anyway. You can forget all about your precious Mr Justice Gravestone and just enjoy Christmas."

She was, as usual, right. I stretched my legs towards the fire and took a gulp of Earl Grey and a large bite of rich, dark cake.

And then I heard a voice call out, a voice from the tomb.

"Rumpole!" it said. "What an extraordinary coincidence. Are you here for Christmas? You and your good lady?"

I turned my head. I had not, alas, been mistaken. There he was, in person – Mr Justice Gravestone. He was wearing a tweed suit and some type of regimental or old school tie. His usually lugubrious features wore the sort of smile only previously stimulated by a long succession of guilty verdicts. And the next thing he said came as such a surprise that I almost choked on my slice of fruitcake.

"I say," he said, and I promise you these were Gravestone's exact words, "this is fun, isn't it?"

II

"I've often wondered what it would be like to be married to Rumpole."

It was a lie, of course. I dare swear that The Honourable Gravestone never spent one minute of his time wondering what it would be like to be Mrs Rumpole. But there he was, having pulled up a chair, tucking in to our anchovy paste sandwiches and smiling at She Who Must Be Obeyed (my wife Hilda) with as much joy as if she had just returned twenty guilty verdicts – one of them being in the case of The Judge versus Rumpole.

"He can be a bit difficult at times, of course," Hilda weighed in for the prosecution.

"A little difficult! That's putting it mildly, Mrs Rumpole. You can't imagine the trouble we have with him in court."

To my considerable irritation, my wife and the judge were smiling together as though they were discussing, with tolerant amusement, the irrational behaviour of a difficult child.

"Of course we mustn't discuss the case before me at the moment," Graves said.

"That ghastly terrorist." Hilda had already reached a verdict.

"Exactly! We won't say a word about him."

"Just as well," Hilda agreed. "We get far too much discussion of Rumpole's cases."

"Really? Poor Mrs Rumpole." The judge gave her a look of what I found to be quite sickening sympathy. "Brings his work home with him, does he?"

"Oh, absolutely! He'll do anything in the world for some ghastly murder or other, but can I get him to help me redecorate the bathroom?"

"You redecorate bathrooms?" The judge looked at Hilda with admiration as though she had just admitted to sailing round the world in a hot air balloon. Then he turned to me.

"You're a lucky man, Rumpole!"

"He won't tell you that." Hilda was clearly enjoying our Christmas break even more than she had expected. "By the way I hope he wasn't too rude to you in court."

"I thought we weren't meant to discuss the case." I tried to make an objection, which was entirely disregarded by my wife and the unlearned judge.

"Oh, that wasn't only Rumpole being rude. It was Rumpole trying to impress his client by showing him how fearlessly he can stand up to judges. We're quite used to that."

"He says," Hilda still seemed to find the situation amusing, "that you threatened to report him for professional misconduct. You really ought to be more careful, shouldn't you Rumpole?"

"Oh, I said that," Graves had the audacity to admit, "just to give your husband a bit of a shock. He did go a little green, I thought, when I made the suggestion."

"I did not go green!" By now I was losing patience with the judge Hilda was treating like a long-lost friend. "I made a perfectly reasonable protest against a flagrant act of premature adjudication! You had obviously decided that my client is guilty and you were going to let the jury know it."

"But isn't he guilty, Rumpole? Isn't that obvious?"

"Of course he's not guilty. He's completely innocent. And will remain so until the jury come back into court and convict him. And that is to be their decision. And what the judge wants will have absolutely nothing to do with it."

I may have gone too far, but I felt strongly on the subject. Judge Graves, however, seemed completely impervious to my attack. He stood, still smiling, warming his tweed-covered backside at the fire and repeated, "We really mustn't discuss the case we're involved in at the moment. Let's remember, it is Christmas."

"Yes, Rumpole. It is Christmas." Hilda had cast herself, it seemed as Little Lady Echo to his Lordship.

"That's settled then. Look, why don't I book a table for three at dinner?" The judge was still smiling. "Wouldn't that be tremendous fun?"

"What a perfectly charming man Judge Graves is."

These were words I never expected to hear spoken, but they contained the considered verdict of She Who Must be Obeyed before we settled down for the first night of our Christmas holiday. The food at dinner had been simple but good. (The entrecôte steak had not been arranged in a little tower swamped by tomato coulis and there had been a complete absence of roquette and all the idiocy of smart restaurants.) The Gravestone was clearly on the most friendly of terms with "Lorraine", the manageress, and he and Hilda enjoyed a lengthy conversation on the subject of fishing, which sport Graves practised and on which Hilda was expert after her study of the back number of *Country Life* in the residents' lounge.

Now and again I was asked why I didn't go out on a day's fishing with Hilda's newfound friend the judge, a question I found as easy to answer as "Why don't you take part in the London Marathon wearing nothing but bikini bottoms and a wig?" For a greater part of the dinner I had sat, unusually silent, listening to the ceaseless chatter of the newfound friends, feeling as superfluous as a maiden aunt at a lovers' meeting. Soon after telling me how charming she had found The Gravestone, Hilda had sank into a deep and contented sleep. As the moonlight streamed in at the window and I heard the faraway hooting of an owl, I began to worry about the case we hadn't discussed at dinner.

I couldn't forget my first meeting in Brixton Prison with my client, Hussein Khan. Although undoubtedly the author of the fatal letter, he didn't seem, when I met him in the company of my faithful solicitor Bonny Bernard, to be the sort who would strike terror into the heart of anyone. He was short and unsmiling with soft brown eyes, a quiet monotonous voice, and unusually small hands. He wasn't only uncomplaining, he seemed to find it the most natural thing in the world that he should find himself locked up and facing the most serious of all charges. It was, he told us early in the interview, the will of Allah, and if Allah willed, who was he, a twenty-two-year-old undergraduate in computer studies, to ask questions? I was, throughout the case, amazed at the combination, in my inexplicable client, of the most complicated knowledge of modern technology and the most primitive and merciless religious beliefs.

"I wrote the letter. Of course I did. It was not my decision that she should die. It was the will of God."

"The will of God that a harmless woman should be shot for writing something critical in a book?"

"Die for blasphemy, yes."

"And they say you were her executioner, that you carried out the sentence."

"I didn't do that." He was looking at me patiently, as though I still had much to learn about the faith of Hussein Khan. "I knew that death would come to her in time. It came sooner than I had expected."

So, was I defending a man who had issued a death threat which had then been obediently carried out by some person or persons unknown in the peaceful precincts of a south London university? It seemed an unlikely story, and I was not looking forward to the murder trial which had started at the Old Bailey during the run-up to Christmas.

At the heart of the case there was, I thought, a mystery. The letter, I knew, was clear evidence of Hussein's guilt, and yet there was no forensic evidence – no bloodstains on his clothing, no traces of his having fired a pistol with a silencer (there must have been a silencer, because no one in the building had heard a shot). This was evidence in Hussein's favour, but I had to remember that he had been in the university building when the murder had taken place, although he'd already been sent down for writing the letter.

As the owl hooted, Hilda breathed deeply. Sleep eluded me. I went through Hussein Khan's story again. He had gotten a phone call, he said, when he was at his parents' restaurant. (He had answered the phone himself, so there was no one to confirm the call.) It had been, it seemed, from a girl who said she was the senior tutor's secretary and that the tutor wanted to meet him in the university library at ten o'clock that evening to discuss his future.

He had got to the William Morris building at nine forty-five and had told Mr Luttrell, the man at the main reception area, that he was there to meet the senior tutor at the library. He said that when he had arrived at the library, the tutor wasn't there and that he had waited for over an hour and then went home, never going near Honoria Glossop's office.

Of course the senior tutor and his secretary denied that either had made such a telephone call. The implication was that Hussein was lying through his teeth and that he had gone to the university because he had known that Professor Glossop worked in her office until late at night and he had intended to kill her.

At last I fell into a restless sleep. In my dreams I saw myself being prosecuted by Soapy Sam Ballard who was wearing a long beard and arguing for my conviction under Sharia law.

I woke early to the first faint flush of daylight as a distant cock crowed. I got up, tiptoed across the room, and extracted from the bottom of my case the papers in *R. v. Khan*. I was looking for the answer to a problem as yet undefined, going through the prosecution statement again, and finding nothing very much.

I reminded myself that Mr Luttrell, at his reception desk, had seen Honoria and her husband arrive together and go to her office. Ricky Glossop had left not more than fifteen minutes later, and later still he had telephoned and couldn't get an answer from his wife. He had asked Luttrell to go to Honoria's office because she wasn't answering her phone. The receptionist had gone to her office and found her lying across her desk, her hand close to the bloodstained letter.

Next I read the statement from Honoria's secretary, Sue Blackmore, describing how she had found the letter in Honoria's university pigeonhole and taken it to Honoria at her home. On Honoria's reaction at receiving it, Ms Blackmore commented, "She didn't take the note all that seriously and wouldn't even tell the police." Ricky Glossop had finally rung the anti-terrorist department in Scotland Yard and showed them the letter.

None of this was new. There was only one piece of evidence which I might have overlooked.

In the senior tutor's statement he said he had spoken to Honoria on the morning of the day she had died. She had told him that she couldn't be at a seminar that afternoon because she had an urgent appointment with Tony Hawkin. Hawkin, as the senior tutor knew, was a solicitor who acted for the university, and had also acted for Honoria Glossop in a private capacity. The senior tutor had no idea why she had wanted to see her solicitor. He never saw his colleague alive again.

I was giving that last document some thought when Hilda stirred, opened an eye, and instructed me to ring for breakfast.

"You'll have to look after yourself today, Rumpole," she told me. "Gerald's going to take me fishing for grayling."

"Gerald?" Was there some new man in Hilda's life who had turned up in the Cotswolds?

"You know. The charming judge you introduced me to last night."

"You can't mean Gravestone?"

"Don't be ridiculous. Of course I mean Gerald Graves."

"You're going fishing with him?"

"He's very kindly going to take me to a bit of river he shares with a friend."

"How delightful." I adopted the ironic tone. "If you catch anything, bring it back for supper."

"Oh, I'm not going to do any fishing. I'm simply going to watch Gerald from the bank. He's going to show me how he ties his flies."

"How absolutely fascinating."

She didn't seem to think she'd said anything at all amusing and she began to lever herself briskly out of bed.

"Do ring up about that breakfast, Rumpole!" she said. "I've got to get ready for Gerald."

He may be Gerald to you, I thought, but he will always be the Old Gravestone to me.

After Hilda had gone to meet her newfound friend, I finished the bacon and eggs with sausage and fried slice – which I had ordered as an organic, low calorie breakfast – and put a telephone call through to my faithful solicitor Bonny Bernard. I found him at his home talking over a background of shrill and excited children eager for the next morning and the well-filled stockings.

"Mr Rumpole!" The man sounded shocked by my call. "Don't you ever take a day off? It's Christmas Eve!"

"I know it's Christmas Eve. I know that perfectly well," I told him. "And my wife has gone fishing with our sepulchral judge, whom she calls 'Gerald'. Meanwhile, have you got any close friends or associates working at Hawkin's, the solicitor?"

"Barry Tuck used to be our legal executive – moved there about three years ago."

"A cooperative sort of character is he, Tuck?"

"We got on very well. Yes."

"Then get him to find out why Honoria Glossop went to see Tony Hawkin the afternoon before she was shot. It must have been something fairly urgent. She missed a seminar in order to go."

"Is it important?"

"Probably not, but it just might be something we ought to know."

"I hope you're enjoying your Christmas break, Mr Rumpole."

"Quite enjoying it. I'd like it better without a certain member of the judiciary. Oh, and I've got a hard time ahead."

"Working?"

"No," I told my patient solicitor gloomily. "Dancing."

"Quick, quick, slow, Rumpole. That's better. Now *chassé*. Don't you remember, Rumpole? This is where you *chassé*."

The truth was that I remembered little about it. It had been so long ago. How many years could it have been since Hilda and I had trod across a dance floor? Yet here I was in a dinner jacket, which was now uncomfortably tight round the waist, doing my best to walk round this small area of polished parquet in time to the music with one arm round Hilda's satin-covered waist and my other hand gripping one of hers. Although for much of the time she was walking backwards, she was undoubtedly the one in command of the enterprise. I heard a voice singing, seemingly from far off, above the music of the five-piece band laid on for the hotel's dinner dance. It was a strange sound and one that I hadn't heard for what seemed many years – She Who Must be Obeyed was singing. I looked towards my table, rather as someone lost at sea might look towards a distant shore, and I saw Mr Justice Gravestone smiling at us with approval.

"Well done, Hilda! And you came through that quite creditably I thought, Rumpole. I mean, at least you managed to remain upright, although there were a few dodgy moments coming round that far corner."

"That was when I told him *chassé*. Rumpole couldn't quite manage it."

As they were both enjoying a laugh I realized that, during a long day by the river which had, it seemed, produced nothing more than two fish so small that they had had to be returned to their natural environment, Mrs Rumpole had become "Hilda" to the judge, who had become "Gerald".

"You know, when you retire, Rumpole," the judge was sounding sympathetic in the most irritating kind of way, "you could take dancing lessons."

"There's so much Rumpole could do *if* he retired. I keep telling him," was Hilda's contribution. "He could have wonderful days like we had, Gerald. Outdoors, close to nature and fishing."

"Catching two small grayling you had to put back in the water?" I was bold enough to ask. "It would've been easier to pay a quick visit to the fishmongers."

"Catching fish is not the point of fishing," Hilda told me. Before I could ask her what the point of it was, the judge came up with a suggestion.

"When you retire, I could teach you fishing, Rumpole. We could have a few days out together."

"Now then. Isn't that kind of Gerald, Rumpole?" Hilda beamed and I had to mutter, "Very kind," although the judge's offer had made me more determined than ever to die with my wig on.

It was at this point that Lorraine the manageress came to the judge with a message. He read it quickly and then said, "Poor old Leslie Mulliner. You know him, don't you, Rumpole? He sits in the chancery division."

I had to confess I didn't know anyone who sat in the chancery division.

"He was going to join us here tomorrow but his wife's not well."

"He said on the phone that you'd do the job for him tomorrow." Lorraine seemed anxious.

"Yes, of course," Graves hurried to reassure her. "I'll stand in for him."

Before I could get any further explanation of the "job", the music had struck up a more contemporary note. Foxtrots were out, and with a cry of "Come along Hilda," Graves was strutting the dance floor, making curious rhythmic movements with his hands. And Hilda, walking free and unfastened from her partner, was also strutting and waving her arms, smiling with pleasure. It wasn't, I'm sure, the most up-to-date form of dancing, but it was, I suppose, a gesture from two sedate citizens who were doing their best to become, for a wine-filled moment on Christmas Eve, a couple of teenagers.

Christmas Day at Cherry Picker's Hall was uneventful. The judge suggested church, and I stood while he and Hilda bellowed out "Come, all ye Faithful". Then we sat among the faithful under the Norman arches, beside the plaques and monuments to so many vanished rectors and country squires, looking out upon the holly round the pulpit and the flowers on the altar. I tried to understand, not for the first time, how a religious belief could become so perverted as to lead to death threats, terror, and a harmless professor shot through the head.

We had lunch in a pub and then the judge announced he had work to do and left us.

After a long and satisfactory sleep, Hilda and I woke around teatime and went to the residents' lounge. Long before we got to the door, we could hear the excited cries of children, and when we went in we saw them crowded round the Christmas tree. And there, stooping among the presents, was the expected figure in a red dressing gown (trimmed with white fur), Wellington boots, a white beard, and a long red hat. As he picked up a present and turned towards us, I felt that fate had played the greatest practical joke it could have thought up to enliven the festive season.

Standing in for his friend Mulliner from the chancery division, the sepulchral, unforgiving, prosecution-minded Mr Justice Gravestone, my old enemy, had become Father Christmas.

On Boxing Day, I rang a persistent, dogged, ever useful private eye detective who, sickened by divorce, now specialized in the cleaner world of crime – Ferdinand Ian Gilmour Newton, known in legal circles as "Fig Newton". I told him that, as was the truth, my wife Hilda was planning a long country walk and lunch in a distant village with a judge whom I had spent a lifetime trying to avoid. And I asked him, if he had no previous engagements, if he'd like to sample the *table d'hôte* at Cherry Picker's Hall.

Fig Newton is a lugubrious character of indeterminate age, usually dressed in an old mackintosh and an even older hat, with a drip at the end of his nose caused by a seemingly perpetual cold – most likely caught while keeping observation in all weathers. But today he had shed his outer garments, his nose was dry, and he was tucking in to the lamb cutlets with something approaching enthusiasm. "Bit of a step up from your usual pub lunch, this, isn't it Mr Rumpole?"

"It certainly is, Fig. We're splashing out this Christmas. Now this case I'm doing down the Bailey . . ."

"The terrorist?"

"Yes, the terrorist."

"You're on to a loser with that one, Mr Rumpole." Fig was gloomily relishing the fact.

"Most probably. All the same, there are a few stones I don't want to leave unturned."

"Such as what?"

"Find out what you can about the Glossops."

"The dead woman's family?"

"That's right. See what's known about their lives, hobbies, interests. That sort of thing, I need to get more of a picture of their lives together. Oh, and see if the senior tutor knows more about the Glossops. Pick up any gossip going round the university. I'll let you know if Bonny Bernard has found out why Honoria had a date with her solicitor."

"So when do you want all this done by, Mr Rumpole?" Fig picked up a cutlet bone and chewed gloomily. "Tomorrow morning, I suppose?"

"Oh, sooner than that if possible," I told him.

It was not that I felt that the appalling Hussein Khan had a defence – in fact he might well turn out to have no defence at all. But something at the children's Christmas party had suggested a possibility to my mind.

That something was the sight of Mr Justice Graves standing in for someone else.

III

Christmas was over, and I wondered if the season of goodwill was over with it. The Christmas cards had left the mantelpiece, the holly and the mistletoe had been tidied away, we had exchanged green fields for Gloucester Road, and Cherry Picker's Hall was nothing but a memory. The judge was back on the bench to steer the case of *R. v. Khan* towards its inevitable guilty verdict.

The Christmas decorations were not all that had gone. Gerald the cheerful dinner guest, Gerald the energetic dancing partner of She Who Must be Obeyed, Gerald the fisherman, and, in particular, Gerald as Santa Claus had all gone as well, leaving behind only the old thin-lipped, unsmiling Mr Justice Gravestone with the voice of doom, determined to make a difficult case harder than ever.

All the same there was something of a spring in the Rumpole step. This was not only the result of the Christmas break but also due to a suspicion that the case *R. v. Khan* might not be quite as horrifyingly simple as it had appeared at first.

As I crossed the hall on my way to Court Number One, I saw Ricky Glossop – the dashingly handsome husband of the murdered professor – with a pretty blonde girl whom I took to be Sue Blackmore, Honoria's secretary, who was due to give evidence about her employer's reception of the fatal letter. She seemed, so far as I could tell from a passing examination, to be a girl on the verge of a nervous breakdown. She lit a cigarette with trembling fingers, then almost immediately stamped it out. She kept looking, with a kind of description, towards the door of the court, and then turning with a sob to Ricky Glossop and choking out what I took to be some sort of complaint. He had laid a consoling hand on hers and was talking in the sort of low, exaggeratedly calm tone that a dentist uses when he says, "This isn't going to hurt".

The medical and police evidence had been disposed of before Christmas and now, in the rather strange order adopted by Soapy Sam Ballard for the prosecution, the only witnesses left were Arthur Luttrell, who manned the reception desk, Ricky Glossop, and the nervous secretary.

Luttrell, the receptionist, was a smart, precise, self-important man with a sharp nose and a sandy moustache who clearly regarded his position as being at the centre of the university organization. He remembered Hussein Khan coming at nine thirty that evening, saying he had an appointment with the senior tutor, and going up to the library. At quarter to ten the Glossops had arrived. Ricky had gone with his wife to her office, but had left about fifteen minutes later. "He stopped to speak to me on the way," Luttrell the receptionist told Soapy Sam, "which is why I remembered it well."

After that, the evening at William Morris University followed its horrible course. Around eleven o'clock, Hussein Khan left, complaining that he had wasted well over an hour, no senior tutor had come to him, and that he was going back to his parents' restaurant in Golders Green. After that Ricky telephoned the reception desk saying that he couldn't get any reply from his wife's office and would Mr Luttrell please go and make sure she was alright. As we all know, Mr Luttrell went to the office, knocked, opened the door, and was met by the ghastly spectacle which was to bring us all together in Court Number One at the Old Bailey.

"Mr Rumpole." The judge's tone in calling my name was as aloofly disapproving as though Christmas had never happened.

"All this evidence is agreed, isn't it? I don't suppose you'll find it necessary to trouble Mr Luttrell with any questions."

"Just one or two, my Lord."

"Oh very well." The judge sounded displeased. "Just remember, we're under a public duty not to waste time."

"I hope your Lordship isn't suggesting that an attempt to get to the truth is a waste of time." And before the old Gravestone could launch a counterattack, I asked Mr Luttrell the first question.

"You say Mr Glossop spoke to you on the way out. Can you remember what he said?"

"I remember perfectly." The receptionist looked personally insulted as though I doubted his word. "He asked me if Hussein Khan was in the building."

"He asked you that?"

"Yes, he did."

"And what did you tell him?"

"I told him 'yes'. I said Khan was in the library where he had an appointment with the senior tutor."

I allowed a pause for this curious piece of evidence to sink into the minds of the jury. Graves, of course, filled in the gap by asking if that was my only question.

"Just one more, my Lord."

Here the judge sighed heavily, but I ignored that.

"Are you telling this jury, Mr Luttrell, that Glossop discovered that the man who had threatened his wife with death was in the building, then left without speaking to her again?"

I looked at the jury as I asked this and saw, for the first time in the trial, a few faces looking puzzled.

Mr Luttrell, however, sounded unfazed.

"I've told you what he said. I can't tell you anything more."

"He can't tell us any more," the judge repeated. "So that would seem to be the end of the matter, wouldn't it, Mr Rumpole?"

"Not quite the end," I told him. "I don't think it's quite the end of the matter yet."

This remark did nothing to improve my relations with his Lordship, who gave me a look from which all traces of the Christmas spirit had been drained.

The jury may have had a moment of doubt during the receptionist's evidence, but when Ricky Glossop was put in the witness box, their sympathy and concern for the good-looking, appealingly modest, and stricken husband was obvious. Graves supported him with enthusiasm.

"This is clearly going to be a terrible ordeal for you, Mr Glossop," the judge said, looking at the witness with serious concern. "Wouldn't you like to sit down?"

"No, thank you, my Lord. I prefer to stand," Ricky said bravely. The judge gave him the sort of look a commanding officer might give to a young subaltern who'd volunteered to attack the enemy position single-handed. "Just let me know," Graves insisted, "if you feel exhausted or overcome by any part of your evidence, and you shall sit down immediately."

"Thank you very much, my Lord. That *is* very kind of your Lordship."

So with formalities of mutual admiration over, Ricky Glossop began to tell his story.

He had met Honoria some ten years before when they were both cruising round the Greek Islands. "She knew all the classical legends and the history of every place. I thought she'd never be bothered with an under-educated slob like me." Here he smiled modestly, and the judge smiled back as a sign of disagreement. "But luckily she put up with me. And, of course, I fell in love with her."

"Of course?" Soapy Sam seemed to feel that this sentence called for some further explanation.

"She was extremely beautiful."

"And she found you attractive?"

"She seemed to. God knows why." This answer earned him smiles for his modesty.

"So you were married for ten years," Ballard said. "And you had no children."

"No. Honoria couldn't have children. It was a great sadness to both of us."

"And how would you describe your marriage up to the time your wife got this terrible letter?" Ballard was holding the letter out, at a distance, as though the paper itself might carry a fatal infection.

"We were very happy."

"When she got the letter, how did she react to it?"

"She was very brave, my Lord," Ricky told the judge. "She said it had obviously been written by some nutcase and that she intended to ignore it."

"She was extremely brave." The judge spoke the words with admiration as he wrote them down.

So Ricky Glossop told his story. And when I, the representative, so it appeared, of his wife's murderer, rose to cross-examine, I felt a chill wind blowing through Number One Court.

"Mr Glossop, you said your marriage to your wife Honoria was a happy one?"

"As far as I was concerned it was very happy." Here he smiled at the jury and some of them nodded back approvingly.

"Did you know that on the afternoon before she was murdered, your wife had consulted a solicitor, Mr Anthony Hawkin of Henshaw and Hawkin?"

"I didn't know that, no."

"Can you guess why?"

"I'm afraid not. My wife had considerable financial interests under her father's will. It might have been about that."

"You mean it might have been about the money?"

"Yes."

"Did you know that Anthony Hawkin is well known as an expert on divorce and family law?"

"I didn't know that either."

"And you didn't know that your wife was considering proceedings for divorce?"

"I certainly didn't."

I looked at the jury. They were now, I thought, at least interested. I remembered the frightened blonde girl I had seen outside the court and the hand he had put on her as he had tried to comfort her.

"Was there any trouble between your wife and yourself because of her secretary, Sue Blackmore?"

"So far as I know, none whatever."

"Mr Rumpole, I'm wondering, and I expect the jury may be wondering as well, what on earth these questions have to do with your client's trial for murder."

"Then wonder on." I might have quoted Shakespeare to Graves: "Till truth makes all things plain." But I did not do that. I merely said, "I'm putting these questions to test the credibility of this witness, my Lord."

"And why, Mr Rumpole, are you attacking his credibility? Which part of this gentleman's evidence are you disputing?"

"If I may be allowed to cross-examine in the usual way, I hope it may become clear," I said, and then I'm afraid I also said, "even to your Lordship."

At this, Gravestone gave me the look that meant "you just wait until we come to the summing up, and I'll tell the jury what I think of your attack on this charming husband", but for the moment he remained as silent as a block of ice, so I soldiered on.

"Mr Glossop. Your wife's secretary delivered this threatening letter to her."

"Yes. Honoria was working at home and Sue brought it over from her pigeon-hole at the university."

"You've told us that she was very brave, of course. That she had said it was probably from some nutcase and that she intended to ignore it. But you insisted on taking the letter to the police."

"An extremely wise decision, if I may say so," Graves took it upon himself to note.

"And I think you gave the story to the Press Association so that this death threat received wide publicity."

"I thought Honoria would be safer if it was all out in the open. People would be on their guard."

"Another wise decision, the members of the jury might think." Graves was making sure the jury thought it.

"And when the letter was traced to my client, everyone knew that it was Hussein Khan who was the author of the letter?"

"He was dismissed from the university, so I suppose a lot of people knew, yes."

"So if anything were to have happened to your wife after that, if she were to have been attacked or killed, Hussein Khan would have been the most likely suspect?"

"I think that has been obvious throughout this trial." Graves couldn't resist it.

"My Lord, I'd really much rather get the answers to my questions from the witness than receive them from your Lordship." I went on quickly before the judge could get in his two pennies' worth. "You took your wife to the university on that fatal night?"

"I often did. If I was going somewhere and she had work to do in her office, I'd drop her off and then collect her later on my way home."

"But you didn't just drop her off, did you? You went inside the building with her. You took her up to her office?"

"Yes. We'd been talking about something in the car and we went on discussing it as I went up to her office with her."

"He escorted her, Mr Rumpole," the sepulchral voice boomed from the bench. "A very gentlemanly thing to do."

"Thank you, my Lord." Ricky's smile was still full of charm. "And what were you discussing?" I asked him. "Was it divorce?"

"It certainly wasn't divorce. I can't remember what it was exactly."

"Then perhaps you can remember this. How long did you stay in the office with your wife?"

"Perhaps five, maybe ten minutes. I can't remember exactly."

"And when you left, was she still alive?"

There was a small silence.

The witness looked at me and seemed to catch his breath. Then he gave us the invariably charming smile.

"Of course she was."

"You spoke to Mr Luttrell at the reception area on your way out?"

"I did, yes."

"He says you asked him if Hussein Khan was in the building?"

"Yes, I did."

"Why did you do that?"

"I suppose I'd heard from someone that he might have been there."

"And what did Mr Luttrell tell you?"

"He said that Khan was in the building, yes."

"You knew that Hussein Khan's presence in that building was a potential danger to your wife."

"I suppose I knew. Yes."

"I suppose you did. And yet you left and drove off in your car without warning her?"

There was a longer silence then and Ricky's smile seemed to droop.

"I didn't go back to the office. No," was what the witness said.

"Why not, Mr Glossop? Why not warn her? Why didn't you see that Khan left before you went off?"

And then Ricky Glossop said something which changed the atmosphere in court in a moment, even silencing the judge.

"I suppose I was in a hurry. I was on my way to a party."

After a suitable pause I asked, "There was no lock on your wife's office door, was there?"

"There might have been. But she never locked it."

"So you left her unprotected, with the man who had threatened her life still in the building, because you were on your way to a party?"

The smile came again, but it had no effect now on the jury.

"I think I heard he was with the senior tutor in the library. I suppose I thought that was safe."

"Mr Glossop, were you not worried by the possibility that the senior tutor might leave first, leaving the man who threatened your wife still in the building with her?"

"I suppose I didn't think of that," was all he could say.

I let the answer sink in and then turned to more dangerous and uncharted territory.

"I believe you're interested in various country sports."

"That's right, my Lord." The witness, seeming to feel the ground was now safer, smiled at the judge.

"You used to go shooting, I believe."

"Well, I go shooting, Mr Rumpole." A ghastly twitch of the lips was, from the bench, Graves' concession towards a smile. "And I hope you're not accusing me of complicity in any sort of a crime?"

I let the jury have their sycophantic laugh, then went on to ask, "Did you ever belong to a pistol shooting club, Mr Glossop?" Fig Newton, the private eye, had done his work well.

"When such clubs were legal, yes."

"And do you still own a handgun?"

"Certainly not." The witness seemed enraged. "I wouldn't do anything that broke the law."

I turned to look at the jury with my eyebrows raised, but for the moment the witness was saved by the bell as the judge announced that he could see by the clock that it was time we broke for lunch.

Before we parted, however, Soapy Sam got up to tell us that his next witness would be Mrs Glossop's secretary, Sue Blackmore, who would merely give evidence about the receipt of the letter and the deceased's reaction to it. Miss Blackmore was, apparently, likely to be a very nervous witness, and perhaps his learned friend Mr Rumpole would agree to her evidence being read.

Mr Rumpole did not agree. Mr Rumpole wanted Miss Sue Blackmore to be present in the flesh and he was ready to cross-examine her at length. And so we parted, expecting the trial of Hussein Khan for murder to start again at two o'clock.

But Khan's trial for murder didn't start again at two o'clock or at any other time. I was toying with a plate of steak and kidney pie and a pint of Guinness in the pub opposite the Old Bailey when I saw the furtive figure of Sam Ballard oozing through the crowd. He came to me obviously heavy with news.

"Rumpole! You don't drink at lunchtime, do you?"

"Yes. But not too much at. Can I buy you a pint of stout?"

"Certainly not, Rumpole. Mineral water, if you have to. And could we move to that little table in the corner? This is news for your ears alone."

After I had transported my lunch to a more secluded spot and supplied our Head of Chambers with mineral water, he brought me up to date on that lunch hour's developments.

"It's Sue the secretary, Rumpole. When we told her that she'd have to go into the witness box, she panicked and asked to see Superintendent Gregory. By this time, she was in tears and, he told me, almost incomprehensible. However, Gregory managed to calm her down and she said she knew you'd get it out of her in the witness box, so she might as well confess that she was the one who had made the telephone call."

"Which telephone call was that?" Soapy Sam was demonstrating his usual talent for making a simple statement of fact utterly confusing.

"The telephone call to your client. Telling him to go and meet the senior tutor."

"You mean . . .?" The mists that had hung over the case of Khan the terrorist were beginning to clear. "She pretended to be . . ."

"The senior tutor's secretary. Yes. The idea was to get Khan into the building whilst Glossop . . ."

"Murdered his wife?" I spoke the words that Ballard seemed reluctant to use.

"I think she's prepared to give evidence against him," Soapy Sam said, looking thoughtfully towards future briefs. "Well, she'll have to, unless she wants to go to prison as an accessory."

"Has handsome Ricky heard the news yet?" I wondered.

"Mr Glossop has been detained. He's helping the police with their enquiries."

So many people I know, who help the police with their enquiries, are in dire need of help themselves. "So you'll agree to a verdict of not guilty of murder?" I asked Ballard, as though it was a request to pass the mustard.

"Perhaps. Eventually. And you'll agree to guilty of making death threats in a letter?"

"Oh, yes," I admitted. "We'll have to plead guilty to that."

But there was no hurry. I could finish my steak and kidney and order another Guinness in peace.

"It started off," I was telling Hilda over a glass of Château Thames Embankment that evening, "as an act of terrorism, of mad, religious fanaticism, of what has become the new terror of our times. And it ends up as an old-fashioned murder by a man who wanted to dispose of his rich wife for her money and be free to marry a pretty young woman. It was a case, you might say, of Dr Crippen meeting Osama Bin Laden."

"It's hard to say which is worse." She Who Must be Obeyed was thoughtful.

"Both of them," I told her. "Both of them are worse. But I suppose we understand Dr Crippen better. Only one thing we can be grateful for."

"What's that, Rumpole?"

"The terrorist got a fair trial. And the whole truth came out in the end. The day when a suspected terrorist doesn't get a fair trial will be the day they've won the battle."

I refilled our glasses, having delivered my own particular verdict on the terrible events of that night at William Morris University.

"Mind you," I said, "it was your friend Gerald Graves who put me onto the truth of the matter."

"Oh really." Hilda sounded unusually cool on the subject of the judge.

"It was when he was playing Father Christmas. He was standing in for someone else. And I thought, what if the real murderer thought he'd stand in for someone else. Hussein Khan had uttered the death threat and was there to take the blame. All Ricky had to do was to go to work quickly. So that's what he did – he committed murder in Hussein Khan's name. That death threat was a gift from heaven for him."

One of our usual silences fell between us, and then Hilda said, "I don't know why you call Mr Justice Graves my friend."

"You got on so well at Christmas."

"Well, yes we did. And then he said we must keep in touch. So I telephoned his clerk and the message came back that the judge was busy for months ahead but he hoped we might meet again eventually. I have to tell you, Rumpole, that precious judge of yours does not treat women well."

I did my best. I tried to think of The Old Gravestone as a heartbreaker, a sort of Don Juan who picked women up and dropped them without mercy, but I failed miserably.

"I'm better off with you, Rumpole," Hilda told me. "I can always rely on you to be unreliable."

The Temp

by René Appel

The plump woman in the pale-blue smock introduced herself as Anja. She looked around and giggled shyly, as if she wasn't sure exactly how to handle the situation. A man wouldn't have laughed like that.

"Ki—." I caught myself and turned it into a cough. "Marjolein."

We shook hands. "I'll take you around and show you the ropes," she said. The corners of her mouth inched tentatively upward. "These are the cash registers, of course, and upstairs" – she pointed at a narrow door set into the far wall and led me off in that direction – "is the, well, we call it the lounge. You can eat your lunch there, hang up your coat. Did you get your code yet? No? Well, I'll give it to you later."

Anja punched in her own code, and the door clicked open. At the top of the stairs, she indicated another door, also closed but without the metal locking mechanism. "This is Mr Hovenkamp's office. The boss." She glanced at me meaningfully, but I had no idea *what* meaning I was supposed to attach to the look.

She knocked and went in without waiting for a response, her steps heavy, as if she was loaded down with suitcases. I followed close behind. Hovenkamp looked up from the papers on his desk in surprise, like he'd seen a ghost. Maybe there were secrets buried in his pile of paperwork, or perhaps we'd caught him paging through an issue of *Playboy*.

"This is Marjolein," said Anja, "the new temp."

"Temp?" asked Hovenkamp, still preoccupied with his papers.

"Don't you remember? Today's her first day."

Hovenkamp stood up. "Fine, fine, we definitely need the help. All summer long, this place is a madhouse. Three times as many customers as in the off-season. You'll take care of her, Anja, yes? Get her all settled in?" He wiped his forehead with an oversized handkerchief. "Warm in here, isn't it?"

"I'm on it," said Anja.

We left the office, crossed the narrow hallway and entered a sterile little room holding nothing but a table, a couple of chairs, and a half-dozen pale-blue smocks on hooks screwed into one dingy wall.

I'd told Anja over the phone that I needed the job because I was practically broke. "I've got a little tent over at the campground, I thought I'd brought enough money to make it through the summer, but you know how it goes. You splurge a little on a nice dinner, you have a couple of drinks too many at the disco, and pretty soon your pockets are empty. You've been there yourself, I bet."

"Actually," she said, "I've been saving every cent." Again a little laugh escaped her. "I'm getting married next year."

"Congratulations! What's his name?"

"Gerard."

"Marriage, wow. Not for me! But, anyway, I can't use my debit card, my account's pretty much overdrawn. So I need a job, because I *do* want to stick around for the rest of the summer. I met this guy, Marcel . . ."

I wondered if that was giving away too much.

"Anyway, I used to work in a supermarket in Rotterdam, so I've got plenty of experience. I can start right away."

A supermarket in Rotterdam, that was vague enough.

Anja explained a bit about the store's practices and procedures, how to handle possible register problems and what they did with the money.

". . . and it winds up in Mr Hovenkamp's office. The safe's in there, an old-fashioned one, no time lock or anything" – she laid a hand on my arm confidentially – "but you didn't hear that from me." She wore a ring, probably an engagement ring. They'd had a big party, I figured, lots of presents from their families and friends to get them started in their little life together. I did my best to look interested.

This was obviously a more primitive neck of the woods than Rotterdam. Their busy season lasted ten weeks, tops, and then the place went into hibernation, which probably suited Hovenkamp and Anja just fine.

"Just to be safe," said Anja, "not that anything like this would ever happen here, knock on wood" – she rapped her knuckles on the tabletop, just like she'd rapped on Hovenkamp's office door earlier – "but if the place was to get robbed, you just hand over everything that's in your register, no argument. Here, look, it's in the rulebook." She opened the mimeographed sheaf of pages she'd laid on the table between us and pointed to a paragraph.

I read a few lines about "the safety of the employees and customers".

"So," she said, pulling a smock down from the wall and handing it over, "you ready to get started?"

Anja stood right behind me for a while, explaining this and that. It didn't take me long to get into the swing of things. After half an hour, she left me on my own. There was nothing to it: every transaction followed pretty much the same pattern.

"Have you got 13 euro cents, ma'am?"

"Here you go."

"Thanks very much. Have a nice day!"

I'd been instructed to wish each customer a nice day. The only variation on the theme came when one punky girl of sixteen with two little silver hoops in her lower lip shot back, "You don't give a shit what kind of day I have."

I didn't argue with her.

I'd ordered myself not to look too often at my watch, but it had to be getting close to the end of my shift when I noticed a young man hanging around in the area behind the registers, over by the empty cardboard boxes and the bulletin board for local announcements and advertisements. He was wearing mirrored sunglasses. Despite the summer heat, he had on a leather jacket. Just looking at him made me sweat. He stuck his hands in his pockets and hurried towards me with long strides.

Marcel looked at his watch. Quarter past five. Another hour to wait. He stretched like a cat, then reached for the bottle of beer that stood in the umbrella's shade and took a refreshing swallow.

Meeting her had been like winning the lottery. He'd noticed her right away at DaDa Dance. She'd been standing by herself in a corner, just scoping out the scene. He'd gone and stood next to her. They'd checked each other out, and they'd each liked what they saw.

From the way she'd acted, he knew he'd better not try anything that first night. She wasn't that kind of girl, that was obvious. They'd made a date for the next evening, and just thinking about that second encounter made him hard. Damn, she knew what she had and how to use it. Obviously she'd never gone back to her stupid campground. No, his *casa* had quickly become her *casa*. This was going to be a summer to remember, with a hefty payoff at the end. She was definitely something, coming up with the whole plan on her own.

He emptied his beer. Ten months of the year, it was beyond boring here, but this would make up for a lot. No, this would make up for *everything*.

The guy in the leather jacket seemed to hesitate, turned his head towards the other registers, but then took another step toward me.

"Can I . . . can I, um, ask you something?" he stammered.

I ignored him and scanned a bottle of Coke and two bags of crisps for a man with a sunburned forehead and a T-shirt that read NO BULLSHIT in big letters. "That'll be €16.44," I told him, wondering if that was a catchphrase between him and his wife – and if he was the one who said it to her or the other way around.

Out of the corner of my eye, I watched the kid in the leather jacket shift nervously from foot to foot. Why didn't he just go to another register? What did he need *me* for? Maybe he was getting up the nerve to pull something and could tell I was new to the store and less ready to handle problems and emergencies. Here's your chance, man, she doesn't know what she's doing, take her down! Shit, this was all I needed under *any* circumstances, and least of all now.

"Can I—?" he said again. He was actually blushing. Oh, this was just perfect – on top of everything else, he's *shy*?

I waved him off, as NO BULLSHIT handed me a twenty-five-euro note.

"Have you got two euros, sir?"

He searched his pockets and came up empty. I glanced around the store, but no one was paying us the least attention. Anja was ringing up groceries as if her life depended on it, and the other girl, Rachida, was finishing up a sale. I handed the man his change, counting out the coins slowly.

When I was finished, I turned to Leather Jacket. "Yes?"

He smiled, revealing an irregular row of teeth. "I wanted to ask you something."

"Well, go ahead," I said impatiently. "There are people waiting." I glanced at the woman who was next in line. Her face was red from the sun, and her overdone makeup emphasized the tiredness in her eyes instead of concealing it. She blew a strand of hair off her face, like a girl in a TV commercial.

"Those boxes." He pointed to the pile of empty cartons across from the registers. "Can I – if you're not going to use them, can I have some of them? I'm moving, see, and I—"

"Go ahead," I cut him off. "Take as many as you want."

He smiled his gratitude and nodded. I wouldn't have been surprised if he'd tried to kiss my hand, the creep. He was missing a couple of teeth, I noticed.

"Poor kid," said the woman with the red face, as I returned my attention to her. "He's probably on welfare. Our taxes at work. I guess that's just the way things are, nowadays . . ."

I nodded silently and reached for her first item.

The rest of the afternoon, I was pretty much on autopilot. I wasn't sure how long I could keep this up. But it was for a good cause, the *best* cause. My own cause. Dozens of litres of soda, bags of crisps, packages of peanuts, bottles of wine, six-packs of beer, boxes of cookies passed over my scanner. Sometimes it seemed like these people never ate an actual *meal*, just snacked and boozed. A blond woman with a fat little boy riding in her cart set bread, vegetables, a package of four hamburgers and a bunch of bananas on the belt, but when the child – stabbing an eager finger at the candy rack – let out a bloodcurdling cry, she added a couple of Mars bars to her pile, tore the wrapper off another one and shoved it into his fist. He looked triumphant.

By the time I handed the register off to the next shift, I was dead on my feet. My fingers wanted to keep right on scanning, and coins and banknotes danced before my eyes. I blinked them away. All I had to do was throw my smock back on its hook, and then I could go home to Marcel, who'd be waiting for me. I punched in the code Anja had given me and went upstairs. Just outside the lounge, I felt an unexpected hand on my shoulder and stifled a scream.

"Marjolein," said Hovenkamp. "It's Marjolein, right?"

I nodded.

"I need you to fill out a couple of forms. Can you step into my office for a minute?"

I followed him. The seat of his trousers, I noticed, hung loosely over his flat ass. No butt on him, but the unmistakeable beginnings of a beer belly, barely contained by his tight striped shirt. Why did that happen so often to men, all their weight on the wrong side of their bodies?

"Have a seat." He indicated a chair, laid a form on the table in front of me and bent over me. I could feel his breath on the back of my neck and smell a sad mixture of perspiration, aftershave and an ashtray that hadn't been emptied in way too long. Probably because I'd quit smoking myself a couple of months earlier – which had been harder than I'd expected it to be – that last component of his odour was the most annoying.

I filled in the form. "This is my home address, obviously," I said, "not my vacation address. I mean, I can't really put down the campground, can I? I don't imagine the taxman would approve."

"I understand." Hovenkamp moved a step closer to me and put his hand back on my shoulder. Even through the smock and my T-shirt I could feel how hot and sweaty his heavy paw was. "And your tax number right there." He indicated the place.

"Oh, gosh, I don't know it by heart. Is it okay if I fill that in tomorrow?" I gave him my sweetest smile, though in my imagination I was smashing his face in with my elbow. Lots of blood, his nose broken, his body doubled over in pain. He kneaded my shoulder lightly, his touch so gentle I could barely notice it. I heard him sigh and thought of Mrs Hovenkamp, wherever she was.

"No problem," he said.

I stood up. "Then I'll be off."

Our faces were very close.

"Maybe," Hovenkamp began, "maybe sometime we can—"

But then there was a knock at the door.

Anja stood in the doorway. "Wendy's sick," she said. "She needs to go home. Maybe Marjolein could—?"

"Me? No, honestly, I can't. I'm beat, and anyway I have a date." I looked at Hovenkamp beseechingly. "My boyfriend, I can't keep him waiting."

"Well, then we'll . . . we'll have to think of something else," said Hovenkamp. "I may just need to work the register myself. Is it busy?"

Anja nodded.

"Good night, Mr Hovenkamp," I said, as friendly as possible. "See you tomorrow."

"Tomorrow, yes."

I was at Marcel's by 5:30. His parents were spending a month in the south of France, he'd told me, so he had their place all to himself. He was stretched out in a chaise longue in the back yard. Three empty beer bottles were on the table beside him. Sure, *he* could hang out and drink, while *I* took care of business. Well, it'd be his turn soon enough.

When I stepped through the kitchen door into the yard, he got to his feet. We hugged. His hands insinuated themselves down inside my jeans, searching and stroking. His fingers seemed to want to travel deeper.

I clenched my cheeks to push him off, but he ignored the signal. Maybe he thought I was trembling in ecstasy.

"No," I said firmly, "not now. I'm exhausted. I need to freshen up and have a drink. This is not fun, you know. Do you understand that? Eight hours behind that freaking register."

He nodded, as if he actually *did* understand. But I knew that a little rich boy like Marcel, who'd never had to do anything more challenging than slack his way through high school and a bit of university, didn't have a clue what I was saying.

"I can't take much more of this," I said. "One more day, tops." Why not speed things up? The longer I stuck around here, the worse it was likely to get. "Tomorrow, okay? The boss is already nagging me for my tax number."

"Okay, fine," said Marcel, "we'll do it tomorrow."

My second day at the market was pretty much a rerun of Day 1. To Rachida and Anja, this was normal – they didn't know anything else. I was already beginning to climb the walls, though.

For one thing, the temperature was a few degrees higher than yesterday, and that had at least two effects on the customers. They had less patience, grew irritated quicker. At one point, Hovenkamp himself had to break up a fight between two guys, one of whom grabbed the last package of beer nuts just as the other one was reaching for it – or, depending on who you believed, snatched it right out of the other jerk's hands. The second effect was that customers came into the store wearing less clothing. Fat bald men with hairy chests and arms appeared at the registers in nothing but a Speedo. I wondered how much hotter it had to get before the first topless woman would walk in. Hovenkamp would probably eat that with a spoon.

During my lunch break, he sat beside me in the lounge and droned on about the exciting world of supermarketry. The things you could learn about humanity, its idiosyncracies and behaviour! (As if I gave a damn – especially since the idiosyncracies seemed flat and simple, especially when it came to groceries.) How to incorporate design elements to give the store its own ambiance, to make it attractive to its customers. How all the employees were one big happy family, and he'd be glad if I felt myself a part of it. He laid a hand on my arm, and I just managed not to pull away from his touch or slap him. No, I had to stay on Hovenkamp's good side, at least for another couple of hours.

After lunch, I soldiered on behind my register, knowing that the more seriously I took the job, the faster the time would seem to pass. Around 3:30 – getting close to the end – a young man of about twenty-five eyed me narrowly as I rang him up. "Don't I know you from somewhere?" he asked.

"I don't think so," I said, not looking up.

"I talked to you in Night Town," he insisted, "a few weeks ago. What's your name again? Something with a K?"

I shook my head and tapped the nameplate Anja had given me that morning.

"Marjolein? Well, you've got a twin out there, then," he said, handing me his money.

"Interesting." I gave him his change.

At a few minutes to four, I began to feel nervous, understandably enough.

And at four on the dot, I took a deep breath and shut down my register.

As I punched in my code, he suddenly materialized beside me. "I'm going upstairs with you," he said in a threatening whisper.

"But—"

"Do what I tell you."

He closed the door behind us, grabbed my arm and pushed me up the stairs. At the top, he pulled a ski mask over his head and took a pistol out of his pocket and held it to my temple. The metal felt cold against my skin. I lowered my gaze: he was wearing red Nikes. Stupid, to wear shoes that stood out like that. I could probably use that later on, though.

With a powerful push, he shoved me into Hovenkamp's office. At first, the boss didn't seem to realize what was happening. "What—?" He started to get up, but then slumped back into his chair.

"The money – let's have it. Otherwise, she gets it, then you. Understand?"

He sounded very convincing.

He yanked the telephone cord out of the wall and then, pointing his pistol right into the boss' face, demanded the key to the safe. Jesus, Hovenkamp was sweating like a pig. I knew his type. Typical asshole, lived in a new condo, drove an Opel Corsa. Wife and kiddies either waiting patiently for Daddy to come home or spending the day at the beach.

As Hovenkamp filled two plastic shopping bags – which I noticed were stamped with one of our competitors' logos – with paper money, he tried to say something.

"Maybe we can—"

"Shut the fuck up or I'll shoot you in the balls."

He seemed to get a kick out of using that kind of language, seemed to use it to keep the boss off-balance, keep him praying that he wouldn't lose it and start blasting. Technically, you're supposed to fire a shot into the ceiling at times like this, but that wouldn't be all that great an idea with *that* gun, since it was just a toy.

"But," I said.

"You too, bitch." He swung the gun back over his shoulder, as if he was about to smash me in the face with it.

I shrank away from him and cowered against the wall, my hands covering my face, sobbing uncontrollably. "No, please!"

He backed out of the office with the two full bags and locked the door from the outside.

I held my breath. Hovenkamp hesitated for a moment, as if he was afraid that the robber might come back. Then it seemed like he was about to begin banging on the door, but I threw myself into his arms, pushed myself close, wrapped my arms around his sweaty back, pressed my head into his shoulder.

"I'm scared! He'll shoot us – I'm so afraid!" I kept it up. "Oh, Mr Hovenkamp, hold me, please. I'm so scared!" I considered peeing my pants – that'd slow things down a while longer – but decided that pissing myself was ickier than I really wanted to get. I'd've loved to have seen Hovenkamp's face, though, if I did it.

"Calm down," he said, stroking my back tenderly with his fat hands. "Be still. He's gone. You're okay."

"Oh, Mr Hovenkamp! If he – if he comes back, then—"

"He won't come back," he said soothingly, then added, "My name is Theo."

"Theo," I repeated, sniffling.

After about five minutes, when I finally settled down, Hovenkamp starting banging on the door like a madman. Then he remembered his computer and sent off a quick e-mail. Soon after that, Anja came up. She had to search for the spare key, and it was 4:30 by the time she found it and released us.

Hovenkamp called the police from the phone in the lounge. The overprotective Anja offered me water, coffee, Coke, cookies, you name it. I called Marcel's house to tell him I'd be late. He told me he'd had a hunch I might be.

It took almost fifteen minutes for the cops to arrive: two young officers with healthy beach tans. They questioned me about the robbery, friendly and empathetic. I told them how the robber had appeared beside me the second I'd punched in my code. Had I seen his face? No, he was wearing a ski mask. "Three little holes, two for his eyes and one for his mouth." Had anything about him caught my attention, any distinguishing characteristics? "No, I'm sorry, nothing."

"And he threatened you with a pistol?"

"Yes, and he—" The memory was suddenly too much for me. I buried my face in my hands and let tears well up from deep inside.

Hovenkamp put a fatherly arm around my shoulder. "Hasn't she been through enough?" he protested. "She's only been working here a couple of days, and now this happens. This is the first time we've ever been robbed. Holland's getting more dangerous every day."

I didn't like the way that sounded, me new to the store and suddenly it gets robbed. I hoped the cops wouldn't draw any conclusions from the coincidence.

"It's all over now," one officer said.

"But if he—" My sentence trailed off into more tears.

After half an hour of that, they let me go. The store was closed. Anja and Rachida stared at me with wide-eyed compassion. "And this was just your second day," Anja said.

The cops gave me a ride. I hoped Marcel would see me get out of the police car, but he was sitting at the kitchen table, drinking a beer. I decided not to mention his sneakers.

He hugged me.

"Where?" I demanded.

"Just like you said. The freezer."

He couldn't understand how she'd managed it. Or maybe it was all just a coincidence. In any case, she'd gotten away clean, with almost all of the money. They'd catch up with her, sooner or later.

He paced the length of his cell, back and forth, glaring angrily at his feet, now encased in old white jailhouse sneakers. His damned red Nikes, they'd given him away. Stupid to have worn them. She hadn't said a word about them.

Sure, he could have gone on denying it, but the ski mask, in freaking August, there was no way to get around *that*. A second dumb mistake. He should have tossed it in a dumpster, duh.

Through the barred window high overhead, he could see the sun. In his mind's eye, he saw himself catching some rays in his parents' back yard, in his chaise longue, a beer on the table beside him.

Fuck, how long would it be before he could get back to that world?

The sun in Spain was much better than in Holland. I stretched luxuriantly and gazed across the table at Ivo. We were on the terrace at Alfonso's. I'd arrived three days earlier, and met Ivo yesterday at the disco. His father was rich, a Dutch fatcat who'd retired here to live a life of money and status.

Ivo leaned towards me. "Want to go out tonight?"

"Maybe."

He smiled. Last night he'd tried to lure me up to his apartment, but I'd politely put him off. "I don't have many principles," I'd said, "but there's *one* rule I never break: don't ever go to bed with a man the first night you meet him."

"And the second night?" he'd asked.

"Well," I'd said, "that depends."

"On what?"

"You'll find out."

I sipped my Perrier. Ivo's eyes met mine. We laughed. I had him, I could feel it.

He had to work that afternoon, till 10 p.m. When he got off, we met back at Alfonso's terrace. He ordered a rum and Coke, I had a nice glass of white wine. I kept him in suspense for a while, but eventually we wound up at his apartment. First we stopped at my hotel.

"Not bad," said Ivo, glancing around my suite.

"I can afford it."

Later, when I lay in his arms – the sex wasn't anything to write home about, but you can't have everything – we engaged in some pillow talk. Some guys fall asleep as soon as they're finished, but others were talkers, I'd learned. Marcel, for instance. He could talk till the cows came home, that one. And I'd just lay there listening, my head on his shoulder, my hand on his belly.

I let Ivo brag about his work, his ambitions, his grand plans. Then I told him about *my* life, and I couldn't resist a little bragging. Once I'd started the story, I figured I might as well spill it all. Maybe because I could see in Ivo's eyes how fascinated he was. I wanted him to admire me, and it was easy to get there. And now he would certainly trust me.

"So I set it all up with him – Marcel, his name is. He went upstairs with me. Nothing to it. No, it wasn't a real gun, just a toy, but of course the boss didn't know that."

What *Ivo* didn't know was that I'd brought the gun with me. It was in my suitcase, in my hotel room. You don't leave a moneymaker like that behind unless you really have to. The beach police had had plenty of clues without it. Besides, I was pretty sure Marcel wouldn't last long under interrogation.

"So they caught him?"

"With a little help from me. The idiot wore red Nikes, so on my way out to the airport I made an anonymous call, told the cops

I'd seen a suspicious-looking guy in red sneakers coming out of such-and-such an address. I didn't want to get involved, I said, but it was my civic responsibility to call it in – and they pulled up like five minutes later and hauled him in for questioning. Seemed a shame to leave all that beautiful money behind, so I brought most of it with me. You have any idea how weird cash feels when it's frozen?"

I rolled over and gave Ivo a deep soul kiss. His sigh of satisfaction had something almost animalistic to it.

"I left a *little* behind for Marcel, but I wonder if he'll ever get the chance to spend it . . ."

Ivo sat up. "You want another drink, Aletta?"

"White wine," I said.

He got out of bed and went off to the kitchen. He acted tough, but I could tell from the way he walked that he'd be as easy as Marcel.

Yes, he'd do for a while.

And it'd be nice to have a temp with money of his own for a change.

Translation by Josh Pachter

Serum

Jo Nesbø

Somewhere a bird screeched. A harsh, ugly sound. Or maybe it was some other animal. Ken didn't know. He held the glass tube up towards the white sun, stuck the needle through the plastic seal, and drew up the plunger, so that the yellowish liquid was sucked into the syringe. A drop of sweat found its way between his bushy eyebrows, and he cursed under his breath when the salt burnt in his eye.

The buzz of insects, which had always been deafening, now seemed to increase. He looked at his father, sitting with his back against a grey tree trunk. His skin seemed to become one with the bark. Splotches of light played over his face and khaki shirt, as if he were sitting under a disco ball in one of Ken's favourite clubs in London. In fact, he sat beside a river in eastern Botswana, and stared up into the crown of the tree, where the sun was being filtered through the quivering leaves, of what Ken Abott did not know was an *Acacia xanthophloea*, a fever tree. Ken Abott didn't know very much of anything about the burning hot, green and nightmarish world surrounding him. He knew only that he had very little time left to save the life of the person he valued most here on earth.

Stan Abott had never made big plans for his son. He had seen far too many tragic examples of what the pressure of upper-class expectations did to the children. He didn't need to look far from home. He didn't even need to look as far as his boarding school friends who hadn't become as successful as hoped. The ones who had emptied bottle after bottle, in order to dare to make the jump from their penthouse apartments in Kensington or Hampstead,

five storeys down to the pavement. A pavement that was just as
hard there as in Brixton and Tottenham. He didn't even have
to look as far as Archie, a nephew he had last seen tangled in
blood-spotted sheets, and disposable syringes, in a hotel room in
Amsterdam. Archie had already had the look of one who had been
kissed on the mouth by the angel of death. He refused to return
home and had carelessly pointed a revolver in Stan's direction,
but in such a way that Stan had understood Archie couldn't have
cared less where it had been pointed when he pulled the trigger.

No, Stan did not need to look far. It was enough to look in the
mirror.

For nearly thirty years, he had been an unhappy publisher
who issued books written by idiots, which were about idiots,
and were purchased by idiots. There seemed to be enough
idiots out there, too, for Stan had managed to triple what had
already been a substantial family fortune, in the course of
his career. This had pleased his wife, Emma, far more than it
had himself. He could well remember the warm summer day
in Cornwall when they had wed, but he had forgotten why.
Perhaps she had just been at the right place at the right time
and from the right type of family. It hadn't been long before
he had wondered what interested him least: the money, the
books or his wife. He had brought up the topic of divorce,
and three weeks later she had joyously announced to him that
she was pregnant. Stan had felt a deep, internal pleasure that
lasted for the next ten days. By the time he sat in the waiting
room of St Mary's Hospital, however, his unhappiness had
returned. The child had been a boy. They had named him Ken
after Stan's father, handed him over to a nanny, sent him to
boarding schools and then suddenly one day he had stood in
his father's office asking for a car.

Stan had looked up in surprise and studied the young man
in front of him. He had inherited his horse-like face and lipless
mouth from his mother, but the rest was undeniably from his
father. The long, narrow nose, with his father's dense eyebrows
above, formed a "T" in the middle of his face, and there were two
bored, blue eyes on either side. They had taken for granted that
his childhood blondness would eventually darken to his mother's
mousy grey, but that had not happened. Ken had already
developed the droll, rather self-satirical sense of humour that

makes the British seem so charming, and it had been dancing lustily in his eyes when he saw his father's confusion.

It occurred to Stan that even if he had meant to make ambitious plans for his son, he would never have managed it. How was it possible that his son had been able to grow up without him even noticing? Had he been too busy being unhappy, being the person he thought everyone around him expected him to be? And if this was the case, how could this persona not include being a father to his only son? It pained him. Or maybe not. He paused to take stock. Yes, he had to admit, it actually caused him a great deal of pain. He had lifted his hands in a powerless shrug.

Whether or not Ken had foreseen his father's bad conscience, is difficult to say, but in any case he had gotten the car.

By the time Ken had turned twenty the car was gone. He had lost it in a bet, with a fellow student, over who could drive back to campus the fastest from one of the boring pubs in Oxford. Now, it must be said that Kirk had had a Jaguar, but Ken had been convinced he had still had a chance.

The following year he had lost his entire yearly stipend, from the education fund his father had set up for him, during a drunken night of poker with the heir to the Rolands' fortune. He had had three jacks in his hand and thought he had had a chance.

When he was twenty-four, he had, miraculously, obtained the right papers attesting to his knowledge of English literature and history, and had, without any trouble, gotten himself a job as a trainee in an English bank. The bank was of the old school, where the management understood the value of a man from Oxford, who knew his Keats and Wilde, and which anticipated that the ability to read accounts or evaluate the credit rating of a customer was something that someone with Ken's background was born with, or could at least learn along the way.

Ken landed in the stock market, where he became an undisputed success. He telephoned important investors every day keeping them updated on the market's latest trends, took even more important investors out to dinner and to strip clubs, and the very most important investors he took down to his father's country estate, where he got them drunk, and when the rare opportunity presented itself, screwed their wives.

The bank's management had considered moving Ken up the ladder and giving him a managerial position in the trading division, when it was discovered that he had incurred losses totaling just under fifteen million pounds, by trading in orange juice futures with the bank's money, and without authorization. He had been called into the board room where he had explained that he had thought he had had a chance. Rather than being moved up, he had been removed – from the bank, the city, and the entire financial world.

He had begun drinking, but had never really gotten the swing of it, so he had started going to the dog races, even though he never could stand dogs. It was from this point that his gambling had begun to take on enormous proportions. Not in actual money, because, in spite of his name, Ken was no longer able to obtain credit, and it would have been difficult for him to top his orange juice deal, anyway. His gambling had come to consume all of his time and energy. It had rapidly sucked him into a maelstrom of compulsive gambling where he had fallen weightless towards a black bottom. That is, it was a supposed bottom. In actuality, the fall had not yet ceased, so if one were an optimist, one might assume that that meant there was no bottom.

Ken Abott financed his accelerating gambling addiction by going to the one person he knew who had not seemed to grasp what was happening: his father. His son had discovered something about Stan Abott, and that was that he had a wonderful ability to forget. Each time Ken had come knocking, his father had looked at him as though it were the very first time he had stood there asking for money, or maybe even the first time he had stood there at all.

Ken pulled the syringe's needle out of the plastic cover.

"Do you remember how to do it?" His father's voice was just a hoarse whisper now. Ken tried to smile. He had never been able to stand needles, otherwise he would probably not have stopped at cocaine, but continued on to the harder drugs. Right now he had no choice. It was a matter of life or death.

"Try to find a vein?" he answered.

His father shook his head.

"Forget about veins. Just make the injection close to the bite. Small injections, three or four shots. And then one in the thigh, so that it's closer to the heart than to the bite, understand?"

"Are you sure that it was an Egyptian cobra, father? Can't it have been a . . .?"

"A what?"

"I don't know . . . a boomslang or something like that."

Stan Abott tried to laugh, but it just turned into coughing.

"A boomslang is a little green devil that hangs around in the trees all day long, Ken. This one was black and slithered along the ground. And the boomslang has a haemotoxin poison, it would have caused bleeding from my mouth, ears and anus. Don't you remember? We went all through this."

"I just want to make sure before I make the injection."

"Of course. I'm sorry." He closed his eyes. "I just hope that you don't think these weeks were a total waste of time."

Ken shook his head and meant it. Yes, he had hated each and every second of the four weeks he had been here. Hated the long, hot days he had trudged around the snake farm in his father's footprints, and the grey-haired, Negro caretaker whose parents had, most likely in a moment of weird humour, decided to call Adolph. Their monotonous chant-like voices had gone in one ear and right out the other. They droned on about green and black mambas, poison fangs in the front and back of the mouth, about which ones could bite you even if you held them upside-down by the tail, and about which ones ate mice and which ate birds. He couldn't give a damn about whether a cobra came from Egypt or Mozambique, he only knew that there were too many of them, and that his father must have been out of his mind when he bought this farm.

In the evenings they had sat on the front veranda, his father and Adolph each with a pipe, while they listened to the animal noises all around them and Adolph told legends about them as they presented themselves. When the moon had come up and the hyenas cold laughter made Ken shiver, Adolph told about the Zulus who believed that snakes were the spirits of the dead and let them come into their homes. He told about the tribes in Zimbabwe that wouldn't kill pythons, because it would cause long-lasting drought. When Ken had laughed over these superstitious beliefs, his father had told him about how in some rural areas in northern England people still practised an old snake ritual: if you saw an adder, you had to kill it right away, draw a ring around it, and then draw a cross within the ring. When that was done you had to read from psalm sixty-eight.

Ken had looked at his father in shock when he stood up and yelled into the night-darkened jungle:

"Let God arise, let his enemies be scattered:
let them also that hate him flee before him.
As smoke is driven away, so drive them away:
as wax melteth before the fire, so let the wicked perish
    in the presence of God."

The bird screeched again. It sat in the top of the tree. It was white with a long beak and a red comb on its head, almost like a rooster.

"Isn't it strange how little you and I know about each other, Ken?"

This made Ken jump. It was as though his father read his thoughts and spoke them aloud.

His father sighed, "We never managed to get to know one another. I . . . was never there was I? It's sad when fathers aren't there." The last sentence was left hanging in the air, demanding a response, but Ken didn't answer.

"Do you hate me, Ken?"

The insects stopped their buzzing abruptly, as though they too were holding their breath a second.

"No." He held the syringe pointing upwards, pushing the plunger a little to get the air out, and a drop escaped down the needle. "Hate has nothing to do with it, father."

Stan Abott had woken up very early one morning, looked at his sleeping wife as if to remember who she was, gotten up and walked to the open window. He had looked at the trees in the park whose black branches were desperately splayed towards a winter-grey sky, and at the asphalt below. It glittered wetly in the light from the lampposts that seemed to be hunched against the wind.

These were bad times, times requiring consolation. People wanted cheap lies and dreams, and since he sold the cheapest of them, his publishing firm was doing extremely well. An American company had made a bid to buy it. The publishing firm had been run by the family for three generations. Stan Abott had smiled. He had climbed up onto the window ledge, and a gust of wind had twisted the curtain around his foot, almost causing him to fall. By grasping the gutter, he had been able to, shakily, pull himself up to his full height. The rain coming from one side had struck his skin like needles of ice. He had opened his mouth. It had tasted like ashes. He had known it was time to take a huge leap. He then closed his eyes.

When he had reopened his eyes, he divorced Emma. She now had the name of Ives, not her maiden name, but the name of the new husband, who had moved in where Stan had moved out, as the divorce settlement stipulated that she was to retain the house. The Americans had taken down the Abott sign above the entrance to the publishing firm. They had decided to use their own name, and Stan was fundamentally glad that his family name would no longer be blemished by association with the things that were produced there. Through a friend, he had purchased a snake farm in Tuli, in the eastern part of Botswana. He knew nothing about snake farms, except that they provided snakes to reptile parks and to laboratories that produced serums which saved the lives of people bitten by snakes, and that it was not a very lucrative business.

Three weeks after he had opened his eyes, he had tried to squeeze them shut again, as well as he could. The sun had hung, like an oversized reading lamp, above the taxi area outside the international airport, in the not-so-international capital of Botswana. It was a smaller town which, according to his airline ticket, was called Gaborone. He had taken a taxi into it, and after a week of running through bureaucratic corridors, he was able to leave it, having obtained all the required licences, signatures, and stamps. He hadn't been back there since. And as Gaborone had the country's only international airport, it meant he had not been outside of Botswana.

What business did he have anywhere else? As quickly and instinctively as he had come to hate Gaborone, he had fallen in love with Tuli. The farm consisted of three old, but well-kept concrete buildings, where the four people who worked there, lived with eight hundred, more or less, deadly poisonous snakes. The buildings stood on a plateau surrounded by buffalo bushes and mongonga trees on low tapering hillsides. The farm was seldom visited, except by elephants, who had gotten lost on their way to the river, jackals on the lookout for garbage and outdated shoes, or the weekly jeep that collected the snakes and snake venom, and brought provisions down the nearly impassable road. On a horizon of green hilltops, dead trees pointed their witch-fingers towards the sky, but aside from that there was nothing here reminiscent of London.

When the dry season arrived, herds of impalas collected on the plains so they could be near the water, and they were accompanied by their faithful friends the baboons. Soon zebras and kudus also appeared. Lions hunted night and day, as it was party time for all the savannah's hunters. In the short period of twilight each day, they could see the sun flame up in the west and then disappear, and later hear the lions' deep roar throughout the night, while groups of moths collected like small snowstorms around the outdoor lights.

There was only one time that he had had doubts about whether or not this was the place he belonged. There had been a hatching of *naja nigricollis*, or black-necked spitting cobra, and Stan had watched the young being eaten alive, one by one, by their own father, until they had managed to fish him out of the cage. Adolph had already told him that smaller snakes were a natural part of the cobras diet, but his own young? It had caused such a sense of disgust in him, such an aversion to the animal's nature that it forced him to question whether he could stand to continue. Then one evening Adolph had shown him a dead tiger snake, bitten to death by its own young, and explained that the course of nature didn't allow for family ties. It was eat or be eaten, everywhere. It was not evil, or immoral, to eat one's own offspring, or parents. On the contrary, it was the fulfilment of nature's course. It was what Africa was all about: survival, at any price. And after a while it had become instinctive for Stan Abott, a thing he had accepted and even come to admire as a part of the merciless order of things. It was the consistent logic that balanced all of nature and gave the animals and people here their justification for existence. As a result he slowly got back something he had been missing for so long: his fear of dying. Or more accurately stated: his fear of not living.

Then the wet season had arrived. He would never forget that first time. He had gone to sleep listening to the first rain one night, and when he awoke in the late morning of the next day, and looked out at the plains, it was as though a mad painter had gone amok on the greyish-yellow canvas. In the course of a day or two, the plains had been transformed into a rolling landscape of strong smells, and a psychedelic display of colour and of insects which had buzzed low over the carpet of petals and the growing, brown river.

And so he had thought, what could be better than this?

Six months after his arrival he had sent a letter to Ken. He waited six months for an answer, and receiving none, wrote one more. He had ended his monologue the following year with a Christmas card, and, having heard through the grapevine that Ken had not managed to find anything meaningful to do in London, an offer of permanent employment on the farm.

He had not expected an answer, and had not received one. Until three years had passed.

Ken liked almost everything about cocaine. He liked the way it affected him, the people around him liked the effect it had on him, he was never hung over from it, and he saw no signs of becoming addicted to it. The only thing he didn't like about it was the cost. That was why, after a financial crisis caused by two terrible weeks at the dog races, he went over to the poor man's alternative – amphetamines. Then a flighty female acquaintance, an ugly, surprisingly dumb, health freak, whom he had only slept with a couple of times because he had hoped he could get her to loan him some of her father's money, had told him that amphetamines were synthetic drugs. And that the human body could never completely break down synthetic drugs. This meant that when one had taken amphetamines one would always have the by-products in one's body. Those were two words Ken hated – always and never – so he had stopped immediately. He had sworn never to take anything but healthy, organic drugs, like cocaine, and had had to admit to himself that he needed money. In a hurry.

His chance came one day, when he had gone to visit an old colleague from the City, with the intention of freshening up the friendship, so that the next time they met he could ask to borrow money. They had been in the colleague's office. Just for the fun of it, his ex-colleague had shown Ken an illegal bet on the World Cup final in football, between France and Brazil. A couple of big stockbrokers had been doing some bookmaking, using coded pages on the Reuters' monitors. When the ex-colleague had gone to make more tea, and forgotten to log out, Ken had been quick to act. He had closed his eyes, pictured Ronaldo's dinosaur thighs, typed in his own name and address, keyed over to the wager box, closed his eyes one more time, imagined Brazil's yellow-clothed heroes raising the trophy, and typed one million pounds sterling. Enter. He had held his breath while he waited for an answer, knowing that his name was not registered, and that his bet was too high, but also that in the world of Reuters, people traded every second for ten times that amount without anyone asking who sat at the other end of the line. He had thought that he had had a chance. And then a message was returned: "CONFIRMED".

Had Ronaldo not, that very same night, had an epileptic episode brought on by the excessive use of his Playstation, Ken might not have had to worry about his future cocaine financing nor, as things developed, his immediate health. Two days later, however, early in the morning, in this case sometime before eleven a.m., the doorbell had rung. Outside stood a man wearing a black suit, sunglasses and carrying a baseball bat. He had explained to Ken the unpleasant consequences that would result if Ken did not manage to have one million pounds sterling ready within fourteen days.

Four days later, late in July, Stan Abbot had received a telegram acknowledging the Christmas greetings, accepting the job offer and asking him to meet his son at the airport in Gaborone, in five days. He had included a bank account number where the money for the tickets could be wired, as soon as possible. Stan had been very pleased about everything, except that he would have to go to Gaborone again.

Ken looked at his wrist-watch, a Weiler watch, which, with its South African gold and Swiss precision, was ticking towards judgment day.

The day had begun as all the other twenty-six had. Ken had woken up wondering where in the hell he was and why. He had remembered the why first. Money. This should have made him think of his creditors in London, but instead made him think of the white powder, a woman he didn't seem to have such a platonic, non-committed relationship to anymore. The symptoms were classic, but in his opinion, the irritation and sweats, could just as easily have been blamed on this God-forsaken place that was full of poisonous creeping things, insects that were everywhere, and Negroes who lacked respect. They seemed to have forgotten who had colonized, and tried to civilize the place. However, the depressions had been something new. The hours that suddenly became a dark place where he lost contact with his surroundings, even the floor seemed to disappear and he fell into a bottomless hole. All he could do was wait until they passed.

"Snake hunt," his father had said at breakfast.

Ken had tried to seem interested, he really had. Like when his father had shown him the test tubes with the serum and with their codes and blue plastic caps, and the tubes with poison that had their own codes and red plastic caps. Or was it the other way around? He had had a problem concentrating as well, and when his thoughts had sailed away, and his pen stopped taking notes, his father had just looked at him grumpily, not commenting on his lack of note-taking.

They had driven for a half-hour, on something that vaguely resembled a road, through alternating scenery. There was the dense, green, bush-like vegetation, the half-metre deep mud puddle, and the dried out moonscape. At one place, that to Ken seemed chosen totally at random, his father had stopped the car and jumped out, taking with him three cloth sacks and a long pole with a wire loop on the end.

"Put these on." His father had tossed him a pair of swimming goggles.

Ken had looked at him in confusion.

"Spitting cobra. Nerve poison. They can hit you in the eye from a distance of eight metres."

They had begun to search. Not on the ground, but up in the trees.

"Watch the birds," his father had said. "If you hear them screeching, or see them hopping from branch to branch, you can be quite certain that there is a boomslang or a green mamba nearby."

"I don't think . . ."

"Hush! Do you hear those clicking sounds? Those are polecats hunting. Come on!" His father had run towards the sounds with Ken dawdling after, against his will. He had suddenly stopped, giving the signal that Ken should approach carefully. There on a large flat stone lay a two-metre long, black beast sunning itself. His father had snuck around the stone until he was directly behind it, manoeuvered the pole above the stone and carefully drawn the wire loop over the snake's narrow, but distinctive, head. He had then tightened it. The snake had thrashed about and opened up in a life-threatening yawn, showing the light red colouring inside its mouth.

"Can you see that the venom fangs are in the front of the mouth?" his father had yelled enthusiastically.

"Yeah?"

"So what do we have here?"

"Please, father, let's get finished first. I'm nervous about this."

He had released the snake into the bag that Ken had held open.

"Black mambo," his father had said while shading his eyes as he squinted up into the trees.

Whatever, Ken had thought and shivered when he felt the snake writhing in the sack.

After one half-hour in the blazing sun, Ken decided to take a cigarette break. He had stood with his back against one of the trees his father had tried to teach him the name of, and had begun to think about the rifle in the car, and that this was probably as good a chance as he was ever going to get, when he heard his father's scream. It had not actually been a scream, but more of a short bark, but Ken had known what had happened right away. Perhaps because he had dreamt it, thought about it, or just unconsciously hoped for it. He had put out his cigarette on the tree trunk. If he was very lucky, this might just save him a lot of trouble.

He had shaded his eyes, and there, over by the river bank, he had seen his father's back, hunched over in the waist-high, stiff grass.

"Damn! Ken, I've been bit, and I didn't get a chance to see what kind of snake it was! Help me to look for it!"

"I'm coming."

His father had hesitated a moment, maybe because of the tone of his son's answer.

Ken had vaguely remembered something his father had said that if you weren't able to identify the snake, you had a choice between forty different serums, and that if you tried the seemingly safe solution of injecting all of them, you would die quicker from the serum than from the poison. He had also remembered something his father had said about not stamping hard when looking for snakes, because they felt the vibrations through the ground and took off. Ken had stamped as hard as he could.

"I've got it!" his father had yelled as he dove down into the grass. Another sentence to remember: the risk of being bitten again is less than not knowing what bit you.

Ken had silently cursed.

Poor bastard, Ken had thought as he watched his father swing the sack, again and again, against the tree trunk. He had not been thinking about the snake, nor about his father. A picture of the man in his doorway, holding the baseball bat, had appeared in his mind again. He had been thinking about Ken Abott.

His father had sunk down beside the tree trunk by the time Ken had gotten to him. His skin was grey and his breathing was coming in heaving gasps.

"You can check what it is," he had whispered and tossed the sack to him. Ken had coughed in the dust that whirled up from the dry ground, opened the sack and reluctantly stuck his hand down into it.

"Don't . . ." his father managed to say.

Ken had felt the rough, dry scaly skin against his palm. He had touched more of them than he liked to think about over the last few weeks. This one seemed no different. Not until it occurred to him that the oscillations he had felt under the scales came from muscles, and that the animal was not dead. Nowhere near dead. He had screamed, more from fear than from pain, when the fangs had broken through the skin of his arm. He had drawn his arm up, seen two circular punctures just under his elbow, and screamed again. Quick as lightning, he put his mouth to the wound and feverishly began to suck.

"Stop that." His father's voice had been weak and disappointed. "That only helps in films about the wild west. I've told you that before."

"Yes, but . . ."

"And the other thing I have told you, is that you never put your hand into a sack with snakes in it, whether you think they are dead or not. You turn the sack upside-down and make sure your legs are out of the way. Always."

"Always" and "never" in the same preachy sentence. Not strange that Ken had repressed it.

"Empty the sack." The snake had fallen to the ground with a soft thud and coiled up, paralysed by the sunlight.

"Well, what do you think, Ken? Cape cobra?"

Ken hadn't answered, just stared, wide-eyed, at the snake.

"Sand snake? Gabon viper?"

The hyper-sensitive tongue had slid out of the snake's mouth, and in a second had oriented the snake using taste and smell.

"Don't let it get away, Ken."

But Ken had let it get away. He had had neither the energy or the nerve to touch a snake again, let alone the one that had just shortened his expected lifetime to twenty-six years.

"Shit!" his father had said.

"You're kidding!" Ken had answered. "You saw it just as well as I did, and you know all the snakes in God damned Africa by heart. Don't tell me you don't know . . ."

"Of course I know which snake it was," his father had said, and looked at Ken with an expression on his face Ken hadn't been able to read. "And that's why I said 'shit'. Hurry up and get the brown bag from the car."

"But shouldn't we get back to . . ."

"That was an Egyptian cobra. Our central nervous systems would be paralysed before we got even halfway. Now, do what I say."

Ken had finally reacted and come back with a large doctor bag made of brown buffalo skin.

"Open it," his father had said. "Quickly". His body had twisted, his mouth open as though he wasn't able to get enough air.

"I feel all right, father, why . . ."

"Because I got the first bite. It contained five times the amount of poison in the second one. It means I have approximately one half-hour, and you have two and a half. What do you see?"

"There are a bunch of tubes fastened to the sides in here."

"We always bring the serums for the snake poisons we know we don't have time to go back for. Egyptian cobra, did you find it?"

Ken's eyes had rushed across the labels on the tubes.

"Here it is, father."

"I have to have it right away. Hopefully, I'll be clear-headed enough to point out the way back, while we drive, and we'll make it back to the farm, with time to spare, before you start to have problems. You'll find the syringes laying in the bottom. You know what to do, son."

Ken stuck the tip of the needle in just above the bite marks. He breathed deeply through his nose as he slowly pressed the plunger down. He watched the yellow liquid until there were about two-thirds of it left. Then he drew back the plunger a little, withdrew the needle and followed the same procedure a little farther up.

"How does it feel?" Ken asked.

"Sad," his father whispered. His chin had sunk down onto his chest.

Ken pulled the needle out and used a ball of cotton to dry off a little blood from the needle marks on his arm.

"Well. If it is any comfort, it hurt like hell," he said, and looked at his watch. "Comfort for the last few minutes you have left to live, old man."

His father lifted his head with great effort.

"Why, Ken? In the name of God, why?"

Ken sat himself down beside his father and put an arm around his shoulders.

"Why? Why do you think? For the same reason I have carried around that rifle, waiting for a situation to arise, where I could blame a shooting accident, a misfire or whatever you call it. Money, father. Money."

Stan's head tipped forward again. "So, that's why you came? To collect your inheritance?"

Ken patted his father on the back with his good arm. A pulsing, half-paralyzing pain had begun to spread itself around the bite and the needle marks on the other arm.

"I read a discouraging article about the older generation in the *Guardian*. Do you know what the life expectancy is for middle-class men, between the ages of fifty and fifty-five, who have never had heart trouble or cancer? Ninety-two years. I have a few creditors who are not willing to wait that long, father. But I believe it will calm them down immensely, when I, as sole heir, arrive home with your death certificate."

"You could just have asked for the money."

"A million pounds? There are limits for even my shamelessness, father."

Ken laughed out loud, and the sound was immediately answered from the other side of the river, where a pack of grey-brown hyenas had appeared and were watching them curiously. Ken shuddered instinctively.

"Where did they come from?"

"They can smell it," said Stan.

"Smell? You haven't started to smell, yet."

"Dead. They recognize it in the air. I've seen it before."

"Well. They are ugly, they are dumb, and they are on the other side of the river. I hate them."

"That's because they are our moral superiors." Ken looked at his father, shocked, while he continued, "Without choice, lacking morality, you probably think. But if choice means being able to force one's nature, and morality involves wanting to, why are we so unhappy?" Stan Abott lifted his head again and smiled sadly. "It's because we convince ourselves that we could have done things differently. We believe we are creatures with souls and that we have the ability to do something other than that which, in the end, would benefit ourselves. But we can't. The proof is that we are here, that we continue to exist. We eat our parents, or our children, when we must, not because of hate, but because of a love of life. Yet we still believe we will burn in hell for it. And maybe we will. That's why a cobra is morally superior to us, when it decides to eat its offspring. It doesn't feel even an instant of shame, because there is no sin, just a burning will to live. You understand. Your only saviour is yourself, and you are saved only by doing what you have to, to survive."

Ken should have answered, but a sudden pain in his chest took his breath away.

"Something wrong?" his father asked.

"I . . ."

"Have pain in your chest," said his father, with a normal voice, now. "That's how it starts."

"Starts? What . . ."

"Egyptian cobra. You should remember. We went through it all."

"But . . ."

"Nerve poison. First there's burning pain around the bite, which gradually spreads to the rest of the body. The skin around the bite becomes discoloured. The arms and legs swell, and this is followed by sleepiness. Now, towards the end there's increased heart rate, runny eyes and mouth, and paralysis of the throat, something that makes it hard to talk and breathe. The final stage occurs when the poison paralyses the heart and lungs, and you die. It can take hours and is extremely painful."

"Father!"

"You sound surprised, son. Weren't you paying attention during your lessons?"

"But you . . . you seem much . . . better."

"No, you must not have been paying much attention," said his father with a thoughtful expression. "Otherwise, you would have seen the difference between an Egyptian cobra and an African stone python."

"African stone python?"

"Aggressive and unpleasant, but not poisonous." His father straightened himself up and limbered up his neck. "You're right, I'm totally fine, but how are you? Can you feel your throat beginning to close, son? In a little while you'll begin to cramp up, not something to look forward to . . ."

"But we . . ."

"Were bit by the same snake? Mysterious, isn't it? Perhaps you've gotten something in your system that I haven't."

It finally dawned on Ken. He looked at the empty, glass tube on the ground, and tried to stand up, but his legs wouldn't obey. He had such intense pain in his armpits.

"Had you paid attention during your lessons, you would have looked at the plastic seal on the tube before you gave yourself the injections, Ken."

Red, thought Ken. Red seal. He had injected himself with poison.

"But there were no other tubes for Egyptian cobra. I checked them all. None with blue seals. No serum . . ."

His father shrugged. Ken gasped for air. The buzzing of the insects had become a constant pressure against his eardrums.

"You knew it all along. You knew . . . why . . . I came."

"No, I didn't know. But I'm not dumb, so I didn't count it out either. And I would have stopped you if you had tried to give me the injection."

Ken couldn't feel the tears that ran down his cheeks.

"Father . . . drive me back, now. Time . . ."

But his father didn't hear him. He had gotten up and gazed towards the other side of the river.

"Adolph says that they're good swimmers, but I've never seen it myself."

He looked up at the sky. The sun hung well over the trees on the hilltops, but he knew that when seven o'clock came, it would be as though someone had cut an invisible thread. The sun would dive, in free-fall, behind the horizon, and it would be pitch black in less than a quarter of an hour.

The white bird screeched one last time, then took to the air.

"It's time to be getting home. Adolph should have dinner ready soon."

Ken knew that he didn't have a chance.

Translation by Susan Loyd

Huxley

Chad Taylor

Angela Bane gave her first violin performance aged five at her parents' second wedding. Her father braced himself when he saw her mount the podium with her tiny stride, but in fact she turned out to be quite good. That night when she was asleep Angela fell out of bed and broke her chin, and so couldn't hold the violin for months afterwards. Her practice fell away and she didn't play again, although she could still read music now.

Angela's parents divorced again five years later. Phillip went overseas and Louise kept Angela and her baby brother Ben. Their first nanny was quite good but she got pregnant after a year and was replaced by a widow named Diane Crawley. Diane looked after Angela for eight years, and so naturally Angela trusted her with money.

"Diane was like a parent to me," Angela told me as she lit up in the gazebo. "Phillip would send me cash from Hong Kong or the islands or wherever he was working, I think because he felt guilty, and I didn't want to tell Louise about it so I would just put it away in one of my jewellery boxes. I also felt guilty about it, so when Diane found it and offered to help me keep it secret, naturally I was relieved. And of course there were no records of it, and Phillip doesn't remember now, with the drinking."

It always sounded odd to me when children used their parents' first names.

"Do you remember how much money it was?" I said.

"Oh sure. Like eight thousand," Angela said, blinking her bright blue eyes. "And this was nine years ago, for whatever the money was worth then."

"And Diane refuses to give it back."

"I didn't even ask for it. When Louise told her that we wouldn't be needing a nanny any more because I'm an adult now, I just asked Diane for clarification – no pressure or anything – and she went through the roof and started yelling. So I had to tell mum and she fired Diane and now Diane's threatening legal action for unfair dismissal. Her sister is a lawyer. And Louise being a corporate manager and everything, a court case would really damage her."

Angela sucked in her lower lip. Her jaw curved to the left where it had healed. The break was what doctors call a guardsman's fall, when you land without extending your hands. The asymmetrical bite lent her the air of breeding. That, along with the house that could have contained my apartment three times. The Bane house was architect-designed and curved in a U around the pool. The pool was not quite long enough to swim a length and the grounds weren't quite big enough to run around, but you can't have everything, I guess.

Angela also complained that the gazebo was draughty but we could talk there in private. Louise was out but the Banes seemed to operate an open-door policy: two parties Angela described as friends had appeared in the lounge and waved to us through the glass in the hour we had been talking. We could also light up in the gazebo, as Angela had pointed out before she produced a joint the size of a cigarillo. As the little room filled with smoke some of it curled away through a gap under the doors and betrayed the ventilation she had talked about.

"I think it's cool that you smoke," she said. "I thought a cop might not be into it."

"I wasn't with the police for very long." I winced as I stretched my knees. "Besides, this is medicinal."

"My little brother Ben plays rugby," she said, brightly.

"I saw the photos." There were two framed portraits on the wall in his room. I played his school many moons ago. They had matching jerseys and we borrowed their scales for the weigh-in. "So what do you want me to do about Diane?"

"Louise just can't know, ay," Angela said. "She's stressed out enough about it already."

"So you're the client?"

"I can afford it." Angela inspected the roach and sniffed. "I just think if someone talked to Diane, then she would come round. It's a clash of personalities."

"Do you know if she's working for anyone else?"

"No. She's gone to ground, I think."

"Did she leave a number?"

"Only the phone we gave her. She was a live-in."

"And her sister?"

"I think she's in the book."

"Then I'll get one of my men on to it."

"Do you work with a partner?"

"No. I shook my head. That was a joke. I hate working with other people."

"I thought you were a team player."

I shrugged. "It's just the nature of the job. You're the only person you can rely on."

Angela stood up, suddenly.

"Would you like a swim, Huxley?"

"I think I should get started."

But she was already peeling off her jeans. "Come on, then."

She stripped down to her T-shirt and her briefs and disappeared in a well-trained arc.

Fortunately I was wearing boxers. The water was cold: when I came up my ears were buzzing and my skull rang like a bell. I spluttered and snorted and rubbed my eyes. Angela enjoyed that. She laughed. And she of course saw my tattoo: Jim Morrison's head and shoulders, almost life-size, stretched between my shoulders and my waist. His long hair flowed outside the picture frame: above his head was a clear white brigantine, a reference to "The Crystal Ship" from their debut album. The caption below the frame, inked in the same green as the rest of the portrait, said "Riders on the Storm". The lines had spread a little over the decades but the stare remained bold. I had thought about getting it touched up but Ricky who inked it died and it didn't seem right letting someone else do it. It took four nights for him to cut it and months more to heal.

"Who's that?" Angela said.

"Jim Morrison."

"Do you like him?"

Diane's son Ivan was an auto electrician. His garage was in Papatoetoe. The yard was filled with cars, but silent. The only noise in his office came from the aquarium pump. It wasn't working very well: the axolotls were barely visible inside the tank. Their dark skin was flaking off in patches.

"I've gotta fucking clean that, ay," Ivan Crawley said. He was a barrel of a man with a short leg and a worried look. "They're the wife's."

"I was actually looking for your mother," I said, trying to make the statement not sound like a challenge. He had one better leg than me even with the limp.

"Is it about money?" he winced.

"Pretty much."

"It fucking always is." He opened the cheque book on his desk. The broken stubs were smudged with oil. "How much?"

"More than that."

"You want to take a car?"

I looked at the vehicles in the yard. "Are they yours?"

"I can always write one off, ay. People hate paying for fucking electrical."

"So you don't know where she is?"

"No."

"Fair enough."

"It fucking is," he said. "Out."

Angela had described Diane's sister as a lawyer but her Ponsonby Road chambers looked more like a collective or a government shop. Marsha Crawley did a lot of social work as well as representing a wildlife organization and a company that wanted to save the mangroves but the vehicle in her parking space was a four-wheel drive. Not that there's anything wrong with that. Marsha also smoked. I watched her sharing a cigarette on the sidewalk with her colleagues or maybe a client, blowing smoke into the spring air. Marsha was rail thin and dressed entirely in black, which made her look thinner. There was no point in talking to her yet.

I was watching Marsha from the passenger seat of my car. It was less conspicuous than sitting behind the wheel. Two spaces in front of me a man in a cut-down Commodore was using the same trick. Marsha dropped her cigarette and stepped on it and went back inside, still talking, oblivious to all the attention she was getting. The man in the Commodore pretended not to look at me in the passenger mirror and I pretended not to look at him as I got out and walked up to the car and tapped the window.

Sonny Tewera's gold tooth flashed when he smiled and his eyes were pink. He was keeping his shoulder down with cortisone so he could coach his boy's sevens every other weekend.

"So who hired you, Sonny?" I said.

"The mother." He looked puzzled. "What about you?"

"The daughter."

"The little stoner chick? Cheers to that, bro."

"Yeah, yeah."

"For true, man. She's cute."

"She's young enough to be my daughter, Sonny."

"Richer, but," he said. "Made a move on her yet?"

Sonny and I stopped off at the sports bar on College Hill. The shutters were down against the sun and the Roosters game was on. We got a standing table which hurt me more after twenty minutes than it did him. His Nikes were as big as a loaf of bread. Sonny watched the game with a cheerful expression. Every surface of his face was either pushing out or pushed in: his grin was the only thing that was flat. It stayed on his face if he was hitting people or being hit himself. He had gone to the trouble of getting a gold front tooth but he still had two missing on the side. Sonny was that sort of guy. His ears were pierced but he wore nothing in them.

"So how much is she paying you?" he said.

"The usual fee."

"You give her a quote?"

"Standard rate."

"Everyone wants a quote now."

"Times are tight."

"I'll say. Can you imagine having a nanny for ten years?"

"Nine years," I said. "And they had two."

"Nice pool."

"The gazebo is draughty," I said.

"Mum told me the house shifted ten years after it was built."

"Architect designed."

"Fuck that shit," he said. "You want another round?"

"I should get going."

"You found the nanny yet?"

"Have you?"

"Nah. Call me if you do, though, hey? We could save money if we team up."

"I don't do teams."

"I could do some running for you."

"I can run."

"To the bathroom, maybe."

"Listen." I put my hand on his shoulder and felt the muscles I used to have. "Maybe after I talk to her, I'll give you a tinkle."

"Sweet." Sonny drained his glass, chuckling and swallowing at the same time.

Her knock was as loud as a man's. I opened the door.

Diane Crawley was taller than her sister, with wide cheekbones and a narrow nose. Her skin was maybe a little pale, but freckled. She was holding a slightly battered briefcase – she had an easy grip on the handle. Her hair was medium length, tied back. Her pants suit was a pants suit.

"As you can see, I'm not hiding," she said. "And I want you to stop bothering my son." Her tone of speaking was low and steady. It was put on, I thought: the manner you'd adopt to calm a child. I rubbed my eyes. It was late.

"Late in the morning," she corrected me. "What are you doing still sitting round? Why aren't you out? Don't you work?"

"Gentleman's hours." I smiled. She did not.

"I won't bother you by coming in," she said. "I didn't come here to have a conversation. I need you to leave my son alone. He has quite enough to deal with as it is, running a business with his disability."

"I wouldn't like to go up against him."

"You would not. He does well for his size, and his means. But my concerns are not his and I want you to leave him alone."

"I understand Angela Bane lent you some money."

"Angela Bane is a darling girl but quite the fantasist. She is prone to clinical depression, like her mother, and is a drug user. I expect an ex-policeman would have determined that."

I raised my eyebrows.

"It was simple enough to find out," she said. "Ivan took down your registration and my sister looked it up. Anyone can be a detective nowadays, Mr Huxley."

"And I count on it," I said. "Angela has financial records—"

"She does not."

"—But you do, so she can demand an audit, and it will take a long time, and it will be dull, and your reputation will be harmed, as will your sister's if she's daft enough to follow you into the small claims court."

It was a good speech, but Diane was already turning away.

I stood outside my door in my boxers. The elevator opened and she stepped inside after glancing back at me with something like pity.

"She's such a cow," Angela said, waving her hand across her face. The gazebo was totally filled with smoke. She might as well have been trying to scoop a hole in the swimming pool. "So is that it?"

"No, it's an update. I wanted you to know where I was. Client briefing and so on." I closed my eyes and let my head fall back for a minute. "I'm going to go to her place and have a look-see."

"You're going to burgle Diane's apartment?"

"I'm going to see if there's any evidence of her financial status in plain view," I said. "Or just out of plain view." I sat forward again. "I'm just going to grab it."

"Isn't that illegal?"

"I'm pretty sure, yes."

"So we can't use the evidence in a court case or anything."

"This isn't TV," I said. "It's never going to go to court. The amount's just too small. A few thousand dollars over several years – anyone can hide that. There's no record, no legal solution. Even the police will tell you that."

"They did tell me that."

"Did you tell me that they told you that?"

"I don't remember."

"Neither do I." I frowned. This was very good shit. "Never mind. What I need is for you to call a meeting with Diane, on a certain night, so I know she's not home, and text me when she's there, and not, and – you know." I wiggled my hand. "Stuff."

"What do you do, normally? Do you just hit people?"

"No. Not at all." I felt a little offended by the idea. "I menace them."

"With your bad knees."

"Nobody else knows they're bad. When I was playing I could cover half a field in ten seconds."

"Ten?"

"Maybe twelve. But I was good. I could bring any man down, and I never dropped the ball."

"You still look fit, Huxley."

"Ha."

"I mean it. I wouldn't mind."

"Don't be silly."

"It's my job. I'm a silly little rich girl. That's what you think, isn't it? Here." She held out the joint.

"Ta. I don't think that."

"Not even a little bit?"

"Maybe the rich part." I held my breath. "But I could tell that from the house."

She held her nose and giggled. "Don't make me laugh."

"I'm not."

She guffawed. She slapped my chest with her hand. She had small, lovely hands. Even her slap was soft.

Angela sent me a text: *she's here now*. A few minutes later she sent me another. It said: *she's here now*. Then she sent me another one, which said: *she's here now*. By the third time the phone rang I was halfway into Diane's little second floor apartment, clambering over the dividing wall between the downstairs units and gripping the rails. Diane lived in a cute little retirement block in Mission Bay: I had worked out who was home by counting the blaring TV sets. I wondered whether I should put the cell on vibrate but everybody in the block was deaf so I left it on ring.

My knees didn't hurt to climb but when I landed on my feet I could have screamed. I crouched there for a moment to catch my breath and let the pain ebb. Diane had left her lights on. The unit was modern but the decor was homespun bordering on fussy: thick carpet, crocheted hangings, hand-turned planters. The balcony was lined with feeder pots, two sets of hanging chimes and random crystals. The deck furniture was woven cane: a faux glass fishing float in a string bag. The aluminium slider doors were latched. I unlatched them.

The place smelled like instant coffee. I could have done with a cup but I put that out of my mind and started taking the place apart – gently, piece by piece, and then putting the pieces back. Diane was a tidy widow. She kept the books. I took them. I was standing on the balcony putting the sliding doors back on the latch when my cell phone rang.

"You want to fucking get that?" said Ivan Crawley, looking up from the lawn.

"It's okay," I called down. "I can guess what it says."

He grinned. "You want to climb down, or shall I come up?"

"I'd like to see you leg it. You could do with the exercise."

"You prick."

"Come on up and say that."

He was already climbing the fence hand-over-hand. He gripped the railing. I stood my boot on his knuckles.

"Aw, don't be fucking juvenile," he said.

He was right. I unlatched the sliding door, stepped inside and was latching it from the inside as he made it up on the deck. I waved. He swore again. As he fumbled with the latch – mustn't break mother's door, now – I walked across the apartment and was headed out by the time he entered, shutting the door behind me on its helpful deadlock. He doubtless had a key. I walked as briskly down the stairs as injury would allow, got into my car and turned the key.

It didn't start.

"He's an auto-electrician, remember," said Sonny, leaning on the window. "I watched him pull the distributor while you were inside."

"Anyone could do that."

"But he did it so quick, bro," Sonny said. "He's a natural."

"Did Angela's mother send you out here?"

"Sent me a text."

"Those girls need to get their shit together."

"Maybe they have, bro." He cocked his head. "I mean, are you going to take him on by yourself?"

Ivan was storming out of the downstairs entrance, silhouetted by the glow of the safety light.

"I reckon I could," I said.

"In the eighties, maybe."

I sighed. It was true. "I've got her accounts," I said.

Ivan was coming round the car towards us both.

"Sixty-forty?" Sonny said.

"Don't be a dick. Finder's fee."

"Sweet."

Sonny drummed his fingers on the car door and turned just as Ivan dropped with the intention of taking him square in the chest. Which is how I would have done it, I thought, wincing, but better from the side of Sonny's bad shoulder. It was not a short fight, but it was fast.

"Angela should not have engaged your services without telling me about it, Mr Huxley. The last thing any mother wants is to disempower her daughter but naturally, I had to move to protect her interests."

Louise Bane stood in her white kitchen stirring her *espresso* at a graceful angle, like an oarsman. Angela must have got her fine bones from her father. Louise spoke in the same bright tone as her daughter but the effect was more controlling than of good cheer. I imagined she talked the same way whether she was standing in the boardroom or the kitchen. A gardener in overalls was outside cleaning the pool. It was taking him a lot longer than it had to cut the lawn.

"Well, I'm feeling a little disempowered myself," I told her.

"I was acting on the concerns of your ex-employers. They advised that you might need someone to watch your back, what with your injuries and the lifestyle."

"I think I'm in pretty good shape, Louise."

"Mrs Bane."

"Mrs Bane." I dropped a sugar lump into my coffee and splashed it everywhere. I left the tiny cup alone. "Basically, I feel that I have a right to know when my client pays a someone else to shadow me, especially when it's a man like Sonny Tewera. It's unprofessional."

"The Chinese have a saying, Mr Huxley: 'The greatest managers let people work without letting them know they're being managed at all.' Built-in redundancy is the secret to successful project management. I'm sorry if your nose was put out of joint."

"Ivan's moved a little."

"Well, indeed." She shook her gold watch around her wrist and frowned. "I don't know where Angela's got to. She did promise she'd be here. I'm sorry I can't offer you the same hospitality. *Biscotti?*"

"I think I'll lay off the sweets."

"Ben was very excited to know you'd played at a senior level."

"Club level, yes. Is he good, your son?"

"Apparently, yes."

"You don't watch?"

"It's a question of time. Would you like payment now? I assume cash will do." She counted it out from a bank roll in her purse.

"That's a lot to be carrying round."

"It's so convenient."

"I guess there's always more where it came from."

She handed me the money and smiled. "That's right, Mr Huxley. There is."

Sonny was at the pub. He did a double-take when I dropped the bills on the table.

"Cash?" he said.

"It must be nice being a Bane."

"For sure."

Parramatta were playing so we watched them lose for a bit. My cell was on vibrate. I felt it shake my pocket once, twice, then three times.

"You gonna pick that up?" Sonny said.

I just kept quiet about it.

Among Partisans

Carmen Korn

The screw-cap dropped to the table when Arie pulled the bottle towards himself to drip olive oil onto a crust of bread. It was the first sound at the table since a quarter of an hour. Before they had just sat there in silence looking out into the deep black of the night beyond the terrace. Listening to the cicadas.

They were tired. Building houses from the ruins exhausted their bodies, although none of them was over forty. But only Arie was used to this hard work. He had already finished his house. The house on whose terrace they were sitting on in silence.

Arie had been the first to come to the deserted village with its crumbling houses. The houses with the dry stone walls that had been built two hundred years ago and had been left behind two decades ago by people who had gotten tired of carrying the fresh figs to the markets on the coast in August and picking the olives from the trees in November.

Deep down in the valley a siren was to be heard, its precipitant sounds tumbling over one another. An ambulance, perhaps. The Carabinieri. Jos glanced at Arie, as he always glanced at his friend when sirens ripped the air. That had been so in Germany and in the days in Holland, and it hadn't changed since they were settled here in Testa di Lucio, the paltry hamlet in Liguria.

The only one at the table who belonged here was old Bixio, who had come to Testa at the age of eighteen with the partisans. At the time there had been no road leading to the settlement, only a bumpy trail. People coming uphill from Genova got no glimpse of Testa with its odd dozen houses. To this day, Bixio didn't understand how the Nazis had been able to find it in May 1944. Only he and two others had managed to escape.

Arie noticed Jos' glance, as he always did. But he just stared into the candle that stood in an old olive jar and kept on chewing his piece of bread. Only when the valley had fallen silent again did he raise his head and smile at Jos.

They knew each other since Arie had been sixteen and Jos thirteen years old. Neighbourhood kids. The elder had looked after the younger. Jos had been a dishevelled bird at the time. He had lived alone with his father, who wanted to fall apart because Jos' mother had gone off and away with another man. Jos had acted out his pain from the loss of his mother in wildness. Wildness that had almost broken his neck. He had fallen off of a tall tree, and Arie had been standing there below and just caught the slight boy.

"*Ancora di vino?*" Bixio asked. He had brought a threadbare shopping-bag when he came over early in the evening from his cottage that had been the only intact building in the hamlet before Arie had come and built his. Bixio stood up, bent down to his bag and brought forth another bottle. Without a label, the cork only pressed in by hand. A red wine from Piedmont, behind the mountains to the north. It was good for the young people, gave them strength for the work in the ruins. Bixio was endlessly glad he was no longer alone up here, and he liked to bring up wine from his cellar, where the only other things he kept were the old German army rifle he had captured in the war, and a box with photos and letters his comrades had written from prison before they were shot.

Bixio poured the dark wine into the glasses, and only Hanna pulled hers away, one of the two women who were with them. Hanna, the saint. What she wanted up here no one knew. She had just been there one day. Maybe she considered the remoteness as cloistral. Hanna was afraid of the world. That was clear to all of them, and they all had a heart for people who had gone astray.

Every day, Hanna carried away the rubble they found in the houses' cellars. Carried it in buckets down the road to the first bend, where she dumped it in the nettles. On her way back, she always stopped at the old shrine of the Virgin Mary beside the bend. The picture of the Virgin might have been painted in garish colours, but now it was long since bleached out by rain and sun. Only the blue of the Madonna's mantle still glowed. Sometimes Hanna placed some small white bellflowers that grew beside the road on the stone still of the small altar. She always stood still for a long time, and most of the times she prayed.

"Maybe your house will be finished tomorrow," Arie said to the Dutchman who a year before had driven to the land registry office in Genova together with him to initiate the purchase of the six ruins with their piece of land. Pioneers of the first hour. Testa di Lucio belonged to the two of them. Them and Bixio. "The windows will be delivered tomorrow," Arie said.

The Dutchman shrugged his shoulders, a sceptic who no longer believed that things happened at the time they ought to happen. It wasn't his dream he was fulfilling here, it was his wife Jeltje's dream.

Jos had become addicted to Jeltje the day they met. Because of the soft sedate tone with which she spoke German. His mother had sounded just the same.

"They'll come on time," Jeltje said, giving Jos a loving glance, as if he could guarantee the arrival time of the windows. She was the youngest of them all and nonetheless willing to be their shepherd.

Arie squinted, as if he could illuminate the night beyond the terrace. It was his land down there. He of all people had become a landowner. One and a half hectares that belonged to the Dutchman and himself. A mockery of fate. Hadn't he fought against the propertied class?

With all means, Arie thought, twisting his face into a painful grimace. He took the bottle Bixio had put on the table and poured himself wine. He emptied the glass in big gulps and again felt Jos' gaze. Arie knew that Jos tormented himself even more than he did.

Later, as they undressed in the room that they shared as long as the others were still sleeping in the house, Jos asked Arie what he had been thinking about when he had distorted his face in pain.

"You know what it is," Arie said, full of reluctance.

"The pictures in my mind are getting more terrible every day," Jos said. "I'm dreaming of them almost every night."

"You weren't even there," Arie said, "don't start assuming blame you don't have."

"I didn't stop you."

"I didn't ask you," Arie said. He stretched out on the cot and pulled the sheet up to his chin. A signal that he no longer wanted to talk.

"Good night," Jos said and lay down on his bed.

Arie listened to the long regular breaths intended to make him believe Jos was sleeping. Jos was not sleeping. Both of them would lay awake for a long time, listening to their consciences.

The windows arrived at a quarter to eight, even though the carpenter had to drive almost an hour on his way up from the coast. Italy remained a land of miracles. The morning shone blue like the mantle of the Virgin Mary, the shadows of the night seemed to have left Jos, too, and Jeltje was happy. The windows were a perfect fit.

At noon Jeltje wiped the old table they had found in one of the cellars one more time and then set it with six plates. The sunlight danced on the thick white china. Soon it would become too hot inside the house, but Jeltje didn't want to close the shutters yet, because she enjoyed the view through the shiny new panes so much.

Only when they had drunk to the new house and the spaghetti they had carried over from Arie's kitchen was on the plates did Jeltje get up to close the shutters that first jammed a bit and then loudly snapped shut.

The next disturbing sound came from Jos' fork that had slipped from his hand and dropped on to the edge of his plate.

"I was just startled," Jos said. The others passed over this jumpiness, but Arie was worried. Jos was becoming a bundle of nerves.

In the afternoon, when they both stood in the smallest of the ruins looking up to the sky largely visible through the broken roof, Arie said: "It's been years since."

"Why are you telling me that?" Jos asked.

"Because it's over. None of the dead will come back to life if you crack up now."

"I'm afraid they're going to come and get you," Jos said. Arie shook his head.

"That the Carabinieri will track you down, just as the SS did with Bixio and his people." Jos' voice sounded breathless, as if he had been running up a hill.

"You can't compare that," Arie said softly. "Bixio's people were innocent."

"They also killed, for a holy cause," Jos said.

Arie laid his hands on Jos' shoulders. "Calm down," he said. "There's nothing holy about killing a man just because he has power, and two others along with him who just happened to be nearby."

"He had abused his power." Jos was almost pleading.

Arie sighed and glanced up at the sky. The roof looked as if the last tiles were ready to fall today.

They startled when they heard steps behind them. Jos turned first and saw Hanna standing in the opening that once been the door.

"I'm bringing Holy Water," she said.

"Thanks," Arie said, "we don't need an exorcist."

"This is going to be my house," Hanna said. "I want God to live in it." She brandished a blue plastic bottle that still carried the label of Acqua Nori.

"You can't have walked all the way to Valesa to get Holy Water," Arie said, "it would have taken you hours."

"The Virgin Mary sanctified it for me," Hanna said, "down by the bend of the road. I put the bottle before her."

"Tomorrow we'll start with your house," Arie said, unsure if he wanted Saint Hanna to move into it. He was busy enough with Jos.

Only when they had reached the old mule trail on their way to check if the creek still carried water farther down did he start to talk again, and what he said made Jos stop abruptly and contemplate his old friend.

"Thou shalt not murder," Arie said.

"It seems that Hanna is driving you crazy," Jos said.

Arie climbed up a grassy knoll and looked out across the olive trees. He looked as he was going to deliver a sermon. Then he only said: "Violence is shit. Look what's happening in Palestine."

"What you wanted back then was different."

Arie snorted. "Shooting at a big shot?" he asked.

"I can't stand you kicking at the framework I've built for myself," Jos said.

"Your framework is only patchwork," Arie said. They had arrived at the creek that was now merely a trickle. They were going to be short of water this August. Arie stepped over the creek without difficulty. In better days it had been wide enough to swim two strokes in crossing it.

"What is that supposed to be, the Rubicon or the Sea of Galilee?"

"I don't get it." Arie said.

"Caesar or Jesus?"

Arie understood. "There's not enough water to walk upon," he said.

"By crossing the Rubicon, Caesar started a civil war," Jos said.

"Do you want me to start a civil war?"

"I want you to be a hero, not a murderer."

Arie looked at him in concern. "My boy," he said and returned to the other bank of the creek with a big step. He felt like taking Jos into his arms.

"I would like to catch you once more if you were to jump from the tree," he said. The memory of the wild kid Jos had been at thirteen still softened his heart. But Jos quickly freed himself from Arie's embrace.

"Since that day you shot them my breath stops every time I hear a siren," he said.

"Yes," Arie said. "That was horrible. Whenever I look out into the black landscape at night, I see them lying there on the street. All three of them."

"And I only think that they'll be coming to get you, and they won't care that you've renounced violence. They'll treat you like they did the poor guys down in Genova who opposed globalization."

"Stop it," Arie said. "let's not burden this day so much. We've completed the second house today."

He started walking up the mule trail.

"Jeltje has taken the Vespa down to Valesa to buy grilled chickens. To celebrate the day," Jos said. Thinking of Jeltje soothed him.

His mother came to his mind. She had ignominiously deserted him, but nonetheless she had been the first person that came to his mind, back then when he was looking for a hideaway for Arie. But Nijmegen had been too small to hide a wanted terrorist, and too close to the German border. His mother had been put to the test for hardly a day. She had had only a short meeting with Arie and had given him as little attention as she had her son.

Then the flat in Scheveningen had already become available, provided by an unknown supporter. It had surely been a help that Jos spoke Dutch. Otherwise, Arie would have been even more conspicuous than he was. No town in Holland was big enough to make him invisible. Jos had sighed with relief when they left the country. Suddenly he had become the man who drove the getaway car. It had been a very high tree that Arie had jumped off that time, and catching him had been almost too hard for Jos.

"I hope she's going to Rosario's," Arie said, "he has the best chickens."

"She always goes to Rosario's," Jos said.

When they got near the houses, they heard Jeltje's transistor radio blaring at full power.

"*Anche gli angeli si sporcanno*," Dalla and Morandi sang. Even angels dirty their hands. Jos had been in his early twenties when he first heard that song, during a seaside vacation in Alassio. Arie had not shot anyone at the time, and Jos would have laughed out loud at the idea that the two of them would one day take refuge up in the hills of Liguria, for better or for worse. Would he really have laughed out loud? Hadn't Arie's political activities already begun to show? His rigorousness?

Arie cast a glance into Hanna's ruin before they went on to the Dutchman's house. It would take a lot of work to give the crazy woman a lodging.

Hanna was sitting on the steps in front of Jeltje's kitchen door cleaning salad greens. The leaves of the home-grown romaine lettuce had grown big and tough in the hot July sun.

"You have to take down the portrait of Padre Pio," Arie said. Hanna raised her head and looked at him aversely.

"Or do you want him to put up with a construction site?" Arie asked.

"*Padre Pio. Un uomo cangiante*," Bixio said behind them. Even an old communist soul was inclined to call the priest revered by half the population of the country at least a chatoyant figure. Arie noticed that Bixio's shopping-bag seemed to be even heavier than usual. Soon Jos would have to drive to Piedmont with Bixio to buy new wine. There, there were still vintners who sold wine in bulk. Hardly anyone could afford Ligurian wines these days.

The three men pushed by Hanna and entered Jeltje's house. The Dutchman had been lugging furniture while his wife had been down to Valesa to get grilled chickens. A sideboard stood in the kitchen, an heirloom from Jeltje's grandmother that, like all their other furniture, had been kept in Arie's house up to now. The plates stood ready on the sideboard, there was a stack of paper napkins with an anemone design, and there was a glass jug full of a reddish liquid.

"We've got to stop Jeltje," the Dutchman said, "otherwise she's going to start hanging up drapes." Jeltje's laugh came from the next room. "Try the punch", she said, "as long as it's cold." She entered the kitchen and saw Bixio. *"Bevi, Bixio. Oggi è una festa."*

She took glasses from the draining-board of the stone sink and filled them. "Nothing sinister," she said, "only white wine with peaches and a bit of brandy."

"You've been on a shopping spree," the Dutchman said, "and brought everything home on the Vespa." He loved Jeltje; he admired her. That's why he was willing to fulfil her dreams. Dreams that weren't his own.

"To our houses," Arie said, "and to our future. He looked at Jos and raised his glass. Jos smiled, but in the same moment turned towards Jeltje again. "I'll set the table," he said.

He did it carefully. Folded the napkins, placed candles. Then he went outside to cut olive twigs to decorate the table.

It was a feast, just as Jeltje had promised. Arie was the one who once in a while reminded them that hard work was waiting for them the next day. But he exercised no more moderation in drinking than the others, and finally Bixio's shopping-bag was empty, and Bixio the most drunk of them all.

Arie and Jos almost had to carry the small old man when they brought him home. And Bixio hardly felt tired, only his legs would no longer support him.

Bixio sat at the window of his bedroom for a long time looking at Venus and the Big Dipper, pondering, as he had so often done during all the years, who had been the Judas back then in May of 1944.

A lot of carrying was done the next day. The roof of Hanna's ruin had to be cleared, and it was slow work. Their heads and bodies were still heavy with the past night's alcohol.

Finally they succeeded in lowering the rotten ridgebeam, but Arie failed in his attempt to load it on his back and carry it off alone.

"That's about how Jesus must have felt beneath the cross," he said and was grateful when Jos came to help him, and they carried the heavy trunk to the shed together, where they would later cut it up. The beam would still render good firewood.

Hanna kept creeping around the ruin and wasn't much help.

But at noon, when they had moved the table on Arie's terrace into the shade of the old fig tree to have their lunch of bread and cheese and tomatoes, Hanna greatly surprised Arie by laying a bundle of banknotes next to his plate. "For the roof beams," she said.

"Where have you got the money from?" Arie asked. For him, Hanna had always been the poor saint to whom he gave shelter.

Hanna shrugged. "I brought it from home," she said, seemingly unwilling to tell more.

"If you want to live with us, you must tell us about yourself," Arie replied.

"Do you tell everything?" Hanna asked.

Arie broke himself a piece of bread and reached for the olive oil. "Do as you like," he said. "After lunch, we'll drive over to Acqui Terme to buy the wood. You're coming along, Hanna. You might want to chose something better than pine." He looked at the bundle of money. "Oak," he said, "you could afford it."

Now also Jeltje and her husband looked at Hanna curiously.

Arie turned to Jos. "Is the Fiat running?" he asked.

Jos had become the wagon master for the old vehicle that was parked beyond the bend in the road because it had trouble making the last hundred metres of the steep stony grade up to the houses.

"It'll start or it won't start," Jos said.

"See to it that it starts," Arie said.

"Maybe we ought to buy a small truck," the Dutchman said. Arie and he knew that nothing would become of that. Buying the land had depleted their resources. Both of them were short on cash.

But the Fiat did start up, and Jos drove it to Acqui Terme without mishap. Hanna chose expensive oak and placed the banknotes into the timber merchant's hand.

It was Jos who then paid for a couple of cartons of wine.

"Have you seen Bixio yet today?" Arie asked.

"No," Jos said, succeeding at starting the Fiat at his fourth try, "but now it occurs to me that his shutters were still closed when we left."

"*Porca Madonna*," Arie said. It was the worst Italian oath he knew. He was surprised that Hanna didn't react to it.

They already saw from far away that Bixio's door stood open. Was that a good sign? Arie and Jos were out of breath when they entered the house. In the bedroom they found Jeltje sitting on Bixio's bed stroking his hand.

"*Sto gia meglio*," Bixio said.

Was he really doing better already?

"He was feeling slightly feeble," Jeltje said. "He's a bit too old for binges like yesterday's."

Bixio smiled. What a godsend that had brought him these children. Jeltje. Wonderful Jeltje. Arie and Jos. Who would have dreamed that in his old days he would have a deep friendship with two Germans? Hadn't it been the triumph of his life having fought against them? The men in the field-grey uniforms of the Wehrmacht, in the black dress of the SS? Bixio still saw them, coming up the hill, back in 1944. He would not die before he knew who had betrayed the partisans of Testa di Lucio. Was it Albo, the truck driver? Silvio, the sixteen-year old boy born here in Testa? Besides himself they had been the only survivors. Bixio shook his head. No.

Jeltje looked at him full of concern. Maybe Bixio's crisis wasn't over yet.

"Shall we call a doctor?" Jos asked, having seen Jeltje's worried look.

"*Niente medico*," Bixio said, "*sto gia meglio*." He was sure of himself.

Jeltje left to cook some soup. Jos went to get the wine from the car to store it in Bixio's cool cellar. Arie stayed, and Bixio told him why they needn't worry about him. Death would only come for him when he had learned the name of the traitor.

Jos heard about this, as he and Arie were on their way to the small ruin. "How would that come about? Learning the name of the traitor?" he asked. "After more than sixty years?"

"Perhaps it will no longer be that important to Bixio during his last days, and Bixio will find peace without knowing the name."

They had arrived at Hanna's house and looked up at the sky, and Arie thought about the roof truss he was going to start building the next morning.

"To find peace," Jos said.

"I wish you'd do that too," Arie said.

Jos kicked at the small stones that covered the floor. Remnants of the rubble.

"Everything I'm doing here makes no sense if I have to think of you as a murderer," Jos said.

"You knew about it from the beginning. Three people dead. I killed them, and at least two of them were innocent."

"Brenner wasn't." It was the first time he pronounced the name. "If a tyrant won't step down, he has to be removed by force."

Arie looked at him sadly. Could it be that Arie was now beginning to get entangled in the old ideas?

"Sometimes I dream they're coming up the mountain to get you. In my dreams I feel relieved then."

"It's up to you. Go to the Carabinieri. They'll still find my name in their lists."

Jos shook his head. "No," he said.

But that night he dreamt exactly that. Arie woke Jos because he couldn't stop sobbing in his sleep. He held him like one holds a child who has had a nightmare. Hadn't Jos always been like a kid brother to him, and wouldn't he remain that as long as they both lived? Jos was sleeping more calmly again, and Arie covered him carefully and got up to go to the window.

What had Jos said that evening? Sometimes I dream that they're coming up the hill to get you. Maybe he himself would be relieved, too. Then, it would be accomplished. Why were images from the bible always coming to his mind these days? Perhaps it was Hanna's holy nearness, Arie thought.

Before going to bed he had come past the room downstairs in which she slept. Hanna hadn't been there. For a moment he had hesitated on the doorstep, constraining himself not to go in. But he had looked around the sparsely furnished room. There was a small suitcase underneath the old iron bed Hanna had dragged from the rubble in the cellars. But Hanna's other baggage was in the cellar. He was sure about that. Could it be the small suitcase was full of bundles of money?

The thought made Arie grin, and he left.

"Arie," Jos said.

Arie turned. Jos had awakened and sat up. "Come here," he said.

Arie sat down on the edge of the bed. "You were dreaming pretty heavily," he said. Jos nodded.

"Thank you," Jos said and then did what he hadn't done often in the life of Arie and himself. He kissed him.

"Tomorrow we'll tackle the roof truss," Arie said. The kiss had embarrassed him. "I don't want to have Hanna here in the house much longer. I don't trust her."

"The bundle of money?"

"Would you bundle your money?"

"It wouldn't be worth the trouble." Jos smiled. "Hanna is harmless," he said. "All that might happen is that you and I join the order of the Capuchins and get Holy Wounds on our Hands. Like Padre Pio. I guess we're both susceptible to any kind of madness."

Arie got up and let himself fall on to his own cot.

"Let's forget the past," he said.

It took a while before Arie got an answer.

"I'm so damned fond of you," Jos said softly.

Never before had Arie erected a roof truss as quickly as that of Hanna's house. Even taking into account that it was the smallest, it was a record, having been completed within a single day.

That he wanted to have Hanna out of his house wasn't the only reason. The good wood that had been delivered in the morning had a stimulating smell. Yes, it had been a joy, building that truss into the sky.

Only in the evening, when they were sitting around his table, did Arie feel what he had accomplished. Already the first glass of wine made him feel heavy as a stone, and he thought he would never manage to get up from his chair again. Bixio appeared juvenile by comparison. Dusk set over the land in front of them, enshrouding the olive trees whose small hard fruit would be picked in November.

A dog barked further down in the valley. Otherwise it was quiet, except for the clinking of the glasses when the wine bottle touched them when wine was poured. Except for the breaking of the bread that had become too hard. Except for an occasional word.

Then they heard the sirens. Hurried sounds tumbling over another. The sirens were coming up the hill, towards Valesa. But not stopping there. Continuing up the hill on bumpy trails. Negotiating the last bend and the final hundred metres up to the hamlet. The police cars' headlights bathed the houses of the village in blinding light.

Arie was surprised that the Carabinieri were armed with Berettas. Carrying pistols to capture a wanted terrorist, not machine guns.

Jos got up. "There he is," he said and went towards Arie.

He thought he was in his own dream.

"*Ecco lui,*" Jos said. He couldn't help it.

Hanna stood frozen as the handcuffs clicked around her wrists. "*Assalto ad una banca*" is what the other five thought they heard. Hanna, a bank robber who had paid the timber merchant with registered banknotes.

Maybe it was because Arie had to laugh so loudly and violently that he was almost shaking. Maybe it was because one of the Carabinieri was so young and inexperienced and excitedly brandished his Beretta when Arie got his attack of laughter.

The shot just went off. By mistake. An accident.

The Carabinieri had had no idea who he was. They only found it out later. By then, Arie had already been dead for six days.

Bixio lived another ten years and died without learning who had been the Judas, back in 1944.

Translation by Peter C. Hubschmid

Ethnic Cleansing

Dominique Manotti

Day 1

"Twenty thousand now," says the fat, greasy-haired man in a cheap brown suit, his forehead and upper lip covered in perspiration. He repeats: "Twenty thousand now," as if to convince himself of the amount, and taps his desk drawer. "Cash. And twenty thousand when the job's done, if it all goes well, no discussion. Again, cash." Breaks out into a fresh sweat. I'm handing over forty thousand euros to a guy whose name I don't even know. He mops his forehead with the cuff of his brown suit jacket, which is nice and absorbent, as if he does it all the time. It's come to this . . . This or fleeing abroad. This and fleeing abroad?

The guy standing in front of him – athletic body, well-groomed, shaved head, smooth, tanned, tight black T-shirt, black jeans, black leather boots, not far off forty, from the slight slackening of the skin and the stomach – wordlessly extends an open hand across the desk. The fat man hesitates for a moment, opens the drawer and tosses an envelope onto the desk. The other guy picks it up, counts the notes in no hurry, and slips them into his underpants, under his jeans, pulling in his stomach.

"How long?"

"A week, max."

"Fine."

He automatically hitches up his jeans and leaves. Does his sums as he goes down the stairs (avoid lifts, potential hazard). Forty thousand, not exactly a fortune. But I'm not getting any younger . . . Besides, it's not the riskiest job. That's why it's worth it, don't want to stick my neck out, or share. Not bad. He's back in the street. Little wink at the copper plate by the entrance to the building. Alfred Poupon Property Agent, Staircase A, 3rd floor, left. Old Poupon was sweating, he reeked of fear. Not used to this type of operation. Is that a good thing for me or dangerous?

Hidden behind a third-floor window, Alfred Poupon watches the man walk off down the street with the wad of notes in his underpants. He turns the corner, calm and assured. That's it, he's gone.

End of a suffocatingly muggy August day. Zé leaves Paris at the wheel of his white, five-year-old, all-purpose Clio. He turns off the *périphérique* onto a very wide main road alongside a chaotic sprawl of showy office blocks. This new business district is the big city's latest growth spurt. At this hour, and in the middle of August, it's completely deserted, quite sinister. Zé cruises slowly. He's approaching the A86 motorway which is becoming the second Paris orbital, spots the slip road, turns onto it, goes even slower. The target's there, set back from the road below him, a few metres from the security barrier. Zé's on the alert, eyes sharp, neurons buzzing: take it all in at a glance, clock everything, don't risk a second drive-by. An isolated five-storey building of dirty, greyish brick, with a long crack running diagonally from window to window. All the openings, which must have been bricked up once, are now gaping. Behind the building, a huge overgrown waste ground dotted with loose stones, apparently empty, sloping down to a canal where there's little activity.

But the building in the middle of this wilderness is teeming with life. At ground level, on the strip of beaten earth between the façade and the motorway slip road, there's a whole crowd of black men in jellabas or brightly coloured shirts coming and going amid the dust – squatting, sitting on wooden packing cases, standing around, chatting, playing cards and doing business. An old man in a long, immaculately white robe sitting motionless on a chair against the wall, face upturned, eyes closed, seems to be drinking in the light of the orange sunset which makes his face glow.

Through the cracks in the wall, glimpses of a central wooden staircase, women in flowing boubous busy around makeshift fires surrounded by hordes of children jostling and running. The upper floors look very animated too. Zé thinks he catches a whiff of the familiar smell of groundnuts and spices simmering. That's the real thrill of the chase, when the hunter feels this close to his prey. Get a grip. Professional. Loads of squatters, all looking alike. No hope of passing unnoticed with your white mug, even with a deep tan. He pulls out onto the motorway and accelerates.

Day 2

In a midnight-blue tracksuit, Zé jogs along the former towpath beside the canal. A few warehouses, silos and barges line the quay. Not a soul. He draws level with the Africans' squat. A fence, broken in several places. Still nobody about. He pulls his tracksuit hood over his shaved head and slips through to the waste ground. A series of stony humps and dips overgrown with brambles, like a field of ruins dominated by the grey brick building, obscured at the bottom by brambles. From this side, everything looks dead. The ground- and first-floor windows are still bricked up with concrete breeze blocks and on the upper floors only a few small holes have been made here and there. Clearly the squatters are wary of the waste ground and are trying to keep it out.

Zé moves slowly and noiselessly, camouflaged by the undergrowth, and comes across a whole network of paths and hidey-holes dug into the ground, protected by cardboard, planks, and sometimes carpeting. You can bet that after dark, this sort of wild garden, so close to the dormitory suburbs, will be teeming with people. Zé looks for a hole that appears to be empty and finds one on an area of high ground near the motorway from which he can watch the building. He clears some space for himself with a few flat stones, wedges himself in and waits. The building looks deserted. In the late afternoon, Zé distinctly hears the noise of people flocking back to the squat and going about their usual business. In the openings of the façade he's watching, he sees lights flickering. Then darkness falls and the waste ground comes alive. Life rises up from the canal, floats above the ground, as if immaterial. Rustling, whispering, half-glimpsed flames. Zé hopes he's not in the path of the main tide of people and focuses on the façade. Sniff out any clandestine contacts between the squat and the waste ground. That's his way in. He lights a joint, to blend in, and pulls his hood down over his eyes.

As the night's very dark, for a few hours he concentrates on the sounds so as to chart the comings and goings, and thinks he's identified more intense activity under the brambles at the farthest corner of the building. He doesn't budge. He waits. Around 4 a.m., life begins to flow back towards the canal and dissolves into the night by osmosis.

Zé uncurls himself, dives under the brambles closest to the building and finds a clear path running its entire length. At ground level, the five bricked-up basement windows must open into the cellars. Zé stops in front of the fifth one, bricked up like the others, and prods the breeze blocks. Finding they're loose, he pulls a knife from his pocket and inserts the blade between the rubble stones. They're a snug fit, but not cemented in. Zé moves away quickly, and hides in a dip in the ground, keeping still again. Take time to think. I've found the front door. No doubt I'm sharing it with dealers I know nothing about. So I don't know what I might find behind it. Don't want to know. Too great a risk of being seen. Come back tomorrow, properly equipped, and give it a go, blind.

Around 5.30, the lights begin to come on again in the squat. Between the dealers leaving and the squatters waking, I have got a good half hour to act undisturbed. That's plenty. Zé too makes his way back to the canal.

Day 3

Back to the waste ground, same time, same clothes, to find the same hole and wait there. The routine, in other words. Zé's brought an old ruck-sack, crammed full, and a sleeping bag. The hours tick by. Nothing out of the ordinary. Only, around midnight, a kid who's already well out of it and really wants to hang out with "a grown-up" and "possibly more". Zé frightens him off with a few curses in Serbo-Croat and the kid doesn't insist.

4.20 a.m. Zé gets up, walks quickly over to the fifth basement window. Crouching in front of it, from his rucksack he pulls a pair of rubber gloves, a balaclava and night-vision goggles, which he puts on. He inserts a flat hook between the breeze blocks and loosens them just like that, throws his rucksack through the window and drops down into the cellar. First surprise, he hits the ground sooner than expected. A huge underfloor space rather than a cellar. Barely room to stand up. Senses a presence in a corner: a horizontal shape beginning to sit up. In two strides, Zé's on top of him, pinning him to the floor. He knocks him out with a punch to the chin. He finishes him off with a stone picked up from the ground. Quick, find the trap door leading up to the ground floor.

Torch. Some kind of flimsy wooden partition gives way to his touch. Piles of rubbish. Towards the centre of the building, a few wooden cases full of wire jewellery, wooden statuettes and leather belts, street hawkers' wares no doubt, wonderfully flammable material. And the trap door. A gentle push: it yields easily; glance around, I'm just under the main staircase.

The wooden staircase. Perfect. Zé lets the trap door close, hurriedly goes over to the body, drags it under the trap door, piles up the planks from the partition, the boxes full of stuff, the guy's sleeping bag, syringe, needle, tourniquet, spoon, cotton wool, bottle of water and even a dose of smack: do the job properly. Sprinkles several litres of methylated spirits over the whole lot. Then takes a spirit stove out of his rucksack, lights it, throws it onto the sleeping bag and opens the trap door. The fire catches immediately. Zé picks up his rucksack, runs to the window, clambers up into the open air with no difficulty. He walks quickly down to the canal without looking back. He must get as far away as he can before the fire spreads to the upper floors. As he walks, he stuffs the balaclava, gloves and goggles into his rucksack, reaches the towpath and breaks into a run, like an early-morning jogger. He watches the building out of the corner of his eye. Judging by the façade, nothing's happening. The fire hasn't caught, did it burn itself out in the cellar? Not enough meths? He carries on jogging, keeping up the same pace. Just as the outline of the building vanishes behind the carcass of an abandoned cement silo, he hears a rising scream. Don't turn around. Hot flush. That's it, you did it. They chucked you out of their place, you chuck them out of yours. Nice work.

He keeps on running. A kilometre further on, the rucksack will sink to the bottom of the canal, in two kilometres, he'll be back in his Clio and will drive straight down to Marseille. Tomorrow, he'll be out of the country. The fire engulfs the cellar, a magnificent blaze sucked towards the stairwell, which grows scorchingly hot before the staircase bursts into flames in several places, crackling. The dangling naked electric wires catch fire and give off a smell of burning rubber which masks that of the corpse being slowly burned to cinders. Wreaths of grey and black smoke billow from the ground floor, spread over the motorway, rise to the roof. Men abruptly roused emerge to see what's going on just as the first flight of stairs collapses in a shower of sparks. Screams. In a few seconds, the alarm's raised and the whole building resounds with panic-filled shouts, jostling, stampeding. The fire spreads to the upper storeys – there's little to hinder it, the doors have been ripped off and the curtains replacing them catch fire at the slightest gust. The women and children gather by the windows at either end of the building, the men try to halt the progress of the flames by blocking any opening with everything they can get their hands on; it's a ludicrous battle which only feeds the flames. Gas stoves explode here and there. Women jump out of first-floor windows clutching their children. Others on the fourth and fifth floors fling bundles of clothes out of the windows, hover over the void, scream for help. The distraught squatters scatter onto the motorway slip road where traffic is at a standstill.

The fire brigade arrives, sirens wailing, three fire engines, just as the roof over the staircase collapses. They extend their ladders, evacuate the inhabitants, attack the flames. Four more engines arrive. Then the police show up. Two police stations have been mobilized, plus a brigade of riot police. The area is cordoned off. Nobody's allowed near. Not onlookers, friends or family. Orders are clear: avoid any demonstration of support for the victims, no breaches of the peace. All the uninjured squatters are herded into big buses: immediate removal to a municipal sports centre placed at the disposal of the disaster victims. The dead are taken to the morgues in ambulances and the burned and the wounded to various hospitals, as and when the fire-fighters are able to drag them out of the blaze. Some people manage to slip through the police cordon and run off across the waste ground.

By 6 a.m., in the building where the fire's still smouldering, only a few bodies are left, along with the fire-fighters still battling the flames and drowning what's left of the squat under gallons of water. According to the police bulletin, 123 people were living in this squat, seven are dead and fifteen others injured, three of whom are critical; 101 people are in the municipal sports centre where identity checks are being carried out. The plan is to escort any illegal immigrants to the border and rehouse those whose papers are in order. The investigation should establish whether the fire is of criminal or accidental origin.

Two Years Later

A twelve-storey steel and glass structure hugs the curve of the A86 motorway slip road, which has been concreted over and where at this very moment a garden is being laid out. The façade overlooking the canal has reflective glass echoing the changing hues of the weather, blue sky, clouds, storms, in an arresting mirror effect. A vast paved esplanade stretches down to the canal. In the centre is a circular, white stone fountain with geometric sculptures. On either side, a row of lime trees in front of two multilevel apartment blocks. Terraced gardens that will soon be verdant slope down to the canal. An old-fashioned bandstand has been installed on the quayside, which has been turned into a promenade.

It's summer, the weather's very hot, the whole complex is still empty, a few finishing touches yet to be added. The Bâtimo construction company is holding a party to celebrate the completion of the works before the August holidays. White marquees have been set up along the canal and a throng of men in dark suits and a few women in light dresses are crowded around the buffets piled with refreshments and champagne. Entrepreneurs and politicians big and small, of all persuasions, mingle and rub shoulders.

When the mayor arrived, flanked by his deputy, he was a little tense. The tragedy that took place here two years ago is on everyone's mind, he was thinking. Granted, the police investigation concluded it was an accident following a fight between dealers who had broken into the basement of the squat. But eight dead . . . Granted, the city council rehoused all the legal immigrants. But not locally, not together, a long way from Paris . . . and the illegal immigrants were deported before they'd had time to recover. Granted, some immigrant support organizations were invited to this inauguration of the new canal district. But only those with close ties to the mayor's office. What if the others, the ones the police repressed with some brutality during the fire

and afterwards, were to decide to come and spoil the party . . .
Then he relaxes a little more with each glass of champagne. And
whisky. After all, the fire, the dead, you're probably the only one
still thinking about it. Too sensitive . . .

Marchal, the CEO of Bâtimo, has invited Louvois, the big boss
of the construction group that bears his name and which owns
Bâtimo. The big boss hasn't come, but he's sent his son. And
Marchal is blowing his own trumpet.

"With this scheme completed, we'll be pitching to the mayor
and the regional authorities for the renovation of the entire
canal area. We're the experts in mixed business and residential
developments. This is the way forward."

The mayor, who's perked up, glass in hand, explains to the
Paris and regional authorities: "We need to change the image of
social housing. There's a high demand for quality social housing
here. Among our council employees alone . . ."

Louvois junior gazes after a tubby man in a navy blue suit,
panting and sweating profusely, who's drinking too much,
steering between groups, always on his own. A man who looks
completely out of place. He leans towards Marchal. "Who's that
guy? Do you know him?"

"Yes. Alfred Poupon, a property agent. He's got an extraordinary
nose for sniffing out new sites. He's the one who discovered this
one, under the most difficult circumstances." A pause. "The
old buildings were occupied, and the mayor wouldn't hear of
expulsions, of course." A fresh silence, no questions. "He made
a lot of money from the deal, but he's a sad case. Everything he
makes, he loses on the horses."

Translation by Lulu Norman and Ros Schwartz

A Really Shitty Day

Camilla Läckberg

"Fatso!"

"Hey! Stupid idiot!"

"God damn, you're so disgusting!"

The words hit him like needles, as he walked across the school grounds. He should have gotten used to it by now, because he had heard such words for years, but they still caused him pain. A lot of pain.

"Hey fatso, tell us if you want us to help you walk. Maybe we could push."

Five of the toughest boys in the school sat on benches and made very sure that Maria and Ellen heard what they said. These girls were officially recognized as the prettiest in the school, and they radiated the knowledge of this, as they glided past the boys on the benches.

Each eager to be the most impressive, the boys increased their efforts and yelled their taunts so that they almost drowned each other out.

"Nice boobs you got there, Wilbur!"

Wilbur, after his maternal grandfather. As if it weren't enough that he was fat.

With the taunts and insults ringing in his ears, he slowly approached the school. There was nothing enticing him to enter within its walls. It was as though he was a wandering target, or a vent for all the other teenagers' frustrations about their existence. Life seemed so much better when one realized that at least one wasn't Wilbur. Kicking him gave a few moments respite from one's own anxiety, and gave a feeling of power that was otherwise utterly lacking, in a world that was governed by parents', teachers', and other grown-ups' rules and laws. He wasn't stupid. He understood all of this. Understanding just didn't make it any easier.

After drawing a deep breath, he strode through the doors to the school, or the gates to hell, as he tended to call them, in his more ironic moments. There wasn't really any need for irony though, it was more a case of cold, hard fact. For him they really were the gates to hell. Not that things were any better at home. That was a hell, too, but of a different type.

Wilbur stole along the wall towards his locker. The trick was to make oneself as invisible as possible. Not an easy task with his height, but there were days when it seemed to work . . . Days when everyone seemed to look straight through him, as though he was made of air. Today was no such day.

"Hey, Wilbur, how you doin'?" A falsely friendly tone of voice came from Martin, one of the boys in his class. Wilbur considered him suspiciously.

"Fine, thanks," he said, groping for words, and all the time on guard for the direction from which the next attack would come, be it verbal or physical.

"I'm thinking of going camping this weekend," Martin said, then paused.

"Oh . . .?" answered Wilbur, hesitantly. He had no illusions that there was a possibility for this conversation to continue with the exchange of simple pleasantries.

"Yeah. I wondered if I could use your pants – you know – as a tent." Martin, and everyone else standing around, laughed loudly, extremely satisfied with what they thought was an especially humorous exchange. Wilbur just sighed, opened his locker and took out his books for the first lesson. He'd heard a lot worse. Martin wasn't the sharpest knife in the drawer, and his insults were never very sophisticated.

With dragging feet, Wilbur went to math class. Just another long day to get through.

Patrick Hedstrom stared at the paper before him. He had no desire to work. He had no desire to do anything. Occasionally, he wondered what the point was with it all, and today was really one of those days. He, who had always loved his job, now had to drag himself out of the house and to the station in the morning. Not that things were much better at home, either. If only he could put his finger on what it was that was wrong. He had thought that he and Karen had it great together, but in the last few months she had pulled away from him, more and more. Well, he believed so, anyway. Sometimes he didn't know. Sometimes things felt normal and he wondered if he was just imagining everything.

With a deep sigh, he picked up one of the files in front of him. A name he had seen many times before, was written on the report, but as usual, a note had been added to the file saying that the charges had been withdrawn. Just what he needed today, another case of abuse that would never lead to any consequences for the abuser. It was all so damned meaningless.

Patrick reached for the phone to call Karen. She had felt ill this morning and had stayed home from work. But his hand stopped halfway. He suddenly didn't know what he wanted to say. They had had a really spectacular quarrel, before he left, about what he couldn't remember any longer, and the bitterness still hung in the air between them. If he called now, he'd be forced to apologize, and he didn't feel he was ready for that, yet. If he was totally honest, he didn't know what he should apologize for. The quarrel had popped up out of thin air and seemed to be about everything and nothing.

Anne's voice, from out in the corridor, interrupted these gloomy thoughts. The new Chief, Bert Mellberg, had called another one of his countless meetings. He mostly held them in order to make long monologues about his earlier successes with the Gothenburg police. Patrick's mood sank to an even lower level.

When math class was finished, he tried to steel himself to go out into the corridor. These fifteen-minute breaks, by definition, lasted only fifteen minutes, but to Wilbur they seemed to last for hours. He had no one to be with during the breaks, no little group to hang around the lockers with. No one was interested in hearing what he had to say.

Most often he tried to find the most remote corner he could, squeeze himself into it and spend the rest of the break trying not to make eye contact with anyone. Eye contact was always problematic. It meant he was noticed, and that someone might see the possibility of feeling superior, by humiliating him in front of an appreciative public. He should have known that on this particular day, nothing was going to go his way. He hadn't even gotten through the door out of the classroom, before a foot shot out right in front of him. With his arms full of books and pens, he tripped and landed face down in the corridor. He felt sharp pain in one of his elbows, but pretended he didn't, as he stood up and tried to get away. He didn't manage it. Another foot shot out in front of him and this time he landed badly on his knees. Wilbur felt how tears of anger and frustration burned behind his eye lids, but he fought against them, not wanting to give the onlookers the supreme satisfaction of seeing him cry. But it was too late. A single tear rolled down his round cheek and was immediately seen by those around him.

"Look at him bawling," said a boy who was in the ninth grade, the grade above him. He continued with baby talk, "Did wittle Wilbur hurt his wittle self? Is wittle Wilbur gonna wun home to his mama and cwy?"

Everyone had a good laugh. A small crowd had gathered in the corridor to watch the scene unfolding. This was entertainment at its pinnacle.

Wilbur looked around desperately. All he could see were jean-clad legs and feet in dirty jogging shoes. Sweat running down his forehead, he feverishly gathered up his things, and managed to shoot out through a small hole in the wall of onlookers. This time they let him go, but their laughter followed him all the way to the room for his next class. He carefully tried the door. He was lucky and it was unlocked. He hastily checked the faces around him. No one seemed to be looking as he snuck inside. Thank God. Maybe he'd get to have a few minutes of peace.

This was his favorite class, not that he would ever admit that to anyone. Liking French was not something that would diminish his "jerk" status. Anyway, he liked it for quite other reasons, as well. Nina, a girl in his grade, also took French. She was the most wonderful creature he had ever seen. She was petite and blonde, with long hair that she often put up in a ponytail. She was so beautiful that it made his heart hurt when he saw her. She wasn't one of the nasty ones, either. Not that she talked to him nicely, but she was never among those girls who joined in when the boys harassed him. In his world this was something unheard of and fantastic.

A few minutes later, she was one of the first to come wandering into the room. She didn't even cast a glance at him, when she sat down in the row in front of him, but that didn't matter. Now he could study her neck without interruption and drink in the image of her hair where it fell down her back, gathered with a blue band. His heart was beating so hard that he thought everyone in the room must be able to hear it. His mouth felt dry and he had to work to get the saliva to moisten it. He watched her, spellbound, as she got out her books, and turned to the page with her vocabulary homework.

"Difficult words we got this time, huh?" He couldn't believe it, himself. The words had just slipped out. Where had he found the courage to speak to her? Time went into slow motion, he watched as she began to turn her body in his direction to answer him – to talk to him! The enormity of it made him gasp for air. But just then some of the others entered the room, and the magic moment came and went. She turned her attention to them and once again he had to be satisfied with staring at her back. In spite of this, he was content. For a fraction of a second she had recognized his existence. The day might not turn out as bad as he had thought.

He would soon find out how wrong he was.

The meeting felt like it would never end. Mellberg had droned on and on about how they had to raise their standards, about how they had to be more professional, and about how they mustn't slacken their pace, or think that they could sashay around just because they lived in a small community. He said he was used to a much higher standard than he had seen at this station, and that he did not plan to tolerate laziness, or sloppiness with the rules.

Everyone had listened, nodded and strained to look interested. Everyone had pretended, except Ernie Lundgren, who had immediately identified Mellberg as a man who would be susceptible to ass-kissing, and therefore devoted himself eagerly to the job.

Patrick had spent the meeting contemplating his life as an outsider might. The picture that came to mind was far from uplifting. Things were falling apart at home, and being forced to sit here being lectured by a pompous idiot from Gothenburg, made him wonder, once again, if there was any point to it all.

"How're things?" asked Martin Molin, the youngest police officer at the station.

"Fine, thanks," answered Patrick, in a way that discouraged further conversation. The kid was pleasant, but still wet behind the ears, and he had no desire to confide either his private, or job-related, worries to him.

"Ok, ok, I just asked to be polite," Martin said and went into his office with a wounded expression. Damn it! Patrick thought to himself. He hadn't meant to take out his frustration on the kid. Martin was green, but he worked hard and didn't deserve to be snapped at. No. Perhaps the best thing to do, would be to take an hour to go home and grab some lunch, and see how Karen was feeling, at the same time. And if it was necessary for him to apologize for something he had no idea about, it would be worth it, as long as they ended up on good terms again.

It only took a few minutes to drive to the house he shared with Karen, and park out front. Thinking that she might be sleeping, and not wanting to wake her if that were the case, he crept quietly into the house. The bedroom door was closed, so at first he thought he'd been right, but when he heard voices from inside, he thought she must be lying in bed watching the television. He walked rapidly to the door.

As he touched the handle, and began to turn it, another thought suddenly occurred to him. When he heard how it abruptly got quiet within, his brain was already working on what was now a certainty. What he saw when the door swung open, only verified what he had come to understand the instant before. So many things cascaded into place. All the small signs he had managed to ignore, were now written with huge letters, impossible to misunderstand, and he couldn't believe how stupid he had been. All the abruptness, all the withdrawal, all the anger and regret, all the hints she had given him, consciously or unconsciously, were all clearly explained in the sweaty, naked, lusty blend of fondling hands and intertwined legs. He could see that she had opened her mouth to say something, but she must have realized, as he did, that there wasn't anything to say.

Patrick carefully re-closed the door. He was completely empty inside. The only thing he wanted, was to breathe fresh air. He fled.

*   *   *

The lesson was finished way too quickly and he looked longingly at her back, as she disappeared through the door. It was an impossible dream.

Because the first hour had been a free period, it was now time for lunch. Wilbur plodded off to the cafeteria, casting watchful glances in all directions. He felt a wave of relief when he saw that he was the last in line to get his food. In the cafeteria he was usually left alone. Of course, he always sat by himself, but the serving women and the teachers' watchful eyes did him the favor of allowing him to eat without having to worry about where the next attack would be coming from. Maybe that's why he missed the signs that something was in the works. The signs he could usually read so well in these situations. He was so looking forward to digging into his large portion of spaghetti and meat sauce, that he didn't hear the giggling behind him. He also forgot to check his seat before he sat down, something he usually did reflexively.

The pain he felt was worse than anything he had ever experienced before. It made him howl in desperation and throw his tray of food into the air. Slowly, it and its huge portion of spaghetti, flew across the room. Even in his shock and pain, Wilbur was aware of Nina turning to see what was happening. With a decisively disgusting sound, the plate landed on her, covering her with food. It suddenly got very quiet. Wilbur's scream had died out and everyone was looking at them, mouths open and eyes sparkling. Then he heard Nina's voice, as she slowly turned her spaghetti covered self to face him.

"You, you, you . . . disgusting, God-damned, FATSO!"

The devastation he felt, as his heart broke, overpowered the pain in his buttocks, caused by all the staples that had jabbed into his skin when he sat down. Short pictures, of various moments, flashed by in his head. His father with a raised fist, the nasty sound of his mother's head hitting a wall. Himself, alone in his room, the space under his bed filled with candy and empty wrappers. The taste of chocolate that filled his mouth, filled the hole in his heart, and dampened the sound of the beatings and arguments that came from the floor below. One image flew by, and came back, insisting on his attention. His father's gun cabinet. The hunting rifle his father loved more than he had ever loved Wilbur or his mother. The lessons in the forest in an attempt "to make a man of him". The sound of bullets hitting the body of an animal.

The answer to all his problems suddenly seemed so simple. That was exactly what they were to him. Animals. Without feeling, and without intelligence, because they wouldn't be able to treat him like this if they were human, would they?

As he ran out of the cafeteria, several staples still painfully stuck in the tender meat of his ass, he had no thought or consciousness. The only thing he felt was pure, red hate. The wish to do something bad, and cause the same kind of pain he had had to go through, day in and day out.

He ran up the hillside and felt the air burning in his lungs. This didn't cause his decisiveness to waver, though, just the opposite. But at the bus stop, on the top of the hill, his endurance ran out. He sat down to catch his breath before he ran the rest of the way home. It wasn't until his heart rate began to slow down, that he realized someone else was already sitting there. A person who looked just about as bad as he felt, himself. His first impulse was to get up and continue on home, to complete the task that was now pounding in his head like a mantra. But just as he was about to stand up, the man beside him spoke.

"You've got it good," Patrick said to the young man who had sat down beside him at the bus stop. Why he had decided to sit here, after his world had imploded, was a mystery to him. Perhaps it was just that he had nowhere else to go. He couldn't go to the station, and when he'd be able to go home again, he didn't know. Hopefully, Karen had enough sense to be packing right now and disappearing somewhere. He had no idea where she'd go, and he didn't care, either. Just so he never had to see her or her things ever again.

"Your biggest problem is that you're not allowed to buy booze, or that you have to be in by ten o'clock instead of eleven. Enjoy it while you can, is all I'm saying. Before you know it, you'll come home and find your wife in bed with another man." He laughed bitterly and looked at the young man for the first time. He immediately regretted his outburst. The boy couldn't have been more than fourteen or fifteen, and was looking at him in shock. Patrick realized at once how he must seem. A grown man who sat at a bus stop, blurting out strange tirades.

"Oh, God, I'm sorry. I should have enough sense to keep my mouth shut. A few stupid things have happened lately . . ." He quit talking and saw that the kid was looking at him with a weird look in his eyes. Impulsively he stuck out his hand.

"Patrick Hedstrom." The boy took his hand, but didn't say anything, so Patrick decided to help him a little. "And you're . . .?"

"Wilbur," the boy answered without elaboration, but now studied Patrick with a measure of curiosity.

"Is everything okay?" asked Patrick. He had just seen something in the boy's eye that had made him ask the question. Wilbur looked aside and laughed an odd, little laugh that made Patrick's skin crawl.

"Sure, everything's just fine. Why wouldn't it be? I have nothing more to worry about than that I can't buy booze, or stay up past ten o'clock, isn't that what you said?" And again the strange, little laugh.

"Look, I'm really sorry. I apologize," said Patrick. He felt like such an idiot for having ranted like he had. Great example he set for the neighborhood's youth. Sitting here like some freaky, old man, mumbling to himself.

"Oh, it's okay," the boy answered, waving away the apology, but something he'd said must have been dumb, because suddenly the boy seemed deflated.

"Are you sure?" Patrick said, uneasy. "Because I'm a policeman, not some weirdo, or pervert, if that was what you were thinking . . ."

"Policeman!" said Wilbur, and laughed out loud.

"What's so funny about that," said Patrick a little confounded and insulted that his vocation was seen as something humorous.

"Nothing, absolutely nothing," the boy said and got up. "Listen, I have to go now. Good luck with . . . your wife, and all that stuff."

"Uh, thanks" said Patrick dumbly, and followed the boy with his eyes, as he strolled across the road. There was something unsettling about the boy, something he couldn't quite put his finger on. It was probably just his imagination. Patrick looked at his watch. The others were more than likely wondering where he was. Either he could sit here feeling sorry for himself, or he could go back to the station and at least try to do something worthwhile. If he could only, for one instant, convince himself that he made a difference to someone. Everything was meaningless. He didn't matter. To anyone.

*   *   *

All the hate had run out of him. The anger was still there, but it was more of the resigned sort. The kind that didn't act, but more just contemplated and observed. The same anger he was used to. The other anger, the hate, had felt so wonderful for a few minutes, so freeing. But it was the kind that couldn't stand contemplation, so the talk with Patrick, the policeman, had forced it to slow down, waver and fall apart. In some ways he missed it.

He found himself feeling a little sorry for that man. Poor bastard. It seemed like he had had an even worse day than he'd had himself, and that gave things, undeniably, another perspective.

Wilbur plodded home. The days until graduation stretched forever in front of him, but he would have to take them one at a time. Like he always had.

Patrick rose and walked slowly in the direction of the station. He could still see the boy, a ways in front of him, walking towards a housing development. It was the same neighborhood he lived in, and which Karen was in the process of leaving.

Something in their talk had worried him, but he finally shook it off. He didn't have the strength to worry about someone else's shitty day. He had enough with his own mess.

Ironically, work was the only thing he had left. The only thing that could give his existence meaning. If only he could have known that he'd made a difference in someone's life. If only in a small way. He realized the vanity in this hope. He'd never make a difference to anyone.

Patrick looked for the boy, Wilbur, again, but he was gone.

Translation by Susan Loyd

That Fat, Sadistic Bastard

José Carlos Somoza

"There's something you should know," Karl said to me one morning. "We're here to kill the woman."

"Yeah, I know," I smiled back.

"You don't understand," he replied, giving his head a shake. "I'm not kidding. It won't be faked."

I looked at him straight. He had a weakness for "funny" jokes whenever he got hungry, but by this time in the morning we'd already filled our stomachs, and this joke besides was weird, even for Karl.

"Ha, ha," I said! "I'm splitting my sides. Go jump in the lake."

"Listen," he insisted, "it's for real. They've already shot a test short using another victim. He's got it in his trailer."

Now it was my turn to give my head a shake. Not that I couldn't believe what Karl was saying, but the guy's naivety was incredible, every little rumour instantly transformed into gospel. He must have read my mind, as he looked slightly miffed:

"Come on, Louie, smell the coffee. What d'you *think* we've been hired for? We're not actors, we're thugs. What else in God's name would we be doing on this film?"

"We're extras, Karl, walk-on parts, or whatever the fuck they're called."

"That's what I thought until a short while ago, but Vince and Todd have convinced me it's not so. They told me all about the short."

"Vince and Todd are a couple of idiots who are scared shitless half the time, and I'm surprised you pay them any attention, Karl. We're here to work, and that's what we're going to do."

This got me a sceptical glance.

"You know exactly who we're working for, Louie, and he's no normal director. He's a fat, sadistic bastard . . ."

"That's enough, Karl."

For a minute neither of us spoke, each nursing his own slight. I'd known Karl a couple of months, and we'd got along fine, although I knew he could be a hothead. I, on the other hand, was more the icy type, even when we had to do a difficult job with blood all over the place. I warmed to his fiery nature, but didn't approve the way he used it to torch our director.

On the other hand, this director was certainly an odd bird. Serious yet jokey, distracted and at the same time completely on the ball; when he looked at you, it was never clear what was going on under that smooth, bald pate. At the same time, he had a certain aura which he wore like one of those royal cloaks with a long train for others to take care of. Yes, he was a big shot all right, obsessed with his own navel (contemplating hardly difficult in his case) – but then what Hollywood director wasn't?

I have a certain amount of experience in showbiz, like my father, and since the late fifties have worked in various circuses, festivals, and films, always as an extra. I can confidently assert I've known enough bastards and sadists to fill the entire LA phonebook. I've also done everything – I mean *everything* – to please others along the way. But I never killed anyone. Never that. That was murder, and murder is a big word.

Karl leaned over towards my ear.

"Tomorrow they'll continue shooting by the lake, and we've got the whole day free. Why don't we meet up at three-thirty at the director's trailer?"

"But what for?"

"I've already told you," he gave an impatient grimace: "that's where he keeps the short."

"What short?"

"Oh for God's sake, Louie. Have you perforated your goddamned ear-drums? Perhaps you didn't hear what I said. Hitch has got a short he made which shows a blonde being savagely murdered . . ."

I gave him a cold look:

"Karl, what the hell did you have for breakfast? Bourbon?"

"I swear it's the truth . . .!"

"Have you *seen* this short?"

"No, but Vince and Todd . . ."

"Oh, sure, I might have guessed," I snorted: "Yahweh and his holy prophet."

We'd only known Vince and Todd since they'd begun shooting the film. They were always larking about, and had lots of success with the fair sex, but I'd be damned if this explained Karl's belief in everything they told him as if it was the sacred word of his parents, or of our boss, Mr Berwick himself.

"Look at it this way," insisted Karl: "would they make up that short if it wasn't for real?"

"Look at it this way, Karl: we're working on a film." We were perched on a fence next to the stables. In front were painted sets, real ones as well as fantasy. I nodded towards them. "Look around you: facades of houses that don't exist, cameramen, sound technicians, carpenters, make-up artists . . . It's a film, Karl. As fake as a $3 bill. No one here dies for real." I paused to collect my thoughts. "And even if it *were* to happen, by some awful stroke of ill-luck . . . it would be an accident."

As soon as the phrase was out, I looked up to qualify it, but he'd already jumped on it, nodding grimly:

"They want it to *look* like an accident, Louie. That's the plan."

"Oh come on, Karl . . . You've worked in too many films."

Karl had been in front of the lens more often than I had, and was proud of his experience. Directors like John Huston or John Ford had shot him in various group scenes, and he couldn't say two words to anyone on set without alluding in some way to "*the time Mr Ford wanted* . . ." It made him an incorrigible romantic, seeing grisly murders in every scene and a sadist inside every director. But beneath this facade of being right in the thick of things was a timid, impressionable soul. I certainly wasn't ready to believe it just because he said so.

"The other day I heard a conversation between the boss and that fat, sadistic bas . . ."

"Leave it out, Karl," I cut him short. "You already told me. And you're getting paranoid."

But then, while I was moving away, I heard him say something else:

"Do you think you'd kill someone if they ordered you to, Louie?"

I think of myself as neither good nor bad. I am what I am, and pay my own way. In Hollywood we're all like that. My grandfather Fred told me I'd become a cardboard cutout, and he maybe had a point. But then my grandfather was from the country, and I'm "city" nowadays. I prefer hanging out in glamorous joints, where you meet beautiful girls and people treat you with respect, not like an animal good for nothing but a kick in the belly. Having said that, I'd be lying if I didn't admit Karl's question at the end of the conversation left me thinking: "Do you think you'd kill someone if they ordered you to, Louie?"

My father used to say that every question has just one answer: the truth. In this case, I was startled by what my answer might be, so to quell my conscience, I decided to accept Karl's hare-brained plan for the following midday. When the crew moved off to the lake to shoot the boat scene, we likewise made our way to Hitch's roomy trailer, bang in the centre of things and highly visible. Along the way we bumped into the bewitching Ms Suzanne Pleshette who was having words with the director's assistant, Peggy Robertson. We spotted each other some way off, and Ms Pleshette gave us a wave, a fairly friendly one it seemed. I was more concerned with Ms Robertson though. Seeing Peggy hanging round meant Hitch couldn't be far off, and I shared my concern with Karl.

"It's just what we need," he replied.

"Huh?"

"What were you thinking? That we were going to fiddle around with his expensive projectors and break them? No, we'll wait under a window until that fat . . ."

"OK, you already said that. How do you know he'll come?"

"He comes every afternoon, together with the boss and Mr Boyle, and they go over the murder short again and again."

"What about us?"

"We'll be right there at the window so you can see it."

The plan was Karl to a "T": naïve, passionate, and very stupid.

"And what if they find us?"

His wounded pride made him scowl:

"Are you kidding, Louie? We're better than that."

So we stationed ourselves by the window ledge, and kept our eyes peeled to make sure no one would catch us. From this spot we also had a good view into the interior: a spacious salon with all the furnishings of a typical VIP pad, a large screen, a projector and some reels piled high on a table. There was also a strong smell of the cigars Hitch puffed, plus a director's chair with his full name embroidered on the back, just so everyone would know that *that* was where Mr Alfred Hitchcock sat.

"That's it," said Karl pointing: "the one with a red 'X' on top. Can you see it?"

I nodded, spotting a reel set aside from the rest. But now that we were fully committed to our "crime", I was beginning to feel nervous.

"And if they don't play the reel today?"

"We'll come back tomorrow, Louie." Karl had started on a snack bar to keep himself occupied. "But you'll see. They've been planning the scene for quite some time."

"And . . . who do they want to . . . kill? Ms Pleshette?"

"The blonde," replied Karl poker-faced. "And don't say 'who do they want to kill', but 'who do they want *us* to kill'."

"Oh, but that's . . ."

"They're here now!" he said in a stage whisper.

The sound of the door and voices gave me a turn. I'm easily unnerved, but have managed to get the better of it on most occasions. My father used to say that fear, like scx, is only good if experienced at the proper moment. He got that about right, but at this point an overpowering curiosity, much stronger than fear, kept me glued to the window.

We kept completely quiet, raising our heads just enough to peer in without calling attention to ourselves. Sure enough, what I saw was Hitch, Boyle and Berwick jabbering away, though when I listened carefully, I realized the last two were simply replying to what the first had asked. Sometimes the reply might contain a question in turn but Hitch, unlike the others, hardly ever replied. I guessed that was the definition of being important within one's field.

And, of course, they screened the short.

We saw it fairly well, taking turns to raise our heads. When it was over, we managed to slip away without anyone being the wiser.

"Convinced now?" asked Karl, anxiously.

I didn't know what to say. On the one hand, I felt like laughing. On the other, well there *was* something creepy about the whole thing.

"It was . . . just a dummy, Karl. It wasn't a real woman."

"But it'll be real on the day they shoot," insisted my pal.

Worst of all, there was a ghost of a smile hovering on his lips.

It was March, and in the Californian seaside town where we were shooting spring seemed everywhere, filling every little corner with its fresh and heady aroma. The very sea smelt vaguely of flowers and blossom, and under any other circumstances, I'd have been glad to be alive with the excellent food, friendly locals and light workload. But instead I spent my days obsessed with the scene in the short. True, the figure was a dummy, but the murder itself was cruel and utterly merciless. The victim's eyes popped out as if on springs, her dress was torn to shreds, and the joints of her outer limbs broke as if they were dry stalks. Simply remembering it made me want to throw up, as did Hitch's voice floating calmly above all the horror: "Let's place her closer to the wall . . . No, no, Bob: I want her to receive the first wounds when she raises her arms . . ."

"*Do you think you'd kill someone if they ordered you to?*"

"It would depend who gave the order," I thought. I could hardly imagine the kindly Mr Berwick asking anything of the sort. It wasn't as if I particularly liked the blonde, either. She was pleasant enough and had long legs, but it happened that I was much more interested in Ms Pleshette. Still, the blonde was a woman, not a dummy. I'd never harmed a woman in my life, and had no intention of changing things on that score. But . . . what would I do if Mr Berwick ordered me . . .?

"*Do you think you'd kill someone if . . .?*"

It's today, Karl told me bluntly one fine day. "We're doing it today."

We were sitting on the same fence as our first conversation, a bad omen in itself as far as I could see. I stared at my friend wide-eyed.

"Berwick will give us instructions," he continued soberly. "And you know as much as me that you'll do it, just like you know I'll do it, Louie. We're here to do whatever they say, like everyone else in Hollywood. We're just cogs in the machine. We'll do it – and you'll see how – the moment we receive the order from that fat, sadi— . . ."

"To the set, boys," snapped Todd, hurrying past.

I followed him feeling ever more unsettled, as did Karl. Mr Berwick was waiting for us on a piece of smooth ground, together with the rest of the crew. Any last-ditch hope that this was all a gigantic farce (at the end of the day, wasn't cinema just that?), evaporated into thin air when the blonde appeared, attractive as ever but as terrified as we were, and the boss explained what we were all supposed to do.

Karl was right about one thing: we did it.

And how, my God.

Even now, after a certain amount of time has passed, the memory of it all remains more than I can bear. I would call it "inhuman", but the expression is not nearly cruel enough. After the appalling act, I never saw Karl again, and I never worked again in the movies. I went back to the circus, as it paid well and other jobs were hard to come by. I now have children, and although they're very young, they bring joy to my days. It can't be said I live any worse than before, but the nightmares are what torment me. The memory of what I did, of what *we* did, just won't leave me in peace.

The blonde survived our terrible attack, I suppose, but the fact is I saw her sobbing for real, heard screams that weren't faked, and received some of the frantic blows with which the poor girl tried to keep us at bay. As if that weren't enough (and I admit this without any hesitation, although I doubt I'll ever be brave enough to tell my own children), I was one of those who, confused and disoriented by the savage violence inflicted on her by our coach, slashed her left arm leaving deep incisions in her skin.

The poor woman's wounds may now be nothing more than scars, but they still remain fresh in my heart. After that day I swore never again to work in movies.

My only wish now is to grow old in peace, and also to give up the circus as soon as I can. It is one of life's paradoxes, but I've recently begun to feel nostalgic about my country childhood, and when work and my new boss allow, I like to spread my black wings and fly as high as possible, leaving the world of men far behind.

Strange to say, flying is when I feel more human than ever.

Translation by Martin Davies

The Strawberry Tree

Ruth Rendell

1

The hotel where we are staying was built by my father. Everyone assures me it is the best in Llosar and it is certainly the biggest and ugliest. From a distance it looks as if made of white cartridge paper or from hundreds of envelopes with their flaps open. Inside it is luxurious in the accepted way with sheets of bronze-coloured mirrors and tiles of copper-coloured marble and in the foyer, in stone vessels of vaguely Roman appearance, stands an army of hibiscus with trumpet flowers the red of soldiers' coats.

There is a pool and a room full of machines for exercise, three restaurants and two bars. A machine polishes your shoes and another makes ice. In the old days we used to watch the young men drink *palo* out of long thin bow-shaped vessels from which the liquor spouted in a curving stream. Now the hotel barman makes cocktails called *Mañanas* that are said to be famous. We tried them yesterday, sitting on the terrace at the back of the hotel. From there, if you are not gazing at the swimming pool as most people do, you can rest your eyes, in both senses, on the garden. There the arbutus has been planted and flourishes, its white flowers blooming and strawberry fruits ripening at the same time, something I have heard about but never seen before, for it is October and I was last here all those years ago in summer.

We have rooms with envelope balconies and a view of the bay. There are no fishing boats any more, the pier of the old hotel with its vine canopy is gone and the old hotel itself has become a casino. But the harbour is still there with the statue of the Virgin,

Nuestra Doña de los Marineros, where, swimming in the deep green water, Piers and Rosario and I first saw Will sitting on the sturdy stone wall.

All along the "front", as I suppose I must call it, are hotels and restaurants, souvenir shops and tourist agencies, cafés and drinking places, where once stood a string of cottages. The church with its brown campanile and shallow pantiled roof that used to dominate this shore has been almost lost among the new buildings, dwarfed by the gigantic Thomson Holiday hotel. I asked the chambermaid if they had had jellyfish at Llosar lately but she only shook her head and muttered about *contaminación*.

The house we were lent by José-Carlos and Micaela is still there but much "improved" and extended, painted sugar-pink and surrounded by a fence of the most elaborate wrought ironwork I have ever seen, iron lace for a giant's tablecloth around a giant's child's iced cake. I would be surprised if Rosario recognized it. Inland, things are much the same, as far as I can tell. Up to now I have not ventured there, even though we have a most efficient rented car. I climb up a little way out of the village and stare at the yellow hills, at the olive trees and junipers, and the straight wide roads which now make seams across them, but I cannot see the little haunted house, the *Casita de Golondro*. It was never possible to see it from here. A fold in the hills, crowned with woods of pine and carob, hides it. The manager of our hotel told me this morning it is now a *parador*, the first on Majorca.

When I have performed the task I came here to do I shall go and have a look at it. These state-run hotels, of which there are many on the mainland, are said to be very comfortable. We might have dinner there one evening. I shall propose it to the others. But as for removing from here to there, if any of them suggest it, I shall make up my mind to turn it down. For one thing, if I were staying there I should sooner or later have to rediscover *that* room or deliberately avoid it. The truth is I no longer want an explanation. I want to be quiet, I want, if this does not sound too ludicrous, to be happy.

My appointment in Muralla is for ten o'clock tomorrow morning with an officer of the *Guardia Civil* whose rank, I think, would correspond to our detective superintendent. He will conduct me to see what is to be seen and I shall look at the things and try to remember and give him my answer. I haven't yet made up my mind whether to let the others come with me, nor am I sure they would want to come. Probably it will be best if I do this, as I have done so much in the past, alone.

2

Nearly forty years have passed since first we went to Majorca, Piers and I and our parents, to the house our Spanish cousin lent us because my mother had been ill. Her illness was depression and a general feeling of lowness and lethargy, but the cause of it was a lost child, a miscarriage. Even then, before there was real need, my parents were trying to have more children, had been trying to have more, although I was unaware of this, since soon after my own birth thirteen years before. It was as if they knew, by some sad superstitious prevision, that they would not always have their pigeon pair.

I remember the letter to my father from José-Carlos. They had fought side by side in the Spanish Civil War and been fast friends and sporadic correspondents ever since, although he was my mother's cousin, not my father's. My mother's aunt had married a Spaniard from Santander and José-Carlos was their son. Thus we all knew where Santander was but had scarcely heard of Majorca. At any rate, we had to search for it on the map. With the exception of Piers, that is. Piers would have known, Piers could have told us it was the largest of the Balearic Islands, Baleares Province in the western Mediterranean, and probably too that it covered something over fourteen hundred square miles. But one of the many many nice things about my clever brother, child of good fortune, was his modesty. Handing out pieces of gratuitous information was never his way. He too stood and looked over our father's shoulder at Goodall and Darby's University Atlas, a pre-war edition giving pride of place to the British Empire and in which the Mediterranean was an unimportant inland sea. He looked, as we did, in silence.

The tiny Balearics floated green and gold on pale blue, held in the arms of Barcelona and Valencia. Majorca (Mallorca in brackets) was a planet with attendant moons: Formentera, Cabrera, but Minorca too and Ibiza. How strange it now seems that we had never heard of Ibiza, had no idea of how to pronounce it, while Minorca was just the place a chicken was named after.

José-Carlos's house was at a place called Llosar. He described it and its setting, deprecatingly, making little of the beauty, stressing rustic awkwardnesses. It was on the north-west coast, overlooking the sea, within a stone's throw of the village, but there was not much to the village, only a few little shops and the hotel. His English was so good it put us to shame, my father said. They would have to brush up their Spanish, my mother and he.

The house was ours for the months of July and August, or for us children's school holidays. We would find it very quiet, there was nothing to do but swim and lie in the sun, eat fish and drink in the local tavern, if my parents had a mind to that. In the south-east of the island were limestone caves and subterranean lakes, worth a visit if we would entrust ourselves to the kind of car we would find for hire. Tourists had begun to come, but there could not be many of these as there was only one hotel.

Llosar was marked on our map, on a northern cape of the island. The capital, Palma, looked quite big until you saw its letters were in the same size print as Alicante on the mainland. We had never been abroad, Piers and I. We were the children of war, born before it, confined by it to our own beleaguered island. And since the end of war we had been fated to wait patiently for something like this that would not cost much or demand a long-term plan.

I longed for this holiday. I had never been ill but now I dreaded some unspecified illness swooping down on me as the school term drew to its close. It was possible. Everyone, sooner or later, in those days before general immunization, had measles. I had never had it. Piers had been in hospital for an operation the previous year but I had never so much as had my tonsils out. Anything could happen. I felt vulnerable, I lived in daily terror of the inexplicable gut pain, the rash appearing, the cough. I even began taking my temperature first thing in the morning, as my poor mother took hers, although for a different reason. They would go without me. Why not? It would be unfair to keep four people at home for the sake of one. I would be sent, after I came out of hospital, to stay with my Aunt Sheila.

What happened was rather different. We were not to be a member of the party fewer but to be joined by one more. José-Carlos's second letter was even more apologetic and this time, in my view at least, with justice. He had a request. We must of course say no at once if what he asked was unacceptable. Rosario would very much like to be at the house while we were there. Rosario loved the place so much and always stayed there in the summer holidays.

"Who is he?" I said.

"He's a girl," my mother said. "José-Carlos's daughter. I should think she must be fifteen or sixteen by now."

"It's one of those Spanish names," said my father, "short for Maria of the something-or-other, Maria del Pilar, Maria del Consuelo, in this case Maria of the rosary."

I was very taken aback. I didn't want her. The idea of a Spanish girl joining us filled me with dismay. I could imagine her, big and dark, with black flowing hair and tiers of skirts that would swing as she danced, a comb and mantilla, although I stopped at the rose between her teeth.

"We can write to José-Carlos and say it's not acceptable." This seemed perfectly reasonable to me. "He says we are to, so we can. We can do it at once and she'll know in plenty of time not to be there."

My mother laughed. My father did not. Now, so long afterwards, I can look back and believe he already understood the way I was and it worried him. He said gently but not smiling, "He doesn't mean it. He's being polite. It would be impossible for us to say no."

"Besides," said Piers, "she may be very nice." That was something I could never consider as possible. I was wary of almost everyone then and I have changed very little. I still prepare myself to dislike people and be disliked by them. Their uncharitableness I anticipate, their meanness and envy. When someone invites me to dinner and tells me that such-and-such an acquaintance of theirs will be there, a man or a woman I shall love to meet, I invariably refuse. I dread such encounters. The new person, in my advance estimation, will be cold, self-absorbed, malicious, determined to slight or hurt me, will be handsome or beautiful, well-dressed and brilliant, will find me unattractive or stupid, will either not want to talk to me or will want to talk with the object of causing humiliation.

I am unable to help this. I have tried. Psychotherapists have tried. It is one of the reasons why, although rich beyond most people's dreams and good-looking enough, intelligent enough and able to talk, I have led until recently a lonely life, isolated, not so much neglected as the object of remarks such as:

"Petra won't come, so there is really no point in asking her," and "You have to phone Petra or write to her so far in advance and make so many arrangements before you drop in for a cup of tea, it hardly seems worth it."

It is not so much that I am shy as that, cold myself, I understand the contempt and indifference of the cold-hearted. I do not want to be its victim. I do not want to be reduced by a glance, a laugh, a wounding comment, so that I shrivel and grow small. That is what the expression means: to make someone feel small. But another phrase, when someone says he wants the earth to open and swallow him up, that I understand, that is not something I long for but something which happens to me daily. It is only in this past year that the thaw has begun, the slow delayed opening of my heart.

So the prospect of the company of Rosario spoiled for me those last days before we left for Spain. She would be nicer to look at than I was. She would be taller. Later on in life the seniority of a friend is to one's advantage but not at thirteen. Rosario was older and therefore more sophisticated, more knowledgeable, superior and aware of it. The horrible thought had also struck me that she might not speak English. She would be a grown-up speaking Spanish with my parents and leagued with them in the great adult conspiracy against those who were still children.

So happy anticipation was spoiled by dread, as all my life it has been until now.

If you go to Majorca today special flights speed you there direct from Heathrow and Gatwick and, for all I know, Stansted too. It may well be true that more people go to Majorca for their holidays than anywhere else. When we went we had to take the train to Paris and there change on to another which carried us through France and the night, passing the walls of Carcassonne at sunrise, crossing the frontier into Spain in the morning. A small, light and probably ill-maintained aircraft took us from Barcelona to Palma and one of the hired cars, the untrustworthy rackety kind mentioned by José-Carlos, from Palma to the north.

I slept in the car, my head on my mother's shoulder, so I absorbed nothing of that countryside that was to grow so familiar to us, that was to ravish us with its beauty and in the end betray us. The sea was the first thing I saw when I woke up, of a deep, silken, peacock blue, a mirror of the bright cloudless sky. And the heat wrapped me like a shawl when I got out and stood there on dry pale stones, striped with the thin shadows of juniper trees.

I had never seen anywhere so beautiful. The shore which enclosed the bay was thickly wooded, a dark massy green, but the sand was silver. There was a skein of houses trailed along the shore, white cottages with flat pantiled roofs, the church with its clean square campanile and the hotel whose terrace, hung with vines and standing in the sea, was a combination of pier and tree house. Behind all this and beyond it, behind *us* the way we had come, a countryside of yellow hills scattered with grey trees and grey stones, stretched itself out and rolled up into the mountains. And everywhere stood the cypresses like no trees I had ever seen before, blacker than holly, thin as stems, clustered like groups of pillars or isolated like single obelisks, with shadows which by evening would pattern the turf with an endlessly repeated tracery of lines. Upon all this the sun shed a dry, white, relentless heat.

Children look at things. They have nothing else to do. Later on, it is not just a matter of this life being full of care and therefore worthless if we have no time to stand and stare. We have no time, we cannot change back, that is the way it is. When we are young, before the time of study, before love, before work and a place of our own to live in, everything is done for us. If we have happy childhoods, that is, and good parents. Our meals will be made and our beds, our clothes washed and new ones bought, the means to buy earned for us, transport provided and a roof over our heads. We need not think of these things or fret about them. Time does not press its hot breath on us, saying to us, go, go, hurry, you have things to do, you will be late, come, come, hurry.

So we can stand and stare. Or lean on a wall, chin in hands, elbows on the warm rough stone, and look at what lies down there, the blue silk sea unfolding in a splash of lace on the sand, the rocks like uncut agate set in a strip of silver. We can lie in a field, without thought, only with dreams, gazing through a thousand stems of grasses at the tiny life which moves among them as between the tree trunks of a wood. In a few years' time, a very few, it will be possible no more, as all the cares of life intrude, distract the mind and spoil the day, introducing those enemies of contemplation, boredom and cold and stiffness and anxiety.

At thirteen I was at the crossing point between then and now. I could still stand and stare, dawdle and dream, time being still my toy and not yet my master, but adult worries had begun. People were real, were already the only real threat. If I wanted to stay there, leaning on my wall, from which hung like an unrolled bolt of purple velvet the climber I learned to call the bougainvillea, it was as much from dread of meeting José-Carlos and his wife Micaela and Rosario, their daughter, as from any longing for the prolongation of my beautiful view. In my mind, as I gazed at it, I was rehearsing their remarks, designed to diminish me.

"Petra!"

My father was calling me, standing outside a white house with a balcony running all the way around it at first floor level. Cypresses banded its walls and filled the garden behind it, like spikes of dark stalagmites. There was a girl with him, smaller than me, I could tell even from that distance, small and thin and with a tiny face that looked out between great dark doors of hair, as through the opening in a gateway. Instead of guessing she was Rosario, I thought she must be the child of a caretaker or cleaner. Introductions would not be made. I scarcely glanced at her. I was already bracing myself for the coming meeting, hardening myself, emptying my mind. Up through the white sunlight to the house I went and was on the step, had pushed open the front door, when he said her name to me.

"Come and meet your cousin."

I had to turn and look then. She was not at all what I expected. People never are and I know that – I think I even knew it then – but this was a knowledge which made no difference. I have never been able to say, wait and see, make no advance judgments, reserve your defence. I managed to lift my eyes to hers. We did not shake hands but looked at each other and said hallo. She had difficulty with the H, making it too breathy. I noticed, close up beside her, that I was an inch taller. Her skin was pale with a glow behind it, her body as thin as an elf's. About the hair only I had been right and that not entirely. Rosario's hair was the colour of polished wood, of old furniture, as smooth and shining, and about ten times as long as mine. Later she showed me how she could sit on it, wrap herself in it. My mother told her, but kindly, meaning it as a compliment, that she could be Lady Godiva in a pageant. And then, of course, Piers, who knew the story properly, had to explain who Lady Godiva was.

Then, when we first met, we did not say much. I was too surprised. I must say also that I was gratified, for I had expected a young lady, an amalgam of Carmen and a nun, and found instead a child with Alice in Wonderland hair and ankle socks. She wore a little short dress and on a chain around her neck a seed-pearl locket with a picture of her mother. She preceded me into the house, smiling over her shoulder in a way unmistakably intended to make me feel at home. I began to thaw and to tremble a little, as I always do. Her parents were inside with my mother and Piers, but not to stay long. Once we had been shown where to find things and where to seek help if help were needed, they were to be off to Barcelona.

We had been travelling for a day and a night and half a day. My mother went upstairs to rest in the big bed under a mosquito net. My father took a shower in the bathroom which had no bath and where the water was not quite cold but of a delectable cool freshness. Piers said,

"Can we go in the sea?"

"If you like to." Rosario spoke the very correct, oddly-accented English of one who has been taught the language with care but seldom heard it spoken by an English person. "There is no tide here. You can swim whenever you want. Shall we go now and I can show you?"

"In a place like this," said my brother, "I should like to go in the sea every day and all day. I'd never get tired of it."

"Perhaps not." She had her head on one side. "We shall see."

We did grow tired of it eventually. Or, rather, the sea was not always the sweet buoyant blessing it appeared to be that first afternoon. A plague of jellyfish came and on another day someone thought he saw a basking shark. Fishermen complained that swimmers frightened off their catch. And, as a day-long occupation we grew tired of it. But that first time and for many subsequent times when we floated in its warm blue embrace and looked through depths of jade and green at the abounding marine life, at fishes and shells and the gleaming tendrils of subaqueous plants, all was perfect, all exceeded our dreams.

Our bodies and legs were white as fishes. Only our arms had a pale tan from the English summer. Piers had not been swimming since his illness but his trunks came up just high enough to hide the scar. Rosario's southern skin was that olive colour that changes only a little with the seasons but her limbs looked brown compared to ours. We sat on the rocks in the sun and she told us we must not leave the beach without covering ourselves or walk in the village in shorts or attempt to go in the church – this one was for me – with head and arms uncovered.

"I don't suppose I shall want to go in the church," I said.

She looked at me curiously. She wasn't at all shy of us and what we said made her laugh. "Oh, you will want to go everywhere. You will want to see everything."

"Is there much to see?" Piers was already into the way of referring back to the textual evidence. "Your father said there would only be swimming and a visit to the caves."

"The caves, yes. We must take you to the caves. There are lots and lots of things to do here, Piers."

It was the first time she had spoken his name. She pronounced it like the surname "Pearce". I saw him look at her with more friendliness, with more warmth, than before. And it is true that we are *warmed* by being called by our names. We all know people who hardly ever do it, who only do it when they absolutely must. They manage to steer conversations along, ask questions, respond, without ever using a first name. And they chill others with their apparent detachment, those others who can never understand that it is diffidence which keeps them from committing themselves to the use of names. They might get the names wrong, or use them too often, be claiming an intimacy to which they have no right, be forward, pushy, presumptuous. I know all about it for I am one of them.

Rosario called me Petra soon after that and Piers called her Rosario. I remained, of course, on the other side of that bridge which I was not to cross for several days. We went up to the house and Rosario said,

"I'm so happy you have come."

It was not said as a matter of politeness but rapturously. I could not imagine myself uttering those words even to people I had known all my life. How could I be so forward, lay myself open to their ridicule and their sneers, *expose* myself to their scorn? Yet when they were spoken to me I felt no scorn and no desire to ridicule. Her words pleased me, they made me feel needed and liked. But that was far from understanding how to do myself what Rosario did, and forty years later I am only just learning.

"I'm so happy you have come."

She said it again, this time in the hearing of my parents. Piers said,

"We're happy to be here, Rosario."

It struck me then, as I saw him smile at her, that until then he had not really known any girls but me.

3

My brother had all the gifts, looks, intellect, charm, simple niceness and, added to these, the generosity of spirit that should come from being favoured by the gods but often does not. My mother and father doted on him. They were like parents in a fairy story, poor peasants who know themselves unworthy to bring up the changeling prince some witch has put into their own child's cradle.

Not that he was unlike them, having taken for himself the best of their looks, the best features of each of them, and the best of their talents, my father's mathematical bent, my mother's love of literature, the gentleness and humour of both. But these gifts were enhanced in him, he bettered them. The genes of outward appearance that met in him made for greater beauty than my mother and father had.

He was tall, taller at sixteen than my father. His hair was a very dark brown, almost black, that silky fine dark hair that goes grey sooner than any other. My father, who was not yet forty, was already grey. Piers's eyes were blue, as are all the eyes in our family except my Aunt Sheila's which are turquoise with a dark rim around the pupils. His face was not a film star's nor that of a model posing in smart clothes in an advertisement, but a Pre-Raphaelite's meticulous portrait. Have you seen Holman Hunt's strange painting of Valentine rescuing Sylvia, and the armed man's thoughtful, sensitive, gentle looks?

At school he had always been top of his class. Examinations he was allowed to take in advance of his contemporaries he always passed and passed well. He was destined to go up to Oxford at seventeen instead of eighteen. It was hard to say whether he was better at the sciences than the arts, and if it was philosophy he was to read at university, it might equally have been classical languages or physics.

Modern languages were the only subjects at which he failed to excel, at which he did no better and often less well than his contemporaries, and he was quick to point this out. That first evening at Llosar, for instance, he complimented Rosario on her English.

"How do you come to speak English so well, Rosario, when you've never been out of Spain?"

"I learn at school and I have a private teacher too."

"We learn languages at school and some of us have private teachers, but it doesn't seem to work for us."

"Perhaps they are not good teachers."

"That's our excuse, but I wonder if it's true."

He hastened to say what a dunce he was at French, what a waste of time his two years of Spanish. Why, he would barely know how to ask her the time or the way to the village shops. She looked at him in that way she had, her head a little on one side, and said she would teach him Spanish if he liked, she would be a good teacher. No English girl ever looked at a boy like that, in a way that was frank and shrewd, yet curiously maternal, always practical, assessing the future. Her brown river of hair flowed down over her shoulders, rippled down her back, and one long trees of it lay across her throat like a trailing frond of willow.

I have spoken of my brother in the past – "Piers was" and "Piers did" – as if those qualities he once had he no longer has, or as if he were dead. It is not my intention to give a false impression, but how otherwise can I recount these events? Things may be less obscure if I talk of loss rather than death, irremediable loss in spite of what has happened since, and of Piers's character only as it was at sixteen, making clear that I am aware of how vastly the personality changes in forty years, how speech patterns alter, specific learning is lost and huge accumulations of knowledge gained. Of Piers I felt no jealousy but I think this was a question of sex. If I may be allowed to evolve such an impossible thesis I would say that jealousy might have existed if he had been my sister. It is always possible for the sibling, the less favoured, to say to herself, ah, this is the way members of the opposite sex are treated, it is different for them, it is not that I am inferior or less loved, only different. Did I say that? Perhaps, in a deeply internal way. Certain it is that the next step was never taken; I never asked, where then are the privileges that should be accorded to my difference? Where are the special favours that come the way of daughters which their brothers miss? I accepted and I was not jealous.

At first I felt no resentment that it was Piers Rosario chose for her friend and companion, not me. I observed it and told myself it was a question of age. She was nearer in age to Piers than to me. And a question too perhaps, although I had no words for it then, of precocious sex. Piers had never had a girlfriend and she, I am sure, had never had a boyfriend. I was too young to place them in a Romeo and Juliet situation but I could see that they liked each other in the way boys and girls do when they begin to be aware of gender and the future. It did not matter because I was not excluded, I was always with them, and they were both too kind to isolate me. Besides, after a few days we found someone to make a fourth.

At this time we were still, Piers and I, enchanted by the beach and all that the beach offered: miles of shore whose surface was a combination of earth and sand and from which the brown rocks sprang like living plants, a strand encroached upon by pine trees with flat umbrella-like tops and purplish trunks. The sea was almost tideless but clean still, so that where it lapped the sand there was no scum or detritus of flotsam but a thin bubbly foam that dissolved at a touch into clear blue water. And under the water lay the undisturbed marine life, the bladder weed, the green sea grass and the weed-like trees of pleated brown silk, between whose branches swam small black and silver fish, sea anemones with pulsating whiskered mouths, creatures sheathed in pink shells moving slowly across the frondy seabed.

We walked in the water, picking up treasures too numerous to carry home. With Rosario we rounded the cape to discover the other hitherto invisible side, and in places where the sand ceased, we swam. The yellow turf and the myrtle bushes and the thyme and rosemary ran right down to the sand, but where the land met the sea it erupted into dramatic rocks, the colour of a snail's shell and fantastically shaped. We scaled them and penetrated the caves that pocked the cliffs, finding nothing inside but dry dust and a salty smell and, in the largest, the skull of a goat.

After three days spent like this, unwilling as yet to explore further, we made our way in the opposite direction, towards the harbour and the village where the little fishing fleet was beached. The harbour was enclosed with walls of limestone built in a horseshoe shape, and at the end of the right arm stood the statue of the Virgin, looking out to sea, her own arms held out, as if to embrace the world.

The harbour's arms rose some eight feet out of the sea, and on the left one, opposite *Nuestra Doña*, sat a boy, his legs dangling over the wall. We were swimming, obliged to swim for the water was very deep here, the clear but marbled dark green of malachite. Above us the sky was a hot shimmering silvery-blue and the sun seemed to have a palpable touch. We swam in a wide slow circle and the boy watched us.

You could see he was not Mallorquin. He had a pale freckled face and red hair. Today, I think, I would say Will has the look of a Scotsman, the bony, earnest, clever face, the pale blue staring eyes, although in fact he was born in Bedford of London-born parents. I know him still. That is a great understatement. I should have said that he is still my friend, although the truth is I have never entirely liked him, I have always suspected him of things I find hard to put into words. Of some kind of trickery perhaps, of having deep-laid plans, of using me. Ten years ago when he caused me one of the greatest surprises of my life by asking me to marry him, I knew as soon as I had recovered it was not love that had made him ask.

In those days, in Majorca, Will was just a boy on the watch for companions of his own age. An only child, he was on holiday with his parents and he was lonely. It was Piers who spoke to him. This was typical of Piers, always friendly, warm-hearted, with no shyness in him. We girls, if we had been alone, would probably have made no approaches, would have reacted to the watchful gaze of this boy on the wall by cavorting in the water, turning somersaults, perfecting our butterfly stroke and other hydrobatics. We would have *performed* for him, like young female animals under the male eye, and when the display was over have swum away.

Contingency has been called the central principle of all history. One thing leads to another. Or one thing does not lead to another because something else happens to prevent it. Perhaps, in the light of what was to come, it would have been better for all if Piers had not spoken. We would never have come to the *Casita de Golondro*, so the things which happened there would not have happened, and when we left the island to go home we would all have left. If Piers had been less than he was, a little colder, a little more reserved, more like me. If we had all been careful not to look in the boy's direction but had swum within the harbour enclosure with eyes averted, talking perhaps more loudly to each other and laughing more freely in the way people do when they want to make it plain they need no one else, another will not be welcome. Certain it is that the lives of all of us were utterly changed, then and now, because Piers, swimming close up to the wall, holding up his arm in a salute, called out,

"Hallo. You're English, aren't you? Are you staying at the hotel?"

The boy nodded but said nothing. He took off his shirt and his canvas shoes. He stood up and removed his long trousers, folded up his clothes and laid them in a pile on the wall with his shoes on top of them. His body was thin and white as a peeled twig. He wore black swimming trunks. We were all swimming around watching him. We knew he was coming in but I think we expected him to hold his nose and jump in with the maximum of splashing. Instead, he executed a perfect dive, his body passing into the water as cleanly as a knife plunged into a pool.

Of course it was done to impress us, it was "showing off". But we didn't mind. We *were* impressed and we congratulated him. Rosario, treading water, clapped her hands. Will had broken the ice as skilfully as his dive had split the surface of the water.

He would swim back with us, he liked "that end" of the beach.

"What about your clothes?" said Piers.

"My mother will find them and take them in." He spoke indifferently, in the tone of the spoiled only child whose parents wait on him like servants. "She makes me wear a shirt and long trousers all the time," he said, "because I burn. I turn red like a lobster. I haven't got as many skins as other people.

I was taken aback until Piers told me later that everyone has the same number of layers of skin. It is a question not of density but of pigment. Later on, when we were less devoted to the beach and began investigating the hinterland, Will often wore a hat, a big wide-brimmed affair of woven grass. He enjoyed wrapping up, the look it gave him of an old-fashioned adult. He was tall for his age which was the same as mine, very thin and bony and long-necked.

We swam back to our beach and sat on the rocks, in the shade of a pine tree for Will's sake. He was careful, fussy even, to see that no dappling of light reached him. This, he told us, was his second visit to Llosar. His parents and he had come the previous year and he remembered seeing Rosario before. It seemed to me that when he said this he gave her a strange look, sidelong, rather intimate, mysterious, as if he knew things about her we did not. All is discovered, it implied, and retribution may or may not come. There was no foundation for this, none at all. Rosario had done nothing to feel guilt about, had no secret to be unearthed. I noticed later he did it to a lot of people and it disconcerted them. Now, after so long, I see it as a blackmailer's look, although Will as far as I know has never demanded money with menaces from anyone.

"What else do you do?" he said. "Apart from swimming?"

Nothing, we said, not yet anyway. Rosario looked defensive. After all, she almost lived here and Will's assumed sophistication was an affront to her. Had she not only three days before told us of the hundred things there were to do?

"They have bullfights sometimes," Will said. "They're in Palma on Sunday evenings. My parents went last year but I didn't. I faint at the sight of blood. Then there are the Dragon Caves."

"*Las Cuevas del Drach*," said Rosario.

"That's what I said, the Dragon Caves. And there are lots of other caves in the west." Will hesitated. Brooding on what possibly was forbidden or frowned on, he looked up and said in the way that even then I thought of as sly, "We could go to the haunted house."

"The haunted house?" said Piers, sounding amused. "Where's that?"

Rosario said without smiling, "He means the *Casita de Golondro*."

"I don't know what it's called. It's on the road to Pollença – well, in the country near that road. The village people say it's haunted."

Rosario was getting cross. She was always blunt, plain-spoken. It was not her way to hide even for a moment what she felt. "How do you know what they say? Do you speak Spanish? No, I thought not. You mean it is the man who has the hotel that told you. He will say anything. He told my mother he has seen a whale up close near Cabo del Pinar."

"Is it supposed to be haunted, Rosario?" said my brother.

She shrugged. "Ghosts," she said, "are not true. They don't happen. Catholics don't believe in ghosts, they're not supposed to. Father Xaviere would be very angry with me if he knew I talked about ghosts." It was unusual for Rosario to mention her religion. I saw the look of surprise on Piers's face. "Do you know it's one-thirty?" she said to Will, who had of course left his watch behind with his clothes. "You will be late for your lunch and so will we." Rosario and my brother had already begun to enjoy their particular rapport. They communicated even at this early stage of their relationship by a glance, a movement of the hand. Some sign he made, perhaps involuntary and certainly unnoticed by me, seemed to check her. She lifted her shoulders again, said, "Later on, we shall go to the village, to the lace shop. Do you like to come too?" She added, with a spark of irony, her head tilted to one side, "The sun will be going down, not to burn your poor skin that is so thin."

The lace-makers were producing an elaborate counterpane for Rosario's mother. It had occurred to her that we might like to spend half an hour watching these women at work. We walked down there at about five, calling for Will at the hotel on the way. He was sitting by himself on the terrace, under its roof of woven vine branches. Four women, one of whom we later learned was his mother, sat at the only other occupied table, playing bridge. Will was wearing a clean shirt, clean long trousers and his grass hat, and as he came to join us he called out to his mother in a way that seemed strange to me because we had only just met, strange but oddly endearing,

"My friends are here. See you later."

Will is not like me, crippled by fear of a snub, by fear of being thought forward or pushy, but he lives in the same dread of rejection. He longs to "belong". His dream is to be a member of some inner circle, honoured and loved by his fellows, privileged to share knowledge of a secret password. He once told me, in an unusual burst of confidence, that when he heard someone he knew refer to him in conversation as "my friend", tears of happiness came into his eyes.

While we were at the lacemakers' and afterwards on the beach at sunset he said no more about the *Casita de Golondro*, but that night, sitting on the terrace at the back of the house, Rosario told us its story. The nights at Llosar were warm and the air was velvety. Mosquitos there must have been, for we all had nets over our beds, but I only remember seeing one or two. I remember the quietness, the dark blue clear sky and the brilliance of the stars. The landscape could not be seen, only an outline of dark hills with here and there a tiny light glittering. The moon, that night, was increasing towards the full, was melon-shaped and melon-coloured.

The others sat in deckchairs, almost the only kind of "garden furniture" anyone had in those days and which, today, you never see. I was in the hammock, a length of faded canvas suspended between one of the veranda pillars and a cypress tree. My brother was looking at Rosario in a peculiarly intense way. I think I remember such a lot about that evening because that look of his so impressed me. It was as if he had never seen a girl before. Or so I think now. I doubt if I thought about it in that way when I was thirteen. It embarrassed me then, the way he stared. She was talking about the *Casita* and he was watching her, but when she looked at him, he smiled and turned his eyes away.

Her unwillingness to talk of ghosts on religious grounds seemed to be gone. It was hard not to make the connection and conclude it had disappeared with Will's return to the hotel. "You could see the trees around the house from here," she said, "if it wasn't night," and she pointed through the darkness to the south-west where the mountains began. "*Casita* means 'little house' but it is quite big and it is very old. At the front is a big door and at the back, I don't know what you call them, arches and pillars."

"A cloister?" said Piers.

"Yes, perhaps. Thank you. And there is a big garden with a wall around it and gates made of iron. The garden is all trees and bushes, grown over with them, and the wall is broken, so this is how I have seen the back with the word you said, the cloisters."

"But no one lives there?"

"No one has ever lived there that I know. But someone owns it, it is someone's house, though they never come. It is all locked up. Now Will is saying what the village people say but Will *does not know* what they say. There are not ghosts, I mean there are not dead people who come back, just a bad room in the house you must not go in."

Of course we were both excited, Piers and I, by that last phrase, made all the more enticing by being couched in English that was not quite idiomatic. But what returns to me most powerfully now are Rosario's preceding words about dead people who come back. It is a line from the past, long-forgotten, which itself "came back" when some string in my memory was painfully plucked. I find myself repeating it silently, like a mantra, or like one of the prayers from that rosary for which she was named. Dead people who come back, lost people who are raised from the dead, the dead who return at last.

On that evening, as I have said, the words which followed that prophetic phrase affected us most. Piers at once asked about the "bad" room but Rosario, in the finest tradition of tellers of ghost stories, did not admit to knowing precisely which room it was. People who talked about it said the visitor knows. The room would declare itself.

"They say that those who go into the room never come out again."

We were suitably impressed. "Do you mean they disappear, Rosario?" asked my brother.

"I don't know. I cannot tell you. People don't see them again – that is what they say."

"But it's a big house, you said. There must be a lot of rooms. If you knew which was the haunted room you could simply avoid it, couldn't you?"

Rosario laughed. I don't think she ever believed any of it or was ever afraid. "Perhaps you don't know until you are in this room and then it is too late. How do you like that?"

"Very much," said Piers. "It's wonderfully sinister. Has anyone ever disappeared?"

"The cousin of Carmela Valdez disappeared. They say he broke a window and got in because there were things to steal, he was very bad, he did no work." She sought for a suitable phrase and brought it out slightly wrong. "The black goat of the family."

Rosario was justly proud of her English and only looked smug when we laughed at her. Perhaps she could already hear the admiration in Piers's laughter. "He disappeared, it is true, but only to a prison in Barcelona, I think."

The meaning of *golondro* she refused to tell Piers. He must look it up. That way he would be more likely to remember it. Piers went to find the dictionary he and Rosario would use and there it was: a whim, a desire.

"The little house of desire," said Piers. "You can't imagine an English house called that, can you?"

My mother came out then with supper for us and cold drinks on a tray. No more was said about the *Casita* that night and the subject was not raised again for a while. Next day Piers began his Spanish lessons with Rosario. We always stayed indoors for a few hours after lunch, siesta time, the heat being too fierce for comfort between two and four. But adolescents can't sleep in the daytime. I would wander about, fretting for the magic hour of four to come round. I read or wrote in the diary I was keeping or gazed from my bedroom window across the yellow hills with their crowns of grey olives and their embroidery of bay and juniper, like dark upright stitches on a tapestry, and now I knew of its existence, speculated about the location of the house with the sinister room in it.

Piers and Rosario took over the cool white dining room with its furnishings of dark carved wood for their daily lesson. They had imposed no embargo on others entering. Humbly, they perhaps felt that what they were doing was hardly important enough for that, and my mother would go in to sit at the desk and write a letter while Concepçion, who cleaned and cooked for us, would put silver away in one of the drawers of the press or cover the table with a clean lace cloth. I wandered in and out, listening not to Rosario's words but to her patient tone and scholarly manner. Once I saw her correct Piers's pronunciation by placing a finger on his lips. She laid on his lips the finger on which she wore a ring with two tiny turquoises in a gold setting, holding it there as if to model his mouth round the soft guttural. And I saw them close together, side by side, my brother's smooth dark head, so elegantly shaped, Rosario's crown of red-brown hair, flowing over her shoulders, a cloak of it, that always seemed to me like a cape of polished wood, with the depth and grain and gleam of wood, as if she were a nymph carved from the trunk of a tree.

So they were together every afternoon, growing closer, and when the lesson was over and we emerged all three of us into the afternoon sunshine, the beach or the village or to find Will by the hotel, they spoke to each other in Spanish, a communication from which we were excluded. She must have been a good teacher and my brother an enthusiastic pupil, for he who confessed himself bad at languages learned fast. Within a week he was chattering Spanish, although how idiomatically I never knew. He and Rosario talked and laughed in their own world, a world that was all the more delightful to my brother because he had not thought he would ever be admitted to it.

I have made it sound bad for me, but it was not so bad as that. Piers was not selfish, he was never cruel. Of all those close to me only he ever understood my shyness and my fears, the door slammed in my face, the code into whose secrets, as in a bad dream, my companions have been initiated but I have not. Half an hour of Spanish conversation and he and Rosario remembered their manners, their duty to Will and me, and we were back to the language we all had in common. Only once did Will have occasion to say,

"We all speak English, don't we?"

It was clear, though, that Piers and Rosario had begun to see Will as there for me and themselves as there for each other. They passionately wanted to see things in this way, so very soon they did. All they wanted was to be alone together. I did not know this then, I would have hated to know it. I simply could not have understood, though now I do. My brother, falling in love, into first love, behaved heroically in including myself and Will, in being polite to us and kind and thoughtful. Between thirteen and sixteen a great gulf is fixed. I knew nothing of this but Piers did. He knew there was no bridge of understanding from the lower level to the upper, and accordingly he made his concessions.

On the day after the jellyfish came and the beach ceased to be inviting, we found ourselves deprived, if only temporarily, of the principal source of our enjoyment of Llosar. On the wall of a bridge over a dried-up river we sat and contemplated the arid but beautiful interior, the ribbon of road that traversed the island to

Palma and the side-track which led away from it to the northern cape.

"We could go and look at the little haunted house," said Will.

He said it mischievously to "get at" Rosario, whom he liked no more than she liked him. But instead of reacting with anger or with prohibition, she only smiled and said something in Spanish to my brother.

Piers said, "Why not?"

4

They were very beautiful, those jellyfish. Piers kept saying they were. I found them repulsive. Once, much later, when I saw one of the same species in a marine museum I felt sick. My throat closed up and seemed to stifle me, so that I had to leave. *Phylum cnidaria*, the medusa, the jellyfish. They are named for the Gorgon with her writhing snakes for hair, a glance at whose face turned men to stone.

Those which were washed up in their thousands on the shore at Llosar were of a glassy transparency the colour of an aquamarine, and from their umbrella-like bodies hung crystalline feelers or stems like stalactites. Or so they appeared when floating below the surface of the blue water. Cast adrift on the sand and rocks, they slumped into flat gelatinous plates, like collapsed blancmanges. My kind brother, helped by Will, tried to return them to the water, to save them from the sun, but the creeping sea, although nearly tideless, kept washing them back. It was beyond my understanding that they could bear to touch that quivering clammy jelly. Rosario too held herself aloof, watching their efforts with a puzzled amusement.

By the following day a great stench rose from the beach where the sun had cooked the medusas and was now hastening the process of rot and destruction. We kept away. We walked to the village and from there took the road to Pollença which passed through apricot orchards and groves of almond trees. The apricots were drying on trays in the sun, in the heat which was heavy and unvarying from day to day. We had been in Llosar for two weeks and all that time we had never seen a cloud in the sky. Its blueness glowed with the hot light of an invisible sun. We only saw the sun when it set and dropped into the sea with a fizzle like red-hot iron plunged into water.

The road was shaded by the fruit trees and the bridge over the bed of the dried-up river, by the dense branches of pines. Here, where we rested and sat and surveyed the yellow hillsides and the olive groves, Will suggested we go to look at "the little haunted house" and my brother said, "Why not?" Rosario was smiling a small secret smile and as we began to walk on, Will and I went first and she and Piers followed behind.

It was not far to the *Casita de Golondro*. If it had been more than two kilometres, say, I doubt if even "mad tourists", as the village people called us, would have considered walking it in that heat. There was a bus which went to Palma but it had left long before we started out. Not a car passed us and no car overtook us. It is hard to believe that in Majorca today. Of course there were cars on the island. My parents had several times rented a car and a driver and two days afterwards we were all to be driven to the Dragon Caves. But motor transport was unusual, something to be stared at and commented upon. As we came to the side road which would lead to the *Casita*, an unmetalled track, a car did pass us, an aged Citroën, its black bodywork much scarred and splintered by rocks, but that was the only one we saw that day.

The little haunted house; the little house of a whim, of desire, was scarcely visible from this road. A dense concentrated growth of trees concealed it. This wood, composed of trees unknown to us, carob and holm oak and witches' pines, could be seen from Llosar, a dark opaque blot on the bleached yellows and greys, while the house could not. Even here the house could only be glimpsed between tree trunks, a segment of wall in faded ochreish plaster, a shallow roof of pantiles. The plastered wall which surrounded the land which Piers called the "demesne" was too high for any of us to see over, and our first sight of the *Casita* was through the broken bars and loops and curlicues of a pair of padlocked wrought iron gates.

We began to follow the wall along its course which soon left the road and climbed down the hillside among rocky outcroppings and stunted olive trees, herb bushes and myrtles, and in many places split open by a juniper pushing aside in its vigorous growth stones and mortar. If we had noticed the biggest of these fissures from the road we might have saved ourselves half a kilometre's walking. Only Rosario objected as Will began to climb through. She said something about our all being too old for this sort of thing but my brother's smile – she saw it too – told us how much this amused him. It was outside my understanding then but not now. You see, it was very unlike Piers to enter into an adventure of this kind. He really would have considered himself too old and too responsible as well. He would have said a gentle "no" and firmly refused to discuss the venture again. But he had agreed and he had said, "Why not?" I believe it was because he saw the *Casita* as a place where he could be alone with Rosario.

Oh, not for a sexual purpose, for making love, that is not what I mean. He would not, surely, at that time, at that stage of their relationship, have thought in those terms. But only think, as things were, what few opportunities he had even to talk to her without others being there. Even their afternoon Spanish lessons were subject to constant interruption. Wherever they went I or Will and I went with them. On the veranda, in the evenings, I was with them. It would not have occurred to me not to be with them and would have caused me bitter hurt, as my brother knew, if the most tactful hint was dropped that I might leave them on their own. I think it must be faced too that my parents would not at all have liked the idea of their being left alone together, would have resisted this vigorously even perhaps to the point of taking us home to England.

Had he talked about this with Rosario? I don't know. The fact is that she was no longer opposed to taking a look at the "little haunted house" while formerly she had been very positively against it. If Piers was in love with her she was at least as much in love with him. From a distance of forty years I am interpreting words and exchanged glances, eyes meeting and rapturous looks, for what they were, the signs of first love. To me then they meant nothing unless it was that Piers and Rosario shared some specific knowledge connected with the Spanish language which gave them a bond from which I was shut out.

The garden was no longer much more than a walled-off area of the hillside. It was irredeemably overgrown. Inside the wall a few trees grew of a kind not to be seen outside. Broken stonework lay about among the myrtles and arbutus, the remains of a fountain and moss-grown statuary. The air was scented with bay which did not grow very profusely elsewhere and there were rosy pink heathers in flower as tall as small trees. Paths there had once been but these were almost lost under the carpet of small tough evergreens. In places it was a battle to get through, to push a passage between thorns and bay and laurels, but our persistence brought us through the last thicket of juniper into a clearing paved in broken stone. From there the house could suddenly be seen, alarmingly close to us, its cloisters only yards away. It was like being in a dream where distance means very little and miles are crossed in an instant. The house appeared, became visible, as if it had stepped out to meet us.

It was not a "little" house. This is a relative term and the people who named it may have owned a palace somewhere else. To me it seemed a mansion, bigger than any house I had ever been in. José-Carlos's villa in Llosar and our house in London could have both been put inside the *Casita* and lost somewhere among its rooms.

Its surface was plastered and the plaster in many places had fallen away, exposing pale brickwork beneath. The cloisters were composed of eight arches supported on pillars Will said were "Moorish", though without, I am sure, quite knowing what this meant. Above was a row of windows, all with their shutters open, all with stone balconies, a pantiled over-hang, another strip of plaster, carved or parged in panels, and above that the nearly flat roof of pink tiles.

Within the cloister, on the left-hand side of a central door, was (presumably) the window that Carmela Valdez's cousin had broken. Someone had covered it with a piece of canvas nailed to the frame, plastic not being in plentiful supply in those days. Will was the first of us to approach nearer to the house. He was wearing his grass hat and a long-sleeved shirt and trousers. He picked at the canvas around the broken window until a corner came away, and peered in.

"There's nothing inside," he said. "Just an old empty room. Perhaps it's *the* room."

"It's not." Rosario offered no explanation as to how she knew this.

"I could go in and open the door for you."

"If it's *the* room you won't come out again," I said.

"There's a table in there with a candle on it." Will had his head inside the window frame. "Someone's been eating and they've left some bread and stuff behind. What a stink, d'you reckon it's rats?"

"I think we should go home now." Rosario looked up into Piers's face and Piers said very quickly,

"We won't go in now, not this time. Perhaps we won't ever go in."

Will withdrew his head and his hat fell off. 'I'm jolly well going in sometime. I'm not going home without getting in there. We go back home next week. If we go now I vote we all come back tomorrow and go in there and explore it and then we'll *know*."

He did not specify exactly what it was we should know but we understood him. The house was a challenge to be accepted. Besides we had come too far to be daunted now. And yet it remains a mystery to me today that we, who had the beaches and the sea, the countryside, the village, the boats which would take us to Pinar or Formentor whenever we wished to go, were so attracted by that deserted house and its empty rooms. For Piers and Rosario perhaps it was a trysting place but what was there about it so inviting, so enticing, to Will and me?

Will himself expressed it, in words used by many an explorer and mountaineer. "It's *there*."

On the following day we all went to the *Cuevas del Drach*. Will's parents, whom our parents had got to know, came too and we went in two cars. Along the roadside between C'an Picafort and Arta grew the arbutus that Will's mother said would bear white flowers and red fruit simultaneously in a month or two. I wanted to see that, I wondered if I ever would. She said the fruit was like strawberries growing on branches.

"They look like strawberries but they have no taste."

That is one of the few remarks of Iris Harvey's I can remember. Remember word for word, that is. It seemed sad to me then but now I see it as an aphorism. The fruit of the arbutus is beautiful, red and shiny, it looks like strawberries but it has no taste.

The arbutus grew only in this part of the island, she said. She seemed to know all about it. What she did not know was that these same bushes grew in profusion around the little haunted house. I identified them from those on the road to C'an Picafort, from the smooth glossy leaves that were like the foliage of garden shrubs, not wild ones. Among the broken stones, between the junipers and myrtle, where all seemed dust-dry, I had seen their leaves, growing as green as if watered daily.

On our return we inspected the beach and found the jellyfish almost gone, all that remained of them gleaming patches on the rocks like snail's trails. Piers and Rosario sat on the veranda doing their Spanish and Will went back to the hotel, his shirt cuffs buttoned, his hat pulled well down.

"Tomorrow then," Piers had said to him as he left and Will nodded.

That was all that was necessary. We did not discuss it among ourselves. A decision had been reached, by each of us separately and perhaps simultaneously, in the cars or the caves or by the waters of the subterranean lake. Tomorrow we should go into the little haunted house, to see what it was like, because it was *there*. But a terrible or wonderful thing happened first. It was terrible or wonderful, depending on how you looked at it, how *I* looked at it, and I was never quite sure how that was. It filled my mind, I could scarcely think of anything else.

My parents had gone to bed. I was in the bedroom I shared with Rosario, not in bed but occupied with arranging my mosquito net. This hotel where we now are is air-conditioned, you never open the windows. You move and dress and sleep in a coolness which would not be tolerated in England, a breezy chill that is very much at odds with what you can see beyond the glass, cloudless skies and a desiccated hillside. I liked things better when the shutters could be folded back against the walls, the casements opened wide, and the net in place so that you were protected from insects, yet in an airy room. The net hung rather like curtains do from a tester on an English four-poster and that morning, in a hurry to be off to the *Cuevas*, I had forgotten to close them.

Having made sure there were no mosquitoes inside the curtains, I drew them and switched off the light so that no more should be attracted into the room. Sentimentally, rather than kill it, I carried a spider in my handkerchief to the window to release it into the night. The moon was waxing, a pearl drop, and the stars were brilliant. While dark, with a rich clear somehow shining darkness, everything in the little walled garden could clearly be seen. All that was missing was not clarity but colour. It was a monochrome world out there, black and silver and pewter and pearl and lead-colour and the opaque velvety greyness of stone. The moon glowed opal-white and the stars were not worlds but light-filled holes in the heavens.

I did not see them at first. I was looking past the garden at the spread of hills and the mountains beyond, serrated ranges of darkness against the pale shining sky, when a faint sound or tiny movement nearer at hand drew my eyes downwards. They had been sitting together on the stone seat in the deep shade by the wall. Piers got up and then Rosario did. He was much taller than she, he was looking down at her and she up at him, eye to eye. He put his arms round her and his mouth on hers and for a moment, before they stepped back into the secretive shadow, they seemed to me so close that they were one person, they were like two-cypresses interwined and growing as a single trunk. And the shadow they cast was the long spear shape of a single cypress on moon-whitened stone.

I was very frightened. I was shocked. My world had changed in a moment. Somewhere, I was left behind. I turned away with the shocked rejecting movement of someone who has seen a violent act. Once inside my mosquito net, I drew its folds about me and lay hidden in there in the dark. I lay there rigid, holding my hands clasped, then turned on to my face with my eyes crushed into the pillow.

Rosario came upstairs and into our room and spoke softly to me but I made her no answer. She closed the door and I knew she was undressing in the dark. In all my life I had never felt so lonely. I would never have anyone, I would always be alone. Desertion presented itself to me as a terrible reality to be confronted, not to be avoided, and the last image that was before me when sleep came was of getting up in the morning and finding them all gone, my parents and Piers and Rosario, the hotel empty, the village abandoned, Majorca a desert island and I its only wild, lost, crazed inhabitant. Not quite the last image. That was of the twin-trunked cypress tree in the garden, its branches interwoven and its shadow a single shaft.

5

We entered the little house of desire, the little haunted house (*la casita que tiene fantasmas*) by the front door, Rosario going first. Will had climbed in through the broken window and opened the door inside the cloisters. It had the usual sort of lock which can be opened by turning a knob on the inside but from the outside only with a key. Piers followed her and I followed him, feeling myself to be last, the least there, the unwanted.

This, of course, was not true. The change was in my mind, not in outward reality. When I got up that morning it was not to find myself deserted, abandoned in an alien place by all those close to me, but treated exactly as usual. Piers was as warm to me as ever, as *brotherly*, my parents as affectionate, Rosario the same kind and interested companion. I was different. I had seen and I was changed.

As I have said, I could think of nothing else. What I had seen did not excite or intrigue me, nor did I wish not to have seen it, but rather that it had never happened. I might have been embarrassed in their company but I was not. All I felt, without reason, was that they liked each other better than they liked me, that they expressed this in a way neither of them could ever have expressed it to me, and that, obscurely but because of it, *because of something he did not and could not know*, Will too must now prefer each of them to me.

On the way to the *Casita* I had said very little. Of course I expected Piers to ask me what was the matter. I would have told him a lie. That was not the point. The point was that I was unable to understand. Why, why? What made them do that, behave in the way I had seen them in the garden? Why had they spoiled things? For me, they had become different people. They were strangers. I saw them as mysterious beings. It was my first glimpse of the degree to which human beings are unknowable, my first intimation of what it is that makes for loneliness. But what I realised at the time was that we who had been a cohesive group were now divided into two parts: Piers and Rosario, Will and me.

Yet I had not chosen Will. We *choose* very few of the people we know and call our friends. In various ways they have been thrust upon us. We never have the chance to review a hundred paraded before us and out of them choose one or two. I knew nothing of this then and I resented Will for being Will, cocky, intrusive, with his red hair and his thin vulnerable skin, his silly hat, and for being so much less nice to know than either my brother or Rosario. But he was for me and they were not, not any more. I sensed that he felt much the same way about me. I was the third best but all he could get, his companion by default. This was to be my future lot in life – and perhaps his, but I cared very little about that. It was because of this, all this, that as we entered the *Casita*, Piers and Rosario going off into one of the rooms, Will making for the hall at the front of the house, I left them and went up the staircase on my own.

I was not afraid of the house, at least not then. I was too sore for that. All my misery and fear derived from human agency, not the supernatural. If I thought of the "bad room" at all, it was with that recklessness, that fatalism, which comes with certain kinds of unhappiness: things are so bad that *anything* which happens will be a relief – disaster, loss, death. So I climbed the stairs and explored the house, looking into all the rooms, without trepidation and without much interest.

It was three storeys high. With the exception of a few objects difficult to move or detach, heavy mirrors on the walls in gilded frames, an enormous bed with black oak headboard and bedposts, a painted wooden press, it was not furnished. I heard my brother's and Rosario's voices on the staircase below and I knew somehow that Piers would not have remained in the house and would not have let us remain if there had been furniture and carpets and pictures there. He was law-abiding and responsible. He would not have trespassed in a place he saw as someone's home.

But this house had been deserted for years. Or so it seemed to me. The mirrors were clouded and blue with dust. The sun bore down unchecked by shutters or curtains and its beams were layers of sluggishly moving dust that stretched through spaces of nearly intolerable heat. I suppose it was because I was a child from a northern country that I associated hauntings with cold. Although everything I had experienced since coming to Llosar taught otherwise, I had expected the *Casita de Golondro* to be cold inside and dark.

The heat was stifling and the air was like a gas. What you breathed was a suspension of warm dust. The windows were large and hazy dusty sunshine filled the house, it was nearly as light as outside. I went to the window in one of the rooms on the first floor, meaning to throw it open, but it was bolted and the fastenings too stiff for me to move. It was there, while I was struggling with the catch, that Will crept up behind me and when he was only a foot away made that noise children particularly associate with ghosts, a kind of warbling crescendo, a howling siren-sound.

"Oh, shut up," I said. "Did you think I couldn't hear you? You made more noise than a herd of elephants."

He was undaunted. He was never daunted. "Do you know the shortest ghost story in the world? There was this man reached out in the dark for a box of matches but before he found them they were stuck into his hand."

I pushed past him and went up the last flight of stairs. Piers and Rosario were nowhere to be seen or heard. I saw the double cypress tree again and its shadow and felt sick. Somewhere they were perhaps doing that again now, held close together, looking into each other's eyes. I stood in the topmost hallway of the house, a voice inside me telling me what it has often told me since, when human relations are in question: don't think of them, forget them, stand alone, you are safer alone. But my brother . . ? It was different with my brother.

The rooms on the top floor had lower ceilings, were smaller than those below and even hotter. It sounds incomprehensible if I say that these attics were like cellars, but so it was. They were high up in the house, high under the roof, but they induced the claustrophobia of basements, and there seemed to be weighing on them a great pressure of tiers of bricks and mortar and tiles.

What happened to me next I feel strange about writing down. This is not because I ever doubted the reality of the experience or that time has dimmed it but really because, of course, people don't believe me. Those I have told – a very few – suggest that I was afraid, expectant of horrors, and that my mind did the rest. But I was *not* afraid. I was so unafraid that even Will's creeping up on me had not made me jump. I was expectant of nothing. My mind was full of dread but it was dread of rejection, of loneliness, of others one by one discovering the secret of life and I being left in ignorance. It was fear of losing Piers.

All the doors to all the rooms had been open. In these circumstances, if you then come upon a closed door, however miserable you may be, however distracted, natural human curiosity will impel you to open it. The closed door was at the end of the passage on the left. I walked down the passage, through the stuffiness, the air so palpable you almost had to push it aside, tried the handle, opened the door. I walked into a rather small oblong room with, on its left-hand wall, one of those mirrors, only this one was not large or gilt-framed or fly-spotted, but rather like a window with a plain wooden frame and a kind of shelf at the bottom of it. I saw that it was a mirror but I did not look into it. Some inner voice was warning me not to look into it.

The room was dark. No, not dark, but darker than the other rooms. Here, although apparently nowhere else, the shutters were closed. I took a few steps into the warm gloom and the door closed behind me. Hindsight tells me that there was nothing supernatural or even odd about this. It had been closed while all the others in the house were open which indicates that it was a "slamming" door or one which would only remain open when held by a doorstop. I did not think of this then. I thought of nothing reasonable or practical, for I was beginning to be frightened. My fear would have been less if I could have let light in but the shutters, of course, were on the outside of the window. I have said it was like a cellar up there. I felt as if I was in a vault.

Something held me there as securely as if I were chained. It was as if I had been tied up preparatory to being carried away. And I was aware that behind me, or rather to the left of me, was that mirror into which I must not look. Whatever happened I must not look into it and yet something impelled me to do so, I *longed* to do so.

How long did I stand there, gasping for breath, in that hot timeless silence? Probably for no more than a minute or two. I was not quite still, for I found myself very gradually rotating, like a spinning top that is slowing before it dips and falls on its side. Because of the mirror I closed my eyes. As I have said, it was silent, with the deepest silence I have ever known, but the silence was broken. From somewhere, or inside me, I heard my brother's voice. I heard Piers say,

"Where's Petra?"

When I asked him about this later he denied having called me. He was adamant that he had not called. Did I imagine his voice just as I then imagined what I saw? Very clearly I heard his voice call me, the tone casual. But concerned, for all that, caring.

"Where's Petra?"

It broke the invisible chains. My eyes opened on to the hot, dusty, empty room. I spun round with one hand out, reaching for the door. In doing so I faced the mirror, I moved through an arc in front of the mirror, and saw, not myself, *but what was inside it.*

Remember that it was dark. I was looking into a kind of swimming gloom and in it the room was reflected but in a changed state, with two windows where no windows were, and instead of myself the figure of a man in the farthest corner pressed up against the wall. I stared at him, the shape or shade of a bearded ragged man, not clearly visible but clouded by the dark mist which hung between him and me. I had seen that bearded face somewhere before – or only in a bad dream? He looked back at me, a look of great anger and malevolence. We stared at each other and as he moved away from the wall in my direction, I had a momentary terror he would somehow break through the mirror and be upon me. But, as I flinched away, holding up my hands, he opened the reflected door and disappeared.

I cried out then. No one had opened the door on my side of the mirror. It was still shut. I opened it, came out and stood there, my back to the door, leaning against it. The main passage was empty and so was the side passage leading away to the right. I ran along the passage, feeling I must not look back, but once round the corner at the head of the stairs I slowed and began walking. I walked down, breathing deeply, turned at the foot of the first flight and began to descend the second. There I met Piers coming up.

What I would best have liked was to throw myself into his arms. Instead, I stopped and stood above him, looking at him.

"Did you call me?" I said.

"No. When do you mean? Just now?"

"A minute ago."

He shook his head. "You look as if you've seen a ghost."

"Do I?" Why didn't I tell him? Why did I keep silent? Oh, I have asked myself enough times. I have asked myself why that warning inner voice did not urge me to tell and so, perhaps, save him. No doubt I was afraid of ridicule, for even then I never trusted to kindness, not even to his. "I went into a room," I said, "and the door closed on me. I was a bit scared, I suppose. Where are the others?"

"Will found the haunted room. Well, he says it's the haunted room. He pretended he couldn't get out."

How like Will that was! There was no chance for me now, even if I could have brought myself to describe what had happened. My eyes met Piers's eyes and he smiled at me reassuringly. Never since in all my life have I so longed to take someone's hand and hold it as I longed then to take my brother's. But all that was possible for me was to grip my own left hand in my right and so hold everything inside me.

We went down and found the others and left the house. Will pinned the canvas back over the broken window and we made our way home in the heat of the day. The others noticed I was unusually quiet and they said so. There was my chance to tell them but of course I could not. Will had stolen a march on me. But there was one curious benefit deriving from what had happened to me in the room with the closed shutters and the slamming door. My jealousy, resentment, insecurity I suppose we would call it now, over Piers and Rosario had quite gone. The new anxiety had cast the other out.

Nothing would have got me back to the *Casita*. As we walked across the hillside, among the prickly juniper and the yellow broom, the green-leaved arbutus and the sage, I was cold in the hot sun, I was staring ahead of me, afraid to look back. I did not look back once. And later that day, gazing across the countryside from my bedroom window, although the Casita was not visible from there, I would not even look in its direction, I would not even look at the ridge of hillside which hid it.

That evening Piers and Rosario went out alone together for the first time. There was no intention to deceive, I am sure, but my parents thought they had gone with me and Will and Will's mother to see the country dancing at Muro. It was said the *ximbombes* would be played and we wanted to hear them. Piers and Rosario had also shown some interest in these Mallorquin drums but they had not come with us. Will thought they had gone with my parents to see the Roman theatre, newly excavated at Puerto de Belver, although by then it was too dark to see anything.

When we got home they were already back. They were out on the veranda, sitting at the table. The moon was bright and the cicadas very noisy and of course it was warm, the air soft and scented. I had not been alone at all since my experience of the morning and I did not want to be alone then, shrouded by my mosquito net and with the moonlight making strange patterns on the walls. But almost as soon as I arrived home Rosario got up and came upstairs to bed. We hardly spoke, we had nothing to say to each other any more.

Next evening they went out together again. My father said to Piers,

"Where are you going?"

"For a walk."

I thought he would say, "Take Petra", because that was what he was almost certain to say, but he did not. His eyes met my mother's. Did they? Can I remember that? I am sure their eyes must have met and their lips twitched in small indulgent smiles.

It was moonlight. I went upstairs and looked out of the window of my parents' room. The village was a string of lights stretched along the shore, a necklace in which, here and there, beads were missing. The moon did not penetrate these dark spaces. A thin phosphorescence lay on the calm sea. There was no one to be seen. Piers and Rosario must have gone the other way, into the country behind. I thought, suppose I turn round and there, in the corner of this room, in the shadows, that man is.

I turned quickly and of course there was nothing. I ran downstairs and to while away the evening, my parents and I, we played a lonely game of beggar-my-neighbour. Piers and Rosario walked in at nine. On the following day we were on the beach where Will, for whom every day was April Fool's Day, struck dismay into our hearts with a tale of a new invasion of jellyfish. He had seen them heading this way from the hotel pier.

This was soon disproved. Will was forgiven because it was his next but last day. He boasted a lot about what he called his experiences in the "haunted room" of the *Casita* two days before, claiming that he had had to fight with the spirits who tried to drag him through the wall. I said nothing, I could not have talked about it. When siesta time came I lay down on my bed and I must have slept, for Rosario had been on the other bed but was gone when I awoke, although I had not heard or seen her leave.

They were gone, she and my brother, when I came downstairs and the rest of us were preparing to go with Will and his parents in a hired car to see the gardens of a Moorish estate.

"Piers and Rosario won't be coming with us," my mother said, looking none too pleased, and feeling perhaps that politeness to the Harveys demanded more explanation, "They've found some local fisherboy to take them out in his boat. They said, would you please excuse them."

Whether this fisherboy story was true or not, I don't know. I suspect my mother invented it. She could scarcely say – well, not in those days – "My son wants to be alone with his girlfriend." Perhaps there was a boy and a boat and perhaps this boy was questioned when the time came. I expect everyone who might have seen or spoken to Piers and Rosario was questioned, everyone who might have an idea of their whereabouts, because they never came back.

6

In those days there were few eating places on the island, just the dining rooms of the big hotels or small local *tabernas*. On our way back from the Moorish gardens we found a restaurant, newly opened with the increase of tourism, at a place called Petra. Of course this occasioned many kindly jokes on my name and the proprietor of the *Restorán del Toro* was all smiles and welcome.

Piers and Rosario's evening meal was to have been prepared by Concepçion. She was gone when we returned and they were still out. My parents were cross. They were abstracted and unwilling to say much in front of me, although I did catch one sentence, an odd one and at the time incomprehensible.

"Their combined ages only add up to thirty-one!"

It is not unusual to see displeasure succeeded by anxiety. It happens all the time. *They're late, it's inexcusable, where are they, they're not coming, something's happened.* At about half-past nine this change-over began. I was questioned. Did I have any idea where they might be going? Had they said anything to me?

We had no telephone. That was far from unusual in a place like that forty years ago. But what use could we have put it to if we had had one? My father went out of the house and I followed him. He stood there looking up and down the long shoreline. We do this when we are anxious about people who have not come, whose return is delayed, even though if they are there, hastening towards us, we only shorten our anxiety by a moment or two. They were not there. No one was there. Lights were on in the houses and the strings of coloured lamps interwoven with the vine above the hotel pier, but no people were to be seen. The waning moon shone on an empty beach where the tide crawled up a little way and trickled back.

Apart from Concepçion, the only people we really knew were Will's parents and when another hour had gone by and Piers and Rosario were not back my father said he would walk down to the hotel, there to consult with the Harveys. Besides, the hotel had a phone. It no longer seemed absurd to talk of phoning the police. But my father was making a determined effort to stay cheerful. As he left, he said he was sure he would meet Piers and Rosario on his way.

No one suggested I should go to bed. My father came back, not with Will's parents who were phoning the police "to be on the safe side", but with Concepçion at whose cottage in the village he had called. Only my mother could speak to her but even she could scarcely cope with the Mallorquin dialect. But we soon all understood, for in times of trouble language is transcended. Concepçion had not seen my brother and cousin that evening and they had not come for the meal she prepared for them. They had been missing since five.

That night remains very clearly in my memory, every hour distinguished by some event. The arrival of the police, the searching of the beach, the assemblage in the hotel foyer, the phone calls that were made from the hotel to other hotels, notably the one at Formentor, and the incredible inefficiency of the telephone system. The moon was only just past the full and shining it seemed to me for longer than usual, bathing the village and shoreline with a searching whiteness, a providential floodlighting. I must have slept at some point, we all must have, but I remember the night as white and wakeful. I remember the dawn coming with tuneless birdsong and a cool pearly light.

The worst fears of the night gave place in the warm morning to what seemed like more realistic theories. At midnight they had been dead, drowned, but by noon theirs had become a voluntary flight. Questioned, I said nothing about the cypress tree, entwined in the garden, but Will was not so reticent. His last day on the island had become the most exciting of all. He had seen Piers and Rosario kissing, he said, he had seen them holding hands. Rolling his eyes, making a face, he said they were "in lo-ove". It only took a little persuasion to extract from him an account of our visit to the *Casita* and a quotation from Piers, probably Will's own invention, to the effect that he and Rosario would go there to be alone.

The *Casita* was searched. There was no sign that Piers and Rosario had been there. No fisherman of Llosar had taken them out in his boat, or no one admitted to doing so. The last person to see them, at five o'clock, was the priest who knew Rosario and who had spoken to her as they passed. For all that, there was for a time a firm belief that my brother and Rosario had run away together. Briefly, my parents ceased to be afraid and their anger returned. For a day or two they were angry, and with a son whose behaviour had scarcely ever before inspired anger. He who was perfect had done this most imperfect thing.

Ronald and Iris Harvey postponed their departure. I think Iris liked my mother constantly telling her what a rock she was and how we could not have done without her. José-Carlos and Micaela were sent for. As far as I know they uttered no word of reproach to my parents. Of course, as far as I know is not very far. And I had my own grief – no, not that yet. My wonder, my disbelief, my panic.

Piers's passport was not missing. Rosario was in her own country and needed no passport. They had only the clothes they were wearing. Piers had no money, although Rosario did. They could have gone to the mainland of Spain. Before the hunt was up they had plenty of time to get to Palma and there take a boat for Barcelona. But the police found no evidence to show that they had been on the bus that left Llosar at six in the evening, and no absolute evidence that they had not. Apart from the bus the only transport available to them was a hired car. No one had driven them to Palma or anywhere else.

The difficulty with the running away theory was that it did not at all accord with their characters. Why would Piers have run away? He was happy. He loved his school, he had been looking forward to this sixth form year, then to Oxford. My mother said, when Will's mother presented to her yet again the "Romeo and Juliet" theory,

"But we wouldn't have stopped him seeing his cousin. We'd have invited her to stay. They could have seen each other every holiday. We're not strict with our children, Iris. If they were really that fond of each other, they could have been engaged in a few years. But they're so young!"

At the end of the week a body was washed up on the beach at Alcudia. It was male and young, had a knife wound in the chest, and for a few hours was believed to be that of Piers. Later that same day a woman from Muralla identified it as a man from Barcelona who had come at the beginning of the summer and been living rough on the beach. But that stab wound was very ominous. It alerted us all to terrible ideas.

The *Casita* was searched again and its garden. A rumour had it that part of the garden was dug up. People began remembering tragedies from the distant past, a suicide pact in some remote inland village, a murder in Palma, a fishing boat disaster, a mysterious unexplained death in a hotel room. We sat at home and waited and the time of our departure from the island was due, came and went. We waited for news, we three with José-Carlos and Micaela, all of us but my mother expecting to be told of death. My mother, then and in the future, never wavered in her belief that Piers was alive and soon to get in touch with her.

After a week the Harveys went home, but not to disappear from our lives. Iris Harvey had become my mother's friend, they were to remain friends until my mother's death, and because of this I continued to know Will. He was never very congenial to me, I remember to this day the *enjoyment* he took in my brother's disappearance, his unholy glee and excitement when the police came, when he was permitted to be with the police on one of their searches. But he was in my life, fixed there, and I could not shed him. I never have been able to do so.

One day, about three weeks after Piers and Rosario were lost, my father said,

"I am going to make arrangements for us to go home on Friday."

"Piers will expect us to be here," said my mother. "Piers will write to us here."

My father took her hand. "He knows where we live."

"I shall never see my daughter again," Micaela said. "We shall never see them again, you know that, we all know it, they're dead and gone." And she began crying for the first time, the unpractised sobs of the grown-up who has been tearless for years of happy life.

My father returned to Majorca after two weeks at home. He stayed in Palma and wrote to us every day, the telephone being so unreliable. When he wasn't with the police he was travelling about the island in a rented car with an interpreter he had found, making enquiries in all the villages. My mother expected a letter by every post, not from him but from Piers. I have since learned that it is very common for the mothers of men who have disappeared to refuse to accept that they are dead. It happens all the time in war when death is almost certain but cannot be proved. My mother always insisted Piers was alive somewhere and prevented by circumstances from coming back or from writing. What circumstances these could possibly have been she never said and arguing with her was useless.

The stranger thing was that my father, who in those first days seemed to accept Piers's death, later came part of the way round to her opinion. At least, he said it would be wrong to talk of Piers as dead, it would be wrong to give up hope and the search. That was why, during the years ahead, he spent so much time, sometimes alone and sometimes with my mother, in the Balearics and on the mainland of Spain.

Most tragically, in spite of their brave belief that Piers would return or the belief that they *voiced*, they persisted in their determination to have more children, to compensate presumably for their loss. At first my mother said nothing of this to me and it came as a shock when I overheard her talking about it to Iris Harvey. When I was fifteen she had a miscarriage and later that year, another. Soon after that she began to pour out to me her hopes and fears. I cannot have known then that my parents were doomed to failure but I seemed to know, I seemed to sense in my gloomy way perhaps, that something so much wished-for would never happen. It would not be allowed by the fates who rule us.

"I shouldn't be talking like this to you," she said, and perhaps she was right. But she went on talking like that. "They say that longing and longing for a baby prevents you having one. The more you want the less likely it is."

This sounded reasonable to me. It accorded with what I knew of life.

"But no one tells you how to stop longing for something you long for," she said.

When they went to Spain I remained behind. I stayed with my Aunt Sheila who told me again and again she thought it a shame my parents could not be satisfied with the child they had. I should have felt happier in her house if she had not asked quite so often why my mother and father did not take me with them.

"I don't want to go back there," I said. "I'll never go back."

7

The loss of his son made my father rich. His wealth was the direct result of Piers's disappearance. If Piers had come back that night we should have continued as we were, an ordinary middle-class family living in a semi-detached suburban house, the breadwinner a surveyor with the local authority. But Piers's disappearance made us rich and at the same time did much to spoil Spain's Mediterranean coast and the resorts of Majorca.

He became a property developer. José-Carlos, already in the building business, went into partnership with him, raised the original capital, and as the demands of tourism increased, they began to build. They built hotels: towers and skyscrapers, shoe-box shapes and horseshoe shapes, hotels like ziggurats and hotels like Piranesi palaces. They built holiday flats and plazas and shopping precincts. My father's reason for going to Spain was to find his son, his reason for staying was this new enormously successful building enterprise.

He built a house for himself and my mother on the north-west coast at Puerto de Soller. True to my resolve I never went there with them and eventually my father bought me a house in Hampstead. He and my mother passed most of their time at Puerto de Soller, still apparently trying to increase their family, even though my mother was in her mid-forties, still advertising regularly for Piers to come back to them, wherever he might be. They advertised, as they had done for years, in the *Majorca Daily Bulletin* as well as Spanish national newspapers and *The Times*. José-Carlos and Micaela, on the other hand, had from the first given Rosario up as dead. My mother told me they never spoke of her. Once, when a new acquaintance asked Micaela if she had any children, she had replied with a simple no.

If they had explanations for the disappearance of Piers and Rosario, I never heard them. Nor was I ever told what view was taken by the National Guard, severe brisk-spoken men in berets and brown uniforms. I evolved theories of my own. They *had* been taken out in a boat, had both drowned and the boatman been too afraid later to admit his part in the affair. The man whose body was found had killed them, hidden the bodies and then killed himself. My parents were right up to a point and they had run away together, being afraid of even a temporary enforced separation, but before they could get in touch had been killed in a road accident.

"That's exactly when you would know," Will said. "If they'd died in an accident that's when it would have come out."

He was on a visit to us with his mother during the school summer holidays, a time when my parents were always in England. The mystery of my brother's disappearance was a subject of unending interest to him. He never understood, and perhaps that kind of understanding was foreign to his nature, that speculating about Piers brought me pain. I remember to this day the insensitive terms he used. "Of course they've been bumped off," was a favourite with him, and "They'll never be found now, they'll just be bones by now."

But equally he would advance fantastic theories of their continued existence. "Rosario had a lot of money. They could have gone to Spain and stopped in a hotel and stolen two passports. They could have stolen passports from the other guests. I expect they earned money singing and dancing in cafés. Spanish people like that sort of thing. Or she could have been someone's maid. Or an artist's model. You can make a lot of money at that. You sit in a room with all your clothes off and people who're learning to be artists sit round and draw you."

Tricks and practical jokes still made a great appeal to him. To stop him making a phone call to my mother and claiming to be, with the appropriate accent, a Frenchman who knew Piers's whereabouts, I had to enlist the help of his own mother. Then, for quite a long time, we saw nothing of Ronald and Iris Harvey or Will in London, although I believe they all went out to Puerto Soller for a holiday. Will's reappearance in my life was heralded by the letter of condolence he wrote to me seven years later when my mother died.

He insisted then on visiting me, on taking me about, and

paying a curious kind of court to me. Of my father he said, with his amazing insensitivity,

"I don't suppose he'll last long. They were very wrapped up in each other, weren't they? He'd be all right if he married again."

My father never married again and, fulfilling Will's prediction, lived only another five years. Will did not marry either and I always supposed him homosexual. My own marriage, to the English partner in the international corporation begun by my father and José-Carlos, took place three years after my mother's death. Roger was very nearly a millionaire by then, two-and-a-half times my age. We led the life of rich people who have too little to do with their time, who have no particular interests and hardly know what to do with their money.

It was not a happy marriage. At least I think not, I have no idea what other marriages are like. We were bored by each other and frightened of other people but we seldom expressed our feelings and spent our time travelling between our three homes and collecting seventeenth century furniture. Apart from platitudes, I remember particularly one thing Roger said to me:

"I can't be a father to you, Petra, or a brother."

By then my father was dead. As a direct result of Piers's death I inherited everything. If he had lived or there had been others, things would have been different. Once I said to Roger,

"I'd give it all to have Piers back."

As soon as I had spoken I was aghast at having expressed my feelings so freely, at such a profligate flood of emotion. It was so unlike me. I blushed deeply, looking fearfully at Roger for signs of dismay, but he only shrugged and turned away. It made things worse between us. From that time I began talking compulsively about how my life would have been changed if my brother had lived.

"You would have been poor," Roger said. "You'd never have met me. But I suppose that might have been preferable."

That sort of remark I made often enough myself. I took no notice of it. It means nothing but that the speaker has a low self-image and no one's could be lower than mine, not even Roger's.

"If Piers had lived my parents wouldn't have rejected me. They wouldn't have made me feel that the wrong one of us died, that if I'd died they'd have been quite satisfied with the one that was left. They wouldn't have wanted more children."

"Conjecture," said Roger. "You can't know."

"With Piers behind me I'd have found out how to make friends."

"He wouldn't have been behind you. He'd have been off. Men don't spend their lives looking after their sisters."

When Piers and Rosario's disappearance was twenty years in the past a man was arrested in the South of France and charged with the murder, in the countryside between Bedarieux and Lodeve, of two tourists on a camping holiday. In court it was suggested that he was a serial killer and over the past two decades had possibly killed as many as ten people, some of them in Spain, one in Ibiza. An insane bias against tourists was the motive. According to the English papers, he had a violent xenophobia directed against a certain kind of foreign visitor.

This brought to mind the young man's body with the stab wound that had been washed up on the beach at Alcudia. And yet I refused to admit to myself that this might be the explanation for the disappearance of Piers and Rosario. Like my parents, Roger said, I clung to a belief, half fantasy, half hope, that somewhere they were still alive. It was a change of heart for me, this belief, it came with my father's death, as if I inherited it from him along with all his property.

And what of the haunted house, the *Casita de Golondro*? What of my strange experience there? I never forgot it, I even told Roger about it once, to have my story received with incomprehension and the remark that I must have been eating some indigestible Spanish food. But in the last year of his life we were looking for a house to buy, the doctors having told him he should not pass another winter in a cold climate. Roger hated "abroad", so it had to be in England, Cornwall or the Channel Islands. In fact no house was ever bought, for he died that September, but in the meantime I had been viewing many possibilities and one of these was in the south of Cornwall, near Falmouth.

It was a Victorian house and big, nearly as big as the *Casita*, ugly Gothic but with wonderful views. An estate agent took me over it and, as it turned out, I was glad of his company. I had never seen such a thing before, or thought I had not, an internal room without windows. Not uncommon, the young man said, in houses of this age, and he hinted at bad design.

This room was on the first floor. It had no windows but the room adjoining it had, and in the wall which separated the two was a large window with a fanlight in it which could be opened. Thus light would be assured in the windowless room if not much air. The Victorians distrusted air, the young man explained.

I looked at this dividing window and twenty-eight years fell away. I was thirteen again and in the only darkened room of a haunted house, looking into a mirror. But now I understood. It was not a mirror. It had not been reflecting the room in which I stood but affording me a sight of a room beyond, a room with windows and another door, and of its occupant. For a moment, standing there, remembering that door being opened, not a reflected but a real door, I made the identification between the man I had seen, the man at the wheel of the battered Citroën and the serial killer of Bedarieux. But it was too much for me to take, I was unable to handle something so monstrous and so ugly. I shuddered, suddenly seeing impenetrable darkness before me, and the young man asked me if I was cold.

"It's the house," I said. "I wouldn't dream of buying a house like this."

Will was staying with us at the time of Roger's death. He often was. In a curious way, when he first met Roger, before we were married, he managed to present himself in the guise of my rejected lover, the devoted admirer who knows it is all hopeless but who cannot keep away, so humble and selfless is his passion. Remarks such as "may the best man win" and "some men have all the luck" were sometimes uttered by him, and this from someone who had never so much as touched my hand or spoken to me a word of affection. I explained to Roger but he thought I was being modest. What other explanation could there be for Will's devotion? Why else but from long-standing love of me would he phone two or three times a week, bombard me with letters, angle for invitations? Poor Roger had made his fortune too late in life to understand that the motive for pursuing me might be money.

Roger died of a heart attack sitting at his desk in the study. And there Will found him when he went in with an obsequious cup of tea on a tray, even though we had a housekeeper to do all that. He broke the news to me with the same glitter-eyed relish as I remembered him recounting to the police tales of the little haunted house. His voice was lugubrious but his eyes full of pleasure.

Three months later he asked me to marry him. Without hesitating for a moment, I refused.

"You're going to be very lonely in the years to come."

"I know," I said.

8

Never once did I seriously think of throwing in my lot with Will. But that was a different matter from telling him I had no wish to see him again. He was distasteful to me with his pink face, the colour of raw veal, the ginger hair that clashed with it, and the pale blue bird's-egg eyes. His heart was as cold as mine but hard in a way mine never was. I disliked everything about him, his insensitivity, the pleasure he took in cruel words. But for all that, he was my friend, he was my only friend. He was a man to be taken about by. If he hinted to other people that we were lovers, I neither confirmed nor denied it. I was indifferent. Will pleaded poverty so often since he had been made redundant by his company that I began allowing him an income but instead of turning him into a remittance man, this only drew him closer to me.

I never confided in him, I never told him anything. Our conversation was of the most banal. When he phoned – I *never* phoned him – the usual platitudes would be exchanged and then, desperate, I would find myself falling back on that well-used silence-filler and ask him,

"What have you been doing since we last spoke?"

When I was out of London, at the house in Somerset or the "castle", a castellated shooting lodge Roger had bought on a whim in Scotland, Will would still phone me but would reverse the charges. Sometimes I said no when the operator asked me if I would pay for the call, but Will – thick-skinned mentally, whatever his physical state might be – simply made another attempt half an hour later.

It was seldom that more than three days passed without our speaking. He would tell me about the shopping he had done, for he enjoys buying things, troubles with his car, the failure of the electrician to come, the cold he had had, but never of what he might understand love to be, of his dreams or his hopes, his fear of growing old and of death, not even what he had been reading or listening to or looking at. And I was glad of it, for I was not interested and I told him none of these things either. We were best friends with no more intimacy than acquaintances.

The income I allowed him was adequate, no more, and he was always complaining about the state of his finances. If I had to name one topic we could be sure of discussing whenever we met or talked it would be money. Will grumbled about the cost of living, services bills, fares, the small amount of tax he had to pay on his pension and what he got from me, the price of food and drink and the cost of the upkeep of his house. Although he did nothing for me, a fiction was maintained that he was my personal assistant, "secretary" having been rejected by him as beneath the dignity of someone with his status and curriculum vitae. Will knew very well that he had no claim at all to payment for services rendered but for all that he talked about his "salary", usually to complain that it was pitifully small. Having arrived – without notice – to spend two weeks with me in Somerset, he announced that it was time he had a company car.

"You've got a car," I said.

"Yes," he said, "a rich man's car."

What was that supposed to mean?

"You need to be rich to keep the old banger on the road," he said, as usual doubling up with mirth at his own wit.

But he nagged me about that car in the days to come. What was I going to do with my money? What was I saving it for, I who had no child? If he were in my place it would give him immense pleasure to see the happiness he could bring to others without even noticing the loss himself. In the end I told him he could have my car. Instead of my giving it in part exchange for a new one, he could have it. It was a rather marvellous car, only two years old and its sole driver had been a prudent middle-aged woman, that favourite of insurers, but it was not good enough for Will. He took it but he complained and we quarrelled. I told him to get out and he left for London in my car.

Because of this I said nothing to him when the lawyer's letter came. We seldom spoke of personal things but I would have told him about the letter if we had been on our normal terms. I had no one else to tell and he, anyway, was the obvious person. But

for once, for the first time in all those years, we were out of touch.
He had not even phoned. The last words he had spoken to me, in
hangdog fashion, sidling out of the front door, were a truculent
muttered plea that in spite of everything I would not stop his
allowance.

So the letter was for my eyes only, its contents for my heart
only. It was from a firm of solicitors in the City and was couched
in gentle terms. Nothing, of course, could have lessened the shock
of it, but I was grateful for the gradual lead-up, and for such
words as "claim", "suggest", "allege" and "possibility". There
was a softness, like a tender touch, in being requested to prepare
myself and told that at this stage there was no need at all for me
to rush into certain conclusions.

I could not rest but paced up and down, the letter in my hand.
Then, after some time had passed, I began to think of hoaxes,
I remembered how Will had wanted to phone my mother and
give her that message of hope in a Frenchman's voice. Was this
Will again? It was the solicitors I phoned, not Will, and they
told me, yes, it was true that a man and a woman had presented
themselves at their offices, claiming to be Mr and Mrs Piers
Sunderton.

9

I am not a gullible person. I am cautious, unfriendly, morose
and anti-social. Long before I became rich I was suspicious.
I distrusted people and questioned their motives, for nothing had
ever happened to me to make me believe in disinterested love. All
my life I had never been loved but the effect of this was not to
harden me but to keep me in a state of dreaming of a love I had
no idea how to look for. My years alone have been dogged by a
morbid fear that everyone who seems to want to know me is after
my money.

There were in my London house a good many photographs
of Piers. My mother had cherished them religiously, although I
had hardly looked at them since her death. I spread them out
and studied them, Piers as a baby in my mother's arms, Piers
as a small child, a schoolboy, with me, with our parents and me.
Rosario's colouring I could remember, her sallow skin and long
hair, the rich brown colour of it, her smallness of stature and

slightness, but not what she looked like. That is, I had forgotten her features, their shape, arrangement and juxtaposition. Of her I had no photograph.

From the first, even though I had the strongest doubts about this couple's identity as my brother and his wife, I never doubted that any wife he might have had would be Rosario. Illogical? Absurd? Of course. Those convictions we have in the land of emotion we can neither help nor escape from. But I told myself as I prepared for my taxi ride to London Wall that if it was Piers that I was about to see, the woman with him would be Rosario.

I was afraid. Nothing like this had happened before. Nothing had *got this far* before. Not one of the innumerable "sightings" in those first months, in Rome, in Naples, Madrid, London, the Tyrol, Malta, had resulted in more than the occasional deprecating phone call to my father from whatever police force it might happen to be. Later on there had been claimants, poor things who presented themselves at my door and who lacked the nous even to learn the most elementary facts of Pier's childhood, fair-haired men, fat men, short men, men too young or too old. There were probably ten of them. Not one got further than the hall. But this time I was afraid, this time my intuition spoke to me, saying, "He has come back from the dead," and I tried to silence it, I cited reason and caution, but again the voice whispered, and this time more insistently.

They would be changed out of all knowledge. What was the use of looking at photographs? What use are photographs of a boy of sixteen in recognising a man of fifty-six? I waited in an ante-room for three minutes. I counted those minutes. No, I counted the seconds which composed them. When the girl came back and led me in, I was trembling.

The solicitor sat behind a desk and on a chair to his left and a chair to his right sat a tall thin grey man and a small plump woman, very Spanish-looking, her face brown and still smooth, her dark hair sprinkled with white pulled severely back. They looked at me and the two men got up. I had nothing to say but the tears came into my eyes. Not from love or recognition or happiness or pain but for time which does such things to golden lads and girls, which spoils their bodies and ruins their faces and lays dust on their hair.

My brother said, "Petra," and my sister-in-law, in that voice I now remembered so precisely, in that identical heavily-accented English, "Please forgive us, we are so sorry."

I wanted to kiss my brother but I could hardly go up to a strange man and kiss him. My tongue was paralysed. The lawyer began to talk for us but of what he said I have no recollection, I took in none of it. There were papers for me to see, so-called "proofs", but although I glanced at them, the print was invisible. Speech was impossible but I could think. I was thinking, I will go to my house in the country, I will take them with me to the country.

Piers had begun explaining. I heard something about Madrid and the South of France, I heard the word "ashamed" and the words "too late", which someone has said are the saddest in the English language, and then I found a voice in which to say,

"I don't need to hear that now, I understand, you can tell me all that later, much later."

The lawyer, looking embarrassed, muttered about the "inevitable ensuing legal proceedings".

"What legal proceedings?" I said.

"When Mr Sunderton has satisfied the court as to his identity, he will naturally have claim on your late father's property."

I turned my back on him, for I knew Piers' identity. Proofs would not be necessary. Piers was looking down, a tired, worn-out man, a man who looked unwell. He said, "Rosario and I will go back to our hotel now. It's best for us to leave it to Petra to say when she wants another meeting."

"It's best," I said, "for us to get to know each other again. I want you both to come to the country with me."

We went, or rather, Rosario and I went, to my house near Wincanton. Piers was rushed to hospital almost before he set foot over my threshold. He had been ill for weeks, had appendicitis which became peritonitis, and they operated on him just in time.

Rosario and I went to visit him every day. We sat by his bedside and we talked, we all had so much to say. And I was fascinated by them, by this middle-aged couple who had once like all of us been young but who nevertheless seemed to have passed from adolescence into their fifties without the intervention of youth and middle years. They had great tenderness for each other. They were perfectly suited. Rosario seemed to know exactly what Piers would want, that he only liked grapes which were seedless, that although a reader he would only read magazines in hospital, that the slippers he required to go to the day room must be of the felt not the leather kind. He disliked chocolates, it was useless bringing any.

"He used to love them," I said.

"People change, Petra."

"In many ways they don't change at all."

I questioned her. Now the first shock and joy were passed I could not help assuming the role of interrogator, I could not help putting their claim to the test, even though I knew the truth so well. She came through my examination very well. Her memory of Majorca in those distant days was even better than mine. I had forgotten – although I recalled it when she reminded me – our visit to the monastery at Lluc and the sweet voices of the boy choristers. Our parents' insistence that while in Palma we all visited the *Mansion de Arte*, this I now remembered, and the Goya etchings which bored us but which my mother made us all look at.

José-Carlos and Micaela had both been dead for several years. I could tell she was unhappy speaking of them, she seemed ashamed. This brought us to the stumbling block, the difficulty which reared up every time we spoke of their disappearance. Why had they never got in touch? Why had they allowed us all, in such grief, to believe them dead?

She – and later Piers – could give me no reason except their shame. They could not face my parents and hers, it was better for us all to accept that they were dead. To explain why they had run away in the first place was much easier.

"We pictured what they would all say if we said we were in love. Imagine it! We were sixteen and fifteen, Petra. But we were right, weren't we? You could say we're still in love, so we were right."

"They wouldn't have believed you," I said.

"They would have separated us. Perhaps they would have let us meet in our school holidays. It would have killed us, we were dying for each other. We couldn't live out of sight of the other. That feeling has changed now, of course it has. I am not dying, am I, though Piers is in the hospital and I am here? It wasn't just me, Petra, it was Piers too. It was Piers's idea for us to – go."

"Did he think of his education? He was so brilliant, he had everything before him. To throw it up for – well, he couldn't tell it would last, could he?"

"I must tell you something, Petra. Piers was not so brilliant as you thought. Your father had to see Piers' headmaster just before you came on that holiday. He was told Piers wasn't keeping up with his early promise, he wouldn't get that place at Oxford, the way he was doing he would be lucky to get to a university at all. They kept it a secret, you weren't told, even your mother wasn't, but Piers knew. What had he to lose by running away with me?"

"Well, comfort," I said, "and his home and security and me and his parents."

"He said – forgive me – that I made up for all that."

She was sweet to me. Nothing was too much trouble for her. I, who had spent so much time alone that my tongue was stiff from disuse, my manners reclusive, now found myself caught up in her gaiety and her charm. She was the first person I have ever known to announce in the morning *ideas* for how to spend the day, even if those notions were often only that I should stay in bed while she brought me my breakfast and then that we should walk in the garden and have a picnic lunch there. When there was a need for silence, she was silent, and when I longed to talk but scarcely knew how to begin she would talk for me, soon involving us in a conversation of deep interest and a slow realization of the tastes we had in common. Soon we were companions and by the time Piers came home, friends.

Until we were all together again I had put off the discussion of what happened on the day they ran away. Each time Rosario had tried to tell me I silenced her and asked for more about how they had lived when first they came to the Spanish mainland. Their life at that time had been a series of adventures, some terrible, some hilarious. Rosario had a gift for story-telling and entertained me with her tales while we sat in the firelight. Sometimes it was like one of those old Spanish picaresque novels, full of event, anecdote, strange characters and hairsbreadth escapes, not all of it I am afraid strictly honest and above-board. Piers had changed very quickly or she had changed him.

They had worked in hotels, their English being useful. Rosario had even been a chambermaid. Later they had been guides, and at one time, in a career curiously resembling Will's scenario, had sung in cafés to Piers's hastily improvised guitar-playing. In her capacity as a hotel servant – they were in Madrid by this time – Rosario had stolen two passports from guests and with these they had left Spain and travelled about the South of France. The names of the passport holders became their names and in them they were married at Nice when he was eighteen and she seventeen.

"We had a little boy," she said. "He died of meningitis when he was three and after that no more came."

I thought of my mother and put my arms round her. I, who have led a frozen life, have no difficulty in showing my feelings to Rosario. I, in whom emotion has been something to shrink from, can allow it to flow freely in her company and now in my brother's. When he was home again, well now and showing in his face some vestiges of the Piers I had known so long ago, I found it came quite naturally to go up to him, take his hand and kiss his cheek. In the past I had noticed, while staying in other people's houses, the charming habit some have of kissing their guests good night before everyone retires to their rooms. For some reason, a front of coldness perhaps, I had never been the recipient of such kisses myself. But now – and amazing though it was, I made the first move myself – I was kissing both of them good night and we exchanged morning kisses when we met next day.

One evening, quite late, I asked them to tell me about the day itself, the day which ended so terribly in fear and bright empty moonlight. They looked away from me and at each other, exchanging a rueful nostalgic glance. It was Rosario who began the account of it.

It was true that they had met several times since that first time in the little haunted house. They could be alone there without fear of interruption and there they had planned, always fearfully and daringly, their escape. I mentioned the man I had seen, for now I was sure it had been a man seen through glass and no ghost in a mirror, but it meant nothing to them. At the *Casita* they had always found absolute solitude. They chose that particular day because we were all away at the gardens but made no other special preparations, merely boarding the afternoon bus for Palma a little way outside the village. Rosario, as we had always known, had money. She had enough to buy tickets for them on the boat from Palma to Barcelona.

"If we had told them or left a note they would have found us and brought us back," Rosario said simply.

She had had a gold chain around her neck with a cameo that they could sell, and a gold ring on her finger.

"The ring with the two little turquoises," I said.

"That was the one. I had it from my grandmother when I was small."

They had sold everything of value they had, Piers's watch and his fountain pen and his camera. The ring saved their lives, Piers said, when they were without work and starving. Later on they became quite rich, for Piers, like my father, used tourism to help him, went into partnership with a man they met in a café in Marseille, and for years they had their own hotel.

There was only one question left to ask. Why did they ever come back?

They had sold the business. They had read in the deaths column of a Spanish newspaper they sometimes saw that Micaela, the last of our parents, was dead. Apparently, the degree of shame they felt was less in respect to me. I could understand that, I was only a sister. Now I think I understood everything. Now when I looked at them both, with a regard that increased every day, I wondered how I could ever have doubted their identities, how I could have seen them as old, as unutterably changed.

The time had come to tell Will. We were on speaking terms again. I had mended the rift myself, phoning him for the first time ever. It was because I was happy and happiness made me kind. During the months Piers and Rosario had been with me he had phoned as he always did, once or twice we had met away from home, but I had not mentioned them. I did not now, I simply invited him to stay.

To me they were my brother and sister-in-law, familiar loved figures with faces already inexpressibly dear, but he I knew would not know them. I was not subjecting them to a test, I needed no test, but the idea of their confronting each other without preparation amused me. A small deception had to be practised and I made them reluctantly agree to my introducing them as "my friends Mr and Mrs Page".

For a few minutes he seemed to accept it. I watched him, I noticed his hands were trembling. He could bear his suspicion no longer and burst out:

"It's Piers and Rosario, I know it is!"

The years could not disguise them for him, although they each separately confessed to me afterwards that if they had not been told they would never have recognized him. The red-headed boy with "one skin too few" was not just subsumed in the fat red-faced bald man but utterly lost.

Whether their thoughts often returned to those remarks the solicitor had made on the subject of legal proceedings I cannot say. When mine did for the second time I spoke out. We were too close already for litigation to be conceivable. I told Piers that I would simply divide all my property in two, half for them and half for me. They were shocked, they refused, of course they did. But eventually I persuaded them. What was harder for me to voice was my wish that the property itself should be divided in two, the London house, the Somerset farm, my New York apartment, literally split down the middle. Few people had ever wanted much of my company in the past and I was afraid they would see this as a bribe or as taking advantage of my position of power. But all Rosario said was,

"Not too strictly down the middle, Petra, I hope. It would be nicer to *share*."

All I stipulated was that in my altered will I should leave all I possessed to my godchild and cousin, Aunt Sheila's daughter, and Piers readily agreed, for he intended to leave everything he had to the daughter of his old partner in the hotel business.

So we lived. So we have lived for rather more than a year now. I have never been so happy. Usually it is not easy to make a third with a married couple. Either they are so close that you are made to feel an intruder or else the wife will see you as an ally to side with her against her husband. And when you are young the danger is that you and the husband will grow closer than you should. With Piers and Rosario things were different. I truly believe that each wanted my company as much as they wanted each other's. In those few months they came to love me and I, who have loved no one since Piers went away, reciprocated. They have shown me that it is possible to grow warm and kind, to learn laughter and pleasure, after a lifetime of coldness. They have unlocked something in me and liberated a lively spirit that must always have been there but which languished for long years, chained in a darkened room.

*   *   *

It is two weeks now since the Majorcan police got in touch with me and told me what the archaeologists had found. It would be helpful to them and surely of some satisfaction to myself to go to Majorca and see what identification I could make, not of remains, it was too late for that, but of certain artefacts found in the caves.

We were in Somerset and once more Will was staying with us. I suggested we might all go. All those years I had avoided re-visiting the island but things were different now. Nothing I could see there could cause me pain. While I had Piers and Rosario I was beyond pain, it was as if I was protected inside the warm shell of their affection.

"In that case," Will said, "I don't see the point of going. You know the truth. These bits of jewellery, clothes, whatever they are, can't be Piers's and Rosario's because they sold theirs, so why try to identify what in fact you can't identify?"

"I want to see the place again," I said. "I want to see how it's changed. This police thing, that's just an excuse for going there."

"I suppose there will be bones too," he said, "and maybe more than bones even after so long." He has always had a fondness for the macabre. "Did the police tell you how it all got into the caves?"

"Through a kind of pothole from above, they think, a fissure in the cliff top that was covered by a stone."

"How will you feel about going back, Piers?" asked Rosario.

"I shan't know till I get there," he said, "but if Petra goes we go too. Isn't that the way it's always going to be?"

10

When I woke up this morning it was with no sense of impending doom. I was neither afraid nor hopeful, I was indifferent. This was no more than a chore I must perform for the satisfaction of officials, as a "good citizen". For all that, I found my room confining in spite of the wide-open windows, the balcony and view of the sea, and cancelling my room service order, I went down to breakfast.

To my surprise I found the others already there in the terrace dining room. It was not quite warm enough to sit outside so early. They were all unaware of my approach, were talking with heads bent and close together above the table. I was tempted to come up to them in silence and lay a light loving hand on Rosario's shoulder but somehow I knew that this would make her start. Instead I called out a "good morning" that sounded carefree because it was.

Three worried faces were turned to me, although their frowns cleared to be replaced in an instant by determined smiles on the part of my brother and his wife and a wary look on Will's. They were concerned, it appeared, about *me*. The effect on me of what they called the "ordeal" ahead had been the subject of that heads-together discussion. Horrible sights were what they were afraid of, glimpses of the charnel house. One or all of them should go with me. They seemed to believe my life had been sheltered and perhaps it had been, compared to theirs.

"I shan't be going into the caves," I said as I ordered my breakfast. "It will be some impersonal office with everything spread out and labelled, I expect, like in a museum."

"But you'll be alone."

"Not really. I shall know you're only a few miles away, waiting for me."

The table was bare except for their coffee cups. None of them had eaten a thing. My rolls arrived and butter and jam, my fruit and fruit juice. I suddenly felt unusually hungry.

"Let's see," I said, "what shall we do for the rest of the day? We could take the boat to Formentor for lunch or drive to Lluc. This evening, don't forget, we're having dinner at the Parador de Golondro. Have we booked a table?"

"I'm sorry, Petra, I'm afraid I forgot to do that," Piers said.

"Could you do it while I'm out?" A little fear struck me. I was going to say I don't know why it did, but I do know. "You *will* all be here when I get back, won't you?"

Rosario's voice sounded unlike her. I had never heard bitterness in it before. "Where should we go?"

The car came for me promptly at ten. The driver turned immediately inland and from the road, just before he took the turn for Muralla, I had a sudden bold sight of the *Casita*, glimpsed as it can be between the parting of the hills. It seemed a deeper brighter colour, an ochreish gold, an effect either of new paint or of the sun. But when does the sun not shine? The yellow hills, with their tapestry stitches of grey and dark green, slipped closed again like sliding panels and the house withdrew behind them.

I was right about what awaited me at Muralla, a new office building made of that whitish grainy concrete, which has defaced the Mediterranean and is like nothing so much as blocks of cheap ice-cream. Inside, in what I am sure they call the "atrium", was a forest of plastic greenery. There was even a small collection, in styrofoam amphorae, of plastic strawberry trees. I was led via jungle paths to a room marked *privado* and then and only then, hesitating as two more policemen joined us and a key to the room was produced, did my heart misgive me and a tiny bubble of panic run up to my throat so that I caught my breath.

They were very kind to me. They were big strong macho men enjoyably occupied in doing what nature had made them for, protecting a woman from the uglinesses of life. One of them spoke tolerable English. If I would just look at the things, look at them very carefully, think about what I had seen and then they would take me away and ask me one or two simple questions. There would be nothing unpleasant. The bones found in the cave – he apologised for their very existence. There was no need for me to see them.

"I would like to see them," I said.

"They cannot be identified after so long."

"I would like to see them."

"Just as you wish," he said with a shrug and then the door was opened.

An empty room. A place of drawers and bench tops, like a dissecting room except that all the surfaces were of light polished wood and at the windows hung blinds of pale grey vertical strips. Drawers were opened, trays lifted out and placed on the long central table. I approached it slowly, holding one of my hands clasped in the other and feeling my cold fingertips against my cold damp palm.

Spread before me were two pairs of shoes, the woman's dark blue leather with sling backs and wedge heels, the man's what we call trainers now but "plimsolls" then or "gym shoes"; rags, gnawed by vermin, might once have been a pair of flannel trousers, a shirt, a dress with a tiny pearl button still attached to its collar; a gold chain with pendent cross, a gold watch with bracelet and safety chain, a heavier watch with its leather strap rotted, a child's ring for a little finger, two pinhead turquoises on a gold band thin as wire.

I looked at it all. I looked with indifference but a pretence of care for the sake of those onlookers. The collection of bones was too pitiful to be obscene. Surely this was not all? Perhaps a few specimens only had found their way to this room. I put out my hand and lifted up one of the long bones. The man who had brought me there made a movement towards me but was checked by his superior, who stood there watching me intently. I held the bone in both my hands, feeling its dry worn deadness, grey and grainy, its long-lifeless age, and then I put it down gently.

I turned my back on the things and never looked at them again.

"I have never seen any of this before," I said. "It means nothing to me."

"Are you quite sure? Would you like some time to think about it?"

"No, I am quite sure. I remember very well what my brother and my cousin were wearing."

They listened while I described clothes that Piers and Rosario had had. I enumerated items of jewellery. There was a locket I remembered her wearing the first time we met, a picture of her mother in a gold circlet under a seed pearl lid.

"Thank you very much. You have been most helpful."

"At least I have eliminated a possibility." I said, knowing they would not understand.

They drove me back to Llosar. The fruit on the strawberry trees takes a year to ripen. This year's flowers, blooming now, will become the fruit of twelve months' time. And immediately it ripens they pick it for making fruit pies. I had this sudden absurd yearning to see those strawberries in the hotel garden again, to see them before the bushes were stripped. I opened the car door myself, got out and walked up to the hotel without looking back. But instead of going up the steps, I turned aside into the shady garden, the pretty garden of geometric paths and small square pools with yellow fish, the cypresses and junipers gathered in groups as if they had met and stopped to gossip. To the left of me, up in the sun, rose the terrace and beyond it was the swimming pool, but down here grew the arbutus, its white blossom gleaming and its red fruits alight, as shiny as decorations on some northern Christmas tree.

Piers and Rosario were up on the terrace. I am not sure how I knew this for I was not aware of having looked. I felt their anguished eyes on me, their dread communicated itself to me on the warm, still, expectant air. I knew everything about them, I knew how they felt now. They saw me and read into my action in coming here, in coming immediately to this garden, anger and misery and knowledge of betrayal. Of course I understood I must put an end to their anguish at once, I must go to them and leave adoration of these sweet-scented snowy flowers and strawberry fruits until another day.

But first I picked one of the fruits and put it in my mouth. Iris Harvey had been wrong. It was not tasteless, it tasted like some fresh crisp vegetable, sharp and strange. It was different, different from any other fruit I had tasted, but not unpleasant. I thought it had the kind of flavour that would grow on me. I walked up the steps to the terrace. Will was nowhere to be seen. With the courage I knew they had, their unconquered brave hearts, they were waiting for me. Decorously, even formally, dressed for that place where the other guests were in swimming costumes, they were nevertheless naked to me, their eyes full of the tragedy of long wretched misspent lives. They were holding hands.

"Petra," Piers said. Just my name.

To have kept them longer in suspense would have been the cruellest act of my life. In the time they had been with me I had learned to speak like a human being, like someone who understands love and knows warmth.

"My dears," I said. "How sad you look. There's nothing wrong, is there? I've had such a stupid morning. It was a waste of time going over there. They had nothing to show me but a bundle of rags I've never seen before and some rubbishy jewellery. I don't know what they expected – that all that was something to do with you two?"

They remained there, quite still. I know about the effects of shock. But slowly the joined hands slackened and Rosario withdrew hers. I went up to each of them and kissed them gently. I sat down on the third chair at the table and smiled at them. Then I began to laugh.

"I'm sorry," I said. "I'm only laughing because I'm happy. Children laugh from happiness, so why not us?"

"Why not?" said Piers as if it was a new thought, as if a new world opened before him. "Why not?"

I was remembering how long long ago I had heard my brother ask that same rhetorical question, give that odd form of assent, when Will proposed going into the *Casita* and Rosario had demurred. For a moment I saw us all as we had been, Will in his grass hat, long-legged Rosario with her polished hair, my brother eager with love. I sighed and turned the sigh to a smile.

"Now that's behind me," I said, "we can stay on here and have a holiday. Shall we do that?"

"Why not?" said Piers again, and this time the repetition of those words struck Rosario and me as inordinately funny and we both began to laugh as at some exquisite joke, some example of marvellous wit.

It was thus, convulsed with laughter, that we were found by Will when, having no doubt been watching from some window up above for signs of good or ill, judged the time right and safe to come out and join us.

"Did you book that table at Golondro?" I said, hoarse with laughter, weak with it.

Will shook his head. I knew he would not have, that none of them would have. "I'll do it this minute," he said.

"Don't be long," I called after him. "We're going to celebrate. I'm going to order a bottle of champagne."

"What are we celebrating, Petra?" said Rosario.

"Oh, just that we're here together again," I said.

They smiled at me for I was bestowing on them, on both of them, the tender look I had never given to any lover. And the feeling which inspired it was better than a lover's glance, being without self-deception, without illusion. Of course I had never been deceived. I had known, if not quite from the first, from the third day of their appearance, that they were not my brother and his wife. For one thing, a man is not operated on twice in his life for appendicitis. But even without that I would have known. My blood told me and my bones, my thirteen years with a brother I was closer to than to parent or any friend. I knew – always – they were a pair of imposters Will had found and instructed. I knew, almost from the beginning, it was a trick played on me for their gain and Will's.

But there is another way of looking at it. I have bought them and they are mine now. They have to stay, they have nowhere else to go. Isn't that what Piers meant when he said being together was the way it always would be? They are my close companions. We have nothing more to gain from each other, we have made our wills, and the death of one of us will not profit the others.

They have made me happier than I have ever been. I know what people are. I have observed them. I have proved the truth of the recluse's motto, that the onlooker sees most of the game. And I know that Piers and Rosario love me now as I love them, and dislike Will as I dislike him. No doubt they have recompensed him, I don't want to know how, and I foresee a gradual loosening of whatever bond it is that links him to us. It began when I sent him back into the hotel to make that phone call, when Rosario's eyes met mine and Piers pursed his lips in a little *moue* of doubt.

Am I to end all this with a confrontation, an accusation, casting them out of my life? Am I to retreat – and this time, at my age, finally, for good – into that loneliness that would be even less acceptable than before because now I have seen what else is possible?

I have held my dear brother's bone in my hands. I have seen his clothes that time and decay have turned to rags and touched the ruin of a shoe that once encased his strong slender foot. Now I shall begin the process of forgetting him. I have a new brother and sister to be happy with for the rest of my life.

Will has come back, looking sheepish, not understanding at all what has happened, to tell us we are dining at the Parador de Golondro, the little house of desire, at nine tonight. This is the cue, of course, for some characteristic British complaining about the late hour at which the Spanish dine. Only Rosario has nothing to say, but then she is Spanish herself – or is she?

I resolve never to try to discover this, never to tease, to lay traps, attempt a catching-out. After all, I have no wish to understand the details of the conspiracy. And when the time comes I will neither listen to nor make deathbed confessions.

For I saw in their eyes just now, as I came to their table to reassure them, that they are no more deceived in me than I am in them. They know that I know and that we all, in our mutual love, can accept.

Out of the Blue

Carla Vermaat

His dinner had gone cold. By now, the food was spoiled. Bea had finished hers hours ago. She knew she'd have to throw his away, but something held her back.

She frowned. The sour smell of the spinach was beginning to irritate her. She knew that reheated spinach wasn't any good. She really *ought* to throw it away, but that seemed like such a waste. She could certainly warm up the three leftover meatballs, and the potatoes would be fine. But the spinach?

She finally began to clear the table. She piled the dishes next to the sink; the washing up could wait for morning.

The cuckoo on the wall announced that it was 11 o'clock. She went to the window and drew the curtains shut. Aart wouldn't be home tonight.

It was strange waking up in an empty bed, but on the other hand not really. Bea rolled over onto her side and laid a tender hand on the unmussed pillow. Aart's job kept him away from home several nights a week. When he was on the road, he stayed in hotels or bed and breakfasts. He was always home by Friday, though, and every Saturday morning she woke up with him beside her. Except today.

She sighed. 7:15. She suddenly realized how small and confining her world had become. And now it was even worse. Aart was never coming back. Never.

She couldn't make herself feel grief for her loss, just a bottomless bitterness over what had happened to her. And consternation over what she had done, although that feeling didn't go very deep. It was as if her emotions were being kept at a distance by an invisible wall.

There was emptiness, too, but that was nothing new. The emptiness had been there for years, though perhaps she'd never really been quite aware of it. She had simply borne it. Now, though, she began to realize that it was entirely her own fault that she'd never done anything truly worthwhile with her life. If she were asked to write her memoirs, she wouldn't need more than half a page. Born, engaged, married, chief cook and bottle washer for a small household, her maternal instincts never fulfilled . . . and now alone. Her life in a nutshell, a life without high points.

Until now.

It was impossible, but she had actually done it. She had stepped up to the plate. Her behaviour was so at odds with her usual meek character that she could barely believe it of herself.

Restless, she got out of bed and went into the bathroom. No need to look at herself in the mirror. She knew what she would see reflected in the glass: a grey mouse with vaguely blue-green eyes, pale skin and greying dark-blond hair. She was almost fifty, and life had had its usual way with her skin and her shape.

In the shower, she tipped her head back and let the water rain onto her face and wished it could wash her life down the drain with her tears.

It was an ordinary Saturday. It *must* be, because everything and everyone seemed completely normal. At the farmer's market, Bea stood next to a chattering married couple and listened in on their good-natured discussion about which cheese to buy. Had she and Aart ever talked like that? She thought not. She couldn't remember the last time they'd gone shopping together. How odd to think of that now. It was as if, somewhere inside her head, the volume had been turned up to a level she could finally hear.

Bea dawdled. What was she *doing* here? Aart was gone. There was no point buying his favorite cheese.

"Can I help you, ma'am?"

"A pound of Edam, please."

The cheeseman nodded. He knew exactly what she wanted, because she made the same selection every week. He didn't need to offer her a sample to taste – he knew she would politely refuse.

"Nice day," he said.

"Yes."

She watched his dexterous hands wrap the brick of cheese in wax paper. She would put it in the fridge, as if nothing had changed. At the nut stand, just like every week, she would buy two little bags of nuts, salted cashews for Aart, unsalted almonds for herself.

The train sped across a more or less empty landscape of green meadows dotted with sheep and the spring's first lambs. Doetinchem. What in the world would bring anyone to Doetinchem?

Bea didn't really have a plan. After wandering aimlessly around the market, she had walked to the station on impulse and bought a round-trip ticket. When she changed trains in Amsterdam, she still had no clear idea of what she meant to accomplish in Doetinchem. She walked uncertainly through the busy station hall. When the salesgirl at the newsstand offered her a book of crosswords, she took it. She never did crosswords, but she paid for it anyway. Then she boarded the new train and stared blankly out the window till after they'd passed Utrecht.

The night before, something had awakened inside her. A realization that she hadn't yet quite settled into the waiting room for the dead. She wasn't even 50. Now that Aart was gone, she was free to do as she pleased. She could buy whatever she wanted, even take vacations to all the places he'd always been quick to criticize. She'd never wondered at the fact that he wouldn't suggest an alternate plan. Only now did she finally understand.

Unconsciously, she sat up a bit straighter. With much noise, the train passed a slower local one, and for the briefest of moments she saw her face reflected in its windows.

A man had taken the seat opposite her. She turned from the window and met his gaze. There was something hard and cold in his eyes, and she looked hastily away.

To give herself something to do, she pulled the book of crosswords from her shoulder bag. Frowning, she studied the first page. She knew that she wouldn't be able to concentrate on the puzzle. But she didn't want to have to continue to avoid the man's stare.

She got out at Doetinchem. She was nervous. The impulse that had driven her from her home in Zaandam to the station had long since given way to regret. She had continued with the journey only because, having once bought the ticket, her natural thriftiness forbade her to throw it away unused. She felt she should turn around and go home, yet that seemed wrong somehow. Now that she was here, she ought at least to have a look at the house. Just this once.

She bought a city map and studied it in a corner of a restaurant, where she ordered nothing but a simple cup of tea. Her stomach rumbled, but she knew she wouldn't be able to eat anything. When she left the restaurant, she was surprised to see that it was already dusk. For some reason, the lateness of the hour set her in motion. The new development she was looking for was naturally on the edge of the city. She didn't take a bus, because she had the vague idea that, walking, it would be easier to change her mind and turn back.

She didn't know how long she'd been walking. A long time. Her feet were swollen, her shoes pinched, and her calves were sore from the unusual exercise. Her bag wasn't heavy, but the longer she carried it the more it began to weigh her down. She suddenly noticed that she'd begun to giggle at the thought of the piece of cheese she'd bought for Aart. It was in the bottom of her bag, with the two bags of nuts, a pack of string beans and four bananas.

As she approached the new development, she came to a halt. She looked around her nervously. By now it was almost dark. It must be late, because her mouth was dry and her stomach protested loudly. She had eaten two of the bananas as she walked, and made a start on the almonds.

There was the car. The light from a streetlamp made the metallic blue paint glitter unnaturally. She had assumed that she would find the car parked in a driveway. She felt a stab of disappointment, because now she had no way of knowing which house it was. Silly that she'd remembered the name of the street, but not the number of the house.

As if in a trance, she walked up to the car and laid her hand almost tenderly on the glittering hood.

Somewhere, a dog barked. A flood of hysteria welled up inside her. This was crazy. Here she was, standing giggling like a fool in a deserted parking lot in a suburb of Doetinchem, when she ought to be home, crying.

Suddenly she dug into her shoulder bag, in the side pocket where she kept the spare set of keys. Of course, why hadn't she thought of them before?

She opened the door on the driver's side. She had gotten a license at Aart's insistence, but she'd never really taken to driving. It was more comfortable just to relax in the passenger seat beside him and enjoy the ride, without constantly having to worry about the unpredictable behaviour of the other drivers.

Her hands trembled on the steering wheel. The keys were on her lap. She hadn't planned it this way, but it was a good idea. She slid the key into the ignition. Could she do it? It had to be two years since her last experience behind the wheel.

Of course, the whole situation was bizarre. Her life had been turned upside down. She set her mouth in a thin, grim line, conscious that the events of the last few hours had had an enormous impact on her personality.

With one last cautious look at the row of houses, she started the car and backed away slowly. For a moment, she thought she saw a curtain move, but she decided it was probably her imagination. Nothing happened. No door flew open, no cry of protest that she was driving off in the car.

Proud of the cool and confident way she turned the wheel and worked the gas and brake and clutch, she pulled out of the parking space and traversed the streets of Doetinchem until she spotted a road sign that directed her out to the highway.

Somewhere in her subconscious mind, she must have come up with the glimmer of an idea. Otherwise, why had she taken this unnecessary detour? The empty asphalt road stretched out endlessly before and behind her. To one side, a grassy dike protected the highway from weather, wind and sea. On the other side of the road, the black sky dissolved seamlessly into the blackness of the lake.

What was she supposed to do with the car? Why had she taken it? It had to disappear, just as Aart had disappeared.

The water.

She glanced off to the side. In the distance, she could make out tiny pinpricks of light. Was that the opposite shore, or were there ships closer to hand?

It wouldn't be a bad idea, she thought. The water. But not here. Not by this godforsaken dike alongside the Ijsselmeer. She would have to find somewhere else, nearer to civilization, someplace from which she could return home without the car.

A canal. She giggled. She'd always been too frightened to park beside a canal. What if the emergency brake wouldn't hold, and the car was gone when she came back from shopping? Or if she accidentally stepped on the gas and drove herself over the edge? Now, though, a canal struck her as a fine solution.

At the end of the dike, she followed the signs for the city center. She thought the city was Enkhuizen, but she was concentrating so intensely on driving that she hadn't paid close enough attention to the signs. Carefully, she kept an eye out for a spot that was suited to her plan. An industrial park was bordered by a narrow canal. The water was a dark green, and the orange lights that illuminated the outsides of the warehouses were reflected in its calm surface.

Without a moment's hesitation, she parked the car facing the water. The trees which lined the canal were far enough apart, and luckily there was no protective low iron fence. As she stared at the dark water, she could feel her heart pounding in her chest. She felt a bit lightheaded, but that she attributed to pure tension. She could scarcely believe that the events of the last few hours had really happened. She had metamorphosed from a virtuous housewife to a resolute woman who was coolly and deliberately covering her tracks. How could this be? Was it all truly only set in motion so recently, when she had so suddenly decided that there was only one possible resolution: that Aart had to die? It hadn't even been all that difficult. Cleaning up the various loose ends was much more complex. She had to think of literally everything. Everything had to be carefully planned and considered, down to the smallest details.

She felt a momentary twinge of doubt, and asked herself if she was doing the right thing – but that was soon replaced by other, stronger emotions. She took her shoulder bag, made sure that her wallet was inside, and switched off the engine. The headlights blinked out abruptly.

She had no idea how deep the canal was, but that was a chance she'd have to take. It was lucky that the night was so dark. She stepped out of the car and leaned in to release the emergency brake. She left the door open, went behind the car and faced away from it and pushed against it with the weight of her body. It didn't take long before the car slowly began to roll towards the water. At first she had to walk the car forward, but then gravity or inertia took over and quickly finished the job for her. She jumped away and found it hard not to burst out laughing: had she not been careful, she would have followed the car into the water.

Her heart beating wildly, she stood there and watched the blue colossus dive over the edge of the canal. Its front end hit the water, which immediately streamed inside. Little eddies and air-bubbles formed strange patterns on the peaceful surface of the dark water. For a moment, she panicked. What in the name of God was she *doing*? She – Aart's virtuous, obedient little woman, the stupid housewife – had just purposely driven a car into a canal. The dumb, aloof creature who had endured twenty-five years of married life with Aart had now done things she'd only previously read about in books. Eaten up by hate and bitterness, but just as coolly as she'd pushed the car over the edge of the canal, she had taken away Aart's very existence. His life. He no longer *was*. What she was doing now was wiping away the tracks he had left in the world. It had to be like this.

She didn't wait until the car had gone completely under. With calm and collected movements she returned the spare set of keys to the side pocket of her bag and began to walk through the deserted streets of Enkhuizen.

As Bea – tired and hungry – stepped over the threshold of her silent house, the telephone shrilled. She hurried to the living room, noticing almost subliminally that the newspaper lay on the little table in the foyer. Had she left it there? Her heart again began to pound, and she stood for a moment with her hand not quite touching the receiver to get her breathing back under control.

"Hi, Bea. It's not too early to call, is it?"

Rein, her neighbor. He'd moved in next door five years ago, after he'd buried his wife and couldn't take the emptiness and especially the memories that filled the home they had shared. "No, of course not, Rein."

Had he heard something? Seen something?

"I'm sorry to bother you so early, Bea. I stopped by last night." There was a hint of accusation in his voice.

"I – yes. We were out, Rein."

"Oh, nice. Movie?"

Bea swallowed. She hadn't expected this. Her body was heavy with exhaustion, her head was splitting. She needed time to rest, to think.

"No, just – out. Shopping, you know?" She felt satisfied that her answer had been generic enough to be convincing.

"Aart and you together? I had the impression Aart wasn't much of a shopper." There was unmistakable surprise in his tone, and Bea's mouth stretched into a thin line. Couldn't the man mind his own business? What difference did it make to him whether or not Aart was a shopper?

"Is that so hard to believe?" she replied snappishly.

"No, of course not. Sounds great, Bea."

"Ah, why *are* you calling, Rein?"

"I was just wondering if you two were home."

She swallowed. "I am, yes." Was this it, then? What in God's name could she come up with if he were to ask for Aart?

"Actually, I was expecting a package yesterday, and I was hoping that the mailman might have left it with you. I ordered something, and I don't understand why it's taking so long to get here."

She frowned, distracted. Mailman? Yesterday? "Did he leave a note that he'd delivered it here?"

"No, but I was hoping. Well, never mind, Bea. It'll probably get here next week."

"Sure." She replaced the receiver and rested her head against the back of the chair. She was so tired! It seemed that, as the tension waned, her tiredness waxed. She was bone tired, and her headache was worse. There must be an aspirin somewhere. She needed time to work things out.

Aart was gone. But how could she explain that? God, she needed time to *think*!

She had to be careful to avoid even the smallest contradiction in her story. She needed an explanation she could stick to, one that wouldn't entangle her in a web of lies and evasions.

But she was so terribly tired! Her head felt stuffed full of cotton balls. Her ears buzzed, as if she'd been listening to loud music for hours, and her eyes burned with lack of sleep. Worst of all, she was famished and horribly thirsty.

She gasped. She raced back to the foyer, where she'd dropped her shoulder bag at the foot of the coat-rack. A brick of cheese. Salted cashews. But no string beans. As if illuminated by a searchlight, she saw the pack of string beans wrapped in a sheet of newspaper, in a little plastic shopping bag on the floor of the car.

She told herself to calm down. No one in his right mind would connect a package of string beans in a car in a canal with Aart's disappearance.

Coffee.

She needed strong black coffee with lots of sugar. After that, she would find a piece of paper and write her story down, so that later on she could read through it carefully and commit every detail to memory.

Bea breathed deeply as she stared at her neighbor, refusing to glance down at the dead-white feet sticking out from his blue striped pajamas. His hand gripped the belt of his old brown bathrobe tightly, as if he was afraid it might spontaneously fly open.

"Rein, I'm sorry to bother you so early, but I just don't know what to do!"

His white feet shuffled slowly backwards. "Come in, Bea. Calm down and tell me what's wrong."

"I – I feel so *guilty*." Like an abandoned dog tied to a tree in a forest, she began to whimper pitifully.

"What is it? Is something wrong with Aart?"

"Yes! He's – gone. Just disappeared."

"Nonsense. As if Aart would ever leave you."

For a moment it was silent, and each of them listened to the echo of those last words.

"Something must have happened to him, Rein, but what? Last night, he said he felt dizzy and – he had a terrible headache, he was burning up. He went to bed early, really sick."

"That doesn't sound like Aart."

"No, it doesn't. I went up later and felt his head, and his fever had come down some. So I just went to bed myself, and this morning I woke up and–and—"

"Don't tell me he's dead!"

Bea shook her head quickly. Too quickly? "No, he was just – *gone*. I'm so afraid something's happened to him, Rein. I don't know why, but I think – well, he was dizzy, and he had such a headache – maybe he's really ill, and he's in a ditch somewhere. . . ."

"Is he on foot?"

"No, he took the car."

"Did you try his cell?"

"I've been calling and calling, but I just get his voicemail." She paused. "I can't think what else to do, Rein. He was so – dazed. Maybe he's forgotten who he is, where he lives."

"I think we'd better go to the police," said Rein decisively. "Wait here. I'll throw some clothes on, and then I'll drive you to the station."

Through the pebbled glass of the front door, Bea made out two human shapes on the front stoop. She intuitively knew who they were. Police.

A few days ago, the concerned Rein had taken her to the station to report Aart as missing. And now they had come to her house. What would they have to tell her?

She wiped her clammy hands on her hips, fighting the impulse to flee out the back door.

"Mrs Driehuis?"

Her eyes slid searchingly across their earnest faces. A young officer with smooth cheeks, little more than a boy. The woman was older and bulkier, wearing an expression of professional friendliness.

"I'm Brigadier Hilbrink. Are you Mrs Driehuis?" The woman held up an identification card. Bea barely had time to examine the photo, let alone read the name. A detective, not an ordinary police officer.

"Yes, that's me."

"May we come in?"

She took a step back. "Yes, of course – I'm sorry."

She didn't ask them why they were there. It was obvious that they must have news about Aart, and the fact that it was not good news was written on their serious faces. In the living room, she indicated the colorful sofa and politely offered them coffee or tea.

"No, thank you. Ah, the news isn't good, ma'am."

So they'd found him. And now they were here to arrest her. Perhaps it was for the best. The suspense that had been keeping her awake through the long nights was practically unbearable.

She sat on the edge of a chair and folded her hands in her lap.

The woman detective looked around the room. "Are you alone, Mrs Driehuis?"

"Yes. My neighbor will be back later. He had some errands to run, and he's picking up some bread and cold cuts for me. It's strange, but life goes on, you know? Aart's gone, but I still have to eat."

She watched the woman frown slightly. Why was she rattling on so foolishly? What did these police people care that Rein was off doing her shopping for her? She lowered her gaze to the carpet and added, more calmly, "Are you sure I can't make you some coffee or tea?"

"There's no need to trouble yourself." Her visitors exchanged a quick look. "A few days ago, you reported the disappearance of your husband, correct?"

She swallowed with difficulty. "Yes."

"We've found someone who seems to fit the description you gave us."

At a barely discernible signal from the woman, the young man took a photograph from his jacket pocket. He laid it on the table, facing her. "Is this your husband, Mrs Driehuis?"

She didn't look at it. Not yet.

"Is he dead?"

"I'm afraid so, ma'am. Would you take a good look at the picture and tell us if it's your husband?"

She couldn't bring herself to pick it up. "I gave you a photo of him when I reported him missing."

Again the detectives glanced at each other. "Yes, I know. But it was several years old, you said, and the condition of the body is . . . well . . . it's not very nice."

Bea understood that she couldn't put it off any longer. She could feel them watching her. Were they simply concerned for her, or was there suspicion in their experienced police eyes?

"Take your time," the woman said sympathetically. "We know this is difficult for you."

Her colleague flipped open a thin black notebook. "The man we found was between forty and fifty years old. Dark hair, blue-grey eyes. No other distinguishing characteristics."

Illogically, Bea suddenly realized that she wasn't wearing any shoes. She leaned forward and felt under her chair, as she slowly thought that she must be reacting badly. She hadn't asked what had *happened* to her husband. Where he'd been found. How. When. What. Why. As she slipped her feet into her shoes, she watched their serious faces.

"Would you rather wait until your neighbor gets here, Mrs Driehuis?"

Bea clasped her hands together. "No. I'm fine."

With trembling fingers, she reached for the photograph, but at the last moment she changed her mind and didn't touch the glossy rectangle. "I – what happened to him?"

"We think it was a hit and run, ma'am." The young man seemed unsurprised by her delayed question.

"Where was he found?"

"Just outside the city. Near the Nauerna dike. We think someone ran him down and then just kept driving. He was found in a ditch by the side of the road."

That made no sense. Aart dead in a ditch? At the bottom of a dike? How in God's name could that be possible?

"But he's been missing for *days*," she said, almost accusingly. "How can you just have found him now?"

"He was lying in the weeds, ma'am, almost impossible to spot him from a passing car. A man on a bicycle had a flat tire and stopped by the side of the ditch and happened to see him."

"Oh."

"Sometimes it's better to know for sure," said the woman sympathetically.

Bea swallowed. For some reason it bothered her that all of her reactions and movements were being followed by the watchful eyes of the two detectives. Could she ask them to leave her alone with the photo?

Again she reached her trembling hand towards it. She stared at the blank face with short dark hair. She examined the unnatural features, the pale cheeks, the dark beard stubble, the stubby nose and small, rather pointy ears. She saw the dark eyebrows, the greying temples, and studied the crinkles at the corners of the eyes and the deeply etched lines that ran from the outsides of his nostrils to the corners of his mouth. But mostly she focused on the terrible damage that had been done to the face, the strangely misshapen jaw, as if the bottom half of the head had been cruelly wrenched out of alignment.

How in the name of God was this possible? How had he wound up in a ditch by the dike?

She swallowed several times in a row and wiped her eyes. She didn't notice the tears that had spotted her dress.

"Ma'am, is there someone we can call, so we don't have to leave you here alone?"

"No, I'm all right. I'll be fine." She wiped her hand across her eyes again. "I can go next door to Rein's. The neighbor."

A solemn nod, and then the formal question: "Mrs Driehuis, is this your husband?"

"Yes." Suddenly, she raised her head and looked straight at the policewoman. "Yes, it's him," she mumbled hoarsely.

"Ma'am?"

"Sorry." Her voice sounded strange and high-pitched, but it wasn't shaking any more. "Yes," she said firmly, "that's my husband, Aart Driehuis."

"Thank you. That's all we need for now."

"Do – do I need to fill in any paperwork? I don't—"

"The formalities can wait a while," answered the woman gently.

Bea hoped they wouldn't offer to stay until Rein got back. She wanted to be alone. She needed time and quiet, she had to think, and she had to write down everything she'd said as soon as possible.

Funny, she'd never before realized that it was harder *not* to lie than to lie.

"Bea speaking."

Silence on the other end of the line.

"This is Bea," she said again.

"I have to talk to you."

She gasped. "What?"

"You heard me, Bea. We need to talk."

"This – you – this isn't possible."

"Of course it's possible. I've been—"

She slammed down the receiver, cutting him off. She couldn't catch her breath, and all around her she saw black spots and blinding flashes of light. That voice! It was exactly as she remembered it, maybe just a tone deeper.

But it wasn't possible. He was *dead*. It had to be someone else. Someone who knew what she had done.

The phone rang.

She wouldn't speak to him. Never, never again.

But Rein was in the kitchen, making coffee, and of course he would want to know why she hadn't answered the phone. She had to regain her composure before he came out of the kitchen.

Rein, who had so unexpectedly turned out to be a true friend, a source of comfort. He'd been so wonderful throughout the two weeks since she'd laid Aart in his final resting place.

She reached out a trembling hand and lifted the receiver. "Yes?"

Her voice sounded very weak.

"Bea? Bea, is that you?"

"What do you want?"

"To talk."

"There's nothing left to say!"

"I think there is. You can't just—"

"You're dead, Aart," she said slowly and calmly. "We buried you two weeks ago."

"I was on vacation, Bea. With Ellie. Ellie and I were in Greece, you knew that, I told you before we left." He paused for a moment. "Bea, what have you done?"

"What have *I* done?" Her laugh was high, hysterical. "You're the one who *did* something, Aart. You moved in with her, didn't you? With that whore, in Doetinchem?"

"Ellie's not a whore. She's my girlfriend. I love her, Bea."

"What's your address?"

"I gave it to you the last time. Why?"

"I want to send you a card. Your own funeral card, Aart."

She heard him draw a breath, but also heard Rein's footsteps approaching, stepping carefully so as not to spill their coffee.

"Hello?" Her voice was suddenly different. "Would you please stop pestering me?"

"Don't hang up, Bea, I have to—"

"I don't have anything to say to you!"

"I'll call back another time, Bea. I can't just—"

But she had already cradled the receiver. Her face was as cold as ice, and droplets of perspiration pearled her upper lip. A muscle twitched in her right cheek.

"Who was that? Crank call?" asked Rein, concerned.

She looked up with a start. Worry traced itself across his face. How lucky she was to have such a wonderful neighbor, such a dear friend. He was so different from Aart, who had run her whole life for her. Who was still trying to run her life.

She smiled tightly. "Some insurance salesman."

He set the local newspaper on the table. "Sometimes I pity these people," he said casually, waving a hand at the paper.

She stared at him, perplexed. What was he talking about?

"These Russians," he explained. "They keep trying to emigrate to the West. They must think things are so much better here. Otherwise, why would they go through so much hardship to get here?" He picked up the paper and unfolded it, looking for the article that had attracted his attention. He showed her a page with two photographs on it. "Little while back, these two tried it. They hid themselves in the cargo hold of an airplane that was flying from Moscow to Amsterdam. Only they didn't realize how cold it gets at 30,000 feet."

"How awful." She tried with all her might to focus her mind on what he was saying.

"Yeah. Did you see the headline? 'Russian lands in Russian Town.' What a coincidence, eh? Look, the pilot let down his landing gear, and this Russian who was hiding in the cargo hold and had already frozen to death – well, of course he couldn't hold on any more, so he fell out of the plane. He landed on the roof of an old shed in Russian Town in Zaandam, bounced off, and rolled into the gutter. What a coincidence! A Russian fell, out of the blue, into Russian Town."

He folded back the page and handed it to her. "Put your glasses on, Bea, so you can see it."

Annoyed by his bossy tone, she ignored his comment about her glasses and stared at the two photos without them. Her eyes were good enough to make out the features of the two men's faces.

She would have recognized those pointy little ears anywhere.

She cleared her throat with some difficulty. "Did they both land in Russian Town?"

"No, of course not – that would have been too much of a coincidence! They haven't found the other one yet."

"How do they know there were two of them?"

"They found a duffel bag in the cargo hold. With two passports."

The ringing of the telephone sounded very far away.

Bea stared at Rein, who smiled back at her with the innocent look of someone who'd just robbed a bank and had stashed the money somewhere safe.

She couldn't move.

She realized that Rein hadn't brought up the Russians randomly, that he hadn't shoved the newspaper with those passport photos under her nose for no reason.

He must have heard them that Friday evening when Aart had announced he was leaving her to move in with Ellie, with the woman who had been his mistress for more than ten years, the mother of his eight-year-old daughter. Rein must have heard her screams of anguish, her bitter rage.

Her dull eyes silently watched him as he slowly lowered himself into Aart's chair.

"If that man calls again, trying to sell you insurance – or bother you with anything else – you just pass him over to me, dear Bea," he said calmly. "I'll take care of him for you."

He smiled possessively. "From now on, I'll take care of everything for you."

Translation by Josh Pachter

Wedding in Voerde

Gunter Gerlach

1

The noise of the motor is suddenly different.

I sit up, startled. "Where are we?"

Something's scratching and scraping under the hood. An animal, trying to get out.

"The coolant's overheated," says Ulrich. He's sweating behind the wheel. His plaid suit's gotten too small for him over the last four years. The pants are too short. His stomach rubs against the steering wheel. And the shirt buttons are about to pop. There's a red light blinking on the dashboard.

Ulrich turns on the warning flasher and begins to look for a parking lot.

"Dinslaken," he says. "We've almost made it."

He opens yet another button on his light-blue shirt. Then he guides the car into an empty parking space and turns off the motor. I unfold the street map.

"That's the road to Voerde," says Ulrich. "That's it all right." He wipes the sweat off his forehead with the back of his hand.

"Why didn't you take the autobahn?" I ask.

"Because the coolant's overheating."

"How long?"

"Since Bochum."

I take a deep breath. Ulrich pats the air in a soothing gesture, palms toward me.

"Calm down. It's my car. And I want to get to that money just as fast as you do." He gets a rag from underneath the driver's seat. We get out. Ulrich takes off his jacket and rolls up the sleeves of his shirt, then opens the hood.

A thin hiss of steam rises from a hose. Ulrich grips the radiator cap with the rag and turns it. The cap jumps from his hand. Steam spurts out and envelops him. He emerges dancing and swearing, blowing on his arm.

I shake my head. "End of the line."

I go to the trunk and open it. "We're in luck; we've got everything here." I take out the heavy wire cutters. Bicycles are leaning against the fence around a building. I pick out two and cut through the locks.

"It's not far," I said. "Is it?"

2

The cool shade of the woods lines both sides of the road. It's too warm for Ulrich. He's riding in his shirtsleeves, his jacket rolled into a bundle on the bicycle's back rack. "Why do you have gears on your bike and I don't?" he shouts.

"Because you weigh more," I say. "That means more pressure on the pedals."

The district called Möllen is just along here, after the woods. It belongs to Voerde. There are houses on both sides of the street. But no people.

"We're too late," says Ulrich.

"We're also not invited."

My backside hurts. When you've spent four years in prison, you're not used to riding a bicycle. I stop, get off, and pull my pants out of my crotch. Ulrich leans his bicycle against a fence. He gasps for air, the corners of his mouth turned down, like a fish on land.

"All this just because of your car," I say. "Even though you had four years to get it fixed." It's supposed to be a joke. Ulrich growls. "If Heinz doesn't have the money, I'll kill him." He shows me his arm. The scalded spot is swelling into a red egg. As he climbs on the bike again, his foot slips off the pedal and his toes ram the asphalt. He flings the bike away and hops around on the other leg, his teeth clenched.

"What's the matter?" I ask.

"Nothing," he hisses, and climbs on the bike again. I ride ahead. After a while he catches up. "God help him if he doesn't have the money," he says, his eyes small and red.

3

We find City Hall and push our bicycles into a bike stand.

"Have you ever noticed that everything's purple here?" asks Ulrich.

"Sure," I say, and point to the scalded spot on his arm.

"Nonsense," he says. "I mean the streetlights, the signs, the bike stand. That's purple, isn't it? Or is it dark violet?"

A woman comes out of the building. I ask where the registry office is. She laughs, tilts her head and looks us up and down. "A friend of ours is getting married today," Ulrich tries to explain. I think she thinks we're gay.

The registry office, we learn, isn't in Voerde's City Hall, it's in "Haus Voerde," which is a castle with a moat. The woman tells us how to get there. Then she takes a little town map out of her bag and gives it to us. Meanwhile Ulrich is sitting on a bench and has taken off his right shoe and sock. The nail of his big toe is swimming in blood.

"Have you hurt yourself?" asks the woman.

"He's always bleeding from somewhere or other," I say.

Ulrich taps carefully on the nail and sucks in air through his teeth. "That hurts right down to the bone!"

The woman walks slowly away across the plaza and turns to look at us.

"Do you have to tell everyone why we're here?" I smack my forehead with my hand. "It's a small town. By tomorrow everybody'll know. That's why everything's purple. It's a warning color. The gossip zone."

Ulrich dabs at his toe. Then he tries to put on his sock and shoe again. Everything's too small, too tight, his arms are too short. Sweat oozes from his hair. "I want my money," he whines. "And then we're outta here."

4

"We've gotta be careful," I say.

The castle glows whitely between the trees lining the road. We can hear voices and loud laughter. We push the bicycles into the shrubs on the side of the road and walk toward Haus Voerde. There are several wedding parties there. A large group is having a photo taken in front of the castle as a smaller party makes its way up the path.

"Out of here, move!" I push Ulrich back toward the street.

He limps and groans with every step. "The pain's making me crazy," he says.

We hide behind a tree. The bridal couple poses for a photo on a bridge over the moat. The bridegroom is Heinz. With his gray face and black suit, he looks just like a waiter from a basement nightclub that never sees the light of day. Next to him is his blond bride in a yellow dress. She probably tends bar in the same nightclub. Someone hands her a white bouquet of flowers. Just for the photo.

"Let's just walk in," says Ulrich.

"And if it gets serious? There are too many of them."

Down by the street, Heinz's wedding party gets into three cars.

"Let's go." I grab my bike. "We can't afford to lose them."

Ulrich turns to go and promptly runs into a tree.

5

"Stupid bikes," I say. We're riding through a field, directly into the wind.

"I want my money," moans Ulrich. I turn to look at him. A drop of blood from the scrape on his forehead is running up into his hair, driven by the wind.

We find the cars on a parking lot in Götterswickerhamm, in the next part of town. The wedding party is sitting in a restaurant with a view of the Rhine. We put the bikes in a rack. Heinz is just coming out of the restaurant with another man. They light cigarettes. When they inhale, their faces become bony, their eyes seem to recede in the sockets.

"Let's go get the money," says Ulrich, his face like a puffer-fish. He limps toward the restaurant. Heinz recognizes him and his eyebrows shoot upward. He leaves the other man standing there and comes toward us.

"You're out?"

"We want the money," Ulrich sings out.

"Sure. You'll get it."

I shake Heinz's limp hand. "Congratulations."

"How do you know about the wedding?"

"*Some* people got a wedding announcement."

"I didn't know . . ." Heinz spread his arms. "Well, I've got to get back." He shows his yellow teeth.

"We're coming with you," says Ulrich.

Heinz curls his upper lip. You can see the narrow stumps of his teeth. They have cavities.

"Nope," he says. "It's a wedding party. If I'd known you were out, I'd have sent you an invitation, honest."

6

"If he doesn't have the money, I'm going to kill him!" Ulrich is behind me, sweating. We're pedaling through the fields again. I let him catch up with me. The noises he's making sound just like the bicycle seat squeaking and the chain scraping.

"You could have used those four years to lose a few pounds," I say.

"I want my money," he says, as if he's drunk with the exertion. On the little town map, Heinz has marked the neighborhood where he lives. Friedrichsfeld am Markt. By the time we get there, Ulrich is completely exhausted. He drops heavily into a chair at the café and orders a cherry ice cream sundae. He eats it, choking and coughing. I order espresso.

"You get stomach cancer from that – and those deep lines from your nose to your chin," says Ulrich, pointing at the tiny espresso cup.

"I've had those lines all my life."

Ulrich eats another ice cream sundae, this time with strawberries. I order cappuccino. Heinz doesn't turn up.

"Let's go, we're going to his place," says Ulrich. "I want my money. And then I'm going to kill him."

"It's his wedding day."

"So what."

We get up and walk to the bikes. The front tire on Ulrich's bike is almost flat. I give him my pump. His hand slides off the valve and he catches his little finger in the spokes. I pump up the tire for him.

Heinz emerges from one of the apartment buildings. So that's where he lives. He waves us over to the middle of the plaza. He looks around him and talks softly.

"Listen, I can't get my hands on the money right away. It'll take a while. Can't you come back in a few days?"

Ulrich shakes his head and sucks on his little finger.

I explain to Heinz about the car trouble. We follow him to an ATM. Five hundred, the machine won't give him any more than that.

7

"Why didn't I just kill him?" Ulrich's little finger is swollen. He spreads his fingers on the handlebars as he rides.

"It's his wedding night," I say. "We'll get the money."

We're on our way through the fields again, pedaling back to Voerde. There's a hotel at the train station there. Heinz called and booked us a room. Ulrich rides slower and slower. He says he ate too much ice cream. He begins to weave and wobble and his face glows in the twilight as if it's sunburned. He says his stomach is pulling him from one side to the other. I let him ride ahead and set the pace, but just then his front wheel runs into a pothole and gets stuck. The bicycle tips over and Ulrich sails, arms outstretched, into a cornfield. I help him up, dust him off. His shirt has pulled out of his pants.

"Just look at that," he says, and pulls the shirt up higher. He has blood on his belly.

"I want my money," he says.

I wipe his belly clean with a Kleenex. A sliver of glass from a broken bottle is still sticking out of his skin. I pull it out.

"You should be glad you're so fat," I comfort him. "This was just stuck in a layer of blubber."

Ulrich sits by the side of the road, his hand pressed on the wound. I kneel down in front of him and look directly at him.

"I'm going to die," he says. He looks almost as if the beads of sweat are tears.

"Heinz is just bullshitting us," he says. "We should go back right now and demand the money."

"Tomorrow," I say, and point to the sky. "It's getting dark."

"No. Now," says Ulrich. "Tomorrow I'll be dead."

He braces himself and gets to his feet.

"You know what, we're going to kidnap him and extort the money from his wife. She knows where it is, I'll bet. That's why she married him. I mean, a guy like that, he looks like death. Why else would anyone marry him?"

8

"We had an accident," I say into my mobile phone. "Ulrich's hurt. We're down here in front of the building."

"I'll come down," says Heinz.

There are four apartments in the building. Heinz's name isn't on any of the buzzers, just his wife's. We station ourselves on both sides of the door to the street. When Heinz comes out, Ulrich hits him on the forehead with a flat rock. I catch Heinz, and together we pull him back into the house, to the door to the cellar. I search through his pants pockets for the key. I can tell he's gotten thin. Just skin and bones. The pores in his face are much larger than they used to be.

"You killed him," I said. Heinz's eyes are open, but he doesn't say anything or move. I try all the keys in the cellar door until I find the right one. Ulrich tips Heinz over his shoulder. There's an old sofa in the cellar. We lay him down on it and tie him up with an extension cord.

"I'll go upstairs," says Ulrich.

"Let me do that," I say. "You'll just scare her." I point to his belly. It hasn't stopped bleeding. His whole shirt is bloody.

"Hurry up," he says. "I don't have much blood left."

9

"Congratulations," I say. "I'm a friend of Heinz's."

"My husband will be right back." She laughs. "That sounds strange: 'my husband'."

She asks me to come in. In the living room there's a bottle of champagne with two glasses. She laughs again. For no reason. Up close, she's older than I thought. Giggling, she introduces herself as Elisabeth and gets a third glass from the kitchen.

"I used to work with Heinz," I say.

"You mean when he was with the security service?" She laughs again. "I've never had a job," she laughs.

I tell her the story of the armored car. The whole story of the heist; of Ulrich, Heinz and me. And then I say: "We've kidnapped Heinz. If you don't give us the money he owes us, then . . ." I drew my hand across my throat.

She smiles, bends forward and asks, "Another glass?" And then she just pours. I think she wasn't even listening, or maybe she's not right in the head and doesn't understand what I'm saying.

"Did you understand what I just said?"

"Yes. No." She laughs. "Heinz, that is, my husband, will be here in a minute."

"No, he won't." I stand up and bend over her, so close that I can feel her breath. "We've kidnapped Heinz," I shout. "We want our share. One hundred thousand euros. There's got to be that much left. And if you call the police, I'll tell them all over again about the armored car. Because we've done our time. Heinz hasn't."

She kissed me on the nose.

"You're sweet," she says. "But I don't know where he gets his money."

10

"She doesn't know anything," I say.

In the dim light of the cellar, Ulrich and Heinz look Chinese.

"She doesn't know anything," says Heinz.

"I want my money," says Ulrich. He's holding his left hand.

"What happened?"

Heinz tries to sit up. "He mangled his fingers in that cabinet over there," he says. I go over to the cabinet and open it. There's wine in a rack inside.

"Open a bottle," says Heinz.

I use a screwdriver to push the cork down into the bottle, and drink a few mouthfuls. Then I give the bottle to Ulrich. He drinks and then holds the bottle up to Heinz's mouth.

"You're gonna knock out my teeth," Heinz complains.

"Where's the money?" I ask.

"Come on, tell us. You can see I'm dying," says Ulrich. "Shot in the gut. You can see. But first you talk." The wound on his belly looks like it's still bleeding.

"I changed the money into small notes, just a little at a time, and then I buried it. There's a transformer station behind the water tower. With three big fat insulators." He laughs. "A hundred thousand volts for a hundred thousand euros. Easy to remember. It's lying a couple of feet underground. But you can't get to it. It's live, see. They only turn off the power once every three years to inspect the place. And you can only dig it up then. So you'll have to come back in three years."

"Nice story," I said. "Okay then, we'll do that. Of course, you won't mind if we take your sweet little wife with us. We'll bring her back in three years, just a little the worse for wear."

"That's enough!" says Heinz. He closes his eyes and presses his lips together.

"You can kill him now," I say to Ulrich.

Heinz begins to tug against the extension cord. "Okay. I took all the money and bought a snack bar. Honest. Ask Elisabeth."

11

Heinz has a lump on his forehead. It's getting bigger.

Elisabeth opens the garage door in the dark. Inside, a black station wagon gleams faintly.

"No money, you said? So where'd the car come from?" I ask.

"We got it for picking up supplies," says Elisabeth. "We buy the sausages directly from the factory."

Ulrich wants to drive, but as he walks around the car his pants get caught on something. The fabric tears.

"Not you," I say. "Get in the back with Heinz."

"I'll drive," says Elisabeth.

"Let me smell your breath," I say to her. She puts her arms on my shoulders and licks the tip of my nose. "Do you know today's my wedding night?" she asks. She tries to kiss me but I pull away from her.

"I'll drive," I say.

Ulrich pushes the still-tied-up Heinz onto the back seat and climbs in next to him. Elisabeth guides me onto a federal highway. After a short while we turn back toward Voerde.

"You're already past it," laughs Elisabeth. "You should have turned off back there." I turn around and drive back. A dark road.

"Stop," says Elisabeth. Through the windows of a car we can see the snack bar on the other side of the road. Closed. Dark except for a neon tube twitching faintly over the counter.

"You have to see it by daylight," says Heinz. "It's a super place."

Paint is peeling everywhere. There's grass growing in front of the entrance. I look at Heinz, my mouth fallen open. "This dump?"

"It's lots bigger inside," he says.

"I'm going to kill him," says Ulrich.

12

I don't want to get out. We all stay in the car, and Heinz tells us that he bought the snack bar a year ago from an old couple.

"They're only turning it over to me now. Next week," he says. "And there's a snack wagon, too. The old man used to take it to the farmer's markets. But then he went and died. And the old lady's sick and doesn't have anyone else. That's why it's been closed for two months now. I mean, what can you do? But we'll get the place into shape."

I look at Ulrich. He sits sunken into a heap on the back seat, his too-short arms and legs dangling from his body. Slowly he closes his eyes.

"You can make a first-class eatery out of it," says Heinz. "I'll hire a cook and the thing is practically the golden goose."

"It's a dump," I say.

"Bad location," says Ulrich. He shakes his head.

"They took you for a ride," I say.

"Shitty," says Ulrich.

"No, no, it just looks that way. I'll take the wagon to the markets and Elisabeth will run the snack bar here. In three years you'll have your money. With interest. It's really a good investment."

Elisabeth has gotten out of the car and is standing in front of the snack bar, arms outstretched, turning slowly in circles. We follow her and look through the windows. It's filthy.

"I want champagne," says Elisabeth. "How come they're not open?"

I untie Heinz. "I feel sorry for you." Ulrich kicks the bicycle rack in front of the snack bar. He swears and hops around on the other leg. His face glows redly. Then he makes a fist and hits one of the glass panes in the door. It shatters.

"Let's get out of here," I say.

In the car, Ulrich winds the safety belt around his hand. He has a cut on the back of it.

"Idiot," I say. There's a packet of Kleenex lying on the dashboard. I toss them over the back of the seat to him.

13

We take Heinz and Elisabeth home and drive the car back to the hotel by the train station in Voerde.

In our room, I unroll toilet paper and wind it around Ulrich's belly, fingers, hand and big toe.

"At least we've got the car," he says.

"Won't get much for it if we sell it." I take off my clothes and get into bed. It's too warm for Ulrich under the covers. He lies on top of the bed like a lump of dough. "Tomorrow I'm going to kill him," he says.

I turn out the light.

"You know," I say after a while, "there oughta be a sign for the snack bar out on the highway."

"And a couple of flags out in front of the place," says Ulrich.

"Did you see, they didn't even have ice cream."

Ulrich tosses restlessly. "You can't get by these days just on sausages," he says. "You've got to have Turkish *döner* sandwiches and hamburgers, that's what works. And soup – you've got to have soup, too."

"How do you know?"

"I used to work in a snack bar."

"Honest?"

"Yeah. That was a good time. You've got to have salads, too. I was good at those. They're easy. And I even introduced lunch plates. The place was really hopping then! But then I spilled the fryer grease all down my leg, and quit."

"You can do all that?"

"Sure. And crêpes, you need crêpes. Those are really good, lemme tell you."

I reach for the switch and turn the light on again.

"Listen, Ulrich," I say.

"I know," he says. "We'll take the snack bar."

Translation by Mary W. Tannert

When He Finally Came

Inger Jalakas

Okay! So I'm no angel. It's not like I'm exactly evil either. I just have this anger inside of me. I don't really know where it comes from. Maybe it's my damned father haunting me. He's just the way he is and he could drive anybody crazy.

I don't know.

I suddenly just get really mad sometimes. When I get provoked, the anger bubbles up and takes control of my thoughts. Once in a while, I might have a tendency to go too far. But between my bouts of anger, I'm as gentle as a lamb. I really am.

Anyway, what happened this summer might have been a bit too much. I guess I crossed the line. Yes, I did. I have to admit it. But the gods know I had good reason. Damned workmen! I have to say it.

You know, I live alone. I always have. I've had a relationship or two over the course of the years, you understand. But they just ran out of steam. Or, more accurately, I did away with them when they showed their true, feeble-minded sides. I ended the relationships, I mean, not murdered them or anything.

"You have to take the bad with the good," a girlfriend of mine used to say. She's married. I'm not. Never in my life would I stand to be bullied like she is. Nope, it's best to keep to oneself. Definitely. Just as long as I have peace, I'm as serene as can be. Harmonious. I like to stick to my normal routines. And the incident this summer would never have happened, if the ventilation system hadn't broken down in the house where I live.

It's a beautiful old house from the turn of the previous century. I have a wonderful apartment on the top floor, with a view out over the roof tops. On clear days, I can see all the way across town. Although I don't know how much shoddy work they did when the house was renovated. In any case, things are breaking down all the time, and this summer the ventilation went. In July. In the middle of the worst heat wave. We had more than thirty degrees, both inside and out. And for once there wasn't even a breeze, so it didn't help to have a window open, either. Yes. You must remember how hot it was.

"A thunderstorm blew out the system," the real estate manager explained, when I finally located his cell phone number and got ahold of him. He was on vacation.

"Oh, yeah?" I said. "And why don't you get the fan turned on again?" I was entitled to wonder, don't you think? Yes. He promised to take care of it, even though he was on vacation. Someone would come. And soon.

I was satisfied with that, and returned to the sofa, and my life of panting.

And so that day passed. And the next. I hadn't seen hide nor hair of any repairman. And it was still just as hot. It was impossible to do anything during the day, and impossible to sleep at night.

That I am a writer, is relevant to the story. You see, I sit at home and write. Normally, anyway. In that heat it was impossible. I mostly lay around, suffering, with a wet cloth covering my face.

Finally, I dragged myself off the sofa, and called the real estate manager again. This time I was a bit more harsh with him. And with every right, if you ask me.

"It's in the middle of summer holidays," he said. "It's difficult to find a repairman."

"Yes, but my God! This is an acute situation. It's more than thirty degrees in here!" I pointed out to him.

The damned idiot had the nerve to say that he was suffering with me.

"You are? Really?" I replied. "In that case, perhaps you'll do something to fix the problem. Immediately."

But no one came.

After one more sleepless night, I called again. This time I got mumbling and vague answers, when I asked if he'd been able to reach any repairmen. Of course he hadn't. Now, I was beginning to get really irritated. I have better things to do than nag such people day after day. In the end he promised to contact someone as soon as we hung up.

So I hung up and waited. Fruitlessly. No repairman in sight that day, either. I was getting desperate, by now. A week in a baking hot sauna had really worn me out. So I called to complain again.

"Where are you?" I asked. "You seem to have it nice and cool."

I could hear happy voices in the background and the tinkling of a glass with ice cubes in it, which he must have been holding in his hand. The question seemed to make him nervous. He was hesitant to answer it, anyway. Instead, he swore that he would immediately see to it that a repairman came out.

Believe it or not, the next morning my doorbell rang. Outside of it stood the strangest looking little man, with wild hair and extremely thick glasses. He asked me to open the door to the fan room.

"It's locked," he told me.

The request was astonishing, in my opinion. Why did he think I had the key? It would be the real estate manager that had that. I'm no real estate manager. And when I had gotten so far in my explanation, he turned around and left.

"Hello!" I yelled after him. "Wait! Don't go! Let's call him," but he got into the elevator and disappeared.

So, of course I called, myself. You understand. A woman answered. The wife, presumably. Or maybe it was his mother, how would I know. At least, she had the same last name. She lied, anyway, that much I'm certain of. When I asked for the real estate manager, she maintained that he wasn't there. I didn't believe her. In any case, I explained the situation to her, and she didn't seem very interested. She was short with me, in fact. Rather dismissive.

Her snotty attitude irritated me to such a degree that I threw the phone on the floor. That was pretty dumb, you understand, because it broke. As a result, I had to go out into that tropical heat and buy a new one.

When I got home again, I pondered about what I was going to do. I suddenly remembered that I have a friend who works for the phone company, and that the real estate manager's cell phone had a number she could trace. I called her right away, and promised her the moon and stars if she would do it. You can do that nowadays. The telephone company can see where the signals come from. You must know about that. Of course, it isn't legal, but we're friends, and all. No matter, she did it. The phone was

located in a summer cottage area a ways outside of town. As soon
as I got the address, I drove there.

What a ruckus. I found him in a lawn chair with a large whisky
within his reach. He wasn't happy. The fact is, he was terribly
rude. Went on and on about how I was harassing him during
his well-deserved vacation, and threatened to have me charged
with disturbing the peace. That was the dumbest thing I had ever
heard and I told him so.

"Do you really think I would drive all the way out to these
obscure boondocks if I didn't have to? It's your own damned
fault. If you had done what you promised, I wouldn't be standing
here. Fix the problem!" I said.

Loudly.

After that I went back to my car and drove home. And wonder
of wonders, that little man stood outside my door again the next
morning. With the key.

"I'm going up to fix it now," he said. And he did. In a way.
That strange little man is certainly clever at something, but
ventilation systems weren't it. The fan came on again, but the
only speed it had was maximum. It was impossible to adjust it
or turn it off. The result was that I now had a hurricane in my
apartment.

It was so bad that I almost preferred the heat.

I went up to the fan room to tell him about the mistake, but the
door was locked, and the light was switched off. I could see this
when I peeked through the keyhole. He'd already left.

There was nothing to do but call my dear real estate manager
again. I used the code to hide my number, just in case he was
screening his calls. He, himself, answered and moaned when I
presented myself. I ignored the moan, told him how things stood,
and calmly wondered if it might have been better to send a
competent repairman. He didn't appreciate the question.

"Why don't you try to find a repairman, yourself, in the middle
of the summer," he hissed at me.

"Gladly," I replied. "Will you come here and open the door, if
I do?"

He hung up on me. Endlessly rude, if you'll pardon my saying
so. I was so indignant that I fainted. Well, almost, anyway. I
collapsed to the floor, hitting my head on the computer keyboard,
as I went down.

It happened to be turned on, I had obviously forgotten to turn it off, after my last attempt to write a few lines. Unfortunately, I managed to hit the delete button. An entire chapter was erased. A week's work. That did nothing to improve my mood.

After that the days passed in much the same way. I called and complained. He lied and played for time, had worthless explanations, or couldn't be bothered to answer my questions. I couldn't even think about working. I have to have peace and quiet when I create.

The nights were worse than the days. Now, I couldn't sleep because of all the noise. Hour after hour, I lay tossing and turning, never able to fall asleep.

Two weeks passed before the real estate manager returned to work from his wonderful vacation. By then I was totally worn out. I realized he was back when it suddenly got quiet. At least for a little while. Then the racket started up again.

I carefully opened my door and listened up the stairs. Yes, heavy wooden shoes could be heard tramping around up in the fan room. I had soft slippers on my own feet. I would never have considered disturbing my neighbors with wooden shoes.

I'm not an evil, or bad person, as I've said before.

Just when I stood there, weighing whether or not to drag myself up the stairs, the tramping stopped. I waited and listened. But no, he had stopped walking around. The only sound was the roaring of the fan. Now, I had no choice. I had to go up and see what he was up to.

I quietly snuck up the stairs. There he lay sleeping, slumped against the green fan housing. He was tanned and bloated and reeking of several days' drunkenness. His tool box was by his feet and there were tools spread out all over the floor. Screwdrivers and wrenches, measuring sticks and hammers. Everything in a big mess. There was nothing orderly about the man.

"What are you doing?" I asked him. "Have you fixed the problem?"

He jumped and blinked drowsily.

"Fell asleep, I guess," he muttered. "I'm tired."

"Tired! When you finally come, you're tired? What in the hell do you think I am? I haven't been able to sleep in weeks?" I said. Quietly, so as not to disturb the neighbors.

Then I beat him to death with his hammer.

* * *

Interrogation ended 2:27pm, 8 September, 2003.
  Interrogating officer: Criminal Inspector Margaret Nordin, District Police in Gothenburg.

Translation by Susan Loyd

An Angel Is Speaking

François Rivière

Today, 14 January 2003, I am celebrating the fifteenth anniversary of my death. A somewhat solitary and even derisory celebration as I am the only one to be actually surprised that I am still alive ... but you must find me rather confusing and I will try and clarify matters for you.

Let's start at the beginning. My name is Anthony Valleau, but since the winter of '86 I am better known as "Little Tony". Yes, you remember now: Little Tony who drowned one sad evening in the Seugne, that muddy tributary of the Charente river, a three-year old innocent victim in a mighty drama that fed the French judicial chronicle for months, if not years ... What? Tony Valleau isn't dead! What are you talking about? Well, what I am talking about, dear friends, is a ballad of the forgotten, the remains of a terrible case, over which still hangs a troubled mystery scotched with mad rumours, an affair that over the years has become as notorious as those of the Dominici farm or Bruay-en-Artois.

The Valleau Affair, also known as the Tragedy of the Seugne, or again the Abominable Crime in the Charente-Maritime. You all know most of it: on the morning of 15 January 1986, a shopkeeper from the town of Rochefort-sur-Mer walking by the shores of the Seugne river, near the Tarsay hamlet, caught sight of my small body floating across the colourless waters of the unremarkable stream. The police were called and concluded that I had reached my death by drowning in the icy water. Very soon, a forensic examiner uncovered much worse: the three-year old little boy found in the Seugne had previously been strangled. It did not take the policemen long to identify the small body: as soon as they got back to the station which stood at the top of the only hill in the region – these were flatlands full of salty marshes ever lashed by a sharp winter wind – they came across my desolate parents who had come to report my disappearance during the course of the previous night. I had been put to bed around nine o'clock, and then later everyone in the house had gone to sleep only for my mother to discover, around eight in the morning, my horrifying disappearance. At any rate, that is the story that quickly spread throughout the region that morning, causing much consternation and, already, commentary.

Of course, matters were not that simple.

The weeping faces and halting words of my dear parents could only lead the police to believe this version of my "disappearance" soon followed by the possibility of a "kidnapping" and soon after of a murder. (The medical examiner at least quickly reassured people that there had been no sign of sexual abuse, which would have made matters even worse.) Earlier I referred to people's comments, maybe I should have said "gossip", as the tittle-tattle soon spread like wildfire. But before I return to the unofficial version, which soon took hold thanks to the gutter press which rapidly turned the whole situation into the Valleau Affair, which all France, both with excitement and disgust, would feast on for a long time, I must supply some necessary additional details so that you might better understand what happened in 1986.

When the drama occurred, in the eyes of the public, our family situation was already a tad spicy. Let us have a look at the protagonists. My father, Maurice, had just turned thirty. My mother, Josyane, and he had been married for seven years, and she had only become pregnant once – I was born in 1983. Papa, who had long worked as a clerk in the town hall, was out of work. Everyone around knew it was because he was an alcoholic. Mama had worked as a cleaner since she was sixteen and also looked after old people. There was talk around Tarsay that her devotion to Madame Duchemin, a childless notary's wife, was not unrelated to the fact that she had a strong chance to inherit a large share of the woman's wealth.

My father had a brother, Germain, who was two years older than him, with whom Josyane had been much in love before settling for the lazier of the two Valleau brothers. Ever since an awkward childhood, there had been bad blood between the brothers: my grandfather, an unscrupulous animal trader well known in the region for his excessive drinking and his boisterous sexual activities, treated both of them even worse than his flock ever since they had been tiny. So, you see how bad my heredity was!

In the past, the two brothers had always seemed to be quarrelling about one thing or another and, needless to say, Josyane Valleau's pregnancy had not made matters any better. However, from the very moment the midwife who had assisted in my delivery had left the house, the situation outwardly appeared to improve. Although the brutal bike accident in which Madame Brun, the midwife, succumbed shortly after certainly clouded the event. Some, in town, would later refer to it as a sign of destiny.

Our house—since sold to a tobacconist couple evidently fascinated by the "Affair" – had been built with the help of half the inheritance from grandmother Valleau; the other half had been used by Germain to build a strictly identical house just 300 meters from the Seugne river. A graceless little stream, though much loved by local fishermen who enjoy hunting for slimy eels that I just find totally disgusting.

But back to our story, which is no less slimy. I was telling you about my mother: she was something of a tart, and my father and uncle had never quite managed to agree what their respective relationships were with such an openly sensual and versatile woman. Do you get my point? There were strong doubts amongst the family as to who was actually responsible for the much-awaited pregnancy, which had suffered long delays sometimes attributed to the sterility of Josyane Valleau's husband, Maurice, who was still deeply jealous of his brother despite the outcome of the duel that had opposed them over the body of my mother. In my solitude, I had already often noticed how she personally enjoyed keeping the fires burning between the two Valleau brothers, with a look here or a word there to keep the situation tense.

So we come to 1986, and the sudden storm that was about to make the Tarsay hamlet the very epicentre of a malevolent earthquake that the region still hasn't recovered from. I am referring to my death by strangulation, followed by my night-time immersion which rapidly bloated my floating body to horrifying proportions, a sight for sore eyes for the few passers-by who managed to bypass the cops and feast on the spectacle. I once even

witnessed for myself, leafing through a book published shortly
after the case, perusing the only photograph ever published of
my battered body.

The prosecuting judge in charge of the case soon attracted
attention to himself, "put himself on display" as grandmother
Valleau put it, a loud and ferocious woman who would become
the family spokesperson in front of the press – a gaggle of
hysterical, vulgar and even louder than her Parisian journalists.
Roger Dupin, a small-minded bourgeois with an exaggerated
sense of his self-importance, thought my uncle was the killer,
listening as he did to all those venomous local tongues hidden
behind falsely contrite features. In all the affray that followed the
announcement of the imminent arrest of Germain, my father
even attempted to shoot him with a rifle, which didn't make
the situation any better. Papa was also arrested and imprisoned
in Saintes, and newspaper speculation continued, fed daily by
so-called revelations from sources allegedly close to the Valleau
family, in truth folk who were mistaking their desires for reality.

Even though I'd survived this unjust and absurd death, I was
naturally unaware of what was happening all around me. I was
still only a small child, relatively innocent, but then I knew no
better!

If you're about to tell me that my story makes no sense, just
hold your fire. How could I have died – and in such a horrific
manner – and kept on living no doubt in a dream from purgatory,
observing life on earth and the terrible consequences of my
drowning from high on above? As you well know, soon it was my
mother who was accused of my murder, and who was poisoned
on a cold desolate day in March, after a crazy female novelist
from Paris, here to report on the case for a left-wing newspaper,
had conjured up dreadful accusations against her: "Don't go
looking too far afield; it's the mother who drowned him!" In the
meantime, a second prosecuting judge had taken over from the
one who almost got my uncle killed.

It took only a few weeks for poor little Tony's legend to be
forged, blending often contradictory facts and theories – or should
I say woolly unfounded speculations – haphazardly constructed
by journalists and other so-called criminal experts. One of them,
an Englishman called Peter Grale, had arrived on the scene very
early in the day, with a view to investigating matters discreetly

on his own behalf. Six months following the affair, he published a book in London called *Killing to Survive*, in which he cleverly developed the theory that a family plot was responsible for my death, my poor innocent soul having been sacrificed on the altar of rage and the incapacity of the members of the Valleau clan to resolve their hopelessly entangled psychological problems without resort to blood. The person I now live with translated the book, which was never published in French, for me word for word a few months ago, which is probably why I was motivated to begin this short tale; although I know that in the future I might provide further revelations on the whole affair.

I must confess that I have long been solidly sheltered by her, and she now means the world to me. To the extent that it was only after reading the Peter Grale book that I truly came to understand the complexity of the tragedy that took place in the Tarzay hamlet in 1986. Of course, the Englishman never knew the truth, but he got very close to it, which has quietly comforted my friend and I.

This truth that I am now about to reveal to you, as only I could truly know it, the miscellany of facts I could not be aware of having been reported to me by my friend in question, who happened to be a privileged observer of what took place in 1986.

First of all, may I apologise to you for all this fairytale trickery about my "death" and ensuing "survival". Of course, it wasn't actually my body which was recovered from the waters of the Seugne, but that of a nameless child, my very own twin brother, brought up in a broom cupboard by my mother – our unworthy mother. And he was truly nameless, because the poor soul my parents referred to for three long years as "zozo" had never been baptised and almost never left the small room where he was being held. It might appear bizarre that no other family member was ever aware of the existence of my blood brother, but that was truly the case. The alleged bike accident that happened to the midwife was in all likelihood the second crime committed by my parents, united as they were by an insane desire to eliminate the only witness to our two births.

I have come to understand that for the conflicted couple formed by Josyane and my father, "zozo" was like a curse, the end result of the love of my mother for Germain. For them, he was more than an illegitimate son, the living proof of an unforgivable sin and had to be kept hidden. Was Germain aware? Most likely he was, but then he was himself a male Valleau, no more than a kid formed by the twisted morality of the clan, led by the angry matriarch that grandmother Valleau was. The sacrifice of "zozo" was just the stepping stone to a mighty drama which my parents, marginalized and naive as they were, could never get to grips with. Nonetheless, they kept their burdensome secret, and bravely resisting all interrogations, they accepted their brief sojourns in prison as a necessary evil.

But what became of me, you no doubt ask. Well, Josyane had thought of everything. Barely one hour before the terrible deed was committed – both my parents were closely involved: one had strangled "zozo", the other had drowned him – I was taken to the house of madame Duchemin, which my mother had the key to. Needless to say, the notary's widow was in on the plot. To the extent that . . . and allow me a moment to catch my breath before I break the news to you . . . I am still today living with her and have never wanted to leave.

Alice Duchemin is only seventy-two, and she assures me she doesn't look her age. We are in love, Alice and I, and I clearly intend to look after her, much as she so affectionately did with me for such a long time, for which I can never thank her enough. I, small Tony Valleau whom everyone thought was dead and whose supposed death created such a torrent of ink.

I will not tell you more about our love – you have no doubt read Colette's *Le Blé en Herbe* or seen the marvellous *Harold and Maude*, a movie I never tire of watching on video.

A couple of days after the "tragedy", Alice and I left her house and travelled to the flat she owns in Biarritz, and it was there, in the old-fashioned atmosphere of a city which is still synonymous with happiness for me, that I grew up, watching the fury of the incoming ocean waves, tucked in every single night by the most loving person I had ever known since my birth.

We only returned to the large grey-stoned house and its slate roof and tall metal gables when I was twelve years old. By then, who could have recognized the thin and gracious adolescent Alice introduced as her grandson Adrien, as the long believed dead Tony Valleau? And so, my singular life continued, in a spacious room overlooking the marshes and the Seugne river, and in the well-appointed library of the widow Duchemin, whom most people in the region considered to be just an amiable eccentric.

My mother no longer came to clean the Erables house, which surprised no one.

I am now in my twentieth year, and Alice and I will soon be leaving the house in Tarzay for Bordeaux where I shall begin a more orthodox education. However, I don't feel in any way deprived or lacking in knowledge, as Alice has always been particularly cultured, keen on literature and many other disciplines. Before she met Edouard Duchemin and wed him only to find themselves childless, she had obtained a degree in literature and another in history back in Paris. With the help of the immense wealth accumulated by her husband, she firmly intends to make a complete man of me.

Which will definitely be a first in my family.

Translation by Maxim Jakubowski

Table Talk, 1882

Boris Akunin

After the coffee and liqueurs, the conversation turned to mystery.

Deliberately not looking at her new guest – a collegiate assessor and the season's most fashionable man – Lidia Nikolaevna Odintsova, hostess of the salon, remarked, "All Moscow is saying Bismarck must have poisoned poor Skobelev. Can it really be that society is to remain ignorant of the truth behind this horrible tragedy?"

The guest to whom Lidia Nikolaevna was treating her regulars today was Erast Petrovich Fandorin. He was maddeningly handsome, cloaked in an aura of mystery, and a bachelor besides. In order to inveigle Erast Petrovich into her salon, the hostess had had to bring off an extremely complex intrigue consisting of many parts – an undertaking at which she was an unsurpassed mistress.

Her sally was addressed to Arkhip Giatsintovich Mustafin, an old friend of the house. A man of fine mind, Mustafin caught Lidia Nikolaevna's intention at the first hint and, casting a sideways glance at the young collegiate assessor from beneath his ruddy and lashless eyelids, intoned, "Ah, but I've been told our White General may have been destroyed by a fatal passion."

The others at the table held their breath, as it was rumored that Erast Petrovich, who until quite recently had served in the office of Moscow's Governor-General as an officer for special missions, had had a most direct relation to the investigation into events surrounding the death of the great commander. However, disappointment awaited the guests, for the handsome Fandorin listened politely to Arkhip Giatsintovich with an air suggesting that the words had nothing whatever to do with him.

This brought about the one situation that an experienced hostess could not permit – an awkward silence. Lidia Nikolaevna knew immediately what to do. Lowering her eyelids, she came to Mustafin's assistance. "This is so very like the mysterious disappearance of poor Polinka Karakina! Surely you recall that dreadful story, my friend?"

"How could I not?" Arkhip drawled, indicating his gratitude with a quick lift of an eyebrow.

Some of the party nodded as if also remembering, but most of the guests clearly knew nothing about Polinka Karakina. In addition, Mustafin had a reputation as a most exquisite raconteur, such that it would be no penance to hear even a familiar tale from his lips. So here Molly Sapegina, a charming young woman whose husband – such a tragedy – had been killed in Turkestan a year ago, asked with curiosity, "A mysterious disappearance? How interesting!"

Lidia Nikolaevna made as if to accommodate herself to her chair more comfortably, so also letting Mustafin know that she was passing nourishment of the table talk into his capable hands.

"Many of us, of course, still recall old Prince Lev Lvovich Karakin," – so Arkhip Giatsintovich began his tale. "He was a man of the old sort, a hero of the Hungarian campaign. He had no taste for the liberal vagaries of our late Tsar, and so retired to his lands outside Moscow, where he lived like a nabob of Hindi. He was fabulously wealthy, of an estate no longer found among the aristocracy of today.

"The prince had two daughters, Polinka and Anyuta. I beg you to note, no Frenchified *Pauline* or English *Annie*. The general held the very strictest of patriotic views. The girls were twins. Face, figure, voice, all were identical. They were not to be confused, however, for right here, on her right cheek, Anyuta had a birthmark. Lev Lvovich's wife had died in childbirth, and the prince did not marry again. He always said that it was a lot of fuss and he had no need – after all, there was no shortage of serving girls. And indeed, he had no shortage of serving girls, even after the emancipation. For, as I said, Lev Lvovich lived the life of a true nabob."

"For shame, Archie! Without vulgarity, if you please," Lidia Nikolaevna remonstrated with a stern smile, although she knew perfectly well that a good story is never hurt by "adding a little pepper," as the English say.

Mustafin pressed his palm to his breast in apology, then continued his tale. "Polinka and Anyuta were far from being horrors, but it would also be difficult to call them great beauties. However, as we all know, a dowry of millions is the best of cosmetics, so that in the season when they debuted, they produced something like a fever epidemic among the eligible bachelors of Moscow. But then the old prince took some sort of offense at our honored Governor-General and withdrew to his piney Sosnovka, never to leave the place again.

"Lev Lvovich was a heavyset fellow, short-winded and red-faced, a man prone to apoplexy, as they say, so there was reason to hope that the princesses' imprisonment would not last long. However, the years went on, Prince Karakin grew ever fatter, flying into ever more thunderous rages, and evinced no intention whatsoever of dying. The suitors waited and waited and in the end quite forgot about the poor prisoners.

"Although it was said to be in the Moscow region, Sosnovka was in fact in the deep forests of Zaraisky district, not only nowhere near the railroad, but a good twenty versts even from the nearest well-traveled road. The wilderness, in a word. To be sure, it was a heavenly place, and excellently established. I have a little village nearby, so that I often called on the prince as a neighbor. The black grouse shooting there is exquisite, but that spring especially the birds seemed to fly right into one's sights – I've never seen the like in all my days. So, in the end, I became a habitué of the house, which is why the entire tale unfolded right before my eyes.

"The old prince had been trying for some time to construct a belvedere in his park, in the Viennese style. He had first hired a famous architect from Moscow, who had drawn up the plans and even started the construction, but then didn't finish it – he could not endure the prince's bullheaded whims and so had departed. To finish the work they summoned an architect of somewhat lower flight, a Frenchman named Renar. Young, and rather handsome. True, he was noticeably lame, but since Lord Byron our young ladies have never counted this as a defect.

"What happened next you can imagine for yourselves. The two maidens had been sitting in the country for a decade now, never once getting out. They both were twenty-eight years old, with absolutely no society of any sort, save for the arrival of the odd fuddy-duddy such as myself, come to hunt. And suddenly – a handsome young man of lively mind, and from Paris at that.

"I have to say that, for all their outward similarity, the two princesses were of totally different temperament and spiritual cast. Anyuta was like Pushkin's Tatyana, prone to lassitude, a touch melancholic, a little pedantic, and, to be blunt, a bit tedious. As for Polinka, she was frolicsome, mischievous, 'simple as a poet's life, sweet as a lover's kiss', as the poet has it. And she was far less settled into old-maidish ways.

"Renar lived there a bit, had a look around, and, naturally enough, set his cap at Polinka. I watched all this from the sidelines, rejoicing greatly, and of course not once suspecting the incredible way in which this pastoral idyll would end. Polinka besotted by love, the Frenchie giddy with the whiff of millions, and Anyuta smoldering with jealousy, forced to assume the role of vessel of common sense. I confess that I enjoyed watching this comedy at least as much as I did the mating dance of the black grouse. The noble father, of course, continued to be oblivious of all this, because he was arrogant and unable to imagine that a Princess Karakina might feel attracted to some lowly sort of architect.

"It all ended in scandal, of course. One evening Anyuta chanced ... or perhaps there was nothing of chance about it ... Anyuta glanced into a little house in the garden, found her sister and Renar there in flagrante delicto, and immediately informed their father. Wrathful Lev Lvovich, who escaped apoplexy only by a miracle, wanted to drive the offender from his estate immediately. The Frenchman was able only with the greatest difficulty to plead to be allowed to remain at the estate until the morning, for the forests around Sosnovka were such that a solitary night traveler could well be eaten by wolves. Had I not intervened, the malefactor would have been turned out of the gates dressed in nothing but his frock coat.

"The sobbing Polinka was sent to her bedroom under the eye of her prudent sister, the architect was sent to his room in one of the wings to pack his suitcase, the servants scattered, and the full brunt of the prince's wrath came to be borne precisely by your humble servant. Lev Lvovich raged almost until dawn, wearing me out entirely, so that I scarcely slept that night. Nevertheless, in the morning I saw from the window how the Frenchman was hauled off to the station in a plain flat farm cart. Poor fellow, he kept looking up to the windows, but clearly there was no one waving him farewell, or so his terribly droopy look seemed to say.

"Then marvels began to occur. The princesses did not appear for breakfast. Their bedroom door was locked, and there was no response to knocks. The prince began to boil again, showing signs of an inevitable apoplexy. He gave orders to splinter the door, and devil take the hindmost. Which was done, everyone rushed in, and . . . Good heavens! Anyuta lay in her bed, as if in deepest sleep, while there was no sign of Polinka whatsoever. She had vanished. She wasn't in the house, she wasn't in the park . . . it was as if she had slipped down through the very earth.

"No matter how hard they tried to wake Anyuta, it was to no avail. The family doctor, who had lived there on the estate, had died not long before, and no new one had yet been hired. Thus they had to send to the district hospital. The government doctor came, one of those long-haired fellows. He poked her, he squeezed her, and then he said she was suffering from a most serious nervous disorder. Leave her lie, and she would awake.

"The carter who had hauled off the Frenchman returned. He was a faithful man, his whole life spent at the estate. He swore to heaven that he had carted Renar right to the station and put him on the train. The young gentle-lady had not been with him. And anyway, how could she have gotten past the gate? The park at Sosnovka was surrounded by a high stone wall, and there was a guard at the gate.

"Anyuta did wake the following day, but there was no getting anything from her. She had lost the ability to speak. All she could do was weep, tremble, and rattle her teeth. After a week she began to speak a little, but she remembered nothing of that night. If she were pressed with questions, she would immediately begin to shudder and convulse. The doctor forbade such questions in the very strictest terms, saying that it endangered her life.

"So Polinka had vanished. The prince lost his mind utterly. He wrote repeatedly to the governor and even to the Tsar himself. He roused the police. He had Renar followed in Moscow – but it was all for naught. The Frenchman labored away, trying to find clients, but to no avail – nobody wanted a quarrel with Karakin. So the poor fellow left for his native Paris. Even so, Lev Lvovich continued to rage. He got it into his head that the villain had killed his beloved Polinka and buried her somewhere. He had the whole park dug up, and the pond drained, killing all his priceless carp. Nothing. A month passed, and the apoplexy finally came. The prince sat down to dinner, gave out a sudden wheeze, and *plop!* Facedown in his soup bowl. And no wonder, really, after suffering so much.

"After that night it wasn't so much that Anyuta was touched in the head as that her character was markedly changed. Even before, she hadn't been noted for any particular gaiety, but now she would scarcely even open her mouth. The slightest sound would set her atremble. I confess, sinner that I am, that I am no great lover of tragedy. I fled from Sosnovka while the prince was still alive. When I came for the funeral, saints above, the estate was changed beyond recognition. The place had become dreadful, as if some raven had folded its black wing over it. I looked about and I remember thinking, *This place is going to be abandoned*. And so it came to be.

"Anyuta, the sole heir, had no desire to live there and so she went away. Not to Moscow, either, or some place in Europe, but to the very ends of the earth. The estate manager sends her money to Brazil, in Rio de Janeiro. I checked on a globe to find that Rio is absolutely on the other side of the world from Sosnovka. Just think – Brazil! Not a Russian face to be seen anywhere!" Arkhip Giatsintovich ended his strange tale with a sigh.

"Why do you say that? I have an acquaintance in Brazil, a former c-colleague of mine in the Japanese embassy, Karl Ivanovich Veber," Erast Petrovich Fandorin murmured thoughtfully, having listened to the story with interest. The officer for special missions had a soft and pleasant manner of speaking, in no way spoiled by his slight stammer. "Veber is an envoy to the Brazilian emperor D-Don Pedro now. So it's hardly the end of the earth."

"Is that so?" Arkhip Giatsintovich turned animatedly. "So perhaps this mystery might yet be solved? Ah, my dear Erast Petrovich, people say that you have a brilliant analytic mind, that you can crack mysteries of all sorts, like so many walnuts. Now here's a problem for you that doesn't seem to have a logical solution. On the one hand, Polinka Karakina vanished from the estate – that's a fact. On the other hand, there's no way she could have gotten out of the garden, and that's also a fact."

"Yes, yes," several of the ladies started at once, "Mr Fandorin, Erast Petrovich, we so terribly want to know what really happened there!"

"I'm prepared to make a wager that Erast Petrovich will be able to resolve this paradox quite easily," the hostess Odintsova announced with confidence.

"A wager?" Mustafin inquired immediately. "And what are you willing to wager?"

It must be explained that both Lidia Nikolaevna and Arkhip Giatsintovich were avid gamblers whose passion for making wagers sometimes approached lunacy. The more insightful of the guests glanced at one another, suspicious that this entire interlude, with a tale supposedly recalled solely by chance, had been staged by prior agreement, and that the young official had fallen victim to a clever intrigue.

"I quite like that little Bouchet of yours," Arkhip Giatsintovich said with a slight bow.

"And I your large Caravaggio," the hostess answered him in the same tone of voice.

Mustafin simply rocked his head a bit, as if admiring Odintsova's voracious appetite, but said nothing. Apparently he had no qualms about victory. Or, perhaps, the stakes had already been decided between them in advance.

A bit startled at such swiftness, Erast Petrovich spread his hands. "But I have not visited the site of the event, and I have never seen the p-participants. As I recall, even having all the necessary information, the police were not able to do anything. So what am I to do now? And it's probably been quite some time as well, I imagine."

"Six years this October," came the answer.

"W-well then, you see . . ."

"Dear, wonderful Erast Petrovich," the hostess implored, "don't ruin me utterly. I've already agreed to this extortionist's terms. He'll simply take my Bouchet and be gone! That gentleman has not the slightest drop of chivalry in him!"

"My ancestors were Tartar *murza*, warlords!" Arkhip Giatsintovich confirmed gaily. "We in the Horde keep our chat with the ladies short."

However, chivalry was far from an empty word for Fandorin, apparently. The young man rubbed the bridge of his nose with a finger and muttered, "Well, so that's how it is . . . Well, Mr Mustafin, you . . . you didn't chance to notice, did you, what kind of bag the Frenchman had? You did see him leave, you said. So probably there was some large kind of trunk?"

Arkhip Giatsintovich made as if to applaud. "Bravo! He hid the girl in the trunk and carted her off? And Polinka gave the meddlesome sister something nasty to drink, which is why Anyuta collapsed into nervous disorder? Clever. But alas . . . There was no trunk. The Frenchman flew off as light as an eagle. I remember some small suitcases of some sort, some bundles, a couple of hatboxes. No, my good sir, your explanation simply won't wash."

Fandorin thought a bit, then asked, "You are quite sure that the princess could not have won the guards to her side, or perhaps just bribed them?"

"Absolutely. That was the first thing the police checked."

Strangely, at these words the collegiate assessor suddenly became very gloomy and sighed, then said, "Then your tale is much nastier than I had thought." Then, after a long pause, he said. "Tell me, did the prince's house have plumbing?"

"Plumbing? In the countryside?" Molly Sapegina asked in astonishment, then giggled uncertainly, having decided that the handsome official was joking. However, Arkhip Giatsintovich screwed his gold-rimmed monocle into one eye and looked at Fandorin extremely attentively, as if he had only just properly noticed him. "How did you guess that? As it happens, there *was* plumbing at the estate. A year before the events that I have described, the prince had ordered the construction of a pumping station and a boiler room. Lev Lvovich, the princesses, and the guest rooms all had quite proper bathrooms. But what does that have to do with the business at hand?"

"I think that your p-paradox is resolved." Fandorin rocked his head. "The resolution, though, is awfully unpleasant."

"But how? Resolved by what? What happened?" Questions came from all sides.

"I'll tell you in a moment. But first, Lidia Nikolaevna, I would like to give your lackey a certain assignment."

With all present completely entranced, the collegiate assessor then wrote a little note of some sort, handed it to the lackey, and whispered something quietly into the man's ear. The clock on the mantel chimed midnight, but no one had the slightest thought of leaving. All held their breath and waited, but Erast Petrovich was in no hurry to begin this demonstration of his analytic gifts. Bursting with pride at her faultless intuition, which once again had served her well in her choice of a main guest, Lidia Nikolaevna looked at the young man with almost maternal tenderness. This officer of special missions had every chance of becoming a true star of her salon. Which would make Katie Polotskaya and Lily Yepanchina green with envy, to be sure!

"The story you shared with us is not so much mysterious as disgusting," the collegiate assessor finally said with a grimace. "One of the most monstrous crimes of passion about which I have ever had occasion to hear. This is no disappearance. It is a murder, of the very worst, Cain-like sort."

"Are you meaning to say that the gay sister was killed by the melancholy sister?" inquired Sergey Ilyich von Taube, chairman of the Excise Chamber.

"No, I wish to say something quite the opposite – gay Polinka killed melancholy Anyuta. And that is not the most night-marish aspect."

"I do beg your pardon! How can that be?" Sergey Ilyich asked in astonishment, while Lidia Nikolaevna thought it necessary to note, "And what might be more nightmarish than the murder of one's own sister?"

Fandorin rose and began to pace about the sitting room. "I will try to reconstruct the sequence of events, as I understand them. So, we have two p-princesses, withering with boredom. Life dribbling through their fingertips – indeed, all but dribbled away. Their feminine life, I mean. Idleness. Moldering spiritual powers. Unrealized hopes. Tormenting relations with their high-handed father. And, not least, physiological frustration. They were, after all, young, healthy women. Oops, please forgive me. . . ."

Conscious that he had said something untoward, the collegiate assessor was embarrassed for a moment, but Lidia Nikolaevna let it pass without a reprimand – he looked so appealing with that blush that suddenly had blossomed on his white cheeks.

"I would not even dare to imagine how much there is intertwined in the soul of a young w-woman who might be in such a situation," Fandorin said after a short silence. "And here is something particular besides – right there, always, is your living mirror image, your twin sister. No doubt it would be impossible for there not to be a most intricate mix of love and hatred between them. And suddenly a young handsome man appears. He demonstrates obvious interest in the young princesses. No doubt with ulterior motive, but which of those girls would have thought of that? Of course, an inevitable rivalry springs up between the girls, but the ch-choice is quickly made. Until that moment everything between Anyuta and Polinka was identical, but now they were in quite different worlds. One of them is happy, returned to the land of the living and, at least to all appearances, loved. While the other feels herself rejected, lonely, and thus doubly unhappy. Happy love is egoistical. For Polinka, no doubt, there was nothing other than the passions that had built up through the long years of being locked away. This was the full and real life that she had dreamed about for so many years, the life she had even stopped hoping for. And then it was all shredded in an instant – indeed, precisely at the moment when love had reached its very highest peak."

The ladies all listened spellbound to the empathetic speech of this picture-perfect young man of beauty, all save for Molly Sapegina, who pressed her slender fingers to her décolletage before freezing in that pose.

"Most dreadful of all was that the agent of this tragedy was one's very own sister. We may agree, of course, to understand her as well. To endure such happiness right alongside one's own unhappiness would require a particular cast of the spirit which Anyuta obviously did not possess. So Polinka, who had only just been lounging in the bowers of Paradise, was cast utterly down. There is no beast in this world more dangerous than a woman deprived of her beloved!" Erast Petrovich exclaimed, a tad carried away, and then immediately grew a bit muddled, since this sentiment might offend the fairer half among those present. However, there came no protests – all were greedily waiting for the story to continue, so Fandorin went on more briskly, "So then, under the influence of despair, Polinka has a mad plan, a terrible, monstrous plan, but one that is testament to the enormous power of feeling. Although, I don't know, the plan might have come from Renar. It was the girl who had to put the plan into action, however ... That night, while you, Arkhip Giatsintovich, were nodding drowsily and listening to your host pour out his rage, a hellish act was taking place in the bedroom of the princesses. Polinka murdered her sister. I do not know how. Perhaps she smothered her with a pillow, perhaps she poisoned her, but in any event, it occurred without blood, for otherwise there would have remained some trace in the bedroom."

"The investigation considered the possibility of a murder." Mustafin shrugged, having listened to Erast Petrovich with unconcealed scepticism. "However, there arose a rather sensible question – what happened to the body?"

The officer of special missions answered without a moment's hesitation, "That's the nightmarish part. After killing her sister, Polinka dragged her into the bathroom, where she cut her into bits and washed the blood away down the drain. The Frenchman could not have been the one to dismember her – there is no way he could have left his own wing for such a long time without being noticed."

Waiting out a true storm of alarmed exclamations, in which "Impossible!" was the word most often heard, Fandorin said sadly, "Unfortunately, there is no other possibility. There is no other solution to the p-problem as p-posed. It is better not even to attempt to imagine what went on that night in that bathroom. Polinka would not have had the slightest knowledge of anatomy, nor could she have had any instrument more to the purpose than a pilfered kitchen knife."

"But there's no way she could have put the body parts and bones down the drain, it would have plugged!" Mustafin exclaimed with a heat quite unlike him.

"No, she could not. The dismembered flesh left the estate in the Frenchman's various suitcases and hatboxes. Tell me, please, were the bedroom windows high off the ground?"

Arkhip Giatsintovich squinted as he tried to recall. "Not especially. The height of a man, perhaps. And the windows looked out on the park, in the direction of the lawn."

"So, the remains were passed through the w-window, then. Judging by the fact that there were no traces left on the window sill, Renar passed some kind of vessel into the room, Anyuta took it into the bathroom, put the body parts in there, and handed these to her accomplice. When this evil ferrying was done all Polinka had to do was scour out the bathtub and clean the blood from herself . . ."

Lidia Nikolaevna desperately wanted to win her bet, but in the interests of fairness she could not remain silent. "Erast Petrovich, this all fits together very well, with the exception of one circumstance. If Polinka indeed committed so monstrous an operation, she certainly would have stained her clothing, and blood is not so simple to wash away, especially if one is not a washerwoman."

This note of practicality did not so much puzzle Fandorin as embarrass him. Coughing slightly and looking away, he said quietly, "I im-imagine that before she began dismembering the b-body, the princess removed her clothing. All of it . . ."

Some of the ladies gasped, while Molly Sapegina, growing pale, murmured, "Oh, *mon Dieu . . .*"

Erast Petrovich, it seemed, was frightened that someone might faint, so he hastened to finish, now in a dry tone of scientific detachment. "It is entirely probable that the extended oblivion of the supposed Anyuta was no simulation, but rather was a natural psychological reaction to a terrible tr-trauma."

Everyone suddenly began speaking at once. "But it wasn't Anyuta that disappeared, it was Polinka!" Sergey Ilyich recalled.

"Well, obviously that was just Polinka drawing a mole on her cheek," the more imaginative Lidia Nikolaevna explained impatiently. "That's why everyone thought she was Anyuta!"

Retired court doctor Stupitsyn did not agree. "Impossible! People close to them are able to distinguish twins quite well. The way they act, the nuances of the voice, the expressions of their eyes, after all!"

"And anyway, why was such a switch necessary?" General Liprandi interrupted the court doctor. "Why would Polinka have to pretend that she was Anyuta?"

Erast Petrovich waited until the flood of questions and objections ebbed, and then answered them one by one. "Had Anyuta disappeared, Your Excellency, then suspicion would inevitably have fallen on Polinka, that she had taken her revenge upon her sister, and so the search for traces of the murder would have been more painstaking. That's one thing. Had the besotted girl vanished at the same time as the Frenchman, this would have brought to the forefront the theory that this was a flight, not a crime. That's two. And then, of course, in the guise of Anyuta, at some time in the future she might marry Renar without giving herself away. Apparently that is precisely what happened in faraway Rio de Janeiro. I am certain that Polinka traveled so far from her native land in order to join the object of her affections in peace." The collegiate assessor turned to the court doctor. "Your argument that intimates are able to distinguish twins is entirely reasonable. Note, however, that the Karakins' family doctor, whom it would have been impossible to deceive, had died not long before. And besides, the supposed Anyuta changed most decidedly after that fateful night, precisely as if she had become someone else. In view of the particular circumstances, everyone took that as natural. In fact, this transformation occurred with Polinka, but is it to be wondered at that she lost her former animation and gaiety?"

"And the death of the old prince?" Sergey Ilyich asked. "Wasn't that awfully convenient for the criminal?"

"A most suspicious death," agreed Fandorin. "It is entirely possible that poison may have been involved. There was no autopsy, of course – his sudden demise was attributed to paternal grief and a disposition to apoplexy, but at the same time it is entirely possible that after a night such as that, a trifle like poisoning one's own father would not much bother Polinka. By the way, it would not be too late to conduct an exhumation even now. Poison is preserved a long while in the bone tissue."

"I'll bet that the prince was poisoned," Lidia Nikolaevna said quickly, turning to Arkhip Giatsintovich, who pretended that he had not heard.

"An inventive theory. And clever, too," Mustafin said at length. "However, one must have an exceedingly active imagination to picture Princess Karakina carving up the body of her own sister with a bread knife while dressed in the garb of Eve."

Everyone again began speaking at once, defending both points of view with equal ardor, although the ladies inclined to Fandorin's version of events, while the gentlemen rejected it as improbable. The cause of the argument took no part in the discussion himself, although he listened to the points of both sides with interest.

"Oh, but why are you remaining silent?!" Lidia Nikolaevna called to him, as she pointed at Mustafin. "Clearly, he is arguing against something perfectly obvious simply in order not to give up his stake. Tell him, say something else that will force him into silence!"

"I am waiting for your Matvey to return," Erast Petrovich replied tersely.

"But where did you send him?"

"To the Governor-General's staff headquarters. The telegraph office there is open around the clock."

"But that's on Tverskoy Boulevard, five minutes' walk from here, and he's been gone more than an hour!" someone wondered.

"Matvey was ordered to wait for the reply," the officer of special missions explained, then again fell silent while Arkhip Giatsintovich held everyone's attention with an expansive explanation of the ways in which Fandorin's theory was completely impossible from the viewpoint of female psychology.

Just at the most effective moment, as Mustafin was holding forth most convincingly about the innate properties of the feminine nature, which is ashamed of nudity and cannot endure the sight of blood, the door quietly opened and the long-awaited Matvey entered. Treading silently, he approached the collegiate assessor and, with a bow, proffered a sheet of paper.

Erast Petrovich turned, read the note, then nodded. The hostess, who had been watching the young man's face attentively, could not endure to wait any longer, and so moved her chair closer to her guest. "Well, what's there?" she whispered.

"I was right," Fandorin answered, also in a whisper.

That instant Odintsova interrupted the lecture. "Enough nonsense, Arkhip Giatsintovich! What do you know of the feminine nature, you who have never even been married! Erast Petrovich has incontrovertible proof!" She took the telegram from the collegiate assessor's hand and passed it around the circle.

Flabbergasted, the guests read the telegram, which consisted of three words:

"Yes. Yes. No."

"And that's it? What is this? Where is it from?" Such were the general questions.

"The telegram was sent from the Russian mission in Br-Brazil," Fandorin explained. "You see the diplomatic stamp there? It is deep night here in Moscow, but in Rio de Janeiro right now the mission is in attendance. I was counting on that when I ordered Matvey to wait for a reply. As for the telegram, I recognize the laconic style of Karl Ivanovich Veber. This is how my message read. Matvey, give me the paper, will you? The one I gave you."

Erast Petrovich took the paper from the lackey and read aloud, " 'Karl, old boy, inform me the following soonest: is Russian subject born Princess Anyuta Karakina now resident in Brazil married? If yes, is her husband lame? And does the princess have a mole on her right cheek? I need all this for a bet. Fandorin.' From the answer to the message it is clear that the pr-princess is married to a lame man, and has no mole on her cheek. Why would she need the mole now? In far-off Brazil there is no need to run to such clever tricks. As you see, ladies and gentlemen, Polinka is alive and well, married to her Renar. The terrible tale has an idyllic ending. By the by, the lack of a mole shows once again that Renar was a witting participant in the murder and knows perfectly well that he is married precisely to Polinka, and not to Anyuta."

"So, I shall give orders to fetch the Caravaggio," Odintsova said to Arkhip Giatsintovich with a victorious smile.

Translation by Anthony Olcott

Dead End

Julián Ibáñez

I took the wallet where he kept his papers and ID, and removed twelve banknotes for my pocket. Then I shooed off the flies and put the wallet back.

On the Audi's seats I found clothes and toiletries. No books, maps, or any other papers. Just silk shirts, a dozen pairs of yellow socks, some flashy Italian shoes, badger-hair brushes and cartons of Chester cigarettes.

I returned to the Ford, and drove towards a garden that could be seen in the distance.

After parking in the shade, I went through a gate and pressed the doorbell. A few seconds later I heard a woman's voice:

"Who is it?"

"Someone passing by." I was about to ask for a glass of water, but realized the priority was to inform the Guardia Civil. "Do you have a phone?"

"A telephone? . . . I'm afraid not . . . In the village. We'll send someone. What's it for?"

"Nothing." I then remembered that the Ford's tank was almost empty. "Do you have a car?"

"A car? No, I'm sorry . . . We have horses, though. I'll get one saddled up for you."

I glanced round. It was a modern house with a large, carefully tended garden.

I was about to return to the car when the front door opened. A woman of indefinite age was standing in the frame, very slim, with perfect corkscrew curls and a golden fringe that just brushed the tops of her eyebrows. She was wearing a very thin green dress which looked like silk.

"Is something wrong?"

"Nothing of importance."

I evidently passed muster.

"Would you . . . would you like a cup of tea?"

"A cup of tea?"

"It's just about ready . . . Why don't you come in?" she said, drawing back from the frame. I squared my shoulders, removed the hands from my pockets, and went in. "You don't mind if I serve you myself. The maid's just changing the rooms upstairs."

Nothing was to be heard, and little more to be seen. The temperature in the dim hall was ten degrees cooler.

I followed her in, my fingertips grazing the passage walls. We entered the living room, a faint light filtering in through the slats of the blinds.

"Take a seat, please . . . A little dark?" she said, gesturing towards an armchair. "Make yourself at home."

I sat down. She left the room.

Dusty pictures on the walls; moth-eaten zebra skins on the floor, silver deities on the shelves of a glass display cabinet. A spider web hung above my head.

I stood up. Through a chink in the blinds I could see a truck drawn up on the road. Two men were walking towards the Audi.

She returned with a laden tea tray, and set it on a side table made of pinkish marble.

"Cigarette?"

I reached for my packet, but she stopped me with a gesture.

"Virginia blend?"

". . . Fine . . ." I looked at her. "Chester, by any chance?"

"Chester? Yes, of course."

She proffered a small box made of black wood. I took a cigarette and she did the same, inserting hers into a long marble holder.

For a few minutes we sat there, blowing smoke and sipping tea.

"What do you want from life?" she asked suddenly, sliding her bare foot over the settee's damask surface.

". . . Something like this, I guess. A peaceful chat and a nice quiet smoke."

She smiled, then took a long drag and turning her head blew the smoke into my face. I breathed it in, not quite sure what to think.

She suddenly sat up.

"Excuse me."

She set the holder down in the ashtray, and bumped into a couple of armchairs before disappearing through a door.

I cleaned my nails with a toothpick, then went over to the window. There were now a half dozen cars by the Audi. Three or four Guardias were bent over the corpse. A couple of local farmers were gesturing with their heads in the direction of the house.

On her return, she bumped into the sofa, and a silver-mounted frame came crashing down on a side table. She flopped onto the settee, and I sat down again.

"Fancy a drink?"

I seemed to be wrapped in her fragrant breath.

"Only if you'll join me."

"What would you like?"

". . . Anisette, with a little ice."

"Really?" She looked at me with interest, arching her brows. "What colour do you prefer?"

". . . Yellow."

She gave a snort, and then couldn't stop laughing for a while. When she finally regained control, she shook her head making the corkscrew curls dance, and then pointed to a small bar.

"But if you don't mind . . . *you* can fix the drinks."

I made the drinks and we sat there drinking them. For several minutes she spoke to me about her life as a young girl. She'd drained her glass in one gulp. Then she fell silent. Eventually, she looked at me with moist lips.

". . . Sit down here, by my side . . ."

I drained my glass and picked up hers.

"First let's have another round. I'll give these a rinse."

I went into the kitchen. It was spacious, with copper pans hanging from the walls. I looked for the sink. In the bucket was the knife, over a foot long, for cutting serrano ham. Very sharp. The blade and handle were covered in blood. I put down the glasses, turned on the tap and washed it carefully. After drying it, I put it in a drawer, washed and dried the glasses, and returned to the living room.

She had her eyes closed. Her chin was pointed up at the ceiling.

". . . Sit down here . . ."

I fixed the drinks. The doorbell rang.

"I'll get it," I said.

The bell rang again. I paused in the hall, listening. It rang once more. I waited without moving, until I heard footsteps receding. Then I peeped through the spyhole. Two Guardias and a farmer were walking back towards the road. One of the Guardias turned to look back at the door.

I returned to the living room.

"Who was it?"

"A driver asking for directions."

I handed her one of the glasses, sat down, and took a sip from mine. She did the same.

"Do you know . . . do you know how to play écarté?" she asked.

"I could learn."

". . . Let's have a game before dinner . . . Then we'll go for a stroll . . . I love walking barefoot on the grass."

I put down my drink.

"I'd like to take a shower."

She opened her eyes.

"Oh . . . please excuse me . . . Where are your suitcases?"

"In the car. I'll get them later."

"Yes, do . . . There's a bedroom upstairs . . . You'll find bathrobes and towels . . . Have a cold shower, it's terribly hot."

I went up and had a shower. The bedroom was a mess, bed unmade, wardrobe open and empty. There was nothing but a pair of Italian shoes, men's shoes, on the dressing table, and a message in chalk on the mirror: "Goodbye, darling. The ones you bought me were too big. Enjoy shining them." I put away the shoes and wiped off the message with a damp towel.

I went down to the living room, and found her sitting at the card table with a pack in her hands. She looked relaxed.

"Please have a seat . . . By the way, what's your name?"

"Juan."

"You deal, Juan."

I shuffled and began to deal the cards. After a bit, there was a sound of chiming bells, but by then I was completely immersed in the game.

Translation by Andrew Davies

Die Wanderung

Michael Gregorio

The three men would be executed at dawn the following morning.

After reading out the death sentence, I took off my black cap and slipped the robe from my shoulders, watching as the prisoners were taken away to the cells, waiting while the large crowd filed out of the court-room. My thoughts were heavier than the hanging of a band of feckless Prussian rogues might have justified. I was thinking of an incident which had happened more than twenty years before.

Later that afternoon, I walked home along the dusty lane beneath the city walls. I paused when I reached my own gate. I could hear the voices of my wife and children in the garden at the rear of the house, but I did not go to join them. Nor did I announce that I was home. Instead, I slipped in through the side entrance like a thief, made directly for my study, and locked the door behind me. After taking down the Dutch clock from the mantelpiece, I removed the key which is hidden inside the case, and used it to unlock the bottom drawer of my desk. There I keep the leather-bound diary which accompanied me on the foreign travels of my youth.

I began to search through the pages until I found what I was looking for. It was a brief account of an episode which had taken place in Italy. When I wrote those lines, I was an untried student of jurisprudence, not the seasoned magistrate that I have since become. I had been a witness to a tragic event for which I could find no explanation at the time. And as every investigator knows, where there is no apparent motive for a crime, only the mystery remains. Still, after what I had heard in court that morning, I believed that I might be able to explain the fate of Enrico De Pretis to my own satisfaction.

The first time that I travelled outside East Prussia, I was twenty-three years old. It was the beginning of July, 1792, I had come into my allowance, and European politics had momentarily settled down in the aftermath of the French Revolution. The French had been forced back towards Paris by a united force of Austrians and Prussians; it was possible to travel through the German states. I was young, and I was restless. Despite the violence of my father's opposition, and the subtler persuasion of my mother's tears, I declared one day that I meant to go a-wandering. My plan was hastily devised and badly formed. No one would come with me. My brother, Stefan, was pursuing his short-lived career in the army (he would be dead within a few months). Various friends had expressed the will to join me, but they had not the means to do so. In a fit of stubbornness, I decided that I would go alone. My intention was to travel southwards by public coach, stopping off wherever I wished, continue on through Switzerland (where a paying passenger must walk up the mountains if he goes by public stages), then cross into the Kingdom of Lombardy. There, I would take account of how much money I had spent, and decide how much farther south I might still venture.

I had been frugal in my expenses, and so I pressed on, leaving Milan behind me.

Shortly after noon on 23 October, 1792, having come from Arezzo by way of Cortona, following the rolling wooded hills above the sparkling shores of Trasimeno Lake, the coach deposited me in Corso Vannucci, which is the main thoroughfare of the city of Perugia. All was brilliant light. There was not a shadow to be seen. The sky above my head was cerulean blue. Perugino, the painter after whom the Corso was named, had rendered the Umbrian sky to perfection, as I was soon to understand. I found comfortable lodgings in a *pensione* called *La Rosa*. Which is to say, I was accompanied there.

I was no longer alone.

No traveller ever is alone, unless he chooses to remain aloof. In the coach which carried twelve passengers from Zurich to Milan, I had made the acquaintance of Enrico De Pretis. He was reading the works of Goethe, and I, of course, declared my own fond admiration for the poet. As we were crossing the Alps that night, he suddenly dropped the window-sash and leant right out, intoning a line which was a particular favourite of my own. It is from the well-known passage which begins: "It is night. I am alone, forlorn on the hill of storms."

"Rise moon from behind thy clouds!" he cried. *"Stars of the night, arise!"*

Though the moon and stars refused to emerge at his bidding, Enrico De Pretis and I became firm friends. He was returning home to Rome after having spent three years as an apprentice clockmaker "in the company of prudes and Zwinglians". The city of Zurich, as he described it, "woke up before dawn, and went to bed before sunset". He had never liked the city, or its inhabitants. It was hellishly expensive, he said, though there was nothing on which to spend one's money.

"Except for clocks," he chuckled.

He had a predilection for a paradox.

Having deposited our bags, we wandered around Perugia for the rest of the day, and visited all the most notable sights. I was particularly impressed by the *Scuola del Cambio* where Perugino's sky is always blue, the countryside peaceful and welcoming, and by the ornamental fountain which stands in front of the cathedral of S. Lorenzo. As the evening drew on, the shops were closed, the churches were shut up for the night, and we sat down to dine in a *locanda* called *Il Grifo* – a dish of salted quails and lentils, served with rich red wine. Afterwards, fresh fruit was brought to end the meal. Enrico picked up an apple on the point of his knife, waved it at me and declared with a grin: "Once I have paid for dinner, I'll be eating apples all the way to Gianicolo."

He had a coach ticket which would take him on to Rome, but no remaining cash.

"I'll pay tonight," I offered. "That will be my parting gift."

"Parting?"

As we were travelling down through the Kingdom of Tuscany and into the Papal state of Umbria, I had slowly been coming to a decision. If I travelled any further south – I had set my heart on seeing the ancient ruins of Rome by moonlight – it would be too late in the season for me to safely cross the Alps again.

"Once winter comes," I reasoned, "I'll be obliged to stay in Italy. But if I turn back now, I will be able to travel westwards, perhaps as far as Paris, before I am forced to turn my sights on home again."

Enrico was a warm-hearted soul. "I'll be sad to see you go," he said. "When are you thinking of leaving?"

"Tomorrow morning," I replied. Having made a decision, I act upon it. "I'd have liked to visit the basilica in Assisi, but . . ."

There, *that* was why I had decided to leave without delay. The temptations were endless, I knew myself too well. If I travelled to Assisi and Giotto, I would then be drawn to Pintoricchio in Spello, Benozzo Gozzoli in Montefalco, Filippo Lippi in Spoleto, the spectacular Marmore falls on the River Nera, Orvieto and the Devils of Signorelli, the list kept growing. Three days more of travelling would take me all the way to Rome, and then it would be too late to turn back. I would be obliged to winter there.

"If you have made up your mind," Enrico said, "what can I do to alter it?"

I smiled without answering, but he had not finished.

"When two friends part," he went on, raising his glass, savouring his wine, "likely to see each other never again, they should share some experience, some manifestation of the Sublime, which is known to themselves alone, and to no one else. A bond of friendship, let us call it, which will forever link them in the days and weeks and years to come."

I had to smile. He spoke Swiss-German with a strong Roman inflection. It made everything that he said seem knowing and original.

"And what would you suggest?" I asked.

"I have a little money, thanks to you," he said. "I intend to treat you to a spectacle that you and I may carry in our hearts all the way to the grave."

"Now you insult me," I cut in. "If you would do such a thing for me, why should I not do the same for you? I have money. Not a vast amount, I admit, but I don't suppose you're speaking of a fortune. How much were you thinking of?"

"A tip for the doorkeeper," he said.

"Doorkeeper?"

He smiled, but he would not speak any further.

"What is this spectacle?" I insisted.

"You must wait and see," he replied. "In every place on earth there is a mystery waiting to reveal itself to a receptive soul."

"Here's to mystery!" I said, raising my glass.

Shortly afterwards, I paid the bill and we left the *locanda*.

An unseen bell tolled the half-hour as we began to wind our way through the narrow streets and medieval alleys. Via Gatti, Via Luna, Via Cupa, Piazza Drago. The names were all peculiar. The Street of Cats, Moon Street, Melancholy Lane, Dragon Square, as I translated them. It was very dark, the lamps were few, the lanes stank of cats and dogs, and goodness knows what else. There was a sharp icy wind that night, and I was very glad of it – it carried off the noisome smell – until, at last, we stepped once more onto the broad expanse of the Corso, which was now completely deserted.

"Not long," Enrico said with a grin. "Not far."

"You've been here before, I think."

"On my way to Switzerland I stayed in Perugia for a month," he replied. "I learnt to make pendulums from a craftsman who had his shop in Via della Tartaruga. That's Tortoise Street to you. He took me to see the . . . the place where we are going."

Halfway down the Corso, Enrico De Pretis took off his cap, raised his fist, and knocked on a large double door.

At last, the door swung back, a lantern was held up, a man's dark face stared out at us. "*Sì?*" he asked, suspiciously.

"Offer him money," De Pretis said to me with a wink.

He turned again to the Italian, raised his forefinger and pointed upwards.

The man smiled, nodded, took the coins from my fingers, stepped back, and let us enter a cold, stone vestibule. With a careless wave of his hand, he indicated a broad stone staircase.

"He is our Virgil," Enrico whispered, "we must follow him."

The flights of stairs seemed endless, turning back and forth upon themselves, growing narrower and narrower as we climbed ever upwards. Stone became brick, then brick became wood, the stairs grew steeper, narrower. Underfoot I crushed something soft. By our guardian's light I saw the glinting eye of a dead pigeon, dull feathers, dark blood. And still we climbed.

At last, the man stopped before a small door on a landing. He caught his breath, then turned a key and threw the door open, waving at us to go through it. He put his hands together as if he were grasping an axe, then made a violent movement – up and down, up and down.

"What does he mean?" I asked.

"He has a job to do," Enrico said.

This all sounded very mysterious. And the mystery reverberated in my mind as we stepped out onto a covered terrace. We were standing in the bell-tower of the *Palazzo dei Priori*, which is the tallest, highest building in the whole of the city. The man who had brought us there was the guardian of the bell-tower, whose duty it was to ring the hours and the half-hours throughout the night.

"What a view!" Enrico exclaimed, running between the stone balustrades, looking to all four points of the compass. "You can see the whole of Umbria from here. And by the light of the moon. There is the lake that we passed this morning."

It was exceptionally cold, and I was not heavily dressed.

I looked where he pointed, seeing the effects of the moonlight on the countryside that we had admired earlier that day. Lake Trasimeno was a flat expanse like a large sheet of solid ice. The gentle brown hills of the day were now black waves, fold upon fold of them, like an undulating sea concealing monsters. The sky was pitch-black, limitless, the stars a speckled ceiling of unimaginable profundity.

I felt awed, even frightened, by what I saw.

"Is it not Sublime? he asked.

"It is," I said uncertainly, "the most memorable sight that I have ever . . ."

At that instant, there was a loud creak of wood.

The bell-trees began to groan and shift.

Beneath us the keeper tolled the first of the twelve chimes of midnight.

The tower seemed to quiver with each clang of the hammer against the massive rolling bells. The tolling drilled its way inside my brain, my sight blurred, my ears ached painfully, as stroke followed stroke followed stroke.

Sublime?

Against my will, I turned away and vomited.

Lentils, quails and rich red wine spilled out into the chasm of the night.

Before the twelfth note sounded, I had retired indoors again, pressing my hands to my ears, trying to block out that terrible sound. If Enrico had intended to make that night a memorable one, he had succeeded. But while he was alive with excitement, I felt drained by an anxiety which would not set me free.

"I must go to bed," I said, trying to excuse my strange reaction to the pounding bells. "I am tired out, I suppose. Perhaps it was the food and drink. In any case, tomorrow morning I must leave quite early."

"I will stay a while yet," he said. "I'd like to see the sun come up."

"If you can stand the cold so long," I warned him. I was shivering violently, involuntarily clenching my teeth. "I think I may have caught a chill."

"Until tomorrow morning, then," he said.

I clattered down the stairs, and met the bell-ringer in the lower hall.

I thrust more money into his hand, and said: "*Buona notte, signore.*"

By the time the hour of one was struck, I had entered the *pensione*, claimed my candle from the landlord, climbed the stairs, and was warm inside my narrow bed. I was still awake as the clock struck two, but Enrico did not return. Would he really sit up all night and see the sunrise? I intended to catch the coach for Cesena; it would be leaving at half-past six the following morning. If Enrico De Pretis had returned by then, I would say goodbye. If not, I would remember him as a fine young man who had wished to share an experience with a friend. I had not been the ideal companion for the expedition that he had proposed, I thought ruefully. The harmless, fun-loving Roman clockmaker was a more adventurous Romantic than this faint-hearted Teuton would ever be!

Five minutes more, and I was fast asleep.

I missed the morning coach, but not because I had overslept.

I was wakened by a loud banging at my door.

"Night watch! Open up!"

It was not yet dawn. Three men were standing there with cudgels in their hands. Before I could resist them, they had pushed the door inwards very hard, and carried me along with it. No formal introductions were made. I did not dare to ask who they were as I was pressed against the wall, and a cudgel held in two hands was crushed hard against my windpipe.

"Where were you last night?"

I spoke a little Italian, so I told them.

"Who were you with?"

I answered the question. What had I to hide?

"Enrico De Pretis? Is that his name?"

I nodded.

One of the men was an ex-Papal trooper as I soon learnt, and he spoke German. There were many men like him in Umbria, soldiers who had once been employed by the Pope, men who had stayed when the terms of their service ended. "What time did you see him last? Why did you not wait for him? Was he carrying money in his purse?"

I answered all these questions honestly, then asked a question of my own.

"Where is Enrico? What has he done?"

"He is dead," the Swiss replied. "That's what comes of roistering at night, and in a strange town. If he died in sin," the man said, crossing himself, "he'll be warming up in Hell now."

"Can I see him?"

I did not need to ask, they were going to take me to identify the body.

It was a quick run through the empty town. A stone plaque on the wall identified the building which we entered as the Faculty of Medicine. A note had been pinned to the door which the officers pushed open. "*Dissection – 10 am.*" The large room was built like a theatre-in-the-round without a stage. Rows of pews looked down on a wooden table in what might have been the stalls. And on that table was a naked body. Knives, drills and a selection of surgical saws were laid out beside it on a tray.

"Is this him?"

Enrico's face was as white as snow. His long black hair fell straight back from his brow like a thundering waterfall. A river of blood had drained out from a hole beneath his heart. The wound was a round, black, crusted stain. Clearly, he had bled to death.

"Where was he found?" I asked.

"On the steps of the fountain in the Corso."

"Did no one see what happened?"

"No one."

Later that day, keeping close in my room, condemned to wait until the following morning for the coach which would take me away from the city, I wrote this note in my diary: *Enrico De Pretis, died before dawn on the morning of 24 October, 1792, Perugia, Italy. Murdered. But not by my hand. The authorities are convinced of it.*

My landlord met me coming in at one o'clock, or thereabouts. The bell-ringer of the Palazzo dei Priori let Enrico out at half past three. I had paid for both of us, the man remembered me.

I saw his body. Apart from the fatal wound, he was virtually untouched. The knuckles of his right hand were full of cuts, however, as if he had been holding a sword, fending off another man's attack. But where would Enrico get a sword? He was unarmed when we went out. In conversation he had told me that he would never allow himself to be drawn into a fight. He would rather apologise, right or wrong, and take a beating if he must. He said that he had never held a blade in all of his life.

Who killed him?

Why?

Back home in Ruisling, having spent three months in France, I suppressed my memories of the incident. That is, while my sense of dismay slowly faded away, I was careful not to mention what had happened to my mother or my father. I locked my diary away in a desk-drawer and I hid the key inside the Dutch clock. And when, a short time later, I completed my studies and married my childhood sweetheart, Helena Jordaenssen, I carried the desk, the drawer and key to Lotingen, where I had been appointed as a junior magistrate on the western circuit, making sure that lock and key should never be united. Children came – three, then four, then three again, when Anders died – and all that time, for all those years, the mystery of Enrico De Pretis lay locked inside my desk as safe as any rotting corpse inside a forgotten funeral vault.

Until today . . .

The last Friday of the month is the day of the assizes in Lotingen. Three men were brought before me on a charge, and a strange-sounding charge it was when Knutzen, my clerk, read it out in public. "*That they had all three, and concurrently, murdered Jacob Gregorius, a wandering Jewish pedlar, 37, and the father of six children, with a duelling-rapier.*"

"How," I asked the defendants, "can three men kill with a single rapier?"

I had asked them this question while they were in the gaol, and I knew the answer. But in a public trial for murder, it is important to demonstrate the facts before a sentence can be pronounced and carried out. The principal defendant's name was Dieter Winnig. He had been a lance-corporal in the King's

Own regiment before they drummed him out. Now, he was a scoundrel, a prodigious drinker, a man who never settled his bills or paid his debts, except by challenging his creditors to a duel. Perhaps he thought by telling me the technicalities of the matter, he might get off with a lighter sentence. Whatever the reason, he was prepared to speak before the court. He was the son of a minor aristocrat, it was evident in his manner of speaking, his style of dress, and his evident disdain for what any person there might think of him.

"Winnig, speak up!" I snapped.

He was chubby, turning to fat, his chins doubled up against his collar as he turned to me with a smirk of superior knowledge. "Very well, Herr Procurator Stiffeniis," he began, his eyes two bright pinpricks, "this is how it was. We were in a tavern making no trouble, when a chap called Johann out over a wench . . ."

"Called him out?" I challenged. "Please explain yourself."

"A duel, sir. That man insulted Johann," he pointed to the man beside him in the dock. "Said that Johann had been ogling the fellow's wife. He told him to be waiting in the meadow beyond the West Gate at six o'clock next morning."

"Go on," I said, "and keep it simple."

"As simple as an oath," he swore. "The problem was . . . you see how young he is?"

"How old are you, Johann Goltz?" I asked the other man.

"Nineteen, Herr Magistrate." His voice was thick, drunken, though none of the men had touched a drop in the week that I had kept them in the cells. "I'd never fought a duel before, sir."

"Needed practice, didn't he?" Winnig went on. "Still the worse for drink, he needed warming up. Needed a taste of blood, he did . . ."

"And then the Jewish pedlar came along."

"We didn't know what race he was . . ."

"Regardless of his religion," I opposed, "the man is dead."

"Johann killed him!" Winnig cried, suddenly turning on his friends. "Adam had a sword, he forced that man to take it."

The dock exploded. Fists were thrown, curses were uttered, each man shouting louder than the next, accusing the other two, excusing his own part in the murder.

"It changes nothing," I said. "I intend to sentence all three of you to the gallows. You put the sword in his hand, Adam Schmidt.

You ran him through, Johann Goltz. And you egged them on, Dieter Winnig."

"And wiped the sword clean," one of the other two chipped in.

It had all been for nothing. The other duellist had not appeared for the appointment. He had left town that night, and never been seen again. A father of six had died, and that was that.

As I donned the black cap and passed sentence, my thoughts were far away.

In Perugia, Italy. Twenty years before. With Enrico De Pretis, clockmaker.

I did not know who had killed him, but I had an inkling how he might have died.

Had some Italian duellist needed warming up?

Pot Luck

by Lisa Allen-Agostini

She always left him, wandering off like a cat without provocation or explanation, returning just as suddenly and without comment after a day or a week or a month. He loved her, but it was hard to keep track of where he stood in her life. He kept her clothes neatly stacked in a chest of drawers and hoped for the best.

One day she just didn't come back. He only found out by accident after six weeks that she had actually moved in with another man in his – their – neighborhood. It was a guy he knew well. They had smoked together and that made them friends of a sort. Not very good friends, evidently, as this guy had had no problem taking his woman away.

After that Trey lost his appetite, partly because eating usually meant buying ingredients at the shop at the corner opposite her new home in Diego Martin's mostly working-class suburb of Rich Plain Road. He saw her through the fence sometimes in a tiny pair of white short pants, new ones that she didn't have when she lived with him, hanging kitchen towels out to dry on the lines strung outside. The pants were skintight and he recognized the imprint of her labia through their dense denim folds. The lower curve of her round ass hung just under the frayed hem. Instead of wanting to eat potatoes and corned beef, he'd taste her memory, salty sweet. He grew thin.

Tabanca like that has two cures – new love or exorcism. He chose the latter, only because he saw her in the face of every woman he met and feared that any new partner would also prove fickle and desert him for another man.

Leaving her clothes in the drawers and her compact of cheap brown face powder on the dresser, the only things she had left behind, Trey took off from Diego Martin's close houses and cramped streets and headed north.

Trey pored over the small pile of dark green herb in his left palm. Nimbly, he shredded the sticky, soft leaves and brown flowers hidden in the mass, picking out the polished black seeds and putting them aside. When the mix was cleaned to his satisfaction, he reached into the front pocket of his colorful nylon shorts and extracted a balled-up piece of white paper. This he unfolded into a two-inch square and poured the cleaned herb onto it. Behind his ear was a single cigarette. Trey pulled it from its nesting spot and broke off about half an inch. He sprinkled the tobacco onto the herb on the paper, then placed the end of the cigarette on the smoothed-out sheet. Rolling the herb into the shape of the cigarette, he meticulously straightened the emerging cylinder. When it was perfectly flush, he wrapped the paper around it, put it to his lips, and licked the flap shut.

"Danny!" Trey called to a similarly clad young man lying on the beach in front of him. Danny had dozed off, his long, pencil-thin dreadlocks trailing in the golden sand. The hair was almost as light as the sand itself, in contrast to the owner of the hair who was midnight black. Danny jerked up, only to subside nearly immediately. "Danny," Trey said on an intake, "you want some of this, man?" He extended the joint and held in the smoke to better absorb the THC into his lungs. Danny stretched out his hand and took the cigarette without opening his eyes. He put it to his lips and drew deep. It was his turn to hold in the smoke. As they sucked in the heady marijuana, passing the joint back and forth, the sea roared in the background. "Good stuff," Trey murmured, his eyes reddening and narrowing as the weed took effect.

"Yeah, I get it from a partner in the village. Not the usual suspect," Danny replied. He sat up and looped his waist-length dreadlocks with one hand, tucking them into a knot. He looked over at his cousin, his eyes as red as Trey's. "This man have it sick, horse. Only quality weed he supplying. No compress, only fresh." He took another hit. "I trying to get him to sell me some more but he brakesing. Say the man who he getting it from gone away for a week."

The waves continued to roll up on the sand. Trey's orange surfboard, leaning on the fisherman's shed next to him, cast a

long shadow across his deeply tanned face. His olive skin was
freckled across the bridge of his nose, complemented by his
short, nappy Afro, the color of brown sugar. Full lips curved into
a slight smile as he contemplated the surf. His hand reached out
to lightly caress the board, which was rough with a thick coat of
wax. "You going and hit that again before it reach cigarette?"
he asked Danny, who shook his head and passed it back to him.
Trey nursed the joint until the weed was burned off and passed
the rest of the funk back to Danny. "I ent feeling for no cigarette
right now." They were quiet for a few minutes. "Thinking of
going back." Danny said nothing. "Two months in the jungle is
enough, man." Danny smoked without comment. The murmur
of the waves continued. "I go have to call them men to pick back
up a little end in work."

"Is so you is a work jumbie, boy?" Danny finally replied. "Two
months of surf, weed, and country food, and you ready to go
back in the rat race?" He shook his head again. "Me, I wouldn't
rush back to go and work in no factory assembly line."

"Is not no assembly line," Trey snapped. "I tell you, I is a
technician. Is skilled work, man. And the two months was good,
partner, but is time I go back. I have things to do."

"Like what? Tack back by that slut?" Danny rolled onto his
knees and to his feet.

"Don't talk about she so."

"But she's a slut, Trey. She leave you for your partner. How she
go play you like that?"

Trey's golden eyes, about the color of his skin, gave him a
ghostly appearance. Right now they were cloudy with weed and
budding rage. "She make a mistake, all right? That don't make
she a slut."

Danny sucked his teeth in disgust and grabbed his own board
from the sand. "I heading up the road. Later." He flicked the butt
of the cigarette into the blue ocean. "Tasha real chain you up,
boy," he muttered as he walked up the track leading to the main
road. "If I was you, I would have shoot both of them."

Trey scowled and lit another cigarette from a pack in his
pocket. "Is not Tash, is Garvin. That man is the one who is to
blame," he told his cousin's broad back. Danny wasn't listening,
focused instead on scaling the rocky path without dropping
or dinging his board on the huge stones on either side of the

track. "Is Garvin who pull she in!" Trey swiftly sucked on the cigarette. "Is he, not she. Is he fault."

Danny's blond locks disappeared over the top of the steep path. Trey was left alone with the rocks and the waves, the sand and the fisherman's hut.

Beyond the road, the Sans Souci forest towered, dim and green and forbidding. In two months, Trey had only been in the forest twice, both times with his cousin. They had gone to find a certain spring which Danny swore had the sweetest water in the world, but they had become lost in the undergrowth and never found it. They made do with the chlorinated water piped in by the public utility, but Trey craved the fresh, untreated water of the spring. He stubbed the cigarette out in the sand and rose, grabbing his board and heading toward the forest in bounding strides.

Bareback and barefoot, his lean, muscular body quickly maneuvered the path. His calloused feet barely registered the bumpy pitch of the Toco Road before he was in the cool mulch of the forest. It was rainy season, but the ground wasn't sodden, only damp and spongy with fallen leaves and topsoil. He had no idea where he was going, but with a quick glance around for a landmark, Trey moved into the woods. He passed a giant immortelle tree, a clump of stunted cocoa trees, a dead one stretched across what could have been a track. The gloom deepened as he walked, the trees becoming larger and taller, the ground softer and cooler despite the mid-afternoon heat.

The light changed. It was somehow brighter, more airy. A sloped clearing appeared full of lime-green, leafy shrubs about a head taller than his six feet. "To ras!" he breathed, breaking into the space gingerly and leaving his surfboard behind.

The weed was planted in even rows, smelling pungent, sweet, musky. As far as he could see, marijuana trees were coming into bloom, their small orange flowers just starting to show – plants ripe for the picking. Making his way through the rows, Trey tenderly brushed the leaves and stems. He almost missed the hut in the center of the field, stumbling when he noticed the galvanized steel sheeting that made up its walls and roof. The double gate, also corrugated sheets of steel, bore a heavy iron padlock threaded through a thick steel chain looped into a pair of holes in the gates. The message was clear: *Keep out.* To Trey that was as good as an invitation.

He walked the entire field until his feet were sore and covered in mud. There wasn't a soul in sight. He picked his way back to the galvanized shed and peered through the holes in the gate. It was dark inside and he couldn't see much, just large hanging shapes. The smell, however, was unmistakable – it was exactly the same weed he had just been cleaning. Trey turned and ran for the road, leaving his surfboard behind as a bright orange marker to light his way back to paradise.

Jimmy the maxi-taxi driver was cagey, driving extra slowly on the winding country road. Though a large banner on the back windscreen proclaimed it *Jah Bus*, the real owner was a Christian who wanted no part of Rastafari. A keen businessman, he recognized that popular culture glorified all that was Rasta, from dreadlocks to Bob Marley and marijuana use, so he latched onto the trend to make his business popular. He warned his drivers, the men he hired to work the vehicle on a twenty-four-hour rotation, that he wasn't going to allow weed smoking on the job. What they did in their own time was their affair, but behind the wheel of *Jah Bus* they were to be clean and sober.

It was close to ten and Jimmy, an occasional Rasta, had finished his last trip with only $100 in pocket after oil, gas, and the $300 child maintenance he had to pay his ex-girlfriend every two weeks for their three sons. When Trey and Danny flagged him down and put their unusual proposition to him, Jimmy had been of two minds, thinking about the maxi's owner and the prospect of being out of a job. But the offer of a bonus payment was irresistible. It wasn't every day that someone offered to rent your maxi for five pounds of weed. Though he doubted the resurrection of Haile Selassie I, the late Ethiopian emperor whom Rastas acknowledge as the descendant of Christ, he certainly agreed that smoking weed was an ideal part of livity. Five pounds of it – a whole black bin liner full of the stuff – would keep him high for quite some time.

Trey and Danny directed the driver to a small house on a hill off the main road. It was where Danny lived and where Trey had been hiding out from the world for two months. The house was like most of the others around it, a humble concrete dwelling with a small front porch, a neat garden behind a chain-link fence, and three pot hounds skulking around the yard. "Rambo!" Danny shouted affectionately at the first brown mongrel to reach his feet as he pushed open the rusty gate. Hiding behind a lush ixora was a black bitch, marked like a Doberman pinscher but with none of the grace of the breed, and lounging on the front steps, just below the porch, was a dog that resembled both its parents, half-brown and half-black. Trey shot a warning look at the one behind the bush. Sarah was prone to snapping at strangers and Jimmy was already nervous enough. "Come nah, Princess," Danny was urging the dog on the step, nudging her aside with his foot. "Move and let people pass. You feel this is your house, eh, girl?" Trey stayed in the yard between Jimmy and the growling bitch.

"That is you, Danny?" a woman's voice called from the house. Aunty Zora leaned over the bottom half of the Dutch door leading to the kitchen. Her arms were covered in flour up to the elbows. Jimmy eyed her long salt-and-pepper dread-locks with admiration. "Full some water and bring it for me, nah. This pipe giving trouble again." Trey's maternal aunt glanced at Jimmy with little curiosity. The boys were always bringing friends home. "Good evening," she said mildly before disappearing back into the kitchen.

Danny changed direction, going around the house instead of through the front door. "Give me a minute, man," he tossed over his shoulder as he headed to the kitchen, reemerging in a moment with a plastic pail in each hand. As he filled the buckets at the standpipe outside the kitchen, Jimmy edged closer to Trey.

"So, where the thing?" Jimmy asked, lighting a cigarette and peering around the yard.

"Cool yourself, nah," Trey muttered. "We go handle it. Let the man see about he queen first."

"Scene," Jimmy agreed, swiping his brow with one finger and flicking the stream of sweat off to the side. "What she making?" he asked Trey, sniffing the fragrant air that smelled of vanilla.

"Sweetbread."

"So much'a sweetbread? Is all up by she elbow I see flour. Allyuh have a bakery or what?"

Trey was growing testy. "She does make and sell. Sweetbread, cake, drops. All of that."

"Which part she does sell it?" Jimmy was a talker. Trey was tired of it already.

"In the village there. In the shop."

"Scene," Jimmy nodded. The loaves of sweet coconut bread, full of raisins and cherries, were very popular. Aunty Zora was quite the businesswoman and had placed her products on shelves all up the Toco Road, a string of communities that curved in a rough semicircle around the northeastern tip of Trinidad from Valencia to Matelot. Danny, when he wasn't surfing, delivered the goods in their old beat-up Land Rover.

After their visit to Aunty Zora's, they stopped by the fisherman's hut on the beach to load the maxi to the roof with stuffed black garbage bags. Then they drove off to town in *Jah Bus*.

Trey lay on his back in his dusty bedroom surrounded by bulging black garbage bags. His bloodshot eyes and slack expression told his mother the story when she opened the door. That, plus the unique aroma of twenty pounds of fresh weed.

"So, is so you come home and ent offer nobody nothing?" His mother sized him up. "Didn't see your mother two months and you haven't said a word. Smoking inside here by yourself." She crossed her arms over her slender chest, tossing aside long dreadlocks with an angry flick.

Wordlessly, Trey reached into an open bag and grabbed a handful of weed. "Here, Mammy. Smoke. Have a time." When she saw the quality of the herb, she smiled.

"Where allyuh get this? Danny farming now?"

Trey shook his head. "The less you know about this ganja, the better. Trust me."

His mother hesitated, her smile slipping slightly. "Is tief you tief the weed, Tracy?" Trey took a pinch of herb from the same bag and started building a spliff. He didn't answer. "So when they come looking for you, what we go do?" Her voice grew shrill.

"Let me study that. Besides," he flicked aside a seed, "that ent go happen. The place was deserted and we didn't tell nobody nothing. Is one man know and he ent go say nothing. That is the maxi man. And we pay he off good." She looked skeptical.

"I hope you know what you doing." She paused, watching him lick the spliff and light it. "And what you going to do with all this weed?" There were five or six bags, each two feet high and two feet wide.

"Don't you worry about that," Trey said through a cloud of smoke.

*   *   *

From the time Trey let it be known, through a hint dropped at the corner shop, that he had product to sell, the calls started coming. *Man, hook me up with some of that* was what he heard every ten minutes on the phone. Then there were the customers, mostly men, who drove or walked up to the house at all hours asking for a ten-piece or a five-piece, conveniently measured buds rolled into tinfoil fingers, just enough for a spliff or two. His neighbors were smokers themselves, so there was little chance they would turn him in to the police. As long as he kept things quiet, he would be fine.

The talk of Trey's new hustle had to come back to Garvin, a man whose appetite for weed was exceeded only by his appetite for luxury. Lying in bed next to Tasha, Garvin inhaled the smoke from his fat, short joint. He passed her the channa pack, a marijuana cigarette resembling the paper cones vendors used to wrap channa in years before, when boiled chickpeas were a popular snack. Tasha took the cone and drew deep. The room was silent. The fifty-two-inch plasma TV was muted, showing images of gyrating bodies, rappers, and singers. Silk sheets slid noiselessly from her naked body as Tasha rose and padded across the plush white carpeting to the bathroom.

She surveyed herself in the mirror as she washed her hands after using the toilet. Same full breasts Trey loved. Same high, round butt. Same long, jet-black legs. Better makeup, definitely a better weave. Garvin wasn't pretty but he was generous to a fault. And that fault was stupidity.

Sliding back into bed next to him, she asked, "So what now?" Garvin frowned, shrugged. He smoked some more. "Antonio coming back in five days," she said pointedly. "He going to want to know where the weed is." Again, Garvin shrugged. "What you going to tell him?" She didn't wait for him to shrug again. "You going to tell him you lost five pounds of weed? Just so? Like magic?" Garvin looked genuinely troubled. His pale brow wrinkled, his thin lips folded into a scowl, even his nearly transparent ears looked upset, blushing bright red. "You forget how he get on the last time—"

"How I go forget?" Garvin snapped. "Is my ass he shoot!" Reflexively he grabbed for his flat behind, finger dipping into the round scar of the bullet wound. It was still pink and raw, a fresh reminder that he shouldn't tamper with his big brother's stock.

But was it enough to stop him from "redistributing" over two Ks of compressed, high-grade Vincy weed while Antonio was on a buying trip to St Vincent? Nope. Garvin frowned again, wiggling yellowish toes until their joints popped, a habit Tasha loathed.

She thought of Garvin's pale body against hers and shuddered. No doubt Trey, that honey-dipped lover of her past, was twice the man in all respects. Trey was smarter and more complex too. But he was also poor. He lived with his mother, he worked in a factory, and his only ambition was to surf, smoke, and "reason" with the other Rastas on the corner, talking religion and livity late into the night and leaving her home alone. Flicking a glance at her $200 pedicure as she kicked off the covers impatiently, she knew that Trey's was the wrong family for her.

Garvin's, on the other hand, was perfect. Behind the modest façade of their house was an upscale, even posh home, equipped with every modern convenience and luxury, all paid for by Antonio's job as a marijuana agent. He imported and wholesaled the stuff, keeping a relatively small amount for recreation, bribes, and retail sales. The boys lived on the proceeds of Antonio's part in the lucrative marijuana trade, sharing everything except women.

Living around the corner from them, and buying weed from Garvin, who handled the retail trade for Antonio, she had gotten to know the brothers well. It wasn't hard to see that they liked the chase, both of them, so she teased them into wanting to steal her away from her undeserving man. Though it was Garvin who took the bait first, it was Antonio she really wanted. As rich as he was, he would be able to afford a lifetime supply of the Baby Phat jeans, Timberland boots, and Gucci bags that Tasha craved. If she never wore another knockoff it would be too soon.

Sitting at the edge of the bed, she sucked her teeth in disgust. Antonio had balls. He was no Trey, who had too much damned integrity, but Antonio was a strong man who knew his responsibilities. Antonio would never have grabbed and sold his brother's weed to take her on a shopping spree. *Idiot*, she thought, tossing an annoyed look at Garvin.

"You think I want him to shoot me again? I can't take that pain. Besides, he might kill me this time." He wasn't joking. Antonio had a wicked temper, hence the bullet wound, an emblem earned a few weeks before when Garvin had accidentally-on-purpose forgotten to give him a bag of cash. Antonio had come looking for him with a grim look and a gun. When Garvin lied, Antonio hit him in the buttocks to remind him who was in charge. Although the wound was still healing, the lesson had already been lost. Garvin imagined he could take Antonio in a fight. The poor fool.

"So what you going to do about it?" she repeated. Garvin thought for a minute, sucking on the joint.

"I go have to replace it."

"With what? You feel weed does grow on trees?"

Garvin grinned. "Well, yes. Besides, you ent hear your exman have a new sideline?"

She was slow to respond. When it hit her, she did a double take. "Trey selling now?"

Garvin nodded. "And I hear is some real high-grade." Tasha's eyes lit up.

Danny called Trey with bad news. "The man come back. He asking questions."

Trey wasn't sweating. "Jimmy irie, right? We ent have nothing to worry about, brethren. Is cool. Nobody ent see we and nobody don't know nothing."

"They don't have to know nothing to lick we up," Danny said cagily. "He only have to suspect is me and my ass is grass."

Trey laughed at the unwitting pun. "Don't fret yourself, cousin. We safe like Selassie I briefcase, man."

On the other end, Danny was bitting his lip. "Man . . ."

Trey, blowing out a thick cloud of smoke, repeated his assurances.

Danny wasn't appeased. "I coming down. We have to deal with this man or he go find we and mess we up bad bad, brother. I coming down tonight."

Trey hung up the phone just as a voice called, "Good afternoon," from outside the house. Ambling to the door in shorts and a plain white undershirt, he jumped visibly when he saw his visitors – Garvin and Tasha. He walked to the gate.

"What going on?" Trey greeted Garvin. "Tasha." He couldn't help his eyes, which drank her in. She smiled lightly and held Garvin's arm tighter.

"Trey, my brother!" Garvin was all fake good cheer but his eyes were flint. His grip around Tasha's waist contracted. "I hear you have some excellent smoke. I was wondering if you could make a deal with us. I need two kees. Will you give it to me?"

"I don't know about give," Trey said coolly. "But I could certainly sell it to you if you want." Garvin was half-listening. His eyes were busily roaming the facade of the house, trying to bend around the corner to see what lay on the other side. In time, his brain churned the information around. "How much?" he asked. Trey called his price. Garvin whistled. "Even with the employee discount that sounding high," the drug pusher said with a small, cold laugh. Tasha stood up taller, bristling.

Trey was casually taking out a sample for them. "Smoke that and tell me it not worth it."

Garvin rubbed the thick, fragrant leaves between his fingers, pulling them apart to feel the stickiness of the plant. It was perfectly dried, and full of illegal goodness. He didn't have to smoke it to know it would be a sweet, potent ride.

They were standing at the gate in the fence surrounding the yard, Trey on one side and Garvin and Tasha on the other. Garvin jerked his head in farewell and pulled Tasha down the road after him into a black Lexus SUV.

Tasha was livid. "What the hell was that? You don't have to pay he for that weed! Just take it!"

Garvin sucked his teeth and drove faster. "Hush your stupid mouth, nah," he mumbled threateningly. "What you think I planning to do?" They reached his house, drove through the electronic gate past the half-dozen dozing Rottweilers, parked, and walked through the triple-locked front door with its alarm system. "But I had to find out if he had the weed. No sense robbing he for a ounce. And look, he have it. Nice grade too." Tasha waited in silence for him to get to the point. "So while you bulling him to distract him, I go find the weed and take it."

She recoiled instantly. "What you mean?" She pushed a finger into his face. "What you take me for? Some kinda ho?"

"Aye, take it easy. What, you can't bull the man one more time? I sure when you was living there allyuh wasn't playing patty-cake when the night come. What is one more, for this? For me?" He paused, giving her a canny look. "Or I know what it is. You want me to get lick up. You want Antonio to shoot me."

Tasha's face grew hot. She slapped him hard. "Don't be an ass, Garvin. I done tell you already, me ent no ho."

Rubbing his face, he cut her a sideways look and lifted his hand to hit her but stopped. "Why you always have to slap me, Tasha? I tell you don't do it. One of these days I will slap you down."

Instantly contrite, Tasha snuggled a hand on the reddened cheek. "Sorry, darling."

He sucked his teeth in disgust. "Anyway, you go have to distract him somehow. Whether you sex him or not is your choice. Me ent business with that. Just make sure he don't come out. I go handle it from this end."

But she doubted Garvin could. "Why you don't distract him and let me tief it?" Garvin shook his head, but before he could speak, she interjected, "I know the house better than you. I know where he does like to hide things. It make more sense this way, Garvin." She pressed her round breasts into his chest and thrust her hips forward until their pelvic regions touched. By the time she kissed him, Garvin had changed his mind.

"No scene." He couldn't maintain a blood flow to both his brain and his penis, so he aimed low.

The knock was soft. It was close to midnight. This time Trey wasn't surprised to see Garvin outside his window. "What's the scene, man?" Trey asked.

Garvin grinned. "I come to do the deal, partner." Trey rubbed his eyes. He had been napping before the visit. He yawned and stretched as he closed the window and went to open the front door. His nemesis was still grinning. "Two kilos, man. Look, the money there," Garvin said, gesturing at a small package on the steps of the front porch.

Trey didn't move from the doorway. Something felt wrong. "Look, man, I change my mind. I not selling you again." As he moved to close the door, Garvin sprang forward with surprising grace and speed.

"How you mean you ent selling me? Man, don't talk foolishness now. Two kilos. Go and bring it."

Trey shook his head. "Nah, partner. I done. You go have to get that someplace else—"

The report of the gunshot silenced them both. Blood drained from Garvin's face and he was as white as the wall he had to lean against to keep from falling.

Leaving him standing there, Trey ran to the back of the house
from where the noise had come. Tasha's still body was sprawled
on the ground by the kitchen door. Danny was standing in the
doorway, dazed, a .38 in his hand. Trey rushed to his side and
grabbed the gun.

"She was picking the lock, Trey. She was coming to tief the
weed . . ."

"Boy, you mad or what? What we going to do now? Eh?" He
turned to his dead ex-girlfriend. Knowing she had probably been
trying to steal the ganja was no consolation. He stooped and
stroked her silky, dark cheek. It was still warm, unblemished, and
as soft as it had been in life.

Danny sprang to action. "Boy, we don't have no time for that.
We have to move she."

Trey nodded. At least he had some garbage bags at hand.

When Garvin got home he was trembling and pale. Antonio
found him there, still jittery and sickly yellow, four days later.
Tasha was gone, and so were two kilograms of product. Antonio
wanted an explanation and he wanted one quickly.

"Is-is-is Trey!" Garvin stammered, breath cut short by the
fingers tightening around his throat. "He trust the weed and then
tell me he don't have the money." Antonio relaxed his grip. *Trust
the weed? Why would Trey want two kilos of weed on credit?* Antonio
glared at his brother, but Garvin just gave an anxious smile.

They pulled up at Trey's gate in Antonio's Lexus SUV, a
shiny black monster that Antonio probably loved more than he
did his whiny, dishonest little brother. It was nearly one in the
morning.

"Trey!" Garvin bawled at the top of his lungs. "Trey!" There
was no answer. Antonio leaped from the van and strode up to
the house. Kicking in the front door, he entered. There were no
signs of life or weed, except for endless ashtrays overflowing with
cigarette and spliff butts.

Garvin murmured weakly, "Like they gone."

Antonio, a stronger, larger version of Garvin, was not amused.
He pulled his Magnum Desert Eagle from his waistband and put
it to his brother's temple. "You go find them, right? And find my
weed. If I only find out you had anything to do with this—"

"But how you go say that, Antonio?" Garvin whined.

"You like to tief too damn much. You feel I don't know you?" Antonio flicked off the gun's safety and rubbed the chrome muzzle against Garvin's cheek. "If I only find out," he repeated. Then he uncocked the gun and stuck it back into his waistband. He turned to look at the contents of the house again. It was on the dresser in Trey's bedroom that he found what he was looking for—a block of board wax wrapped in a plastic bag labeled, *Zora's Sweetbread and Cakes, Toco Road, Sans Souci*. He grinned. There was no humor in the smile.

Once again, Trey was surrounded by black garbage bags. This time they were empty. Danny, sprawled in a beanbag next to the bed, was nearly unconscious. Trey was feeling no pain himself. It was the last of the weed, a nearly impossible amount to smoke out in three days, but with dedication and a lot of help from their friends, mothers, and Jimmy, they had done it. The evidence was up in smoke. Mostly, anyway. Aunty Zora had seen her way to baking a most excellent batch of sweetbread with an unusually strong herbal kick.

Trey stumbled to his feet and zigzagged to the bathroom. As he let a stream of urine hiss urgently into the toilet bowl, he vaguely heard a car pull up outside in the silence of the Sans Souci night. Moving to the window, he saw the moonlight bouncing off the glossy surface of a familiar black Lexus. "Shit," he muttered. Danny was bleary-eyed when Trey tried to shake him awake. "Danny, boy, get up. Garvin and he brother come looking for we."

This was instantly sobering. Danny shook his head to clear it. "What the hell we go do?" he asked in a whisper.

Trey was down on his hands and knees, avoiding the windows. "Well, first thing is to get to ras out of here."

They slipped silently out the back door as Garvin and Antonio walked through the front gate. The three dogs, rushing at the strangers, kept them occupied, and at first they didn't see the two figures running down the road. It was Garvin, shaking Sarah off his left ankle, who spotted them.

"Look them running!" Antonio and Garvin gave chase into the bush. But the dark night, even lit by a full moon, confounded them. They were soon lost. There was a rustling to their right. Garvin, who had never been in a forest before, whimpered, "Antonio, what was that?"

Antonio sucked his teeth and kicked at the undergrowth. "What you get me in here, Garvin? You's a real clown, boy. I don't know why I does trust you with anything." They kept walking for about an hour, drifting further and further into the bush. Then they spotted it—a sloped clearing planted with lush marijuana trees higher than their heads. Garvin was the first to rush in.

"So, is here he get it!" he exclaimed. In the quiet forest, his voice was a cannon.

"What you talking about?" Antonio asked, fingering a leaf with admiration. Even in the dark he recognized it was good weed.

"Trey. This is where he get the—"

Too late, he realized his mistake. But Antonio already had the gun to his head.

"I thought you say he tief the weed from we."

Garvin gave a sickly smile. "Well . . ."

"I tell you already, I go kill you for tiefing from me."

"But Antonio, listen, this is the weed, man! I smoke it myself!"

Neither of them heard the footsteps behind them. A pair of gunshots shattered the quiet of the night. Antonio never had time to turn and fire a single bullet.

The tall, bald-headed man with the smoking gun spat on the two bodies before turning on his heel, saying, "Come back to tief my weed again, you bitches. Not one fart of that."

In the fisherman's hut on the beach, Trey and Danny shivered for a few hours until dawn before creeping back to the house. Garvin and Antonio never came back for the Lexus, so eventually it replaced the battered Land Rover as Zora's delivery van. And in Zora's backyard, a new bed of ixora bloomed unusually well that year.

Angel Child

Tove Klackenberg

It had been her job to hold the piglets when it had been time to
castrate them. She could still feel the hard little body struggling
in her lap, the scream that penetrated her every pore. The child's
scream was unpleasant, but quite bearable. The small, chubby
arms that flailed weren't even an inconvenience. She had a
good grip on the little head and stuck the nail a few centimeters
into the left ear, then scraped around thoroughly. The girl's
screaming became stronger, but she didn't hesitate a second.
Instead, she turned the head and repeated the procedure in
the other ear. Castrating the pigs had been necessary. This,
too, was necessary. Nothing strange about that. Soon it would
be over – this time. The howling had stopped and turned into
hiccupping sobs.

Swollen. Fulfilled. She was something, for the first time in her life.
A kind of power came from her belly, and it almost allowed her
to float along past the rows of plastic boxes, that were filled with
candy. Red frogs, pink mushrooms, and small, sour cola bottles.
Not licorice, that disgusted her. Her belly gave her the right to eat
whatever she wanted. Eat as many sweets as she wanted. There
was nothing strange about it. She was just as valuable as anyone
else, in fact more valuable. Thanks to her belly.
    She prepared herself carefully. On the shelf above the towel
hooks in the bathroom, all the pacifiers were lined up in a row
One with Mickey Mouse, one with Dumbo, and two pink ones
with little hearts on them – in case it was a girl. The pram had
been purchased, and it had been expensive, but her child wasn't
going to have anything used.

The days passed with a comfortable tempo. She had to be careful, she knew that. It was not just a time of waiting, but more a condition. A kind of happiness.

It ended on one of those medium-gray days in March. She'd been five days overdue, and suddenly it was time. Everything went as planned and the little, red-faced, baby-doll lay in her crib. Now, she would never again have to be lonely, she had her child to take care of. The child needed her and she needed the child. Such relationships are called "symbiotic" and were encouraged on the maternity ward.

The child, who was baptized Angelica, was gifted with angel hair and big, naive, blue eyes, but she also had vocal resources that could compete with the best smoke detector. The child always found something to screech about, but she took care of her responsibilities, as a mother should, and was quick to read from a book she'd gotten about babies. She prepared herself thoroughly for each new stage of development. And how she loved to comb the gleaming hair. The small tufts of it turned into petit braids. She fastened them with the kind of rubber bands that were covered and didn't damage the hair. They were also decorated, most often with tiny hearts.

The woman on the other side of the desk leaned forward and her voice hardened.

"We have some concerns," she repeated. "The child's need for security and stimulation . . . Can you describe how you satisfy . . . No, perhaps I've started at the wrong end. Tell me a little about yourself, your childhood and such."

Her gaze had fastened just above the caseworker's left shoulder. Her lips moved when she read one of the messages on the notice board: "*The most important thing about life is not where we're standing, but in which direction we're headed.*" She had to ask the caseworker to repeat the question, and the woman's voice cracked as she nearly shouted, "I asked you to tell me about your childhood!"

After a moment of silence, she answered, "Normal. It was normal. Just like everyone else's, just about."

*   *   *

She saw the pen move a little helplessly above the notebook without leaving any marks. Wrong answer, obviously.

"What assistance do you think you need?"

"Do I need help, you mean . . .? A little something extra for Angelica's birthday would be nice, you know. I was thinking of having a real party, with all the children getting a bag of candy to take home. That can get expensive, you know."

The caseworker suddenly smiled encouragingly, and shoved the candy dish on her desk forward, as though in reward. "Good. Excellent. That's more like it. A social network. Tell me more, please, who had you thought to invite to the party?"

The inquiry had resulted, six months later, in a "Care Plan" including "Assistance" that she accepted without the slightest resistance. The "Assistance" came in the form of her very own At-Home-Aid, a large breasted creature, with a wide open embrace, who loved children, all children, but especially an angel child such as Angelica. It felt so good to be able to let go and let the Aid take control. She enjoyed being able to stay in bed while the Aid pottered about. Angelica's jarring screams, that had been impossible to get away from, earlier – even in the shower with the little, turquoise radio turned up to full volume – were handled by the Aid's steady hand. This was practical, as the child seemed to cry more often as she got older.

The Aid was also clever at organization, at getting past busy health clinic receptionists, emergency room nurses and foreign-born doctors who were unwilling to make referrals. During her second year of life, Angelica had developed into a frequent client of the Health Care System. The Aid was concerned, but happy in secret. Each new visit to the doctor gave her an extra kick of self-esteem. She was "The Child's Mother". She alone guaranteed its regular intake of penicillin and insured recovery. Her knowledge of the intimate details of ear inflammation, often exceeded that of the various "white-coats" they met. Things like plastic tubes and resistance to antibiotics – life revolving around the never-ending ear problems – were all so much simpler for her.

Everyone around her, in the conference room, was serious. Some looked sad, one looked indignant. The dirty, yellow walls seemed to be closing in. When she was faced with the words on the paper in front of her, she laughed, but no one smiled with her. A memory, of a teacher from her years in college, popped up. He hadn't had long to go until his retirement, and had gotten bored with tenses, word classifications and burnt out teenage students, long ago. Instead, he spent class time reading aloud. Baron Von Münchausen came riding on a cannonball in her mind's eye, as she attempted to make her way through the meaning of the words on the papers, that everyone seemed so eager for her to understand. Her lawyer tried to explain them, but she wasn't listening. She just felt so tired.

"Have to get home to Angelica," she mumbled and rose to leave. She sank back down into her chair when a woman with horse teeth, and big earrings took command, and obviously decided to speak in simple terms:

"Angelica is no longer in your home. She will be living with your At-Home-Aid until further notice. Think how good . . . it is for her, to be staying with someone she knows. Angelica has not fared well, and is at risk of further injury if we do not do this. You don't want that, do you?"

She didn't understand anything. Hurt Angelica? They didn't believe that she could injure her own angel child? Through her confusion, she tried to understand what they were thinking, but no one would meet her eye. She protested, albeit weakly, but "horse teeth" just continued: "It is quite understandable that you lack understanding of what you did, at this time. It's actually part of the diagnosis. Not strange at all. One could almost call it normal."

It went slowly. Angelica managed to walk long distances on her own. She only had to carry the child when they had to cross marshy areas and when the terrain angled steeply uphill. Occasionally, the path was blocked by trees, blown down by the wind. Angelica crawled up onto the trunks, waited impatiently for her to climb over, then threw herself into her arms, laughing heartily. Steam rose from the ground, where the sun succeeded in reaching it through the spruce trees. There were smells of moss and spruce needles, and there was a trace of something musty from the puddles. Here and there, patches of dirty snow had survived in the protection of the trees' shadows. Spring sometimes needed help along the way, so they kicked apart some of the sad, little snow drifts. Both wore their blond hair collected in braids down their backs. They were finally on their way. The Social Services waiting room, saturated with its sense of powerlessness, lay far behind them. They were going to save themselves, work together, and take care of each other.

The forest became lighter, the knotty birches, more frequent. She could see the rust-spotted roof of the cabin, and felt the strength returning to her legs.

She opened her eyes when someone touched her shoulder. The sun still warmed her face. Motes of dust played in the light that fell through the unwashed window. The corridor looked like the one on the maternity ward, though this one had locked doors. It wasn't the newborn who screeched here, either.

"The verdict has come," the voice said, and its owner patted her a bit carefully. "I thought maybe you'd like to read it yourself. I'll sit here beside you in case it gets difficult."

She didn't feel anything. The words marched past, rhythmically, and she didn't stop until she came to page fourteen:

The Court has passed the following judgment: in the preliminary work regarding legislation pertaining to non-consensual intervention, the classification "Lack of Care" shall be applied. Under this classification, the situation is defined as occurring when a child is exposed to improper care, due largely to negligence, to the extent that the child's health is at risk. In the case which is under consideration, a witness, in the person of an At-Home-Aid, testified that not only was Angelica neglected by her mother, she was also actively injured by her. The case was referred to Dr Jeanette Pilsäther-Roos, Senior Physician of the Children's Clinic at Central Hospital. In a document supported by Social Services, Dr Pilsäther-Roos writes that the mother's behavior falls under the little-known diagnosis "Münchausen Syndrome by Proxy" (MSP). MSP is a compulsive disorder which involves a parent repeatedly ensuring that his or her child experiences some sort of medical affliction, thereby compelling the child to undergo medical treatment. The strains of motherhood have, in this instance, caused a shallow and self-centered personality to develop the actual disorder. According to Pilsäther-Roos, the correct diagnosis was obtained thanks to the exemplary cooperative efforts of concerned personnel in both the Health Care and Social Services sectors.

Based upon the above-mentioned medical document, the Court therefore finds that there is an obvious risk that the child's health and/or development is being damaged. Preparations should therefore be made to care for Angelica outside of her current home. Taking into consideration the child's safety, it is clear that the necessary care cannot be given under present conditions, in a voluntary manner.

She gently rocked Angelica in her arms and hummed a little. The crying had stopped and the girl's body suddenly seemed heavier. She carefully moved a lock of golden hair to make sure the child was truly asleep. Slowly, slowly she rose from the sofa and carried the child in to her bed. The room had been made ready a long time ago. There were dried flowers on the top shelf of a white book case. The next shelf held stuffed animals lined up in a row. Further down, there were books, puzzles, and a toy vacuum cleaner made of plastic. The curtains were thin and let in most of the weak, February light.

She stood for a while, enjoying just looking at the sleeping child. The angel child. She was growing and would soon start to talk. She'll learn to call me Mamma, she thought, and felt something soft and warm roll through her body.

She returned to the kitchen, then continued into the hall. She picked up the handbag that rested against the bench under the mirror. After digging around in the center pocket, the one with the zipper, she pulled out the nail. It was four inches long. A single, golden-yellow hair was stuck to its pointed tip. Absent-mindedly, she scraped it away with her thumbnail and went back into the kitchen. The nail disappeared into the recycling container for metal, under the sink. She'd always been meticulous about sorting her garbage.

"We don't need that anymore, Angelica," she mused aloud, and chuckled to herself. The restlessness she had carried in her body for so long had vanished. Even her breasts, the things she'd carried around like a kind of useless ballast, seemed lighter. More meaningful. Being able to quit the At-Home-Aid job was a relief, too. She could no longer stand to deal with all the incompetence, all the weakness, and all the inconvenience that had surrounded her. Her goodwill no longer extended to anyone other than herself – and Angelica, of course. She would never have to be alone again, thanks to her angel child.

She filled the coffeemaker, sat at the kitchen table and was satisfied.

Translation by Susan Loyd

All For Bergkamen

Sebastian Fitzek

A lot of people think I am an asshole. Most likely I am one. But very few individuals can really judge that. They usually meet me in situations in which it is impossible to make friends. Not in a friendly crowd over beer, not at sports and definitely not at a party but always through my work. And my work is death.

Death does not follow regular working hours so I don't have an office. I am more like a representative, a travelling sales man. I track people of whose existence you don't want to know. Psychopaths who carry the severed finger of a child which they want to suck on after end of shift around in their lunch box. Sociopaths who observe with interest as their paralysed wives starve to death. You know, people next door. Mostly I am too late. Like today, in Bergkamen.

When I got the call on my emergency mobile I was in the process of making a Hello-Kitty watch disappear before the eyes of my daughter. Lisa was celebrating her seventh birthday and my ex-wife Tania had engaged me of all people to be the magician for the children's party.

Now she would have to struggle with the children who were all waiting for the promised magic trick on her own, while I was on the B61 to meet a mental case in Bergkamen.

"Old Dobkowitz was the first to discover him," the leader of the task force informed me on the phone.

Dobkowitz. SEK*-chief Hartmann had emphasized the name of the old lady as if she was a local celebrity. To me she was as a foreign as every single one of the host of local police, media

*SEK Spezialeinsatzkommando, a German Special Forces group

or rubbernecks who pressed themselves into the pedestrian zone of Nordberg and despite the pouring rain could barely be held back from the crime scene by the uniformed officers.

The chief looked exactly like I had imagined him based on his asthmatic voice: overweight, with thinning hair and a butcher nose. When I shook his wet hand I kind of expected an invitation to beer and roast.

"You have brought shit weather with you!"

Like me he didn't wear either a hood or an umbrella. But on his feet he was wearing massive, police green wellington boots. If that was really his shoe size I could later take him to Lisa's birthday party as a clown.

Two of his men cut a path for me behind the crime scene tape.

"Can you explain why he would only speak to you?"

"No idea," I said and shrugged my shoulders.

It would have sounded very arrogant if I had told the chief that all he had to do was google my name. How could I explain to somebody who didn't know me that I was the best? And I wasn't even a trained police psychologist. I studied law and at some point got stuck at the Bundeskriminalamt*.

"The BKA said you are actually a profiler and not a negotiator," said Hartmann. He didn't sound suspicious but just interested. Up until now he obviously didn't think I was a bastard. Well, that would change quickly once he noticed who would take over command in a moment.

"True. Usually I try to get into the pathological thought structure of serial killers," I said. "But that also helps me in negotiations with hostage takers. Conflict de-escalation is something of a hobby for me."

They led me to the red brick building of the Bergkamen-Bönen bank that was located about thirty meters across from the crime scene. "Not a bad idea," I nodded at Hartmann. They had set up their headquarters behind the bullet-proof glass of the bank with a direct line of sight on to the psychopath in the shop window on the other side.

"Has he made his demands?" I asked while I was walked into the open plan office of the bank in Hartmann's wake. The officer

---

*Bundeskriminalamt or BKA, Federal Criminal Police Office, the national investigative police agency of Germany.

sat down behind an empty desk and told me to pull up a chair. A short while later we both stared at a computer screen. The bank's security cameras we now pointed towards the shopping street opposite and threw a sharp colour picture onto the monitor in front of us.

"Demands?" Hartmann shook his head and spread some rain drops across the keyboard. A computer mouse disappeared under his hands and the camera zoomed closer to the crime scene. The image became slightly blurry.

"Can you read that?"

I had paid too much attention to the masked man on the wooden chair behind the dirty shop window so I hadn't noticed the small cardboard sign in front of the perpetrator's Doc Marten's boots up until now. Hartmann pressed a fresh colour copy into my hands which showed a much enlarged part of the shop window.

"Seven hundred euros or the city dies!" I read the text written in black capital letters on the cardboard sign. "You called me here for this laughable sum?"

Hartmann nodded slowly. "Gertrud Dobkowitz was walking her dog and was the first to see him sitting in the window. First she thought he was a mannequin. But then the guy in the ski mask moved and the mutt started yapping."

"So she walked inside?"

"Yes. It is not without reason that the old biddy Dobkowitz is the most popular tour guide in Bergkamen. She knows everything and everyone in the city and if there is anything new she is the first to investigate."

"What did the man say to her?"

"Not much more than what is written on the sign. He wants 700 euros otherwise the city dies. So Gertrud told him to stop this rubbish and better start working and he only laughed and asked for you."

"And why didn't you just go in and get him if even a pensioner can just walk in and out of there?" I asked.

"Because he gave this to Dobkowitz."

Hartmann passed me a clear bag with something in it that looked like the grey children's plasticine Lisa used last year to make me an ashtray. The slight smell of nitro coming from the bag was unmistakable.

"Semtex", I said and passed the explosives back to Hartmann. "That would explain what is blinking over there." I pointed to the flickering red dot above the breast pocket of the olive green outdoor vest worn by the perpetrator.

"Possible, perhaps he is wired." Hartmann blew his nose. "Now he is not letting anybody else inside. The explosives dogs cannot scent through the closed door. Hey, where are you going?"

He jumped up anxiously when he realized that I had left my seat and was walking through the open plan office towards the exit.

"Where do you think?" I asked with a slightly cynical undertone. It was time that I took control. "He wants to talk to me. So I am going to pop over to see him."

Obviously Hartmann would not let me go unprepared. He set me up with a bulletproof vest and a remote which was now in my left ear and which he used to stay in contact with me before he let me march across to the shop window while grinding his teeth. I knew he would have preferred to replace me with a negotiator from his own team but then he would have had to explain to the media hyenas with their cameras and broadcasting vans behind the crime scene tape why he had stopped me from talking directly to a perpetrator who only wanted to speak to me. If the man blew himself up in front of witnesses while Hartmann sent me home, a transfer for disciplinary reasons would be the least of his problems.

I walked slowly and with raised hands towards the shop window and came to a halt ten meters away next to a lamp post. The wind shook a poster that was attached to the lamp post with grey wire and on which a confidently smiling Roland Schäfer was asking for re-election. I loosened the wire, pulled a Sharpie out of my leather jacket and wrote a sequence of numbers on the mayor's high forehead. Then I turned the poster to the shop window. Only seconds later my mobile rang.

"Hello Adam."

The man in the ski mask spoke with the voice of a friend as if we had known each other for a long time. I had the speaker on so Hartmann could hear as well through the transmitter in my ear.

"Hello," I answered. "Now that I am aware that you know my name will you tell me yours?"

"Of course," he said and pulled the mask off his head.

"Oh shit," Hartmann hissed in my ear. "It's Benny."

All around me the electric motors of dozens of digital cameras hummed to life. Luckily the press were so far obeying the flash light prohibition.

"Benjamin," confirmed the long-haired guy who was now loosening his flattened mane through excessive head shaking. As far as I could see through the streaming rain he looked like he was grinning. Quite obviously he enjoyed all the attention everyone was paying him today.

"May I come closer, Benjamin?" I asked cautiously.

He nodded.

"Thanks, that way I can stand dry." I stepped under the canopy of the shop that had to have been a stationery shop at one point. There was an ad for ink cartridges still stuck to the door.

"Benny Senner is a harmless nutcase," the chief was telling me from afar. "He is twenty-four years old, studying eco management with a major in renewable energies and is an environmental activist. Three years ago he occupied a high-rise and demanded free rent for people on welfare."

I asked myself if by high-rise Hartmann meant the ugly, empty concrete tower block opposite the town hall but then went back to more important questions.

"What do you want, Benny?"

"You know what I want. It's all on here!" Benny obviously did not take it amiss that I was trying to build up a relationship by using the pet name version of his name. He bumped the sign at his feet with his boot. Only now did I see that directly under his chair lay a stopwatch. Its hand was moving.

"Seven hundred euros? That's not a lot of money for all this palaver," I said with forced casualness. I kept my left hand with the palm open to him to signal that I wasn't hiding anything from him.

"You haven't understood anything! You're only swimming with the flow."

I blinked. "What do you mean, Benny?"

The smile disappeared from the acne-scarred face of the young student. Suddenly he looked like somebody who worried that nobody was listening to him when he had something very important to say.

"Did you know that Bergkamen has dropped by twenty-five meters over the years?" he asked me.

"No."

"That's where the wind blows," Hartmann growled in my ear. "The damages of mining."

I nodded. I had noticed the cracks in the roads and houses on the way in. I grew up in Lünen and we had received compensation from the mining company. At least until my father was killed in '67 in the mine disaster at *Minister Achenbach* and my mum moved to Cologne with me.

"Fucking coal," muttered Benny and for a moment I thought he wanted to spit on the sign. "They took out everything, the whole fucking hard coal for the fucking power stations and their fucking electricity. Without any bloody care for anything. And there you are! We are going down. But not only the roads, meadows, fields and houses but the rivers as well. Do you know what that means?"

"I can imagine."

"The fucking rivers will soon run backwards! There's no possibility for the rivers to run off properly. Guess how many pumping stations there are in Bergkamen to stop us all from drowning?"

I shrugged my shoulders.

"Nine! Over the last years they have flooded the higher lying rivers and lakes, for example the Emscher, with 22.3 billion litres of water. 22.3 million cubic metres."

"In a moment he is going to start a lecture on the eternity damages," Hartmann informed me through the radio and he would be right in the end.

"Those are the infinite eternal damages left behind by mining. It costs twenty-five million euros every year to fight against the masses of water. Until the end of our days. As long as Bergkamen is inhabited the pumps have to run otherwise we're flooded. On top of that the water table in the shut down pits is rising and contaminating our ground water. That costs another one hundred million, you understand? Over 150 million every year until Final Judgment. All this money that the bigwigs from the mining companies had not planned for."

"Okay," I interrupted the student's heated flood of words. "And with this protest you want to raise awareness for these environmental problems?"

"No," said Benny. "It's too late for that. The damage has already been done. The pits here were shut down far too late."

"What do you want then?"

"Look at my sign," he repeated and he sounded nearly sulky. "Seven hundred euros."

"Fine, I'll go over to the cash machine, pull a few notes and this kerfuffle is over?"

"I don't think there will be enough money in the cash machine."

"Why?"

"Do you know how much 22.3 billion litres of water represents?" he countered with another question. "I will tell you: it is 700 litres per second pouring through our pumps so we don't drown. And that is exactly my exchange rate – 700 euros for every second we are negotiating."

He picked up the stopwatch from under his seat. "And that is now already four minutes and forty-seven seconds gone. Over my big thumb that makes over 200,000 euros with a tendency to increase."

"And why should we pay you this sum?" I asked.

"Because I am giving you no other choice."

He got something out of the chest pocket of his jacket that looked from afar like a plastic lighter with the big difference that it had a blinking diode at its end.

"Should you make me wait too long for the money I will ignite the fuse." Benny grinned. "And, at the latest, after one hour, meaning at 2,520,000 euros."

I registered hectic movement behind me. I knew Hartmann had positioned a number of snipers on the opposite roofs and behind the opened doors of police cruisers parked in a V-shape at a secure distance from the row of shops.

"Benny, we have already cleared the whole pedestrian area as well as all the surrounding houses," I said calmingly avoiding negative words like *death, dying* or *hostage*. "When you press that button you will only hurt yourself."

Benny laughed as if I'd made the joke of the century.

"You are so wrong. You all think I am the one all cabled up, eh? Ok, right, I am. But I am not the only one who's going to die. Oh no, the whole city will go to pot."

"That you will have to explain to me please," I asked. "How are you going to achieve that?"

Benny sniffed up the snot in his nose. "Listen to me, man. I have installed a number of explosive charges at critical points. When they go off all nine pumps will break down. Irreparably. At once. After the floods of the last few days the run off is filled to the brim. Ask the mayor how long it will take for Bergkamen to drown."

He laughed again.

"You may have enough time to evacuate the city. But nobody will be able to come back. That would make no sense with everything having been destroyed. So hurry up, Adam. If I don't get my money in one hour at the latest I will turn Bergkamen into a second New Orleans. It just will be a little wetter."

After Benny had ended the conversation I returned to the bank where Hartmann welcomed me with a facial expression I had seen once before on Tania's face. When she showed me the earring she had found between the seats of our couch. Sadly it was not one that she had been missing.

"What kind of fucking shit is going on here?" Hartmann asked and now he even sounded like my ex-wife. One of his assistants passed me a lukewarm coffee. I took off my dripping jacket and hung it over the back of an office chair.

"You tell me," I answered and looked at the plasma screen TV on the wall which usually showed filmed ads or silent stock market news to the waiting customers. Now jerky aerial pictures of the pedestrian zone flickered across the machine. The pictures must have come from the news helicopter which right this second was hovering high above our heads.

"Is it true what Benny has told us? Can he really drown the city?"

"Theoretically he can!"

I turned to the new voice at my back and looked at a familiar face. Roland Schäfer smiled like on his campaign poster, shook my hand and sat down with us.

"You want to know if he can take the whole city hostage."

I nodded.

"I am afraid I have to say he can. It has been raining for a week non-stop now. If the pumps in Beverbach Rünthe or even the one in Kuhbach break down we are screwed. Whole city blocks will be flooded possibly all the way down to Hamm. The cellars will be flooded for sure and the houses will become uninhabitable over time. Obviously depending on whether the terrorist has found a way to disable the pumps for good."

"For example if he blows them up?" I asked and had a sip of the ochre-coloured coffee.

"We are currently checking all the stations," said Hartmann. "We haven't found anything suspicious so far." He rubbed his eyes with the thumb and index finger of his right hand and I wondered if he suffered from migraines or wore contact lenses. Maybe he'd just had a bad night's sleep.

"What are you suggesting?" he asked without looking up. I waited a few seconds before I answered.

"Well, here we have the very special case of a suicide provocation combined with the threat of a terrorist attack. The perpetrator wants to blow himself up and at the same time make more than 50,000 people homeless. Oddly enough he is making no effort to hide his identity which normally hints at an idealistic, political motivation. Still, he is making clear financial demands. Is he actually organized in a cell?"

"No, not that we are aware. As I said, amongst us Benny Senner was always called Benny Nutter." Hartmann put a pencil advertising the bank in the corner of his mouth. "Illegal entry of someone's house, disorderly conduct and disturbance of the peace, those are the things he would normally do. But he has never harmed any humans."

"But somehow our harmless little Benny has managed to get hold of Semtex," I reminded him.

"Yes, but I don't believe that he would put others in danger and has hidden bombs around the pump stations."

I nodded. "I actually agree with you on that."

Hartmann's pencil moved to the other corner of his mouth and he raised his eyebrows with surprise. "So he is only bluffing?"

"No, I believe he has placed the bombs somewhere else."

I saw how the mayor wanted to say something but I wouldn't let him interrupt me.

"I have just spoken a few words with Benny but in the short time he has repeatedly used the words "electricity" and "run" and has cursed the "power plants". On top of that he has been working on renewable energy as part of his studies." I rose and now alternately spoke to Hartmann and the mayor. "Obviously he is not just after the money. Of course he wants to make a statement. That's what all this sensationalist production is all about. And he doesn't just want to hit Bergkamen but also the "bigwigs" as he calls them. That's why I am going on the assumption that he will hit two birds with one stone." I paused knowing that all the other officers in hearing distance were giving me their full attention. "Through his studies he knows very well how a power station works. He will interrupt the electric current to the pump stations. Probably he will just blow up some power masts, destroy overhead cables or make transformer stations break down."

Hartmann paled. One could practically see how the thought of all the potential targets was working through his brain.

"And what are we supposed to do now? His ultimatum runs out in thirty-two minutes." The mayor grabbed a calculator. "So in 1,344,000 euros."

I threw a confirming look at the greenish display of the calculator. Schäfer was just about to calculate the maximum amount up to the end of Benny's sixty-minute-ultimatum and reached 2.52 million euros.

Hartmann grabbed the radio and rose as well.

"Team A, how is it looking?" he asked and turned his back to me. Behind the window I could see a wrapped-up SEK agent standing in the forecourt raise his hand briefly.

"Good to go," was the quiet response from Hartmann's radio. "All men are in position."

"I wouldn't do that," I wished to avoid a possible storming. Hartmann turned to me and threw me an irritated look. "You have just told me that you think the perpetrator is dangerous. Should I wait until he puts his threat into action?"

"No."

"So what?"

"Give him the money."

Now Hartmann was laughing as if I had suggested giving Gertrud Dobkowitz a machine gun so she could lead the storming.

"You have lost your mind," he said in the familiar tone of voice of my ex-wife.

"Listen to me," I said as calmly as possible. "The offender is very methodical and follows a plan. That means he is no impulsive psychopath. But we have one clear advantage. He has no clear exit strategy."

"Which means . . .?"

"Which means that he cannot do anything with the money. Look at him." I pointed to the security monitor which was still capturing the shop window. Benny was just rolling up the right leg of his trousers. Even from here one could see that his fingers were shaking.

"That is no killer. He is unsure and getting more and more nervous. He has never done anything this big. I am sure I can negotiate him out of this. But to do that I need time. And I will only get that if I have something up my sleeve the next time I go to him."

Twenty-two minutes and therefore 924,000 euros later I approached the shop window again. I hadn't been wrong. Benny was sweating, his Palestinian scarf lay carelessly next to his chair and he was no longer grinning when he saw me. Even though I was carrying a black briefcase and he had to know what was in it. He nervously touched his neck and started slowly to massage it. With the other hand he pulled his mobile from his trouser pocket. Shortly after my phone rang.

"How much?" he asked shortly.

"Nearly two million. The bank couldn't get more together at such short notice."

That was no lie. It was a miracle that even so much had come together. All branches of the area surrounding the Nordberg had put their money transporter into the field in the last twenty minutes.

"Aha," said Benny in a tone of voice that gave no indication if he agreed or was just about to pull the plug. After all, with this sum we were more than 100,000 euros behind his demands and the stopwatch at his feet was still running.

"What do we do now?" I asked as friendly as possible.

"Take the radio from your ear."

"Shit," commented Hartmann on Benny's order. It was the last thing I was going to hear from the chief over the radio.

"It's done," I confirmed and lifted the briefcase. "Do you want me to come to you now?"

"Yes. But first take your mobile and remove the battery."

I could practically feel how behind me Hartmann was pummelling his desk furiously.

"Don't piss yourselves, boys," I said before I hung up. "I am the one walking into danger." I pulled the batteries from the phone and put both on the wet walkway. Then I walked slowly with raised hands towards the shop window. The two million had been split up into six bundles that weighed no more than a small paperback book. Still the briefcase pulled my arm down as if it was dumbbell.

The shop door was open. On the inside the empty shop greeted me with a smell of dust, sweat and fear. Now, close up I realized that Benny would not last another five minutes. Child's play for a negotiator like me.

"How is it going?" I asked him.

"Not so good." He answered and cleared his throat. "Is the money really in there?"

"Yes." I opened the briefcase. For the first time movement came into his skinny body. He walked to the window and pressed a small switch on the frame of the window without leaving me out of his sight. There was a creaky noise and the outside shutters came down.

"Enough with the theatrics," he said and waved at the headquarters across the road.

When nobody could see us from the outside he turned to me and nervously pushed his hand through his hair. "Ok, and what do we do now?"

"As planned," I said and looked at my watch. Then I put the briefcase at his feet and took out the first bundle of money.

"Turn around," I ordered him and put it in one of his many outside pockets.

"As soon as I have put the dosh into your pockets you walk outside and wait until all the cameras have you in their sights."

"I understand; I want everybody to hear what I have to say."

"Exactly."

Luckily, Benny was only manically nervous but not totally nuts. We had been over all of this for hours. For weeks. The whole world would find out about the damage done by mining, damage that would last forever and from which you could not avert your eyes. Not now when in China an even worse ruinous exploitation with a complete disregard for humans and the environment was taking place.

"As soon as you have put yourself into position in front of the press call this number." I stowed away the last bundle of money and then passed him the piece of paper on which I had written Hartmann's number.

"What should I say?"

"Say: 'I am doing all this for Bergkamen'," I demanded. "Nothing else. For anything else there will be enough time later when they are interrogating you. Then you give them back the two million and tonight at the latest everybody will know that you are neither a terrorist nor a thief."

"And the whole world will know the exchange rate," grinned Benny. "Seven-hundred litres of water every second. Man, it is really time that somebody wakes up before they build more coal power stations."

"That it is."

I closed the briefcase and gave him a hug.

"Man, this has been real fun," he laughed nervously. "Thank you for helping me to pull this off. I will be glad when I can take this bomb dummy off again. It itches furiously under the tee-shirt."

I grinned and ruffled his hair. During the year of preparation I had grown fond of this nut case. Of course it was no coincidence that he approached me. There are not many police negotiators whose fathers had been killed in a mining accident.

"The ultimatum is running out," I told him and pointed at the door. "Go outside and finish it."

For a moment I had the impression that he was moving away from me in slow motion. Slowly, gangly but with an energetic walk. He was a warrior walking into his final battle; an idealist who despite his young age carried so much anger that he would sacrifice his whole future for a war that could not be won. I respected his courage, courage that I would never be able to show. But I did what I could, showing them where their mining has led them. The mining that had killed my father.

While Benny opened the door and stepped out into the pouring rain I moved further back into the shop. There was no back door through which I could have escaped. Only a little shed with a sink and a toilet. I felt that Benny was just about to dial Hartmann's number when I crouched under the sink. Then I looked at the watch. Only ten seconds then the ultimatum would run out.

Outside I heard how Benny screamed the agreed sentence.

"I am doing all this for Bergkamen."

Then, two seconds early, a massive explosion not only shredded the shutters and the shop window but also the upper half of Benjamin Senner.

Later, after the initial chaos had died down, the few injured onlookers had been looked at and the death of the obviously mentally ill offender had been officially established I was on my way back to Lisa's birthday. With a little luck I would make it for coffee and cake. The magic trick I would not perform. I had done enough of those today. Obviously the burnt money found on the suicide attacker had not been the full sum. While Benny had had his back turned to me I had put the same bundle over and over again into his pockets. Benny had been far too nervous to realize that he didn't even have 100,000 euros on him, of which a few notes had been flying very effectively through the pedestrian zone after the detonation. The images would rule the news tonight: environmental activist blows himself up in protest against mining damages.

I switched on the indicator for the motorway junction and happily felt for the money bundles in my jacket pocket. Nearly two million for four hours of work. How lucky that this idealist had asked me of all people if I would support him in this mad protest. His biggest worry had been that he would be taken out by the special forces before he could say his thing to the cameras. And he hadn't been so wrong as it had taken all my persuasive skills to stop Hartmann from storming the shop.

I switched on the radio on and sped up to *The Winner Takes It All*.

Well yes, many think I am an asshole. Quite possibly I am one.

But please don't say now that I didn't warn you in the beginning.

Translation by Tina Everitt

An Urban Legend Puzzle

Norizuki Rintarō

1.

"What would you think of a message that said, 'Aren't you glad you didn't turn on the light?' This wasn't spoken, but a sentence written by hand."

" '. . . didn't turn on the light' . . .?" Rintarō cocked his head. "I've heard that phrase somewhere. Is this a quiz or something?"

"No, it concerns a homicide I'm investigating. Late Monday night, a university student was stabbed to death in a one-room apartment in Matsubara, Setagaya Ward. Those words were inscribed in blood, in an unsteady hand, on the wall of the crime scene. Of course it was the victim's blood."

"Letters in blood on the wall of the crime scene?"

Inspector Norizuki nodded, his expression serious. It was a weekend night and he'd changed into his pajamas and was enjoying his after-dinner cigarette.

Rintarō shook his head. "Come on! You can't fool me that that's a case you're working on now. It's a famous urban legend."

"A famous what?"

"Urban legend. That's what sensational rumors that are spread by word of mouth are called. People claim that they're true stories heard from a friend of a friend. Some of these are standard occult or ghost stories, while others have their roots in celebrity scandals or strange cases involving vicious crimes. The story you've heard is one of the more popular ones, Father."

"Wait a second." Inspector Norizuki looked bewildered. "You've actually heard tell of such a case before this?"

"Yes, I have. And when you say 'actually,' I think you're just trying to pretend innocence because I've blown your cover."

"This isn't one of your novels, Rintarō. I wouldn't do something so roundabout. Tell me about this rumor."

"You're a harsh critic, Father. All right, then. The story I've heard goes like this:

"Ms A, a college student, went to a party at B's apartment with other members of her club. B was a year ahead of her at college. They had a good time drinking. A little after midnight, the party ended, and A left the apartment along with a friend.

After walking for a while, A realized that she had left her handbag at the apartment and decided to part with her friend and go back to retrieve her bag. When she returned to the apartment, the lights were already out and there was no response when she rang the doorbell. It appeared that B had already gone to bed. Feeling dejected, A tried turning the doorknob and it opened. B must have forgotten to lock the door.

The apartment's one room was pitch dark. But she remembered where she had left her bag and felt bad about waking the soundly sleeping B. Without turning on the light, A whispered, 'I came to pick up what I forgot,' as she groped for her bag. She left the apartment as she had entered it."

"Hmm, that's very interesting," Inspector Norizuki mused. The expression on his face was deadly serious, in contrast to the seeming nonchalance of the statement. Unaware that the lengthening ashes of his cigarette were about to drop onto the table, he asked, "And then?"

"The next day, A, concerned that she hadn't seen B on campus, went to his apartment. When she arrived, a police car was parked in front of the building, and the street was filled with policemen and onlookers.

'Did something happen here?' A asked one of the neighbors clustering around.

'There was a murder here last night. Mr B in Apartment X was killed.'

It seemed that after A and the others had departed, someone

had entered through the unlocked door and stabbed B to death as he was sleeping.

I should have woken him and told him to lock his door when I came back to retrieve my bag, A thought. She was filled with remorse, but no matter how much she regretted her actions, B would not return to life. Nothing could be done for him now.

Starting the next day, the club members who had been drinking with B just before he was killed were called in by the police to give their statements. Feeling somewhat responsible for B's death, A went voluntarily to give her statement to the detective in charge, offering as much detail as she could about the events of the night of the crime. When she'd finished, the detective took out a photograph. Prefacing his question by saying the picture might shock her, he asked, 'This message was left at the scene of the crime. Does it mean anything to you?'

The photograph was of the wall in B's apartment. Smeared on the wall in blood were these words:

'Aren't you glad you didn't turn on the light?'

Upon seeing the photograph, A turned pale and fainted. When A had returned to B's room that night, he had already been killed! If she had turned on the light to try to wake B, she would have come face to face with the killer and A would most certainly also have been killed."

Inspector Norizuki folded his arms across his chest and groaned. "You said it was a popular urban legend. Does that mean quite a large percentage of young people have heard it?"

"I suppose so. Nowadays there are many sites on the Internet dealing with urban legends. Leaving aside whether one believes it to be a true story, it's likely most young people have come across it at least once. There was even a movie last year that dealt with a similar tale."

The inspector opened his eyes wide in wonder. "Even a movie?"

"An American film that was given the title *Rules* in Japan. The original title was *Urban Legend*. It was a horror-suspense B-movie on the subject of urban legends – just as it says. It should be out now on video. The plot sounded interesting – a series of murders made to look like popular urban legends in America, like 'The Backseat Murderer,' 'The Boyfriend's Death,' or 'The

Babysitter and the Man Upstairs' – but it wasn't really very good as a mystery movie. A different version of the story we've been talking about was used."

"By 'a different version' you mean . . .?"

"It's a type known as 'The Roommate's Death.' And it might be closer to the original. The version we were just talking about didn't arise spontaneously. The core of the story must have been translated from an earlier American version. After all, the recent boom in urban legends started in America. What kicked it off was the book *The Vanishing Hitchhiker*, written by the folklore scholar Jan Harold Brunvand, which came out in 1981."

The inspector snorted impatiently and said, "Quit showing off your knowledge. What was the version of the story in the movie *Rules*?"

"I'm sorry, sir," Rintarō apologized. "Details of 'The Roommate's Death' can vary, but in the movie, it goes like this. It's set in a dormitory of a college far from any major city. The heroine's roommate is a dissolute female college student. One night, she enters the room to hear moans from her roommate's bed. Assuming, mistakenly, that her roommate is in the midst of a tryst with her boyfriend, the heroine doesn't turn on the light, but goes directly to her own bed and falls asleep listening to music through her earphones. Waking up the next morning, she discovers her roommate's butchered body in the bed next to hers. On the wall, written in the blood of the victim, are the words, 'AREN'T YOU GLAD YOU DIDN'T TURN ON THE LIGHT?' "

"So again, by not turning on the light, she saved her own life. I see. It's a valuable piece of information. The fact that the film was shown in Japan means that it is possible the murderer may have seen it. If it's out on video, then we should check the video rental shops. If we're lucky, this could help us narrow down the suspects." Inspector Norizuki took out his pocket notebook and jotted down the movie title. He seemed to be serious.

Wondering if he could really be in earnest, Rintarō said, "This isn't just an after-dinner entertainment? Don't tell me that such a strange case has actually occurred?"

"Yes, it has, actually. I've been saying so from the beginning, haven't I? But it's not the movie version. This case is just like the first story of Ms A that you related. We've kept the message written in blood from the media, so it hasn't become a news item."

Rintarō stared wide-eyed at his father. "A copycat murder of an urban legend?"

Frowning deeply, the inspector replied, "It seems like it, from what you have to say."

"Then, please," Rintarō said eagerly, "give me the details and circumstances of the case."

2.

"The victim, or student B," Inspector Norizuki explained, "is Matsunaga Toshiki, a second-year student in the Sciences Department at M—— University. He lived in Room 206 of the Belle Maison Matsubara apartment building at Matsubara 1-chōme. This is a building for students a five-minute walk from Meidaimae Station on the Keiō Line. The name of the building is fancy, but the one-room units are just one rank above low-end apartments. Apparently the soundproofing is thorough, but as the front entrance has no auto-lock system, anyone can freely enter the building, even those who do not live there. Matsunaga's body was found lying on the floor of his room on Tuesday afternoon."

"Who found it?"

"A deliveryman from Yamaneko Delivery Company. It just happened that on Monday, the day before, a package was sent from Matsunaga's family in Shizuoka. The deliveryman rang the door-bell for Room 206, but there was no response. Noticing that the door was unlocked, the deliveryman suspected that Matsunaga was actually there but pretending not to be. It does seem a waste of gasoline to go repeatedly to the same address to try to deliver a package to a student who might be sleeping in until the sun is high in the sky," the Inspector said, seeming to sympathize with the deliveryman. "Just to make sure, he opened the door and peeked into the room to discover the victim lying in a pool of blood on the floor of the eight-tatami-mat-sized room. In a panic, the deliveryman tried to raise him up, but it was obvious that hours had passed since the victim had died. It was one forty-five pm when he called the police emergency number, 110, from the scene on his cell phone."

"It is fortunate that he gave priority to contacting the police over fulfilling his delivery quotas. What was the method used in the crime and the cause of death?"

"Matsunaga died almost immediately from loss of blood, having been stabbed in the chest with a sharply pointed object like a pick. But it wasn't that he was suddenly attacked while he was asleep in his bed. There were signs that he struggled with the assailant. So we should take it that the victim woke up and resisted."

"You say 'a sharply pointed object like a pick'. Could it have been something like a screwdriver?"

"No, we discovered an ice pick left in the sink with blood on the tip that matched the victim's blood. We found out that this ice pick wasn't brought in from elsewhere. It was one that Matsunaga, who liked to drink, frequently used. As the handle had been washed clean with water, we couldn't lift any fingerprints that might have been those of the murderer. According to the Identification Section, the murderer must have washed off most of the victim's blood at the same time."

"I see. The fact that there were signs of struggle and that the ice pick from the crime scene was used seems to indicate that it was an unpremeditated crime. What about the estimated time of death?"

"According to the medical examiner and the results of the autopsy, Matsunaga was killed between eleven p.m. on Monday and one a.m. on Tuesday. But we ascertained from the statements taken from those associated with the victim that he was already dead by about eleven-thirty pm."

"Whom do you mean by 'those associated with the victim'?" Rintarō cut in.

Inspector Norizuki did not respond right away; he appeared to want to tell his story at his own pace. Only after he had reached for a cigarette and taken his time lighting it did he continue.

"Those who were in the same club at the university, of course. I told you it was exactly like the story of Ms A, didn't I? Matsunaga Toshiki was a member of the university Bowling Club. He often invited other members of the club to drinking parties in his apartment. The solid soundproofing had the advantage that even if they became drunk and boisterous, his neighbors would not complain."

"Hmm, and that's why Matsunaga had his own ice pick?"

"Right. Monday, when the crime occurred, was the last day of first-term exams at the university. The Bowling Club members had gathered early in the evening at a pub in Shimokitazawa to celebrate the end of their exams. When that initial party at the pub broke up, the seven members of the club who were an especially close group repaired, as usual, to Belle Maison Matsubara to continue to drink. They said they bought some drinks and snacks at a convenience store on the way and began the second party just after nine p.m."

"Who was at the second party?"

"Four male students, including Matsunaga, and three female students. Here's the list of them."

So saying, the inspector opened to a page in his notebook. The list noted each member's name, major department, university year, gender, and the train station closest to his or her residence.

Matsunaga Toshiki	Sciences	2nd year	male	(Meidaimae)
Nozaki Tetsu	Sciences	2nd year	male	(Machida)
Miyoshi Nobuhiko	Law	2nd year	male	(Yōga)
Nagashima Yurika	Literature	2nd year	female	(Kichijōji)
Endō Fumiaki	Economics	1st year	male	(Tsutsujigaoka)
Hirotani Aki	Literature	1st year	female	(Yoyogi Hachiman)
Sekiguchi Reiko	Economics	1st year	female	(Umegaoka)

"There are two first-year female students, aren't there? Which one played the part of Ms A?" Rintarō asked as he attempted to commit the names on the list to memory.

"It was Hirotani Aki of the Literature Department. But let me tell you the facts in order. At first, the drinking party on Monday night was friendly and lively. But then it veers from your story. Partway through, there was quite a disagreement. Matsunaga and Miyoshi Nobuhiko, also a second-year student, started arguing over some small matter. Disregarding the efforts of the others to calm them down, they continued to revile each other."

"I thought you said it was a close-knit group? Did they dislike each other?"

"Apparently not normally. And though they insulted each other, they didn't actually come to blows. Matsunaga, who was the calmer of them, seemed to enjoy dishing out a string of insults that angered Miyoshi. Since he was drinking, Miyoshi must have overreacted to comments he would have let slide if he had been sober. Isn't that what student gathering have always been like?

Nevertheless, Miyoshi apparently did have a reason to dislike Matsunaga."

"Would that be related to this?" Rintarō extended his little finger, indicating girlfriend problems.

The inspector made a sour face and nodded. "Exactly. What they call a love triangle."

"Did it involve one of the three women there?"

"No, that's not it. It all happened in the past. There was a girl named Sasaki Megumi who had been a member of the Bowling Club. She was in the same year as Matsunaga and Miyoshi and was going out with Miyoshi. Then Matsunaga seduced her. With the trouble that created among the threesome, it became uncomfortable for her and she stopped attending club gatherings. She dropped out of the club, and ultimately her relationship with Miyoshi fell apart."

"I see. It's the kind of story you hear quite often."

"Well, yes. There's a bit more to it, but for now let's go on with the case. The two young men started quarreling shortly after ten p.m. At ten-thirty, Miyoshi said he had drunk too much and didn't feel well, so he would go home. I don't think he was really drunk. He probably felt uncomfortable. No one attempted to keep him there, so he left alone."

"The party didn't break up when Miyoshi left?"

"Not right away," the inspector replied. "But a pall was cast over the party, and those who remained started squirming. For about half an hour they continued with some desultory conversation until they decided to break it up. Matsunaga, the host, had stayed up all night the night before to study for his exam that day, so apparently he was having a hard time keeping his eyes open by then."

"Then perhaps his taunting Miyoshi wasn't out of spite but partly to keep himself awake."

"I wonder about that. In any event, shortly after eleven pm, after cleaning up the cigarette butts, empty bottles, and trash, the five remaining club members (other than Matsunaga) left Belle Maison Matsubara. They divided into two groups. Nozaki Tetsu and Nagashima Yurika, along with Endō Fumiaki, headed for Meidaimae Station. Hirotani Aki and Sekiguchi Reiko, the two first-year coeds, went in the opposite direction to Umegaoka Station on the Odakyō Odawara Line."

"Just a moment, Father." Rintarō broke in. ". . . I can understand why Nagashima Yurika, who lives in Kichijōji, and Endō Fumiaki, who was going to Tsutsujigaoka, would go to Meidaimae on the Keiō Line. But Nozaki Tetsu lives in Machida, doesn't he? Why didn't he go to Umegaoka Station on the Odakyō Line with the two first-year coeds?"

"That's because instead of going home to Machida, Nozaki went to spend the night at Yurika's apartment in Kichijōji," Inspector Norizuki said. "I should have explained earlier that Nozaki and Yurika were an accepted couple within the club. But Yurika asked me to keep this secret from her parents."

"So that's the deal. Sorry I keep interrupting your story. The point isn't that group but the two who headed for Umegaoka, isn't it?"

"Right you are." The Inspector cleared his throat and wet his lips. It was his signal that the story was entering its key stage. "The distance from Belle Maison Matsubara to Umegaoka Station takes about fifteen minutes on foot. When the two women reached the station, Hirotani Aki noticed that she didn't have her cell phone with her. She had received a call during the party, had taken her phone out of her bag then, and had forgotten it in Matsunaga's room. If it had been a different item that she had left, it would not have mattered much. But she couldn't go home without her cell phone, which to her is more valuable than her life. Flustered, Aki decided to go back to Belle Maison Matsubara."

"Did she go alone?"

"That's right. Sekiguchi Reiko did not go with her."

"That's strange. Even though the trains were still running, it was late for a young woman of nineteen to be walking the dark streets alone. That's not safe. Why didn't Sekiguchi Reiko go along with her? Perhaps the two of them weren't such good friends after all?"

Inspector Norizuki shook his head. "No, Aki and Reiko were the best of friends even within the group. This is unmistakable. Your doubts are justified, but there was a valid reason why Aki returned to Matsunaga's apartment alone. Aki borrowed Reiko's bicycle."

"Her bicycle?"

"Yup. Reiko lives in an apartment at Umegaoka 2-chōme, south of Umegaoka Station. She rides her bicycle to the station, where she takes the train. That's why Reiko's bicycle was at the station's bicycle parking lot that day. A distance that takes fifteen minutes to walk one way can be covered in a ten-minute round trip by bicycle. It's practical, isn't it? Reiko handed her bicycle key to Aki and went to the late-night donut shop facing the station to wait for her."

"I see. This is more involved than the urban legend. What happened then?"

"Aki pedaled to Belle Maison Matsubara on the borrowed bicycle. The party had let out after eleven p.m., and they had taken fifteen minutes to walk to Umegaoka Station. Let's say it took a few minutes to arrange to borrow the bicycle and five minutes to bike to Matsunaga's apartment. Aki would have reached the door of Room 206 around eleven-thirty pm. The highlight of the case starts here. Aki rang the doorbell of Matsunaga's apartment, but there was no answer. The light was off as well. As I said before, Matsunaga had stayed up all night the night before the drinking party and seemed quite sleepy by the time everyone left. It would not have been strange if he had turned off the light and crawled into bed as soon as he was alone. Wondering what she should do as she stood outside the door, Aki tried turning the doorknob. Matsunaga must have forgotten to lock his door before he went to bed. The door opened. The room was pitch dark . . ."

"This is just like the story of Ms A. But listening to you, it does sound like a plausible turn of events."

"That may be. After opening the door, Aki hesitated at the entryway. She felt she shouldn't wake the soundly sleeping Matsunaga just for her convenience. Besides, in the worst case, a groggy Matsunaga might mistake her appearance for a seduction and suddenly come at her. So, without turning on the light, she whispered softly, 'It's Aki, I've forgotten my cell phone, so I've come to pick it up.' She crawled on her knees so as not to have to take off her shoes and proceeded into the pitch-dark room. Having been there many times, she remembered the layout. She said she found her cell phone right off when she felt around on the floor where she had been sitting. She backed out the way she had come in without making a sound, quietly closed the door, and quickly left Matsunaga's room. She said it crossed her mind that it was unsafe to leave the door unlocked, but she told herself he would be all right because he was a man. Aki then jumped onto Reiko's bicycle and returned to the station to meet up with Reiko, who was waiting at the donut shop."

"Didn't she notice anything unusual when she entered Matsunaga's room?"

"No, nothing. Her mind must have been taken up with collecting her cell phone. She was convinced that Matsunaga was fast asleep in his bed, and apparently she didn't sense anything or hear any sounds that were eerie."

"I suppose she can't be faulted for that. Say she stayed in Matsunaga's apartment for a few minutes, then it took her about five minutes to return to the station by bicycle, the same amount of time as getting there. In that case, it must have been about eleven-forty when she met up with Reiko at the donut shop."

"Right. During our questioning I had them show me their receipts for the drinks they had ordered. They showed 11:26 for Reiko and 11:41 for Aki, who entered the shop later. The two of them chatted for a while at the donut shop, sobering up. They said they talked about their reactions to the argument between Matsunaga and Miyoshi. As Aki was returning to Yoyogi Hachiman, they left the shop a few minutes before 12:33 am, the departure time for the last train toward Shinjuku, and parted at the ticket gate."

3.

While Inspector Norizuki went to the toilet, Rintarō prepared some cold drinks in the kitchen. The night was deepening, but the discussion about the case was only now entering its crucial phase. His father would be wanting a drink about now.

"Hey, that's considerate." Returning to the living room, Inspector Norizuki took a sip.

Rintarō joined him, just to wet his throat.

Bending his neck sideways to give it a stretch, the Inspector continued, "I got as far as telling you that Hirotani Aki and Sekiguchi Reiko had parted at Umegaoka Station. I don't have to tell you what happened next. It's almost the same end as Ms A's story."

"Almost?"

"There are a few differences. For example, Aki didn't drop by Belle Maison Matsubara the following day, and during her questioning she didn't faint when she found out about the message written in blood. But she turned pale when she heard about it and couldn't stop shaking. It will affect her for quite a while."

"It must have been quite a shock."

"Of course it was. It wasn't only Matsunaga's dead body that was right in front of her eyes in that pitch-dark room but also someone who had just committed murder. She must have been in mortal fear. I sent her home with an officer for protection in case of the worst. I've had her watched ever since. It would be good if she could recall something that might be a clue to identifying the murderer, but I don't have much hope of that. After all, the phrase 'Aren't you glad you didn't turn on the light?' was also a warning aimed at her."

"Can that message be used as physical evidence? The trace of the finger or the handwriting?"

"No, the murderer is quite clever." His expression glum, Inspector Norizuki turned his eyes to the ashtray on the table. "According to the Identification Section, the words in blood were written with a cigarette butt left in the room, by soaking the filter in blood. The victim was a chain smoker. We haven't found the blood-soaked cigarette butt. It must have been flushed down the toilet. We can't rely on the handwriting, either. It is unnaturally faltering, almost as if it were written by a child."

"Does it look as if it was written with the non-dominant hand to hide the penmanship?"

"Yes, that's about it. And now I'd like to have your thoughts. You said there were many versions to the story of Ms A. Are there any that deal with the murderer's character?"

Since his father had chided him earlier for showing off, Rintarō took care not to be pretentious when he answered, "Even if there were some, it probably wouldn't be of any use. In these kinds of rumors, the murders usually end up being committed by an escaped convict or a crazed killer with a screw loose."

"I thought as much. Just for the record, there's been no report of any prison escapes this month," the Inspector said.

Nodding, Rintarō continued, "There's probably the influence of an actual crime committed in America in the motif of a psychotic killer leaving a crime-scene message written in blood. For example, in the 1969 Sharon Tate mass murder, where five people including the actress were butchered by the Charles Manson Family, the word 'Pig' was inscribed with the victims' blood on the wall of the crime scene, and at the scene of another murder they committed that same day, the words 'Helter Skelter' were used."

"I've heard of that one. Weren't those words from a Beatles song?"

"Yes. And even further back, from 1945 to the following year, there was the case of William Heirens, a murderer who killed three females, including a six-year-old girl, for the fun of it. A seventeen-year-old student at the University of Chicago at the time, Heirens left a message written with the victim's lipstick at the crime scene. It said, 'For heaven's sake catch me before I kill more. I cannot control myself.'"

"Hmm. He must have been completely crazy."

"In Heirens's case, it wasn't written in blood, but the memory of these kinds of shocking crimes works on the public's subconscious. And you can see why the 'message written in blood' was made into a symbol of the indiscriminate psychotic murderer. But this is just to say that this was the case for the original urban legend. It doesn't prove definitively that the actual murder at Belle Maison Matsubara was committed by a psychotic, or in the manner of a killer who wantonly knifes passers-by."

Inspector Norizuki rubbed his chin and nodded his satisfaction. "I agree with you on that. As a practical matter, even if we consider just the time factor, I can't conceive that a psychotic with no past connection to the victim would enter Matsunaga's room and kill the occupant."

"What do you mean 'the time factor'?"

"As I explained to you, it was just past eleven p.m. when the club members departed Belle Maison Matsubara. And it was eleven-thirty when Aki, having returned to pick up her cell phone, nearly ran into the murderer in the pitch-dark room. It is much too preposterous to suppose that a total stranger would break into Matsunaga's room and kill him in the span of those thirty minutes, even if he had forgotten to lock his door. I just can't believe that such a thing could happen."

"That is true. In that case, do you think that the message 'Aren't you glad you didn't turn on the light?' was an elaborate trick to make it look as if a wanton psychotic killer was the culprit?"

"Yes. But rather than say it was an elaborate setup, I would say it was done on the spur of the moment. I wasn't sure until I talked to you, but hearing that the phrase is straight out of a popular urban legend, I'm able to have conviction about my theory. That's not all." The Inspector set his glass on the table to stress his next point. "When we consider what went on before and after, there's a high probability that Matsunaga's murderer was one of the members of the drinking party on Monday night."

"The way you say that, it sounds as if you already have an idea who the killer is. Is it because of an alibi?"

At Rintarō's anticipation of the next step, the inspector grinned.

"That's about it. From Aki's statement and the content of the message in blood, there can be no mistake that the murderer was in Matsunaga's room around eleven-thirty. Now, turning to everyone's alibi. We've already discussed Hirotani Aki and Sekiguchi Reiko. I can add that not only do we have the times stamped on the receipts, we also have backing for their statements from an attendant at the donut shop. During the fifteen minutes or so before she met with Aki, Reiko occupied a seat within sight of the shop attendant and did not leave the shop. It was about twelve twenty-five when the two of them left the donut shop."

"Seems airtight. Next?"

"The couple, Nozaki Tetsu and Nagashima Yurika, I just told you about. After they parted from Endō Fumiaki, who was going home to Tsutsujigaoka, on the platform at Meidaimae Station, they went toward Kichijōji on the Inogashira Line, and then to her apartment. They were together until morning, and provide alibis for each other."

"Hmm. We can't discard the possibility that they were accomplices, but . . . What about Endō Fumiaki after he left the other two?"

"He stated that he went home directly, without stopping off anywhere. There isn't any direct proof to back up his statement, but we found out that just at that time a classmate, also in the Economics Department, called Endō's cell phone. According to that classmate's statement, he talked continuously with Endō for about ten minutes from eleven twenty-five."

"I see." Rintarō started and slapped his knee. "That was when Aki was in Matsunaga's room. At that moment, the killer must have been hiding in the dark room after killing Matsunaga. So, regardless of where he was, Endō, who was talking on his cell phone with his classmate, couldn't have been the killer."

"Exactly. As for the last one left, Miyoshi Nobuhiko, he doesn't have a definite alibi. According to his statement, after he left Belle Maison Matsubara alone at ten-thirty, he went to several video-game centers in the area, still in a foul mood from his argument with Matsunaga. He played games for about an hour, and then took the train home to Yōga. He lives with his parents and siblings. The family stated that he returned home shortly after midnight."

"So he got home shortly after midnight. Say he left Matsunaga's apartment after eleven-thirty. If he walked to Matsubara Station, took a train on the Tōkyū Setagaya Line, and changed to the Denentoshi Line at Sangenjaya, he would have had time to reach home by then."

"Right. We're looking for witnesses around the game centers, but so far we have no reports of anyone seeing someone fitting Miyoshi's description around that time. Not only doesn't he have an alibi, but also in terms of motive, since he had an intense argument with the victim during the drinking party, Miyoshi seems suspicious to me," Inspector Norizuki stated emphatically.

It was perfectly natural to suspect Miyoshi from what had been discussed so far. Yet, as he sifted through the alibis, Rintarō felt a slight doubt. Since he couldn't put his finger on what specifically was bothering him, he decided to go along for a while longer with his father's theory.

"We were still in the middle of the story with regard to motive, weren't we? You said that there was a story behind the trouble between Matsunaga and Miyoshi – concerning the former club member Sasaki Megumi. What's that all about?"

"It relates to the victim's conduct. And it's typical of young people these days in that drugs were involved."

Inspector Norizuki let the implication hang and reached for another cigarette.

"One of Matsunaga's relatives is a cousin eight years older than he who is an internist with a psychiatric specialty. Apparently Matsunaga had something on this cousin. It's probably a trite thing, like he knew of the cousin's extramarital affair or something. In exchange for keeping quiet about this secret, Matsunaga hit his cousin up for drugs that are ordinarily hard to get."

"Were they illegal drugs?"

"No. Only Prozac, an antidepressant put out by an American pharmaceutical company. It's not a crime just to possess it. The victim had some fifty green-and-white capsules hidden away. When the crime scene was investigated, the search of Matsunaga's room revealed the pills in a cardboard box in his closet."

"Prozac is a drug said to promote the production of seratonin in the brain and to be very effective in treating depression. I hear that since it came on the market in America, it's sometimes used as a legal 'happy drug' even by healthy people. . . . Does that mean Matsunaga had a tendency toward depression?"

"No, he himself was quite healthy. He may have tried it once or twice, but there's no indication that he was a regular user. It seems Matsunaga was selling the Prozac he got from his cousin to people he knew as a way to earn some spending money."

Rintarō furrowed his brow at this piece of unexpected information. "Just a minute. If the victim was selling drugs, the motive for the crime could have been trouble related to a drug deal. I don't mean to say a drug user is necessarily a psychotic, but doesn't this completely change the nature of the case?"

"I don't think so. We checked into that possibility, but Matsunaga wasn't selling enough to make him a drug dealer. And he didn't have any drugs other than Prozac." He added that Matsunaga used a rough count, and appeared not to have a ledger or list of buyers, either. Having struck down Rintarō's suspicion with one blow, Inspector Norizuki exhaled smoke and continued, "It's also called SSRI – Selective Seratonin Re-uptake Inhibitor – and there is a similar domestic drug on the market. Insurance will cover that one. Prozac hasn't been approved by the Health and Labor Ministry yet. But it's all right for qualified physicians to prescribe it to patients, and it's no longer rare for people to use the Internet to import it on an individual basis."

"You mean it's rather widely available, so selling it can only bring in enough for spending money?"

"Exactly. If he did it too openly, he would be targeted, and if he approached someone in the know he would be taken advantage of. After all, there are plenty of other routes to get hold of it. Unless he was using it as a way to pick up girls, about all he could do was to sell small amounts to naive, earnest coeds as a cure for May post university entry depression."

"May depression isn't so prevalent anymore. But are you suggesting that Sasaki Megumi is one of those who bought Prozac from Matsunaga?"

"Yes. Megumi was an intense, introverted type from the start, so she must have been an easy mark for Matsunaga. She regularly bought the drug from him without letting her boyfriend Miyoshi know about it. If that was all, it would have been one thing, but Matsunaga apparently pressed for a physical relationship in exchange for giving her the drug. He probably didn't actually succeed, but this caused Megumi to become deeply neurotic. She couldn't face Miyoshi, and she may also have suffered a reaction to having become dependent on Prozac. Not only did she stop showing up at the Bowling Club, she also stopped attending her classes. Now she is on leave and recuperating at home."

Disheartened, Rintarō said, "That's abominable. I can't blame Miyoshi for holding that against Matsunaga."

"See? There's no doubting that he had a motive. And as to opportunity, if we consider the crime to have been committed by Miyoshi, the time factor that has been the bottleneck for the case will fit exactly."

"How so?"

"It would go like this. Having had a verbal fight full of recriminations with Matsunaga, Miyoshi left Belle Maison Matsubara at ten-thirty. But instead of going to the game center as he claimed in his statement, he could have wandered around nearby, intending to cool his head. He did this for thirty or forty minutes, but he was still angry, so he went back to the party intending to settle the argument. But when he returned to Belle Maison Matsubara, the party had ended, and Room 206 was quiet. He rang the doorbell, but there was no answer, and it appeared that Matsunaga had already gone to bed. Just as he was about to give up and head home, Miyoshi noticed that the door was unlocked."

Folding his arms across his chest, Rintarō uttered without much enthusiasm, "I see. And then?"

"Miyoshi stole into the room without turning on the light, roused the sleeping Matsunaga, and let loose a string of abuse. The time was between eleven-fifteen and eleven-twenty. At this stage I don't think Miyoshi had any clear intent to kill. But having been woken from his sleep, Matsunaga could hardly have stood for this. Mistaking the intruder for a burglar, he may have swung at Miyoshi without first questioning him. The two of them scuffled, and after several rounds, one of them took hold of the ice pick left in the room. As they grappled for it in the dark, Miyoshi's hand faltered and the stainless-steel tip ended up stabbing Matsunaga's chest. The hands of the clock showed half-past eleven. It was then, as Miyoshi was standing in a daze over Matsunaga's dead body in the darkened room, that Hirotani Aki, who knew nothing of this, came to retrieve what she had forgotten."

Having recreated the crime as if he had seen it happen, Inspector Norizuki jerked his chin up and sought his son's reaction.

Arms still folded, Rintarō absent-mindedly gazed at the ceiling. Finally he said, "You certainly make the time factor fit. Your theory gives a logical explanation for the victim having been killed in less than thirty minutes after he was left alone. However . . ."

Peering at Rintarō dubiously, the Inspector said, "What do you mean, 'However'? Is there something that is unconvincing to you?"

"Yes, a major something. If that were the end of the story, then your theory would hold up. But the problem lies in what comes after that. If we consider Miyoshi to be the murderer, it is inconceivable that he would have written the message in blood. The message 'Aren't you glad you didn't turn on the light?' was not left by Miyoshi."

4.

"I started thinking something was off as I reviewed the alibis of those at the drinking party," Rintarō explained to his father as he unfolded his arms. "I should have realized what it was earlier. Namely, that if Miyoshi were the murderer, then the disadvantage to him of leaving the message in blood far outweighs the advantage of making the crime appear to be like the urban legend."

Inspector Norizuki cocked his head. "Disadvantage?"

"Yes. Let's first look at the advantage. We've been thinking that the message 'Aren't you glad you didn't turn on the light?' was a deliberate trick to make Matsunaga's murder look like a crime committed randomly by a psychotic. However, if you think it over a bit, it's obvious that one couldn't hope to alter the focus of the investigation with such a childish trick. As the phrase is copied straight from a popular urban legend, even if I hadn't told you, sooner or later someone would have noted that fact. Once the message was discovered to be a fake, it is clear that suspicion would fall on whoever harbored hatred toward the victim. The killer would have been able to foresee that much. And even more so from Miyoshi's standpoint, as he had had a confrontation with the victim over a love triangle. To put it another way, there is hardly any advantage for Miyoshi to have left the message in blood."

"What you say makes sense, but isn't it merely a theory born of hindsight?"

"You could say that if we look only at the advantage side. But the disadvantages that come about from leaving the bloody message are even more critical. Can you see? Let's say that, just as you imagined, Miyoshi killed Matsunaga at eleven-thirty pm, and was nearly bumped into by Aki at the crime scene. Under cover of darkness, he succeeded in not being seen by her. In that case, why would he purposely leave a message saying 'Aren't you glad you didn't turn on the light?' which would tell not only Aki but also the police that he had been there at that time?"

The Inspector sucked in air in surprise.

Rintarō continued: "According to your story, Father, Aki wasn't aware that the murderer was hiding in Matsunaga's room until she was told about the bloody message. That means that if the message hadn't been left, no one would have found out that the murderer was at the crime scene at eleven-thirty. The same can be said for the estimated time of death. Without the bloody message, it would have been impossible to specify the time when the crime was committed."

"Yes, what you say is true, but . . ."

"Let's keep this in mind and review the theory that Miyoshi committed the crime. If, as in the initial supposition, he killed Matsunaga at eleven-thirty pm, he should have been the one to most dislike having the time the crime was committed narrowed down. This was because he had no definite alibi from the time he left Matsunaga's apartment at ten-thirty. As he had no way of establishing an alibi after the fact, all Miyoshi could hope for was that suspicion be deflected from him onto others who had attended the party due to there being no precisely estimated time of death. That is, the wider the range of the estimated time of death, the greater the benefit to him. Though he may have been upset immediately after killing Matsunaga, when he calmed down and became more rational, he would have been able to make such a calculation. That is why I wonder about Miyoshi having left the message written in blood . . ."

"Just a minute. Isn't it dangerous to jump to such a conclusion?" Recovering a little, Inspector Norizuki attempted to put the brakes on Rintarō's deduction. "We can't assume that Miyoshi assessed the advantages and disadvantages and acted rationally. It is possible that he may have had his attention only on the less likely advantages and impulsively wrote the message."

"I can't see that happening. After all, you yourself said the killer was exceedingly clever. And if Miyoshi had lost his cool, could he have held his breath in the dark and refrained from killing Aki as well?"

The Inspector's face betrayed acknowledgment of his weak point. Yet he seemed not to be entirely convinced, and said, as if he were poking at the crumbs left in a lunchbox, "Your argument certainly makes sense, but to me it is, after all, founded on extremely passive grounds."

"What do you mean?"

"The reasoning your theory attributes to Miyoshi is entirely passive. For no matter how much the estimated time of death is broadened, it doesn't change Miyoshi's not having an alibi, does it? Wouldn't he be pushing his luck to sit back and do nothing and expect to avoid being suspected?"

Nodding at this commendable objection, Rintarō replied, "Naturally, you would have such a rebuttal. But go back to what you said about passive grounds. If Miyoshi were the culprit, he would also have had an active reason for leaving the scene without writing the message in blood."

"And what would that be?"

"As I said before, if there had been no message in blood, when Aki returned at eleven-thirty to pick up what she had forgotten, no one would have found out that the killer, that is, a third person other than Aki and the victim, had been there. In fact, she had visited the victim's apartment entirely alone within the limits of the estimated time of death. This meant that the first person to be suspected would be none other than Aki herself. If the message hadn't existed, would the police have taken her statement as the truth? I can't think that would be the case. If Miyoshi had been there, I'm sure he would have thought the same way – that he had motive and no alibi. And that by quitting the scene without leaving evidence that someone else had been there he would be helping to shift the suspicion of murder to Aki, who had the misfortune to have shown up at the scene of the crime. This wouldn't at all be an unnatural way to think."

Rintarō stopped to wait for his father's response. The theory of Miyoshi Nobuhiko as murder suspect was about to go under.

Still, the Inspector seemed to persist in promoting his own theory. With a jut of his chin he said, "It might be that Miyoshi was in love with Aki. Weighing the fact that Aki would be suspected versus the fact that his crime would be exposed, what if he deliberately chose to leave a message that would be disadvantageous to himself?"

Shaking his head firmly, Rintarō countered, "That is an impossibility. If Miyoshi loved Aki, he wouldn't have left a message written in blood that would frighten her. It could result in her becoming deeply traumatized, just like Sasaki Megumi. I'm sorry, Father, but you have no more escape routes. The Miyoshi-as-culprit theory is now completely disproved. He is not the one who killed Matsunaga."

"Mmm." Letting out a moan of defeat, the Inspector, having nothing else to do, lit a cigarette. He smoked it wordlessly for a while, but then he slapped himself on the forehead. "All right. I agree. I'll take back my suspicions about Miyoshi. But this means the investigation is back to square one. If it wasn't Miyoshi, then who the hell killed Matsunaga?"

"There's no need to go back to square one."

The inspector raised his eyebrows. "Does that mean you have an idea who the real murderer is?"

"Yes. All we have to do is to look at our argument from the opposite direction. We should ask what conditions would allow for the disadvantage of leaving the message in blood to work contrarily, to favor the killer. In other words, who would gain the most from the existence of the message 'Aren't you glad you didn't turn on the light?' That's what we need to look at."

His cigarette still at his lips, Inspector Norizuki suddenly glared.

"Do you mean Hirotani Aki? You just said that if there had been no message in blood, she would undoubtedly have been the first to be suspected."

"Just as you say. The reason Aki's statement was recognized as being true to fact was due to the message in blood. What if, though, her statement was a boldfaced lie? What if, when she went back to Belle Maison Matsubara to retrieve her cell phone, Matsunaga was still alive, and no one was hiding in the darkened room?"

"Then the message saying 'Aren't you glad you didn't turn on the light?' was . . ."

"Of course, Aki herself wrote it."

"What?! I can't buy that."

But Rintarō persisted. "Let's start from where her story begins. When Aki went back to Matsunaga's apartment, did she really not turn on the light? Her own statement is the only thing to back this up. You mentioned that in her statement she said one of the reasons she didn't turn on the light was that in the worst case, a groggy Matsunaga might mistake her appearance for a seduction and suddenly attack her. What if this statement wasn't hypothetical but what actually happened, and Aki let it slip out?"

"What actually happened? You mean Matsunaga tried to assault Aki?"

"It's not impossible. After all, Matsunaga had made a prior attempt at seducing a friend's girlfriend. Returning to Matsunaga's apartment to retrieve her cell phone after the party, Aki entered the unlocked room and turned on the light, waking the soundly sleeping Matsunaga. Drunk and half-asleep, Matsunaga seized the chance of Aki having come back alone and tried to take advantage of her. Of course Aki resisted. Desperate to protect herself, Aki grabbed the ice pick used during the party, which was within reach, and stabbed Matsunaga in the chest. I doubt she had any intention to kill him, but that one stab was fatal, and he slumped to his death."

"That section is similar to the Miyoshi-as-murderer theory."

"Is that sour grapes?" Rintarō grinned. "It goes without saying that Aki was shaken up. Coming to her senses with difficulty, she considered how she might conceal her crime. Her problem was Sekiguchi Reiko, who was waiting for her return at the donut shop. The police would eventually find out from Reiko that Aki had returned alone to Matsunaga's apartment to reclaim what she had forgotten. At that point, she would be the first to be suspected. Was there some way she could avoid this predicament? At that moment, what flashed across her mind like a revelation was the story she had heard from someone of Ms A and the murderer who had left a message written in blood. She might be able to thwart the police investigation if she acted the part of Ms A, who narrowly evaded becoming a second victim of the person who had just killed a fellow university student in the dark. Having thought this up on the spot, Aki copied the urban legend and left the message 'Aren't you glad you didn't turn on the light?' Then she turned off the light, left the apartment, and rode the bicycle she had borrowed from Reiko back to the donut shop as though nothing had happened."

"If that were the case," said Inspector Norizuki doubtfully, "what about her reaction when she saw the message during her questioning?"

"Of course that was an act."

"But I can't believe it was."

"That's likely because you had a preconception as to what her reaction would be."

"I wonder. It's not as though I've learned nothing during the many years I've spent in the interrogation room. If she had fainted on the spot like Ms A did, I would admit that Aki had faked it. But her reaction was the real stuff. And even if my perception is wrong, your theory has holes in it."

Rintarō sat up so as to squarely face his father's counterattack. "What holes?"

"It's a time problem. As the donut shop receipts show, there were at most fifteen minutes when Aki was alone after she parted from Reiko. And ten of those minutes were taken up bicycling round-trip between Umegaoka Station and Belle Maison Matsubara. Even with a liberal estimate, Aki could have been in Matsunaga's room for only five minutes. Just think about it: five minutes is only 300 seconds. On your theory, in just that short amount of time, Aki began to struggle with Matsunaga, who tried to take advantage of her," as he continued, the Inspector counted the points off on his fingers, "stabbed him with the ice pick, then, barely recovering from the shock of killing someone from over-defensiveness, she immediately thought up the brilliant idea to make it seem like a copycat of the urban legend, wrote the message in blood with a cigarette filter, flushed the filter down the toilet, washed the blood from the ice pick and her hands at the sink, made certain she left nothing, and quickly left the scene of the crime. And that's not all. She would have needed time to straighten out her appearance, which must have become disheveled during her struggle with the victim, so that Reiko wouldn't suspect anything. This might be possible in one of your novels, but in actuality, do you think she had enough time to do all of that in just five minutes? What's more, Aki is a nineteen-year-old college student, not a professional killer. She couldn't possibly have remained calm enough to complete all that so quickly and efficiently immediately after she had unexpectedly killed someone."

The tables had turned. Uncharacteristically red-faced, Rintarō dejectedly scratched his head. "I have to admit that the time factor is rather difficult . . . But what if Aki used an illusion as a trick, causing Reiko's sense of time to be off, and was able to squeeze out more than five minutes?"

"Hardly. What about the times stamped on the donut shop receipts?"

"Maybe she pilfered another customer's receipt and switched it with hers or Reiko's receipt?"

Inspector Norizuki gave a snort. "Now you're forcing an improbability. I told you we have corroboration from the donut shop attendant regarding the alibis for Hirotani Aki and Sekiguchi Reiko. There are no holes in their statements. I say there is no chance that Aki killed Matsunaga."

5.

Still, Rintarō was unable to give up on his theory that Aki had committed the crime. Various possibilities branched out in his head. Somewhere there must be a shortcut that would clear the time obstacle . . .

After a while, he spoke. "What if we look at it this way? The crime committed on Monday night wasn't spontaneous, but planned out to the smallest detail."

"You mean Aki planned it? But Aki had no reason for killing Matsunaga, did she?"

"Maybe she did. Just as with Sasaki Megumi, drugs may have been involved. Aki may have regularly obtained Prozac from Matsunaga, but there was some trouble over the deal. When that became a big problem, Aki decided to kill Matsunaga."

"Hmm. Trouble regarding Prozac deals," Inspector Norizuki said, without much enthusiasm. "But I wouldn't think that would lead to murder – though it can't be ruled out completely. Well, what then?"

"In her murder plan, Aki decided to use the rumour about the murderer leaving a message written in blood at the crime scene. It goes without saying that her objective was to deflect suspicion by playing the role of Ms A. So, on Monday night, she didn't happen to forget her cell phone in Matsunaga's room; she had planned it. This was to create a natural reason for returning to Belle Maison Matsubara after the drinking party was over – she may have already taken the ice pick with her at that time. And it was probably Aki who suggested that she borrow Reiko's bicycle in front of Umegaoka Station. If Reiko had gone back with her, she would have hindered Aki's committing the crime. At the same time, arranging to meet her at the donut shop must have been done with the purpose of creating an alibi."

"Why was the door to Matsunaga's apartment unlocked when Aki returned to Belle Maison Matsubara? It's too convenient to have been a coincidence."

"Of course, it wasn't a coincidence. She must have secretly told the victim before the party that she would return alone later. I don't know what kind of reason she gave, but Matsunaga was waiting for her without going to sleep, unaware that she had murderous intentions. Aki pedaled the bicycle as fast as she could back to Belle Maison Matsubara. As soon as she entered Room 206, she stabbed Matsunaga in the chest with the ice pick when he welcomed her – with no hesitation."

"Wait. There was evidence on Matsunaga's body that indicated he had struggled with his assailant."

"Aki faked the evidence afterward. As she had planned, after she dipped the cigarette filter in his blood, wrote the message 'Aren't you glad you didn't turn on the light?' and quickly took care of all those things that you just counted off, Aki hurriedly left the room. With a plan firmly in place, it wouldn't be impossible to complete all of these steps within five minutes. In actuality, there was no grappling with the victim, so her hair and clothes were not messed up. After this, Aki again pedaled full speed to the station and met up with Reiko at the donut shop as if nothing had happened. How about that, Father? I would think that it was quite possible for Aki to kill Matsunaga even if she only had about five minutes."

The response from the Inspector was not favorable. Blowing a lungful of smoke at Rintarō's face, he retorted, "It might be possible – as a desktop plan. But your theory has a fatal flaw."

"Oh?"

"Let's say she did plan Matsunaga's murder," the Inspector said cuttingly. "Why would she need to fake it as an urban legend in order to accomplish it? If it were a spontaneously committed crime, I could understand – Aki's random behavior happened to coincide with the story of Ms. A and became the impetus for leaving the bloody-lettered message. But if the murder was premeditated, nowhere is there a reason to embellish it with the urban legend motif. There are many other ways to set it up, so why would she have concocted such a convoluted, intricate plan? Such a plan, which mistakes the means for the end, could only be entertained in the abstract by someone lacking a real necessity for committing the crime."

Rintarō was forced into silence. He had to admit it was exactly as his father said.

6.

"This makes it a draw between us in terms of injuries." Inspector Norizuki spoke as if to encourage the despondent Rintarō. He had just returned from the kitchen, fresh drinks in hand. He set the glasses on the table and sat down heavily.

"Don't be so discouraged. The night is still young. Let's rethink the case one more time, going back to our first assumptions. I don't buy your identifying Hirotani Aki as the murderer, but I don't think the direction of your reasoning was wrong. As you suggested, Matsunaga's killer was someone who would benefit from leaving the message 'Aren't you glad you didn't turn on the light?' "

Sighing deeply as he reached for his glass, Rintarō said, "The problem then becomes the nature of the benefit, doesn't it?"

•

"Yeah. But I don't have any bright ideas on that. Shall we go over the list of those at the party one more time? It's not unusual in a race in which the front-runner and its rival horse fall for a dark horse that no one had paid attention to to carry off the victory."

So saying, the Inspector drew lines through the names listed in his notebook.

~~Matsunaga Toshiki~~	~~Sciences~~	~~2nd year~~	~~male~~	~~(Meidaimae)~~
Nozaki Tetsu	Sciences	2nd year	male	(Machida)
~~Miyoshi Nobuhiko~~	~~Law~~	~~2nd year~~	~~male~~	~~(Yōga)~~
Nagashima Yurika	Literature	2nd year	female	(Kichijōji)
Endō Fumiaki	Economics	1st year	male	(Tsutsujigaoka)
~~Hirotani Aki~~	~~Literature~~	~~1st year~~	~~female~~	~~(Yoyogi Hachiman)~~
Sekiguchi Reiko	Economics	1st year	female	(Umegaoka)

"Of the four remaining, can we exclude the two who have solid alibis for eleven-thirty pm – Endō Fumiaki and Sekiguchi Reiko? If so, we can look at the couple – Nozaki Tetsu and Nagashima Yurika. As you pointed out before, if these two had colluded and concocted a false alibi . . . Huh? What is it, Rintarō?"

While the Inspector was speaking, Rintarō suddenly looked up at the ceiling, his jaw dropping open. From his lips escaped the whisper, ". . . a solid alibi."

He did not stir at all for a time, until eventually his eyes began to shine brightly. All of a sudden, he slammed both of his hands on the table.

"That's it! That's the only possibility! I've been blind!"

Inspector Norizuki was dumbfounded at this turnaround. "Hey, are you all right?"

"Sure I am, Father. Actually I should say I've finally come to my senses. The answer has been right in front of our noses all along, and I didn't even notice it."

"In front of our noses?"

"Yes. The clue to the truth was something I said when we were discussing the Miyoshi-as-killer theory. Didn't I say that if there had been no message in blood, it would have been impossible to pin down the time the crime was committed?"

"Yeah, I remember hearing something like that."

"That's exactly the advantage gained by leaving the message in blood. It's a simple but extremely effective alibi trick. Can

I explain? The medical examiner estimated the victim's time of death to be between eleven pm on Monday and one am the following day at its broadest. This means that the actual crime could have been committed before eleven-thirty or after that time. But the murderer used Aki's statement and left the message 'Aren't you glad you didn't turn on the light?' to plant the impression that the crime was committed at eleven-thirty – despite the fact that the murderer was not in Matsunaga's room at that time. To put it another way, the person who benefited from the existence of this message, that is, the real killer of Matsunaga, had to be someone who had a solid alibi for eleven-thirty pm."

Rintarō had rushed on without pausing for breath. As if his son's excitement had transferred to him, Inspector Norizuki was now on the edge of his seat. "I see. The trick of using preconception as a counterattack. In that case, the couple Nozaki Tetsu and Nagashima Yurika, whose alibi isn't limited to eleven-thirty don't fit the criterion. The ones who have a solid alibi for eleven-thirty pm are Endō Fumiaki and Sekiguchi Reiko, but—"

"Endō isn't the killer. I can say that because he doesn't meet the other criterion necessary for leaving the message in blood."

"What other criterion?"

"In order to leave that message in blood, the person had to know not only that Aki went back to Matsunaga's apartment to retrieve what she had forgotten, but also the fact that she left the room *without ever having turned on the light*. Without knowing that, it would be meaningless, impossible, really, to leave the message 'Aren't you glad you didn't turn on the light?' Endō was not in a position to have known in advance about the details of Aki's actions. Therefore, he is not the killer."

Solemn-faced, Inspector Norizuki said, "That leaves one person . . ."

"Sekiguchi Reiko. She meets both criteria that I just set out. One: At eleven-thirty pm Reiko was at the donut shop at Umegaoka Station and had a solid alibi. Two: Reiko met up at the donut shop with Aki, who had returned from Matsunaga's apartment, and had the chance to hear from her the details of what happened in his room."

"Hmm. Most likely Aki told her about it right off. The two of them left the donut shop around twelve twenty-five am. That means that after parting with Aki at the station's ticket gate, Reiko went back to Belle Maison Matsubara. What was her reason for that?"

"This is just my supposition, but I think it involves the Prozac that Matsunaga had. Let's say Reiko purchased the drug periodically from Matsunaga. He may have charged more than the normal rate, and Reiko may have had difficulty paying up. But that night, Reiko heard from Aki about Matsunaga's room – that he was fast asleep with the door unlocked."

Stroking his chin, Inspector Norizuki said, deep in thought, "I get it. And I wouldn't be surprised, from the impression I got talking to her, if she were taking Prozac. She seemed to be kind of a highly-strung type, one of the best students from the countryside. That's the type who sometimes do bad things on the spur of the moment, though they don't look like they would. On your supposition, then, Reiko crept into Matsunaga's apartment while he was asleep and tried to steal some Prozac, which was put away somewhere."

"When we look at it that way, everything fits into place. It took five minutes for her to return to Belle Maison Matsubara from the station on her own bicycle. She entered Room 206 just after twelve-thirty. Leaving the room dark so she wouldn't wake the sleeping Matsunaga, Reiko began to search the apartment, feeling around with her hands. But she must have tripped on something in the dark, making a loud noise. Woken up by the noise, Matsunaga noticed Reiko's presence. He must have realized right away that she had come for the Prozac. Angered, Matsunaga hurled himself onto Reiko and grappled with her. Here our familiar ice pick comes into play and Reiko stabs Matsunaga dead... At the least, this all happened before twelve forty-five."

"That's just barely within the range of the estimated time of death. Then what?"

"With Matsunaga's body in front of her, Reiko probably couldn't think of anything for a while. Her initial aim of stealing the Prozac must have flown out of her mind. But she had plenty of time to come to her senses and devise a cover-up. She could bicycle back to her place in Umegaoka, so she didn't need to be concerned about the time of the last train. As her breathing returned to normal in the dark, while she gazed at Matsunaga's dead body, Reiko remembered that Aki had returned to Matsunaga's apartment to retrieve what she had forgotten. That led quite naturally to her recalling the rumor of the message in blood that she had heard from someone. If she set it up so that it seemed Aki had narrowly avoided bumping into the murderer . . . Of course, at the time that Aki actually went back to Matsunaga's apartment, he was still alive, fast asleep, unaware of her presence. But, if Reiko created conditions in which it would appear that Matsunaga had already been killed and the killer was hiding in the room, her alibi of being at the donut shop in front of the station at that time would clear her of suspicion. Reiko must have smiled slightly at her idea. She stood up and found Matsunaga's cigarette lighter to use for a light. Then, picking up a cigarette butt, she dipped it into the blood flowing from the victim's wound. Holding this in her non-dominant hand, she wrote the message on the wall – 'Aren't you glad you didn't turn on the light?' " "

A while later, postcards, always with the same message, began arriving once a week for Ms A. They were sent by Ms C, who had been her best friend and a member of the same club. The sender's address was the medical correctional institution in Hachiōji. When Ms A moved, the deliveries would stop for a while, but someone must have been secretly looking up her address, for soon the postcards, with the same message, would start arriving at the new address. Written on the back of the postcard, always in red pencil, in an unsteady scrawl, were the words, "Why didn't you turn on the light?"

Every time she read these words, Ms A felt a chill go up her spine. She also felt that she could never get rid of her regret – if, that night when she had returned to his room, she had turned on the light and woken B, then he would not have been killed! And her best friend, Ms C, would not have been so burdened by her guilt that she went insane.

Translation by Beth Cary

The Duel

Jacob Vis

My wife sleeps with open eyes. She lies on her back and stares at the ceiling with half-open eyes. She seems to be dead. I bring my mouth to her ear and whisper: "I am going to kill you."

She stays motionless. She breathes lightly, with long, irregular pauses. I whisper again, a little louder: "Elaine, I am going to kill you."

She moves her lips. Suddenly she closes her eyes. She sits straight, clings to me and screams: "He wants to kill me! He wants to kill me!" She shrieks her night breath in my face. I pull her head against my shoulder and say: "Relax! Nothing happened. It was only a dream."

She shocks as if she is being electrocuted. She slowly relaxes, but she holds me tight. "He wanted to kill me," she says in a childish little voice. "The bastard wanted to kill me."

"What bastard?"

"That man." Suddenly she looks at me, wide-awake. "He looked like you."

"Freudian," I say. "Let's go back to sleep. Do you want to lay with me?"

She nods. I move over a bit and Elaine nestles her warm body against mine. Her head fits into the little hole of my shoulder. She sighs and puts her thigh on my crotch. This is the way we have been laying for twenty-three years. Every night she wakes up from some kind of dead sleep and every night I soothe her back to sleep.

She licks my nipple. My cock swells, despite my intention to stop sex with Elaine. She feels it too. She lifts her leg and puts my cock straight ahead. "Sleep," she murmurs, but she goes on licking, pushing her soft thigh against me and my lust grows. She puts out her nightgown, catches my trousers with her toes and pulls it down. The elastic sticks. Elaine giggles. She releases my cock and leads it with a thousand-fold repeated routine to the place where it belongs in her opinion. Afterwards she lies with me.

"Wester?"

"Yes?"

"He really looked like you."

"Then who was it?"

"Don't know. Some guy. He could be your brother."

"I have no brother."

She giggles. "Imagine me thinking that your brother is visiting me at night."

I do not answer. She is a good fuck, but that moaning afterwards is getting boring. "Let us go back to sleep. I have to rise early."

"Where are you going?"

"I have a seminar in Driebergen."

"Do you have to do something there yourself?"

"No, this time I only have to listen."

"Who is coming there?"

"The usual. Specialists, hospital directors, people from the government."

"Will Stan be there?"

I laugh. "Stan is where the food is."

Elaine laughs too. "Give him my love. What is it about?"

"Cutback in ophthalmology."

"The best cutback is to drop the seminar."

I grin in the dark. "I'll suggest it tomorrow."

"Good. Kiss."

I kiss her. She nestles in my arms. After a while her head becomes heavy. My shoulder goes tense. I pull her to her place. She murmurs: "He really looked like you," and falls asleep.

The seminar is boring, as I expected. A Japanese professor tells an inarticulate story. When he is finished Lord Curr asks with stiff upper lip: "Who ever understood this lecture may now ask questions." and after some seconds the laughter bursts out. The Japanese bows and disappears. His face is motionless.

Halfway through the question hour Stan Smits and I do a bunk for a sandwich. He is a fellow student from Utrecht. We spent a year together with Hagen in Gottingen and have been friends ever since. Stan is in employment with the hospital, just as I am. We do not earn as much as the free specialists, but we don't have to work like hell for our pension. And a seminar is a not an expensive trip, it is simply part of our job.

Stan stuffs his mouth. Since my years as a student I never saw someone eat a ham sandwich so greedily.

"How are you doing?" he asks with his mouth full.

"Fine," I say.

"Elaine too?"

"Fine, fine."

He rinses the last bite with a glass of milk and gives me an inquisitive look. "You have grown thin."

"Right." I pat my belly which sounds unpleasantly hollow. "I lost ten kilos."

"Good boy. Advice of your doctor?"

"No, my own advice. I looked down and missed my cock."

He laughs. "That is a good reason."

"Would be good for you too."

"I haven't seen it in years. Only use it to piss. What should I care?"

"We are not that old, Stan."

"Fifty-four. Another six years. What are you going to do then?"

"I'll buy a camper and go traveling."

"I thought Elaine does not like camping."

"Who says that I will go traveling with Elaine?"

He gives me another look. "I thought the two of you were good friends."

"We are, but Elaine hates my way of traveling. She only wants to stay in a hotel."

"Maybe you could try it her way."

"Not with my pension. If I buy that camper, nothing else will be possible for a long time."

Stan shakes his head. "What are you going to do? Shall we have another sandwich?"

"Not me, but please, go ahead."

He smiles. "You became ascetic, Wester. I don't recognize you. What happened to the man of the double rice table?"

"Suffocated in his cholesterol."

"Nonsense."

The question time is over and everyone rushes to the sandwiches. Stan presses his fat body through the crowd. Colleagues hold him and start small talk. I am a bit lost aside. Stan is popular. I am not. Normally I don't care, but at a seminar it is disturbing. People stare at me, wondering who that long fellow is with the scar on his chin and why he does not have it removed. After a while the hungry crowd subsides. I grip Stan's arm and lead him to the half-open garden doors. It is unusually mild for the end of February.

"Stan, did you ever kill someone?"

He is flabbergasted. "What!"

"I ask if you ever killed someone." I shake my head. "Oh no, not you, of course. I should not have asked you."

"You can't ask anyone that question," he says. "Are you mad? People will think you are insane."

"I am insane."

Again the searching look. "Let us go for a walk. The start of the afternoon program is bullshit anyway."

We walk through the park around the Congress Center. Old trees, shaven greens, raked little footpaths. Congress people are walking everywhere. Stan greets, nods, shakes hands, but as soon as we are together again his face gets an unusually serious look. "What is going on, Wester?" he asks when we are alone in the park forest.

"I am in love."

He looks at me. "Is that all?"

"It is fucking more than enough."

"Calm down, man. When you are in love you only want to make love as I remember well. I do not understand what murder has to do with love."

"Everything," I say. "Elaine does not want this, so she has to die."

"Okay, that makes sense. You are in love, not with Elaine, so she is an obstacle that has to be removed."

"I am glad you understand."

"Asshole!"

I look at him. Stan has a round face that normally shines with kindness, but now his eyes are hard and gloomy. "This is outrageous, Wester. The mere thought of it makes you a bastard. I don't recognize you."

I shrug my shoulders. "Spare me the morality, please. All this guilt, useless."

Stan sits on a fallen tree and taps on the stem. I sit down beside him.

"Who is the lucky woman?"

"Someone from the hospital."

"Colleague?"

"She is a co-assistant. Does her examinations as a doctor next year."

"Straight from the cradle? How old is she anyway?"

"Twenty-five."

"Twenty-five," he repeats. "You could have been her father and if you had done very well her grandfather. It is almost pedophilia."

"Stan, stop moralizing and give me advice. I am desperate."

"Does Elaine know?"

"No. You know how emotional she is. I told her nothing."

"Women guess these things," he says, gloomy. "And Elaine will for sure. You can't fool her."

"You know her," I mock.

"Not as well as you do," he says quietly. "But as far as I know her it would surprise me if she had not guessed."

"Tonight she dreamt of my look-alike wanting to kill her."

"Freud," Stan says. "What did the old jerk tell us about those kind of dreams?"

"They predict reality."

"Yes, I remember." He looks me straight in the eyes. "Why bother Elaine? Why don't you make love to that child, if necessary, on a holiday? You make up something, a burn out or something like that and then you return to your beloved Elaine."

"Elaine is not my beloved anymore."

"Come on. We all fall in love from time to time, even you. Nothing special. Hard, all those unusual hormones, but if you take care with your diet it will all be all right. Well," he points at my belly. "At least you lost your paunch."

"Stan, the problem is that Elaine must not know because that would mean disaster."

"Is a murder not a disaster?"

"Yes, that too," I admit.

"Tell me about the girl."

"Ellen is twenty-five as I said. Ash blond hair, deep blue eyes, great figure. Intelligent, nice, surprisingly mature for such a young person."

"Kill her," Stan murmurs. "Kill her immediately."

Now it is my turn to be surprised. "What on earth are you talking about?"

"Ideal people should be killed immediately. They are a threat to society. Is she married?"

"No. Not engaged either. I am the only man in her life."

"You hope so. If half of what you say is true then you share her with a thousand other guys"

"I am sure of her."

"What does she want?"

"Me."

"Including house, salary and pension?"

"Only me," I say stiffly.

"Come on Wester. Did you consider discussing it with Elaine?"

"She said that she will kill me if I leave her."

"So you want to be ahead of her. Is it not a bit exaggerated?"

"She is serious."

He nods "She loves you, though."

"Yes."

"And you don't love her anymore?"

"We are friends. Twenty-three years of marriage create a bond of course."

"Do you fuck her?"

"Every night."

"What?" He is surprised. "Have you got enough energy left for your diversion then?"

"Since I minimized food it goes a lot better."

"A good cock is not a fat one." Stan grins and his face regains its normal, pleasant expression. "Forgive me for laughing."

"Please do. As long as you come up with a good idea."

"Fight."

"That is what I am waiting for," I laugh. "This whole setup is meant to avoid a fight."

"Indeed," Stan says. "You want to leave with your young sweetheart, but you are too cowardly to tell your wife. So you want to kill her."

"I am no coward," I mutter.

"You said that Elaine will kill you if you leave her and to avoid that you want to kill her. Be a man and fight."

"How? A duel?"

"Yes. You have done it before."

I stroke my chin. After thirty years the scar of the sabre is a soft, beardless stripe. I greet with my imaginary sabre and stand at attention.

"Not with that," Stan says. "Elaine must have a chance."

I let my weapon down. "What do you mean?"

"I bought a couple of duel pistols in Brugge last month. Beautiful things. Old, maybe from Tjsechov's time. No idea if they still work, but I can have them checked."

"Absurd. This really is ridiculous, Stan."

"Elaine might think differently. Make a proposal. Or don't you dare?"

"It is not a matter of courage. It is weird. Suppose one shoots the other, what do we tell the police?"

"The truth. I will testify."

"It's insane. They'll imprison us all."

But Elaine likes the idea. When she has ceased raging about my love for Ellen, the first woman she finds out about in our long marriage, she gives me the option: it is her or Ellen. In the last case they both have nothing because she will kill me. I tell her that I can't leave Ellen.

"Try!" Elaine says. "Do all you can to save our marriage."

"If you would not be so stern, we could save our marriage."

"I want all of you, or nothing. The idea that you are having an affair is unbearable."

"We'll fight."

She nods. We choose place, date and time: at 12 March at seven pm the duel takes place in our bedroom. Stan will be the witness. Elaine and I write a statement for the notary. I suggest recording the duel on video, but she does not want a second witness, not to mention one with a camera and she rejects it angrily. "Stan is enough," she says. "And if we kill each other the notary will be the second witness."

Elaine hates sports, but now she takes shooting lessons and practises every day in an obscure shooting club in the inner city. I don't have to practise. I am a hunter and a good shot with a stern hand and the speed of reaction of a far younger man. But when I hold Stan's gun for the first time, feel the weight and peer over the long barrel, doubt seizes me. This is ridiculous! Elaine and Stan are deadly serious. They talk about ballistics and trajectories as if they know what they are talking about. Stan proposes some shooting practice. He has the guns checked by an expert. They are really old, but the expert says that we can shoot ten times before the barrel bursts. That is, if we use the right bullets. Heavy bullets with a soft tip that cause horrible wounds.

"I'll aim at your head," Elaine says. "I do not want you to suffer."

"Thank you," I say seriously.

We shoot under the supervision of the expert in the cellar of his house. Elaine has learned at the shooting club. She holds the heavy gun in both hands, arms stretched, a little bow in the knees and she shoots three bullets in succession into the head of the dummy. It strikes me that the expert takes the duel for granted just like Stan and Elaine. A couple does not want to get a divorce and challenges each other for a duel. It has a bizarre beauty.

It really gives Ellen the creeps. She suggested stopping the affair for the time being until peace has returned. She wants to talk, but Elaine refuses to meet her and I convince Ellen that a conversation is useless.

On the 12 March Stan arrives in morning dress. I am also in morning dress. Elaine wears a new black costume that suits her adorably. For the first time in weeks I notice how beautiful she is. What a waste to shoot her.

Stan carries the guns upstairs. We follow him, Elaine first, I follow two steps behind. Stan places the box with the guns on the table near the window. He opens the box. Suitable, solemn gestures. The guns glow. They have a 30-cm barrel, hexagonal on the outside, perfectly round at the inside. They are identical, but Elaine chooses her weapon with care. I get the other gun. Stan loads the weapons. Each gun contains one heavy bullet with a soft tip. Horrible wound. I try not to think of it.

We have a big house. The rooms on the first floor are situated around a gallery. Our bedroom is as long as the house is: fourteen metres. One of the walls consists of a cabinet with mirror doors, which reach to the ground. We push our twin beds aside to create a wide path in the middle. Stan posts us. Elaine and I stand back to back on the path in the middle. As soon as Stan gives the signal we can begin to walk six steps. Then we turn and aim our guns. I am the first to shoot. It has been assigned by fate: heads or tails. Elaine did not move a muscle when the coin fell with my side up. I concentrate. Until tonight I saw it as a joke, but now the weird truth enters my brain in all violence. One of us will be carried out of this room, I thought that it would not be me, but I am not sure any more. Concentrate!

"One, two three, go, for Heaven's sake," Stan says.

We start to walk. Six steps. One, two, three, four, five, six. We turn at the same moment. Each of us holds the gun in front of the breast. Elaine lowers her gun. She stands there with the dignity of Mata Hari in front of the firing squad. Behind her back I see myself, six times in a slightly distorted image.

I shoot. The mirror bursts into splinters. The noise is deafening. Elaine stands there, pale as death, unharmed. I try to control myself, but I start to tremble. My image is in thousands of fragments behind her on the ground. My mouth is dry. I sweat. My heart beats as if it wants to prolong every second of life. I want to say something, scream, beg for forgiveness, but Elaine stands motionless, deaf to my silent appeal and points her gun. I close my eyes.

"Bang," she says.

She unloads the gun and puts it back in the box. I stand as if I am cast in wax. Stan takes the gun out of my hand, cleans it with a cotton rag and puts it next to the other gun in the box. He bows to Elaine. He shakes hands with both of us and leaves with his guns.

Elaine takes my hand and leads me to the bathroom. She takes off my clothes and washes me like a child. Then she takes off her own clothes. We lay down on her bed. She pulls me against her body and says: "You dreamed". My mouth is dry and my voice rasps when I say: "I dreamt that someone wanted to kill me."

I put down my head. It fits in the hole of her shoulder. She hums a song from our childhood, very softly, in such a way that it sounds far away and nearby at the same time.

We fall asleep.

Translation by Josh Pachter

The Deepest South

Paco Ignacio Taibo II

The sun, a perfect, orange-colored ball on the horizon, almost made up for the difficulty the breeze was causing me. I lit the third match and tried to cover the flame with my left hand. Alex had taken off his shoes and was squatting down, in deep conversation with a group of fishermen. He was speaking Spanish at full speed, eating his vowels, charming the three men. Seen from a distance he looked like the best vacuum-cleaner salesman in the world. He wasn't. Halfway through the conversation, the monologue, he looked up and nailed me with those two blue eyes. I was about twenty yards from him, next to his abandoned shoes. I released the smoke from the cigarette in his direction; the wind blew it away.

I was already becoming accustomed to this relationship – distant, yet in a way affectionate – that turned us into phantoms, shadows of each other. Four days before, one of the lawyers who handles his father's business had placed an envelope full of cash in front of me. "Alex will probably travel to Mexico sometime this week. Take care of him," he said.

I didn't like the lawyer's tie, red dots on a metallic blue background, and I didn't like his cross-eyed look. I liked even less his presumption that I knew who Alex was and why I had to take care of him. At any rate, as the sun entered through the cracks in the Venetian blinds in my Los Angeles office, the smoke from my cigarette made me remember a cup of steaming Mexican coffee I had drunk years ago.

Four days later Alex and I were looking at each other while the sun was setting on that beach some miles from Ensenada, in Baja California. If Alex was getting bored, soon we would be able to eat supper (at separate tables, of course) in some restaurant in Ensenada and I would be able to drink the coffee I remembered.

Alex seemed to get my message and, patting the fishermen on the back, walked towards his shoes. I didn't move. Alex approached, reeling like a sailor in a Hollywood musical comedy, and picked up his shoes without looking at me.

"Dinnertime, shadow," he said while speaking to the sea.

We walked toward the automobiles: his, a cherry-red Fleetwood convertible; mine, parked so close that it almost scraped his bumper, a green Oldsmobile that showed its scars and could have used a paint job.

I gave him a few seconds' advantage, tossed my cigarette on the ground, took one last look at the sun which was beginning to set in the sea, and got into the car.

Alex was no vacuum-cleaner salesman on vacation south of the border. He was the only heir to the Fletcher supermarket chain. Not that it mattered to me, but this seemed essential to the lawyer who slipped the envelope with dollars across my desk. He offered me very little else: a photograph of a boy of twenty-three with wild, blond hair that seemed to want to rise into a horn over his forehead, and a little bit of chatter about how "reckless" and "unstable" Alex was, "how sick he had returned from the Pacific," and "how bad it had been for him during the war in one of the Japanese concentration camps in Burma or the Philippines or Malaya." When I tried to determine the exact nature of my obligations as nanny, I couldn't find out anything more concrete. ". . . gets into too much trouble, you know? You can stop him from getting himself stabbed in some bad-luck brothel in Tijuana, that sort of thing." When I asked whether Alex should know that I was following him, he answered, shrugging his shoulders, "Do as you wish. One way or the other, Alex will find out and I'm sure he'll blame me. It's difficult to hide things from Alex, as you'll soon realize."

Monday. Alex fulfilled the lawyer's predictions and went south, first toward San Diego and later following the border to Calexico. He entered Mexico through Mexicali and stopped the Fleetwood right at Revolution Park, a few yards from the borderline. He rubbed his eyes as if he had just woken up and approached my automobile. Through the open window he said, "They told me that a China-Mex jumped that green fence seven times in one day. They captured him all seven times and sent him back to Mexico. He holds the local record. No one saw him, no one seems to know his name, but everyone knows the story. Maybe he never existed. I always wondered why he had to be Chinese. Why choose a Chinese guy for a myth?"

He didn't wait for my answer and walked left toward the Hotel Palacio, carrying a suitcase. By the way he was carrying it, it must have been heavy. We ran into each other a half hour later in the hotel bar. I was weighing the possibilities of a margarita as opposed to a gimlet, when Alex made his appearance on the scene. The ceiling fans seemed to be bothered by arthritic pains. A pair of Central European refugees were sweating copiously while drinking an acid wine, their silent faces fixed on a horizon that must have been thousands of miles away. Just watching them made me hot, the worst kind of hot, sad and exhausting. A girl of about fifteen, probably German, was playing the piano in the corner and humming. Alex came over to me.

"I don't know why the Chinese guy wanted to go to the United States. It's much better down here. We're the ones who ought to be jumping the green fence, not them," he said. Then he sat down at the next table and in Spanish ordered a pitcher of sangria.

Mexicali at that time was a way station for refugees from all over Europe who were seeking permission to enter the United States. It had been, and probably still is, the trampoline for thousands of Mexicans who illegally cross the border to make themselves a few dollars in the north. Above all, it was a languid city; dirt was everywhere; clouds of dust tried to cover the poor tracks of progress and return the city to its ancient desert condition. It was a city where you heard songs in many languages, songs that were almost always melancholy.

That first day on Alex's tracks turned into a pilgrimage that seemed absurd, erratic, but at other times motivated by some obscure design. He entered a shoe store and spent hours trying on Mexican boots, only to end up not buying anything. He stopped by the local newspaper and placed an announcement (for two dollars I got hold of a copy: "I've already arrived, Ana. I'm at the Palacio, Alex."). He visited three doctors. (I duly noted the names and addresses and promised to stop by later on. One of them had a marvelous bilingual sign in the window: "We cure incurable diseases, the others cure themselves.") He went to the fair on the outskirts of the city and with absolute seriousness dedicated himself to winning rounds in the shooting gallery, in between flirting sessions with the gypsy woman who ran the booth.

At the end of the afternoon, with his white linen suit and my black shoes covered with dust, we went walking toward the border, bound for the hotel like a pair of defeated gamblers. As we went inside, he looked at me with curiosity. His two blue eyes were shining with a strange intensity. I entered the bar to kick around some ideas and get rid of the taste of dust with a pair of margaritas.

"Marlowe, you work for that *guero*, that blond guy?" a man at the next table asked me as I was finishing the first drink. I should have looked up before. The tables around him were empty. I never like Mexican police, but Mexicans liked them even less than I did. The man had a big scar that went from his right eye to his throat. Through his open jacket you could see the butt of his .45.

"I don't know. It seems he doesn't like me very much." I laughed.

The policeman smiled. "I don't like him either."

"And me?" I asked, returning the smile and signaling the waiter to bring me the next margarita.

"No, amigo. You're in the business. With you, we always know what's going on, and if we don't, we guess, or we ask. No, the one I don't like is that blond guy. He came here to go crazy. Do you know what he has in that suitcase?"

I kept on smiling. There's nothing like candor when engaged in chit-chat with the police.

"He's carrying a pile of dollars and a Thompson sub-machine gun. *Ta loco el pendejo ese*. That asshole's crazy."

"And why didn't they take it away from him at the border?"

"He must have paid a *mordida*, a bribe. You figure it out."

The heat kept me from sleeping.

The morning of the second day I ran into Alex in the corridor. The bathroom was around the corner and we were both on the way to shave. Alex wasn't wearing a shirt; an enormous whitish scar crossed his back.

"You can call me Alex," he said, turning his back to me, knowing that my eyes were mesmerized by the scar. "I'll call you

Marlowe. It doesn't matter to me if that's your name or not. It's
the name you used to register and that's good enough for me. By
the way, if you talk to the doctors I saw yesterday, they'll tell you
that I have a fatal disease. There's no point trying to cure me; it's
a matter of months." He was speaking without looking at me, not
even granting me a gesture over his shoulder. He presumed that
I, with my towel on my shoulder and my shaving brush and razor
in hand, was following him.

"Try not to cut yourself shaving. There's nothing that bothers
me more than blood in the bathroom sink," I said.

He laughed forcefully. Neither of us could shave. There was
a Mexican in the bathroom, sitting on the toilet and playing the
guitar. He had the face of a man with few friends. Disturbing him
didn't seem like a good idea.

In the afternoon he took off in his Fleetwood at seventy-five
miles an hour down the terrible roads that go to Ensenada,
crossing canyons and desert. Every once in a while, despite the
best efforts of my Oldsmobile, I lost sight of him.

We got to Ensenada as it was getting dark. At the entrance to
town he swerved off the road and drove directly onto the beach. I
took all the time in the world to light a cigarette, because I hadn't
been able to enjoy one during the roadside chase that afternoon.
Alex appeared in between the shadows; he seemed annoyed that
I hadn't followed him.

"I'm in love with a woman who lives around here. Her husband
is a famous Mexican poet. He threatened to kill me if he saw me
near his wife again. What do you plan to do, Marlowe?"

His eyes sparked with fury. He was about to take a walk when
I landed a direct hit on his jaw. He collapsed in silence onto the
white sand. I walked along the beach, guided by the lights of a
cabaña some two hundred and fifty yards away.

"I saw Alex's car a while ago. Did he come with you?" asked
a young man with curly hair who was smoking on the cabaña
porch.

I nodded.

"Are you his doctor?" the man asked.

"No. I'm a kind of nursemaid."

"In my country they're called bodyguards."

"It's specialized work. More like soul guards."

"Raul Cota," he said, extending his hand.

He must have been about forty, with a full beard capped by a moustache. There was a sad look about him.

"Marlowe," I answered, extending my hand. "How do you know Alex?"

"He comes around here; he spends his time roaming around my cabaña and telling everybody that he's in love with my wife. But that would be difficult. I've been a widower for two years. Maybe he knew her before. . . I don't know. I don't think so."

I sat on the porch, pushing the sand around with the tips of my shoes. Cota went inside and returned a little later with two cups of coffee. I could hear the sea. Alex suddenly appeared in front of us, rubbing his jaw. I smiled.

"A cup of coffee?" offered Cota.

Alex nodded.

As the sun came up, Alex drove his Fleetwood north at full speed bound for a port on the Pacific called Rosarito. There we had lobsters with tortillas and frijoles for breakfast. I didn't pay more than two dollars for mine. If things kept going like this, I would never get my expense money from the lawyer in Los Angeles.

Alex began to walk along the beach. I was getting fed up and stayed at the shack where they had served us the freshly captured lobsters. I was ready for a second cup of coffee with cinnamon. Alex, seeing that I wasn't following him, came back looking like an angry child.

"Come, Marlowe, let's walk along the beach and I'll tell you about the caves and the rock drawings."

"What's the hurry, gringo? Let him drink his coffee," the fisherman who had waited on us said.

"We have important things to discuss," Alex said in his rapid Spanish.

I left the coffee to one side. At any rate it was too hot. I lit a cigarette and tried to catch up to Alex, who was walking in a great hurry at the edge of the sea. The doves began to keep us company.

"Miles south of here there are prehistoric caves, full of rock drawings. They were painted thousands of years ago by a tribe of tall men, much taller than the *guaycuras* who later settled in this area. You know what we can do, Marlowe? We can get a couple of good cameras and cross the sierra. The caves are incredible: men of two colors, turning themselves into animals with horns . . ."

He waited an instant for my answer. Then he seemed bored and left me still smoking a cigarette while he went toward the sea, getting his shoes wet every time the cusp of a little wave would reach the shore.

Alex was getting drunk, like a soldier who just realized he had been fighting on the wrong side. Mezcal after mezcal; not even enough time to warm his tongue.

I was sitting at the next table surrounded by the noise of fifty simultaneous conversations and a mariachi band whose cornet player tried to blast my brains out by playing his instrument four inches from my ear. The Club Camalias had been the one and only stop after Tijuana. The Fleetwood, full of dust, was parked outside the den, which was a center for nervous drug addicts, sailors from San Diego, pimps and their merchandise, Mexican workers from a nearby construction company who didn't have the time to remove their hard hats, and a group of policemen headed by my old friend, whose name was Ramirez. After distributing his boys throughout the club, he came to sit at my table. I couldn't make out his words through the noise, only his smile.

Alex took note of the presence of my companion and sent for a double mezcal to welcome him.

"The Mexican police are *putas*, whores," said Alex, looking straight at our table and taking advantage of the break in the mariachi music.

Ramirez smiled, raised his cup, and toasted Alex.

"Your friend is completely crazy. Surely he wants to commit suicide."

"Seems like that to me," I responded.

"Why doesn't he do it on the other side?" asked Ramirez.

I was left looking for an answer. After all, it wasn't such a bad question.

Alex's eyes were glassy; his jaw slightly disconnected. Seeing that Ramirez wasn't reacting, he looked for something else to grab his attention. He found it easily. One of the American sailors was sitting at a nearby table, absolutely enthralled with a prostitute. Alex stood up and walked toward him. The mariachis began to play "La Paloma," possibly the only Mexican song to which I know the lyrics, but Alex gave me no time to enjoy it. He was arguing about something with the sailor. Suddenly Alex slapped the woman in the face. I jumped out of my chair. Ramirez didn't even make an attempt to follow me. The sailor took out a knife and stuck it in the first thing he found – Alex's left hand, resting on the table.

Violence, as always, provoked screams and abandonment. Nevertheless, the mariachis continued to play. I pushed the sailor aside and pulled the knife from the table, freeing Alex's left hand. Blood gushed out profusely. At his table, Ramirez limited himself to a smile.

Alex insisted on being treated in Mexicali, which is how the front seat of my car became full of blood. I knew I should be mad, but I wasn't. Alex's behavior just made me feel melancholy. While he was resting in an overstuffed chair in the waiting room, I spoke to Dr Martinez about Alex's supposedly incurable disease.

"Incurable? It would have been fifty years ago, amigo. Now it's perfectly curable. All he has is a venereal disease, syphilis, and it's not even an advanced case. He's already being treated for it."

The nights in Mexicali are dark. Music lures you, like bait, from several places at once. Every once in a while a group of drunks crosses you, or a taxi driver stops to try to convince you that the doors of his automobile lead to the gates of paradise. There's a sense of asphyxiation, from the dirt in the air, the dry heat. It's a small city, stolen from the desert. Without my hat and jacket, I went walking in the night looking for answers. Maybe the questions applied to me, too. We went down to the south to leave our nightmares there, our worst dreams. Instead, we found ourselves, looking in the mirror, face to face with the dark side of our sadness and our solitude. What fault was it of the Mexicans that Alex had chosen their country to go crazy in?

"If I swim out there for 181 days, I'll be back . . ." Alex said, pointing to some place on the other side of the Pacific where he had left a piece of his soul.

"You should probably wait until your hand is better," was the only thing that occurred to me to say.

We returned to Rosarito, this time the two of us in my Oldsmobile. We were eating lobsters on the beach, and Alex allowed himself to drift off to sleep in the hammock. I decided to fight my drowsiness by walking on the beach. I had a few cigarettes with a group of women and gave them a hand cleaning sea snails. In return they gave me a couple of dozen for supper. When I returned I found that Alex had disappeared from the hammock and from sight. His suitcase was still in the automobile. I opened it.

There really was an old Thompson submachine gun, unloaded and rusty. There were also four or five stacks of Japanese money, printed during the occupation of the Dutch East Indies. Underneath them was a pile of photos of ragged English soldiers, Americans, Australians, and New Zealanders, saluting their flags, probably right after they had been liberated from a concentration camp. Many of them were covered with bandages, or they were on crutches, their hands in slings, with months-old beards, long hair, skeletal bodies consumed by fever, dysentery, and malnutrition.

Alex offered me a match to light the cigarette hanging from my lips. I accepted it.

"They want me to return, but I'm staying here. They want to put me in a cage in Los Angeles. Have you heard the Mexican song 'Jaula de ord', about a cage of gold?"

He started to walk toward the ocean. I tried to take him by the hand, but he freed himself with a quick movement.

"Don't you realize, Marlowe?"

He turned his back to me and continued toward the sea. Then he turned and looked at me with his ice-blue eyes. A wave broke near the shore; the sun was beginning to set.

I saw him hurl himself into the water, swimming madly straight into the horizon, foam rising with every stroke. The sun floated over the sea. Alex was going further and further away. Fifteen minutes later you could hardly see his head in the distance. Then it disappeared.

The sunsets in Baja California are unforgettable. I would have to return the money to the lawyer in Los Angeles. I turned my back to the sea. My joints ached. It must have been the humidity. I walked toward the Oldsmobile.

The first Spanish edition of The Long Goodbye *appeared in 1973. I read it three times. I added it to what I had learned from Simenon, Durenmatt, Hammett, and Le Carré, and was certain that crime literature offered me the best possible scenario for the stories I wanted to tell. Three years later my novel was published. I don't know how much of Chandler was left in it; probably little, because what I was trying to do with* Dias de combate *was launch a new genre, the new crime novel in Mexico, and not simply follow the tradition of the hard-boiled with a change of scenery. But no doubt Chandler was there; in stories built on dialogue and characters and atmospheres, rather than anecdotes, but which still managed to tell a story. For me, influenced by the Mexican baroque and magical realism, neorealism in the style of Chandler was the best option. Maybe no one can find traces of these influences in my books; it's not that important. I know how to recognize my debts; I know that Chandler is there somewhere in my novels, and I'm grateful to him.*

    Paco Ignacio Taibo II

Translation by Barbara Belejack

Escalator Obstructors

Juergen Ehlers

They'd never have got me, if those guys hadn't stood in the way. On the escalator.

"Excuse me," I'd asked. "Could you please let me pass?"

Really friendly, although in truth, of course, I was in quite a hurry. No reaction. Nothing.

"Excuse me," I said again.

No one moved. *Stand on the right, walk on the left* – they should really put up a sign at every escalator, until even the last idiot gets it. Maybe that would have helped back then. Maybe. But there were no signs, and so they got me. The coppers. That's five years ago now, but at last I'm a free man again.

Yes, of course I'm glad to be free again.

"Is something wrong?" asks Monika.

Luckily she still has our old flat. Otherwise I wouldn't have known where to start looking.

"No, everything's fine," I say.

Strange to see that she has also aged five years in the meantime. Somehow I hadn't expected that. We haven't seen much of one another lately.

"Come on, tell me, something is wrong."

Yes, I think, something *is* wrong. But what?

"It was tidier in prison," I say at last.

"Tidy all you like," says Monika.

Actually I thought that she should do that, but of course she's right. I suppose I have more time at the moment than her with her part-time job and the kids. The kids are playing in the living-room. Somehow there are more than when I was home last.

"The blond one is new," I say.

Monika shrugs. "You weren't here."

True. But I still don't like it. Of course Monika sees immediately that I'm not pleased.

"We could put him in the baby hatch," she suggests.

"Nah, I don't know," I say. I don't think that's a good idea. "I don't think they will want him now . . ."

"Why not? He's only three."

Later I realize that Monika is only joking. She gives me a kiss.

"You need a job," she says.

The good old Job Centre is now called Agentur für Arbeit, *Agency for Work*. Nice name. And they've got new furniture, too, since I came here last time. But they don't have any work for me. The interviewer seems annoyed at me for even asking. She takes my details. What have I done last, she wants to know.

"In prison?" I ask.

"No, before."

"Driving armoured cars."

The woman looks up.

"I don't think we've got anything for you," she says coldly.

She doesn't even look into her computer.

I suggest that I could do something else.

What have I learned, she wants to know.

In prison? Loads of things. But I'd better not tell her that. My only other qualification is the measly report I got after the obligatory nine years of school. And my driving licence, of course.

She says that business is a bit on the slow side in security at the moment, and that she can't give me much hope. But I could try the *In-house Service – Education*. She means retraining.

"Nothing for you?" Monika asks as I come back.

"We all got a Father Christmas . . ."

"Couldn't you at least have brought three? For the kids."

"No, nobody got more than one. You can have him, I don't like chocolate. Anyhow, they didn't have any work for me. I suppose we'll have to live off our savings for now."

Monika looks at the Father Christmas.

"Why don't you ask again next time? I'm sure they always have leftovers at the end."

She weighs him in her hand.

"He's hollow," I say.

"Of course, what did you expect? From the Job Centre?"

"A shame it didn't work out. Wouldn't be bad to have a little extra money."

Although we still have our savings. The stuff from the robbery at the jeweller's. Well hidden. No one ever found it. Not even Monika knows where I left the booty back then.

Monika cuddles up to me. She wants something, I think. In the end she says:

"Damn, I haven't told you yet. About Christmas. The children need new animals."

"Yes," I say. "Surely we can get them a used hamster or something from the animal home. Or a cat, if necessary."

"No, I mean cuddly toy animals."

"What?" I ask. "Even more? Their beds are teaming with creatures, aren't they? At least they were when I was here last."

Monika shakes her head.

"All gone. Little Pamela brought home lice from primary school one day. You know, head lice."

"But that's nothing to fret about," I say.

"No, usually not. But when that happens, you have to put all the toys and everything into this quarantine . . ."

"Into what?"

"Quarantine. That's what it's called. But really it's only a bin bag. They have to go in there for a few weeks. The toy animals, I mean. And if there are still lice on them, they die. Because they don't have any heads anymore on which they can graze. So, I put all the animals into the bin bag and tied it up."

I don't know what Monika wants to tell me.

"Well, and then, when everything was over, we made this big thing of opening the bin bag again."

"Good."

"No, not good! – There was nothing but rubbish in the bag."

"Rubbish?"

"Yes. I must have taken out the wrong bag that Tuesday."

"Oh," I say. "That's awful."

"Yes, you can't imagine how the kids cried."

"Oh yes." I also feel like crying. "Is the panther still there?" I ask.

Of course it isn't. Monika shakes her head in silence. I had sewn the jewels into the panther. Now we really are poor.

This is not the last unpleasant surprise of the evening.

"You don't mind Gerd sleeping here tonight, do you?" asks Monika. "After all, he must sleep somewhere."

"That's okay," I say.

Gerd is the father of the little blond one, Frithjof. I gathered that pretty quickly.

"You can take the couch for now," she says.

I say that Gerd could also sleep on the couch.

"Nah," says Monika. "It's better to keep it the way it is now. Gerd is always so easily offended when things don't go his way, and then he gets terribly mean . . ."

Gerd works in St Pauli.

"You don't want to know the details," says Monika.

"Why?" I ask.

"You really don't want to know the details," she insists. "Believe me, it's better that way."

He has to be quite bad then.

Gerd comes home late at night.

"Get rid of that bastard," he tells Monika when he sees me.

But Monika doesn't want to hear any of that. Very decent of her. And brave, too. I don't know what Gerd did with her that night in our bedroom, but they had a fight, and the next morning Monika has a black eye and generally looks a bit battered.

"All that just because of me?" I ask.

Monika nods.

"Perhaps you should find a different place to stay for now after all," she suggests.

"Or you," I say.

"Not so easy," she says.

Wherever she goes, she's scared Gerd will find her.

I go into the bedroom. Gerd is still sleeping.

"Be careful," Monika whispers.

Yes, I'm careful. But I'm not afraid of sleeping men. I search his clothes. Gerd Kubitzki is his name. At least that's what it says in his passport. And he has a pistol. Just as I had thought.

"I'll borrow this for a bit," I say.

"You can't do that," Monika says.

Yes, I can.

"I still have some unfinished business," I say.

Monika laughs. She doesn't think I'm capable of finishing any sort of business. Not with a pistol, at any rate.

"This is a *Glock*," I tell her.

At that moment Gerd coughs. A disgusting, rattling smoker's cough. We leave him alone.

Yes, I really do have some unfinished business. Remember the thing about the escalator obstructors? Well, they'll pay for it, you'll see. I leave the house.

It is chilly outside, and it is snowing a little. I'm cold. Good thing I brought my mittens. For a moment I ponder whether I shouldn't move out of our flat after all. Go away and give it a completely fresh start. But where would I go? No job, no money, no place to live. Impossible. So, I begin to set to work.

The city centre is crowded. The usual Christmas madness. First of all to *Karstadt*, I say to myself. I'm lucky right away. A fat man bustles onto the escalator right in front of me.

"Excuse me," I say.

No reaction.

"Could you, please, let me pass?"

He still doesn't react. So I fire a warning shot. And instantly there is chaos. Women scream, men run away, one even leaps over the handrail. The fat man meanwhile has dropped his shopping bags and stares at me in bewilderment. He puts his hands up in defence. I take his bags, squeeze past him, and a moment later I'm out in the open again. I don't know if anyone tries to follow, but the Mönckebergstrasse is so busy that no one has a chance of getting me anyway.

In *Kaufhof* I'm not quite as successful. I have to go up and down all the escalators at least ten times before I finally find an obstructor. A whole group to be precise. Teenagers. Their bags are probably full of pop music CDs. Just the right thing for our little ones.

"Could you let me pass, please?"

"Shut it, gramps!"

They laugh. Not for long, of course, but this time I need to fire three warning shots, and on the ground floor, as I run for the exit, someone throws a book at me. I shoot his hat off. Forgotten nothing, I think to myself, because you have to be really careful not to accidentally graze the skull instead. But as an ex-armoured car driver I'm quite a good shot.

At the Central Station everything goes smoothly. I could get a suitcase immediately, but that's not what I want. I don't need suitcases, I need Christmas presents. Someone drags along a huge floor lamp. That would be nice for our living-room, I think. But the man makes space for me, as best he can, so he may keep his lamp. However, the man in front does not let me pass. He's got an especially large shopping bag standing next to him, and he makes no attempt to move it. So I shoot again. The acoustics are particularly good in the Central Station. The girl who was just saying "Attention, please, on platform five . . ." stops her announcement. I quickly fire two more shots, just to make clear that I'm not messing about, and then I grab the promising looking shopping bag. It is lighter than I had thought. Never mind. But now I really can't carry any more. And it's time I got out of here. A frail old man blocks my way.

"Hey, are you sure you want to die so shortly before Christmas?" I ask.

No, that's not what he wants. I hurry on. The station police begin to look for the source of all the chaos, but they're right on the other side of the great hall, the south end. They won't get me. I take the underground for one stop, then the bus for a bit, then the underground again, until I am quite certain that no one is following me.

Back home Gerd is still asleep. No harm done. He won't notice that I borrowed his pistol. When he wakes up, eventually, it's time for him to go to work.

"You're still here, are you," he growls.

Yes, I am. And I intend to stay.

And then it's Christmas Eve, at last. Monika has fetched some sprigs of fir tree from the cemetery, and meanwhile I have managed to bypass the electric meter. The flat is ablaze with lights. It's going to be a wonderful Christmas, full of surprises. Although, sadly, without any cuddly toy animals. The parcel I had taken for chocolate turns out to be a box with three rolls of sewing thread in different colours. Frithjof doesn't know what to do with them. So I show him that they are perfect for unwinding.

"And who's going to wind them up again?" Monika hisses.

I show her. It's dead easy. All you need to do is fix the reel to the food mixer with sellotape.

Heidemarie tears the wrapping paper from a book. She is disappointed.

"I can't read yet!"

"Then look at the pictures."

"There are none."

"Then draw some!" Creativity, that's important right from an early age.

Pamela gets a box of cigars.

"Only to play with," I say. "Corner shop and the like."

"What's a corner shop?" Pamela asks.

The biggest present is for Monika, of course.

"Oh, you shouldn't have," she says.

"I'd do anything for you," I tell her.

She tears the paper, and a bin comes out, one of those pedal bins. O dear, I think to myself, that was not such a good idea. But Monika only laughs.

"You little rascal!" she says and gives me a kiss.

Gerd never came back. I've read in the papers that he got arrested in St Pauli. *Gerd Kubitzki – The Central Station Gunman*, that's what the press called him. He denied all charges, but then they compared the bullets with his pistol – for which he didn't have a licence, by the way – and that proved it. And with his criminal record, he'll probably get locked away for quite a while. The papers also wrote that the whole thing might never have come out, if he hadn't lost his passport on the escalator.

The *Agency for Work* is closed over Christmas and New Year. But I'll go right back afterwards and ask whether any job vacancies have come up in the meantime. Or if they at least have any leftover Father Christmases.

If the worst comes to the worst, I'll just have to keep going a bit more. Maybe not quite as spectacular as that day before Christmas, but still in the same style. For, you know, I learnt things in prison. I don't have to shoot. There are other ways. Hamburg is the town of escalators. And if you happen to block my way on one of those escalators, please don't be surprised if you later find that your wallet is gone. Because it's your own fault.

Translation by Ann-Kathrin Ehlers.

Voices in the Head

Altaf Tyrewala

I am an abortionist. I run a nursing home in a seedy by-lane of Colaba. On the steely innards of trains crawling along the Harbour Line, you will find badly-spelled fliers advertising my services. I get one or two customers every day. Sad cases, angry faces, embarrassed women, careless men, swelling tummies, a cut, tears, and we all go home happy. Yes, happy. I spread happiness. Relief. I save families, lives, marriages. Now I need to be saved. From all the unborn-baby voices in my head.

This morning a client walked into my nursing home. Her stomach had just started to stick out. I could see through her cheap nylon *kurta*. Three more weeks and it would have been obvious. But she was safe now. I handed her a form asking for personal information. She filled it out and handed it back to me. I don't talk to my clients. No one talks to anyone in my nursing home. I don't bother to read the forms either. They always lie.

I locked the entrance to my nursing home and nodded to the nurse. She went into the adjoining room to prepare for the operation. It was over in half an hour. Don't. Don't ask me about the foetuses. They stopped registering after my third abortion. Now, I only see them as knots of blood and gore. Abdominal tumours that threaten to wreck the lives of decent, god-fearing people.

I am married. She has the mentality of a farmer. Won't let me touch her willingly. I am violent with her every night. She says she won't give herself to me willingly till I stop harvesting the wombs of mothers. She even has the rhetoric of a farmer. If only she saw the gratitude in my clients' eyes. Like the lady this morning. She kissed my hand before I administered the anaesthesia. When she regained consciousness she wanted to know if it was a boy or a girl, she wanted to know if it was fair or dark, she wanted to know if it was normal or deformed, she wanted to know . . . "Or is it too early to tell? Can you tell? This soon? Tell me, doctor! Am I right? Can you tell this soon?"

I didn't answer her. I don't talk to my clients. No one talks to anyone in my nursing home. I too will have a child some day. I will have several children. Several. I will have a child for each time the doors to my operation room have been sealed. The collective cries of my children will drown out the unborn-baby voices in my head.

This is how my flier reads. Yes, it is badly written, unimaginative, but it gets the message across.

Get Rid of Unwanted Pregnuncy in One Hour
Rupee 300
Absolutely Secrative
Shamma Nursing Home
Opp. Janvi Manzil (Bahind Colaba P.O.)

I wrote it. The nun pun makes me burst into amused hiccups every time I read it. It is the only comic relief in my life. The family dramas that are occasionally staged in my nursing home don't amuse me any more. Their horrible echoes don't die for days. Daughters pleading with incensed fathers, husbands kneeling before heartless wives, brides begging with misogynist mothers-in-law.

I have heard that in America abortion is a source of perennial controversy. If you are pro you are a murderer, cruel, careless. If you are anti you are stupid, religious, but still careless. I am neither.

And I am never careless. You can either be qualified or careful. I am very, very careful. That is why I get repeat business. Mostly from slim, college-going girls of the neighbourhood. There was one who visited me six times in two years. Haven't seen her for three years now. Doubt if I ever will again. Also, married women with their husbands. The first time is shameful and painful. The second time, the routine sets in. Like visiting a dentist to deal with a recurring cavity on a sweet tooth.

In a wilful attempt to decay and self-destruct, I have started smoking. Never in the nursing home. Always on the street, outside the front door. I deliberately don't carry matches or a lighter. Asking for a light is my only excuse to talk to others. Unfortunately, the only people in the by-lanes of Colaba are pimps and German tourists in search of Aryan India – they first want to know if you are Brahmin. The man next door, the one who owns a souvenir shop, doesn't talk to me. He is a Jain, the epitome of non-violence. Won't even eat potatoes because the act of extracting them from the earth deprives and kills underground insects. I am an abortionist and a Muslim to boot.

I have grown used to people avoiding me. Friends and relatives have gradually forsaken me over the years. They avoid me at the mosque. My wife and I are invited to marriages only out of formality. Even then, we are ignored. Treated like well-dressed gatecrashers who can't be ejected (because you never know), but are watched from a distance.

Five years ago, Ma, my mother, had gone to Mecca for Haj. For my sake. Just before boarding her flight, right there in the crowded departure lounge, she had looked at a point about three feet above my head and said, "Oh Allah! I am undertaking this journey to the heart of your home so that you may forgive my son and cause a change of heart in him so that he may find a cleaner occupation and may stop taking the lives of children, so that when he has a child of his own he can love the child with all his heart and realize what a wondrous thing it is to nurture life in all its forms and in all the situations that you may put us in."

When I am in an irreverent mood, I like to believe Ma paid with her life for such convoluted appeals to Allah.

She was trampled while running towards the Satan's pillar at Haj. Of all the physical metaphors that thrive under an otherwise abstract Islam, the Satan's pillar at Mecca is the most potent. On the fifth day, after the morning *namaaz*, as is traditional, two million pilgrims made a dash towards the Satan's pillar. They all wanted to be the first to stone it.

A woman who had been with her told me that Ma ran the fastest that morning. She pushed at the burgeoning crowds the hardest. She cursed the Devil the loudest. Like some hysterical lioness whose cub was being snatched away. But in that crowd, there were people far more desperate than Ma. People whose sons were worse than abortionists. They, too, wanted to attack and vanquish the Devil with all their might. These very people, these desperate, god-fearing fathers and mothers of sinners, were the ones who ran over Ma and pounded her body into the Holy Ground.

Of the 300 Indians who had gone to Haj that year, Ma was the only one who died in the stampede. She and three Nigerians. My father, my wife and I got the news a day later. By then, they'd already buried Ma's two-dimensional remains on the outskirts of Mecca.

When I try to imagine how she died that day in the Holy City, I stop believing in Allah. But only for a short while. I can't afford to remain godless for too long. The only way I can hide from myself is by being religious – or delusional. Call it whatever the hell you want. Ma's voice is now a part of the unborn-baby voices in my head.

Noise.

"Buy the cassettes! For fuck's sake, man, I need the cash. My whole collection for 300 rupees only. Come on dude! Buy the friggin' cassettes . . ."

I didn't say no. I had bought all five audio cassettes from the drunk American who barged into my nursing home six months ago. I didn't ask him what kind of music it was. I didn't care. I wanted him out of my nursing home. He was making my nervous customers (a young couple) even more nervous. It happens all the time: cash-starved foreign tourists randomly barge into places of business in Colaba to sell their personal belongings.

After the couple left, I examined the cassettes I had been forced to buy. They had bizarre covers with outlandish words written on them. Nirvana, Radiohead, Secret Samadhi and so on. English music, unfortunately.

It was the last day of Ramadan. The next day was to be Eid. I was to put on laundered clothes and go to the mosque for the morning namaaz. At the mosque, no one was to give me the three congratulatory hugs that Muslim men are meant to exchange on auspicious occasions. I was to come back home with a dry mouth, jerk my wife out of her sleep, open the cabinet in my hall, insert one of the English cassettes into my old player and rewind it all the way to the beginning. I was to press the play button.

I didn't know I was to rattle with sorrow for the next thirty minutes.

I did. Like a laboratory skeleton dangling in an earthquake. Like a sceptic to whom a saint had revealed his sainthood. I shook and wept tearlessly. The music that bled from the speakers matched the cacophony of unborn-baby voices in my head. Discordant and raw and numbing.

A single baby's voice is beautiful. The collective googoos and gagas of a hundred children is grotesque. But concentrate on these hundred voices long enough and you'll realize the beauty of each infantile voice. So it was with the music bleeding from the speakers. It consisted of singular strands of guitars so exquisite that they unfolded your leaden heart inside out and scraped away the pain and rage coagulating on its inner walls.

But these singular strands weren't what overwhelmed me. Beauty stopped seeming beautiful to me a long time ago. It was the collective noise of ten, hundred, millions of strands of guitars playing together that made my body convulse and my gaze still. Afsana, my wife, stood in a corner of the hall and watched me. Side A reached its end and the player bled silence.

I haven't played any of those English cassettes again. It was enough that I had come across an analogue to the unborn-baby voices. I wasn't going to allow a new cacophony to compete with them. It was the least I could do for my dead mother, whose aural imprints are part of the unborn-baby voices in my head.

And the least I can do for my father? To let him be. He threw out Afsana and me the day Ma's death washed up on our jagged beach. Having never opposed my occupation until then, he had called me a bastard abortionist and told us to vacate in an hour. My wife and I now live in a building nearby. I haven't spoken to my father since.

I see him often. He too works in Colaba. Has been a salesman in a shoe-shop for fifteen years. Sometimes, we take the same train to work. If we spot each other on the platform, we wordlessly board the same compartment and wade towards each other through the working-class crowd. Our actions would seem comic to an acquaintance. A father and son going through all this trouble to be near each other in a packed Harbour Line train, only to not exchange a single word. Like sulky kids.

I want to show him how the circles around my eyes have started invading my cheeks and forehead, making me darker every day. How on the sides of my neck I have started developing raisin-like moles that could prove to be cancerous or could end up as rubbery playthings for my curious grandchildren. My father has remained the same. This is what he wants to display. Black hair. Still a mouthful of teeth. No shrinkage even at sixty-five.

The Harbour Line has slums on either side. Every morning, male slum-dwellers shit on the railway tracks. There's no point hating them for their shamelessness. The route is a busy one, with trains going to and fro every two minutes. For privacy, a slum-dweller would have to wait until nightfall. Only women can bear the wait.

One morning, post-Ma, my estranged father and I were on our way to work. The train was nearing our destination – Victoria Terminus. We moved towards the same exit and fought our way to the front. The signal turned red. The train stopped. My eyes wandered and landed on a woman squatting between two railway tracks. She was facing our train. Her left hand was covering her face. Her right hand was struggling to hide her exposed parts.

The train didn't move for four minutes that morning. The woman remained frozen. She would've been a forgotten freak sight had the train moved on. But with each passing minute, her presence turned piercing, painful like the sun. I craved to watch her as one would a rare animal trapped by a hunter. But her will hurt my eyes and I looked away. My father was standing behind me.

Our fellow-commuters turned restless. In the vast urban landscape visible from the train, this singular sight of a beggarly woman struggling to maintain her modesty took on monumental proportions. Someone from the adjoining First Class compartment flung a full Bisleri bottle at her. It struck her shoulder with a deep *thuck*. A bone had been hit. She toppled over like a bowling pin. But her left hand was still hiding her face. Her right hand was still clutching at her exposed parts. My father winced on the woman's behalf. As he and a few others started abusing the First Class compartment, the train set into motion, its steely innards groaning at the futility of it all. The beggar woman lay there like a fallen queen of the gutter.

That's my father. Taking offence on behalf of others. Feeling free to continually offend his own.

There's no relief in my life. No relief. I can't offer you any. It's one thing to read about a life like mine. It's another thing to live it . . . every relentless day. Why don't I change my occupation? Just shake off this life leeching away at my being. I could easily shut down my nursing home. I'd save on the nurse's wages and the monthly packet of bribes I have to pass on to all those poor Municipal officials. Afsana would start fulfilling her wife's role willingly. And all this pain, rage, and congestion of unborn-baby voices in my head would be out from my system. But people like me, rational, responsible, sane, level-headed, careful, thinking, always thinking, can never take such rash steps.

I'd need a careless fuck-you attitude towards everything around me, including my own body, to throw away everything I have. Or else a greedy, gigantic embrace of everything life has to offer and spend my time doing, getting, doing, getting, getting, getting, getting . . .

No, people like me get the rawest of deals. We do our jobs. Live moderate, upright lives. Don't drink. Don't stone ourselves on bits of paper dipped in hallucinogenic acids. Have no burning ambitions.

People like me preserve our minds and bodies by living tepid, languid lives. Just to end up as cold, brittle artefacts. Like life-sized cut-outs pinned to the floor by the worst of memories. And like ink from a leaking pen, we let the past blot our shining futures. Continually.

The Christmas Present

Jeffery Deaver

"How long has she been missing?"

Stout Lon Sellitto – his diet shot because of the holiday season – shrugged. "That's sort of the problem."

"Go on."

"It's sort of—"

"You said that already," Lincoln Rhyme felt obliged to point out to the NYPD detective.

"About four hours. Close to it."

Rhyme didn't even bother to comment. An adult was not even considered missing until at least twenty-four hours had passed.

"But there're circumstances," Sellitto added. "You have to know who we're talking about."

They were in an impromptu crime scene laboratory – the living room of Rhyme's Central Park West town house in Manhattan – but it had been impromptu for years and had more equipment and supplies than most small-town police departments.

A tasteful evergreen garland had been draped around the windows, and tinsel hung from the scanning electron microscope. Benjamin Britten's *Ceremony of Carols* played brightly on the stereo. It was Christmas Eve.

"It's just, she's a sweet kid. Carly is, I mean. And here her mother knows she's coming over but doesn't call her and tell her she's leaving or leave a note or – anything. Which she always does. Her mom – Susan Thompson's her name – is totally buttoned up. Very weird for her just to vanish."

"She's getting the girl a Christmas present," Rhyme said. "Didn't want to give away the surprise."

"But her car's still in the garage." Sellitto nodded out the window at the fat confetti of snow that had been falling for several hours. "She's not going to be walking anywhere in this weather, Linc. And she's not at any of the neighbors'. Carly checked."

Had Rhyme had the use of his body – other than his left ring finger, shoulders and head – he would have given Detective Sellitto an impatient gesture, perhaps a circling of the hand, or two palms skyward. As it was, he relied solely on words. "And how did this not-so-missing-person case all come about, Lon? I detect you've been playing Samaritan. You know what they say about good deeds, don't you? They never go unpunished . . . Not to mention, it seems to *sort of* be falling on my shoulders, now, doesn't it?"

Sellitto helped himself to another homemade Christmas cookie. It was in the shape of Santa, but the icing face was grotesque. "These're pretty good. You want one?"

"No," Rhyme grumbled. Then his eye strayed to a shelf. "But I'd be more inclined to listen agreeably to your sales pitch with a bit of Christmas cheer."

"Of . . . ? Oh. Sure." He walked across the lab, found the bottle of Macallan and poured a healthy dose into a tumbler. The detective inserted a straw and mounted the cup in the holder on Rhyme's chair.

Rhyme sipped the liquor. Ah, heaven . . . His aide, Thom, and the criminalist's partner, Amelia Sachs, were out shopping; if they'd been here Rhyme's beverage might have been tasty but, given the hour, would undoubtedly have been non-alcoholic.

"All right. Here's the story. Rachel's a friend of Susan and her daughter."

So it was a friend-of-the-family good deed. Rachel was Sellitto's girlfriend. Rhyme said, "The daughter being Carly. See, I was listening, Lon. Go on."

"Carly—"

"Who's how old?"

"Nineteen. Student at NYU. Business major. She's going with this guy from Garden City—"

"Is any of this relevant, other than her age? Which I'm not even sure is relevant."

"Tell me, Linc: You always in this good a mood during the holidays?"

Another sip of the liquor. "Keep going."

"Susan's divorced, works for a PR firm downtown. Lives in the burbs, Nassau County—"

"Nassau? Nassau? Hmm, would they sort of be the right constabulary to handle the matter? You understand how that works, right? That course on jurisdiction at the Academy?"

Sellitto had worked with Lincoln Rhyme for years and was quite talented at deflecting the criminalist's feistiness. He ignored the comment and continued. "She takes a couple days off to get the house ready for the holidays. Rachel tells me she and her daughter have a teenage thing – you know, going through a rough time, the two of them. But Susan's trying. She wants to make everything nice for the girl, throw a big party on Christmas Day. Anyway, Carly's living in an apartment in the Village near her school. Last night she tells her mom she'll come by this morning, drop off some things and then's going to her boyfriend's. Susan says good, they'll have coffee, yadda yadda . . . Only when Carly gets there, Susan's gone. And her—"

"Car's still in the garage."

"Exactly. So Carly waits for a while. Susan doesn't come back. She calls the local boys but they're not going to do anything for twenty-four hours, at least. So, Carly thinks of me – I'm the only cop she knows – and calls Rachel."

"We can't do good deeds for everybody. Just because 'tis the season."

"Let's give the kid a Christmas present, Linc. Ask a few questions, look around the house."

Rhyme's expression was scowly but in fact he was intrigued. How he hated boredom . . . And, yes, he was often in a bad mood during the holidays – because there was invariably a lull in the stimulating cases that the NYPD or the FBI would hire him to consult on as a forensic scientist, or "criminalist" as the jargon termed it.

"So . . . Carly's upset. You understand."

Rhyme shrugged, one of the few gestures allowed to him after the accident at a crime scene some years ago had left him a quadriplegic. Rhyme moved his one working finger on the touch pad and maneuvered the chair to face Sellitto. "Her mother's probably home by now. But, if you really want, let's call the girl. I'll get a few facts, see what I think. What can it hurt?"

"That's great, Linc. Hold on." The large detective walked to the door and opened it.

"What was this?"

In walked a teenage girl, looking around shyly.

"Oh, Mr Rhyme, hi. I'm Carly Thompson. Thanks so much for seeing me."

"Ah, you've been waiting outside," Rhyme said and offered the detective an acerbic glance. "If my friend Lon here had shared that fact with me, I'd've invited you in for a cup of tea."

"Oh, that's okay. Nothing for me."

Sellitto lifted a cheerful eyebrow and found a chair for the girl.

She had long, blonde hair and an athletic figure and her round face bore little makeup. She was dressed in MTV chic – flared jeans and a black jacket, chunky boots. To Rhyme the most remarkable thing about her, though, was her expression: Carly gave no reaction whatsoever to his disability. Some people grew tongue-tied, some chatted mindlessly, some locked their eyes on to his and grew frantic – as if a glance at his body would be the faux pas of the century. Each of those reactions pissed him off in its own way.

She smiled. "I like the decoration."

"I'm sorry?" Rhyme asked.

"The garland on the back of your chair."

The criminalist swiveled but couldn't see anything.

"There's a garland there?" he asked Sellitto.

"Yeah, you didn't know? And a red ribbon."

"That must have been courtesy of my aide," Rhyme grumbled. "Soon to be ex, if he tries that again."

Carly said, "I wouldn't've bothered Mr Sellitto or you. . . . I wouldn't have bothered *anyone* but it's just so weird, Mom disappearing like this. She's never done that before."

Rhyme said, "Ninety-nine percent of the time there's just been a mix-up of some kind. No crime at all . . . And only four hours?" Another glance at Sellitto. "That's nothing."

"Except, with Mom, whatever else, she's dependable."

"When did you talk to her last?"

"It was about eight last night, I guess. She's having this party tomorrow and we were making plans for it. I was going to come over this morning and she was going to give me a shopping list and some money and Jake – that's my boyfriend – and I were going to go shopping and hang out."

"Maybe she couldn't get through on your cell," Rhyme suggested. "Where was your friend? Could she have left a message at his place?"

"Jake's? No, I just talked to him on my way here." Carly gave a rueful smile. "She likes Jake okay, you know." She played nervously with her long hair, twining it around her fingers. "But they're not the best of friends. He's . . ." The girl decided not to go into the details of the disapproval. "Anyway, she wouldn't call his house. His dad's . . . difficult."

"And she took today off from work?"

"That's right."

The door opened and Rhyme heard Amelia Sachs and Thom enter, the crinkle of paper from the shopping bags.

The tall woman, dressed in jeans and a bomber jacket, stepped into the doorway. Her red hair and shoulders dusted with snow. She smiled at Rhyme and Sellitto. "Merry Christmas and all that."

Thom headed down the hall with the bags.

"Ah, Sachs, come on in here. It seems Detective Sellitto has volunteered our services. Amelia Sachs, Carly Thompson."

The women shook hands.

Sellitto asked, "You want a cookie?"

Carly demurred. Sachs too shook her head. "I decorated 'em, Lon – yeah, Santa looks like Boris Karloff, I know. If I never see another cookie again it'll be too soon."

Thom appeared in the door, introduced himself to Carly and then walked toward the kitchen, from which Rhyme knew refreshments were about to appear. Unlike Rhyme, his aide loved the holidays, largely because they gave him the chance to play host nearly every day.

As Sachs pulled off her jacket and hung it up, Rhyme explained the situation and what the girl had told them so far.

The policewoman nodded, taking it in. She reiterated that a person's missing for such a short time was no cause for alarm. But they'd be happy to help a friend of Lon's and Rachel's.

"Indeed we will," Rhyme said with an irony that everyone except Sachs missed.

No good deed goes unpunished . . . .

Carry continued. "I got there about eight-thirty this morning. She wasn't home. The car was in the garage. I checked all the neighbors'. She wasn't there and nobody's seen her."

"Could she have left the night before?" Sellitto asked.

"No. She'd made coffee this morning. The pot was still warm."

Rhyme said, "Maybe something came up at work and she didn't want to drive to the station, so she took a cab."

Carly shrugged. "Could be. I didn't think about that. She's in public relations and's been working real hard lately. For one of those big Internet companies that went bankrupt. It's been totally tense. . . . But I don't know. We didn't talk very much about her job."

Sellitto had a young detective downtown call all the cab companies in and around Glen Hollow; no taxis had been dispatched to the house that morning. They also called Susan's company to see if she'd come in, but no one had seen her and her office was locked.

Just then, as Rhyme had predicted, his slim aide, wearing a white shirt and a Jerry Garcia Christmas tie, carted in a large tray of coffee and tea and a huge plate of pastries and cookies. He poured drinks for everyone.

"No figgy pudding?" Rhyme asked acerbically.

Sachs asked Carly, "Has your mom been sad or moody?"

Thinking for a minute, she said, "Well, my grandfather – her dad – died last February. Grandpa was a great guy and she was totally bummed for a while. But by the summer, she'd come out of it. She bought this really cool house and had a lot of fun fixing it up."

"How about other people in her life, friends, boyfriends?"

"She's got some good friends, sure."

"Names, phone numbers?"

Again the girl fell quiet. "I know some of their names. Not exactly where they live. I don't have any numbers."

"Anybody she was seeing romantically?"

"She broke up with somebody about a month ago."

Sellitto asked, "Was this guy a problem, you think? A stalker? Upset about the breakup?"

The girl replied, "No, I think it was his idea. Anyway, he lived in L.A. or Seattle or some place out west. So it wasn't, you know, real serious. She just started seeing this new guy. About two weeks ago." Carly looked from Sachs to the floor. "The thing is, I love Mom and everything. But we're not real close. My folks were divorced seven, eight years ago, and that kind of changed a lot of things. . . . Sorry I don't know more about her."

Ah, the wonderful family unit, thought Rhyme cynically. It was what made Park Avenue shrinks millionaires and kept police departments around the world busy answering calls at all hours of the day and night.

"You're doing fine," Sachs encouraged. "Where's your father?"

"He lives in the city. Downtown."

"Do he and your mother see each other much?"

"Not anymore. He wanted to get back together but Mom was lukewarm and I think he gave up."

"Do you see him much?"

"I do, yeah. But he travels a lot. His company imports stuff, and he goes overseas to meet his suppliers."

"Is he in town now?"

"Yep. I'm going to see him on Christmas, after Mom's party."

"We should call him. See if he's heard from her," Sachs said.

Rhyme nodded and Carly gave them the man's number. Rhyme said, "I'll get in touch with him. . . . Okay, get going, Sachs. Over to Susan's house. Carly, you go with her. Move fast."

"Sure, Rhyme. But what's the hurry?"

He glanced out the window, as if the answer were hovering there in plain view.

Sachs shook her head, perplexed. Rhyme was often piqued that people didn't tumble to things as quickly as he did. "Because the snow might tell us something about what happened there this morning." And, as he often liked to do, he added a dramatic coda: "But if it keeps coming down like this, there won't be any story left to read."

A half-hour later Amelia Sachs pulled up on a quiet, tree lined street in Glen Hollow, Long Island, parking the bright red Camaro three doors from Susan Thompson's house.

"No, it's up there," Carly pointed out.

"Here's better," Sachs said. Rhyme had drummed into her that access routes to and from the site of the crime could be crime scenes in their own right and could yield valuable information. She was ever-mindful about contaminating scenes.

Carly grimaced when she noticed that the car was still in the garage.

"I'd hoped . . ."

Sachs looked at the girl's face and saw raw concern. The policewoman understood: Mother and daughter had a tough relationship that was obvious. But you never cut parental ties altogether – can't be done – and there's nothing like a missing mother to set off primal alarms.

"We'll find her," Sachs whispered.

Carly gave a faint smile and pulled her jacket tighter around her. It was stylish and obviously expensive but useless against the cold. Sachs had been a fashion model for a time but when not on the runway or at a shoot she'd dressed like a real person, to hell with what was in vogue.

Sachs looked over the house, a new, rambling two-story Colonial on a small but well-groomed lot, and called Rhyme. On a real case she'd be patched through to him on her Motorola. Since this wasn't official business, though, she simply used her hands-free cord and cell phone, which was clipped to her belt a few inches away from her Glock automatic pistol.

"I'm at the house," she told him. "What's that music?"

After a moment "Hark, the Herald Angels Sing" went silent.

"Sorry. Thom insists on being in the *spirit*. What do you see, Sachs?"

She explained where she was and the layout of the place. "The snow's not too bad here but you're right: in another hour it'll cover up any prints."

"Stay off the walks and check out if there's been any surveillance."

"Got it."

Sachs asked Carly what prints were hers. The girl explained that she had parked in front of the garage – Sachs could see the tread marks in the snow – and then had gone through the kitchen door.

Carly behind her, Sachs made a circuit of the property.

"Nothing in the back or side yard, except for Carly's footprints," she told Rhyme.

"There are no visible prints, you mean," he corrected. "That's not necessarily 'nothing.' "

"Okay, Rhyme. That's what I meant. Damn, it's cold."

They circled to the front of the house. Sachs found footsteps in the snow on the path between the street and the house. A car had stopped at the curb. There was one set of prints walking toward the house and two walking back suggesting the driver had picked Susan up. She told Rhyme this. He asked, "Can you tell anything from the shoes? Size, sale prints, weight distribution?"

"Nothing's clear." She winced as she bent down; her arthritic joints ached in the cold and damp. "But one thing's odd – they're real close together."

"As if one of them had an arm around the other person."

"Right."

"Could be affection. Could be coercion. We'll assume hope – the second set is Susan's, and that, whatever happened, at least she's alive. Or was a few hours ago."

Then Sachs noted a curious indentation in the snow, next to one of the front windows. It was as if somebody had stepped of the sidewalk and knelt on the ground. In this spot you could see clearly into the living room and kitchen beyond. She sent Carly to open the front door and then whispered into the microphone, "May have a problem, Rhyme . . . It looks like somebody was kneeling down, looking through the window."

"Any other evidence there, Sachs? Discernible prints, cigarette butts, other impressions, trace?"

"Nothing."

"Check the house, Sachs. And, just for the fun of it, pretend it's hot."

"But how could a perp be inside?"

"Humor me."

The policewoman stepped to the front door, unzipping her leather jacket to give her fast access to her weapon. She found the girl in the entryway, looking around the house. It was still, except for the tapping and whirs of household machinery. The lights were on – though Sachs found this more troubling than if it'd been dark; it suggested that Susan had left in a hurry. You don't shut out the lights when you're being abducted.

Sachs told the girl to stay close and she started through the place, praying she wouldn't find a body. But, no; they looked everywhere the woman might be. Nothing. And no signs of a struggle.

"The scene's clear, Rhyme."

"Well, that's something."

"I'm going to do a fast grid here, see if we can find any clue where she went. I'll call you back if I find anything."

On the main floor Sachs paused at the mantel and looked over a number of framed photographs. Susan Thompson was a tall, solidly built woman with short blonde hair, feathered back. She had an agreeable smile. Most of the pictures were of her with Carly or with an older couple, probably her parents. Many had been taken out-of-doors, apparently on hiking or camping trips.

They looked for any clue that might indicate where the woman was. Sachs studied the calendar next to the phone in the kitchen. The only note in today's square said *C here*.

The girl gave a sad laugh. Were the single letter and terse notation an emblem of how Carly believed the woman saw her? Sachs wondered what exactly the problems were between daughter and mother. She herself had always had a complex relationship with her own mother. "Challenging" was how she'd described it to Rhyme.

"Day-Timer? Palm Pilot?"

Carly looked around. "Her purse is gone. She keeps them in there. I'll try her cell again." The girl did and the frustrated, troubled look told Sachs that there was no answer. "Goes right to voice mail."

Sachs tried all three phones in the house, hitting redial. Two got her directory assistance. The other was the number for a local branch of North Shore Bank. Sachs asked to speak to the manager and told her they were trying to locate Susan Thompson. The woman said she'd been in about two hours ago.

Sachs told this to Carly, who closed her eyes in relief. "Where did she go after that?"

The policewoman asked the manager the question and the woman responded that she had no idea. Then she asked hesitantly, "Are you calling because she wasn't feeling well?"

"What do you mean?" Sachs asked.

"It's just that she didn't look very good when she was in. That man she was with . . . well, he had his arm around her the whole time. I was thinking maybe she was sick."

Sachs asked if they could come in and speak with her.

"Of course. If I can help."

Sachs told Carly what the woman had said.

"Not feeling well? And some man?" The girl frowned. "Who?"

"Let's go find out."

As they approached the door, though, Sachs stopped. "Do me a favor," she said to the girl.

"Sure. What?"

"Borrow one of your mother's jackets. You're making me cold just looking at you."

The branch manager of the bank explained to Sachs and Carly, "She went into her safety deposit box downstairs and then cashed a check."

"You don't know what she did down there, I assume?" the policewoman asked.

"No, no, employees are never around when customers go into their boxes."

"And that man? Any idea who he was?"

"No."

"What did he look like?" Sachs asked.

"He was big. Six-two, six-three. Balding. Didn't smile much."

The police detective glanced at Carly, who shook her head. "I've never seen her with anybody like that."

They found the teller who'd cashed the check but Susan hadn't said anything to her either, except how she'd like the money.

"How much was the check for?" Sachs asked.

The manager hesitated – probably some confidentiality issue – but Carly said, "Please. We're worried about her." The woman nodded to the teller, who said, "A thousand."

Sachs stepped aside and called Rhyme on her cell. She explained what had happened at the bank.

"Getting troubling now, Sachs. A thousand doesn't seem like much for a robbery or kidnapping, but wealth's relative. Maybe that's a lot of money to this guy."

"I'm more curious about the safe deposit box."

Rhyme said, "Good point. Maybe she had something he wanted. But what? She's just a businesswoman and mother. It's not like she's an investigative reporter or cop. And the bad news is, if that's the case, he's got what he was after. He might not need her anymore. I think it's time to get Nassau County involved. Maybe . . . Wait, you're at the bank?"

"Right."

"The video! Get the video."

"Oh, at the teller cage, sure. But—"

"No, no, no," Rhyme snapped. "Of the *parking* lot. All banks have video surveillance of the lots. If they parked there it'll have his car on tape. Maybe the tag number too."

Sachs returned to the manager and she called the security chief, who disappeared into a back office. A moment later he gestured them inside and ran the tape.

"There!" Carly cried. "That's her. And that guy? Look, he's still holding on to her. He's not letting her go."

"Looks pretty fishy, Rhyme."

"Can you see the car?" the criminalist asked.

Sachs had the guard freeze the tape. "What kind of—"

"Chevy Malibu," the guard said. "This year's model."

Sachs told this to Rhyme and, examining the screen, added, "It's burgundy. And the last two numbers on the tag are seventy-eight. The one before it could be three or eight, maybe six. Hard to tell. It's a New York plate."

"Good, Sachs. Okay. It's up to the uniforms now. Lon'll have them put out a locator. Nassau, Suffolk, Westchester and the five boroughs. Jersey too. We'll prioritize it. Oh, hold on a minute . . ." Sachs heard him speaking to someone. Rhyme came back on the line. "Susan's ex is on his way over here. He's worried about his daughter. He'd like to see her."

Sachs told Carly this. Her face brightened. The detective added, "There's nothing more we can do here. Let's go back to the city."

Amelia Sachs and Carly Thompson had just returned to the lab in Rhyme's town house when Anthony Dalton arrived. Thom led him inside and he stopped abruptly, looking at his daughter. "Hello, honey."

"Dad! I'm so glad you came!"

With both affection and concern in his eyes, he stepped toward the girl and hugged her hard.

Dalton was a fit man in his late forties with a boyish flop of salt-and-pepper hair. He wore a complicated ski jacket, straps and flaps going every which way. He reminded Rhyme of the college professors he sometimes shared the podium with when he was lecturing on forensics at criminal justice colleges.

"Do they know anything?" he asked, apparently only now realizing that Rhyme was in a wheelchair – and finding the fact unremarkable. Like his daughter, Anthony Dalton earned serious points with Rhyme for this.

The criminalist explained exactly what had happened and what they knew.

Dalton shook his head. "But it doesn't necessarily mean she's been kidnapped," he said quickly.

"No, no, not at all," Sellitto said. "We're just not taking any chances."

Rhyme asked, "Do you know anyone who'd want to hurt her?"

He shook his head. "I have no idea. I haven't seen Susan in a year. But when we were together? No, everybody liked her. Even when some of her PR clients had done some pretty shady things, nobody had a problem with her personally. And she always seemed to have the particularly nasty clients."

Rhyme was troubled – for reasons beyond the danger to Susan Thompson. The problem was that this wasn't a real case. They'd backed into it, doing a favor for someone; it was a Christmas present, as Sellitto had said. He needed more facts; he needed serious forensics. He'd always felt you run a case 110 per cent or you don't run it at all.

Thom brought more coffee in and replenished the plate of ugly cookies. Dalton nodded at the aide and thanked him. Then the businessman poured coffee from the pot for himself. "You want some?" he asked Carly.

"Sure, I guess."

He poured it and asked, "Anyone else?"

No one else wanted anything. But Rhyme's eyes flipped to the Macallan on the shelf and, lo and behold, without a syllable of protest, Thom took the bottle and walked to Rhyme's Storm Arrow. He opened the tumbler, then frowned. He sniffed it. "Odd, I thought I washed this out last night. I guess I forgot," he added wryly.

"We can't all be perfect, now," Rhyme said.

Thom poured a few fingers into the tumbler and replaced it in the holder.

"Thank you, Balthazar. You can keep your job for now – despite the weeds on the back of my chair."

"You don't like them? I told you I was going to decorate for the holidays."

"The house. Not me."

"What do we do now?" Dalton asked.

"We wait," Sellitto said. "DMV's running all the Malibus with that fragment of a tag number. Or, if we're real lucky, some officer on the street'll notice it." He pulled his coat off a chair. "I gotta go down to the Big Building for a while. Call me if anything happens."

Dalton thanked him, then he looked at his watch, took out his mobile phone and called his office to say he'd have to miss his office Christmas party. He explained that the police were looking into his ex-wife's disappearance and he was with his daughter at the moment. He wasn't going to leave the girl alone.

Carly hugged him. "Thanks, Dad." Her eyes lifted to the window, staring at the swirling snow. A long moment passed. Carly glanced at the others in the room and turned toward her father. In a soft voice she said, "I always wondered what would have happened if you and Mom hadn't broken up."

Dalton laughed, ran his hand through his hair, mussing it further. "I've thought about that too."

Sachs glanced at Rhyme and they turned away, letting the father and daughter continue talking in relative privacy.

"The guys Mom's dated? They were okay. But nobody special. None of them lasted very long."

"It's tough to meet the right person," Dalton said.

"I guess . . ."

"What?"

"I guess I've always wished you'd get back together."

Dalton seemed at a loss for words. "I tried. You know that. But your mom was in a different place."

"But you stopped trying a couple of years ago."

"I could read the writing on the wall. People have to move on."

"But she misses you. I know she does."

Dalton laughed, "Oh, I don't know about that."

"No, no, really. When I ask her about you, she tells me what a cool guy you were. You were funny. She said you made her laugh."

"We had some good times."

Carly said, "When I asked Mom what happened between you, she said it wasn't anything totally terrible."

"True," Dalton said, sipping his coffee. "We just didn't know how to be husband and wife back then. We got married too young."

"Well, you're not young anymore . . ." Carly blushed. "Oh, I didn't mean it like that."

But Dalton said, "No, you're right. I've grown up a lot since then."

"And Mom's really changed. She used to be so quiet, you know. Just no fun. But she's into all kinds of things now. Camping and hiking, rafting, all that out-of-doors stuff."

"Really?" Dalton asked. "I never pictured her going in for that kind of thing."

Carly looked off for a moment. "Remember those business trips you'd take when I was a kid? You'd go to Hong Kong or Japan?"

"Setting up our overseas offices, sure."

"I wanted all of us to go. You, Mom and me . . ." She played with her coffee cup. "But she was always like, 'Oh, there's too much to do at home.' Or, 'Oh, we'll get sick if we drink the water,' or whatever. We never did take a family vacation. Not a real one."

"I always wanted that too." Dalton shook his head sadly. "And I'd get mad when she didn't want to come along and bring you. But she's your mother; it's her job to look out for you. All she wanted was for you to be safe." He smiled. "I remember once when I was in Tokyo and calling home. And—"

His words were interrupted when Rhyme's phone rang. He spoke into the microphone on his chair, "Command, answer phone."

"Detective Rhyme?" the voice clattered through the speaker.

The rank was out of date – a "Ret." belonged with it – but he said, "Go ahead."

"This's Trooper Bronson, New York State Police."

"Go ahead."

"We've had an emergency vehicle locator request regarding a burgundy Malibu and understand you're involved in the case."

"That's right."

"We've found the vehicle, sir."

Rhyme heard Carly gasp. Dalton stepped beside the girl and put his arm around her shoulder. What would they hear? That Sue Thompson was dead?

"Go ahead."

"The car's moving west, looks like it's headed for the George Washington Bridge."

"Occupants?"

"Two. Man and a woman. Can't tell anything more."

"Thank God. She's alive." Dalton sighed.

Heading toward Jersey, Rhyme reflected. The flats were among the most popular places for dumping bodies in the metro area.

"Registered to a Richard Musgrave, Queens. No warrants."

Rhyme glanced at Carly, who shook her head, meaning she had no clue who he was.

Sachs leaned forward toward the speaker and identified herself, "Are you near the car?"

"About 200 feet behind."

"You in a marked vehicle?"

"That's right."

"How far from the bridge?"

"A mile or two east."

Rhyme glanced at Sachs. "You want to join the party? You can stay right on their tail in the Camaro."

"You bet." She ran for the door.

"Sachs," Rhyme called.

She glanced back.

"You have chains on your Chevy?"

Sachs laughed. "Chains on a muscle car, Rhyme? No."

"Well, try not to skid into the Hudson, okay? It's probably pretty cold."

"I'll do my best."

True, a rear-wheel-drive sports car, with more than 400 eager horses under the hood, was not the best vehicle to drive on snow. But Amelia Sachs had spent much of her youth skidding cars on hot asphalt in illegal races around Brooklyn (and sometimes just because, why not, it's always a blast to do one-eighties); this little bit of snow meant nothing to her.

She now slipped her Camaro SS onto the expressway and pushed the accelerator down. The wheels spun for only five seconds before they gripped and sped her up to eighty.

"I'm on the bridge, Rhyme," she called into her headset. "Where are they?"

"About a mile west. Are you—"

The car started to swerve. "Hold on, Rhyme, I'm going sideways."

She brought the skid under control. "A V W doing fifty in the fast lane. Man, doesn't that just frost you?"

In another mile she'd caught up to the trooper, keeping back, just out of sight of the Malibu. She looked past him and saw the car ease into the right lane and signal for an exit.

"Rhyme, can you get me a patch through to the trooper?" she asked.

"Hold on . . ." A long pause. Rhyme's frustrated voice. "I can never figure out—" He was cut off and she heard two clicks. Then the trooper said, "Detective Sachs?"

"I'm here. Go ahead."

"Is that you behind me, in that fine red set of wheels?"

"Yep."

"How do you want to handle this?"

"Who's driving? The man or the woman?"

"The man."

She thought for a moment. "Make it seem like a routine traffic stop. Tail-light him or something. After he's on the shoulder I'll get in front and sandwich him in. You take the passenger side and I'll get the driver out. We don't know that he's armed and we don't know that he's not. But the odds are it's an abduction, so assume he's got a weapon."

"Roger that, Detective."

"Okay, let's do it."

The Malibu exited. Sachs tried to look through the rear window. She couldn't see anything through the snow. The burgundy car rolled down the ramp and braked slowly to a stop at a red light. When it turned green the car eased forward through the slush and snow.

The trooper's voice crackled into her ear. "Detective Sachs, are you ready?"

"Yep. Let's nail him."

The light bar on his Police Interceptor Crown Victoria started flashing and he hit the squeal once. The driver of the Malibu looked up into the rearview mirror and the car swerved momentarily. Then it pulled to a stop on the side of road, bleak town houses on the left and reedy marshes on the right.

Sachs punched the accelerator and skidded to a stop in front of the Malibu, blocking it. She was out the door in an instant, pulling her Glock from her holster and jogging fast toward the car.

Forty minutes later a grim Amelia Sachs walked into Rhyme's town house.

"How bad was it?" Rhyme asked.

"Pretty bad." She poured herself a double scotch and drank down half the liquor fast. Unusual for her; Amelia Sachs was a sipper.

"Pretty bad," she repeated.

Sachs was not, however, referring to any bloody shoot out in Jersey, but to the embarrassment of what they'd done.

"Tell me."

Sachs had radioed in from the roadside to tell Rhyme, Carly and Anthony Dalton that Susan was fine. Sachs hadn't been able to go into the details then, though. Now she explained, "The guy in the car was that man she's been seeing for the past couple of weeks." A glance at Carly. "Rich Musgrave, the one you mentioned. It's his car. He called this morning and they'd made plans to go shopping at the Jersey outlet malls. Only what happened was, when she went out to get the newspaper this morning she slipped on the ice."

Dalton nodded. "The front path – it's like a ski slope."

Carly winced. "Mom always said that she was a born klutz."

Sachs continued, "She hurt her knee and didn't want to drive. So she called Rich back and asked him to pick her up. Oh, the spot in the snow where I thought somebody was looking in the window? It was where she fell."

"That's why he was so close to her," Rhyme mused. "He was helping her walk."

Sachs nodded. "And at the bank, there was no mystery – she really did need something out of the safe deposit box. And the thousand bucks was for Christmas shopping."

Carly frowned. "But she knew I was coming by. Why didn't she call me?"

"Oh, she wrote you a note."

"Note?"

"It said she'd be out for the day but she'd be back home by six."

"No! . . . But I never saw it."

"Because," Sachs explained, "after she fell she was pretty shaken up and forgot to leave it on the entryway table like she'd planned. She found it in her purse when I told her it wasn't there. And she didn't have her cell phone turned on."

Dalton laughed. "All a misunderstanding." He put his arm around his daughter's shoulders.

Carly, blushing again, said, "I'm really, really sorry I panicked. I should've known there was an explanation."

"That's what we're here for," Sachs said.

Which wasn't exactly true, Rhyme reflected sourly. No good deed . . .

As she pulled on her coat, Carly invited Rhyme, Sachs and Thom to the Christmas party tomorrow afternoon at her mother's. "It's the least we can do."

"I'm sure Thom and Amelia would be *delighted* to go," Rhyme said quickly. "Unfortunately, I think I have plans." Cocktail parties bored him.

"No," Thom said. "You don't have any plans."

Sachs added, "Nope, no plans."

A scowl from Rhyme. "I think I know my calendar better than anyone else."

Which wasn't exactly true either.

After the father and daughter had gone, Rhyme said to Thom, "Since you blew the whistle on my unencumbered social schedule tomorrow, you can do penance."

"What?" the aide asked cautiously.

"Take the goddamn decorations off my chair. I feel like Santa Claus."

"Humbug," Thom said and did as asked. He turned the radio on. A carol streamed into the room.

Rhyme nodded towards the speaker. "Aren't we lucky there are only twelve days of Christmas? Can you imagine how interminable that song would be if there were twenty?" He sang, "Twenty muggers mugging, nineteen burglars burgling . . .

Thom sighed and said to Sachs, "All I want for Christmas is a nice, complicated jewelry heist right about now – something to pacify him."

"Eighteen aides complaining," Rhyme continued the song. He added, "See, Thom, I am in the holiday spirit. Despite what you think."

★ ★ ★

Susan Thompson climbed out of Rich Musgrave's Malibu. The large, handsome man was holding the door for her. She took his hand and he eased her to her feet; her shoulder and knee still ached fiercely from the spill she'd taken on the ice that morning.

"What a day," she said, sighing.

"I don't mind getting pulled over by the cops," Rich said, laughing. "I could've done without the guns, though."

Carrying all her shopping bags in one hand, he helped her to the front door. They walked carefully over the three-inch blanket of fine snow.

"You want to come in? Carly's here – that's her car. You can watch me prostrate myself in front of her and apologize for being such a bozo. I could've sworn I left that note on the table."

"I think I'll let you run the gauntlet on your own." Rich was divorced too and was spending Christmas Eve with his two sons at his place in Armonk. He needed to pick them up soon. She thanked him again for everything and apologized once more for the scare with the police. He'd been a nice guy about the whole thing. But, as she fished her keys out of her purse and watched him walk back to the car, she reflected that there was no doubt the relationship wasn't going anywhere. What was the problem? Susan wondered. Rough edges, she supposed. She wanted a gentleman. She wanted somebody who was kind, who had a sense of humor. Somebody who could make her laugh.

She waved goodbye and stepped into the house, pulled the door shut behind her.

Carly had already started on the decorations, bless her, and Susan smelled something cooking in the kitchen. Had the girl made dinner? This was a first. She looked into the den and blinked in surprise. Carly'd decked out the room beautifully, garlands, ribbons, candles. And on the coffee table was a big plate of cheese and crackers, a bowl of nuts, fruit, two glasses sitting beside a bottle of California sparkling wine. The girl was nineteen, but Susan let her have some wine when they were home alone.

"Honey, how wonderful!"

"Mom," Carly called, walking to the doorway. "I didn't hear you come in."

The girl was carrying a baking dish. Inside were some hot canapés. She set it on the table and hugged her mother.

Susan threw her arms around the girl, ignoring the pain from the fall that morning. She apologized for the mistake about the note and for making her daughter worry so much. The girl, though, just laughed it off.

"Is it true that policeman's in a wheelchair?" Susan asked. "He can't move?"

"He's not a policeman anymore. He's kind of a consultant. But, yeah, he's paralyzed."

Carly went on to explain about Lincoln Rhyme and how they'd found her and Rich Musgrave. Then she wiped her hands on her apron and took it off. "Mom, I want to give you one of your presents tonight."

"Tonight? Are we starting a new tradition?"

"Maybe we are."

"Well, okay . . ." Then Susan took the girl's arm. "In that case let me give you mine first." She got her purse from the table and dug inside. She found the small velvet box. "This is what I got out of the safe deposit box this morning."

She handed it to the girl, who opened it. Her eyes went wide. "Oh, Mom . . ."

It was an antique diamond and emerald ring.

"This was—"

"Grandma's. Her engagement ring." Susan nodded. "I wanted you to have something special. I know you've had a rough time lately, honey. I've been too busy at work. I haven't been as nice to Jake as I should. And some of the men I've dated . . . well, I know you didn't like them that much." A laughing whisper. "Of course, I didn't like them that much either. I'm resolving not to date losers anymore."

Carly frowned. "Mom, you've never dated losers. More like semi-losers."

"That's even worse! I couldn't even find a red-blooded, full-fledged loser to date!"

Carly hugged her mother again and put the ring on. "It's so beautiful."

"Merry Christmas, honey."

"Now, time for your present."

"I think I like our new tradition."

Her daughter instructed, "Sit down. Close your eyes. I'm going outside to get it."

"All right."

"Sit on the couch right there."

She sat and closed her eyes tight.

"Don't peek."

"I won't." Susan heard the front door open and close. A moment later she frowned, hearing the sound of a car engine starting. Was it Carly's? Was she leaving?

But then she heard footsteps behind her. The girl must have come back in through the kitchen door.

"Well, can I look now?"

"Sure," said a man's voice.

Susan jumped in surprise. She turned and found herself staring at her ex-husband. He carried a large box with a ribbon on it.

"Anthony . . ." she began.

Dalton sat on the chair across from her. "Been a long time, hasn't it?"

"What are you doing here?"

"When Carly thought you were missing, I went over to that cop's place to be with her. We were worried about you. We got to talking and, well, that's her Christmas present to you and me: getting us together tonight and just seeing what happens."

"Where is she?"

"She went to her boyfriend's to spend the night with him." He smiled. "We've got the whole evening ahead of us. All alone. Just like the old days."

Susan started to rise. But Anthony stood up fast and swung his palm into her face with a jarring slap. She fell back on the couch. "You get up when I tell you to," he said cheerfully, smiling down at her. "Merry Christmas, Susan. It's good to see you again."

She looked toward the door.

"Don't even think about it." He opened the sparkling wine and poured two glasses. He offered her one. She shook her head. "Take it."

"Please, Anthony, just—"

"Take the goddamn glass," he hissed.

Susan did, her hand shaking violently. As they touched flutes, memories from when they were married flooded back to her: his sarcasm, his rage. And, of course, the beatings.

Oh, but he'd been clever. He never hurt her in front of people. He was especially careful around Carly. Like the psychopath that he was, Anthony Dalton was the model father to the girl. And the model husband to the world.

Nobody knew the source of her bruises, cuts, broken fingers . . .

"Mommy's such a klutz," Susan would tell young Carly, fighting back the tears. "I fell down the stairs again."

She'd long ago given up trying to understand what made Anthony tick. A troubled childhood, a glitch in the brain? She didn't know and after a year of marriage she didn't care. Her only goal was to get out. But she'd been too terrified to go to the police. Finally, in desperation, she'd turned to her father for help. The burly man owned several construction companies in New York and he had "connections." She'd confessed to him what had happened and her father took charge of the problem. He had two associates from Brooklyn, armed with baseball bats and a gun, pay Anthony a visit. The threats, and a lot of money, had bought her freedom from the man, who reluctantly agreed to a divorce, to give up custody of Carly and not to hurt Susan again.

But, with terror flooding through her now, she realized why he was here tonight. Her father had passed away last spring.

Her protector was gone.

"I love Christmas, don't you?" Anthony Dalton mused, drinking more wine.

"What do you want?" she asked in a quivering voice.

"I can never get too much of the music." He walked to the stereo and turned it on. "Silent Night" was playing. "Did you know that it was first played on guitar? Because the church organ was broken."

"Please, just leave."

"The music . . . I like the decorations too."

She started to stand but he rose fast, slapping her again. "Sit down," he whispered, the soft sound more frightening than if he'd screamed.

Tears filled her eyes and she held her hand to her stinging cheek.

A boyish laugh. "And presents! We all love presents. . . . Don't you want to see what I got you?"

"We are not getting back together, Anthony. I do not want you in my life again."

"Why would I want someone like *you* in my life? What an ego." He looked her over, smiling faintly, with his placid blue eyes. She remembered this too – how calm he could be. Sometimes even when he was beating her.

"Anthony, there's no harm so far, nobody's been hurt."

"Shhhh."

Without his seeing, her hand slipped to her jacket pocket where she'd put her cell phone. She'd turned it back on after the mix-up with Carly earlier. She didn't, however, think she could hit 911 without looking. But her finger found the send button. By pressing it twice the phone would call the last number dialed. Rich Musgrave's. She hoped his phone was still on and that he'd hear what was happening. He'd call the police. Or possibly even return to the house. Anthony wouldn't dare hurt her in front of a witness – and Rich was a large man and looked very strong. He outweighed her ex by fifty pounds.

She pressed the button now. After a moment she said, "You're scaring me, Anthony. Please leave."

"Scaring you?"

"I'll call the police."

"If you stand up I'll break your arm. Are we clear on that?"

She nodded, terrified but thankful, at least, that if Rich was listening, he would have heard this exchange and probably be calling the police now.

Dalton looked under the tree. "Is *my* present there?" He browsed through the packages, seeming disappointed that there was none with his name on it.

She recalled this too: one minute he'd be fine. The next, completely out of touch with reality. He'd been hospitalized three times when they were married. Susan remembered telling Carly that her father had to go to Asia on month long business trips.

"Nothing for poor me." he said, standing back from the tree.

Susan's jaw trembled. "I'm sorry. If I'd known—"

"It's a joke, Susan," he said. "Why would you get me anything? You didn't love me when we were married; you don't love me now. The important thing is that I got you something. After the scare about what'd happened to you this afternoon I went shopping. I wanted to find just the right present.

Dalton drank down more wine and refilled his glass. He eyed her carefully. "Probably better if you stay snuggled in right where you are. I'll open it for you."

Her eyes glanced at the box. It had been carelessly wrapped – by him, of course – and he ripped the paper off roughly. He lifted out something cylindrical, made of metal.

"It's a camping heater. Carly said you'd taken that up. Hiking, out-of-doors . . . Interesting that you never liked to do anything fun when we were married."

"I never liked to do anything with *you*," she said angrily. "You'd beat me up if I said the wrong thing or didn't do what you'd told me."

Ignoring her words, he handed her the heater. Then he took out something else. A red can. On the side: *kerosene.* "Of course," Anthony continued, frowning, "that's one bad thing about Christmas . . . lot of accidents this time of year. You read that article in *USA Today*? Fires, particularly. Lot of people die in fires."

He glanced at the warning label and took a cigarette lighter from his pocket.

"Oh, God, no! . . . Please. Anthony."

It was then that Susan heard a car's brakes squeal outside. The police? Or was it Rich? Or was it her imagination?

Anthony was busying himself taking the lid off the kerosene.

Yes, there were definitely footsteps on the walk. Susan prayed it wasn't Carly.

Then the doorbell rang. Anthony looked toward the front door, startled.

And as he did, Susan flung the champagne glass into his face with all her strength and leapt to her feet, sprinting for the door. She glanced behind her to see Anthony stumbling backward. The glass had broken and cut his chin. "Goddamn b—!" he roared, starting for her.

But she had a good head start and flung the door open.

Rich Musgrave stood there, eyes wide in shock. "What?"

"It's my ex!" she gasped. "He's trying to kill me!"

"Jesus," Rich said. He put his arm around her. "Don't worry, Susan."

"We have to get away! Call the police."

She took his hand and started to flee into the front yard. But Rich didn't move. What the hell was he doing? Did he want to *fight*? This was no time for any chivalry crap. "Please, Rich. We have to run!"

Then she felt his hand tighten on hers. The grip became excruciating. His other hand took her by the waist and he turned her around. He shoved her back inside. "Yo, Anthony," Rich called, laughing. "Lose something?"

*   *   *

In despair, Susan sat on the couch and sobbed.

They'd tied her hands and feet with Christmas ribbon, which would burn away, leaving no evidence that she'd been bound after the fire, Rich had explained, sounding like a carpenter imparting a construction tip to a homeowner.

It had all been planned for months; her ex-husband was smugly pleased to tell her. As soon as he'd learned that Susan's father had died, he started making plans to get even with her – for her "disobedience" when they were married and then for divorcing him. So he'd hired Rich Musgrave to work his way into her life and wait for an opportunity to kill her.

Rich had picked her up at a shopping mall a few weeks ago and they'd hit it off at once. They'd had a lot in common, it seemed – though Susan realized now that he'd merely been fed information about her from Anthony to make it seem like they were soul mates. Planning the killing itself was tough; Susan led a very busy life and she was rarely alone. But Rich learned that she was taking today off. He suggested they meet in Jersey and go to the malls. Then he'd suggest driving to an inn for lunch. But they'd never make it that far. He'd kill her and dump her body in the flats.

But she'd called Rich this morning, asking him if he'd drive; she'd fallen and hurt her knee. He'd be happy to. . . . Then he'd called Anthony and they'd decided that they could still go ahead with the plan. This worked out even better, in fact, because it turned out that Susan had left the note and shopping list for her daughter on the entryway table after all. When he picked her up that morning he'd pocketed the note and list and slipped them into her purse – to be buried with her – so there'd be no trace of him. Rich had also made sure her cell phone was off so she couldn't call for help if she saw what he was up to.

Then they'd run a few errands and headed toward Jersey.

But it hadn't worked out as planned. Carly had gone to the police and, to Anthony's shock; they'd tracked down Rich's car. Her ex had called Rich from Lincoln Rhyme's apartment, pretending to be talking to a business associate about missing an office party; in fact, he was alerting Rich that the police were after him. Susan remembered him taking a call in the car and seeming uneasy with whatever news he was receiving. "What? You're sh—ing me!" (Rough edges, yep, she'd thought at the time.) Ten minutes later that red-haired cop, Amelia, and the state trooper had pulled them over.

After that incident Rich had been reluctant to proceed with the murder. But Anthony had coldly insisted they go ahead. Rich finally agreed when Anthony said they'd make the death look like an accident – and when he promised that after Susan died and Carly'd inherited a couple of million dollars, Anthony would make certain Rich got some of that.

"You son of a b—! You leave her alone!" Anthony ignored his ex-wife. He was amused. "So she just called you now?"

"Yeah," Rich said. "Hit redial, I guess. Pretty f— smart."

"Damn," Anthony said, shaking his head.

"Good thing I was the last person she called. Not Pizza Hut."

Anthony said to Susan, "Nice thought. But Rich was coming back anyway. He was parked up the street, waiting for Carly to leave."

"Please . . . don't do this."

Anthony poured the kerosene on the couch.

"No, no, no . . ."

He stood back and watched her, enjoying her terror.

But through her tears of panic Susan saw that Rich Musgrave was frowning. He shook his head. "Can't do it, man," he said to Anthony as he stared at Susan's tearful face.

Anthony looked up, frowning. Was his friend having pangs of guilt?

Help me please, she begged Rich silently.

"Whatta you mean?" Anthony asked.

"You can't burn somebody to death. That's way harsh. . . . We have to kill her first."

Susan gasped.

"But the police'll know it's not an accident."

"No, no, I'll just—" He held his hand to his own throat. "You know. After the fire they won't have a clue she was strangled."

Anthony shrugged. "Okay." He nodded to Rich, who stepped up behind her, as Anthony poured the rest of the liquid around Susan.

"Oh, no, Anthony, don't! Please . . . God, no . . ."

Her words were choked off as she felt Rich's huge hands close around her neck, felt them tightening.

As she began to die, a roaring filled her ears, then blackness. Finally huge bursts of light speckled her vision. Brighter and brighter.

What were the flashes? she wondered, growing calm as the air was cut off from her lungs.

Were they from her dying brain cells?

Were they the flames from the kerosene?

Or was this, she thought maniacally, the brilliance of heaven? She'd never really believed in it before. Maybe . . .

But then the lights faded. The roaring too. And suddenly she was breathing again, the air flowing into her lungs. She felt a huge weight on her shoulders and neck. Something dug into her face, stinging.

Gasping, she squinted as her vision returned. A dozen police officers, men and women, in those black outfits you saw on TV shows, gripping heavy guns, were filling the room. The guns had flashlights on them; their beams had been the bright lights she'd seen. They'd kicked the door in and grabbed Rich Musgrave. He'd fallen, trying to escape; it had been his belt buckle that'd cut her cheek. They cuffed him roughly and dragged him out the door.

One of the officers in black and that woman detective, Amelia Sachs, wearing a bulletproof vest, pointed their guns towards Anthony Dalton. "On the floor, now, face down!" she growled.

The shock of the ex-husband's face gave way to righteous indignation. Then the madman gave a faint smile. "Put your guns down." He held out the cigarette lighter near the fuel-soaked couch, a few feet away from Susan. One flick and the couch would burst into a sea of fire.

One officer started for her.

"No!" Dalton raged. "Leave her." He moved the lighter closer to the liquid, put his thumb on the tab.

The cop froze.

"You're going to back out of here. I want everybody out of this room, except . . . you," he said to Sachs. "You're going to give me your gun and we're walking out of here together. Or I'll burn us all to death. I'll do it. I goddamn will do it!"

The redhead ignored his words. "I want that lighter on the ground now. And you face down right after it. Now! I *will* fire."

"No, you won't. The flash from your gun'll set off the fumes. This whole place'll go up."

The policewoman lowered her black gun, frowning as she considered his words. She looked at the cop beside her and nodded. "He's right."

She glanced around her, picked up a pillow from an old rocking chair and held it over the muzzle of her gun.

Dalton frowned and dropped to the couch, started to click the lighter. But the policewoman's idea was a good one. There was no flash at all when she fired through the pillow, three times, sending Susan's ex-husband sprawling back against the fireplace.

The Rollx van was parked at the curb. The Storm Arrow wheel chair, which was devoid of ribbons and spruce, was on the van's elevator platform, lowered to the ground, resting on the snow. Lincoln Rhyme was in the thick parka that Thom had insisted he wear, despite the criminalist's protests that it wasn't necessary since he was going to remain in the van.

But, when they'd arrived at Susan Thompson's house, Thom had thought it would be good for Rhyme to have a little fresh air.

He grumbled at first but then acquiesced to being lowered to the ground outside. He rarely got out in cold weather – even places that were disabled-accessible were often hard to negotiate on snow and ice – and he was never one for the out-of-doors anyway, even before the accident. But he was now surprised to find how much he enjoyed feeling the crisp chill on his face, watching the ghost of his breath roll from his mouth and vanish in the crystalline air, smelling the smoke from fireplaces.

The incident was mostly concluded. Richard Musgrave was in a holding cell in Garden City. Firemen had rendered the den in Susan's house safe, removing the sofa and cleaning up or neutralizing the kerosene Dalton had tried to kill her with, and she'd been given an okay from the medics. Nassau County had run the crime scene, and Sachs was now huddled with two county detectives. There was no question she'd acted properly in shooting Anthony Dalton but there'd still be a formal shooting-incident inquiry. The officers finished their interview, wished her a merry Christmas and crunched through the snow to the van, where they spent a few minutes speaking to Rhyme with a sliver of awe in their voices; they knew the criminalist's reputation and could hardly believe that he was here in their own backyard.

After the detectives left, Susan Thompson and her daughter walked down to the van, the woman moving stiffly, wincing occasionally.

"You're Mr Rhyme."

"Lincoln, please."

Susan introduced herself and thanked him effusively. Then she asked, "How on earth did you know what Anthony was going to do?"

"He told me himself." A glance at the walkway to the house.

"The path?" she asked.

"I could have figured it out from the evidence," Rhyme muttered, "if we'd had all our resources available. It would have been more *efficient*." A scientist, Rhyme was fundamentally suspicious of words and witnesses. He nodded to Sachs, who tempered Rhyme's deification of physical evidence with what he called "people cop" skills, and she explained, "Lincoln remembered that you'd moved into the house last summer. Carly mentioned it this morning."

The girl nodded.

"And when your ex was at the town house this afternoon he said that he hadn't seen you since last Christmas."

Susan frowned and said, "That's right. He told me last year that he was going away on business for six months so he brought two checks for Carly's tuition to my office. I haven't seen him since. Well, until tonight."

"But he also said that the path from this house to the street was steep."

Rhyme took up the narrative. "He said it was like a ski slope. Which meant he had been here, and since he described the walk that way, it was probably recently, sometime after the first snow. Maybe the discrepancy was nothing – he might've just dropped something off or picked up Carly when you weren't here. But there was also a chance he'd lied and had been stalking you."

"No, he never came here that I knew about. He must have been watching me."

Rhyme said, "I thought it was worth looking into. I checked him out and found out about his times in the mental hospitals, the jail sentences, assaults on two recent girlfriends."

"Hospital?" Carly gasped. "Assaults?"

The girl knew nothing about this? Rhyme lifted an eyebrow at Sachs, who shrugged. The criminalist continued. "And last

Christmas, when he told you he was going away on business? Well, that 'business' was a six-month sentence in a Jersey prison for road rage and assault. He nearly killed another man over a fender bender."

Susan frowned. "I didn't know about that one. Or that he'd hurt anybody else."

"So we kept speculating, Sachs and Lon and I. We got a down-and-dirty warrant to check his phone calls and it turned out he'd called Musgrave a dozen times in the last couple of weeks. Lon checked on him and the word on the street is that he's for hire muscle. I figured that Dalton met somebody in jail who hooked him up with Musgrave."

"He wouldn't do anything to me while my father was alive," Susan said and explained how it had been her dad who'd gotten the abusive man away from her.

The woman's words were spoken to all of them, clustered in the snow around the van, but it was Carly's eyes she gazed at. This was, in effect, a stark confession that her mother had been lying to her about her father for years and years.

"When the plan with Musgrave didn't work out this afternoon, Dalton figured he'd do it himself."

"But . . . no, no, no, not Dad!" Carly whispered. She stepped away from her mother, shivering, tears running down her red cheeks. "He . . . It can't be true! He was so nice! He . . ."

Susan shook her head. "Honey, I'm sorry, but your father was a very sick man. He knew how to put on a perfect facade, he was a real charmer – until he decided he didn't trust you or you did something he didn't like." She put her arm around her daughter. "Those trips he took to Asia? No, those were the times in the hospitals and jails. Remember I always said I was banging into things?"

"You were a klutz," the girl said in a small voice. "You don't mean—"

Susan nodded. "It was your father. He'd knock me down the stairs, he'd hit me with a rolling pin, extension cords, tennis rackets."

Carly turned away and stared at the house. "You kept saying what a good man he was. And all I could think of was, well, if he was so damn good, why didn't you want to get back together?"

"I wanted to protect you from the truth. I wanted you to have a loving father. But I couldn't give you one – he hated me so much."

But the girl was unmoved. Years of lies, even those offered for the best of motives, would take a long time to digest, let alone forgive.

If they could ever be forgiven.

There were voices from the doorway. The Nassau County coroner's men were wheeling Anthony Dalton's body out of the house.

"Honey," Susan began. "I'm sorry. I—"

But the girl held up a hand to silence her mother. They watched as the body was loaded into the coroner's van.

Susan wiped the tears from her face. She said, "Honey, I know this is too much for you ... I know you're mad. I don't have any right to ask, but can you just do one thing to help me? I have to tell everybody coming to the party tomorrow that we're canceling. It'll get too late if I have to call them all myself."

The girl stared as the van disappeared down the snowy street.

"Carly," her mother whispered.

"No," she answered her mother.

Her face flooding with resignation and pain, Susan nodded knowingly. "Sure, sweetheart, I understand. I'm sorry. I shouldn't've asked. You go see Jake. You don't have to—"

"That's not what I mean," the girl said bluntly. "I mean, we're not canceling the party."

"We can't, not after—"

"Why not?" the girl asked. There was flint in her voice.

"But—"

"We're going to have our party," Carly said firmly. "We'll find a room in a restaurant or hotel somewhere. It's late but let's start making some calls."

"You think we could?" Susan asked.

"Yes," the girl said, "we can."

Susan too invited the three of them to the party.

"I may have other commitments," Rhyme said quickly. "I'll have to check my schedule."

"We'll see," Sachs told her coyly.

Eyes wet with tears, mouth unsmiling, Carly thanked Rhyme, Sachs and Thom.

The two women returned to the house, daughter helping mother up the steep path. They moved in silence. The girl was angry, Rhyme could see. And numb. But she hadn't walked away from her mother. A lot of people would have.

The door to the house closed with a loud snap, carried through the compact, cold air.

"Hey, anybody want to drive around and look at the decorations on the houses?" Thom asked.

Sachs and Rhyme looked at each other. The criminalist said, "I think we'll pass. How 'bout we get back to the city? Look at the hour. It's late. Forty-five minutes till Christmas. Doesn't the time fly when you're doing good deeds?"

Thom repeated, "Humbug." But he said it cheerfully.

Sachs kissed Rhyme. "I'll see you back home," she said and walked towards the Camaro as Thom swung the door of the van shut. In tandem, the two vehicles started down the snowy street.

Scars

Daniel Walther

Professor K owned the most beautiful collection of scalpels and surgical instruments in Western Europe. It also included surgical saws and tenaculums. One of the instruments had apparently belonged to Jack the Ripper. Inspector Abberline in person had picked it up from the scene of one of England's notorious killer's crimes, which appeared to lend credence to the theory that the Ripper had been a member of the medical establishment.

Some of the instruments were used during the course of operations, and scalpels for dissections, but the average person was confused about the specific use of the implements. K was dismissive of the common man and, often, when he had someone under the knife, he had been sorely tempted to just cut through the thread of life. Atropos was male, a master of destiny. Forensic medicine specialists were not subject to that sort of temptation, but K knew a certain Doctor Malbertus who had been known to enjoy caressing, and even penetrating, the bodies of some of his female patients, something medical morals strongly disapproved of.

The oldest piece in the professor's collection was a blade dating back to the eighteenth century, allegedly once owned by the personal physician to King Louis the Beloved, whom K, deeply republican and a confirmed atheist, referred to as the Royal Pox.

Today was a momentous one: President Hernieux's hip. He loathed President Hernieux and would have gladly disposed of him but that would also mean the end of his career, let alone his life.

To kill the President of the Unilateral (the Unilateral International Bank, UIB) even on an operating table could prove a messy affair. He would have gladly been willing to operate on Hernieux with the brass chisel once used by Hammourabi, perforating his sphincter in one swift movement, bursting his innards. But unfortunately the President of the UIB was not suffering from his prostrate.

K's murderous resentment of Louis-Philippe Hernieux was totally illogical and went back to the times when one of France and Belgium's most admired surgeons had dreamed of a political career. Hernieux had blocked his path – he headed a super-powerful politico-financial mafia – all the while lying through his teeth and pretending he was totally supportive of him. K had been turned down and Hernieux had triumphed. But would a good doctor have made a good politician? Some even affirm that medicine is as different from politics as heaven is to hell.

The President's rotting hip (the cartilage was as worn out as an old sock) was a divine act, K considered, not that he believed in any deity, just himself. Medicine was not always a precise science, far from it, and surgery even more so . . .

He closed his eyes and visualized the President's corroded hip. He dreamed he was going further, sawing through the thoracic cage and plunging his latex-covered hand into the patient's open chest, to pull out the corpus politicum, the very essence of Hernieux's soul. Like an Aztec sacrificial killer from Mexico's glory days before Cortez. *Sic transit gloria mundi*. A shudder coursed through him as he held up Jack's blade and it shone in the sun's light.

He felt like Macbeth the regicide and his vision of a phantom dagger, as the tragedy moved irreparably on. But he also knew that he would save the presidential hip and there would be no fatal forest moving towards the felon's castle, just a lot of speeches and the flow of expensive champagne. Presidential bones are worth a lot of money.

After the necessary repairs, the President would have to undergo lengthy rehabilitation and give up on certain terrestrial pleasures. That's how life went. If the surgery worked, the President would still retain his favourite drug: power. Did the exercise of power actually give you a hard-on? K asked himself and cut into his thumb with Jack's blade. Lightly.

He put the blade back into its box and walked over to his Mercedes and drove off to the clinic. HIS clinic. A jewel of modernity designed exclusively for the rich and the very rich.

Occasionally, to demonstrate he sometimes still had something of a soul, Professor K agreed to treat some poor people. Not quite for free, though. Which gave him a reputation as a) a greedy bastard, b) a ruthless operator, c) a philanthropist, d) the best surgeon, cutter and filer in the country.

By the way: few people know the fact but a lancet, also known as a bistoury comes from the words bistorit, bistorie, which means a dagger. In the past, there had been lancet monsters, doctors in the death camps but also killers who did not wear yellow or green frocks. Wolves whose teeth happened to be surgical instruments.

Truly, as Jules Romains had once pointed out, life was such a bizarre assembly of events, and it was difficult to face it in cold blood. Or something approaching it. His memory was somewhat faulty when it came to literature or philosophy. He enjoyed Jules Romains, a now much out of fashion author who had written interesting things about illness and the healthy.

During the course of the journey between his house and his clinic, he wondered what his driver, monsieur Maxence (as the Spanish maid called him) thought of him. Then he concentrated his mind yet again on how he could dispose of President Hernieux. Without being caught. Of course. Which would mean the operation both succeeding and failing. A post-operation form of trauma could not be blamed on the surgeon.

In an ideal world, the President would be rid of his painful limp and later succumb to a welcome cardiac arrest, a perfect outcome. However, these days, forensic investigations were difficult to foil. There was no way he could find some exotic poison with delayed effect; only in bad mystery books. It would only lead to a humiliating court appearance which would end up with a maximum sentence, however much he might pay a whole retinue of venal lawyers. And you couldn't expect any form of clemency from a jury of everymen pretending to worship men in white when in reality they actually were madly jealous of them.

At the clinic, he was greeted by his whole team of zealots, all welcoming him effusively like a poor man's Greek choir. Anna M, the anaesthetist, a sturdy woman in her forties, was often a pleasant distraction. She would enter his well-lit office, wearing only thin lingerie under her tightly buttoned blouse. He would impatiently peel her knickers off and mount her there and then over the desk's darkly polished wood.

On other occasions, she would kneel in front of him and take him whole in her mouth. She would swallow everything, licking her lips as if it had been the finest caviar. He loved it, even though Anna was nothing more than a sex slave.

He didn't know why a mature professional like her agreed to be his plaything, just like any old whore; maybe she was just a masochist who enjoyed being humiliated by men, even more so when they were powerful and often held power over life and death.

K, naturally, also had a wife. Which had helped both increase his wealth and spread his genetic capital with a son and daughter. The boy was a fool but the girl had her father's intelligence and her mother's beauty. Damn families! Wives no longer cared much in bed and children were so ungrateful. The bucking and blow-jobs by Anna were as a result all the more welcome.

At 7.30, he walked into the operating room.

Everything was set.

Including President Hernieux.

Totally helpless. "You old bastard," K muttered under his breath. "Not in charge any more, hey?"

Had he known what was on the professor's mind, he would no doubt have been scared shitless, not that the operation could in any way be described as life-threatening.

Dr Anna M expedited the President into a dream land where pain no longer existed and the ballet began.

An operation like the one they were about to perform was by necessity bloody and somewhat spectacular from a spectator's point of view, but for K it was all a matter of routine. The bones were sawn with haute couture precision, and as the minutes clocked by, the President slowly regained some of his youth. Surgeons like K were past masters at reviving the inside of bodies. With folk now so reluctant to die at a normal age, the amount of operations on used joints was on a constant growth arc, involving knees, hips, shoulders, etc . . .

It took quite a few extra blood bags to keep the damn bastard's useless life stream on course. Oh, how Hernieux was going to be made to pay for it! But what were a few thousand euros for the President of the Unilateral? For him, a university professor's monthly earnings were just pocket money. Not that he wouldn't notice their expenditure, as in addition to the darkness of his soul, he was also damn mean.

How nice it would be to saw him in half from top to bottom . . .

K was becoming delirious; the hate grew inside him like a rising soufflé; he was daydreaming of the perfect crime; a medically perfect crime.

He took hold of the artificial joint.

Put it in place.

When he was operating on a patient, the subject was always guaranteed the most modern, unbreakable, infusible materials, ceramics or plastics that performed impeccably. No way would they break like the archaic prostheses of our grandparents, causing untenable suffering to the patients, should they not strictly follow the right medical advice. K remembered a patient who had once, shortly after surgery on his hips, wanted to try out some complicated yoga position under the impression it could only have a beneficial effect. The result had been edifying!

It was finished.

Well done, as ever. Although there had been a serious cardiac scare during the surgery.

But the President was alive.

Much to K's regret. And relief, as the bastard had bled like a pig. But now, the artificial hip (guaranteed for life) was in place.

He returned to his study where a pile of mail awaited him, already sorted by his faithful secretary Miss T, an efficient woman, much too ugly to be fucked between surgeries, but totally devoted to him.

Among the letters was one made up of letters cut out of a local newspaper:

You Should Butcher That Fucker Hernieux

He silently agreed with the anonymous writer. Probably some poor bugger who'd been robbed by UIB, that nest of financial terrorists whose minions had done more harm than Al-Quaeda and the Chechen rebels together.

Professor K could now dream freely of the perfect crime, albeit within the frame of the rehabilitation process. There was a knock on the door: his secretary opened it and allowed Dr Anna M to walk into the office.

"A welcome diversion," K thought. "Maybe a bit of fun will provide me with ideas . . ."

"Hello David," Anna said as she moved towards the glass, metal and polished wood bulk of the Professor's desk.

"Lock the door," he said, "I'm sure that old bitch likes to listen behind it."

"What would you do if you were in her place?"

"I wouldn't even guess," he grinned.

She was unbuttoning her dress. On this occasion, she didn't even wear a g-string. Just a pair of dark stockings highlighting her milky skin.

"It always affects me when I see you at work."

To confirm this, she slipped her middle finger deep inside her vulva and then placed it beneath her lover's nose. Was she truly his mistress? At any rate, they had never slept together, nor spent dirty weekends together. Between quickies and blow-jobs theirs was a relationship with neither future nor responsibilities. He didn't even know whether she actually took pleasure from their activities or enjoyed the spectacle of her own degradation.

She leaned over the desk, rump extended to him and he roughly entered her from behind, digging deep into her insides, having briefly greased his cock with spit. He grasped her breasts and savagely kneaded them. K had no subtlety. He fucked like he ate. With greed and speed.

"What did you think of the President?" he asked distractedly shortly after he'd ejaculated.

"Boring," answered Anna. "Truly . . . Can you pass the tissues over, darling, you've spread it all over me."

"Did you enjoy it?"

She sneered:

"I'm unsure whether I do this for you or for me."

"You like it when I fuck you in the arse, Anna?"

"I enjoy being humiliated. I'm a bit of a whore and a masochist."

"My poor darling. I grant you it's uncommon: a doctor being fucked like a dog by a professor . . ."

"I don't think so. It's all in the mind."

All the while she was thinking to herself "and if your cock was longer and thicker I'd be even more a whore and a masochist . . ."

"I was daydreaming I was sawing the bastard in half."

"All part of the job."

"I HATE HERNIEUX."

"And you fantasize about killing him . . ."

"I know I should never be mentioning this to anyone, not even you."

In the meantime, she had cleaned the Professor's penis with a tissue and slipped it between her lips. Anna's mouth secreted an infinite softness and her tongue wrapped itself around his semi-hard member like a soft flannel.

"Oh, oh, oh," said the Professor.

Anna kept on sucking him. The Professor soon was in a good mood again.

K's loins were on fire. Inside his head raced a storm of images and thoughts, but none somehow coalesced. He couldn't quite order them into place, too distracted as he was by what Anna was doing with his cock.

Anna sucked and nibbled.

K came. Moaning.

"So, if you want it so much, why don't you kill him. KILL HIM."

(Like Lady Macbeth encouraging her still hesitant husband.)

"It's not that I don't want to take revenge on that fool, but I am worried about the cops, the judges, and a jail full of hardened criminals."

"My little wolf," Anna said, with a lupine smile, "you're just too faint-hearted. We can deal with the President when he's at the bone rehabilitation centre. I can do it for you. But there would be certain conditions attached, naturally."

(The bitch is going to ask me to divorce and marry her . . .)

"Of course, my dear, of course. Everything has to be paid for . . ."

"Nothing reciprocal, dear friend, just a few things to be agreed with me, your kind Anna."

"Anything you want." And he mumbled "Except divorce, my darling, except divorce."

"I won't ask you to divorce your wife. I have no need of it. All I'd require is a larger participation in the clinic's profits. That is, I'd want to replace W on the board."

(Ah, the bitch! But she was right: she was worth W a hundred times over and, at least, she knew how to make him come hard . . .)

"I'm good," Anna said. "And not only when it comes to matters carnal."

"I know, I know. You're a trooper. A trooper and a whore. I do like you a lot."

His wife's features crossed his mind, and it was with disgust he recalled through the eyes of memory her sad, tired flesh. Sad and tired for him, but maybe not for others. Maybe she spent interesting afternoons in the arms of younger gigolos. She certainly had enough spare cash to procure them.

"I'm exhausted," he said.

"And so am I," she quickly responded.

The rest and rehabilitation centre owned by Dr S was the best and most expensive in the region. S and K were old friends, but did not see each other very often. Which is why S was somewhat surprised to see the internationally-renowned "bone cutter" appear in his office.

"I've come to find out how President Hernieux's health is."

"There are phones . . ."

"Of course, but it happens that I have a favour to ask of you. For a change. I have a friend who's a therapist and needs a job. Can you help?"

"We're full, but if you insist."

"She's a first-class hydrotherapy expert and I hear she sucks cock like a vacuum cleaner."

"OK. We'll see. Send her over."

Hernieux was floating in the water like a lead fish. The staff swore there was nothing better than a good hydrotherapy session. And that some repeated movements underwater would, in due course, cause miracles to happen.

He had heard over the last few days there was a new "girl", a Miss Anyaluisa. She apparently had a hell of an arse and magnificent tits. Not that he should get excited about it, Hernieux reckoned, best concentrate on the repair of his damn hip and wait for everything to strengthen around the prosthesis. K might well be a maniac and bitterly envied for his power but in his own field he was the tops. A scalpel, saw and bone champion extraordinaire. Expensive of course, what with all those exceptional extras he added on, but damn money when you've reached the stage when you can barely walk without your joints screaming like hell.

This was anything but fun and he had to force himself to follow the nurses' instructions. He had never obeyed anyone before, apart from his own father, a domestic tyrant of the worst kind. Who'd ended up in jail when his daughter had gone running to the police to complain that he'd begun touching her up day and night after he had become a widower.

The world was a sack of shit and only the rich and the strong could survive. The men with power.

He had often suspected his sister of having invented his father's attentions in order to take revenge on his fierce severity, but the court had imposed a long sentence, with little chance of parole. Once she had rid herself of her father, Elisa became both hooked on drugs and the most feared lesbian in the city.

Those were his thoughts as his eyes lingered over the beautiful Anyaluisa.

She wore a tight, short uniform.

She was pacing around the swimming pool. He floundered a bit in the water in an attempt to catch her attention, but the pain that raced through him was like a dagger to the heart.

Nonetheless, she noticed him.

"Mister President, I do think you need attention."

And winked at him.

For the past few days, Hernieux had been experiencing some pain on the left side of his chest. but had not mentioned it to the medics. The problem with his hip was trouble enough and, anyway, he'd never had heart scares.

Anyaluisa slipped out of her uniform. Under which she wore a severe black one piece swim suit. She dropped into the pool and approached him.

"Are you in much pain, sir?"

"Yes, rather."

He was not lying. He had been warned. Physical rehabilitation was no bed of roses.

The President had never been a patient man.

Unless it involved orchestrating some fiendish take-over bid.

"You must think of something else," the young woman said. "Try and forget the pain; be stoic, like the Greeks . . ."

An amateur philosopher, just what he needed.

But when she slid her hand under the band of his swimming trunks, he quickly forgot his pain. Anyaluisa's agile fingers were soon tightening around his old shrivelled penis, manipulating it gently, as it slowly but surely reacquired some of its vitality. She quickened her movement and whispered:

"Does that feel better, mister President?"

"OOOH, YES!"

The fires of youth were surging back into his loins. Finally, repressing a scream, he let himself go, right into Anyaluisa's hand.

The pain in his hip had faded, although the one in his chest was still present.

"My heart . . . it hurts . . . in my left arm . . ."

"It'll pass," she said. (No pain can resist me)

But the President's pain persisted.

She helped him move around in the water slightly, as if to justify her actual presence beside him, and said:

"You really are making progress, monsieur Hernieux."

But he was still suffering from the acute pain in his chest.

"Miss Anyaluisa T, our new hydrotherapist," was how she had been introduced to him by the head nurse, himself the very image of a provincial army officer with an overt military stance.

"The woman's methods are unconventional, to be sure, but maybe it's all part of some new foreign form of therapy," he reflected.

Or maybe she had done it all just to present him some form of bill later. All large-arsed and big-titted women were venal bitches. Honest women had small breasts and narrow bums. Of course.

He was impatient to see what might happen tomorrow.

But Anyaluisa was nowhere to be seen. He learned she would not be coming today. And was not given a reason. The pain in his chest returned. It was a dreadful day and an exhausting evening. Full of disgusting dreams, in which ugly, hairy women kept on dragging him towards the fires of hell.

He was awakened by a presence in his room. He was lying on his back, like an insect with too heavy a carapace.

Then, in the dim light of the bedside lamp he caught beautiful Anyaluisa's silhouette. She shed her uniform and appeared fully naked, shining as if she had dipped her whole body in precious oils, like some Egyptian courtesan or historical Olympic performer.

Although, in a rare moment of lucidity, she also reminded him of a mythological figure of vengeance.

The light caught the sharp tips of her nipples and her thick pubic bush.

His heart was beating the light fantastic, but his flesh was still.

She pulled the bed-cover away; undid the cord of his silk pyjamas.

In spite of the powerful erotic impact of her appearance, the President was still not reacting physically. The pain was rising inside him, like a vice constricting his chest.

She climbed onto the bed and squatted across him, rubbing her open sex against his, although careful not to drop her full weight onto his still fragile body.

Sensing that her efforts were in vain, Anyaluisa whispered words of encouragement in his ear. All she got back in response were strangled, grotesque sounds. She changed her position and placed her stomach right across Hernieux's mouth, her lips against his cock.

Slowly, panting like a dog, the President felt his penis disappear inside Anyaluisa's mouth, as venomous fragrances filtered through his nostrils.

"One more effort," the goddess of death said.

And then, theatrically:

"JUST SPIT YOUR DAMN LIFE OUT."

He tried to dig his tongue deeper into the young woman's vulva, but he was out of breath and his throat rattled.

Anyaluisa was busy with her lips, tongue and teeth, until the job was complete.

"*Sic transit fortuna mundi . . .*" she said to herself as she picked up her uniform and slipped out of room number three.

She floated like a shadow down the corridor.

Back in her room, she threw herself onto the bed, still excited by what she had accomplished.

Her first dominant act.

The very first time she had naturally been in charge, instead of all those occasions she had stooped (to conquer, as the Sheridan play would have put it).

She made herself come three times before she fell asleep.

For the record, she remained a few days more at Dr S's rehabilitation centre before resigning her post and returning to the city. No one had actually noticed her absence at Professor K's clinic, as she had officially taken a two-week vacation.

K greeted her effusively in his study, but did not touch her.

He wanted to hear all the details about the execution of the President.

Which she was all too glad to provide.

She even admitted to him that the murder had excited her so much that she had masturbated in her room following the nocturnal expedition.

"Vengeance should not have bothered you so much, my darling, it was my vengeance, not yours."

This disturbed the equanimity in Anna's mind.

She looked at her lover and asked:

"Are you sure?"

"Absolutely certain."

She sniggered and blasphemed:

"Vengeance is mine, said the Lord."

"At any rate, such vengeance is highly enjoyable."

She gulped and felt her heart shiver. Something inside her had just broken.

Anna exited the Professor's office without offering herself over the wood, glass and metal desk.

She felt calm.

Different.

A woman determined to win at all cost.

"What can I expect from K? To get myself repeatedly sodomised like a sow? Down on my knees at his feet, my mouth buried inside his trousers?"

She was gazing at K's collection of surgical implements. This was the first time she had set foot in the Professor's expensive villa. And she was admiring his special gallery.

"And this one, they say, might actually have belonged to Jack the Ripper, the London East End disemboweller in the year of our Lord 1888."

Translation by Maxim Jakubowski

Staring at the Sun

Leonardo Padura

It's been two hours I've been staring at the sun. I like to look at the sun. I can look at the sun for an hour straight, without blinking, without tears.

I'm still staring at the sun, leaning against the wall at the corner, listening to the old women as they come out of the bakery, complaining about how shitty the bread is but eating it anyway cuz they're dying of hunger. On this corner, you can smell the smoke from the buses as they pass by on the avenue, the stink from the many dogs who think they've found something in that awful piece of bread, the bitter stench of desperation, like in that shitty song my mother likes. It's a disgusting corner and I think I like it even more for that very reason; I spend huge chunks of time here, waiting for something to come along, just staring at the sun. I'm singing a little bit of that song and don't notice when Alexis comes up.

"Hey, man, what's going on?" he asks.

"Nothing. You?"

"Hanging."

"Cool," I say, looking at Alexis. I suppose Alexis is my best friend. We've known each other from before we even went to school, from when his father and mine worked together at the Ministry. Later, they fucked over Alexis's dad, but not too much, cuz he had good friends. They didn't even take his car, although they did relieve him of his gun. That, yeah.

"Let's go get a liter," he says.

"Who's got some?"

"Richard El Cao."

"C'mon," I say, and I forget about the sun and the bitter vapors . . . Fuck, it's actually the bitter taste of desperation. Same shit.

El Cao always has liquor. Sometimes it's good. Sometimes he also has pills. He gets them easily: He steals a script from his mother, who works as an administrator at a hospital, and he signs her name, and then they give him the best pills at the pharmacy. Easy, right? But there are no pills today. We took the last ones yesterday, with four liters of liquor. Yesterday was fucked up.

Now we're drinking, not talking. It's always like this: At first, you hardly talk. It's as if your brain goes dead for a while. Later, we talk a bit, especially if we pop some pills. Alexis and El Cao talk the most.

After we've been drinking awhile, Alexis says, "There's a fight today."

"At El Hueco?" El Cao asks.

Alexis nods.

"I don't have any money," El Cao says.

"Me neither," I say.

"I do," Alexis says, and since he's been drinking, he tells the whole story of how he got the cash: There were about twenty liters of oil, the good cooking kind, in the trunk of his father's car, and he stole three. He sold them, so he has money. Three hundred pesos.

"Let's go," says El Cao.

"Let me finish," says Alexis.

We drink a little more. This liquor's pretty good. When we finish drinking, that's when we leave.

When we arrive, the fight hasn't started yet. We're told today it's Yoyo's stanford against Carlitín's boxer. I like the stanford. His name is Verdugo and he's won like twenty fights. He almost always kills the other dog. The boxer is also somewhat famous: His name is Sombra and they say once he clamps down, he doesn't let go. There are already twelve people here, waiting. There are two black guys, with their gold teeth and Santería necklaces around their necks. They must be Carlitín's friends. He's always hanging out with black guys like that. He has business dealings with them, and sometimes he pulls jobs with them too.

The betting begins. Alexis puts his three hundred pesos on Verdugo. I tell him to set aside fifty, for another liter in case he loses. But he says no, that there's still plenty of cooking oil in his father's car and Verdugo's gonna win.

They set the dogs. And everybody's screaming. Myself included. They let them loose. Verdugo sinks his teeth into Sombra's shoulder, drawing blood on the very first bite. It's practically black, this blood. Drops of this practically black blood swirl around Verdugo's mouth and drop on the ground. Then the screaming intensifies. Sombra starts to turn and gets ahold of Verdugo's paw. He's gonna tear it off. Verdugo's gonna leap right over him and Sombra's unaware. Then Verdugo hits his neck. Carlitín and Yoyo jump in to separate them but Verdugo won't let go, and neither will Sombra. They jam sticks in their mouths to control them. Sombra lets go first but comes around the side; Verdugo still won't let go. Yoyo finally pries his mouth open and Sombra drops: Two streams of blood pour from his neck, even blacker and thicker. The boxer's dead. Everybody's still shouting and the losers start to pay up. Carlitín kicks his dead dog. Alexis gets his winnings, two hundred pesos, and tells one of the black guys to pay the hundred they bet. The black guy says the fight was bullshit. Alexis says he doesn't give a shit about that, what matters is his hundred. The black guy says he's not paying shit. Alexis says he can stick it up his ass. The black guy pulls a piece and sticks it in Alexis's face.

"What you say, you little white shit?" the black guy asks, then hits his jaw with the gun's butt.

Alexis doesn't say anything. The other black guy has a knife in his hands and is looking around at everybody else. The two black guys laugh. Nobody moves. Should I do something, given that Alexis is my friend? I make my move.

"Let it be, bro," I yell at the black guy. "Alexis, forget the cash."

"Fine, big guy, you win," Alexis says, and the black guy pushes him and laughs. The other black guy joins him. They leave without turning their backs. I like black guys less and less all the time. I swear to God that's true.

Alexis talks even less than usual. And he drinks more. Between him, me, El Cao, and Yovanoti – that's what we call Ihosvani now – we've downed two liters and a third's almost gone. There's one more. Here, on El Cao's roof, there's no fear: We're encircled by a peerless fence and, even if we get drunk, no one can fall off. Then somebody calls El Cao from the street corner.

"Richard, Richard!" a woman shouts. Or two women.

It's two: Niurka and Betty. El Cao tells them to come up. They come up. They already know the black guys hit Alexis, cuz the whole neighborhood knows. They're thirsty so we start the fourth liter.

"Either of you got anything?" I ask, but they play dumb. These two love to play dumb. "Don't play dumb," I tell them.

"I've got two parkisonil left," Betty says, so I ask her for them. They're two little white pills. I think I wanna have one. But I give them to Alexis, who swallows them with a gulp of liquor.

"Stop thinking about those black guys," I say.

"I'm gonna get them back," Alexis says, then lays down on the ground, closes his eyes, shakes a little, and starts to fly. That little parkisonil is a rocket when it's fueled by liquor.

It's nighttime and, since there's no sun, I stare at the moon. I don't like it as much, but it's better than nothing. Betty is still sucking me off, and though I'm hard and the head is red hot, I don't feel like coming. Sometimes it's like that: It just feels swollen. Alexis is still sleeping on the floor while El Cao is sticking it up Niurka's ass and Yovanoti rests. I think he's singing, softly. I have the seventh bottle from our ordeal in my hand and I take another swallow. Suddenly, I don't wanna be sucked off and I take it out of Betty's mouth.

"Get on all fours," I say, and I start to fuck her up the ass, and I think about movies in which men are sticking it up the ass of some woman. But nothing happens anyway; I'm not gonna come tonight.

"Here, my man," I say to Yovanoti, and he comes over and Betty sucks him.

I start to look at the moon again, take another swallow, and fall asleep.

When I open my eyes, I see the sun. I'm alone on the roof.

I don't know why there are days I like to come to church. Not to pray or to think about God, cuz I never learned to pray and I was spared the whole speech about God and the saints and the angels. I just like to come. My parents don't care anymore if I come, cuz it's not seen as a bad thing anymore. A few years ago it was really bad, and they didn't like it when I came here. You don't believe in squat, they said to me. Don't you know that could get us in trouble? What the hell do you think you'll find in church anyway? they asked. I just shrugged: I didn't know then and I don't know now. Well, I do know one thing: I like it cuz I feel calm. But I don't pray or think about God. I just look at him, nailed up there.

This car runs really well. El Kakín spends the whole day cleaning it, tuning it up, putting little things on it. Whenever El Kakín's father's abroad, he gets the car all day. Sometimes he lets us know. *Everybody, go to the beach*, and then we all go to the beach. Like today. Alexis is still pissed off about what happened with the black guys. He doesn't even wanna get in the water. He just drinks rum and every now and then mutters, Fuck those black guys. Me, El Kakín, Yovanoti, and El Cao all get in the water. The water's wonderful today. We get out and drink a little rum, and then I go back in the water and shit and the turd follows me around. But we go back in. Then we go back out, drink more rum, and Vivi and Annia show up. Since we've been drinking so much, we talk for a while. Annia says she's leaving for La Yuma [the US], her and her entire family. Some people from a church – Jehovah's Witnesses – got them the visas. They go to that church once a week. They sing, they pray a lot, and everybody thinks they really believe in all that, now that they don't smoke, or drink, or curse, or harbor ill will in their hearts, as Annia says. But my brother's always losing his temper, she says later. Well, it doesn't really matter that they don't believe in Jehovah, since what they want is to get to La Yuma, just like a bunch of other people I know. Not me, though. They say there's everything over there, but you have to work like a dog. El Cao says he doesn't wanna go either; he does fine with moonshine and pills no matter where he's at. El Kakín wants to go: He wants his own car, with five-speed transmission, four-wheel drive, eight cylinders, diesel motor, hydraulic suspension, cruise control. He knows that car like he already owns it. Alexis says he wants to go too: He says you kill a black guy over there and they give you a thousand dollars. He's obsessed with black guys.

But the one who likes La Yuma most is Yovanoti. He's always talking about it, about how well everybody lives over there, about his brother who owns the racing track in Miami, and that other cousin who, just two months after arriving, was already sending his mother a hundred dollars a month, and about his ex-brother-in-law who has a restaurant, I think, in New Jersey. He says if he ever gets there, he'll give up alcohol and pills and marijuana, even cigarettes, so he can earn a lot of money. Then he takes another chug of rum. And he talks some more.

Since I haven't taken any pills in two days, I'm gonna have fun now. Vivi has a very narrow little ass. At first, you don't think you can get it in, but she opens up good, tickles herself with her finger, and then takes a deep breath and says, "Put it in me." And then you just push a little and it goes in all the way. The downside is that I wanna go a little longer before coming but I come really fast, and then I can't get it back up. El Cao always gets it up: He's come twice in Vivi and once in Annia. I don't know how El Cao can come so much. He hardly ever eats. Alexis didn't wanna do anything. He wants a pill. It looks like he jerked off and drank some rum so he wouldn't get bored.

"Look," Alexis says, and he shows me a strip of pills.

"Where'd you get that, man?" El Cao asks, dazed.

"I stole them from my grandmother."

El Cao cracks up. "Man, what if something happens to the old lady?"

"She can die, for all I care," Alexis says, and he takes two with a chug of liquor.

He gives me two and hands two over to Richard El Cao and two for Yovanoti and he keeps two more for himself.

The good thing about pills is that you really don't have to keep drinking. They multiply what you already have in your belly, I think, by, like, ten. They're also good cuz if you're not drunk, then you wanna talk, fuck, listen to music. Well, for a while at least. Alexis starts talking.

"I need you to lend me your old man's piece," he says to me.

El Cao cracks up again. "You're gonna kill those black guys over one hundred shitty pesos?"

"Yeah, one hundred shitty pesos and cuz they're mothafuckas, those shit fuckin' black faggots. I need the gun," he says.

"You're crazy, Alexis," I say.

"Fuck crazy. You gonna lend it to me or not?"

"Trouble, man."

"No trouble. Bring it tonight and in three hours I'll have it back to him."

"You don't even know where those black guys live."

"I'll find out – where they live, where they drink their beer, where they bet on cockfights, where they play the lottery, where they smoke pot, where they steal hens. They're two dead black guys. Just lend me the fucking gun. Look," he says, and he sticks his hand in his pocket and pulls out six bullets. He takes another chug of the rum with the last two pills.

"You're crazy, Alexis," I say, but I don't think he hears me.

Yovanoti got a movie and we're gonna watch it in his room on the VCR. First, there are two blondes. It looks like they just got home from work, cuz they're carrying purses and that sort of thing. But they start undressing each other right away and they get a really good lezzie thing going. Just when they're getting hot, a mulatta comes in, pushes them apart, and joins them. The mulatta has a red pussy which is practically hairless and must weigh about ten pounds. The two blondes lick the mulatta all over, until one of them pulls out a dildo and straps it on. She sticks it in the mulatta until she comes. While all that's going on, El Cao is the first to take out his dick and start jerking off. Then me. Then Alexis. Then Yovanoti. Then the other blonde in the movie, so she's not left with nothing to do, starts jerking off too. The worst part of all this is how it smells like jism in the bedroom now. I keep thinking about the mulatta's pussy. Just for a while. Cuz now another movie has started and El Cao has brought out a bottle of liquor.

I wake up during the night. I think I'm still in Yovanoti's room. Alexis is still sleeping, on the bed now. Vanessa is naked and sleeping too. El Cao and Yovanoti are gone. Vanessa, the blonde, is between Alexis and me. That seems odd cuz Vanessa never fucks us, much less without protection. She says we're savages, that we're all gonna die from AIDS and that we leave bruises and what she wants is a Yuma to give her dollars and let her live in Paris. I don't know what her deal is with Paris. But that's Vanessa, and the truth is she's hot. She's got a little lock of blond hair on her fat pussy and two tits that are even hotter. All of a sudden, I get a hard-on. I touch Vanessa but she doesn't even flinch. I stick a finger inside her and realize her crack is all slippery. It seems to be jism. I rub my finger on my dick, to get it wet. Then I shove it in her. She remains the same. How'd she get like this? I keep on fucking her until I get bored and then I pull out. I suck her tits for a while. She laughs, asleep, and I stick it back in her and this time I come. But not much.

I look out the window and see that it's raining. I hadn't noticed. I don't know what time it is. It must be very late cuz there's no one on the corner and I'm a little hungry. There are some burned papers on the floor. Of course, we must have smoked some pot. But I don't remember. There's a liter bottle with three fingers of rum left. I drink it to calm my hunger then lay back down. But beforehand, I suck Vanessa's tits again for a little while, thinking the whole time about the mulatta's pussy.

Since El Kakín hasn't shown up, we take off for the coast, where the water's just fine. The drag here are the rocks on the bottom. One time, I almost cracked my head open. Of course, I dove in drunk. You can still see the scar: They gave me sixteen stitches, and since I was so drunk, the anesthesia didn't take. Better to forget about all that. I drink some more rum and listen to El Cao, who just yaks on like a fucking parrot.

"So I go up to the Yuma and say, *Míster, guat yu guan? Girls, rum, tobacco, marijuana?* And the guy's a little scared. Since he was blond and pink, he got red. *Nosing, nosing,* he tells me, and I say, *No problem, míster, yo tengo lo que yu guan.* And the guy, *Nosing, nosing,* but by then Yovanoti was right behind him and I just landed one, and Yova got one in behind his ear, and I grabbed his backpack and kicked him in the balls so hard, I think one came out his ear . . . I swear! So we took off and when I turned around about a block later, there's the guy still shaking on the ground, so we slowed down a little. We went through the backpack and trashed all the crap, until we found his wallet and realized the sucker was German. And you know how much money he had? Ten miserable dollars. Yovanoti had to hold me back, cuz I just wanted to go back and give him two more kicks. What the fuck is that, all the way from Germany with only ten dollars on him? That's what we used to buy these liters . . ."

We laugh, a lot. And we drink more rum.

Then Yovanoti says, "Let us drink to the solidarity between the German and Cuban peoples!" And we drink some more.

Alexis doesn't drink this time. He says, "So you gonna get me your father's piece?"

"You're still tripping on that?"

"Are you gonna get it for me or not?"

"Fuck, Alexis, you know he doesn't let it out of his sight, not even when he's taking a crap."

"He sleeps with it?"

"Of course not."

"Then . . ."

Alexis laughs when he sees the gun. It's a Makarov and it's so clean, it looks new. I hand it to him and he just stares at it. He really does like pieces like that. Not me.

El Cao and Yovanoti also look it over. "That's a nice one," they say.

Alexis takes out the clip and empties it. He puts in his own bullets, one by one.

"Tomorrow, the whole world should pay me tribute," he says. "There are gonna be two fewer black guys. Let's go," he says, and we leave.

But first we take a couple swallows of rum. Or three.

"I'm sure they're there," Alexis says, and he shows us the house. "That's where they go to drink beer."

And so we wait at the corner. No one speaks. While we wait, I look at the moon. Tonight, it's round and very bright. This corner's shitty, I like mine better. It smells of piss here. Yovanoti is smoking cigarette after cigarette. Richard El Cao is sitting on the ground; he's singing, softly. Alexis just stares at the house.

"That's where those mothafuckas are," he finally says.

The two black guys come out and head for the other corner. We go after them, unhurried. We turn the corner and see them make like they're looking into this one house. They're probably gonna pull something there. All black guys are the same. Well, almost all. My father says not all black guys are thieves but that all thieves are black. And he says black people have five senses, just like whites. Except that they have two for music and three for stealing. He should know, since he's a cop. That's why he laughs so hard when he tells these jokes and when he talks about the black guys they've arrested. When they're in jail, he says, those black guys aren't so tough.

We continue along the sidewalk and when we get near the black guys, they feign indifference and light cigarettes. Even though there's so much moonlight, they don't seem to recognize us. As soon as we're in front of them, we jump them and Alexis shows the piece. The black guy who held the knife sees it first. What a black rat he is. He takes off and that costs him his life: Alexis lets fly some lead and the guy falls to the ground. He starts thrashing, like a rabid dog, and Yovanoti and I kick him and yell at him, Black faggot, you got scared, huh, you black faggot. We do that until he shivers really weird and gets stiff, with his tongue hanging out. The other black guy's just standing there, frozen, seeing how his buddy's dead as a doornail. Alexis stands in front of him.

"Now you're gonna pay me my hundred pesos, aren't you?" he says, and hits him on the nose with the piece.

"Fuck, white boy, no need to be this way," the guy says, and shoves his hand in his pocket.

"Careful!" screams El Cao, and Alexis doesn't think: He shoots him right in the head. The black guy's head explodes and rolls back. Even I get splattered with his blood. It's practically black, like the dog's, although it's got little white dots. Then the black guy falls and Alexis leans down to talk to him, though I don't think the guy can hear him anymore.

"See what happens to tough little black guys like you and your buddy?" He takes the guy's hand out of his pocket. The black guy doesn't have a gun today, just a roll of bills: more than five hundred.

Since everybody on the block's already looking and screaming, we start running. That's when everything gets fucked up: Two cops appear on the corner and Alexis doesn't even give it a thought. He never gives anything a thought. And with the aim he's got. He shoots and downs one, and the other one flees. We run off and no one else comes after us.

*   *   *

If you kill two black delinquents, you get in trouble. But if you kill a cop, then things go from bad to the very worst. We know this, which is why we all agree when El Cao speaks up.

"Let's steal a boat from the river and head for La Yuma, cuz this is really bad now; this is what happens when you hang out with punks like this," he says, taking the gun from Alexis. When Alexis starts to say something, El Cao interrupts him: "Shut up or I'll shut you up."

It's been two hours now I've been staring at the sun. I like looking at the sun. I can look at the sun without dropping my lids, with my pupils intact, and without tears. It's been two hours since the boat ran out of fuel and more than four that we've been without water. It's been at least an hour since Alexis slipped off the side, when he went to drink some sea water and never came back. Yovanoti says a shark probably got him. Then he starts to cry and babble, "I'm glad, I'm glad," and to spit in the water. I don't like that. I think Alexis was my best friend.

I've never worried so much about time passing. Richard El Cao says it'll be dark in two hours, and that this is good. I don't know if it's so good. The best thing would be to be on the corner, listening to the bitching of the old women, singing a little, and staring at the sun. Without water, without food, without rum in the middle of the ocean, yeah, there's nothing better . . . It stinks of vomit and shit. If an American coast guard doesn't show up, we're fucked. And if one does show up, we're even more fucked. I ask myself, What the fuck am I doing on this boat? I wanna throw myself in the water like Alexis, but I control myself.

It's night-time and I fall asleep.

The sun's fucked up, intense. My head hurts a little. I'm really sleepy. It's been awhile since Yovanoti has said anything about what he's gonna do when he gets to La Yuma. He's thrown up so much he doesn't have anything left to throw up. He's just oozing green spit. El Cao says we should think about good things, we shouldn't think about how thirsty we are. That's hard to do. I think about sucking Vanessa the blonde's tits and then I think about being in church and then about the corner. Later, still, I think about the mulatta's pussy, the one from the movie. And, to be honest, I do feel better, I even get a hard-on.

When El Cao speaks up again, he says, "Now it's night-time again."

Yovanoti starts to cry and El Cao slaps him twice. So that he'll calm down. Then Yovanoti throws up a little more. There's not much moon tonight and I can't see anything; I don't stare at anything either.

When I wake up, I see the sun and I see the helicopter. It doesn't look like the Cuban police. From way up there, with a bullhorn, they shout down something in English. When I look around the boat, I see only El Cao, just lying there, fainted, I think. Yovanoti is nowhere to be seen. To think he was the one who most wanted to go live in Miami. Tough luck. I really need a chug of rum right about now. I splash some water in El Cao's face and he wakes up, but he stays down.

"We're saved," I tell him, but I'm very sleepy again. I open my eyes real wide and look up at the sun, just as if I were back on my corner, and I sing a little of that song about the bitter smell of desperation.

Translation by Achy Obejas

The Sword of God

Josh Pachter

In the neighborhood where Mahboob Chaudri grew to manhood, where his beloved wife and children still lived, in the Defense Housing Society a safe distance to the southeast of the incessant clamor of central Karachi, Westerners were an infrequent sight. Oh, dearie me, yes, occasional tourists passed through on their way to the Tuba Mosque, in horsedrawn Victorias hired for a hundred rupees a day with driver, but otherwise the pale-skinned foreigners were scarce.

Here in Bahrain, though, Chaudri had lived among them for six years, and he had developed an amused tolerance of their curious ways. From time to time, of course, they still were able to surprise him. Take this remarkable game of theirs, this – this *golf*, they called it.

There stood Senator William Adam Harding, an eminent statesman, tall and athletic and attractively graying, one of the highest-ranking members of the American government ever to visit the emirate. Chaudri could not recall which of the forty or fifty states the Senator represented, but it was one of the larger ones, that much he knew, one of the more powerful ones, one of the ones with oil and cowboys.

It was oil that had brought the Senator to Bahrain, where he had spent most of the last three days touring the Sitrah refinery and meeting with executives of BAPCO, the Bahrain Petroleum Company.

Yet there he stood, that distinguished gentleman, hunched over a pockmarked orange ball on a square of artificial grass in the middle of the fiery desert, waggling a long metal stick foolishly in his thick hands and fully intending to smite the little ball with the stick, to smash it away into the distance, only in order to trudge after it and place his bit of plastic sward beneath it and hit it away from him once more, again and again until at last he succeeded in tapping it into a metal cup with a flag on a pole sticking out of it, the flag now barely visible through the shimmer of heat which rose from the desert surface several hundred yards away.

This was obviously not recreation for the body, Chaudri mused, as beads of itchy sweat trickled within the blouse of his olive-green uniform. Nor, in its pointlessness, could he conceive of it as recreation for anything but the most limited of minds.

Why, then, did they bother with it, the Senator and his deferential young aide and the two exuberant BAPCO executives? Why were they still hard at it after well over an hour, with the thermometer reading in three figures and the merciless sun overhead and their idiotic balls already tapped into a dozen or more of their idiotic cups?

And how much longer would they go on before returning to the bliss of an enclosed and air-conditioned space?

And why, Chaudri marveled, why in the name of the Prophet must they attire themselves in those outrageous costumes? The Senator, whom he had previously only seen in sedate charcoal-gray suits and rich silk ties, now wore a pair of lime-green trousers, an open-necked canary-yellow shirt with a crocodile at the breast, a peaked mechanic's cap and white shoes with leather tassels flapping at every step and – incredibly – *nails* extending downward from their soles!

Chaudri shook his head sadly. He would never really understand these foreigners, never. They lived in another world; their values were hoplessly other than his own.

Which of them was right? The thought disturbed him. In his heart, he knew that neither culture was right, neither wrong. Each was what it was, neither more nor less, and perhaps this *golf* seemed as normal to the Senator as it seemed normal to Mahboob Chaudri that he should live and work and be lonely in Bahrain while his dearest ones stayed behind in Pakistan and lived in vastly greater comfort off the money he was able to send them from his monthly pay packet than they could possibly have enjoyed had he chosen to remain with them and earn perhaps a tenth as much at home.

Though these thoughts occupied his mind, Chaudri was still the first of them to notice the swirl of sand and the faint rumble of an engine in the distance.

It was a dusty Land Rover with four-wheel drive, and as it approached them the Pakistani recognized its driver as a minor functionary at the American embassy, where he had accompanied the Senator to a brief and apparently purely ceremonial meeting with the ambassador two days earlier. Ostensibly, Chaudri had been assigned to provide the Senator with personal security for the length of his stay, but – given the general peacefulness of the emirate since Saddam Hussein's forces had been pushed back out of Kuwait at the beginning of the 1990s – he considered himself more of a uniformed guide than a bodyguard.

The Land Rover's rear tires swung wildly and threw up a curtain of sand as the vehicle slewed to a stop. The gentlemen from BAPCO seemed scandalized by the interruption, the Senator's aide continued to look as if he were waiting to be switched on, the Senator himself wore suit-and-tie solemnity over his ridiculous golfing garb.

"Sorry, sir," the boy from the embassy blurted, jumping from the hot Land Rover to fumble in his pockets before them. "The ambassador thought you'd want to know. The Suq-al-Khamis Mosque, sir, and four Americans. They're going crazy back there!"

The Senator stepped forward and put out a soothing hand. "Slow down, there, son," he said, his deep voice a velvet command. "What's this about four Americans?"

"Hostages!" the young man gasped. "Some group of terrorists has moved into the Suq-al-Khamis Mosque, and they're holding four Americans hostage, a doctor and three nurses from the American Mission Hospital." He pulled at last a sheet of yellow flimsy from a pocket and unfolded it triumphantly. "They sent this message to Radio Bahrain and both of the national newspapers."

The Land Rover's engine ticked its disapproval and settled into silence. For a long moment, the only sound was the whisper of the heat. Then Senator Harding snatched the slip of paper and his aide handed him a pair of wire-rimmed spectacles. He hooked them over his ears and read the note aloud in the stillness of the desert afternoon.

"The decadent era of Western dominance is at an end," it said. "The Great Satan will be driven far beyond Bahrain's borders.

We will re-establish a true Islamic society and return the land to its former glory as the fourteenth province of Iran. It is written in the Book of Books: "As for the unbelievers, their works are as a mirage in a spacious plain which the man athirst supposes to be water, till, when he comes to it, he finds it is nothing; there indeed he finds God, and He pays him his account in full; and God is swift at the reckoning. *Saifoullah*."

The Senator looked up. "The Great Satan," he scowled. "That's supposed to mean the US of A, I reckon. But who the hell's this *Saifoullah* character? One of them damn ayatullahs, is that the idea?"

"*Saifoullah* is a what, sir," said Mahboob Chaudri, "not a who. I have heard of them before. They have been writing inflammatory letters to the Arabic media, but this is to my knowledge the first time they have been committing an act of political aggression. We are knowing very little about them, but from their demands it would seem that they are Iranians, or at least that they are sponsored by Tehran. Bahrain, you see, was a part of the Persian Empire for almost two centuries previous to 1782, when the first of the al-Khalifas was driving the invaders back to Persia. Whatever else they may be, *Saifoullah* are Shi'ite fundamentalists, and if they—"

"Whatever the hell else they may be," the Senator snarled, "*Saifoullah* are a pack of kidnappin' terrorist dogs, and if they think they can get away with holdin' four Americans hostage they damn well better think again."

"*Saifoullah*." The younger of the gentlemen from BAPCO said the word slowly, tasting it. "You know what it means, officer? I've only been here four months; my Arabic doesn't go much beyond please and thank you."

Mahboob Chaudri nodded. His nut-brown face was drawn with lines of concern. "*Saifoullah* is meaning 'the Sword of God,' " he said.

The American Embassy in Manama was not sequestered behind concrete bunkers and grim Marines – not yet – but the windowless walls of Ambassador Paul Northfield's private office were three feet thick and made of steel; his door was as strong as that of any bank vault and opened only to those few high-ranking members of his staff who were privileged to know the combination to its sophisticated electronic locking mechanism.

Behind the state-of-the-art security, the office itself had been decorated to reflect the informal nature of its occupant. A massive mahogany desk and plush swivel chair dominated the room, two sofas at right angles around a low brass filigreed coffee table formed a pleasant conversation nook in one corner and a well-stocked wet bar stood invitingly in another, there was soft brown carpeting underfoot and an attractive arrangement of paintings on the walls. Mahboob Chaudri sipped gratefully at the cold club soda he had been offered and studied the paintings with feigned interest. Most of them were oils by the emirate's own Abdullah al-Muharraqi, scenes of Arab life in warm reds and oranges, old men hunkered down in the *suq* with their worry beads, fishermen mending their nets by the sea, women in black *abbas* heating up their tambourines before a wedding performance. Under other circumstances, Chaudri's interest would have been genuine. But today he was far too busy eavesdropping on the argument from which he had turned his back in deferential politeness to concentrate on the primitive beauty of the artwork.

"Dammit, Mr Ambassador," Senator Harding was saying, "I take your point, sir – but there's no way in hell you're gonna be able to hush this thing up. The local media already know exackly what's goin' on, and – what with Saddam still makin' noise up there in Eye-Rack – you got your wire-service reporters based right here in Bahrain, you got your *Time* and *Newsweek* boys roamin' around lookin' for stories to file, you got—"

"I know all that, Bill." Like his office, Ambassador Northfield seemed relaxed and comfortable in the midst of chaos. He was a tall bear of a man, with steel-gray hair and a full salt-and-pepper beard and a strong handshake – but he was a tame bear, a teddy bear, not a grizzly. "All I'm saying is I think we need to stay in the background on this thing until we—"

"In the background," the Senator exploded. "But that's just exackly my point, Ambassador! Those damn journalists are on the scene, they're a fact of *life*, and before one hell of a lot more time elapses you're gonna have them bangin' on your door here yellin' for answers. And you and I, sir, are gonna wind up representin' the United States of America in a major media event before a global audience, so I say we damn well better have some answers, and we better have 'em right damn quick!"

Chaudri wondered if it had been with the idea of representing his country in mind that the Senator had insisted on a brief stop at the BAPCO compound in Awali before proceeding to the embassy. He had been gone for less than five minutes, but when he'd returned to the government limousine his gaudy golfing costume had vanished, replaced by the impeccable attire of the statesman.

The ambassador smiled tightly. "A major media event, Bill? A global audience? I see what you're driving at, but I can't help thinking you're exaggerating the importance of what's going on here. I mean, it's only been a—"

"—couple of hours," the Senator finished the bear's sentence in exasperation. "And after all, Bill, we don't even know who these people *are*, just yet." He tossed down the rest of his scotch and water and marched to the bar to fix himself a refill. "Now, you lookie here, Ambassador, I *know* all that. And I know that, with the good Lord's blessin', we may well get our folks out of there before anybody winds up gettin' hurt. And I know I may be just a ignorant ol' country boy and talkin' out of turn, but I'd like to remind you of a couple of things here, Ambassador. I'd like to remind you of that little incident back in Tehran in 1979, for instance. You may remember it, because it lasted 444 days and got a lot of attention on the news. I'd also like to remind you of TWA Flight 847 over there in Beirut a couple years later; that one only lasted seventeen days, but it got a fair piece of play in the media, too. Now, while you and I sit here havin' this cozy discussion over drinks, we got—"

"While you and I are having this discussion, Bill," the Ambassador said firmly, "we have four American citizens held hostage about a mile from this spot, and we're not doing a single thing to help them in their time of need."

He leaned forward and pressed a button on his intercom, and a woman's voice immediately said, "Yes, sir?"

"Carol," Ambassador Northfield instructed, "get me the State Department, would you, please? Priority One."

Senator Harding turned to his waiting aide. "Jerry," he said angrily. It was the first time Mahboob Chaudri had heard the young man's name. "Jerry, you go find yourself a secure phone and get me the White House. Mack, if you can get him; otherwise, I'll settle for the Veep. You know who I *really* want to talk to, but I reckon he's out joggin' or eatin' a Big Mac or some damn thing."

From their vantage point atop the four-story apartment building a quarter of a mile to the south, Mahboob Chaudri and Senator Harding had an unobstructed view of the Suq-al-Khamis Mosque. Its twin minarets gleamed in the twilight, though a closer inspection would have revealed that the towers had been patchily whitewashed and the wooden balconies three-quarters of the way up the height of each spire were in poor repair.

Behind the concrete wall which ringed the compound, the mosque itself was a barren ruin – roofless, floorless, without walls. Of the once-proud temple erected almost thirteen centuries in the past by the Umayyad Caliph Umar bin Abdul Aziz, nothing remained but a scattering of stone columns and crumbling archways, baked by the harsh Middle Eastern sun and scoured colorless by a thousand thousand sandstorms.

"AK-47 assault rifles," Chaudri frowned, passing his binoculars to the Senator. "Kalashnikovs, Russian-made."

An armed guard stood on each of the weathered balconies, framed by the narrow arches leading to the interior of the minarets. Both men wore long white *thobes*, their heads covered with the traditional *ghutra* and thin black *agal*. It was impossible to be sure of their nationalities, but from their set expressions and their weapons Chaudri was convinced they were Iranians.

"Mean-lookin' sons a bitches," the Senator snapped, handing the field glasses on to his aide. "Them *and* their guns. Where you reckon they're holdin' the hostages, officer?"

Chaudri considered the question. "Inside the minarets," he said at last. "It is the only possibility. They are being held on the stone steps within the minarets, trapped between the pair of guards we can see on the balconies above and another pair at the base of the towers, hidden from us behind the wall."

Chaudri accepted the return of the binoculars and raised them again to his eyes. A dozen official vehicles were stationed at twenty-yard intervals around the compound; a hundred officers in the olive-green of the Public Security Force were in position behind the buses and sedans and Land Rovers, some unarmed, others with their useless weapons held loosely, waiting.

And, as the Senator had predicted, a score of reporters milled about with their notepads and their tape recorders and their cameras. They, too, were waiting, waiting for something to happen, for tragedy or resolution, for any scrap of news or human interest with which to still the constant hunger of their editors and readers and viewers, their audience.

Among the assembled policemen, there were sharpshooters present who could easily take out the Arabs on the balconies of the Suq-al-Khamis Mosque's twin spires. Even from this distance, Chaudri could read the frustration on their faces. For, if the guards above were wounded or killed, then their brothers below would surely retaliate – and it was the four American hostages who would suffer.

No, the Public Security marksmen must wait impatiently for the situation to develop, and Mahboob Chaudri knew and shared their emotion. He, too, had used a telephone at the American embassy, not an hour before. He had phoned the Police Fort at al-Qalah and practically begged for reassignment to the team now surrounding the mosque. But his superiors had ordered him to remain with Senator Harding, and the Senator's own superiors in Washington had ordered *him* to stay clear of the scene, to leave any negotiations with the Sword of God to the Bahrainis and any contact with the press to Ambassador Northfield.

"Why the hell don't your people get in there and *do* somethin'?" the Senator demanded. "You just sit around and wait for somethin' to happen – well, by God, when somethin' *does* happen, you may just find out it ain't the somethin' you was hopin' for!"

"And what would you suggest we should be doing, sir?" the Pakistani asked quietly.

Senator Harding glared at him. "Don't you patronize me, son. And, hell, *I* don't know what to do. That's why my damn gummint's got me benched here on the sidelines. Ain't you got somebody you can send in there to make nice with 'em, like Jesse Jackson sweet-talked them grunts out of Kosovo last year? Or, if this bunch's too far gone to cut a deal with, you just send your local SWAT team in and pull a Rambo – that's what I'd do if I's in charge. I'll tell you this much for free: you better do *somethin'*, 'fore them bastards in the white nighties decide to commence usin' them peashooters they're totin'."

Mahboob Chaudri understood very little of the Senator's English. He understood the feelings which boiled beneath the words, though. He understood that Senator Harding, too, was frustrated by his inability to bring a stop to this terrorist madness, to find a way to resheathe the Sword of God before innocent blood was spilled.

Chaudri understood and shared the American's sense of impotence – and wondered if the angry words were only words, or if a man of true courage stood behind them.

As the police and press stood around and did nothing, he made up his mind to find out.

"Senator, sir," he said softly, "I am thinking that perhaps it is time for you and I to talk."

The heavy iron gates had been barred and chained by the terrorists. It was well after sunset, and the moon hung obscured behind heavy clouds – but Public Security floodlights bathed the gateway and the twin minarets towering above it in a harsh illumination which gave the mosque the artificial appearance of a disused film set.

The two armed guards stood motionless on their perches, as they had stood for hours. *Saifoullah* had issued no further demands, had not even asked for food or water to be delivered for themselves or their hostages. It was as if the scene was frozen not only in the glare of the spotlights but in time as well, as if the Sword of God awaited some word from absent leaders – some ineffable sign from its vengeful deity – before proceeding with the next step of its plan.

Behind the compound, all was dark. Mahboob Chaudri and the Senator slipped soundlessly between two government vehicles parked far enough apart to allow them to make their way to the wall surrounding the Suq-al-Khamis Mosque unobserved. They crouched there for a moment to catch their breath, backs pressed against the rapidly cooling roughness of the concrete, hearts pounding with the rush of adrenaline, listening intently to the viscous silence which enveloped them. Far away, a nightbird laughed raucously at the folly of their mission.

"You know what happens if we screw this up, don't you?" the Senator whispered fiercely.

Chaudri's nod went unnoticed in the blackness. "Indeed I do," he answered, his voice barely audible. "You and I are probably being injured, sir, quite possibly being dead – and most certainly being unemployed and disgraced. And the hostages? Our actions may be serving to further endanger their safety, rather than restoring it. Shall we be giving up and going back now, Senator?"

Harding tasted his lower lip. "Hell, no," he decided. "Not if you really think there's a chance we can keep this mess from turnin' into tie-a-yellow-ribbon-'round-the-old-oak-tree."

"I *do* think so, Senator. It is a dim chance, at best, but it is better to act and pray for success, I am thinking, than to do nothing and wait helplessly for failure."

"Them's my sentiments exackly, son. Lead on."

The two dark figures straightened and began to work their way westward in single file, the Pakistani in the lead, each of them tracing the course of their progress along the wall with the tips of his fingers. It was difficult to walk quietly on the loose pebbles which rolled beneath their feet; they took slow and cautious steps to compensate, pausing often to listen for movement around them. When the moon peeked out briefly from behind its blanket of clouds, they stopped completely, and waited without speaking until it once more hid its face from sight.

At last Mahboob Chaudri dropped back a step and put his lips close to the Senator's ear. "We are nearing the opening in the wall," he breathed.

And, at that moment, a shape appeared from the shadows before them, and the clouds parted as if on cue to let the moon show them a long white *thobe* and a pair of burning black eyes and a Kalashnikov assault rifle held at the ready.

"You have reached the opening in the wall," the Arab said coldly, in English, "and you are prisoners of the Sword of God."

O pehan yeh geya, thought Mahboob Chaudri bitterly.

"Holy Kee-rist," the Senator sighed.

They raised their hands above their heads.

The terrorist turned away from him, the back of his *thobe* shimmering like the eyes of a cat in the night. His hands gripped the barrel of the AK-47 tightly, and he swung the rifle high over his shoulder and smashed the butt end down at the head of the figure who lay in the sand at his feet. He battered his unconscious victim again and again, and with every slashing stroke of the rifle butt he screamed, "*Saifoullah! Saifoullah! Saifoullah!*" When he stopped at last, the dead man's head was small and round and drenched with orange blood, its features shattered beyond recognition. The Arab looked around, and the face framed by his checkered *ghutra* and black *agal* was the face of Senator William Harding.

Mahboob Chaudri shuddered at the bloodlust in the Senator's eyes and awakened. It was morning, and somewhere a lone rooster was celebrating the dawn.

Chaudri squirmed around on the stone step where he had slept, trying not to disturb Dr Apostolou two steps above him or Nurse Hewitt two steps below, but it was impossible for him to find a comfortable position. His muscles were cramped and sore from the long hours of sitting, his bottom was numb from the chill of the stone, his throat was cottony with thirst, his stomach rumbled.

"*Merea rabba*," he muttered, then cursed himself for speaking aloud when the young nurse stirred restlessly and a pained whimper escaped her. He held his breath and kept still, and was gratified to see her settle back into an uneasy slumber.

Allah let them sleep, he prayed. Every moment they were sleeping was one less moment they would have to deal with the horror of their situation – unless, of course, they went on dealing with it, as he had, in their dreams.

Had the Arabs who were guarding the minarets been able to sleep? Had they taken turns standing watch, or had they forced themselves to remain alert throughout the night? Chaudri did not know. There was much, he found, that he did not know. What was happening in the other spire, where the other pair of terrorists was holding Senator Harding and Nurses Graham and Gaylor? What was going on outside the compound? Were negotiations to effect their release underway? Were demands being made, being met or rejected? Were his comrades on the Public Security Force aware that there were now *six* hostages within the wall surrounding the Suq-al-Khamis Mosque? And, with the Senator a captive, would the Americans finally involve themselves, or would they continue to leave the situation in the hands of the Bahrainis?

Chaudri did not know the answers to any of these questions, and it was the not-knowing which worried him more than anything else.

When he looked up from his thoughts, the doctor was awake. He was a large-boned man with the look of a boxer gone to seed, his forehead receding into what had once been a full head of thick brown hair. He regarded Chaudri through narrowed eyes, his thin lips pressed together tightly.

"What do we do now, *mahsool*?" he said. His voice was hoarse from disuse. They had spoken together the night before, when Chaudri was first brought into the minaret, and the American's story had been quickly told.

Dr Apostolou had suggested an after-work expedition to the Suq-al-Khamis ruins to his colleagues at the Mission Hospital. Three of the nurses on his shift had agreed to accompany him. The foursome had explored the compound for perhaps half an hour, but the day was hot and there was little to see, and they were on their way back to the doctor's car when the four *Saifoullah* Arabs had burst through the iron gates. There had been much shouting and waving of weaponry, and eventually he and Nurse Hewitt had been deposited halfway up the minaret steps with guards stationed above and below them. The doctor was not sure what had become of the other two women, but there had been no gunfire, and he hoped they were safe within the second tower. It had all happened around three the previous afternoon; it was now almost seven in the morning, and they had been given neither food nor water in all that time. After the initial encounter, they had seen only one of their captors and him only once, when Chaudri had been brought in to join them.

"What do we do now?" Dr Apostolou asked, and the sound awakened Nurse Hewitt, who stretched luxuriously and opened her eyes and shrank back in on herself as she remembered where she was, and why.

"I do not know," said Chaudri, watching helplessly as the pretty young Western woman's shoulders shook with the effort to hold back tears. She seemed about the same age as Shazia, his own dear wife, and – though her complexion was pale and tinged a delicate pink by the sun, where his wife's was a rich and beautiful brown – she had Shazia's jet-black hair and bottomless wide black eyes. His heart went out to her, and to the doctor, and to the other women he had not yet seen. "We must wait and pray," he said, but the words seemed hollow and empty in the narrow confines of the minaret.

"I'm not frightened," Nurse Hewitt insisted. "If they were going to – to hurt us, they'd have done it by now, wouldn't they?" She folded her thin arms across her chest and hugged herself.

"I just wish they'd settle whatever it is they have to settle and let us out of here. If I don't get a hot shower and a decent meal sometime soon, I'm going to scream."

Dr Apostolou grinned and reached down from his place on the step above her to touch her shoulder reassuringly. "You're a trooper, Kate," he said. "I hope Jessie and Sarah are holding up as well as you are."

She pressed his hand and returned his smile, and Chaudri found himself wondering if their relationship was entirely a professional one.

There was no opportunity for him to pursue the thought. The sound of sandals scuffing on stone reached him from below, and the guard who had captured him and the Senator the night before came into view as he ascended the spiral steps toward them. It was difficult to see the man clearly in the dimness of the tower, but it seemed to Chaudri that his expression was less threatening than it had been. His mouth had slackened, his eyelids drooped, his curly black hair was oily and streaked with dust, the Kalashnikov he held cradled in his arms seemed to have taken on extra weight.

He has not slept, the Pakistani realized, and he filed that knowledge away for possible future use.

"*Mahsool*," the terrorist addressed him in liquid Arabic, "I must speak with you."

Perhaps it was only the strain of the long hours of imprisonment, but Chaudri thought he could read a plea in the Arab's penetrating gaze. A plea for what? It was the Sword of God which had the weapons, the Sword of God which controlled the situation. What could they possibly want from *him*, their captive?

"If you must be speaking, then I must be listening," Chaudri replied.

The Arab glanced briefly at the two Americans. He was really no more than a boy, Chaudri saw, at most nineteen or twenty years of age. But even 80, he was old enough to carry a rifle, old enough to know how to use it. He was old enough for that.

"We must have food and water," the boy announced suddenly, "but your government does not approach us. How are we to communicate with them and let them know our demands?"

"What's he saying?" Nurse Hewitt whispered, and the doctor squeezed her shoulder to quiet her, afraid the guard might harm her for interfering.

But the guard ignored them both, his attention fixed on Mahboob Chaudri.

They have no plan, Chaudri recognized, and the thought astounded him. *In the passion of their religious fervor, they determined to take over the Suq-al-Khamis Mosque, but they did not anticipate having to deal with hostages. Now they are holding the shrine, but they are stuck with us as well. This is the first time the Sword of God is doing anything more than writing angry letters to the press, and they have no idea how to proceed.*

Interesting, he thought, *most highly interesting. Does this often lie beneath the heartless exterior of terrorism – this uncertainty, this confusion, this doubt? Is this the way it was aboard the Achille Lauro, aboard Flight 847, at the American embassy in Tehran? Is it possible that the Shi'ite extremists are being as much the victims of their madness as they are being its agents?*

"You ask me to help you," said Mahboob Chaudri slowly, "but how can I be helping you when you treat me as if I am your enemy? I am not your enemy. I am your brother, and these Americans are your brother and sisters."

"You lie," the boy spat. "America is not my brother. America is the Great Satan, the despoiler of Islam, the—"

"I am not speaking of America. I am speaking of these innocent Americans, who came to Bahrain to heal the sick – not just their own people, but all who are in need of their skills. What have they done to deserve your anger, your threats?"

Nurse Hewitt reached for the doctor's hand and held it tightly. A silence hung heavily in the air.

"This is wartime," the Arab boy said at last. "And, in wartime, the innocent must suffer for the sins of their governments. This country was a model of Islamic purity until—"

Chaudri shook his head. "But this is not the answer. I am a Muslim myself, and I am agreeing with you that there are problems in the world, problems here in the Gulf, in Bahrain, problems which can and must be solved. But this—" he indicated the Kalashnikov with a gesture – "this violence, this terrorism, this fanaticism, this is not the answer. Perhaps we have been done injustice, but is it Allah's will that we should be repaying the injustices of others with injustice of our own?" He sighed deeply. "No, that is not the way. As it is written in the Holy Quran, 'Direct us in the right path, in the path of those to whom Thou hast been gracious; not of those against whom Thou art incensed, nor of those who go astray.' Put down your gun, my friend, put it down. Let us find another path to peace."

Again it was silent, and the absence of sound was a living thing which wrapped itself around them and held them for a timeless interval. The doctor, the nurse, the Pakistani, the Arab – the silence entered into each of them and touched them and told them its secrets.

Mahboob Chaudri listened to the beating of his heart, and with great serenity put out his hands to the terrorist, his brother.

The Arab boy licked dry lips and swallowed his uncertainty. "My name is Hamid," he said.

The sun beat down fiercely from its perch in the ivory sky, sucking rivulets of perspiration from Chaudri's forehead and armpits. The columns and archways of the Suq-al-Khamis Mosque squatted patiently in the heat, the twin minarets pointing impassive fingers at Heaven's vastness.

Chaudri stood alone between the spires, his only companions the sun and stone, the oppressive warmth and choking dust. The wooden balconies above were empty; Yousif Falamarzi was waiting with Hamid Yacoob and the two Americans within the tower that had been Chaudri's prison, and the remaining pair of terrorists was hidden from his view on the far side of the second minaret. His Public Security Force comrades and the Western reporters waited beyond the compound wall; although Chaudri could not see them from where he stood, he knew that they were still out there, that they would remain at their posts until the confrontation with *Saifoullah* wound its way to a conclusion.

The Pakistani moved slowly toward the second minaret, the olive-green material of his uniform chafing his arms and legs with every step. Hamid and Yousif had wanted to accompany him, but he had decided it would be best to go alone. If there was trouble, if there was gunfire, he must face it by himself. Uncomfortable as it might be in the summer heat, Chaudri's uniform gave him that obligation.

The Americans had wanted him to take one of the Kalashnikovs, but again he had demurred. He would go alone, he had told them firmly, and he would go unarmed. They had tried to change his mind, had tried to convince him that he was taking too many risks, but Chaudri had been resolute. Alone, he had repeated, and unarmed. That was the way it must be.

A determined fly buzzed circles around his head as he crept closer to his destination, alighting momentarily on his ears, his nose, his lips, then flitting off to safety as he slapped at it uselessly.

He reached the stone base of the minaret and paused for a moment to listen. The heat and the silence closed in on him and made the drawing of every breath an arduous task. Chaudri was tempted just to stand there, to wait, yet he knew that there was nothing to be gained by waiting. He had waited long enough already.

Courage, Mr Chaudri, he told himself. He raised his hands in the gesture of surrender he had used the night before – and realized with clinical interest that the Arabic word for "surrender" is "Islam".

Islam, the surrender to God's will, the surrender to destiny.

With surrender in his heart, he stepped around the base of the minaret and gasped in sudden fear to find himself staring down the barrel of an AK-47.

An eternity passed before he recognized that the rifle was in the hands of Senator William Adam Harding, and one of the two remaining members of the Sword of God lay motionless in the dust at his feet, his *thobe* and *ghutra* in disarray.

"Well, hot damn," the Senator roared, "it's you!" He flung aside the Kalashnikov and pounded Chaudri gleefully on the back. "I shore am glad to see your ugly mug again, there, son. I's afraid they might've—"

"What—?" Chaudri stammered. "How—? How did you—?"

"Well, hell, son, there was only two of 'em," the Senator beamed. "It's not like they had thesselves a damn army or nothin'. I took out this here downstairs one first, while he's around this side of the tower and out of sight of the rest of 'em, anen I snuck upstairs and whomped the other'n. I's just on my way over to take care of your two when you walked into my gun and like to scare the pants offa me." He looked Chaudri up and down with admiration. "But I guess you handled your boys okay on your own, there, din't you? I thought you was kind of runty for a police officer, if you'll excuse me for sayin' so, but you done good, son. I'm right proud of you."

Chaudri looked down at the body lying crumpled and motionless in the dust. "Is he—?"

"Dead?" The Senator chuckled. "Hell, no, he's just takin' hisself a li'l nap, that's all. I din't hardly hit him hard enough to raise a lump. And don't you fret none about the one upstairs, neither. He'll be back on his feet afore the ladies in there stop bawlin'."

"They are not hurt?"

"Naw, they're fine and dandy, son." He jerked his head toward the entrance. "They're inside there havin' thesselves a good old-fashioned cry, but they ain't been hurt none."

Chaudri put a hand to his heart. They were all alive, then, and it was over.

He shook his head in disbelief. It could so very easily have ended in bloodshed and horror. The Senator's solution had been unbelievably rash, had been taken without sufficient thought, had endangered all their lives.

And yet . . .

And yet the man had succeeded, praise Allah, and no one had been hurt.

They were a strange people, these Westerners, and the Americans were the strangest of them all. As strange, in their own way, as that small minority of Muslims who fervently believed that violence was the behavior God demanded of them.

And yet it seemed clear to Mahboob Chaudri that, in a world rocked with acts of senseless terrorism, it was perhaps possible after all for his culture and the Senator's to work together toward the goal of peace. And, if it was possible to live in harmony with the Westerners, then perhaps it might be possible to live in harmony with the likes of *Saifoullah* as well.

Insh'Allah. If only God was willing.

And that, Chaudri decided, as he found the ring of keys in the pocket of the fallen Arab's *thobe* and moved through brilliant sunshine to the gate in the wall which surrounded the Suq-al-Khamis Mosque, would be a very good thing.

Oh, dearie me, yes, that would be a very good thing indeed.

Now Let's Talk About Laura

Andreu Martin

Down at the entrance I press a buzzer for the third floor to avoid giving Wágner advance warning. A woman with a high-pitched voice answers, and I get her to open by murmuring the first thing that comes to mind, "Mail". I take the lift to the sixth and make for the first door, still with no idea what I'm going to do. I simply know that Wágner's there inside.

I press the doorbell. Footsteps. The jeweller approaches whistling. He opens without any idea, in shirtsleeves, tails hanging out, tie half undone, no shoes, eyebrows raised like someone expecting to hear a great joke. There's not even time for him to be surprised.

I press my hand to his chest and push him in. After retreating two steps, he bangs up against the wall, his face clouded with fear. I close the door. My fist is like a sledgehammer backed by my 120 kilos. The jeweller's head bounces off the jamb, and he swivels to fall face down in the middle of the hall. Giddy with panic, he attempts to rise, turning at the same time, but the toe of my shoe strikes him right in the mouth. He collapses and begins to scramble along the narrow passage leading to the large living room. Struggling desperately to get to his feet and make a dash, he's maybe hoping to somehow reach the phone when I grab him by the shoulders and push him headlong onto the sofa.

Drooling, sobbing, and bleeding, he's lost several teeth, and has no idea what to do, or what's going on.

"Now let's talk about Laura," I yell.

I can't understand either what's got into me. I remember reading somewhere that one of the feelings experienced by disaster victims is an arbitrary rage and resentment against society in general. Many who have suffered from catastrophes or who've lost close family in terrorist attacks say that after fate has dealt them such a heavy blow they feel entitled to do exactly as they please, to be as savage with the world as the world has been with them. So perhaps I was convinced on an unconscious level that a terrible injustice had been perpetrated, that I'd been robbed of the most valuable thing I possessed, and was allowed to erupt in fury, granted permission to enjoy watching Wágner receive the full force of that explosion.

"Now let's talk about Laura."

The first talk I had with Wágner was in his jewellery shop. All smart and elegant, he wrinkled his nose when he first saw me, or perhaps smelt me. His doll-house chairs were too small for my bulk, and he shuddered when I sat down on one, as if it might collapse under my weight.

"I shot in self-defence," he said with a brittle sort of firmness. "They came upon me with guns in the parking lot, and told me to hand over the sample case. Every day I carry jewellery worth twenty-five million pesetas. I've already been mugged three times, hence my application for a permit, why I bought the gun. And you know if I'm carrying it, it's not just for show. I wasn't going to stand there and let them rob me all over again. So I handed over the case, sure enough, what with the barrel tucked under my chin. But as soon as I saw them running off, I pulled the weapon out from its harness and pulled the trigger."

He'd killed one of the armed robbers, a certain Bernardo Parada.

". . . The other stooped down and managed to get away, protected by the cars. To be frank, I was terrified, stunned at having killed a man, as you might imagine. I stood rooted to the spot, unwilling to move an inch, much less chase the guy running off."

". . . And for all the mugshots you were shown, you didn't recognize him in any?" Wágner shook his head – no, I'm afraid not. "Nor in the ID parades afterwards?" No never, he regretted that too, deeply it seemed. "So, you killed a man and then remained on the scene, just hoping the police would turn up."

"Yes, that's correct."

It was the fourth time Wágner had had his case grabbed. It was hardly surprising the insurance company needed to remove all doubts, whatever conclusion the police enquiry might reach and despite the full support of Inspector Germán from Armed Robberies. They'd hired me to liaise with the cops, recover the jewellery and clear up their suspicions.

Germán, an old friend, backed Wágner's version to the hilt.

"Arturo Wágner's completely above board. I've known him for years. He's helped us on more than one occasion, far more. Identifying missing gems, keeping tabs on fences, that sort of thing. He's in an ideal position to receive information on goods we might be interested in, and we use him as candy."

Candy? It had slipped out. He immediately hid behind the brandy-spiked coffee, finished his cup and asked the waiter for another. We were in the bar next to police HQ and they all knew him there.

"Again, thanks."

So that was that. Looking as if nothing had popped out by accident, he was already smiling and asking, "What else would you like to know?" But I wasn't going to let it pass: "Didn't you just say 'candy'? What do you mean?"

I don't like narks, although they're obviously indispensable to police work: without the stool-pigeon's gift for being in the right place at the right time, many cases would remain unsolved. But they also form a bridge between the police and the world of crime, one that's easy to cross in both directions, moreover. The best informers are those who occasionally break the law, establishing underworld credentials and gaining the implicit trust of authentic criminals. But you have to be indulgent with them, as that's what makes them collaborate with law-enforcers: those little foibles may have far-reaching benefits. Still, I don't like them, however necessary their role.

"What do you mean?" I asked. "That he has relations with . . . ?" I meant the underworld, the criminal element, the mob.

"No, not at all!" Germán shot back, as if appalled, shocked even. "Simply that he lends a helping hand now and then, nothing more."

I sighed heavily. They never tell you a thing. They can't, anyway.

"And what can you tell me about the dead man? Bernardo Parada, right? Police record?"

Inspector Germán darted a glance at me. He was blinking like mad.

"No, nothing like that. Just a bit dodgy. I don't know if he was involved with other armed robberies, but I'd say it wasn't his style."

"Bit dodgy?"

"Con man. One of those sharp-dressing spivs with gold rings and tie-pins complete with family crest. Seems he had a wealthy background, but went through his entire inheritance in various casinos. Was selling non-existent containers complete with imaginary goods. Took multiple orders and then disappeared, leaving creditors in a line as long as those hooded *nazarenos* at Easter. You know the type. I imagine he was blackmailing someone at least . . . And every last penny ploughed straight back into roulette and baccarat."

"You'd met him before," I said curtly.

Germán shook his head. He hardly knew which way to look.

"Just another rich kid that managed to stay one step ahead of the game."

I breathed out again, and moved in my chair to signal impatience.

"What about the accomplice?" Germán gave another shake. "One of Parada's friends?"

"They've all been checked. Not a sausage. We're still looking, though."

"How about a few names?"

He gave me names, but my first visit, all the same, was to Parada's widow. Laura Mendizábal.

"Now, let's talk about Laura."

Not the most beautiful dame I've seen. Nose far from perfect, could easily shed a kilo or two, no question about that. I've known far more attractive women if we're talking looks and figure. But Laura's advantage over all the others lay in being more than just flesh and bone. Her skin was fine and white, her body generous with curves and folds, her hair chestnut and wavy, her eyes large, perhaps a touch too much, as if surprised to be alive. But no, it was the soul, more than anything, shining out of those big eyes, a soul that gave itself up with total surrender.

From the moment she opened the door and I explained I was a private eye, she seemed to look at me like I was real.

With her tight silk negligee, I could see from the movements that she only had on a bra and panties underneath. She was drinking something that looked like water, and offered me a glass saying it was vodka.

"No thanks."

"On duty?"

I could have killed for a witty response, but didn't dare improvise a joke. People never understand mine.

"Private eyes are always on duty – and we're never on duty, depending how you look at it. I'd like to talk about your husband, if you don't mind."

She glanced up, and I felt a rush of blood. Her eyes were tired from crying, and her sadness surrounded her like a halo, the effect contagious. I had to fight a desire to fold her in my arms and provide soothing consolation.

She seemed frightened and nervous, smoking and drinking compulsively. I didn't fancy talking about her husband, anyway, leastways not straight after myself. Yes, she knew Bernardo had gambling debts, that he needed money urgently, that he was always broke, pawning and redeeming jewellery, hiding from creditors, begging for a few days' grace, promising to set up imaginary businesses. He'd never had a gun at home. Of course, his friends . . . who knows about those "friends", who they were or what they might do. Such things weren't important for Laura just then. What mattered was that Bernardo was dead and, for her, his death was intimately and agonizingly bound up with memory.

"The worst thing about dying is that you lose your memories," she said of a sudden. "I like to believe in the transmigration of souls, in reincarnation, in another life. But what use is it being revived in the next life, if we don't remember anything about this one? It's like starting out from scratch, as if the previous one had never existed."

I wasn't really sure where she was going with all this, and if another person had laid such weird stuff on me I'd have sent them packing. But I felt it was part of an outpouring of pain and helplessness like I'd never seen before. She was simply telling me how much she'd been in love with her husband, and how much she was missing him.

"In heaven, if it exists, we can't keep our memories of this life because we'd otherwise feel nostalgia, and there's no room for nostalgia in paradise. That is the great curse of death: the loss of memory. Without memories we are nothing. Amnesia is the equivalent of death. If you lose your memories, you die and in your place another is born, someone confused, lost, dazed. An unknown person is born in your body. What use is it being remembered by others if we don't even remember anything ourselves? What use is another life to us, however wonderful, if we're going to lose this one utterly and completely?"

I wished I could have replied with something on that level, but I simply said the only thing that sprang to mind:

"You remember a lot about your husband, don't you?"

And she replied, crushed by the certainty that her memory would never restore Bernardo's life:

"How couldn't I?"

What enormous importance those words have for me now, as I grab Wágner's shirt and propel him headlong to the other side of the living room.

"Where is Laura?" I ask.

I deliver a kick.

Where is Laura?

After that day I'd lost all interest in crime investigation, and Laura was all I could think of. I picked up the phone, and my fingers ran over the numbers. I knew hers by heart. But what could I say to her?

I tried speaking with friends of Bernardo Parada, colleagues from gambling dens and shady deals, a partner he'd started a business with which made a tidy profit despite having no basis in the real world. Nobody knew a thing. No one remembered anything. "We weren't close friends," they'd say. "Bernardo didn't have any friends." And a gun? No, no one had ever seen him with a gun in his hands. There was also a woman, the owner of a bar where they'd set up gambling dens from time to time, who hinted that Parada had no friends because his breath was so bad.

"That one had a nice thing going with the fuzz," she told me. In other words, he was a nark, just like Wágner. It even occurred to me he was the one Germán had in mind when he spoke of "candy", not the jeweller. I concluded this was what Germán had been hiding from me.

When I got home that night, an envelope was waiting for me with no sender's name. Inside, a typewritten note, unsigned:

Parada was the secret informer of Inspector Germán. They used to meet up on certain evenings at a private club called El Choclo. Just go there and you'll understand everything.

The paranormal exists. The paper wasn't scented, and there was nothing in its anonymity to make me think of Laura, but holding it in my hands I got an erection. My heart was beating like mad when I rang Germán.

"I've heard Bernardo Parada was your candy," I said.

"Who told you?" he snapped.

He was so sharp I knew right then I'd put my finger on something, but I backed down, making light of the matter.

"Just in case you make out later that I never have a clue what's going on."

I suggested dinner, as if there was something else I needed to discuss. When we met up in a bar by the beach, I played dumb (they say I do it brilliantly in the agency: those jokes that everyone finds hilarious, so long as it's not me telling them). I rambled on about this and that, and made only a couple of vague references to the case. Germán gave me a funny look all the same, and confined himself to monosyllables. We had Martini aperitifs, and then I got him to try some Raimat Abadia, a really fine red. He liked it and, as I was hoping, got pretty plastered. I made sure his glass was never empty. Then Cardhu with the coffee. His head was already weaving a little, but he couldn't turn down the single malt.

Which was when I brought up El Choclo.

"What's that? A tango, isn't it?" he made a stab at resistance.

"A club."

All resistance useless. After a good meal with plenty of booze, friends can never keep secrets or maintain a successful subterfuge.

"Come on, Germán, cut the crap. Why don't you want to tell me that Bernardo Parada was your stooge?"

"Informers are supposed to be secret." It wasn't the reply I was looking for, and I simply nodded to let him know I was waiting for the bottom line. He smiled, and nodded back in imitation. "Because cakes are cakes. Because when you see the cake, you'll think it's something it isn't."

On our way to El Choclo, he told me his version of what was going on. A chain of coincidences. The ingredients of the cake were Bernardo Parada, Arturo Wágner and Laura. But everything was the result of pure chance, "don't think the worst", don't get paranoid, reality is never as fiendishly cunning as fiction. He was doing his best to stop me suspecting the very thing he suspected himself.

The club's name was spelt out in gold letters above a small, dark wooden door, on a ground floor in the San Gervasio district. Germán had a plastic card with a magnetic band that allowed us to gain entrance.

Inside, a woman of a certain age, oozing friendliness and charm, welcomed us with a dazzling array of false teeth. She was delighted to make my acquaintance, and informed Germán that his friends were at the back table, as usual. The police officer then had second thoughts, regretted having brought me, and turned to try and stop me passing through the bead curtain.

Too late. I sidestepped, and went through, making a beeline for the rear. I already knew what I was going to find, and what I saw was merely a confirmation.

Those big sad eyes, expecting me. Laura recognized me, *remembered me*, and I sensed a sigh of infinite relief, as if she were shouting, "At last!" and I knew beyond question that she'd written that unsigned note.

To the immense annoyance of Arturo Wágner, who had his arm round her waist, fingers spread wide, pawing her possessively.

According to Germán it had all been the result of pure chance. As soon as Arturo Wágner joined the El Choclo group, he'd been drawn to Laura, had tried to catch her eye. He'd pursued her and eventually got her by being insistent and charming. These things happen. And from the moment Bernardo Parada first met the jeweller, he'd been toying with the idea of a hold-up. He needed the cash, was a bit of a crook, and it was perfectly natural he'd come up with the idea. If we're a bit twisted, we might also deduce he'd realized Laura would get off with Wágner, providing a further incentive to rob him of his jewels, but that's as far as it went. One shouldn't get carried away.

Germán couldn't accept the obvious because he was the one who'd introduced the jeweller, and he felt guilty towards his informer for having set up the explosive cocktail. He couldn't accept the final disastrous outcome either, because there wasn't any proof and also because it was simply too awful. As far as he was concerned, Laura simply went away somewhere.

Arturo Wágner, on that evening, after the evident shock of seeing me there, put his hand on Laura's shoulder and steered her firmly towards the exit. He excused himself with "We'd better be going," and avoided my eyes.

Did he guess in that split second that Laura had sent me the anonymous note? "That private detective came to El Choclo all thanks to you; he twigged because you betrayed me."

Laura, on the other hand, kept her eyes firmly on mine. She was sending out a desperate signal, a plea for help of which I remained unaware and which I was unable to act on. She was telling me, "How couldn't I remember Bernardo?" and that changed everything. I might have seen her as a two-faced bitch happily throwing herself into the arms of her husband's assassin, if she hadn't said with such sadness: "How couldn't I remember him?" That look and those words about memory and death, and that anonymous note – they changed everything.

Arturo Wágner had acquired her, taken possession of her, and she found herself in his arms with an indifference that might easily have been mistaken for happiness. Many might have seen her as a shameless hussy delighting in Bernardo's death but, if you knew how to listen to her, how to recognize the message of helplessness in her eyes, you would find things weren't quite as straightforward as they might appear. Laura was the prisoner of that artificial, perfumed creature, and I failed to save her life when the two of them walked past me and out of the club with indecent haste.

Words on the tip of my tongue: "She has nothing to do with this; I worked it out with no need for her anonymous note; I'd have come to El Choclo anyway, even if she hadn't sent a thing."

And I can picture that monster back in his flat, beating her with his belt and ordering her to confess: "You told him where he could find us, didn't you?"

I've only seen Laura twice in my life, and I know I'll never see her again, and that is the worst thing that's ever befallen me. It's why I believe I'm entitled to beat up Arturo in a way I've never beaten up another. Who knows, maybe I'm going mad.

"Where is Laura?"

"She dropped me, she left me!"

"You killed her!"

Would *I* have to tell *him* what happened? He, the cynic, claimed he loved her, that he was hopelessly in love with her from the moment he first set eyes on her, that Bernardo found out and for that reason had him at gunpoint and was set on shooting him.

I seize him by the jaw to shut him up, bang his head against the wall, and scream an inch from his face, breathing right into his nostrils and spattering him with saliva:

"He didn't want to kill you! *You're* the one that wanted to kill *him* because he scared you, because you knew he could turn nasty, because you were terrified by the possibility of his finding out about your affair with Laura. So you suggested to Parada that he do a fake hold-up and have the jewellery disappear, so you could claim on the insurance! And when he appeared in the parking lot by himself, with a gun like you said to give the robbery an authentic touch, you shot him."

"He was planning to shoot me."

"You shot him in the back" – I take him by surprise. I throw him in a corner like a rag doll. "You shot him in the back, 'as he was fleeing'. You were frightened, absolutely terrified. Just like you were frightened and terrified the other day, when I came into El Choclo and saw your hand on Laura's waist, and you thought, 'He's got me.' You thought Laura had ratted on you, didn't you? That she'd told me everything because you knew she didn't love you. She stayed with you out of sheer apathy, because thanks to your stupidity her husband had died, and if even that stupidity didn't last, then what a useless death it was. But she didn't love you. She despised you for being a murderer and a coward, and that's why she betrayed you. And you, you coward and murderer, you killed again. Got rid of her. Where is she now?"

All this in a furious rant, accompanied by kicks to his stomach and head. "Where is she?" With great difficulty I stop myself killing him, so that he can lead me to where he buried the corpse. "Where is she?" And I finally convince him by saying that if he tells me where she is, he'll have a chance to escape on the way, while we're heading to wherever it is he says. He'll have at least an hour, two hours to live. A lot of things can happen in two hours.

He admits, finally, that it's all true, that he killed her and buried her, and agrees to take me to the place where he dug the grave.

We're making for the front door when the bell goes. It's none other than the police. "Open up! What's going on? Police! Open up!" We've been making too much noise, and the neighbours have taken fright. Arturo Wágner gives a leap of joy and runs to open the door. I have no choice but to trip him, and he sails headlong onto the floor. Then, perfectly conscious of what I'd doing, with the fanatical awareness of the truly mad, I break his neck. I kill him. I then say:

"Don't run. I'll open it myself."

Inspector Germán will look at me as if some complex message was tattooed on my forehead – in code.

"But in God's name, what's he done to you? Why did you pick a fight with Wágner?"

I'll avoid his gaze, and try to regain my composure, and find some answers. I'll tell my friend that he's right and that I'm in the wrong. What'll she be to me, that poor girl, whom I've only seen twice in my entire life? I'll also think a lot about the size and consequences of catastrophes. But, above all, I'll make an effort to remember Laura, to keep her in my memory. Because if I don't, then who will?

Translation by Martin Davies

My Vacation in the Numbers Racket

Howard Engel

Dear Benny,

I was thinking of you all alone in that hotel room of yours with the frost making leaf-prints on your windows, so I thought I'd see if I couldn't get this cassette machine working long enough to send you a letter. I think I've pushed the right button, but I don't think I've got the courage to try playing it back in case I wipe what I think I've recorded.

You'll be surprised to hear that your father and I are in Sarasota. You thought we were still in Miami, where I meant to send you a postcard, but things just happened too fast to send you a postcard. Right from the beginning this winter hasn't been like any other winter we've ever spent in Florida. I'll try to tell you what happened if I can still remember.

One thing I remember, and I'll start there, is the Red Cap. That's the place your father and I went with Shirl. Do you remember Shirl? She's that blonde that if it wasn't for me I think your father might have been nuts about back a few years. She used to work in his store, and then she started doing her hair up and moved to the millinery shop in the Leonard Hotel. That's where she used to hang out until she met Dave Steiner. He was the first man she ever met who had his shirts made to order. Dave might be a little shady in his business life but he was always generous where Shirl was concerned. We have been visiting them every winter for a few days since we started going to Miami. Which brings me back to the Red Cap, the lounge on the edge of Miami where Shirl and Dave used to take us. It's a kind of bar, but a real joint, if you know what I mean. Even for down there it's a joint. They call it the Red Cap, and it's a sort of Last Chance Saloon because it's open all night and it's so far away from everything. It's located right in the middle of these big, big . . . What-do-you-call-'ems? You know, storage tanks for gas? A huge field of them. And right across the road from the bar is the whole electric whatchamacallit for the whole city of Miami. A power station, not a sub-station or anything like that. And this joint just sits there in the middle of all that gas and electricity with its peeling sign winking on and off like it was something to be proud of.

They have a piano player there, some drunk that comes in all the time. They told me he used to be somebody but you could have fooled me. He leaned into the keyboard like he was protecting it with his body. I don't think I ever saw him look up, not even when the girl replaced his empty glass with a full one. He wasn't the only musician. When they finished their club dates, jazz musicians drop around on their way home. There was always some sort of jam session going on if you came in late enough.

The night I met Stone Eyes was the night it all started to happen. Dave and your father were out looking after some business together and were going to pick us up at the Red Cap. Shirl parked her convertible in back and we walked into that neon haze around the front door. So just before she starts telling jokes with the owner, Shirl tells me not to talk to anybody she doesn't introduce me to first. It's a safety precaution, I know that. But you know me; I'm always the little juvenile delinquent. And so I started talking to this tall guy sitting at the bar. He had eyes that looked like they were made of stone. I'd never in my life seen eyes like that. They looked like they were really made of stone. Anyway, I know you're going to say that we were all pretty stoned and sure, we were, because it was after four in the morning and Dave and Manny were busy like I told you.

So anyway, I looked around and everywhere there's something chipped or faded or falling apart: plastic liquor signs that light up, even neon in the windows writing the name of an American beer backwards. It's a really low place and the people in it . . . let's say that it's not where you expect to find ladies with pearls and twin sets, if you know what I mean. This is 159th Street after all: the last chance. You get all types here, millionaires and crooks. They say the mayor or former mayor used to come here all the time. One time Shirl told me that the guy she'd introduced me to owned half of Miami. Now, Benny, you know what I think of

Miami. If it wasn't for the Canadian winter, they could give it to Castro. When you look at them all sitting there talking over their drinks you can't tell the crooks from the millionaires. And you know me. I couldn't care less which is which. Every crook Shirl ever introduced me to treated me like a lady. Anyway, I always talk to men in bars. You know, I tell them I'm from Canada and that I'm visiting friends in Miami and very soon we're talking. And so I was talking to this tall man in the gray suit with the eyes I was telling you about.

That night the orchestra was not great. In fact it was terrible. I was only listening with half an ear until it started playing "Windmills of My Mind." The guy with the eyes was humming into his drink. I leaned over and said to him, "That's from *Don Quixote*, isn't it?"

"What?" he asks.

"The music: 'Windmills of My Mind.' From the musical."

"Oh," he says, and I look into those stone eyes of his.

"That's Cervantes."

"Naw, that's Voltaire. *Candide*," he says, "I'd know it anywhere. You're thinking of *The Man of La Mancha*. That goes different. It's a better book. Longer, but better. They both got a lotta giggles in 'em." And I can't get over it; in a place like that to be having an intellectual conversation with the man with the stone eyes. So, anyway, I don't agree with him about the music, naturally, but I ask him where he went to university. He looks surprised and smiles and says that he didn't even finish high school. Well, I don't tell him that I dropped out in junior fourth, but I compliment him on his reading.

"Ask me any question," he says.

"Is this a game or something?"

"Naw. Just quiz me about stuff. Try me on the Bible. I specialize on the Bible."

"Who was Malachi?"

"It means 'messenger' and he was the last of the Minor Prophets. He wrote a whole book. That was easy. Try me again."

"Who was Lazarus?"

"Trick question, huh?"

"What do you mean?"

" 'Cause there were two of them. One in the parable of the Rich Man and the other one gets raised from the dead. Right?"

"How am I supposed to know? I just asked the first thing that came into my head." I asked him where he got his education and he started laughing.

"I did twenty years of reading in one stretch when I was in prison."

Well, I could have fallen right off my stool – like the time I broke my coccyx and Charlie Wilson from General Motors picked me up and called a doctor. I guess he could see my surprise. I think I let my mouth go slack.

"You got lots of time for reading in prison," he said. "I guess I've smoked more Bibles that most people have read."

I looked him over, but there was nothing of the jailbird about him except that his hair was cut shorter than you see nowadays. But that doesn't mean anything. His clothes were as good as your father's. So, I try to stop staring at him and ask him what he'd done to get sent to prison for twenty years.

"Name it," he said. My mouth was open again and I snapped it shut. "I guess I've done just about everything one time and another," he said. Then he told me that one of the things he'd done was kill his wife. So there I am sitting and laughing and talking about *Candide, Don Quixote*, and the Bible with a wife-killer. I go into a trance and when I hear what he's saying again he's talking about guns. ". . . too much respect for them to carry one. I hate wearing one under my coat in the heat. And you can get into a lot of trouble with guns. I'm all for gun control, you know. I heard about one old-timer with bad kidneys from Louisiana. His relatives riled him up so bad he took a few warning shots at them with a handgun. When it went off it severed the tube from his dialysis machine and he bled to death. I know another guy who thought he saw a prowler at the foot of his bed and shot his own pecker off. You'll have to forgive my language." I tried to show him that it was all right this time, but that I wasn't used to that kind of talk.

Just then the girl behind the bar with blue spots showing through her pancake make-up comes over with a drink for me. I tell her that I didn't order it and she tells me that he ordered it for me. I explain that I couldn't accept it, and she leans over the bar and tells me that in the three years this guy has been coming in here every night regular, this is the first time he'd ever bought anyone a drink. So, being me, I naturally accepted. He'd spent twenty years in prison for killing his wife and God knows what else he's done, and who ends up on the bar stool next to him? Me! Oh, I know, I'm terrible. But I can still picture those stone eyes of his and remember talking about Cervantes and Voltaire. Isn't that the limit? I mean, look: he could have gotten very ugly with me, you know. You accept a drink from some of these guys and they think they own you. One rye and water and you're bought and paid for.

So, anyway, your father and Dave came back around then. They saw me sitting at the bar and I waved to your father and said: "Manny, come over here, I want you to meet a friend of mine." Dave saw who I was talking to and went over to the table where Shirl was still talking to the owner. Manny and Stone Eyes shook hands but didn't exchange names. After that we left. I think I have a feeling that Stone Eyes knew Dave from someplace. I'm not sure. I know that Dave has never done time. Somebody else would have asked my educated ex-con all about his life in prison but not me. He would have expected that, and I always do the unexpected.

So anyway, after that we go back to Shirl's and Dave's place, which is right there off 159th Street, and have a few more drinks and a few laughs. It's a nice place with patio and pool, and Shirl has fixed it up real cute with lamps she's made from kits you can buy for making colored plastic lampshades. That's about as artistic as she gets. I tried to get her interested in art once when she lived in Grantham, but she thought that the man taking the class was queer. Generally, if they don't have hair on their knuckles, she thinks they're queer. So we have a drink and a few laughs, like I say, because we were trying to cheer her up, take her out of herself after everything she'd gone through, what with the robbery and then the probation thing. Don't get me wrong, Benny, she didn't get probation for a robbery that *she'd* committed. I know they have some pretty strange friends, but apart from the numbers, they're very careful, Shirl and Dave. She isn't really any different from the girl who used to work in your dad's store in Grantham. You should meet Shirl again. She always liked you. Your father says that Shirl and Dave are very careful about the numbers, too. Shirl didn't tell anybody she was mixed up in it. The first few winters we came to Miami we didn't know anything about it.

It was only after we heard about her being out on probation, we got to wondering about the big apartment, the pool, and everything. And she had to tell us when we asked her what it was she was on probation for. Then we remembered about the suitcase every Thursday and Saturday, how she was always taking it to a different motel to count out money and tally lists of numbers.

Well, your father, who as you very well know would never hurt a fly, was fascinated by this. He remembered how he'd carried the suitcase for Shirl on a couple of occasions and how sometimes he'd help her add up the accounts. To him it was no different from doing his books at the store. But I didn't want any part of it. I wondered whether it was the Mafia, but Shirl said it was an independent group. But she gave the Mafia its due. If you want anything done in Miami, including protection, you have to get it from the Mafia. The police, she said, are just a joke. Why when we arrived in Miami this year, what with Shirl being depressed and everything, I have to give her Mafia connections their due. At the airport your father couldn't rent a car anywhere. We phoned Shirl and she said that she'd look after it. Inside of half an hour we had a rent-a-car, and not only that, but the guy turned back the speedometer about two hundred miles so that in the end we had the car for the whole two weeks and it only cost your father eighty dollars. If it wasn't for the saving and a few other things I'm going to tell you about, I'd be putting all this down in ballpoint in a letter instead of on a cassette. You know how I hate writing letters. Your father writes a beautiful letter, but you and your brother take after me. Remember how the camp counselor used to threaten you with no swimming if you didn't write home?

Now I don't want you to get me wrong. Your father and mother have not turned to a life of crime. God forbid. And you may not remember but Shirl is just about the most giving and wonderful person on earth. She's the best friend a girl could have and she's always thought the world of your father. But, to tell you the truth, she has run into a lot of unsavory characters. Even Dave. I once saw Dave shake her, right up against the wall of the patio of her apartment, and demand to have half of the money they got from Lou for not mentioning his name at the trial. Lou has always been good to Shirl. He's the guy who looks after the apartment and her other expenses. I think he was at one time sweet on Shirl. I wouldn't be surprised. Lou gave them fifty thousand for taking the rap for him.

When they got the fifty, Shirl and Dave went through it so fast you'd think that they knew it was going to be discontinued. They spent it like it was sea water. And they both used to live pretty high on the hog even in the old days. It took them less than four weeks to rip through that bank roll. They bought a second color TV with all sorts of Atari games. They got a Polaroid camera, you know, all that stuff. And Shirl got a new mink coat. In that climate! Two mink coats! The old one wasn't three years old and she didn't even have to trade it in.

I don't want you to get us wrong, Benny. The first time we went to Miami, as I was saying, we didn't dream about the numbers. I mean, when I think of all the clues there were: Dave and Shirl were always so careful about being followed, driving around the block to see if there was anybody parked by the apartment. That sort of thing. And, of course, not only did your father help out with the tallying, he even went around with Dave to all those black bars collecting bets and then delivering the money afterwards. How can I defend us to you, Benny? We had no training for getting involved, that's all. Your father has kept books all his life, so naturally he became a little suspicious when he saw books with no names in them. In case you're shocked, let me tell you that we were too. Only we just woke up and found ourselves right in the middle of it.

Oh, they've had the numbers in Florida for years. This bunch was run by a gang from Detroit. The numbers were on short slips of paper, about two inches by four, in bunches held together by elastics. It's all on the up and up. There's no way you can cheat on it because the numbers are a combination of who won the first race at Jamaica or the last race at Santa Anita, or something like that. It's all in the open, and if you win, you know it, and if you don't, you're down two, three bucks. For a two-dollar win, you can get maybe two hundred more if it's a special combination win. It's like slot machines or the lotteries. Most of the time you lose, but if you win, Lou and his bunch can go down a couple of hundred thousand. Dave said once a few years ago Lou was borrowing cab fare one day and he owned the company a week later. Naturally, most of the time they don't lose, but they don't cheat at it. I mean you can't fix all those horse races, can you? For a racket, it's as honest as you can make it.

The robbery and Shirl and Dave taking the rap for Lou when the apartment was raided happened last summer. As she said, we missed the fireworks. We missed the court case, too. All the excitement. When we got back to Miami things were a lot different, more creepy. Dave gave me the willies. Manny liked Dave, but me, well, to be honest, I never much liked the look of him. He was like most of Shirl's men: big, dark fellows. Mediterranean types. They always looked like they were carrying guns under their jackets, but most of them weren't carrying anything more than maybe fifty pounds overweight.

Anyway, after the court case, Shirl and Dave got off. I don't know why they didn't deport Shirl. I don't understand how she stays there. It's this lawyer they've got. I can see why she wouldn't want to leave that place of hers; it's really a beautiful place. And she's got a toy poodle, Maggie, a wonderfully cute, dear little fellow. I adore Maggie, and you know about me and dogs as a rule: we can't stand one another. They know it and I know it. It's never been a problem. But I was telling you about the apartment. Wasn't I? The apartment? It's a palace, that's all. Five bedrooms, patio, pool, and a view over, well, I'm telling you that it wouldn't make it very hard for Manny and me to pack up and move down here and that's for sure. And if you want something, anything, Shirl or Dave or Lou knows somebody who can get it. Oh, it's just marvelous.

Where was I? Oh, the apartment. That's really one for the books. You have to see it. Anyway, the point I was making is that after the robbery, they, Shirl I should say, just let it go to rack and ruin. She lost heart, poor girl. Well, I guess, after all she went through, I mean. It must have been hell. A woman can get frightened of things a man doesn't have to worry about in a situation like that. Oh, the kid went through hell. And Dave? Not a scratch. He wasn't even there. I never trusted Dave. He looks like those movie torpedoes, and he acts like that's the way he wants to look. Tough, he-man. Not that Shirl ever went for the choirboy type. Like I said, she always went for the dark, brawny type with size eighteen necks. And most of them had a mean streak. Not like that boy from out Pelham Road she married out of Commercial. He had a real sweetness about him, but Shirl put him on the worry wagon with a vengeance. She preferred the flashy type: she couldn't help it. When they were loaded, Shirl's men always spent freely. They like Cadillacs in the drive and convertibles, if you please. One, two, make it three. Like Shirl and her minks. Same thing.

The numbers were always collected and counted in a new place every time. Shirl first got to use the apartment because it was used as one of the places. Then they didn't want to have anything in the apartment overnight. Wasn't it a big surprise that the Feds knew about the first time in months that there was stuff linking them to the numbers in the place. That can't have been just bad luck. It's like what it says in the mystery stories I read all night, somebody "shopped" them. Now, not only did they lose the money they were holding, but they are having to fight the tax people, you know, Internal Revenue, who want to count the numbers money as income, and undeclared income at that. I mean they had hundreds of thousands with them and none of it was theirs. There must have been a leak of some kind, because Lou and his cousin before him had been running numbers there without anything happening for years and years.

After the trial came the robbery. Shirl thinks there was something fishy about that too, and I don't blame her. When we came back this winter, Shirl was a different woman. She'd lost her – what's the word? Specialness? The thing that made men turn and look at her. You know I've known Shirl for years and we've been very close. We've gone through rough times together. So there was no fooling Manny and me when we got off that plane.

Shirl thinks the world of your father, Benny, and God bless him, he's not one for sitting around when there's work to be done. Anything before talk. That's your father. So, right away he starts cleaning up the place. She'd let it go downhill quite a bit, though who could blame her after what that kid has been through. I looked after Maggie, the poodle. Manny loves gardening. Me, I have a black thumb, can't make anything grow except that ivy I've been trying to kill off in the kitchen. Wouldn't you know it: if I wanted it to live, it would have died off years ago. But your father has a talent, as you know, and he started in on her place, trimming the hedge and cutting back the rubber plant, and cleaning the dead plants out of the place.

Manny bought some annuals. They have annuals all year round down there. He made a proper garden for the patio like we have at home. Oh, your father's wonderful at that sort of thing, while I sit back with a rye and water. Ha! That's my style. Especially when it comes to work. Shirl adores Manny. Always has, not that she'd try anything. Much more likely that he'd look too far into those baby-blue eyes of hers and fall in. I trust your father, but he's only human. Everybody loves Manny. Everybody. There's something sweet about him. You can smell it on his skin. Me? Well, they think I'm pretty special too, but oh, they all love your father.

Well, he cleaned out the pool, scrubbed it, vacuumed it, and replaced the burnt-out lights in the bottom. When at last the place started to look like something again, Shirl started coming out of herself. You know how she can sound tough, but she didn't have to act that way with us. Not ever. We were always special for her and she never put on a show for us. One night she turned on the night lights in the pool and we all went for a swim. She still looked beautiful in that turquoise light, although she wouldn't wear a bikini any more. When we were all dried off and having a drink I had enough courage to ask her to talk about the robbery.

It was after four in the morning when she came home, parked her Cadillac in the drive, and let herself into the apartment. Dave wasn't with her. When she opened the door, they were inside waiting for her. They grabbed her from behind by the throat and mouth. She only saw stockinged faces and screamed into rubber gloves. They blindfolded her, put adhesive tape over her mouth, and tied her to a chair. She said they talked of raping her right at the start, but she made them understand that she had a heart condition, so they left her alone. Here's an interesting thing: they knew she was wearing a diamond pendant under her turtleneck sweater. Can you beat that? They knew which was her car. They took time collecting everything in the place that was fenceable. I learned that word from Ellery Queen. They made themselves Nescafé and went through every pillow, mattress, upholstered chair in the place with their knives. They even cut up the backs of her pictures. The poor kid! Shirl could hear the birds and the sounds of starting cars next door when they left. She knew that it was getting light on 159th Street. Before they left, they poured acid from the swimming pool shed into the pool. Then they left in her car. They found the Caddy a few days later. The cops, I mean, but they won't find the rest of her stuff. Even the cops told her not to hold her breath until that happened.

The rings! She had a seven-hundred-dollar Pucci and a diamond cut like – well, it was the only one of its kind. But the thing that got her was the swimming pool. Shirl couldn't talk about it too much. It was Dave who told us about the acid in the pool. He said that Shirl was broken up into little pieces when he got home after her call to him in New York. "She was a wreck for about a month, weren't you honey?" he said. "I nearly didn't have the heart to tell her about the pool, but she kept bugging me about why I had it drained. Didn't you, sweetheart? I tried lying to her, but that wasn't no good, so I had to tell her. And that got her started all over again. But she's all right now, huh? How's my little girl?" She was sick about that. If she had tried to go swimming, her skin would have been eaten right off by the acid. It makes you sick just thinking about it. It's funny, they didn't break up the place any in a malicious way, except for what I told you already, but they did that to the pool. I don't understand people doing a horrible thing like that.

The next day, I think it was, the three of us, Shirl, Manny, and I, went shopping. Dave was off on business of some kind. I wanted to get some postcards to let you get a taste of the balmy south to pin to your bulletin board. I knew you were looking after our plants and your brother says he likes to hear from us regularly. Not that either of you'd ever think to drop us a line. So we went into this arcade and were browsing around when suddenly Shirl looks at me, really scared, and says, "I've got to get out of here. I'll see you later." And off she goes into the crowd and out of the other end of the arcade. Well. You could have knocked me over with a lemonade. I looked at your father and he looked at me and for a minute we didn't know what to do. Like, it took us a minute to realize that Shirl had left so fast.

Anyway, I bought about half a dozen cards, got some stamps from the machine, and was sitting writing out one to your brother when Manny gives me a nudge. When I looked up, he nods at two men standing about ten feet away. They were watching us. One is a dumpy guy in a sports jacket and the other is wearing a pale blue nylon windbreaker with a zipper. There was no mistake about it. They were watching us. As soon as they saw that we saw them, the tall one in the windbreaker comes over and asks where Shirl is. How do you like that? I tell him it's none of his business.

"You don't understand," he says, "we're friends of hers. Is Dave with her?" He tried to look friendly and the chubby guy was nodding and tried to look agreeable.

"Well, you just missed her," I said, a little apprehensively. "She had some things to do."

"Well, that's too bad. At least we can give you a lift back to where you're staying."

"That won't be necessary," I said. "Thank you very much."

"We're driving right past 159th Street," the other one added.

"We're just shopping," Manny said, and added, "For the love of Mike!" to show that he was serious.

"I'm afraid I'm going to have to insist," said the first guy, trying to take my arm. He smelled of talcum powder like a baby. "Our car's parked right outside."

Well, I looked at Manny and your father looked at me, and there didn't seem to be anything we could do about it. They both wore smiles and seemed friendly enough. While the short one looked like a thug in the movies, I had to remind myself we weren't in the movies. Things like that don't happen to a couple having a holiday in Miami, for goodness sake. So we went with them to the car which was double-parked at the front of the arcade. There was a man at the wheel and the motor was running.

If I was worried at all, I felt better as soon as I saw that the driver was old Stone Eyes from the Red Cap. The guy I was telling you about? He did a real double-take when he saw me. But he didn't smile or say anything. He just got out of the car and came around to open my door. Manny and I sat in the back with the one in the windbreaker and Stone Eyes and the heavy-set one rode in front. For a while nobody said anything. Manny watched the streets run by the car windows and I kept my eyes on the backs of the necks in the front seat. What was I going to do? I'd never be able to remember where they were taking us. All the streets in Miami look alike to me. Or so I thought. After a while I could see these big gas drums, so I could roughly guess where we were. Stone Eyes ran into an empty parking lot and leaned back and said: "What do you say we all have a little drink?"

The waiter with the broom tried to say that the place was closed, but the men just walked right over him. The place looked different in the daylight. There were no shadowy places. Empty, it looked twice as big. Stone Eyes looked at Manny, but he said to me, "Look, why don't you sit at the bar for a sec. I'll join you after I have a word with my associates." He and the other two sat in the booth and started in on what sounded like the middle of a conversation. After about five minutes, he ambles over and sits next to us at the bar. I was sipping a rye and water and so was Manny. The waiter brought him a drink without even asking.

"My friends and I are a little curious about your plans here in Miami. I mean are you down here on a vacation, a visit, or what? They're a little concerned that maybe you're not on a vacation at all, that maybe you're planning to settle down here and I don't mean in a retirement condominium. It's a friendly argument we're having. A little speculating, sure, but a few words from you can settle the whole thing. What do you say?" I could see the other two leaning this way from their booth, trying to hear as much as they could without getting up, but not making a big thing about not appearing to be listening at all. Manny looked pained, the way he gets when I use the garlic powder from the old house and we've run out of Gelusil. But as usual, it's your mother who opens her big mouth.

"We've been down here for about two weeks. Planning to stay three. You're not from the Department of Tourism or something. So, why the interest?" Of course I knew they weren't tourist inspectors, but I just come out with things. You know me. Stone Eyes thought about this for a minute while he took a slow sip from his drink.

"So, you're going back to Canada in a week, right?"

"That's right."

"And you're not in business down here, right?"

"Of course not."

"Good. Okay, that's all I got to know. Be right back." And over he goes to his pals again for another confab. Manny was looking at his fingernails. He gave me a weak grin. Stone Eyes came back to the bar. Your father just had time to say:

"It's going to be all right. You'll see." Stone Eyes looked at both of us, then reached for his drink. He didn't say anything until the glass was empty. He rubbed his mouth with a red bandanna he carried in his pocket.

"Okay, as soon as you're ready, I'll drive you home." He still didn't smile, I don't think I ever saw him do that. But this time his non-smile was as close to a smile as I ever saw him get. "One thing," he said as I was getting off my stool, "my associates would appreciate it if you didn't mix into Dave's and Shirl's business any more." I started to protest, but Manny had me by the upper arm before I could utter a syllable. "You know how things are in business," Stone Eyes continued, "people are superstitious about outsiders. You follow me? It's like our friend Candide. He got his nose busted a few times putting it into the wrong places. I don't mean this unfriendly. It's just that my friends don't understand people the way I do." We were now going out of the door of the Red Cap, and Stone Eyes held the door for your father and me. He took me to one side in the parking lot: "Look, what you do is this," he said, "you go back to Canada in a week, even sooner wouldn't hurt things none, and you don't say anything about what you've seen. That's all." He looked at me really hard with worry in those cold eyes, then he said, "Come one. I'll drop you at the house."

The ride back to Shirl's was much more relaxed. The short one was telling what his ten-year-old son told him about oil spills in the Gulf of Mexico. All three of them said something about the destruction caused by oil spills. Stone Eyes blamed it on lax shipping registry laws and referred to the Law of the Sea Conference that was going on someplace, and then the blue windbreaker got onto acid rain as we came to a stop in front of Shirl's. The other guy said that he was very impressed with the interest young people have in ecology. "Kids are really great the way they want to protect and preserve stuff." That was the end of it. We got out and said goodbye.

So, we let ourselves into the apartment. We didn't notice anything wrong, but when Shirl got back an hour later and when we told her what happened, she really went into orbit. I mean first of all she gets the shakes when she sees that Dave's stuff is gone from the closet. She checks the dressers and starts to cry. She asks us to describe the men we met and in less than no time we are packing ourselves into a limousine and on our way to the airport. Can you beat that? One minute I'm sitting in the sun with a tall, cool drink on the patio, the next I'm packing and Shirl's trying to smile and not fooling anybody. Shirl went with us

to the airline terminal and gave us both a big hug as we go...
the limo. The last we saw of her she was wiping tears from those
huge blue eyes and slamming the door of her Caddy.

Now isn't that the darndest thing you ever heard? Of course I
figured it all out on the flight to Sarasota. Shirl knew that Dave
was in on the robbery because he knew about the acid in the
swimming pool. How can you tell there's acid in a pool unless
you told somebody to put it there? He pulled the robbery to put
Lou off the scent. He must have been creaming the top off his
numbers money. A lot of them try that. People get greedy, that's
all. So Lou hired those thugs to shake things up to see if any
change rolled out of our pockets that didn't belong to us. It all
started looking like something in a paperback mystery novel. Isn't
there a private eye down here who lives on a houseboat? John
D. something. The whole two weeks sounds like a case he might
have got involved in.

Anyway, your father and I are both well. You can pick us up at
the airport on Tuesday, Flight 604 from Sarasota. And, Benny,
don't forget to water my plants.

Love,
Mother

Night Over Unna

Bernhard Jaumann

The words had only come together with some difficulty. Again and again Priest Nicolai had had to murmur them under his breath before they sounded right and before they could drown the terrors of the day. The rasping gasps of the dying, the toll of the church bells, the clatter of the oxcarts taking the bodies to the meadow. Even his stammers of solace had stayed unheard under the desperate cries of widow Schwartz, who had lost her fourth child to the epidemic.

But now, long after midnight, all was quiet in the streets outside, and Nicolai felt peace returning to him again through the words he had found with God's help. He skimmed across the lines in the glow of the tallow candle, dunked the goose feather quill into the ink pot once more and wrote *Unna, in the year 1597 of our Lord* under the last verse of the chorale.

The flame flickered in the draught of the movement of his arm and Nicolai smiled. He was sure that the light of the Lord would never perish, despite all the suffering and hardship, illness and death. Even he didn't know why God allowed the citizens of Unna to die like flies, but he was sure of one consolation: their souls would find salvation after this earthly vale of tears. Nicolai got up and blew out the candle. Darkness surrounded him, but he was not afraid of death. He carefully felt his way to the door, stepped into the lane and made his way towards the church square. A cool breeze had arisen. It had driven the stink of the plague from the streets and had wiped the clouds from the sky. The great and glorious starry firmament twinkled down on Nicolai.

Nicolai's newly finished song awoke inside him and demanded its right to be heard. At first he hummed it softly to himself, but then, one by one, the words urged themselves into the tune, they battled against the silent dying in the dark huts and houses, they conquered death, and when Nicolai looked to the east and saw a star brighter than all the others glimmering over the rooftops, he sang for all he was worth: "How beautiful the morning star shines/full of the mercy and truth of Our Lord . . ."

"And?" Chief Inspector Henze asked.

He motioned upwards into the night sky.

"A young woman with an infant," Inspector Silvia Frieling said.

"An environmentalist fanatic?"

"A what?" asked Frieling.

"Who but some nutter from Greenpeace would get the idea of chaining themselves to the top of a chimney?"

"We don't know if she has tied herself up there."

"Why hasn't anyone organized some floodlights yet?" Henze asked.

He yawned. Because he was tired. And because sometimes his job got on his nerves.

"We've done that," said Frieling. "But we had to turn them off again immediately."

"Because they would have interfered with the art or what?"

He gazed at the blue neon numbers with contempt. Light artist Mario Merz had decorated the old chimney of the Linden Brewery with them: 1, 1, 2, 3, 5, 8, 13 up to the number 987.

"Because the woman threatened to throw down her child," said Frieling.

"Her own child?"

Henze looked up. In the glare of the neon lights he could see the figure of a woman. She sat on the rim of the chimney and seemed to rock her body back and forth. The bundle on her lap could be a baby. Maybe.

"The chimney is fifty-two metres high," said Frieling, "and the base is partly surrounded by buildings. The boiler house and whatever else. It's completely impossible to secure it with rescue nets."

"What does she want?" asked Henze.

Frieling hesitated. Then she said, "She wants to get the night back."

"Well," said Henze.

He would also like the night back. His night in his bed, his sleep with his own bog standard nightmares, in which he had to flee from some nameless danger without being able to move from the spot. He kicked and turned, until he awoke, disoriented, panicked. For some reason he only calmed down when he read the glowing digits of his alarm clock. As if it weren't totally irrelevant whether they showed him that it was 3.12 am or 4.31 am.

"She demands that all lights in Unna be turned off," said Frieling. "And in all the suburbs as well, in Massen and Königsborn, in Hemmerde, Lünern and Kessebüren, everywhere. She doesn't want to see any street-lamps, no lit adverts, no illumination on the church nor on the ramparts, no light in private homes, not even the flicker of the telly and no headlights on the motorways. She wants absolute darkness. And she has given us three hours." Frieling looked on her watch. "Which means we've still got two hours and thirty-five minutes exactly."

"Total blackout like in an air raid. Is that all?" asked Henze. "And then she'll come down again?"

"At least she'll let the child live then."

Flashing blue lights could be seen rotating on the police cars on Massener Street. The *Schalander* was being vacated. Most of the people who had been in the pub joined the crowd of curious onlookers who had gathered behind the barriers despite the late hour. An old man protested as two uniformed officers took away his torch with which he had tried to make out the madwoman. Henze stared at the neon numbers on the facade of the chimney. He didn't like the fact that same numbers didn't have the same shape. As if some giant had scrawled them on the funnel in an awkward hand. Probably art. Henze preferred the world for which his digital alarm clock stood. A world, in which at 5.55 am three absolutely identical digits reassured him that he had only had a bad dream and that he was himself once more.

"I want to know who she is," he said. "I want a name, a face and a history."

"She's got to be from here," said Frieling. "Otherwise she couldn't have rattled off the names of Unna's suburbs like that."

"And her child can't have dropped out of the blue either." He realized how inappropriate his last remark was in light of the situation, so he added, "I want a list of all births in the last twelve months. Doesn't Müller's wife work at the registry office? He can take on that job."

Frieling passed on the orders. One of the officers whispered back that the directional microphone was now ready.

"Let's see what we can hear then," said Henze.

He made sure the record-button was pressed and put on the headphones. Her voice was surprisingly low. She didn't speak, she sang quietly: ". . . ring-a-ring o'roses, a pocket full of posies. A-tishoo! A-tishoo! We all fall down."

Henze handed the headphones over to Frieling and told the technician to make a dozen copies of the recording as quickly as possible.

"In half an hour at the latest, everyone in Unna has to have heard this voice. My men will help you there."

Henze pointed to a group of uniformed policemen who were just gathering by the entrance of the ZIB. Then he looked back up the chimney. The woman still swayed back and forth. Always the same movement, as if she herself was part of the light installation. Henze focussed on the topmost neon number. 987. The nine seemed a bit long and slightly askew. Why did it have to be 987?

"Sometimes she changes the verse to '. . . a pocket full of tissues, I kiss you, I kiss you . . .' " said Frieling taking off the headphones. She looked at her watch. "We've got two hours and nineteen minutes left. Perhaps we should start to organize the blackout."

"We'll wait," said Henze.

He didn't know what they should wait for. For the woman to come back down and admit that it had all been a big joke?

"Perhaps we should try again to . . ." Frieling stopped mid-sentence.

A uniformed officer stepped forward and said, "I don't know her name, but it could be the voice of this woman I checked up on once or twice. If that is really her, she used to hang out with the junkies by the ramparts."

"Take a few men and collect everyone you can find over there!"

The policeman made off. The good thing about Unna was that everything had its place. Even the things that didn't fit in. Therefore you could be sure to find certain minorities in the city gardens by the former embankment, neatly separated into groups. The gang of Russian Germans met on the benches near the *Güldener Trog*, the junkies and alcoholics by the war memorial and a bit further down the booze drinking, chaos-seeking youths.

After only ten minutes the Chief Inspector was presented with four ragged looking men in the foyer of the ZIB, but it took another three minutes before he had made it clear that it would be in their interest to speak. A bald man with sunken cheeks finally acted as spokesman. He said that the woman was Natascha, that he would never forget her voice, that she was a great lass and that the Constable could bet his life on that. No, he didn't know her surname and – with respect – he and the others didn't give a fuck about surnames. Natascha had only been with them a few times, last autumn, and with a big belly, but she had never come back with her child, which had probably been better anyway. No, he had no idea whether she had a place to live, but he supposed she had had before and had made good money by the looks of her.

"Before?" asked Henze.

"Well, before someone gave her that little brat. I expect she didn't get any punters any more, not with the big belly."

"She would have got some," said one of the others, "but she didn't want them no more."

Henze asked where she had worked as a prostitute, but the men didn't know. At least it was likely now that Natascha was known to the vice squad, the youth welfare office or the public order office. Henze gave instructions to find the relevant officials immediately.

One hour and fifty minutes. The blue neon numbers still glared down from the chimney. Between the number 987 and the black night sky a young woman cradled her baby to sleep. There was no star to be seen, and the sky wasn't really black. More like some sort of dark grey, tinted with the glow of lights from the city. Henze decided to risk something. He gave the technicians on the directional microphone a sign and shouted "Natascha!"

He read the neon numbers 337, 610, 987. He cried again, "Natascha, we can't block off four motorways. Give us some . . ." he stopped. Not only because the crowd behind the barriers began to murmur. It was impossible to negotiate with a madwoman who sat on a chimney, fifty-two metres high.

The technician said, "She reacted to the name. And instead of singing she is now muttering 'Shhh, my little one, keep quiet!' "

Henze nodded. He looked up.

"The numbers on that chimney," he said. "Every one is the sum of the two previous ones."

"A Fibonacci Sequence. A progression of numbers describing development and evolution," said Frieling.

"How do you know these things?"

"Once I've . . ." Frieling trailed off.

Henze's mobile was ringing. Müller had organized the list of births and had gone through it. Five names were left over, five mums who couldn't be found. None of those were called Natascha, but that didn't have to mean anything. Every prostitute had a pseudonym. Henze hadn't even finished the call, when Frieling hustled a forty-something-year old woman before him. Sticking out under her thin coat he could see her pyjama bottoms.

"Mrs Rastenau of the youth welfare office," said Frieling. "She lives round the corner in the Klosterwallgasse. She's got something for us."

"Don't hang up, Müller," Henze said into his mobile.

"I've just been dealing with the loss of custody in this case," Mrs Rastenau said. "It's absolutely impossible for the poor child to grow up with a drug addict prostitute, don't you think? It needs . . ."

"What's the mother's name?"

"Daniela Trochowski," said Mrs Rastenau.

"Hold on a minute!"

Henze asked into the phone whether there was a woman with that name on the list.

"Yes? I want everyone there! Get into the house somehow and pump the neighbours for information!"

They had a name, they had an address and now at least they'd got half the story from Mrs Rastenau.

Daniela Trochowski was not indifferent towards her child. Quite the opposite, she desperately wanted to keep it. She swore she did everything for her little Marc, her darling boy, and she really meant it, but she couldn't cope. Hour after hour the neighbours had heard the baby cry when the mother was out getting drugs, or when men came to the flat, time and again different men. She had behaved completely unpredictably towards the youth welfare officers. When suffering from withdrawal symptoms she could get violent or cry and collapse in a corner of the room. Although the doctor from social services hadn't been able to detect any life threatening signs, he had found indications that little Marc had been neglected, and that was enough to withdraw custody legally. The decision had been made ten days ago, and since then neither mother nor child were to be found anywhere.

Until, that is, she had appeared on the chimney of the Linden Brewery and had yelled down to turn off all the lights in Unna and its surroundings. Henze asked himself why she hadn't demanded restoration of custody. He turned to the technician at the directional microphone.

"Is she still talking to the little one?"

The technician nodded and said, "Rock-a-bye baby on the tree top, when the wind blows the cradle will rock, when the bough breaks . . ."

"I know the words," said Henze.

"It's driving me mad," the technician said. "Always the same idiotic rhyme, and every time she reaches the part at which the cradle falls, I shut my eyes, but it's no good. I still see the child falling, like I'm hallucinating, and then I open my eyes once more when she begins again with 'Rock-a-bye baby' and the same thing again and again. I know she can only have been at it a few minutes, but it feels like days and weeks have passed and . . ."

"Get someone to replace you, man!" said Henze.

"One hour and eighteen minutes," said Frieling. "I'll try and get through to someone from the social services. They should hold themselves in readiness."

"She won't kill her own child," said Henze.

"I'll also get them to prepare the road blocks," said Frieling. "Just in case."

Henze's mobile rang again. Once again it was Müller.

"The landlady, Mrs Reitz, is opening the flat for us now, but she doesn't want to come in with us, because Daniela Trochowski is supposed to have Aids."

"Aids?" Henze signalled to Frieling. The woman from the youth welfare office was standing in the foyer of the ZIB and stared through one of the portholes in the floor.

"Mrs Reitz had the locks to the flat changed immediately when the girl vanished with her child ten days ago," said Müller.

Henze could hear Mrs Reitz protesting in the background. Then she was on the phone herself.

"Listen, Chief Inspector, I'm not a monster, honestly, but I'm not so wealthy either. A good tenant moved out because of her, and Mrs Trochowski herself hasn't paid a cent for three months. I told her: go to the social services. A single mum will surely get support, you only have to fill in a form. But she refused . . ."

Frieling had come back.

"No HIV," she whispered. "At least none that the youth welfare office know of."

". . . she said she'd cope somehow," Mrs Reitz continued. "And she said she had always managed to get by on her own and that she'd pay the rent later, every penny of it, but she never did."

Then Müller was back on the phone and said, "We're not done with the flat yet, but there is a note on the pinboard with the phone number of a Max Trochowski. Seems to be in Bavaria somewhere."

Henze dialled the number immediately. He looked at his watch. They had fifty-seven minutes left to go. At last a sleepy man's voice could be heard at the other end. Henze introduced himself and asked, whether the man was related to Daniela Trochowski in Unna.

"I'm the father. Why? Is something the matter?"

Henze hesitated. He said, "Your daughter is threatening to kill her child."

There was a silence.

"Mr Trochowski?"

"You can't be serious," said Mr Trochowski.

"I'm afraid I am. Daniela is threatening to kill her son."

"Her son?"

To kill? He should have asked. Incredulous Henze said, "You didn't know that Daniela has been a mother these six months?"

"I'm on my way," said Trochowski. "Tell me where . . ."

"Mr Trochowski, you didn't know?"

"We didn't have much contact," he said slowly. "Especially over the last three years since I remarried. I told Daniela that I'd always be there for her. Any time. She'd only have had to pick up the phone. Even in the middle of the night. I wouldn't have minded. But she's always had a will of her own . . ." he broke off, then said, "Let me speak to her."

"We can't get at her," said Henze.

"I'll leave for Unna directly," Mr Trochowski said.

Too late, Henze should have replied. You should have done that years back, he should have said. He said, "Please do, Mr Trochowski!"

The number of onlookers in Massener Street hadn't diminished. An old lady craned her neck from an illuminated window on the first floor. Her head projected a huge pale shadow onto the asphalt by the police barriers. The technician on the directional microphone hadn't got himself a replacement after all. Henze turned to him.

"Is she still speaking?"

"Non-stop. Nursery rhymes, counting-out rhymes, lullabies," said the technician. "But I'm beginning to wonder what is the matter with that child. We haven't heard a sound from him for hours."

"Perhaps he's asleep," said Frieling.

The technician shook his head.

"I have two little kids at home myself. I'm telling you, you're glad when at last there's some peace in the evening. You read them a story or sing to them, but when they finally drop off you don't keep singing for two hours."

Frieling looked at Henze. Henze looked up to the rim of the chimney.

"She doesn't really have a child up there. She's just pretending," said the technician.

If that was true, where was her baby then? Henze pulled his mobile from his pocket to call Müller once more, when someone tapped him on the shoulder. It was a pensioner in a green hunter's jacket accompanied by one of the uniformed officers.

"I've recognized the voice," the pensioner said proudly.

Frieling was visibly annoyed with herself for having forgotten to cancel the search for the woman's identity. She said, "Thanks, but we already know . . ."

"I'm absolutely certain," the pensioner interrupted. He didn't seem to want to go without having had his five minutes of fame. "Yesterday I came across the woman at the West Cemetery . . ."

"When?"

"The West Cemetery is only a hundred metres from here," said Frieling.

"For goodness' sake, talk!" said Henze to the pensioner.

His name was Egon Kuballa and he belonged to a group of volunteers who took turns in guarding the cemetery. On his shift the night before, Kuballa had come across Daniela Trochowski, who had spread her sleeping bag behind one of the gravestones. Of course not just anyone could come along and use the cemetery as a free campsite, but the woman had seemed so forlorn that Kuballa, had turned a blind eye and let her stay the night.

"And her child?"

"She was on her own," said Kuballa. "There was no child."

"What did you speak to her about?" asked Henze.

"Nothing significant really, she was a bit confused. At first she said the cemetery was wonderfully peaceful and a moment later she thought it dark and creepy. She wanted to know who lay buried there, so I told her a few family histories. Even that we bury old bones that are sometimes unearthed in town. Always strictly ecumenical with a Catholic and an Evangelic minister, because you never know what denomination the body belonged to."

"And the woman? What did she say?"

"Not much. Although, wait a minute, there's one question I remember that kept me thinking. Whether I thought grief can save a soul. I said perhaps, but that she should really ask the minister."

Henze and Frieling didn't need any more words to understand. Daniela Trochowski's escape to the cemetery, her confusion, her thoughts on grief and salvation, the fact that the child was nowhere to be found – everything indicated the boy was dead.

"She's singing again," the technician said from behind. His voice was monotonous as he repeated the words, "How beautiful the morning star shines/ full of the mercy and truth of Our Lord . . ."

"The chorale by Philipp Nicolai," said Frieling.

"This morning at seven o'clock I went back," Kuballa said. "She was gone already. Only her sleeping bag still lay behind the grave. And I was rather angry with myself for not having chased her away, because quite plainly she had dug around in the earth. That's vandalism!"

"No," whispered Frieling.

Henze longed for one of his nightmares from which he could awake. He summoned a couple of officers and sent them to the West Cemetery to examine the grave Mr Kuballa would show them. They were to dig, even with their fingernails, until they found the body of a baby boy.

"Surely she wouldn't have murdered her own child." Frieling wiped a hand across her eyes.

"Why else should she bury the body in secret?" asked Henze.

The street-lamps dipped Massener Street into a yellow glow, behind the shop windows the goods were set in an advantageous light, some windows were lit, others were dark, and above the roofs of Unna loomed the church tower, illuminated by blue spotlights. Henze and Frieling stood outside the ZIB, motionless and in silence, until the mobile rang.

"Nothing," said the policeman on the other end. "Someone has been digging here, yes, but there is nothing."

"Dig deeper!" said Henze.

"We're already into solid ground."

"Keep going all the same!" Henze ordered. "And search the area!"

A tiny, ridiculous glimmer of hope emerged that little Marc could still be alive after all, but Henze couldn't believe it. Maybe miracles had happened in the past, but not nowadays. Not in Unna and not in a job like his. No, the child was dead. His own mother had murdered him. And all of a sudden Henze knew where he was. Up there, where chorales, which he would never hear again were being sung to him.

Henze looked up the chimney, saw the blue neon 610 and above that the 987. He asked himself which number one would have to write next into the murky sky. Above the rim of the chimney, above the black figure who sat on it and cradled a bundle on her lap. Henze added the numbers in his head.

"1,597," he said. When Frieling gave him a questioning look he added, "That's the next number in the Fibonacci Sequence."

"1,597," said Frieling, "that's also the year in which Philipp Nicolai wrote the chorale 'How Beautiful the Morning Star'."

Frieling twitched the corner of her mouth. She was not only a good policewoman. Henze glanced at his watch.

"We've still got twenty-one minutes," said Frieling. "And everything's ready."

"What's the use now?" asked Henze.

"She's going to jump," said Frieling.

"She's going to jump no matter what," said Henze.

Frieling looked up the chimney. Fifty-two metres to the top.

"Okay then," said Henze, and Frieling began.

It was only afterwards that Henze actually realized how everything had happened. At this point, he did not realize that Frieling had phoned the people from public services and the clergy. He did not hear the traffic warning on the radio, announcing that all the motorways around Unna had to be blocked due to a bomb threat. He didn't know that the traffic police had shut down all the major arterial roads and encouraged honest citizens to park their cars at important junctions to stop any sort of traffic. He wasn't aware that Unna's organizations, from the shooting club *Hemmerde* to the stamp collection club *Am Hellweg*, from Amnesty International to the evangelical church choir, drummed up their members via telephone chains. And he didn't see that in the centre of Unna dozens of volunteers made sure that not even a lighter would be flicked at minute zero.

Henze just stared into the dark sky above the chimney and imagined how more numbers of the Fibonacci Sequence would grow up into the night. He added them furiously in his head, 1,597, 2,584, 4,181, bigger and bigger numbers, higher and higher up, 6,765, 10,946. He didn't even notice how the people of Unna came streaming in, from Massener Street, from Rembrandt Street, from the West and Northring, all gathering by the Linden Brewery, 17,711, 28,657, how they were filling up the square until not the smallest piece of asphalt could be seen from above, 46,368, how the members of the evangelical church choir positioned themselves in strategic places and memorized the text, 75,025 . . .

Henze only jumped when the bells of the town church and the Katharinen church began to ring and made the pigeons flap excitedly around the towers. Then, all at once, the lights went out: light bulbs, street lamps, illuminations, even the Fibonacci Sequence on the chimney. At first Henze felt almost blinded by the sudden blackout, through which the after-effects of the lights still seemed to flicker. It was as if the retina of his eyes couldn't quite believe that everything was out. However, a deep black slowly began creeping from every corner, flooding the streets, drenching the roofs, rising higher and higher. Unna had got the night back.

Henze imagined what the view of the glittering lights of towns on the horizon would be like from the top of the chimney. With their yellow glow they maybe looked like far off coast lines. Before them a black ocean in which every spark of light had been extinguished and created an almost biblical darkness, like at the beginning of all times, when the stars were born, which now emerged one after the other from obscurity.

Amidst all this darkness, somewhere on the square in front of the Linden Brewery, a bass voice began to sing. Right on cue the church choir joined in and drew the rest of the crowd with them. Hundreds, perhaps thousands of people from Unna sang a chorale, a chorale which had been written here in the year 1597 during the great plague: "How beautiful the morning star shines/ full of the mercy and truth of Our Lord . . ."

They sang for a dead child.

They sang for a woman on a chimney, fifty-two metres up.

They sang the first verse of the chorale and then started from the beginning again, since hardly anyone knew any of the following verses off by heart. And when they praised the morning star for the third time, the shadowy figure on the chimney moved, turned, felt for the topmost of the iron rungs that were fixed to the brickwork, and climbed down. The people of Unna didn't stop singing until she was on the ground.

Henze switched on a torch. Together with Frieling he pushed through the crowd. Without protest Daniela Trochowski handed over the blanket in which the dead boy was wrapped. The crowd stood in silence. Henze asked, "Why did you do this, Mrs Trochowski?"

"I didn't want them to find us," she said, "they were following us, everywhere, they searched the cemetery all night only to take away my son. I don't know if they were people or ghosts, but we had to be terribly quiet, but you know Marc is still so small, and so he cried, and didn't want to stop crying. Perhaps he's cold, I thought, because it got really chilly in the morning, so I covered him with the blanket. I wrapped him from head to toe, tighter and tighter, until he wasn't cold anymore. Then he fell asleep. Maybe he understood that they were after us, because all of a sudden he was really quiet. He even stopped breathing so that no one would hear us."

"Come, Mrs Trochowski," said Frieling.

Henze gave her the torch. Then he looked up once more. He would have liked to know, whether from the chimney he could have seen the morning star on the eastern horizon.

Translation by Ann-Kathrin Ehlers.

The Big Switch

A Mike Hammer story

Mickey Spillane & Max Allan Collins

They were going to kill Dopey Dilldocks at midnight the day after tomorrow.

He had shot and wiped out a local narcotics pusher because the guy had passed Dopey a packet of heroin that had been stepped on so many times, it wouldn't take the pain out of a pinprick. The pusher deserved it. Society said Dopey Dilldocks deserved it, too. The jury agreed and the judge laid on the death sentence. All the usual delays had been exhausted, and the law-and-order governor sure as hell wouldn't reprieve a lowlife druggie like Dopey, so the little schmoe's time to fly out of this earthly coop was now.

Nobody was ever going to notice his passing. He was just another jailhouse number – five feet seven inches tall with seven digits stamped on his shirt. On the records his name was Donald Dilbert, but along the path laid out by snorting lines of the happy white stuff, it had gotten shortened and twisted into Dopey Dilldocks.

A week ago his lawyer, a court-assigned one, had written me to say that Mister Dilbert had requested that I be a witness to his execution. And it seemed Dopey also wondered if I might stop in, ASAP, and have a final chat with him before the big switch got thrown.

In the inner office of my P I agency in downtown Manhattan, I handed the letter to Velda, my secretary and right-hand man, if a doll with all that raven hair and a mountain road's worth of curves, could be so described. I was sitting there playing with the envelope absently while she read its contents. When she was done, she frowned and passed the sheet back to me. "Donald Dilbert. . . . You mean that funny little guy who—"

"The same," I said. "The one they called Mr Nobody, and worse."

She frowned in mild confusion. "Mike – he was only a messenger boy. He didn't even work for anybody important, did he?"

"Probably the biggest was Billy Whistler, that photographer over on Sixth Avenue. Hell, I got Dopey that job because the little guy didn't mind running errands at night."

"You know what he did over there?"

"Sure. Took proofs of the late-night photo shoots over to the magazine office."

Velda gave me an inquistive glance.

I shook my head. "No dirty Gertie stuff – Whistler deals with advertising agencies handling big-ticket household items – freezers, stoves, air conditioners, that sort of thing. Not paparazzi crap."

"Big agencies – so little Dopey was getting large pay?"

"Hardly. You said it yourself. He's been around for decades and started a messenger boy and that's how he wound up."

She arched an eyebrow. "Not really, Mike."

"Huh?"

"He wound up a killer. He'll wind up sitting down at midnight."

"Yeah," I nodded. "And not getting up."

She was frowning again. "Messenger boy isn't exactly big bucks, Mike. How could he afford a narcotics habit?"

"They say if you're hooked," I said, "you'll find a way."

"Maybe by dealing yourself?"

"Naw. Dopey doesn't have the brains for it."

"What kind of pusher would give a guy like that credit?"

"Nobody I know," I admitted. "Something stinks about this."

"Coming off in waves. You going to the execution? You thinking of paying him a visit first?" Her voice had a strange tone to it.

My eyes drifted up from the envelope I was fidgeting with and met hers. We both stared and neither of us blinked. I started to say something and stopped. I reached out and took the letter from her fingertips and read it again.

Very simple legalese. The lawyer was simply passing along a request. It was only a job to him. The state would reimburse him for his professional time, which couldn't have been very much.

Before I could say anything, Velda told me, "You haven't done a freebie in a long time."

"Kitten . . ."

"You could make it a tax deduction, Mike."

"Going to an execution?"

"Giving this thing a quick look. Just a couple of days to you, but to Dopey Dilldocks, it's the rest of his life."

I shook my head. "I don't need a deduction. What's gotten into you? The poor slob has been through a trial, he was declared guilty of first-degree murder and now he's paying the penalty."

Very quietly Velda asked, "How do you know it really was first-degree?"

I shook my head again, this time in exasperation. "There was a squib in the paper."

"No," she said insistently. "Dopey didn't even rate a 'squib'. There was an article on narcotics and what strata of society uses them. It gave a range from high-priced movie stars to little nothings like Donald Dilbert, who'd just been found guilty in his murder trial."

"Wasn't a big article," I said lamely.

"No. And Dopey was just a footnote. Still. . . you recognized his name, didn't you?"

I nodded.

"And what did you think?"

"That Dopey had finally come up in the world."

"Baloney. You were thinking, how the hell could Dopey Dilldocks plan and execute a first-degree murder – weren't you?"

She had me and she knew it. For the few times I had used the schlub to run messages, I had gotten to know him just enough to recognize his limitations. He knew the red light that meant stop was on the top and he wouldn't cross the street until the bottom one turned green, and that type of mentality didn't lay out a first-degree kill.

"So?" she asked.

The semblance of a grin was starting to twitch at her lips and she took a deep breath. The way she was built, deep breathing should have had a law against it.

I said, "Just tell me something, doll. You barely know Dopey. You haven't got the first idea of what this is all about. How come you're on his side suddenly?"

"Because I'd give him a couple of bucks to buy me a sandwich for lunch and he'd always bring the change back in the bag. He never stole a cent from me."

"What a recommendation," I said sourly.

"The best," she came back at me. "Besides, we need to get out of this office for a while. It's a beautiful Spring day, the bills are paid, there's money in the bank, nothing's on the platter at the moment and—"

"And we might pass one of those 'Medical Examination, Wedding Ceremony, One Day' places, right?"

"Could be," she said. "Anyway, we could use a day-trip."

"A day-trip where?"

"Some place quiet upstate."

"A little hotel on the river, you mean?"

"That's right."

Sing Sing.

A looker like Velda could have caused a riot in places that didn't consist of concrete and cells, and anyway the court-appointed lawyer could only arrange for one visitor. So she sat in the car in a lot outside the massive stone facility, while I sat in a gray-brick room in one of several cubicles with phones and wire-reinforced glass.

Dopey was a forty-something character who might have been sixty. He had a gray pallor that had been his before he entered the big house, and his runny nose and rheumy eyes spoke of the weed and coke he'd consumed for decades. Smack was never his scene, as his fairly plump frame indicated. His hair, once blond and thick, was white and wispy now, and his face was a chinless, puffy thing.

"I think they musta framed me, Mike," he said. He had a mid-range voice with a hurt tone like a teenage boy who just got the car keys taken away.

My hat was on the little counter. I spoke into the phone, looking at his pitiful puss. "And you want me to pry if off of you, Dopey? You might have given me more notice."

"I know. I know." Phone to his ear, shaking his head, he had the demeanor of a guy in a confessional. Too bad I wasn't in the sin-forgiving game.

"So why now, Dopey?"

"I just been thinking, Mike. I been going back through my whole life. They say it flashes through your brain, right before you die? But I been going through my life, one crummy photo at a time."

I sat forward. "Is that a figure of speech, Dopey? Or are you getting at something?"

Dopey swallowed thickly. "I never gave nobody no trouble, Mike. I never did crime, not even for my habit. I worked hard. Double shifts. Never made no enemies. I'm a nobody like they used to call me, just a damn inanity."

He meant nonentity, but I let it go.

"So you been thinking," I said. "What have you been thinking?"

"I think it all goes back to me sending that photo to LaSalle."

"LaSalle? You don't mean *Governor* LaSalle?"

The chinless head bobbed. "About six months ago, I ran across this undeveloped roll of film. It was in a yellow envelope marked Phi U 'April Fool's Party'."

Where the hell was this going?

"I remembered that night. Up at Solby College? It was wild. Lots of kids partying – girls with their tops off. Crazy."

"When was this?"

"Twenty years ago – April first, like I said. I was taking pictures all over the frat house. They was staging stuff – lots of fake murders and suicides and crazy stuff right out of a horror movie."

"And you got shots of some of that?"

Dopey's head bobbed again. "I was going around campus taking oddball pictures. I even got some 'peeper' type shots through a sorority house window, where this girl was undressing – then this guy pretends to strangle her. It was very real-looking. Frankly, it scared me silly, it was so real-looking."

"Is that why you didn't develop the film?"

"No, the frat guys never paid me, so I said screw it. But when I ran across that roll of film, I don't know why, I just remembered how pretty that girl was – the one that played at getting strangled? She had her top off and . . . well, I can develop my own pics, you know."

"And you did?"

"I did, Mike. And the guy doing the pretend strangling? He looked just like a young version of Governor LaSalle! So I sent it to him."

I thought my eyes would pop out of my skull. "You *what*?"

"Just as a joke. I thought he might get a kick out of it, the resemblance."

I squinted at the goofy little guy. "Be straight with me, Dopey – you didn't try to blackmail him with that, did you?"

"No! I didn't think it was *really* him – just looked like him."

My stomach was tight. "What if it really was him, Dopey? And what if that wasn't an April Fool's stunt you snapped?"

Dopey swallowed again and nodded. "That was what started me thinking, Mike. That's why I hoped you might come see me."

"You told your lawyer about this?"

"No! How do I know I could trust him? He works for the state, too, don't he?"

But he trusted me. This pathetic little doper trusted me to get him out of a jam only an idiot could get into.

Well, maybe I was an idiot, too. Because I told him I'd look into it, and to keep his trap shut till he heard from me next.

"When will that be, Mike?"

"It won't be next week," I said, and got my hat and went.

Our jaunt upstate didn't last long. I called Captain Pat Chambers of Homicide from the road and he was waiting at our favorite little deli restaurant, down the block from the Hackard Building. Pat was in a back booth working on a soft drink and some fries. We slid in opposite him.

The NYPD's most decorated officer wore a lightweight gray suit that went with the gray eyes that had seen way too much – probably too much of me, if you asked him.

"Okay," he said, with no hellos, just a nod to Velda, "what are you getting me into now?"

"Nothing. You found something?"

Those weary eyes slitted, and this time his nod was for me. "Twenty years ago, April second, a coed from Solby College was found strangled, dumped on a country road."

"And nobody got tagged for it?"

"No. There were some stranglings on college campuses back then – mostly in the midwest – and this one got lumped in as one of the likely unsolved murders that went along with the rest."

"Didn't they catch that guy?"

"Yeah. He rode Old Sparky in Nebraska. But the Solby College murder, he never copped to."

"Interesting."

"Is it?" Pat sat forward. "Mike, do I have to tell you there's no statute of limitations on murder? That no murder case is truly ever closed till somebody falls? If you *have* something . . ."

"I do have something."

"What, man?"

"A hunch."

The gray eyes closed. He loved me like a brother, but he could hate me the same way. "Mike . . . do I have to give you the speech again?"

"No. I got it memorized. Tell me about Governor LaSalle."

The eyes snapped open. Pat looked at Velda for help and didn't get any. "You start with a twenty-year-old murder, chum, and then you ask about. . . . What do you *mean*, tell me about Governor LaSalle?"

"He got elected as a law-and-order guy. How's he doing?"

Pat waved that off. "I stay out of politics."

"Which is why you been on the force since Jesus was a baby and still aren't an inspector. What's the skinny on the Gov?"

His voice grew hushed. "You've heard the stories."

"Have I?"

"I can't say anything more."

"Then you can't confirm that an Internal Affairs investigation into the Governor's relationship with a high-end prostitution ring got shut down because of political pressure?"

"No."

"Can you deny it?"

"No."

"What *can* you tell me, buddy?"

He stared at the soft drink like he was trying to will it into a beer. Then, very quietly, he said, "The word is, our esteemed governor is a sex addict. He uses State Patrol Officers as pimps. It's a lousy stinking disgrace, Mike, but it's not my bailiwick. Or yours."

"What about the rumors that he has a little sex shack upstate? A little cabin in the mountains where he meets with female constituents?"

Pat's grin was pretty sick. "That's impossible, Mike. Our governor's a happily married man."

Then Pat stopped a waitress and asked for a napkin. She gave him one, and Pat scribbled something on it, something fairly detailed. Then he folded the napkin, gave it to me, and slipped out of the booth.

"Get the check, Mike," he said, and was gone.

Velda frowned over at me curiously. "What is it?"

"Directions."

This time I took the drive upstate alone, much to Velda's displeasure. But she knew not to argue, when I said I had something to do that I didn't want her part of.

The shade-topped drive dead-ended at a gate, but I pulled over into the woods half a mile before I got there. I was in a black t-shirt and black jeans with the .45 on my hip, not in its usual shoulder sling. The night was cool, the moon was full and high, and ivory touched the leaves with a picture-book beauty. An idyllic Spring night, if you weren't sitting on Death Row waiting for your last tomorrow.

It was a cabin, all right, logs and all, but probably bigger than what Old Abe grew up in – a single floor with maybe four or five rooms. Out front a lanky state trooper was having a smoke. Maybe I was reading in, but he seemed disgusted, whether with himself or his lot in life, who knows?

I spent half an hour making sure that trooper was alone. It seemed possible another trooper or two might be walking the perimeter, but security was limited to that one bored trooper. And that cruiser of his was the only vehicle. I had expected the Governor to have his own wheels, but I'd been wrong.

Positioned behind a nice big rock with trees at my back, I watched for maybe fifteen minutes – close enough that no binoculars were needed – before the Governor himself, in a purple smoking jacket and silk pajamas right out of Hefner's closet, exited with a petite young woman on his arm. He was tall and white-haired and handsome in a country club way. She was blonde and very curvy, in a blue halter top and matching hot pants. If she was eighteen, I was thirty.

At first I thought she had on a lot of garish make-up, then I got a better look and realized she had a bloody mouth and one of her eyes was puffy and black.

The bastard had been beating her!

She was carrying not a purse but a wallet – clutched in one hand like the lifeline it was, a pro doing business with rough trade like the Gov – and her gracious host gave her a little peck on the check. Then he took her by the arm and passed her to the trooper like a beer they were sharing.

I could hear most of what LaSalle said to his trooper/pimp. "Take Miss So-and-So home, and come pick me up. I want to be back at the mansion by midnight."

The trooper nodded dutifully, opened the rear of the cruiser like the prostie was a suspect not a colleague, and then they were off in a crunch of gravel and puff of dust.

There was a back door and opening it with burglar picks took all of twenty seconds. The Gov wasn't much on security. I came in through a small kitchen, where you could hear a shower on in a nearby bathroom.

That gave me the luxury of getting the lay of the land, but there wasn't much to see. The front room had a fireplace with a mounted fish over it and a couch and an area to watch TV and a little dining area. I spent most of my time poking around in his office, which had a desk and a few file cabinets, and a comfortable wood-and-cushions chair off by a window. That's where I was sitting, .45 in hand, when he came in only in his boxer shorts, toweling his white hair.

He looked pudgy and vaguely dissipated, and he didn't see me at first.

In fact, I had to chime in with, "Good evening, Governor. Got a moment for a taxpayer?"

He dropped the towel like it had turned to flame. He wheeled toward me, his ice-blue eyes wide, though his brow was furrowed.

"What the hell . . . *who* the hell . . .?"

"I'm Mike Hammer," I said. "Maybe you heard of me."

Now he recognized me.

"Good God, man," he said. "What are you doing here?"

"I was in the neighborhood. Go ahead. Sit at your desk. Make yourself comfortable. We need to talk."

His shower must have been hot, because his doughy flesh had a red cast. But the red in his face had nothing to do with needles of water.

"There's a trooper on his way back here right now," the Governor said.

"Yeah, but he has to drop your date off first. Tell me, was that shiner and bloody mouth all of it? Or would I find whip marks under that halter top?"

He had gone from startled to indignant in about a second. Now he made a similar trip from indignant to scared. I waved the gun, and he padded over to the desk and got settled in his leather chair.

"What is this," he said, "a shakedown?"

"You mean, lowlife PI stakes out sex-addict governor and tries for a quick kill? Maybe. Your family has money. Your wife's family has more."

He sighed. The ice-blue eyes were more ice than blue. "You have a reputation as a hard-ass, Hammer. But I don't see you as a blackmailer. Who hired you? One of these little chippies? Some little tramp get a little more than she bargained for? Then she should've picked another trade."

"You know, they been talking about you running for president. You really think you can keep a lid on garbage like this?"

He gestured vaguely. "I can reach in my desk drawer and get a check book, and write you out a nice settlement for your client, and another for you, and we'll forget this happened. I just want your guarantee there will be no . . . future payments."

I shifted a little. The .45 was more casual in my hand now. "I have a client, all right, Gov. His name is Dopey Dilldocks."

He frowned. "Your *client* is a murderer."

"No, Gov. You are. My client is an imbecile who thought you might be amused by what he thought was a gag photo taken years ago, involving either you or more likely some college kid with a resemblance to you. But that was no gag – you really strangled that girl. You hadn't quite got a grip, let's say, on your habit, your sick little sex hobby."

The big bare-chested white-haired man leaned forward. "Hammer, that's nonsense. If this is true, where *are* these supposed photos?"

"Oh, hell. Your boys cleaned up on that front right after you framed Dopey. You've got underworld connections, like so many law-and-order frauds. You can't maintain a sadistic habit like yours without high friends in low places – you're tied in with the call girl racket on its uppermost levels, right?"

"You don't know what you're talking about, Hammer."

I stood. I was smiling. I wouldn't have wanted to be on the other end of that smile, but it was a smile.

"Look, Gov – I'm not after blackmail money. All I want is a phone call from the governor."

He frowned up at me. "What?"

"You've seen the old movies." I pointed at the fat phone on his desk. "You're going to call the warden over at Sing Sing, and you are going to tell him that you have reason to believe Donald Dilbert aka Dilldocks is innocent, and you are issuing the prisoner a full pardon."

"Isn't that easy, Hammer . . ."

"It's just that easy. Then you're calling the Attorney General and inform her that you've made that call, and that the pardon is official."

And that's what he did. Under the barrel of my .45, but he did it. And he was a good actor, like so many politicians. He didn't tip it – sounded sincere as hell.

When he'd hung up after his conversation with the Attorney General, he said, "What now?"

I came around behind the desk and stood next to the seated LaSalle. "Now you get a piece of paper out of your desk drawer. I want this in writing."

His face seemed to relax. "All right, Hammer. If I pardon Dilldocks, this ends here?"

"It will end here."

He nodded, the ice-blues hooded, his silver hair catching moonlight through the window behind him. He reached in his bottom-right hand drawer and came back with the .22 revolver and he fired it right at me.

The click on the empty cylinder made him blink.

Then my .45 was in his face. "I took the liberty of removing that cartridge, when I had a look around in here. Lot of firearms accidents at home, you know."

My left hand came around, gripped his right hand clutching the .22, and swung the barrel around until he was looking cross-eyed at it.

"But there's another slug waiting, Gov," I said, "should the need arise."

And my hand over his hand, my finger over his finger, squeezed the trigger. A bullet went in through his open mouth and the inside of his head splattered the window behind him, blotting out the moon.

"Some sons of bitches," I said to the suicide, "just don't deserve a reprieve."

[Co-author's note: I expanded a fragment in Mickey's files of what might have been intended as a first chapter into this short story, utilizing his plot notes. M.A.C.]

Hitching in the *Lodos*

Feryal Tilmaç

Perhaps all of this still would have happened, even if the city hadn't been caught up in the tempestuous *lodos* that night. But the truth is, that frantic wind, spinner of its own mysteries, provided justifiable motive for transgression. Strange, droning, lukewarm, the *lodos* keeps in its thrall not only the city, but the souls of its people as well. And Cavidan Altan was one of those people. Perhaps what would occur later hadn't even remotely crossed her mind when she left home that day. I say "perhaps," because we can never know for sure what's on a woman's mind. Now, I could pretend that I knew, but I don't want to taint the authenticity of the story by adding to it something I'm not sure about. We can safely assume the same about Tolga Güçel, and say that he, too, never would have guessed that he would experience the things he did that evening, or any other evening, for that matter.

Tolga is a computer engineer in his thirties. A few years ago, he left the company he had been working for to start his own business with a friend. They install data processing systems for companies and provide support services and solutions. Of course, he is an intelligent man – he must be, right? He's a person of high moral standards and principles, a man who likes to do things by the book. He's not married, but he has a girlfriend, a woman he met at his last job. They share a home, though theirs is a constant rollercoaster of break-up and make-up. Yes, that's right, yet another case of passion's demise and habitual routine on the rise! He works in Gayrettepe, lives in Etiler. On the evening in question, in spite of the heavy end-of-the-year workload, he had managed to leave early, thinking he might stop by Akmerkez on his way home and buy a New Year's gift for his girlfriend.

A white cashmere sweater, an elegant laptop bag, or a bottle of perfume – he was still undecided. But then, what difference does it make anyway? Considering that, ultimately, he would buy none of these.

That evening on his way home from work, as he passed Zincirlikuyu and made a right onto the road to Levent, he was listening to the radio program *Women Sing Jazz*. "*Dear listeners, we continue with Ethel Waters' 'Stormy Weather'* . . ." There couldn't have been a more fitting selection. He tapped along on the steering wheel. The invasive wind whistled and shook the colored lights on the trees. Who knows, maybe everything would have panned out in another way if the weather had been different; say, if it had been snowing. After all, the New Year spirit calls for snow; and for love, hope, new beginnings, packages of presents, angels hanging on trees, the cinnamon-spiced scent of mulled wine. But it didn't happen, it didn't snow. Instead, a crazy, wayward wind kept the area convulsing for days on end, making the city slave to its whim. Though the majority suffered only mild headaches and a little shortness of breath in its aftermath, at the time, melancholy ran like a viscous liquid through the streets.

Tolga, for his part, did something he never would have done otherwise: Compelled by the sorrowful music and the feeling of benevolence that the New Year's spirit aroused, he pulled up to the curb, where a woman with shopping bags was trying to flag down a taxi. The woman, Cavidan Hanım, had just finished her shopping at the mall in Levent. On the window behind her, *2007* was written in cotton balls, and adorned with wreaths of mistletoe, yellow, green, and red lights, gold-lacquered pine-cones, and red stars. She was a woman of a certain maturity; she held her hand in front of her face as she tried to protect herself from the wind. Perhaps hitching a ride wasn't her intention at all. Still, when she stooped and saw Tolga, she opened the back door, dropped her bags in the car, and settled onto the passenger seat without hesitation. Obviously she was cold, otherwise why on earth would she have plunged headlong into a stranger's car, especially at that hour?

While we were in Tolga's car, making our way from Levent to Gayrettepe, Cavidan Hanım was checking off items on her shopping list. She had bought a different washing detergent, something other than her usual brand, because it came with a free

bottle of fabric softener. The thin peel of the tangerines had not
been to her taste, and so she picked up some oranges and a few
green apples instead. A bag of sliced whole-wheat bread, tahini
halva, and petit beurre biscuits. Aged *kaşar* cheese, napkins, and
ginger for the New Year's cookies she was planning to bake. In
a last-minute dash, she had added olive oil, clotted cream, and
fresh walnuts to her cart at the checkout. She realized that she
couldn't possibly carry those heavy bags all the way home, and
so she had decided to wait for a cab. It should therefore come as
no surprise that she jumped into the car as soon as Tolga stopped.
He's young enough to be my son, she might have thought as she got
into the car. I'm not sure if I told you: Tolga has the kind of face
that puts even the most jittery of people at ease.

As soon as she was in the car, Cavidan Hanım removed her
beret and scarf. She swung her hips left and then right, settling
into the seat and making herself comfortable. She also made sure
to turn and take a good look at Tolga. He was a young man with
a fair complexion, clean shaven, with longish brown hair and
glasses perched on an arched nose. Cavidan Hanım didn't know
much about automobiles, but still, judging from the smell of fresh
leather rising from the black seats and the wooden details of the
dashboard, this had to be a luxury car. Her savior, she guessed,
was probably a successful young businessman. He must have
been at least twenty years younger than her; Cavidan wondered
if he was married. She glanced to see if he had a ring on his
left hand, but her view was blocked. Tolga's fingers had stopped
tapping and now clung to the steering wheel. If it hadn't been so
dark inside, she could have seen how white his knuckles were.
Wishing she were at least ten years younger, Cavidan Hanım let
out a sigh. Fortunately, it was drowned out by the sound of the
radio. "*Dear jazz fans, our program continues with Billie Holiday:
'Long Gone Blues'* . . ."

Tolga's fingers relaxed and started tapping again. "So you're a
jazz fan," Cavidan Hanım said, in an attempt to make conversation.
Tolga looked at her for the first time, smiled, nodded, and then
turned his attention back to the road. "If you drop me off in front
of Akmerkez, I can walk from there." A sudden gush of wind rattled
the windshield, and shook the car even, or so it seemed to them.

"With all those bags? Out of the question! I'll drive you to your
door."

The young man's polite, soft-spoken manner emboldened the woman. "I love going to the shore and watching the sea during the *lodos*. How about you?"

Oh no! thought Tolga to himself, wishing to rein the conversation back in. But he didn't let on. "I don't know, I never have."

As a veteran school teacher, Cavidan Hanım knew a thing or two about human psychology. This young man was clearly a victim of politeness, one of those poor souls incapable of saying no. "I'm an English teacher," she continued. "Could I possibly have had you in my class? You look familiar." She didn't mention that she was retired. She had read somewhere that the word "retired" immediately killed any spark. It reminded one of the smell of dust, wool underwear, weatherproof socks, dentures leisurely soaking in a glass at night . . .

"Oh please, I really don't think you're old enough to have been my teacher!" So she was a teacher; he should be more respectful.

Cavidan Hanım's tiny giggle drowned out the sorrowful notes coming from the radio. "Thank you, that's the nicest thing anyone's said to me in a long time."

They were in front of Akmerkez now. Tolga slowed down. A brass band was playing a merry dance tune. *Post Brass Band* was written on their red jackets. Was that what encouraged Cavidan Hanım? "How about going to the seaside? If you have time, that is."

The young man thought he must have misheard her. Cymbals were clashing, countless sticks were banging on drums, and a trumpet blared proudly, as the band battled the bellowing of the *lodos*. Is that what confused Tolga? "Do you have a certain place in mind?"

Cavidan Hanım gladly shut the door she had been reluctantly holding ajar. "Yes, drive straight ahead; let's go down the Bebek Slope." The jolly tunes of the brass band gradually faded away. "Cavidan," she said. It was a strange meeting, but she didn't care; she extended her hand.

"Tolga," he responded. It would be rude not to shake her hand; he realized his palms were sweaty and felt embarrassed.

The car jerked and jolted, making slow progress in the bumper-to-bumper traffic. Etiler, with its colorful, bright cafés, restaurants, and stores lining the avenue, was drowning out even the noise of the lodos.

"Would you stop at that corner?" Cavidan Hanım hopped out with the agility of a young girl, ducked into a liquor store, and returned with a black plastic bag full of beer cans.

Surprised, the young man remained optimistic. *Maybe she's planning on drinking them at home tonight,* he thought. *Maybe she's expecting guests.* He made a left turn and drove down the slope. If he hadn't turned, he could have seen his girlfriend buying flowers from a stand by the corner one street down; after all, their place was just a stone's throw away. The slope was completely dark, except for the headlights of passing cars and the blinking New Year's ornaments on the walls of the houses.

Cavidan Hanım took the sights in with a happy smile on her face. All kinds of fantasies played out in her head as she watched the dark retaining walls flow by. *All things considered,* she thought, *I'm lucky to live in this city.*

Tolga was uneasy. He had gone beyond the call of courtesy, and besides, what would he say if his girlfriend called? He could turn off his phone and tell her something like, *I was in Akmerkez, the reception was bad,* but that was hardly believable. His inner voice nagged away at him. (He was right, his girlfriend was worried. She had called his office, and they'd told her he'd already left. She'd thought about calling his cell a few times, and she almost did, and in the end, she would certainly call. Where would a grown man disappear to for so many hours?) And as if all that weren't enough already, Ella Fitzgerald had launched into another song: "Baby, Won't You Please Come Home?"

They hit traffic again once they reached the shore. The car slowed down. "Turn left, toward Asiyan." Cavidan Hanım seemed to be in total control now. She cracked open a can of beer for herself. "Sorry, *you're* driving." At that moment, the young man felt certain this was all just one big nightmare. His knuckles were visibly white, even in the dim light. Truth of the matter was, though, this was only the beginning – he had no idea what was in store for him.

The car obediently cruised forward toward their destination. The young man turned and stopped in front of Bebek Park. Just like every evening, the Bebek meatball vendor was setting up his stand in his white minivan, in spite of the contrary weather. Cavidan Hanım took advantage of their time in stalled traffic to look around, and she did so with gusto. It was crowded, as usual;

even in this weather, all the benches in the park were occupied. Cavidan Hanım took a sizable sip from her beer; it had a sour, acidic taste, and she shivered a little as she swallowed. She reached for the bags on the backseat and took out a package: fresh walnuts. She silently congratulated herself; a prescient last-minute purchase, as it were. This time she offered some to her companion. The traffic stirred a little. They barely made it past the taxi stand in front of the Bebek Café when they had to stop again. The *lodos* did not seem to have impacted the hotel or the seafood restaurants here one bit. The valets were constantly stopping traffic to make way for the cars of customers coming and going. Tolga was quietly eating the walnuts Cavidan Hanım kept offering to him, after removing their delicate shells. She was sure no one had skinned or shelled or peeled anything for this boy and handed it to him, ready to eat, since he was a kid. Now he was smiling too. Finally, the valet impatiently motioned for them to drive on through. "*Dear listeners, how about another tune from Ethel Waters? The woman says it ain't her fault – she's just living her life! That's right, Ethel Waters here and 'Don't Blame Me' . . .*"

They passed Bebek Hotel, Starbucks, Divan Bakery, and then the grocery store. Even if the whole world were to go haywire, the colorful fruit-packed trays of that grocery store would be enough to restore the illusion that everything was A-OK. Cavidan Hanım, turning to her right, pointed to the olive oil specialty shop and asked: "Have you ever shopped there?"

"No," said Tolga, laughing.

Brightly lit windows, the headlights of standing cars, people going in and out of restaurants and liquor stores on both sides all blended together into one big blur; a single, gigantic organism quivering in the wind. They stopped again, where the waterfront houses ended and the sea began. The coats and the scarves of people crossing the avenue were flying in the wind. An old man laughed as he pressed down on his fedora. *Now* that's *a retiree*, Cavidan Hanım thought. She was happy, giddy; she'd never felt younger. The whistle of the *lodos* blew in one window and out the other.

An increasingly contented Tolga pointed to a man selling fish on the shore. "Beautiful, isn't it? How bright and colorful they are, even in this weather . . . Do you like fish?" he asked.

Cavidan Hanım looked at the round wooden trays on the stand and the neat rows of pink, white, and silvery fish displayed on them. Lamps and bundles of garlic suspended from the poles above the vendors' carts swung to and fro in the wind. The fish seller was sprinkling water on lettuce, garden cress, radishes, and lemons. "Yes, I do. I like it a lot, in fact. And how about you? Do you like snapper soup? Red snapper? I should make it for you someday."

"My mom makes delicious snapper soup." As soon as the words came out of his mouth, the young man knew he had said something wrong; he clammed up.

Cavidan Hanım pretended she hadn't heard him. What was the point of embarrassing the poor boy? He already regretted having said it anyway. "I just learned how to make it. But Pygmy loves it."

Curious, Tolga asked: "Pygmy?"

"My cat. She loves my snapper soup." She laughed again. "She's so black, I bet you'd be scared of her if you saw her in the dark; she walks around like a pair of bodiless green eyes."

"Come on, why would I be afraid? I'm sure she's adorable . . ."

Beaten black-and-blue by the wind, the sea churned and foamed. The bus in front of them let out a hiss as it lurched forward, and they followed. Launched from the terrace of one of the seafront houses, an umbrella, a remnant from summer, blew over the road and toward the water. Spared, by the grace of God! The incident brought them closer; it was that special affinity shared by people who have survived an accident together. Just then the young man's cell phone started ringing.

"What's that, Pınar? . . . Yes, I left early, I had a few errands . . . To Akmerkez . . . To buy a present for Mom . . . Unbelievable . . . I couldn't find anything . . . What's that? . . . Pınar, can I call you a little later? I can't hear you . . ." He felt obliged to offer an explanation: "My girlfriend."

Cavidan Hanım found an excuse for joy in this revelation; so he wasn't married after all! "She was worried, I suppose. I can't blame her, I'd be worried about you too." Was that a spark of desire she saw in his eyes? No, it couldn't be, she must be mistaken.

"Should we keep going? Is there any particular place you'd like to stop?" For the first time in his life he felt the comfort of being with an assertive woman, a woman in charge, a woman who made decisions for him. But then, there were many firsts in store for him that evening. Feeling submissive to the core, he waited for an answer.

"There's a parking lot by the water, across from the graveyard. Let's go there. It's always deserted after dark." The traffic abated. She unzipped the jacket of her jogging suit a little further, just to get some air. The medallion hanging from her neck glinted for a brief second, catching the young man's eye; Cavidan Hanım promptly took notice. The *lodos* was blowing through the giant trees along the roadside.

Now that they had left the noisy traffic behind, the sound of the radio came to the fore: "*We've reached the end of tonight's program, dear listeners. We leave you until tomorrow – same time, same place – with Lena Horne and 'Mad about the Boy' . . .*"

Cavidan Hanım felt a tingling in her loins. Don't tell me to give you a break; I'm a human being, and I know human beings have a tendency to lose it every now and then. Actually, it was pretty understandable. She'd never really had much of a sex life, other than a few rather tasteless flings with colleagues, and that was so far in the past now, her conspirators had faded into pale ghosts of her imagination. And throughout those long years, whenever she attempted to satisfy the urges of her body by herself, leaning against the cold walls of her shower stall, it wasn't those inadequate lovers but her male students that she fantasized about. She loved the way they smelled so fresh, how their voices still cracked, their unruly attitudes, and their black-haired arms peeking out from rolled-up sleeves; she loved it all, at least as much as she loved this city. She threw her head back, draining the can of beer in her hand. She'd grown silent, perhaps out of shame for her thoughts.

Tolga slowed down next to the cemetery, turned on his right-turn signal, and then parked by the water. The headlights illuminated the sea one last time before going out; the seagulls, caught in the circles of light, flitted about the sky like giant snowflakes.

"I can have a beer now, too, can't I?"

Without breaking her silence, Cavidan Hanım reached down into the black plastic bag next to her foot. She took out a can, opened it, and handed it to the young man. She had avoided his eyes. The jazz program ended, and Tolga switched the radio off. For a while, they just sat there, listening to the wind howling wildly.

I keep referring to the wind, I know, and perhaps you find it annoying, but there's no way around it, because for me it's the main character of the story. It was bolting through the sky in fits of madness, lunging down and surging back up, sending shivers through the evening lights, absorbing the familiar sounds of the city into its own roar. It dried lips, hurled anything and everything that failed to match its strength, weighed down upon souls, made skin crawl. Tolga sipped on his beer, contemplating Cavidan Hanım's profile, while she contemplated the seagulls lowering themselves toward the sea. One wonders what was on their minds just then. But then, it's not hard to guess. Perhaps a jumble of thoughts coursed through Tolga's mind—how he could possibly explain this delay to his girlfriend; his eleventh grade English teacher; the fact that he had to buy a present for his mother; how awful it would be to be out at sea in this weather; whether or not Cavidan Hanım's medallion was in fact a locket, and if there was a picture in it; his girlfriend again; his mother again; even the project he'd turned in that day, and the likelihood of its success. Though these may not have been his exact thoughts, they were certainly something along those lines. He didn't try to focus on anything in particular, and that was comforting to him somehow.

He leaned back in his seat, took a big gulp from his beer, and got lost in thought again. He was back to pondering the matter of the presents; in fact, he was on the verge of actually making a decision. And he would have, for sure, if only he hadn't felt Cavidan Hanım's hand settle onto his crotch just then. At least he had finally eliminated the perfume, narrowing his options down to two: either the laptop bag or the cashmere sweater.

"Do you mind if I touch you?" she asked nonchalantly, as though asking if she could roll down the window. Moreover, she went ahead and began unzipping the young man's pants, without even waiting for an answer. And unzip them she did.

Tolga looked in amazement at the fingers pulling at his boxer shorts. *Would it be rude to ask her to take her hands off of me?* he wondered. His manhood, though, growing beneath the woman's touch, was betraying him. But she just wanted to feel around a little, right? It was hardly the end of the world now, was it? He slid down a little, made himself more comfortable. The woman's hand was brushing over the heat of his flesh; she had lowered her head and was scrutinizing the thing in her hands with the curiosity of a child observing an insect. Tolga grew uneasy and glanced around. There wasn't another person or car in sight. He tried not to think about the cemetery that extended up the hill on the other side of the road. He cleared his throat and, in a voice he thought sounded normal, asked, "Would you like me to turn on the radio?"

"Oh yes," said Cavidan Hanım, "but find another jazz program, will you?" She lowered her head and began stroking him again, picking up where she'd left off.

His hands shaking, the young man turned the radio on and tuned in to a jazz station. The sound of a rebellious, unrepentant saxophone filled the car. Had to be John Coltrane.

At that moment, Cavidan Hanım lowered her head further and took the young man's penis into her mouth. I know, it sounds almost pornographic when I put it like this, but these things are just a part of life, they come so naturally. And as long as I'm telling you the whole story, why should I succumb to puritanical pressures and skip the details? Okay, so what was Cavidan Hanım thinking all this time? Well, first of all, she was wondering why on earth she had never done this before, and thinking how many more things there were that she had never done before, and how the world was just full of things she had never done before . . . She was intrigued by the taste; he must be a clean man, she thought, because she couldn't detect even the faintest scent of urine. Curious, with the tip of her tongue she touched the clear fluid oozing from the tip of the penis; perhaps it was due to the aftertaste of beer in her mouth, but she found it to be rather sour. She cleansed her tongue on the shaft of the young man's manhood, which was as hard as it could possibly get by now. Its skin, wrinkled at first, was now stretched tight, as if a larva inside was struggling to escape.

Tolga placed his can next to the gear-shift. His hands were in the woman's black hair now.

Cavidan Hanım raised her head and peered up at him. Ignoring the pressure gently pushing down on her head, she sat up. She slipped out of her jogging pants with some difficulty, as she wasn't used to doing this sort of thing. Bodies always seemed to grow larger inside cars, somehow. She kicked off her shoes, letting them drop next to the black plastic bag. She tugged on her panties until she'd peeled herself free. The rebellious notes of John Coltrane mingling with the whistle of the wind and merging with their wetness, Cavidan Hanım climbed onto the young man's lap. She carefully gripped his manhood and placed it between her legs.

For Cavidan Hanım, the young man ceased to exist. For her, there were only the seagulls, radiant against the blackness of the night, the strokes of blue and gray against the canvas of pitch black waters, the sea in its bubbling turbulence, the hell of the *lodos*. She didn't notice how Tolga reached and unzipped her top and removed it. Only when he reached around for the clasp of her bra did she move to help him. She had only her socks and her medallion on now. Her breasts, made soft by time, sagging, defeated by the pull of gravity, lunged forward with yearning and met the young man's mouth. She was rising and falling; she was taking the whole city in. This wasn't an ordinary coupling. She imagined the city's skyline, and went mad with desire. The manhood between her legs was every skyscraper of the city, symbolic bastions of power with blue-tinted windows, and crowns disappearing into heavy, low-lying clouds. That manhood was every intricate street she loved to stroll through, from Beyoğlu to Tünel. As she rose and fell, she whispered Istanbul's name. The young man held onto her hips tightly, trying to help her keep her rhythm. That manhood was the winter evenings falling early on the city, the smell of roasted chestnuts, smog, happy lights of domestic bliss, dim street-lamps, bright signs, decorated trees, shopping centers, polished, shiny, illuminated a thousand and one different ways. "Istanbul." She repeated the word faster and faster. That manhood was all the city's markets with their endless spice displays, delicatessens bulging with *pastırma, sucuk*, wheels of kaşar cheese, bluefish with bloody gills lying on red trays, the vivacious hues of quinces, pomegranates, and dates; tangerines, grapefruits, oranges sold from flatbed trucks, baskets of strawberries sold by the roadside, just right for making jam; the first plums of the season, still green and crunchy in wheelbarrows; green, unripe almonds, yellow and red cherries, again pomegranates, again quinces ... tangerines ... oranges ... Cavidan Hanım let out a subdued scream and collapsed onto the young man. Perhaps she couldn't take it anymore when the warm liquid squirted out of the young man and into her. After all, we're talking about years and years of loneliness, which is easier said than experienced – and not even that easy to say. Supermarkets, convenience stores, butchers, neighborhood markets; bought, sold, cooked. Yarn shops, button shops, haberdasheries; Nişantaşi, Şişli, Osmanbey; bought, sold, knit. TV game shows, entertainment programs, bedlam, bacchanals, emotion-commerce, TV series, movies, distant countries filling one with longing, romance, sorrows, lovemaking of others, watched, until one goes numb. Loneliness is a hard business, known only by those who experience it. Has someone said that before? A sentence so trivial, anybody could have said it. But on a New Year's Eve, an evening in the *lodos*, in a dark park by the shore, in the cramped heat of a car with leather seats, with the seagulls dipping down and rising above the water, and the wind relentlessly battering the windows, in the extension, so alive, of a body, so fresh, loneliness could very well be killed.

Cavidan Hanım was lying on top of Tolga, motionless. Tolga stirred uneasily. "Cavidan Hanım?" No answer. This whole encounter had taken on a rather unexpected shape, granted, but even so, this dose of romanticism was a bit too much for Tolga. He tried to right himself without disturbing Cavidan Hanım. "Thank you." It sounded so raw, he thought, once the words were out of his mouth, but he couldn't think of anything else to say. And besides, the weight of the woman's body was becoming rather annoying. Finally, he became aware of the unsettling quiet. "Cavidan Hanım?" She wasn't breathing. An ice-cold shiver went down Tolga's spine. It just couldn't be, no one could possibly be that unlucky. "Cavidan Hanım?" He stumbled over the words. Just then, his phone, which was lying next to the gearshift, started ringing. He stretched, reaching out as far as the body on top of him allowed: It was Pınar. What if he just didn't answer? He did.

"Hi, sweetie . . . I'm fine, I'm okay . . ." He turned his head, away from the smell of Cavidan Hanım's hair. "Just wanted to get some . . . What's that? . . . Yes, yes, to get some air . . . No . . . I'm upset about some stuff that happened at work, that's all . . . No . . . Okay . . . Okay . . . Yes. Will do . . ." He hung up and took a deep breath. He checked for a pulse. He had to stay calm. He'd tell it exactly the way it happened. They'd believe him. There was nothing not to believe. It could happen. It could have happened. It could happen to anybody. He did his best to control the wave

of panic rising in him, but it was growing too quickly, feeding
off the whistle of the *lodos*, pulling the floor from underneath his
feet. He tried to push Cavidan Hanım off of him. He grabbed her
shoulders and propped her up; her head lolled to one side. In a
final effort, he tried to haul her onto the passenger seat, but his
foot got caught between the seat and the door. He let go of the
body and tried to rescue his foot. At that point, he noticed her
woolen socks. Trying not to gag, he yanked his foot free. Then the
woman's foot got caught on one of the CDs in the door pocket
and sent the CD flying. He deposited Cavidan Hanım's naked
body onto the passenger seat, pulled on his pants, and zipped
up. He was sticky all over. The inside of the car reeked of semen,
but he decided against rolling the window down, with the wind
blowing so forcefully outside. The woman's head first hit the glove
compartment, and then the door. The gearshift stick bruised her
waist. You might think, *Well, what does it matter anyway, now that
she's dead?* It wouldn't matter, of course, if every mark on her
body wasn't later considered evidence of battery. But as you
probably guessed, Tolga wasn't the kind of guy to dump a dead
body – and one which had expired with uncanny timing – on a
pile of wet cold stones and just leave it there, even if it did belong
to someone he didn't know, and even if he would have to pay by
having his own life wrenched to pieces. After all, he had faith in
the justice system.

And then . . .

I won't say what happened next. Not because I don't know,
but because I don't want to bore you any further. Considering
the intimate details I've already provided, I must have heard
all about it from one of the parties involved, and since that
obviously couldn't be Cavidan Hanım (though who knows,
right?), I must have heard it from Tolga. Perhaps I'm Tolga's best
friend, bearer of his secrets, his lawyer, or better yet, perhaps
I'm Tolga himself. If I'm not making all this stuff up, that is.
But what difference does it make anyway? Who says these were
their real names? I probably changed them, right? Especially
since the case still remains to be settled in court! Sharing these
experiences with you – even if I don't actually know you – has,
it seems to me, forged a bond between us. And that bond forces
me to confess: Yes, I changed the names, and I also changed the
professions and the addresses. Unfortunately, these are not real

people except for their genders and ages. The only real thing is that everything unfolded exactly as I have told you. Oh, and the wind! It was every bit as powerful as I have said. Really, what a *lodos* it was!

Translated by Amy Spangler

It's Not True

Diego De Silva

Daniele Dalisi wears his fifty years well, with a ruggedly handsome face that appeals to women inclined to complicate their lives. When he takes off his surgical mask and then the white gown, and meeting Sara's eyes immediately senses her discomfort, the same discomfort that betrayed her at the hospital cafeteria on a Wednesday two and a half years ago, the morning Daniele moved closer to reach for her hand under the table regardless of the people passing by and greeting them, Good morning, Doctor Dalisi, Doctor Vallicelli, while she stared at him appalled and delighted, What on earth are you doing, can't you see they're watching us, and he whispered to her just inches from her mouth, You're trembling, look at yourself, feel my hand, me too; when this moment comes back to him (all they have to do is catch a glimpse of one another, even from opposite ends of the ward, and the bond is tightened before it has even loosened); when acting a role becomes unbearable and he instinctively reciprocates the sense of belonging, convinced that neither of them could ever accept other arms (despite the fact that he has a wife and daughter: Paola's arms, however, though she is his partner in life, have long ago ceased to compete); when this happens, Daniele cannot keep from smiling: like now, when the assistants are so tired that they don't even notice (or, if they do notice, they don't stop and wonder about the intimacy of that smile), unlike the nurse, who as she's gathering up the instruments turns her back and makes a pouting face, because now she's certain of it: there's something going on between the chief surgeon and the young anesthetist whom he so often wants at his side in the operating room.

"You were terrific," Sara tells him softly, moving close to him.

The nurse, just a few steps from them, indulges in a kind of ironic assent which she would probably like the lovers to notice, but Sara and Daniele are too focused on one another to pay any attention to her.

"You too," Daniele replies.

And finally they leave the room.

As they make their way down the hall, they are greeted by nurses, colleagues and patients. Every so often, someone looks at them sideways, disapprovingly. If Campobasso is a small town, the hospital is even smaller.

"Come inside . . . a minute?" Daniele whispers to her a few feet from the door to his office. Sara glances around with a certain discomfiture. "Wouldn't it be better to see each other afterwards?"

"Please."

Sara gives in, flattered by his insistence.

"I always feel I've done so little, after an operation," she remarks, once inside his office. Daniele follows hot on her heels and closes the door.

"Don't be silly," he says. "You're the only one I feel at ease with when I'm operating."

"It's the anonymity complex all anethetists have, you know. We go unnoticed on principle. Nine times out of ten the patient doesn't even know our name."

"And you're complaining? If only you knew how much I'd like to be able to operate incognito."

"You say that because you've never felt overlooked, from that standpoint."

He goes over to her, clearly pretending to continue the conversation, only to change the subject.

"And me?"

"What about you?" she replies, playing along.

"Have I ever overlooked you?"

"I meant professionally."

"I didn't."

Sara is about to let him kiss her when there's a knock at the door.

Daniele goes and sits down at the desk. From the other side of the desk, she begins leafing through the patients' charts.

"Come in."

The door opens.

"Yes, Giovanna?" Daniele looks up.

"Excuse me, Doctor, Rotunno is asking for you," the ward clerk says after acknowledging Sara with a nod.

"Tell him we've just finished in the operating room and we'll be with him shortly," Dalisi replies. He gives Sara a sideways look, almost as if he expected to find her put out.

Not satisfied, the ward clerk lingers in the doorway. "Forgive me, Doctor," she says, somewhat exasperated, "but he hasn't given me a moment's peace all morning."

Sara sighs faintly.

"All right, I'll be right there."

Giovanna breathes easier.

"Thank you, Doctor. You don't know how insistent that guy can be."

"I know," Dalisi attests.

Sara's reproach comes with impeccable timing.

"I don't understand why you're so accommodating."

"It doesn't bother me all that much," he says defensively.

She doesn't say anything more, disappointed by the diplomacy of his remark. Daniele gets up from his chair. "So, are you coming?"

"Actually I'm tired."

"You know he asked me if he could meet you before the operation."

"I'm not required to, am I?"

"I don't get it, first you complain that patients don't even know your name, and now that there's one who wants to meet you, you hesitate?"

Sara stiffens. "It must be that I don't mind the anonymity complex we anesthetists have after all."

"Right," Daniele agrees, as he walks around the desk and goes toward the door, avoiding any contact. "See you tomorrow in the operating room."

"That's it?" Sara says, as he's about to leave the room.

"That's it, what?" Dalisi asks argumentatively.

"Not even 'We'll talk later', or 'I'll see you afterwards'? Just, in the operating room tomorrow?"

"I'm leaving early today," he cuts her off, outright distant now, "Mirella is graduating, I told you."

"You told me."

*   *   *

Carmine Rotunno, approaching sixty, has a sinewy body, coarse features, and small bright eyes that appraise more than just look. Seeing him standing in front of the window in his room, wearing an elegant robe, simply waiting, he appears stronger than his cancer. He doesn't read, doesn't watch TV, doesn't use his cell phone, doesn't leave his room, doesn't have any visitors. He has a battle to face, and he wants to be ready.

Daniele appears annoyed to have answered his summons. "What is it now?"

"I didn't see you today."

"This attitude of yours is beginning to irritate me."

"You have to understand my condition. I have the greatest respect for you."

"No. That's not true."

"So I'm a liar?"

"I don't care what you are, or who you are. I just want you to get off my back."

"I'm a sick man, doctor. I need to see my doctor every day."

"Maybe you haven't noticed, but this place is full of sick people. What do you expect, you think you're the only one I should attend to?"

Rotunno tilts his head a little to one side and raises his eyebrows in a piteous way.

"Do I have to answer that?"

Daniele takes a breath and snaps back: "Listen to me. The operation is tomorrow. I will operate on you with the greatest concentration. But to do that I need to stay calm and not be constantly disturbed. I don't like to operate on patients who make me nervous."

Rotunno's lips twist into a kind of sneer. His beady eyes make a thorough tour of the perimeter of the ceiling, before he replies.

"A good doctor never makes it personal, doctor. Because then if he makes a mistake, the consequences will cost him dearly." Daniele's nostrils flare. He has to make an intense effort to swallow his rage.

There, now he can turn his back and head for the door.

The sharpness of Carmine Rotunno's tone as he calls to him a moment before he goes out has the effect of a conviction notice.

"Doctor."

Daniele turns around. Looks at him.

"You're good, aren't you?"

"So they say."

"And that's the reason I came here. You'll remember it, won't you?" Daniele nods, but holds his gaze.

"One thing."

"Tell me," Rotunno says, all ears.

"Tell those two guys to get away from the entrance to the ward. For visitors, there's a waiting room."

Rotunno hesitates, as if intrigued by the squabble's running into overtime.

"You don't like *them* either, doctor?"

"Even less. Seeing them upsets my nervous system."

"You're easily rattled, doctor."

"Will you get rid of those two, yes or no?"

There's a certain admiration in Rotunno's smile now. He lets the question hang for a few seconds.

"Okay, done."

"Wonderful," Daniele replies with satisfaction.

And finally leaves the room.

Sara is walking across the hospital parking lot toward her car, when she sees Daniele not far away, talking with a man his age, arrogant in appearance, arrogant in style.

She stops.

The man with Daniele gives her a vaguely suggestive look. But only briefly, the time it takes to resume his conversation with Dalisi, which Sara, from that distance, can't hear.

There is a stylish audience in the graduation hall at four in the afternoon. Mirella defends her thesis adeptly. The professors exchange satisfied nods of consent. In the front row, Daniele listens attentively, pleased with his daughter's mastery in dealing with such a classic situation. From time to time, Paola, sitting beside him, takes his hand, moved. Daniele meets her eyes and smiles, thinking how strange it is that he misses Sara so fervently at such a moment. Then he looks at the clock and pictures her wearing the tracksuit that he himself gave her, as she runs, light-footed and luminous, along the gardens of Villa De Capoa, and he seems to see her slow down every so often, or stop, bothered by a recurring thought that won't leave her alone.

In the waiting room outside the operating theater, Rotunno's bodyguards wait in silence. Sara is the first to come out. But her face couldn't be more unsuited to the good news she brings them. She's never been able to stand the sight of those two; all the more reason she wants them to think the opposite.

"Successful," is all she says; and already one of them is moving off down the hall, cell phone pressed to his ear.

After a while, Daniele finds her at a table in the ground floor cafeteria. She seems to be letting the coffee get cold on purpose. He sits down.

"Why didn't you come back in?"

"We were finished, weren't we?"

"You've always waited for me at the end of an operation." Sara remains silent.

"It's over, Sara. He's leaving. Let's forget about it."

Impulsively he covers her hand with his. Realizing his gaffe, he quickly pulls his hand back, as if it had been burned.

"What's the matter, are you ashamed?" Sara asks, in an aggressive outburst.

"What are you talking about," he replies with a pathetic smile.

"Do you think they don't know about us in here? Do you think these things can be kept secret?"

Daniele's features stiffen.

"Lower your voice."

"I'll lower it, I'll lower it," Sara says complying with his request, though the defiant attitude she has assumed doesn't change one iota, "heaven forbid I should cause you any trouble. I'm always on your side, right?"

Daniele swivels his head around. All of a sudden he feels like everyone is looking at them. He gets up from the table.

"I have no intention of staying here and putting up with your nerves."

He turns on his heel and walks away without turning around or slowing down.

Sara follows him with her eyes, and for the first time since she's known him she has the unpleasant impression of having been wrong about him.

When Daniele gets home, Paola and Mirella, still fresh with enthusiasm over the graduation, both welcome him at the door. They have no gifts, nothing to offer him but themselves.

With his daughter's arms around his neck, Daniele finds himself wondering whatever happened to the time when this was all he wanted, and where had he been, when those days ended.

Mirella's cell phone rings in the back pocket of her jeans. She pulls it out, reads the name on the display, and announces it as if it were a higher priority.

"It's Federico."

"The party's over for daddy," Daniele says, resigned.

Paola smiles.

Mirella smacks a kiss on her father's forehead and walks off down the hall, head over heels. Daniele takes off his jacket.

"When does he leave?" Paola asks.

"Tuesday."

"Isn't it too soon?"

"He'll assume the responsibility."

"So much the better."

"Right. Shall we eat?"

"What's wrong?"

"Nothing, why?"

"You look like you just came from the accountant."

"Ha, ha, very funny."

"Will you tell me what's wrong?"

"You know what."

"No. It's not just the operation. There's something else."

"I'm just tired."

Sara is preparing her meal with slow, disjointed gestures. She feels like she's thinking in slow motion. She knows there's something wrong inside, she's acknowledged it. She knows there's nothing to be done about it. It's not over yet, but it's worse. She can only wait, there's no other way to know how things stand. This is the problem with pain you're currently experiencing: you can feel it, but you don't know exactly what it is. She thinks about Daniele. There's an air chamber, in between. She's not sure that what she's feeling right now is his absence. The TV is on, a commentator, her long hair worn loose, is conducting the evening news.

If the executive were to come out of the Senate ordeal unscathed, what at one time would have been called a shift of gears might occur.

She listens to every word, and doesn't understand a thing.

The following month passes slowly. Daniele and Sara tacitly agree to a hopeful separation. They don't talk about what happened, they no longer see each other on the sly, they don't make love. They remain faithful and distant, waiting for it to blow over. Every other day, and sometimes every day, he calls her, frightened and full of hope. Sara always answers him.

"I'm not going anywhere, remember that," he tells her one day in the ward, taking advantage of a moment alone.

The news comes on a Sunday afternoon, while Daniele is shaving in front of the bathroom mirror, barefoot, with a towel knotted around his waist. From the bedroom, Paola shouts for him to come quickly.

Behind the news commentator appears a close-up of a man described as a dangerous fugitive, just arrested in France. He's a Mafia boss promoted in the organization by reason of blood, and his name is Sabato Smeraldo, not Carmine Rotunno, as Daniele knew him. "It appears," the talking head says, "that the man was suffering from cancer and recently received treatment. Investigators are currently working to reconstruct his latest movements, to determine the connections and fronts which the boss, in all probability, must have benefited from."

" 'This majority is crumbling along the way': this is the lapidary phrase with which the spokesman for the opposition noted the diff . . ."

Paola turns down the TV volume and looks at her husband with dismay. "Now what happens?" she asks him.

Daniele does not lose his composure. He points to the cell phone lying on the bedside table.

Paola hands it to him, waiting for him to answer.

"What's supposed to happen? Nothing." And he walks out of the room, as if the news were nothing new.

Paola, bewildered, remains seated on the bed in front of the screen, staring at the speaker's lips as they move, saying who knows what.

Daniele goes back to the bathroom. He locks the door. Taps out a brief message on the cell phone's keypad: "I have to talk to you."

He selects Sara's number and hits send.

Then he continues shaving.

In the morning, the café around the corner from Sara's house provides three newspapers to read, hung on wooden rods, like shirts. It's her daily installment before going to work, a private pleasure in a public place that she has allowed herself each day for some years. The barista doesn't even need to take her order: he sees her come in, waits for her to sit down at a table with the newspaper, and shortly afterwards he serves her. A caffè macchiato and a small croissant.

Sara leafs through the paper.

Who knows why, when she recognizes the man in the picture, she feels like smiling.

Later, at work, she meets a co-worker in the elevator. He seems worried.

"Have you heard?" he asks her.

"Yes."

"Are you concerned?"

"Why should I be?"

"Why? Because we're the ones who operated on that guy."

"So? We can hardly be expected to know a patient's life story, Alfredo."

"I know. But it's the suspicion aimed at us that I can't stand. Already two journalists called this morning."

"They were quick."

"But how could such a thing happen?"

"Search me ... Who knows how many felons, maybe not as dangerous as this one, we've treated without knowing it."

Alfredo sighs as the elevator reaches their floor and stops.

"You know what bothers me the most? That if I were someone reading about this in the newspaper, I would feel justified in doubting the entire department, maybe the whole hospital. It's awful to be a suspect, when you yourself wouldn't believe in your innocence."

Sara's gaze is lost in space.

"That's . . . true."

"What's wrong?"

"Nothing. I was just thinking about what you said."

"Doctor Dalisi?"

The man who has just addressed Daniele, getting up from a chair in the waiting room of the ward where he had been waiting until that moment, is young, though graying; his manner is courteous, his attire tasteful, and his gaze direct.

"Yes."

The man holds out his hand.

"Forgive me for appearing without having made an appointment: I am Commissioner Vanini."

"A pleasure to meet you."

"I need to talk to you. But if you're busy now, I can come back another time."

"No. I was expecting a visit like this at any moment."

"I see."

"I have to go downstairs for a consultation. Do you mind if we talk along the way?"

"Of course not. My fault that I came unexpectedly."

They take the stairs.

"I had no idea who that man was," Daniele says point-blank.

"I see you get straight to the point."

"I operated on him just as I would have on any other patient."

"What did he tell you his name was?"

"He didn't tell me. But on his medical record it's listed as Carmine Rotunno."

"You even remember his first name."

Daniele slows up. Looks him in the eye.

"I even remember the pattern on his dressing gown, for that matter. Do you want me to describe it to you?"

"I didn't mean to be ironic."

"I certainly hope not. Because when you read in the paper one morning that your team has saved the life of a mafia boss, witty remarks are the last thing you want to hear, believe me."

"Of course, I can imagine. What was this gentleman suffering from exactly?"

"Adenocarcinoma."

"That would be a malignant lung tumor, correct?"

"Precisely."

"Was the operation successful?"

"Better than any of us had hoped."

"So then, you didn't know the real identity of this fortunate patient."

"I already answered that question."

"I was just summing up. And do you by chance have any reason to believe that one of your assistants, those who participated in the operation I mean, might have been aware of his identity?"

They reach the entrance to the ward where Daniele is headed.

"Absolutely not. Here we are, Commissioner. Now if you'll excuse me."

"Oh, but of course, thank you, Doctor, you've been very helpful. One last thing."

"If it doesn't take too long."

"Very brief: do you know the attorney Saggese?"

Daniele sighs.

"Am I a suspect, Commissioner? Because if I am, I would prefer you tell me without beating around the bush."

"It generally takes me at least half a day to suspect someone, Doctor. And I've known you for barely a quarter of an hour."

"Keep in mind that the newspapers say that Saggese is one of Smeraldo's lawyers."

"Do you know him or not?"

"If I say yes, you'll feel justified in thinking that I may have arranged with him to have Smeraldo admitted to my unit, right?"

"Oh, I think a lot of things, you see. And if you knew how quickly I change my mind. So don't be too sure about what I'm thinking and don't worry about answering me."

"Yes, I know him. And I also think he can't stand me."

"Seriously? Why is that?"

"Because I was his adversary in a trial, about a year ago."

"His adversary?"

"I was an expert witness for the Public Prosecutor."

"I see."

"Saggese lost the case."

"Still."

"My testimony weighed rather heavily toward his defeat, if you get my point."

"I think your point is very well put."

"Saggese's client was a wealthy contractor. I think that sentence made him take a huge loss. Go and check the proceedings, if you want."

"Yes, maybe I will. Thanks for the tip. And for your time."

"No problem."

"I might be back to bother you again. I have to tell you that, unfortunately."

"Whenever you want."

"Doctor Vallicelli?" Vanini asks Sara when he runs into her on the stairs shortly thereafter.

"Do you think I go around wearing someone else's name badge?" she's quick to retort.

Vanini accepts the clever rejoinder and can barely keep from laughing. "Good one," he says.

"Thanks."

They look at one another.

Maybe it's his awkward start that leaves Vanini at a loss for a witty comeback.

"Were you trying to hit on me or what?" says Sara, when he doesn't say anything. "Now, now, don't be cruel," he holds out his hand. "Stefano Vanini. I'm with the police." Sara takes her hand out of her pocket and shakes his hand.

"A pleasure to meet you."

"What, are you making fun of me?"

Sara smiles. "What shall we do, continue with the comedy routine, or is there something you want to tell me? I have an operation in half an hour."

"Even less will do."

"Then go on."

"Have you heard about the mafioso who was arrested in France?"

"I heard on television that he was a mafia boss. For me, he was a patient whom I had to anesthetize."

"Oh, I see, you too get straight to the point. You people in here really can't wait to talk."

"We make your life easier, aren't you glad?"

"How come I inspire such humor in you, doctor?"

"I apologize."

"Can you tell me if anything happened during the time he was hospitalized, even the smallest detail, that might have made you remotely suspicious?"

"I don't understand your question."

"What don't you understand?"

"If I had had any suspicion about that man I would have gone to the police, don't you think?"

"Of course. So he was a patient like any other: no special treatment, no special privileges."

"That's right."

"Do you remember anyone looking after him, anyone who was close to him, who came to visit him?"

"I don't know about visiting him. But whenever I passed by I always saw two young men, standing between the waiting area and his room. I thought they were his sons."

"What were they like?"

"Let's see . . . Young. Twenty-five or thirty. Dark hair, medium height, dressed casually . . . I repeat, very normal-looking. In fact, I'd even say anonymous-looking."

"No one else?"

"I'm an anesthetist. My contacts with the patients are very few, Commissioner."

"And with your colleagues?"

"Daily."

"May I ask what your relationship is with Doctor Dalisi?"

"I'm the anesthetist he relies on the most."

"And aside from the professional aspect?"

Sara gives him a chilly look.

"You're not obliged to answer me, doctor."

"Because you already know, right? You just want to find out how honest I feel like being with you."

"Bull's eye."

"We're lovers."

"For how long?"

"You want to know if we're a motel couple or the kind that holds hands at sunset?"

"It's an original distinction, but yes, let's say that's what I want to know."

"Then let's say that when we go to a motel we choose a room from which you can watch the sunset."

"This makes matters more difficult for me."

"Why is that?"

"Because people who are in love protect one another. And asking questions becomes pointless. But I'll ask you one just the same: do you think Dalisi knew about Smeraldo, prior to his arrest?"

"Definitely not."

"Because if that were the case he would have spoken to you about him, right?"

"He wouldn't have kept such a thing from me."

"Not even if he thought that you would go to the police and report him?" Sara takes a while to answer.

"Did I put you on the spot?" asks Vanini.

Sara replies to his previous question.

"Not even in that case."

"You don't seem too convinced."

"It's just that I needed a moment to think."

"A moment to think."

"Precisely."

"In other words, you needed to reflect on his trust before confirming it."

"No, no, you're the one who caused my hesitation. Asking me that question point-blank made me imagine, if only for a moment, that Daniele might have concealed the truth from me on purpose. It was a necessary step, in order to respond to you. You just wanted to see how I would react faced with that hypothesis."

"You're an intelligent woman, doctor."

"Just because I realized the game you were playing? Don't be so presumptuous, Commissioner."

"You're right. Maybe it's me who's less intelligent than you. One last thing."

"There's more?"

"Do you know the attorney Saggese?"

"By name."

"Then you've never met him."

"I've never needed any legal assistance, fortunately."

"All right then. Thank you for the talk."

"Sure."

"In any case," Vanini concludes offering her his business card, "if you happen to think of anything . . ." Sara takes the card, looks at it, then looks at him.

"I have a good memory, Commissioner. If I had something to tell you, I would already have told you."

"Sometimes memory surprises us, Doctor. Haven't you ever had a memory crop up suddenly?"

"I don't think so."

"Then go ahead and toss my card, if you want."

And without another word, he walks off.

Sara looks at the card again. She heads for a wastebasket nearby. She hesitates, then slips the card into the pocket of her lab coat, unaware that Commissioner Vanini has been watching her from the stairs below. He now continues on his way down, a crafty smile stamped on his face.

Daniele is keeping an eye on the entrance to the otorhino-laryngology ward. He's keeping tabs on me, Sara thinks.

"Hi."

"Hi."

"I need to talk with you, can we?"

"I have an adenoid procedure."

"I know, in forty minutes."

"I don't like you sticking your nose in my affairs."

"I miss you, Sara."

"Look, now isn't the time."

"Why not? What's happened?"

"I don't feel like talking about it."

"I get it, he came to you too, that policeman, what's his name . . ."

". . . Vanini."

"So he came looking for you?"

"No, he read my name on my badge and stopped me on the stairs."

"What did he want?"

"The same thing he wanted from you, I imagine."

"We have to talk, Sara."

"I can't, I have an operation, you know that."

"Why are you giving me the cold shoulder?"

"I'm not giving you the cold shoulder. It's just that I don't want to get upset when I'm due in the operating room."

"Please, come inside a minute."

"I told you that . . ."

Daniele moves closer to her. He takes her hand. Squeezes it lightly.

"Please."

Sara feels her legs tremble. A symptom that she's quite familiar with, that actually amuses her when she's happy, but that now throws her off-balance. She had thought her feelings had matured a little, that they had stopped being unsettled over so little, but instead there they were, fun-loving and childish as ever.

"All right," she hears herself say.

In a daze, she follows him into his office, and is unprepared for the urgency with which he pulls her against him as soon as he locks the door.

"Hey."

"I can't do it. I can't be without you any more." He seeks her lips. Finds them.

"Daniele."

"Say my name. Say it to me again."

"Please, Daniele, not so fast . . ."

He presses her tightly, a departure from the gentleness to which he has accustomed her, throwing her into confusion. Sara feels his arms, never this tense before, the breathlessness, the thud of his heart against her, and realizes how consenting this yearning hunger, this uncontainable candor, this emotional extortion finds her.

He takes her face in his hands. He kisses her eyes, her lips again, then he crushes her against him once more, his body reclaiming the authority of his love.

Sara strokes his hair.

"Calm down now, all right?"

He controls his excitement.

"Okay."

"Give me a second to breathe."

He rubs his nose with a finger, chuckles and loosens his embrace.

"Of course. Sorry."

"I thought you wanted to talk about the policeman."

"You know I don't give a damn about the policeman."

"It's a problem, Daniele. Or rather, it's our problem. We have to talk about it."

"All right. Let's talk about it."

"I have a surgery now, I told you."

"Tonight then?"

"Tonight?"

"Why, are you busy?"

"It's not that I'm busy, it's just that . . ."

"What?"

"Daniele, please. If we've kept away from each other up till now, there's a reason. We can't just make up like a couple of teenagers."

"Why not?"

Sara closes her eyes. Shakes her head. At first, she feels like laughing.

"Look at you: you're acting as though nothing has happened. As if we didn't have a problem. You have no desire to deal with it. You just want things back the way they were."

"I don't see anything wrong with that."

"But there is. And if you don't see it, there's no point in starting to see each other again."

"All right, but let's talk about it at least. I don't understand what you hold me responsible for, exactly. Can we meet and talk about this goddamned problem that's keeping us apart? Is it asking too much?"

Sara is disarmed, his question is so reasonable. She replies following the level ground of logic, rather than the uneven surface of her thoughts.

"No. It's not asking too much."

"Wow, thank goodness. So, may I have the honor, tonight?"

"Don't be an idiot."

"I just want to know: yes or no."

Sara pauses briefly.

"Yes."

Daniele brightens.

Finding yourself pacing up and down the hallway in your house, dressed and all made up, to please your lover moreover who is about to come and pick you up, full of expectations and tricks which you know he'll use to successfully demolish every last resistance of yours, convincing you that nothing serious happened, and who later will officially return to your bed, and in the sleepy tenderness that follows love-making will ask you if it was really necessary to drag it out so long, calling attention to your naked body coupled with his, which obliterate all the good reasons for the separation which had seemed so solid until the day before … well, finding yourself pacing up and down the hallway can be a far from happy state when you realize that you no longer feel like going out, you don't like the dress you've chosen, and the makeup you're wearing can't disguise the bitterness you feel, because what you'd really like to do now is call the evening off, ruin his plans, say: "I'm not coming down", just like that, "I'm not coming down" and that's it, let him think whatever he wants; how nice it would be to change the course of things, on the spur of the moment, reinstate the conflict, decree it, it's not like you think it is, things aren't resolved by seizing me out of desire, I have to know who I have beside me, what you did, what I'm doing with you; how nice it would be to hear your outraged voice over the intercom, replying or rather demanding: "What do you mean?", and I don't explain, I don't say a thing, I don't feel like it: and that's all there is to it. Instead, when Daniele rings, Sara merely replies: "Coming," and half-annoyed, half-resigned, takes one last look in the mirror.

"What's the matter?"

Daniele takes his eyes off the road and turns to look at her to ask what's wrong.

Sara shrugs. Outside it's dark, the Nigerian women on the prowl are ghosts that appear at the side of the road, they lean their head down and sometimes laugh. Some stand still, nearly in the middle of the road, and only move at the last minute, like deer in the headlights.

"I asked you what's the matter."

"I heard you," Sara says unresponsively.

Daniele's facial muscles stiffen.

"You haven't even unwrapped my gift."

"I can do it at the restaurant."

"Yes, but I would have preferred it if you did it when I gave it to you."

Sara lets her reply wait a while, then retrieves her purse from the back seat, exasperated.

"Okay! I'll open it now, just to make you happy!"

She pulls the package out of her purse, unwraps it nervously, looks inside, closes it again.

"Well. It's exquisite. Thank you."

She places the gift back in her purse, puts the purse back on the seat and looks out the window, rigid.

"If this is how the evening is going to go," he says after a while, "we might as well end it right now."

Sara turns to Daniele, hesitating over his remark.

"Yes, maybe that's a good idea."

"It's come to this, then."

"Could be."

"You're feeling this way because of that policeman this morning, right?"

"If that's what you think, you haven't understood a thing."

"What is it I don't understand?"

"That I can't go on lying. I told Vanini that as far as I'm concerned it was unthinkable that you might have known the truth. Do you have any idea how such a thing makes me feel?" Daniele takes a deep breath. A dispirited sigh escapes him.

"Sara, I'm sorry. I shouldn't have involved you."

"I'm the one who shouldn't have let you."

"But what choice did I have? It was me they wanted. In the end all it meant was operating on a patient."

"Please, at least stop justifying yourself, I can't stand it."

"All right," Daniele bursts out, exasperated, "I bowed my head. I did what they wanted. Do you feel better now that I've told you?"

"No."

Daniele looks at her, mortified.

"I thought you understood me. That you were on my side."

"I thought so too."

Daniele glues his eyes on the road and doesn't say another word. He floors the accelerator to release his frustration.

"I'm sorry," she says after a while.

"You know what, Sara?" Daniele explodes angrily. "Go to the police and tell them everything. Ruin my life and yours, if that makes you feel better!"

"You know very well I won't do that."

"Then what do you want from me? Stop persecuting me and leave me in peace!"

The car speeds along the asphalt. The lights of approaching cars flash by faster and faster. Sara looks around, frightened.

"Slow down," she says.

Daniele doesn't even seem to hear her.

"Daniele, please, slow down," Sara repeats, terrified. She can't even scream when the headlights of the oncoming truck blind her. Daniele brakes at the last minute, avoiding a collision.

The truck's horn is a deafening reproach.

The car flips over and leaps off the road like a spring-action toy.

From the driver's seat, the truck driver stares at the scene in horror, as if counting the ricochets that precede the smash-up.

Sara reopens her eyes in a place flooded with light. The sight of a metal cabinet crammed with medicines, and especially the familiar hospital smell, are comforting to her.

"What happened?" she asks the doctor on duty, who appears relieved to see her come to.

"You were in an accident. But you were very fortunate." Sara jolts up nervously.

"Daniele. How is he. Where is he."

The doctor lowers his eyes.

Sara grabs him by the arm.

"What's happened to him."

The doctor looks at her, uncomfortable.

"I'm sorry."

Who knows how she manages to get through the night. Sara asks for a sedative, her colleague gives it to her and stays with her for a long time, he doesn't seem to trust leaving her alone. She would rather he leave, she tells him she feels fine, that she is able to go home. I would prefer that you remain here at least for tonight, he replies, and Sara doesn't feel up to insisting. And so they talk. The doctor (his name is Giulio) tells her about his daughter, whom he hardly ever sees because of the separation, and about how difficult it's become to brush his teeth in the morning looking at the little girl's toothbrush that has been left in its usual glass, and at first Sara doesn't understand this thing about the toothbrush in the glass and is ashamed to look at him because it seems comical and a little odd to her, but later it hits her with such sadness that she bursts into tears and can't stop crying until Giulio embraces her and whispers words in her ear that she doesn't hear but that do her good, nonetheless.

Then Giulio goes on to talk about other things and she follows him up to a certain point but she is very tired, all she wants is to be alone and not hear any voices or sounds, so she closes her eyes. Giulio then lowers his voice, speaking more and more softly like you do when reading fairy tales to children who are about to slip off into sleep, until he thinks she is asleep, then he goes away. After that Sara gets up, goes to the window and remains standing there watching the sky beyond the glass take all night to turn pale.

She is still at the window when a girl comes in whom she recognizes immediately.

Beautiful, young, grieving and unforgiving. She has almost none of Daniele's features. She doesn't look anything like him, except for her expression, just like his, as she looks around. Sara instinctively pulls her hair back, as if wanting to expose her face before facing an accusation.

Mirella stops in the middle of the room and accuses her with her eyes. Sara offers no resistance.

"I hope you're satisfied now," the girl says curtly, breaking the silence.

"Me?" Sara replies, stunned. "Satisfied?"

"First you took him away from my mother. Now from me. At his best moment."

Sara bites her lip.

"I loved him, Mirella."

"Don't call me by name. We're not friends."

Sara's eyes tear up.

"I'm sorry," she says, mortified.

"You should have been the one to die, not him."

Sara begins to cry.

"Please, don't torment me, leave me in peace . . ."

"You were fighting. That's why he drove off the road, isn't it?"

Sara stares at her, her face streaked with tears, shaken by the certainty of the girl's assertion.

"It was an accident," she replies, in despair.

"It's all your fault."

"Please, just go," Sara sobs, "leave me alone . . ."

Her cry is interrupted by the voice of a young doctor who enters the room.

"What's going on here?"

Mirella turns around and studies him. The man looks at her resentfully.

"Who are you?"

Mirella doesn't answer.

"Alfredo!" Sara exclaims, relieved by the appearance of a friendly face.

The doctor moves past the girl and goes to Sara, taking her hand. Sara pulls him to her and holds him close. He returns her embrace, though without taking his eyes off Mirella, who slowly starts toward the door.

"I asked you who you are," he repeats threateningly.

"Ask your colleague who I am," Mirella retorts harshly.

He's about to answer back, but Sara draws him to her.

"Let her go, Alfredo, please. It's not important."

Mirella leaves.

Alfredo strokes Sara's hair, reassuring her.

"Who is that girl?"

"Daniele's daughter," Sara replies with some effort.

Alfredo's eyes take on a faint gleam, as if he were recalling some resemblance. Then he looks at Sara sympathetically.

"I'm so sorry, Sara."

"Thank you," she says rubbing her eyes with her wrist; then she changes the subject to suppress her emotion.

"I wasn't injured, you see?"

"I see, yes," he replies, as if referring to a lucky escape. "The X-rays too. It's some kind of miracle."

"I'm going home today."

"Would you like me to take you?"

Sara looks at him, pleased by his suggestion.

"It wouldn't upset your day, would it?"

"Don't be silly."

"Look, I have no intention of killing myself," Sara responds with a smile on her lips.

"Forgive me, it's just that I don't trust the way you're accepting this. I'm worried about you."

"I know. But there's no reason to be, really."

"Why don't you come and sleep at our house? Gloria would be very happy to have you."

"No, seriously, thank you . . . It's best if I see it through alone."

She opens the door and is about to step out.

"Sara."

"Yes?"

"The funeral is tomorrow. Did you know?"

She looks at him and doesn't reply.

"If you want, I'll come and pick you up," Alfredo says.

"Thank you, but I'm not going."

"You have every right to be there."

"No, I don't feel up to it. Thank you anyway, Alfredo. You've been very sweet. You know, it's hard to go back home, after a death."

Alfredo rears his head back and narrows his eyes.

"What did you say?" he asks, caught off-guard.

Sara brings a hand to her forehead. A slight dizziness overcomes her.

"I don't know, I don't understand . . . I don't know how such a thing popped into my head," she says, confused. "I'm sorry."

"Sara", Alfredo says, as if he wanted to add something more.

But she is already out of the car, and rapidly heading for the front door.

The funeral takes place with a narrow circle of mourners, in the early afternoon. Sara leaves the house late, and stations herself on the sidewalk in front of the church, when the mass is over. Alfredo had called her several times during the evening to make sure she was okay, and something he said had persuaded her: "You were in hiding for two and a half years, isn't that enough?"

Sara didn't think it would hurt so much to see her colleagues as one by one they came out of the church. Many with their heads lowered, some expressionless, some clearly annoyed by the length of the mass. There is also the town mayor, who awaits Daniele's family in the churchyard.

Alfredo comes out, and seeing her, smiles and goes toward her.

"You could have told me you were coming."

"So you too could stand out here and suffer for no reason?"

"Don't be silly. To begin with I would have come to pick you . . . hey, what's wrong?"

All of a sudden Sara's eyes zoom in, like a bloodhound tracking a scent, on the people lined up to pay their respects to Daniele's family.

"How dare he come here, that guy?" she says, grinding her teeth. The last time she saw the man whom she has just recognized he was talking to Daniele in the hospital parking lot, the day before the Mafia boss's operation. Alfredo turns his head toward the group of people standing in front of the church.

"Saggese, you mean? I don't know. I have no idea. In church we were all embarrassed, in fact."

They both pause to look at him, their eyes taking in the crude elegance, the false nonchalance, the vulgar confidence of his attitude.

"Will you look at that arrogance."

"Ignore him, Sara, it's better that way."

Paola and Mirella, deeply moved, are accepting the attorney's condolences now.

"And to think I was ashamed to come." Sara remarks in disgust.

"You see, I was right, wasn't I?" Alfredo says.

Saggese says goodbye to Daniele's family and starts toward the nearby parking lot.

"You were absolutely right," Sara replies, and staring straight ahead begins following Saggese.

"Wait, where are you going?" Alfredo says.

But Sara doesn't even hear him. Completely unconcerned about the looks from Daniele's family as they notice her presence, she follows Saggese to his car. The attorney turns his head aside as he disconnects the car's burglar alarm with a touch of his thumb on the remote control device.

"Good afternoon, Doctor Vallicelli."

Then he turns around, ready to face her.

Sara looks him in the eye. She's so indignant she can't even speak.

"You're not very good at following people, you know?"

Maybe it's the insolence of his wisecrack that restores her ability to give it right back to him.

"You, on the other hand, know all about subterfuge, don't you?"

Saggese frowns.

"I'll pretend I didn't hear that."

"Where did you get the gall to come here?"

"I always go to the funerals of those who cause me to lose a trial."

"Your irony is inappropriate, attorney."

"And your attitude isn't?"

"I was also in that car."

"I know. In fact I'm glad to see that you're uninjured."

Several of Sara's colleagues pass nearby, also heading toward their cars. Seeing her talking with the lawyer of the mafioso who thrust the hospital into the national spotlight, they exchange disapproving glances. Sara takes note of their attitude, but continues the wrangling.

"Do you know how the accident happened?"

"No, I really don't think I can answer that question."

"Because we were arguing."

"I don't see why you're telling me this . . ."

"Because the argument was about Sabato Smeraldo."

"I don't know why . . ."

"Because Smeraldo, the boss they arrested in France, the one we operated on in our hospital for lung cancer, is an illustrious client of yours. Just think, I administered the anesthesia to him."

"A fact I learned from the newspapers, actually."

"Really."

"What do you expect me to say, doctor?"

"That it was you who planned it all. Choosing a quiet town, far from the glare of publicity, perfect for being admitted to a hospital under a false name; a skilled oncologist, above suspicion since he had been your adversary in a trial a short time earlier . . . by the way, congratulations on the alibi: you really showed foresight; assisted by a team unaware of everything . . . it's only too bad they arrested him, otherwise we would never have known that such a famous patient had been in our hospital."

"Quite a good scenario, doctor. May I ask you a question?"

"Let's hear it."

"Does it really embarrass you so much to have operated on a member of the Mafia?"

"Maybe you're used to not paying much attention to who your clients are, Saggese, but I am."

"Are you being serious? Because if it's a joke it's not funny."

"Should I be proud of having treated a dangerous criminal?"

"Absolutely."

For a moment Sara is confused.

"I didn't know who that man was."

"Whether you knew it or not has no importance whatsoever. What do you do, treat only those with a clean record? When they bring you a patient, do you look at his rap sheet instead of his X-rays?"

"Look Saggese, you're the last person to give me lessons in professional ethics."

"Do you think you're so different from me, doctor?"

"Absolutely."

"You're wrong. We do the same thing, you and I. We're paid to wash our hands of our clients' troubles. We're not called upon to make judgments about their past, or about their present, or their actions, or their choices. We're not asked to concern ourselves with them, but to deal with the problem they have."

"You're very clever about justifying yourself morally. But you know what ruins it? That it's clear you don't believe a word of what you say."

"Whether I believe what I say doesn't count. What counts is that what I say is flawless."

"Your way of thinking is chilling."

"Yours, on the other hand, is merely hypocritical."

"How dare you!" Sara threatens, losing her temper.

She raises a hand to slap him.

Saggese intercepts it in mid-air. He grips her forearm and moves closer, speaking just inches from her face, half-menacing and half-seductive.

"I wondered how much longer it would take you to lose your temper," he says between his teeth, grazing her lips."

"I'll wipe that arrogant smile off your face, so help me God."

The lawyer lets her go.

"That's good to hear. That way I'll get to see you again."

He gets in his car and drives off.

Sara stays where she is, immobilized by frustration.

When she hears someone behind her call her name, it's as if she were being released from a spell.

"Doctor Vallicelli."

Sara turns around. It's Vanini.

"Good afternoon, Commissioner," she says, clearly uneasy about having been seen in Saggese's company.

"How are you?" Vanini asks.

"How do you think I am?"

"It's a routine question, automatic, even though . . . I realize . . ."

"I'm sorry, I'm very tense."

"It's all right. I'm very sorry about the doctor."

"Thank you."

"But I'm glad you're not injured."

"Thank you for that too. Excuse me, I have to go now."

"Doctor."

"Yes?"

"Maybe this is not a good time, but I have to ask you a question."

"You're right, Commissioner. It's not a good time."

"They pay me to be inopportune, doctor. What did you want from Saggese? You seemed somewhat heated, talking with him."

Sara hesitates a moment, then manages to find a plausible explanation.

"I found his presence at the funeral inappropriate, after what happened."

Vanini stops to consider her response.

"He should not have fostered suspicions that he and Daniele were associated, especially not in public," Sara goes on.

"An unexceptionable response," Vanini remarks, not at all convinced.

Sara starts to leave when he throws her a curve.

"However, you told me you didn't know Saggese."

She hesitates again, but quickly recovers.

"I knew him by name, as I already told you. Today I had the chance to introduce myself."

"Uh-huh," he nods, less and less convinced.

"Now may I go, Commissioner?"

The following day, at the hospital, Sara realizes how unpopular she is by the strained greeting of the first colleague she runs into. You can immediately sense the barbed wire that others put up, you feel it surrounding you in the morning. They erect it at night, while you're sleeping. No one lingers to chat with her, they stop her only to ask how she is, or simply greet her as if nothing had happened. Exasperated, she goes in search of Alfredo. She finds him in the ward, headed for the operating room.

"Do you have a minute?"

"Actually, we're about to operate."

"What, are you too ganging up on me now?"

"What do you mean, Sara?"

"What do I mean? Everyone in here is treating me as if I had acted scandalously! May I ask what the hell has come over everybody? What harm did I do?"

Alfredo looks around, a little embarrassed; then he replies with a certain gravity, almost as if he partially agreed with the reasons for the exclusion that Sara is experiencing.

"They saw you talking with Saggese, at the funeral."

"So?"

"Surely you must understand, Sara. It's a difficult time. A judgment heavy as a boulder has come down on us. We operated on a mafioso: go and explain to those who read the newspapers that we knew nothing about it."

"I too am paying a price for this situation, what do you think?"

"And you think you improved matters by going off for a private talk with the Mafia boss' attorney at the funeral of the doctor who operated on him?"

"So that's it . . ."

"No one has anything against you, Sara. Understand?"

"Yes, I see. I see that none of you gives a damn about the fact that we were all accomplices to a crime, even though we didn't know it. That you don't give a damn about the truth. On the contrary, the more it remains concealed, the more comfortable you all feel."

"Fine, and even if that were so? We're not all courageous and passionate about justice like you. We're miserable cowards, so what? What do you want to do, stand up on the altar and preach to us?"

"And if I told you it was Saggese who planned everything?"

"Him or somebody else, what difference does it make? I did my job, like Daniele. Like you. We operated on a patient, that's all. We're not policemen, Sara, we're doctors!"

"So then, we just look away and pretend that nothing happened: is that what you're telling me?"

"I have to operate now," Alfredo replies curtly. And leaves her standing there, alone and confused.

Toothbrush, toothpaste, mouthwash, paper towels, exfoliating sponge, two light bulbs, a package of assorted band-aids. Sara looks at the items she's tossed into the metal basket and smiles.

She has virtually no need of any of the things she's buying. Not just now, at any rate.

Although she's no stranger to spending time in supermarkets for reasons that have nothing to do with a need for supplies, she can't help but feel ridiculous. She's never understood why, ever since she was a little girl, walking around among canned goods and detergents has always had this odd, sedating effect on her, almost as if her thoughts slowed down and stopped scuffling for first place. It could be that modular parade of colors, shapes and sizes, the artificial climate, or the concentrated odor of foodstuffs, which partly attracts and partly nauseates her: what's certain is that all she has to do is cross the threshold of a supermarket and her thoughts are left parked outside like bicycles.

She's just started down the wine aisle when she realizes she's being watched. At first it's just a suspicion, a vague indication which becomes more persistent the more she tries to ignore it. Then the man with the vest gives himself away somehow, between the gaps of the shelving that separates the wines from the household articles. She stores away the detail, hurries to the checkout stand and gets out of there.

It's evening, the sky has let loose a neurotic, biting rain, which empties the streets and ruins people's plans. Sara walks quickly under the overhangs, her eyes fixed on the sidewalk, her fear increased by the downpour. Leaving the supermarket she had relied on the presence of passersby, who are now seeking shelter, pulling out their cell phones to cancel, thinking up an alternative to the errand they had gone out for, too busy to come to her aid should her pursuer attack her.

The rain comes down heavier. Sara can see less and less but continues to walk rapidly. She knows she made a mistake by straying so far away, but by now she's gone too far to correct it. That's how fear works, it attacks you midway. All she had to do was stop in any populated place, call the police or Vanini directly (she has his number, she didn't throw it away), but now she's become a disoriented, accessible prey. There's no one around, nobody will see a thing, no one will intervene. Which moment will the man in the vest choose? Will he grab her from behind or bar her way? Will the harm he wants to do her be quick or slow?

She won't give him the benefit. She's in good running condition. Let him run too, if he wants to catch her.

The sidewalk under her feet feels like burning asphalt.

She gets home in a time of which she has no awareness or memory. She's so tired, and at the same time so excited to be safe, that for a while it seems plausible to her that the man in the vest was a figment of her imagination.

She doesn't go to the window on purpose. When she passes in front of it, and sees him down below, a few feet from the front door, it's comforting in some sense to realize that he exists.

She opens the window trying to see his face, and with arrogant deliberation he turns aside, just enough to keep her from identifying him. An act of such insolent criminal presumption that Sara has to restrain herself to keep from going down to the street and confronting him physically. She retrieves Vanini's business card from her purse and dials the number. He answers at the second ring.

"Commissioner? Sara Vallicelli, I must speak with you."

"Good evening to you too, doctor."

"Forgive me, I don't have time for formalities. I think a man followed me. He's still here, in front of my door."

It takes Vanini a few seconds to absorb this information.

"Are you sure?"

"I think so . . . yes, I'm sure. I was at the supermarket, then it started to rain, and there was a man in a vest who . . ."

"All right, you can tell me about it later. Don't get upset, I'm sending a car for you."

"All right."

"If you can, go to a neighbor's house right away. Or lock the door securely." Sara glances down at the street. The man is gone. She opens the window, leans out. There's nobody.

"Maybe there's no need, Commissioner. I think he went away."

"What?"

"He's gone."

For a moment Vanini is silent.

"Doctor."

"Yes?"

"Are you sure someone followed you?"

"Are you saying you don't believe me, Commissioner? Fine then," Sara reacts, piqued, "if that's what you think, excuse me for calling you. It won't happen again, don't worry."

"Just a minute, doctor," Vanini loses his patience, surprising her, "I'm not an old friend, you know, whom you can summon and dismiss whenever you want. You called me saying that a man followed you? Okay: then I want you to file an official report, here, in my office, tomorrow morning. Because I also have some further questions to ask you. And I advise you to come, do you understand?"

Sara accepts the scolding and after a few seconds replies. "I understand."

"Good. Tomorrow, then. Before twelve thirty," the Commissioner concludes, backing down a little.

They remain silent.

"Are you still there?"

It's he who asks.

"Yes."

"What are you smiling about?"

"And how do you know I'm smiling?" Sara asks, intrigued.

"Am I mistaken, by any chance?"

Sara lets a few seconds tick by.

"No."

"You see."

"See what?"

"That I was right."

"Yes, you were," she admits. "But not about the man who followed me."

"Even more reason to come in and file a complaint."

"I already told you I'll be there."

"Mind you, it was hardly an invitation."

"Right, I didn't think it was."

"I'm not at all proud of my authority when I exert it. But at times I have to do it."

"I realize that."

"So then, I'll expect you tomorrow. And if you should need me, call me. At any hour."

"All right."

They hang up, then Sara undresses, gets into the shower, and closes her eyes under the warm water. Later, she goes back to the window.

The man in the vest.

He seems to be smiling.

The following morning, Sara barges into the courthouse like a fury. She knows exactly where to find him. She called his office that morning, and the secretary reported that he had a hearing and then asked her who she was. She told her her name and hung up on her. Saggese sees her coming as he's walking near a courtroom, surrounded by a pack of obsequious interns, like trained monkeys. Sara's stride is so determined, so military, that the attorney feels a momentary uncertainty about the outcome of the battle that he can clearly expect in a second or two. Just time for his natural arrogance to regain the upper hand.

Sara stops a step away from him and points her finger at him.

"Do you think you can scare me? I'm not afraid of you."

Saggese takes her in from head to toe, and even in such an embarrassing situation, he can't manage to restrain the attraction he's always had for her good looks.

"Gentlemen," he says, ironically addressing his young assistants, who stare at one another uneasily, "Doctor Vallicelli; Doctor Vallicelli, my interns."

"Don't clown around, Saggese. You know exactly what I'm talking about, and why I'm here." The interns look on, appalled, and continue to exchange sideways looks.

Saggese looks first at them, then at her.

"Come again?"

"Who is that thug you sent after me? One of your clients?"

"Are you sure you're feeling well, doctor?" Saggese replies with a sardonic grin.

Sara skirts the question, and comes at him from another direction.

"You know, all in all I expected it. It's typical of people like you to have others do their dirty work. Tell me: have you ever dirtied your own hands?"

One of the interns starts to say something. Saggese checks him with a look. Then he confronts her again.

"Now you're really going too far, doctor. Do you realize the gravity of what you're saying? The risk you're taking?"

"No, why don't you tell me what risk I'm taking. What type of rubout is the bastard you sent after me most skilled at?"

For a moment, the attorney reddens.

"You're nervous system is off-balance, Doctor. Are the hospital administrators aware of it?"

Sara rolls her head from side to side before replying, as if to ridicule the threat she's received.

"Watch out for the mentally ill, Saggese. Sometimes they send people to jail." Saggese rears his head back. He would like to respond, say something, but he can't think of anything to say.

Nothing at all. The interns seem like dummies, their mouths hanging open. Sara spins on her heels and leaves. She doesn't turn around to look at him, but she's confident that if she did she'd find him exactly the way she left him, with the same dazed expression on his face.

She arrives at police headquarters twenty minutes late. Vanini is on the phone. Sara nods at him. He nods in return and motions for her to take a seat across the desk from him. Sara sits down as the phone conversation continues.

"Of course I heard you, I heard you perfectly well," the Commissioner says in a grave tone, keeping his eyes fixed on Sara. She returns his gaze, somewhat puzzled, or maybe not.

"What can I say," Vanini goes on, irritated, giving Sara a long look of disapproval, "I'm sorry I don't share your concern, but no, it doesn't surprise me. It must be the job I do that makes me so cynical, what do you expect."

Sara tilts her head to one side and smiles deviously. Vanini raps her knuckles with a look. She recomposes her lips.

"All right. Whenever you like. It's not necessary that I be the one to take the report, as you well know. What's that? No, look, I'm not being argumentative. And I would appreciate it if we could stop talking about my tone, please. You're welcome. Goodbye."

He hangs up, plants his right elbow on the desk, makes a fist, rests his chin on it and resumes staring at Sara, as if she were a naughty little girl who has been up to some new mischief.

She's almost smiling, and he is too.

"I was beginning to worry," Vanini begins.

"After being barely twenty minutes late, Commissioner?"

"It not like we were going dancing."

"You're right. It's just that there was something I had to do first."

"I know."

"What do you know?"

"Can you guess who I was talking to?"

Sara shakes her head, as if the reference doesn't surprise her.

"He was quick, apparently."

Vanini crosses his arms on the desk and leans forward.

"Do you realize what you've done, doctor?"

"Do you too want to call me mentally unbalanced, Commissioner?"

"Is that what he called you?"

"That's right."

"Well he's not all wrong. You go and make a scene in the courthouse, and in front of the prosecutors, on top of it. Can you tell me what you hoped to gain?"

"Nothing. I was just angry. And I still am. Very."

Vanini takes a deep breath and lets out a sympathetic sigh.

"Listen to me. I don't think Saggese will file a complaint, for the time being. But what happened this morning could constitute a very serious problem for you. Do you know that?"

Sara stares at him, then lowers her eyes.

"This is all so ridiculous," she remarks.

Vanini sighs again.

"Why don't you try being sincere with me?"

"Because when I try, you don't believe me."

"You're wrong."

"If you have no reason to detain me, Commissioner, let me go, please."

"First you have to file that report."

"Oh, right, that's true."

"You can go to the front office."

"Fine."

Sara gets up and goes to the door. Vanini calls her as she's about to go out.

"Doctor."

"What is it?"

"Stay away from that guy."

Sara nods. And for the first time since she met him, she feels that that police officer is on her side.

"Are you all right?"

Guido Marcelli, the surgeon who will soon be operating,

asks Sara a rather alarming question, considering that she is the anesthetist on duty.

"Of course, why?" Sara replies, almost disdainfully.

Marcelli doesn't mince words.

"Because your mind seems to be elsewhere today."

"That might be, so what?"

"I'm not interested in your thoughts," the surgeon sticks to the point, "but if anything, in your concentration."

"Thanks for your interest, but I'm in full control of myself, Guido; and I know exactly how to conduct myself in an operating room, don't worry."

"Fine, then," he says, more skeptical than before.

They enter the operating room. The team begins its preparations while awaiting the patient's arrival. Sara doesn't say a word to anyone. She looks around curiously, as if she has entered a room she's never seen before. Everything she sees attracts her attention, holds her spellbound. Now not only Marcelli, but his assistants as well and even the nurses register her distraction with some concern.

The surgeon asks the nurse to fasten his gown in back, then he takes up a position beside Sara.

"Can you tell me what time it is, please?"

Sara glances at the clock on the wall.

"Four twenty," she replies.

Marcelli levels his eyes on those of the assistant facing him, reluctantly finding the confirmation he expected.

"That is, no, I'm sorry, three twenty," Sara corrects herself. The surgeon turns slowly toward her.

"I would prefer that you not take part in the operation, Sara."

"What?"

"You heard me."

"Come on, Guido," she says, groping for an answer, "I was just distracted. Don't you ever mistake one number for another?"

"Nothing personal, Sara. I have the highest regard for you, you know that. But today I don't feel confident in you. I prefer not having you here, if your mind isn't here."

"There's nothing wrong with my mind! How dare you judge me!" she explodes.

"Sara, please. We have an operation to perform. Will you calm down?"

"You can't just throw me out! I was assigned to this operation! You'll have to explain yourself to my chief!"

"I will, don't worry, I'm well aware of procedure. But right now I'm asking you to leave this room," Marcelli concludes firmly.

Sara looks around infuriated, hoping for some support from a colleague.

"Isn't anyone going to say anything?" she raises her voice, addressing the entire team.

"You all agree with him?" Silence.

There are days when jogging doesn't clear your mind. They're the days when your thoughts act up. And even if you take them out running, trying to exhaust them, there's no way. They keep right at you, like children who persist in repeating the same complaint.

Along the gardens of Villa De Capoa, Sara is pursued by Daniele's death (still too unreal for her to really believe), fear of the man in the vest, Saggese's sardonic grin, and being thrown out of the surgical procedure which, of them all, is curiously the thing that causes her the most pain right now.

"I get it," she seems to say, even turning around from time to time to face them, "you're right, leave me alone, please." Then she stops at a bench, tired of running away.

Sleep is gently claiming her, when she hears voices speaking English. That's not right, she thinks to herself, annoyed. That word means something else.

A little further on, a tourist in a running suit is trying to understand something being said by a girl who is waving her arms about wildly, inventing words.

Sara gets up, and goes over to them.

"I speak English, can I help you?" she says.

The girl doesn't even turn around. The tourist continues trying to interpret her gestures.

"Hey," Sara says, irritated by their lack of response, "did you hear what I said?" The girl outlines an imaginary square with her fingers. The tourist follows her gesture, bewildered.

"*Squa-re. Mu-ni-ci-pal-i-ty,*" she pronounces it in syllables.

"Ohhh," the tourist bursts out, and finally smiles.

Sara takes a step back, appalled.

"Why don't you answer me?" she asks, her voice breaking.

And she continues shrinking back as the girl goes on with her explanation, which the tourist now seems to be starting to understand.

"I'm here," Sara shouts in despair.

But the two strangers don't see her. They don't hear her.

Sara would like to go on screaming but she can't, stifled by a knot that tightens her throat.

Another voice comes, from further off.

"Doctor." And then again: "Sara."

Sara opens her eyes. The hands holding her shoulders, the face watching her up close, the mouth speaking to her, are those of Commissioner Vanini.

"Doctor. Calm down, everything is all right."

Distraught and eager for reality, Sara grasps him tightly, breathing heavily.

Though somewhat uneasily, Vanini takes her in his arms.

"You had a dream, doctor. It was just a dream," he whispers in her ear, and draws her out of the dream without jolting her.

Sara disengages herself from his embrace, embarrassed.

"You were shouting: 'I'm here! I'm here!' "

"I . . . I'm sorry."

"For what?" Vanini says, smoothing his hair back. "Are you feeling better now?"

"Yes, thank you."

"Take a breath. Inhale deeply and then exhale, slowly. There, that's right."

"I must really be exhausted," Sara comments, regaining some color, "if I fell asleep on a park bench. And then too, the nightmares . . ."

"You're under a lot of pressure, doctor. Too many things have happened to you. You should get away for awhile."

"Yes, maybe so. But you, what are you doing here?"

"I tried to call you several times, but your cell phone was turned off. So I went looking for you and, well, I found you. I wanted to let you know that Saggese had come to police headquarters, to issue an injunction against you."

"Issue an injunction against me? What does that mean? Did he file a complaint against me?"

"No, let's say it's a watered-down complaint, a kind of warning. As if he were sending a message warning you never to do that again. And that's the reason I'm here. To tell you not to repeat what happened at the courthouse."

"Why did he do it, if it's not a real complaint?"

"To put his denunciation on record, in case it might be useful someday. A little like keeping the return receipt of a registered letter, if that makes any sense. Lawyers are like that, they always have to have their papers in order."

"It's absurd that he should be the one to have the upper hand," Sara says, practically speaking to herself.

"What do you mean?"

"Nothing. Just that I find him arrogant, that's all."

"Enough with the convenient answers, doctor. Tell me the truth. Why did you accuse him of having you followed?"

"Because I believe he did."

"Why should he have done that?"

"To frighten me."

"Nobody has a reason to frighten someone, unless he himself is afraid of something. What do you know that Saggese doesn't want known?"

"Okay, you're right," Sara replies, driven into a corner by his logic. "Maybe it wasn't Saggese who had me followed. Maybe that man wasn't even following me. Maybe it was my imagination that invented him."

"Why do you continue to be so secretive, Doctor? Do you think I haven't figured out how things stand?"

"You can't prove anything if I don't talk."

"Finally you're being sincere," Vanini says relieved.

And as if she has heard enough, she gets up from the bench and starts to walk away.

"This doesn't change anything," Sara says.

"You're wrong."

"Why?"

"Because now I know that sooner or later you'll tell me the truth." Sara looks at him, puzzled.

"Do you know what's about to begin?" Vanini says, abruptly changing the subject.

"No, what?"

"What! Don't you know what day this is?"

"I've lost track of the days, Commissioner. I can't tell them apart anymore."

"It's Corpus Domini."

Sara brightens.

"Really?"

"It skipped your mind. And yet it's always been a very special day for you."

"How do you know that?" Sara asks, surprised.

Vanini smiles, and goes away without answering.

Sara has loved the procession of the *Misteri* since she was a child. Her grandfather always took her, and explained the Mysteries to her. She watched, with curiosity and fear, and held his hand tightly as all those costumed figures tossed about, suspended in air. Sometimes a child dressed up as an angel passed in front of a window and wanted something to drink. A woman would then give him some water.

"Look at the machines, sweetheart."

"What's a machine, grandpa?"

"It's a trick, but you can see it. Look, it's like a hidden shaft, like on a carousel. It supports the Mysteries."

"And what are the Mysteries?"

"They're angels, or devils. Or saints. or madonnas. They're men and women. Or old people. Above all children. Look, they're swimming through the air. But it's because they're secured with a sling stuffed with cotton-wool and leather, they can't fall."

The procession of the Mysteries would make its way through the old town. Sara followed the passage of the bearers who carried the machines and came to know the painted faces, the bent, crooked bodies, the dangling saints, the devils who jeered at the crowd: she watched and learned, not knowing that they were martyrs and miracles in the flesh, living representations of the Old and New Testaments. Her grandfather explained it all to her, but a little at a time. He wanted her to like it, even before she understood it.

Sara doesn't even go home to change her clothes. She goes straight to the procession just as she is, in her tracksuit and sneakers, so she can see it right away, following the Commissioner's suggestion.

When she joins the crowd, the Mystery of Abraham is passing by.

The old man is standing on the machine. He has a long beard, a sword in his fist, and a little angel clinging to his arm, preventing him from lowering the blade on his son crouched at his feet, whom God has ordered him to sacrifice.

Sara is enchanted. She stares at the baby angel whose frail efforts prevent the killing. Just behind is the lamb meant to take Isaac's place.

It gnashes its teeth as the machine goes by, offering itself to the crowd that lines the street. And she finally realizes what she has to do.

"I don't know what you need it for, doctor, but you'd do best to forget it."

The man Sara has come to see has a workshop just outside the city. He's working as a mechanic again, after having served a sentence for robbery. When Sara called him, after exchanging just a few words with her he asked: "What happened?" And it was plain that he had already known.

"It's pointless for you to try and change my mind," she persists, "I've made my decision. Just tell me yes or no."

"You can ask anything of me after what you did for my daughter, you know that. But if I have to help you ruin your life, I want to at least tell you that what you're doing is an idiotic thing."

"So, it's a yes?"

"You know you're taking a big risk if you don't know how to use it."

"You can teach me."

"Me?"

"You said I could ask anything of you."

The man sighs.

"You must really have a heartfelt interest in this business, doctor."

"You're right. I really do."

The man searches her eyes. Sara holds his gaze unwaveringly.

"Look, if you want I'll do this job for you. Seriously."

"You'd do that?"

"For you, yes."

"You're very kind, but no. It's a personal matter."

The man nods, resigned. And without another word opens the metal tool cabinet, leans forward stretching his calves, removes a false bottom, and takes out a gun.

"Okay, then. Let's get started."

*   *   *

The indicator light blinks intermittently on the face of the telephone. Irritated, attorney Saggese grumbles and picks up the receiver.

"What now?"

"Excuse me, sir," the secretary replies, "there's a call for you. She says it's urgent."

"Who 'says'?" he snaps back impatiently.

"A Doctor Vallicelli. I think she's the same one who called the other day, when you were in court."

Saggese goes silent, you'd think someone had pressed the Hold button.

"Sir?" the secretary asks.

Processing the fact takes a few seconds, evidently.

"Put her on."

The connection is interrupted, followed by a brief sequence of beeps which signal that the call is being put through.

The attorney sits down at his desk.

"Hello?"

"This is Sara Vallicelli."

"Yes. They told me."

"Am I disturbing you?"

"No," he replies shortly. But there's a sense of waiting in that no.

"Well, I . . . thank you."

"For what?"

"I wasn't at all certain that you would take my call."

"You're right. It wasn't at all certain."

Sara lets him enjoy full satisfaction, before she goes on.

"Look, though it may seem inappropriate, I apologize for how I attacked you at the courthouse."

"What is it, did Vanini inform you of the injunction? Mind you, it's not as if I filed a complaint against you."

"Yes, the Commissioner explained that."

"I could have."

"I know."

"And this is what made you change your mind about me?"

"I think so."

Saggese thinks it over a minute.

"You embarrassed me in front of my interns."

"I'm sorry."

"It was very distasteful."

"I know."

"I don't know why I let you get away with it."

"I don't know what to say."

A brief silence ensues.

"I have an idea why," Saggese says.

Sara doesn't speak.

"Do you want to hear it?" he continues.

Sara is gleeful. She didn't think it would be this easy. She can just see him, at the other end of the phone line, arrogant and smug.

"Please, just accept my apologies and we'll say goodbye. I feel too embarrassed to appreciate your kindness."

"Naturally I accept them."

"All right, then . . . thank you. I'm grateful. Really. You've taken a big load off my mind."

"Just a minute. Wait."

Sara clenches her fist. A foot even jerks out, striking the floor involuntarily.

"Yes?"

"There's one condition."

"A condition?"

"That's right."

"And what would that be?"

"I'll accept your apology if you'll accept my invitation to dinner."

Sara shrewdly remains silent.

"Well then?" he asks after a moment.

"I really didn't expect this."

"Just say yes."

Sara takes one last pause.

"Why not?"

The restaurant is a little out of the way, simple, not very crowded. Saggese requested a table at the back of the room. The waiters came over to welcome them with the copious deference that is reserved for special customers. A sparkling prosecco arrives, strictly de rigueur. They toast. Sara can't manage to look at him directly.

"I didn't think I'd ever be having dinner with you."

"Well, me neither you know."

"And to think I had to issue an injunction against you, to persuade you to see me in a different light."

"Yes, it's curious but it was that which made me realize that I had used you as a scapegoat for this entire situation."

"I'm happy to hear you say that. Because I couldn't stand having you hate me."

A brief silence follows, during which Saggese ravishes her with his eyes.

Sara couldn't choose a better time to change the subject.

"Aren't they going to take our order here?" she asks squirming around nervously, as if the chair were suddenly too small for her.

Saggese continues staring at her, confident that he has hit on the path to seduction.

"No, they choose it all. You'll like it."

"If you say so," Sara replies toying with her silverware. "I don't really feel like eating anyway."

"Me neither, you know."

"Then why did you take me to dinner? You like doing things the old-fashioned way?"

Saggese laughs heartily.

"You know, one of the things that has always attracted me to you is that you can be very funny."

"It's instinctive, when I feel uncomfortable."

"So you feel uncomfortable now," the idiot says.

"A little," Sara says, lowering her eyes.

Saggese leans forward, trying to see her face up close.

"Sara."

She doesn't answer. She continues staring at her plate. She bites her lip.

He lowers his voice.

"Look at me, please."

Sara complies, little by little.

"You're so beautiful."

Sara brings a hand to her forehead, pretending to be dizzy.

"Look, I . . . it's all happening so fast, I think . . . I need a breath of air."

"Do you feel all right?"

"Yes, I . . . I just need to go outside a moment, if you don't mind."

"But of course, let's go," Saggese replies, delighted at the idea that dessert may actually precede the antipasto.

Sara picks up her purse and gets up.

Saggese signals to the headwaiter, to request a brief postponement of the dinner service; then he leaves the restaurant to catch up with his conquest, who has meanwhile entered the parking lot.

"Are you feeling better?"

Sara walks a few feet ahead of him. She holds her purse in her right hand. The parking lot is half-empty and poorly lit. Further on, the highway. There's no one around.

"Sara," Saggese repeats.

She continues walking.

"Why don't you answer me?" he says, becoming aware, at that moment, of the unmistakable sensation of having made a gross mistake.

Still ahead of him, Sara opens her purse, pulls out the gun, turns around, drops the purse, and aims the weapon at him, holding it with both hands.

At first, Saggese seems disappointed. A matter of seconds, before anxiety grips him. He turns a moment towards the entrance to the restaurant. It's already too far away.

"That's all it was?" he says, trying to maintain control. "Make me believe you like me so you can shove a gun in my face?"

Sara trembles, but her eyes flash courage.

"Shut up."

"I don't believe you're capable of using it."

By way of response, she cocks the trigger.

Saggese pales.

"What do you think you're doing? Everyone saw us, in the restaurant."

"I don't give a damn."

"Look, is it because of the guy in the vest? I just wanted to scare you, I swear."

"You ruined my life. It's your fault that Daniele is dead . . ."

"I only did what they told me. Smeraldo needed an operation, and I had to find the best way. That's it. I'm a paper pusher, Sara, nothing more."

"You talk like a Nazi camp guard. 'All I did was carry out orders', 'I'm not responsible': you're really despicable, you know that?"

"And Dalisi?" Saggese throws it up to her. "Did you find him despicable too?"

"Don't you even dare speak his name, you bastard!"

"You think he was a hard-ass?" Saggese presses her. "That it was difficult for me to persuade him? As soon as I told him that he was the man who had to operate, he gave in."

"Stop it! I don't want to hear any more of your filthy lies!"

Saggese continues on mercilessly however, probably hoping to make her stop by hammering away at her.

"He could have refused. Or reported it. Done his duty as a citizen. And as a doctor. Instead he was afraid, so he looked the other way. Like everyone else."

He takes a step toward her.

Then another.

"Stay back," Sara orders.

"And you know that's true," Saggese says as he keeps moving forward "don't you?"

Sara's lips tremble. She clenches her teeth and fires.

The silence that follows the shot seems to be the beginning of something.

Saggese looks at his left shoulder, appalled. Then he drops heavily to his knees.

"He was no better than me," he gasps, staring into Sara's eyes. "He obeyed, just like I obeyed. He was my accomplice, whether you like it or not. And you can't change that even if you kill me, you filthy slut!"

Sara's nostrils flare. She takes a breath, shoots again.

This time she hits him in the chest.

Saggese doesn't cry out. The blast knocks him back.

Someone runs out of the restaurant.

Sara approaches Saggese's lifeless body.

She looks at him.

"I know," she tells him. She picks up her purse. Takes out her cell phone, and dials a number.

There's a small group of people milling around now in the area in front of the restaurant.

Sara recognizes the headwaiter. Someone starts to approach, but she keeps the gun in her hand, and nobody comes very close.

Commissioner Vanini answers on the third ring.

"Sara Vallicelli. I just killed Saggese. Yes. Right now. I'm in the parking lot of a restaurant called Mesticanza, are you familiar with it? Fine. Come and take me in."

The parking lot is lit off and on by the flashing lights of police cars. The murder scene is marked by a yellow tape. The agents keep the curious spectators away and perform regulation inspections.

Sara is leaning against a car, with her back to it. In front of her, a resigned Vanini is trying to get a word out of her.

"What did you do," he tells her.

The ambulance arrives. The siren is turned off. The paramedics get out to retrieve the body.

"Who gave you the gun," Vanini asks.

Sara looks at him and doesn't answer.

Vanini sighs.

"Let's go."

They walk over to the waiting car. The agents ask the Commissioner if they should handcuff her. He shakes his head no, opens the back door, lets Sara get in, and then climbs in himself. Two agents get in the front seat.

They get back on the highway.

Sara looks out the window. There's a long silence.

"What do you think you gained by it?" Vanini asks.

Sara doesn't know how to answer.

The Commissioner shakes his head.

"It wouldn't have done any good anyway," he adds, in a curiously confidential tone.

"What? What did you say?" Sara asks him, feeling a sudden oppression.

Vanini looks at her, then turns his head slightly and directs his gaze toward the flashing lights of an ambulance stopped on the opposite side of the road, not far away. There's an overturned vehicle, just off the road.

Sara flattens herself against the seat back, gripped by a flash of horror. She knows it, that car.

"What's that?" Sara asks.

"What do you mean, what's that," Vanini replies. "Don't you know?"

Sara pales.

Vanini taps the shoulder of the agent who is driving.

"Pull over," he says.

They pull up almost opposite the accident scene. A couple of paramedics drag two bodies out of the overturned car.

Sara covers her mouth with her hand.

The first body is that of Daniele.

Vanini puts a hand on her shoulder.

"Sara," he says softly.

She turns her head in slow motion. She looks at him, shaken.

The two agents turn towards her.

Vanini nods his head in the direction of the accident. "They won, don't you see?"

Sara's eyes fill with tears.

"You have nothing to do with it. You did what you could."

"I just wanted to tell the truth."

"I know. But the truth . . . is used to being concealed."

Sara starts to cry.

"That's why they didn't see you, that day in the park," Vanini continues.

Sara looks out the window again. It's hers, the second body that they've just extracted from the twisted metal.

She buries her head against Vanini's shoulder, and gives way to fitful sobbing.

The Commissioner holds her, and strokes her hair.

Sara reopens her eyes. She's lying in an ambulance, connected to a monitor, an intravenous drip in her arm. A paramedic is holding her hand. He has Commissioner Vanini's face. On the stretcher nearby lies Daniele, pale, eyes half-closed, his clothes soaked with blood. Beside him, another paramedic.

She tries to speak. Her voice won't come.

"Don't get upset, miss, try to stay calm," the paramedic says.

Sara can feel her legs trembling spasmodically. She raises her head a little to see them, it seems so strange that they're able to rebel on their own. The siren is deafening. She clings tightly to the hand of the paramedic, who with his other hand, raps loudly against the glass that separates the rear compartment from that of the driver.

"Faster. We're losing her."

The other fellow looks at the monitor, then looks at him, and doesn't say a word.

Howling, the ambulance burns up the road, its hysterical voice imposing a right of way born of desperation. Passersby, hearing it approach, stand stock-still. They stop what they're doing and follow it with their eyes, even if there's nothing to see. Sometimes they wait for it to disappear around the corner. Then they lower their heads, think of something else and slowly continue walking.

Translation © 2009 Anne Milano Appel

Tell Me Who to Kill

Ian Rankin

Saturday afternoon, John Rebus left the Oxford Bar after the football results and decided that he would try walking home. The day was clear, the sun just above the horizon, casting ridiculously long shadows. It would grow chilly later, maybe even frost overnight, but for now it was crisp and bright – perfect for a walk. He had limited himself to three pints of IPA, a corned beef roll and a pie. He carried a large bag with him – shopping for clothes his excuse for a trip into the city centre, a trip he'd known would end at the Ox. Edinburgh on a Saturday meant day-trippers, weekend warriors, but they tended to stick to Princes Street. George Street had been quieter, Rebus's tally finally comprising two shirts and a pair of trousers. He'd gone up a waist size in the previous six months, which was reason enough to cut back on the beer, and for opting to walk home.

He knew his only real problem would be The Mound. The steep slope connected Princes Street to the Lawnmarket, having been created from the digging out of the New Town's foundations. It posed a serious climb. He'd known a fellow cop – a uniformed sergeant – who'd cycled up The Mound every day on his way to work, right up until the day he'd retired. For Rebus, it had often proved problematical, even on foot. But he would give it a go, and if he failed, well, there was a bus-stop he could beat a retreat to, or taxis he could flag down. Plenty of cabs about at this time of day, ferrying spent shoppers home to the suburbs, or bringing revellers into town at the start of another raucous evening. Rebus avoided the city centre on Saturday nights, unless duty called. The place took on an aggressive edge, violence spilling on to the streets from the clubs on Lothian Road and the bars in the

Grassmarket. Better to stay at home with a carry-out and pretend your world wasn't changing for the worse.

A crowd had gathered at the foot of Castle Street. Rebus noticed that an ambulance, blue lights blinking, was parked in front of a stationary double-decker bus. Walking into the middle of the scene, Rebus overheard muttered exchanges of information.

"Just walked out . . ."

". . . right into its path . . ."

"Wasn't looking . . ."

"Not the first time I've seen . . ."

"These bus drivers think they own the roads, though . . ."

The victim was being carried into the ambulance. It didn't look good for him. One look at the paramedics' faces told Rebus as much. There was blood on the roadway. The bus driver was sitting in the open doorway of his vehicle, head in his hands. There were still passengers on the bus, reluctant to admit that they would need to transfer, loaded down with shopping and unable to think beyond their own concerns. Two uniformed officers were taking statements, the witnesses only too happy to fulfil their roles in the drama. One of the uniforms looked at Rebus and gave a nod of recognition.

"Afternoon, DI Rebus."

Rebus just nodded back. There was nothing for him to do here, no part he could usefully play. He made to cross the road, but noticed something lying there, untouched by the slow crawl of curious traffic. He stooped and picked it up. It was a mobile phone. The injured pedestrian must have been holding it, maybe even using it. Which would explain why he hadn't been paying attention. Rebus turned his head towards the ambulance, but it was already moving away, not bothering to add a siren to its flashing lights: another bad sign, a sign that the medics in the back either didn't want or didn't feel the need of it. There was either severe trauma, or else the victim was already dead. Rebus glanced down at the phone. It was unscathed, looked almost brand new. Strange to think such a thing could survive where its owner might not. He pressed it to his ear, but the line wasn't open. Then he looked at it again, noting that there were words on its display screen. Looked like a text message.

TELL ME WHO TO KILL

* * *

Rebus blinked, narrowed his eyes. He was back on the pavement.

TELL ME WHO TO KILL

He scrolled up and down the message, but there wasn't any more to it than those five words. Along the top ran the number of the caller; looked like another mobile phone. Plus time of call: 16.31. Rebus walked over to the uniformed officer, the one who'd spoken to him.

"Larry," he said, "where was the ambulance headed?"

"Western General," the uniform said. "Guy's skull's split open, be lucky to make it."

"Do we know what happened?"

"He walked straight out into the road, by the look of it. Can't really blame the driver . . ."

Rebus nodded slowly and walked over to the bus driver, crouched down in front of him. The man was in his fifties, head shaved but with a thick silvery beard. His hands shook as he lifted them away from his eyes.

"Couldn't stop in time," he explained, voice quavering. "He was right there . . ." His eyes widened as he played the scene again in his head. Shaking his head slowly. "No way I could've stopped . . ."

"He wasn't looking where he was going," Rebus said softly.

"That's right."

"Busy on his phone maybe?"

The driver nodded. "Staring at it, aye . . . Some people haven't got the sense they were born with. Not that I'm . . . I mean, I don't want to speak ill or anything."

"Wasn't your fault," Rebus agreed, patting the man's shoulder.

"Colleague of mine, same thing happened not six months past. Hasn't worked since." He held up his hands to examine them.

"He was too busy looking at his phone," Rebus said. "That's the whole story. Reading a message maybe?"

"Maybe," the driver agreed. "Doing something anyway, something more important than looking where he was bloody well going . . ."

"Not your fault," Rebus repeated, rising to his feet. He walked to the back of the bus, stepped out into the road, and waved down the first taxi he saw.

*　　　*　　　*

Rebus sat in the waiting area of the Western General Hospital. When a dazed-looking woman was led in by a nurse, and asked if she wanted a cup of tea, he got to his feet. The woman sat herself down, twisting the handles of her shoulder-bag in both hands, as if wringing the life out of them. She'd shaken her head, mumbled something to the nurse, who was now retreating.

"As soon as we know anything," were the nurse's parting words.

Rebus sat down next to the woman. She was in her early thirties, blonde hair cut in a pageboy style. What make-up she had applied to her eyes that morning had been smudged by tears, giving her a haunted look. Rebus cleared his throat, but she still seemed unaware of his close presence.

"Excuse me," he said. "I'm Detective Inspector Rebus." He opened his ID, and she looked at it, then stared down at the floor again. "Has your husband just been in an accident?"

"He's in surgery," she said.

Rebus had been told as much at the front desk. "I'm sorry," he said. "I don't even know his name."

"Carl," she said. "Carl Guthrie."

"And you're his wife?"

She nodded. "Frances."

"Must be quite a shock, Frances."

"Yes."

"Sure you don't want that tea?"

She shook her head, looked up into his face for the first time. "Do you know what happened?"

"Seems he was starting to cross Princes Street and didn't see the bus coming."

She squeezed shut her eyes, tears glinting in her lashes. "How is that possible?"

Rebus shrugged. "Maybe he had something on his mind," he said quietly. "When was the last time you spoke to him?"

"Breakfast this morning. I was planning to go shopping."

"What about Carl?"

"I thought he was working. He's a physiotherapist, sports injuries mostly. He has his own practice in Corstorphine. He gets some work from the BUPA hospital at Murrayfield."

"And a few rugby players too, I'd guess."

Frances Guthrie was dabbing at her eyes with a paper tissue. "How could he get hit by a bus?" She looked up at the ceiling, blinking back tears.

"Do you know what he was doing in town?"

She shook her head.

"This was found lying in the road," Rebus said, holding up the phone for her to see. "There's a text message displayed. You see what it says?"

She peered at the screen, then frowned. "What does it mean?"

"I don't know," Rebus admitted. "Do you recognise the caller's number?"

She shook her head, then reached out a hand and took the phone from Rebus, turning it in her palm. "This isn't Carl's."

"What?"

"This isn't Carl's phone. Someone else must have dropped it." Rebus stared at her. "You're sure?"

She handed the phone back, nodding. "Carl's is a silver flip-top sort of thing." Rebus stared at the black, one-piece Samsung.

"Then whose is it?" he asked, more to himself than to her. She answered anyway.

"What does it matter?"

"It matters."

"But it's a joke surely." She nodded at the screen. "Someone's idea of a practical joke."

"Maybe," Rebus said. The same nurse was walking towards them, accompanied by a surgeon in green scrubs. Neither of them had to say anything. Frances Guthrie was already keening as the surgeon began his speech.

"I'm so sorry, Mrs Guthrie . . . we did everything we could."

Frances Guthrie leaned in towards Rebus, her face against his shoulder. He put his arm around her, feeling it was the least he could do.

Carl Guthrie's effects had been placed in a large cardboard box. His blood-soaked clothes were protected by a clear polythene bag. Rebus lifted them out. The pockets had been emptied. Watch, wallet, small change, keys. And a silver flip-top mobile phone. Rebus checked its screen. The battery was low, and there were no messages. Rebus told the nurse that he wanted to take it with him. She shrugged and made him sign a docket to that effect. He flipped through the wallet, finding bank-notes, credit cards, and a few of Carl Guthrie's own business cards, giving an address in Corstorphine, plus office and mobile numbers. Rebus took out his own phone and punched in the latter. The silver telephone trilled as it rang. Rebus cancelled the call. He nodded to the nurse to let her know he was finished. The docket was placed in the box, along with the polythene bag. Rebus pocketed all three phones.

The police lab at Howdenhall wasn't officially open at weekends, but Rebus knew that someone was usually there, trying to clear a backlog, or just because they'd nothing better to do. Rebus got lucky. Ray Duff was one of the better technicians. He sighed when Rebus walked in.

"I'm up to my eyes," he complained, turning away to walk back down the corridor.

"Yes, but you'll like this," Rebus said, holding out the mobile.

Duff stopped and turned, stared at it, then ran his fingers through an unruly mop of hair.

"I really am up to my eyes . . ."

Rebus shrugged, arm still stretched out. Duff sighed again and took the phone from him.

"Discovered at the scene of an accident," Rebus explained. Duff had found a pair of spectacles in one of the pockets of his white lab-coat and was putting them on. "My guess is that the victim had just received the text message, and was transfixed by it."

"And walked out in front of a car?"

"Bus actually. Thing is, the phone doesn't belong to the victim." Rebus produced the silver flip-top. "This is his."

"So whose is this?" Duff peered at Rebus over the top of his glasses. "That's what you're wondering." He was walking again, heading for his own cubicle, Rebus following.

"Right."

"And also who the caller was."

"Right again."

"We could just phone them."

"We could." They'd reached Duff's work-station. Each surface was a clutter of wires, machines and paperwork. Duff rubbed his bottom lip against his teeth. "Battery's getting low," he said, as the phone uttered a brief chirrup.

"Any chance you can recharge it?"

"I can if you like, but we don't really need it."

"We don't?"

The technician shook his head. "The important stuff's on the chip." He tapped the back of the phone. "We can transfer it . . ." He grew thoughtful again. "Of course, that would mean accessing the code number, so we're probably better off hanging on to it as it is." He reached down into a cupboard and produced half a dozen mains adaptors. "One of these should do the trick."

Soon, the phone was plugged in and charging. Meantime, Duff had worked his magic on the keypad, producing the phone number. Rebus punched it into his own phone, and the black mobile trilled.

"Bingo," Duff said with a smile. "Now all we do is call the service provider . . ." He left the cubicle and returned a couple of minutes later with a sheet of numbers. "I hope you didn't touch anything," he said, waving a hand around his domain.

"I wouldn't dare." Rebus leaned against a workbench as Duff made the call, identified himself, and reeled off the mobile phone number. Then he placed his hand over the mouthpiece.

"It'll take a minute," he told Rebus.

"Can anyone get this sort of information?" Rebus asked. "I mean, what's to stop Joe Public calling up and saying they're a cop?"

Duff smiled. "Caller recognition. They've got a screen their end. IDs the caller number as Lothian and Borders Police Forensic Branch."

"Clever," Rebus admitted. Duff just shrugged. "So how about the other number? The one belonging to whoever sent that message."

Duff held up a finger, indicating that he was listening to the person at the other end of the line. He looked around him, finding a scrap of paper. Rebus provided the pen, and he started writing.

"That's great, thanks," he said finally. Then: "Mind if I try you with something else? It's a mobile number . . ." He proceeded to reel off the number on the message screen, then, with his hand again muffling the mouthpiece, he handed the scrap of paper to Rebus.

"Name and address of the phone's owner."

Rebus looked. The owner's name was William Smith, the address a street in the New Town. "What about the text sender?" he asked.

"She's checking." Duff removed his hand from the mouthpiece, listening intently. Then he started shaking his head. "Not one of yours, eh? Don't suppose you can tell from the number just who is the service provider?" He listened again. "Well, thanks anyway." He put down the receiver.

"No luck?" Rebus guessed. Duff shrugged.

"Just means we have to do it the hard way." He picked up the sheet of telephone numbers. "Maybe nine or ten calls at the most."

"Can I leave it with you, Ray?"

Duff stretched his arms wide. "What else was I going to be doing at half past six on a Saturday?"

Rebus smiled. "You and me both, Ray."

"What do you reckon we're dealing with? A hit man?"

"I don't know."

"But if it is . . . then Mr Smith would be his employer, making him someone you might not want to mess about with."

"I'm touched by your concern, Ray."

Duff smiled. "Can I take it you're headed over to that address anyway?"

"Not too many gangsters living in the New Town, Ray."

"Not that we know of," Duff corrected him. "Maybe after this, we'll know better . . ."

The streets were full of maroon-scarved Hearts fans, celebrating a rare victory. Bouncers had appeared at the doors of most of the city-centre watering-holes: an unnecessary expense in daylight, but indispensable by night. There were queues outside the fast-food restaurants, diners tossing their empty cartons on to the pavement.

Rebus kept eyes front as he drove. He was in his own car now, having stopped home long enough for a mug of coffee and two paracetamol. He guessed that a breath test might just about catch him, but felt OK to drive nonetheless.

The New Town, when he reached it, was quiet. Few bars here, and the area was a dead end of sorts, unlikely to be soiled by the city-centre drinkers. As usual, parking was a problem. Rebus did one circuit, then left his car on a double-yellow line, right next to a set of traffic lights. Doubled back on himself until he reached the tenement. There was an entryphone, a list of residents

printed beside it. But no mention of anyone called Smith. Rebus
ran a finger down the column of names. One space was blank. It
belonged to Flat 3. He pushed the button and waited. Nothing.
Pushed it again, then started pressing various bells, waiting for
someone to respond. Eventually, the tiny loudspeaker grille
crackled into life.

"Hello?"

"I'm a police officer. Any chance of speaking to you for a
minute?"

"What's the problem?"

"No problem. It's just a couple of questions concerning one of
your neighbours . . ."

There was silence, then a buzzing sound as the door unlocked
itself. Rebus pushed it open and stepped into the stairwell. A
door on the ground floor was open, a man standing there. Rebus
had his ID open. The man was in his twenties, with cropped hair
and Buddy Holly spectacles. A dishtowel was draped over one
shoulder.

"Do you know anyone called William Smith?" Rebus asked.

"Smith?" The man narrowed his eyes, shook his head slowly.

"I think he lives here."

"What does he look like?"

"I'm not sure."

The man stared at him, then shrugged. "People come and go.
Sometimes they move on before you get to know their names."

"But you've been here a while?"

"Almost a year. Some of the neighbours I know to say hello to,
but I don't always know their names." He smiled apologetically.
Yes, that was Edinburgh for you: people kept themselves to
themselves, didn't want anyone getting too close. A mixture of
shyness and mistrust.

"Flat 3 doesn't seem to have a name beside it," Rebus said,
nodding back towards the main door.

The man shrugged again.

"I'm just going to go up and take a look," Rebus said.

"Be my guest. You know where I am if you need me."

"Thanks for your help." Rebus started climbing the stairs. The
shared space was well maintained, the steps clean, smelling of
disinfectant mixed with something else, a perfume of sorts. There
were ornate tiles on the walls. Flats 2 and 3 were on the first floor.

There was a buzzer to the right of Flat 3, a typed label attached to it. Rebus bent down for a closer look. The words had faded, but were readable: LT Lettings. While he was down there, Rebus decided he might as well take a look through the letter-box. All he could see was an unlit hallway. He straightened up and pressed the bell for Flat 2. Nobody was home. Rebus took out one of his business cards and a ballpoint pen, scribbled the words "Please call me" on the back, and pushed the card through the door of Flat 2. He thought for a moment, but decided against doing the same for Flat 3.

Back downstairs again, he knocked on the door of the young man with the dishtowel. Smiled as it was opened.

"Sorry to bother you again, but do you think I could take a look at your phone book . . .?"

Rebus went back to his car and made the call from there. An answering machine played its message, informing him that LT Lettings was closed until ten o'clock on Monday morning, but that any tenant with an emergency should call another number. Rebus jotted it down and called. The person who answered sounded like he was stuck in traffic. Rebus explained who he was.

"I need to ask about one of your properties."

"I'm not the person you need to speak to. I just mend things."

"What sorts of things?"

"Some tenants aren't too fussy, know what I mean? Place isn't their own, they treat it like shit."

"Until you turn up and sort them out?"

The man laughed. "I put things right, if that's what you mean."

"And that's all you do?"

"Look, I'm not sure where you're going with this . . . It's my boss you need to speak to. Lennox Tripp."

"Okay, give me his number."

"Office is shut till Monday."

"His home number, I meant."

"I'm not sure he'd thank me for that."

"This is a police matter. And it's urgent."

Rebus waited for the man to speak, then jotted down the eventual reply. "And your name is . . .?"

"Frank Empson."

Rebus jotted this down, too. "Well, thanks for your help, Mr Empson. You heading for a night out?"

"Absolutely, Inspector. Just as soon as I've fixed the heating in one flat and unblocked the toilet in another."

Rebus thought for a moment. "Ever had cause to visit Gilby Street?"

"In the New Town?"

"Number 26, Flat 3?"

"I moved some furniture in, but that was months back."

"Never seen the person who lives there?"

"Nope."

"Well, thanks again . . ." Rebus cut the call, punched in the number for Lennox Tripp. The phone was answered on the fifth ring. Rebus asked if he was speaking to Lennox Tripp.

"Yes." The voice hesitant.

"My name's John Rebus. I'm a detective inspector with Lothian and Borders Police."

"What seems to be the problem?" The voice more confident now, an educated drawl.

"One of your tenants, Mr Tripp, 26 Gilby Street."

"Yes?"

"I need to know what you know . . ."

Rebus was smoking his second cigarette when Tripp arrived, driving a silver Mercedes. He double-parked outside number 26, using a remote to set the locks and alarm.

"Won't be long, will we?" he asked, turning to glance at his car as he shook Rebus's hand. Rebus flicked the half-smoked cigarette on to the road.

"Wouldn't imagine so," he said. Lennox Tripp was about Rebus's age – mid-fifties – but had worn considerably better. His face was tanned, hair groomed, clothes casual but classy. He stepped up to the door and let them in with a key. As they climbed the stairs, he said his piece.

"Only reason William Smith sticks in my head is that he pays cash for the let. A wad of twenties in an envelope, delivered to the office on time each month. This is his seventh month."

"You must have met him, though."

Tripp nodded. "Showed him the place myself."

"Can you describe him?"

Tripp shrugged. "White, tallish . . . nothing much to distinguish him."

"Hair?"

Tripp smiled. "Almost certainly." Then, as if to apologise for the glib comeback: "It was six months ago, Inspector."

"And that's the only time you've seen him?"

Tripp nodded. 'I'd have called him the model tenant . . ."

"A model tenant who pays cash? You don't find that a mite suspicious?"

Tripp shrugged again. "I try not to pry, Inspector." They were at the door to Flat 3. Tripp unlocked it and motioned for Rebus to precede him inside.

"Was it rented furnished?" Rebus asked, walking into the living room.

"Yes." Tripp took a look around. 'Doesn't look like he's added much."

"Not even a TV," Rebus commented, walking into the kitchen. He opened the fridge. There was a bottle of white wine inside, open and with the cork pushed back into its neck. Nothing else: no butter, milk . . . nothing. Two tumblers drying on the draining-board, the only signs that anyone had been here in recent memory.

There was just the one bedroom. The bedclothes were mostly on the floor. Tripp bent to pick them up, draping them over the mattress. Rebus opened the wardrobe, exposing a single dark-blue suit hanging there. Nothing in any of the pockets. In one drawer: underpants, socks, a single black T-shirt. The other drawers were empty.

"Looks like he's moved on," Tripp commented.

"Or has something against possessions," Rebus added. He looked around. "No phone?"

Tripp shook his head. "There's a wall-socket. If a tenant wants to sign up with BT or whoever, they're welcome to."

"Too much trouble for Mr Smith, apparently."

"Well, a lot of people use mobiles these days, don't they?"

"They do indeed, Mr Tripp." Rebus rubbed a thumb and forefinger over his temples. "I'm assuming Smith provided you with some references?"

"I'd assume he did."

"You don't remember?"

"Not off-hand."

"Would you have any records?"

"Yes, but it's by no means certain . . ."

Rebus stared at the man. "You'd rent one of your flats to someone who couldn't prove who they were?"

Tripp raised an eyebrow by way of apology.

"Cash upfront, I'm guessing," Rebus hissed.

"Cash does have its merits."

"I hope your tax returns are in good order."

Tripp was brought up short. 'Is that some kind of threat, Inspector?"

Rebus feigned a look that was between surprise and disappointment. "Why would I do a thing like that, Mr Tripp?"

"I wasn't meaning to suggest . . ."

"I would hope not. But I'll tell you what . . ." Rebus laid a hand on the man's shoulder. "We'll call it quits, once we've been to your office and checked those files . . ."

But there was precious little in the file relating to Flat 3, 26 Gilby Street – just a signed copy of the lease agreement. No references of any kind. Smith had put his occupation down as "market analyst" and his date of birth as 13 January 1970.

"Did you ask him what a market analyst does?"

Tripp nodded. "I think he said he worked for one of the insurance companies, something to do with making sure their portfolios didn't lose money."

"You don't recall which company?"

Tripp said he didn't.

In the end, Rebus managed a grudged "thank you", headed out to his car, and drove home. Ray Duff hadn't called, which meant he hadn't made any progress, and Rebus doubted he would be working Sunday. He poured himself a whisky, stuck John Martyn on the hi-fi, and slumped into his chair. A couple of tracks passed without him really hearing them. He slid his hand into his pocket and came out with both phones, the silver and the black. For the first time, he checked the silver flip-top, finding messages from Frances Guthrie to her husband. There was an address book, probably listing clients and friends. Rebus laid this phone aside and concentrated on the black one. There was nothing in its memory: no phone numbers stored, no messages. Just that one text: TELL ME WHO TO KILL. And the number of the caller.

Rebus got up and poured himself another drink, then took a deep breath and pushed the buttons, calling the sender of the text message. The ringing tone sounded tremulous. Rebus was still holding his breath, but after twenty rings he gave up. No one was about to answer. He decided to send a text instead, but couldn't think what words to use.

Hello, are you a hired killer?

Who do you think I want you to kill?

Please hand yourself in to your nearest police station . . .

He smiled to himself, decided it could wait. Only half past nine, the night stretching ahead of him. He surfed all five TV channels, went into the kitchen to make some coffee, and found that he'd run out of milk. Decided on a walk to the corner shop. There was a video store almost next door to it. Maybe he'd rent a film, something to take his mind off the message. Decided, he grabbed his keys, slipped his jacket back on.

The grocer was about to close, but knew Rebus's face, and asked him to be quick. Rebus settled for a packet of sausages, a box of eggs, and a carton of milk. Then added a four-pack of lager. Settled up with the grocer and carried his purchases to the video store. He was inside before he remembered that he'd forgotten to bring his membership card; thought the assistant would probably let him rent something anyway. After all, if William Smith could rent a flat in the New Town, surely Rebus could rent a three-quid video.

He was even prepared to pay cash.

But as he stared at the rack of new releases, he found himself blinking and shaking his head. Then he reached out a hand and lifted down the empty video box. He approached the desk with it.

"When did this come out?" he asked.

"Last week." The assistant was in his teens, but a good judge of Hollywood's gold dust and dross. His eyes had gone heavy-lidded, letting Rebus know this film was the latter. "Rich guy's having an affair, hires an assassin. Only the assassin falls for the wife and tops the mistress instead. Rich guy takes the fall, breaks out of jail with revenge in mind."

"So I don't need to watch it now?"

The assistant shrugged. "That's all in the first fifteen minutes. I'm not telling you anything they don't give away on the back of the box."

Rebus turned the box over and saw that this was largely true. 'I should never have doubted you," he said.

"It got terrible reviews, which is why they end up quoting from an obscure radio station on the front."

Rebus nodded, turning the box over in his hands. Then he held it out towards the assistant. 'I'll take it."

"Don't say I didn't warn you." The assistant turned and found a copy of the film in a plain box. "Got your card?"

"Left it in the flat."

"Surname's Rebus, right? Address in Arden Street." Rebus nodded. "Then I suppose it's OK, this one time."

"Thanks."

The assistant shrugged. "It's not like I'm doing you a favour, letting you walk out with that film."

"Even so . . . you have to admit, it's got a pretty good title."

"Maybe." The assistant studied the box for *Tell Me Who to Kill*, but seemed far from convinced.

Rebus had finished all four cans of lager by the time the closing credits rolled. He reckoned he must have dozed off for a few minutes in the middle, but didn't think this had affected his viewing pleasure. There were a couple of big names in the main roles, but they, too, tended towards drowsiness. It was as if cast, crew and writers had needed a decent night's sleep.

Rebus rewound the tape, ejected it, and held it in his hand. So it was a film title. That was all the text message had meant. Maybe someone had been choosing a film for Saturday night. Maybe Carl Guthrie had found the phone lying on the pavement. William Smith had dropped it, and Guthrie had found it. Then someone, maybe Smith's girlfriend, had texted the title of the film they'd be watching later on, and Guthrie had opened the message, hoping to find some clue to the identity of the phone's owner.

And he'd walked out under a bus.

TELL ME WHO TO KILL.

Which meant Rebus had wasted half a day. Half a day that could have been better spent . . . well, spent differently anyway. And the film had been preposterous: the assistant's summary had only just scratched the surface. Starting off with a surfeit of twists, there'd been nowhere for the film to go but layer on more twists, deceits, mixed identities, and conspiracies. Rebus could not have been more insulted if the guy had woken up at the end and it had all been a dream.

He went into the kitchen to make some coffee. The place still held the aroma of the fry-up he'd amassed before sitting down to watch the video. Over the sound of the boiling kettle, he heard his phone ringing. Went back through to the living room and picked it up.

"Got a name for you, sorry it took so long."

"Ray? Is that you?" Rebus checked his watch: not far short of midnight. "Tell me you're not still at work."

"Called a halt hours ago, but I just got a text message from my friend who was doing some cross-checking for me."

"He works odder hours than even we do."

"He's an insomniac, works a lot from his house."

"So I shouldn't ask where he got this information?"

"You can ask, but I couldn't possibly tell you."

"And what is it I'm getting?"

"The text message came from a phone registered to Alexis Ojiwa. I've got an address in Haddington."

"Might as well give it to me." Rebus picked up a pen, but something in his voice had alerted Ray Duff.

"Do I get the feeling you no longer need any of this?"

"Maybe not, Ray." Rebus explained about the film.

"Well, I can't say I've ever heard of it."

"It was news to me, too," Rebus didn't mind admitting.

"But for the record, I do know Alexis Ojiwa."

"You do?"

"I take it you don't follow football."

"I watch the results."

"Then you'll know that Hearts put four past Aberdeen this afternoon."

"Four-one, final score."

"And two of them were scored by Alexis Ojiwa . . ."

Rebus's mobile woke him an hour earlier than he'd have liked. He blinked at the sunshine streaming through his uncurtained windows and grabbed at the phone, dropping it once before getting it to his ear.

"Yes?" he rasped.

"I'm sorry, is this too early? I thought maybe it was urgent."

"Who is this?"

"Am I speaking to DI Rebus?"

"Yes."

"My name's Richard Hawkins. You put your card through my door."

"Did I?"

Rebus heard a soft chuckle. "Maybe I should call back later . . ."

"No, wait a sec. You live at Gilby Street?"

"Flat 2, yes."

"Right, right." Rebus sat down on his bed, ran his free hand through his hair. "Thanks for getting back to me."

"Not at all."

"It was about your neighbour, actually."

"Will Smith?"

"What?"

Another chuckle. "When he introduced himself, we had a laugh about that coincidence. Really, it was down to me. He called himself "William", and it just clicked: Will Smith, same as the actor."

"Right," Rebus was trying to gather himself. "So you've met Mr Smith, talked to him?"

"Just a couple of times. Passing on the stairs . . . He's never around much."

"Not much sign of his flat being lived in either."

"I wouldn't know, never been inside. Must have something going for him though."

"Why do you say that?"

"Absolute cracker of a girlfriend."

"Really?"

"Just saw her the once, but you always know when she's around."

"Why's that?"

"Her perfume. It fills the stairwell. Smelled it last night actually . . ."

Yes, Rebus had smelt it, too. He moistened his lips, feeling sourness at the corners of his mouth. "Mr Hawkins, can you describe William Smith to me?"

Hawkins could, and did.

Rebus turned up unannounced at Alexis Ojiwa's, reckoning the player would be resting after the rigours of the previous day. The house was an unassuming detached bungalow with a red Mazda sports car parked in the driveway. It was on a modern estate, a couple of neighbours washing their cars, watching Rebus with the intensity of men for whom his arrival was an event of sorts, something they could dissect with their wives over the carving of the afternoon sirloin. Rebus rang the doorbell and waited. A woman answered. She seemed surprised to see him.

He showed his ID as he introduced himself. "Mind if I come in for a minute?"

"What's happened?"

"Nothing. I just have a question for Mr Ojiwa."

She left the door standing open and walked back through the hall and into an L-shaped living area, calling out: "Cops are here to put the cuffs on you, baby." Rebus closed the door and followed her. She stepped out through french windows into the back garden, where a tiny, bare-chested man stood, nursing a drink that looked like puréed fruit. Alexis Ojiwa was wiry, with thick-veined arms and a tight chest. Rebus tried not to think about what the neighbours thought. Scotland was still some way short of being a beacon of multiculturalism, and Ojiwa, like his partner, was black. Not just coffee-coloured, but as black as ebony. Still, probably the only question that would count in most local minds was whether he was Protestant black or Catholic black.

Rebus held out a hand to shake, and introduced himself again.

"What's the problem, officer?"

"I didn't catch your wife's name."

"It's Cecily."

Rebus nodded. "This is going to sound strange, but it's about your mobile phone."

"My phone?" Ojiwa's face creased in puzzlement. Then he looked to Cecily, and back again at Rebus. "What about my phone?"

"You do have a mobile phone, sir?"

"I do, yes."

"But I'm guessing you wouldn't have used it yesterday afternoon? Specifically not at 16.31. I think you were still on the pitch at that time, am I right?"

"That's right."

"Then someone else used your phone to send this message." Rebus held up William Smith's mobile so Ojiwa could read the text. Cecily came forward so she could read it, too. Her husband stared at her.

"What's this all about?"

"I don't know, baby."

"You sent this?" His eyes had widened. She shook her head.

"Am I to assume that you had your husband's phone with you yesterday, Mrs Ojiwa?" Rebus asked.

"I was shopping in town all day . . . I didn't make any calls."

"What the hell is this?" It appeared that the footballer had a short fuse, and Rebus had touched a match to it.

"I'm sure there's a reasonable explanation, sir," Rebus said, raising his hands to try to calm Ojiwa.

"You go spending all my money, and now this!" Ojiwa shook the phone at his wife.

"I didn't do it!" She was yelling too now, loud enough to be heard by the car-polishers. Then she dived inside, producing a silver mobile phone from her bag. "Here it is," she said, brandishing the phone. "Check it, check and see if I sent any messages. I was shopping all day!"

"Maybe someone could have borrowed it?" Rebus suggested.

"I don't see how," she said, shaking her head. "Why would anyone want to do that, send a message like that?"

Ojiwa had slumped on to a garden bench, head in hands. Rebus got the feeling that theirs was a relationship stoked by melodrama. He seated himself on the bench next to the footballer.

"Can I ask you something, Mr Ojiwa?"

"What now?"

"I was just wondering if you'd ever needed physio?"

Ojiwa looked up. "Course I need physio! You think I'm Captain Superman or something?" He slapped his hands against his thighs.

If anything, Rebus's voice grew quieter as he began his next question. "Then does the name Carl Guthrie mean anything to you . . .?"

"You've not committed any crime."

These were Rebus's first words to Frances Guthrie when she opened her door to him. The interior of her house was dark, the curtains closed. The house itself was large and detached and sited in half an acre of grounds in the city's Ravelston area. Physios either earned more than Rebus had counted on, or else there was family money involved.

Frances Guthrie was wearing black slacks and a loose, low-cut black top. Mourning casual, Rebus might have termed it. Her eyes were red-rimmed, and the area around her nose looked raw.

"Mind if I come in?" Rebus asked. It wasn't really a question. He was already making to pass the widow. Hands in pockets, he walked down the hallway and into the sitting room. Stood there and waited for her to join him. She did so slowly, perching on the arm of the red leather sofa. He repeated his opening words, expecting that she would say something, but all she did was stare at him, wide-eyed, maybe a little scared.

He made a tour of the room. The windows were large, and even when curtained there was enough light to see by. Rebus stopped by the fireplace and folded his arms.

"Here's the way I see it. You were out shopping with your friend Cecily. You got to know her when Carl was treating her husband. The pair of you were in Harvey Nichols. Cecily was in the changing room, leaving her bag with you. That's when you got hold of her phone and sent the message." He paused to watch the effect his words were having. Frances Guthrie had lowered her head, staring down at her hands.

"It was a video you'd watched recently. I'm guessing Carl watched it, too. A film about a man who cheats on his wife. And Carl had been cheating on you, hadn't he? You wanted to let him know you knew, so you sent a text to his other phone, the one registered to his fake name – William Smith." Smith's neighbour had given Rebus a good description of the man, chiming with accident victim Carl Guthrie. "You'd done some detective work of your own, found out about the phone, the flat in town . . . the other woman." The one whose perfume had lingered in the stairwell. Saturday afternoon: Carl Guthrie heading home after an assignation, leaving behind only two glasses and an unfinished bottle of wine.

Frances Guthrie's head jerked up. She took a deep breath, almost a gulp.

"Why use Cecily's phone?" Rebus asked quietly.

She shook her head, not blinking. Then: "I never wanted this . . . Not this . . ."

"You weren't to know what would happen."

"I just wanted to do something." She looked up at him, wanting him to understand. He nodded slowly. "What . . . what do I do now?"

Rebus slipped his hands back into his pockets. "Learn to live with yourself, I suppose."

That afternoon, he was back at the Oxford Bar, nursing a drink and thinking about love, about how it could make you do things you couldn't explain. All the passions – love and hate and everything in between – they all made us act in ways that would seem inexplicable to a visitor from another planet. The barman asked him if he was ready for another, but Rebus shook his head.

"How's the weekend been treating you?" the barman asked.

"Same as always," Rebus replied. It was one of those little lies that went some way towards making life appear that bit less complicated.

"Seen any good films lately?"

Rebus smiled, stared down into his glass. "Watched one last night," he said. "Let me tell you about it . . ."